THE DIARY OF
JOHN EVELYN

Mrs. Godolphin. By Matthew Dixon (?)

THE DIARY OF
JOHN
EVELYN

Now first printed in full from the
manuscripts belonging to Mr. John Evelyn
and edited by

E. S. DE BEER

In six volumes

Volume IV

KALENDARIUM, 1673–1689

OXFORD
AT THE CLARENDON PRESS
1955

Oxford University Press, Amen House, London E.C.4

GLASGOW NEW YORK TORONTO MELBOURNE WELLINGTON
BOMBAY CALCUTTA MADRAS KARACHI CAPE TOWN IBADAN

Geoffrey Cumberlege, Publisher to the University

PRINTED IN GREAT BRITAIN

DIGNITARIES AND OFFICE-HOLDERS

EVELYN habitually designates dignitaries and office-holders in church and state not by their names but by their dignities. For most readers the dignities mean very little; what is required is the names. It would, however, be impracticable to identify all the persons thus designated whenever they occur; the present list is therefore provided to enable the reader to identify the persons most frequently mentioned in this way in the present volume; those who are thus mentioned only rarely in it are identified on all occasions.

Lord Chancellor
    1672–3. SIR ANTHONY ASHLEY COOPER, earl of Shaftesbury.
    1685–8. SIR GEORGE JEFFREYS, Baron Jeffreys of Wem.

Lord Keeper
    1682–5. SIR FRANCIS NORTH, baron of Guilford.

Lord High Treasurer
    1672–3. SIR THOMAS CLIFFORD, Baron Clifford of Chudleigh.
    1673–9. SIR THOMAS OSBORNE, earl of Danby.
    1685–7. LAWRENCE HYDE, earl of Rochester.

Lord President of the Council
    1685–8. ROBERT SPENCER, earl of Sunderland.

Lord Lieutenant of Ireland ('Lord Deputy')
    1685–7. HENRY HYDE, earl of Clarendon.

Lord Chamberlain (of the Household)
    1674–85. SIR HENRY BENNET, earl of Arlington.

Archbishop of Canterbury
    1663–77. DR. GILBERT SHELDON.
    1678–91. DR. WILLIAM SANCROFT.

Archbishop of York
    1683–6. DR. JOHN DOLBEN.

Bishop of Bath and Wells
    1685–91. DR. THOMAS KEN.

Bishop of Chichester
    1685–9. DR. JOHN LAKE.

Bishop of Durham
  1674–1721. DR. NATHANIEL CREW, Baron Crew of Stene
  from 1697.

Bishop of Ely
  1684–91. DR. FRANCIS TURNER.

Bishop of London
  1675–1713. DR. HENRY COMPTON.

Bishop of Rochester ('our Bishop')
  1666–83. DR. JOHN DOLBEN.
  1684–1713. DR. THOMAS SPRAT.

Bishop of St. Asaph
  1680–92. DR. WILLIAM LLOYD (here distinguished as 'the
  apocalyptic').

Bishop of Salisbury
  1689–1715. DR. GILBERT BURNET.

Vicar of Deptford ('our Vicar', &c.)
  1673–1702. RICHARD HOLDEN.

PRINCIPAL CONTENTS OF THIS VOLUME

Throughout this volume Evelyn generally lived at
Sayes Court, Deptford

The text of this volume to about p. 359 was transcribed by Evelyn from his original notes probably in 1682–3; there are a number of interpolations made by him in the course of transcription. From about p. 359 to the end of the volume the text consists of Evelyn's contemporary entries.

Mrs. Godolphin. By Matthew Dixon (?). By kind permission of John Evelyn, Esquire, of Wotton   *Frontispiece*

KALENDARIUM
My Journal &c:
[1673–1689]

1673. *Jan:* 1. After pub: Prayers in the Chapell at *W:hall*, & my humble supplication to God for his blissing the Yeare now entering, I went to see ☆ not well,[1] & so returned home, having my lately deceased Servant to bury, & some neighbours to entertaine: ⟨5⟩[a] To *Lond:* Dr. *Colebrand*[2] Sub-deane of his *Majesties Chap:* preaching on   *meeke, & sitting on an Asse* &c: I received the *B: Sacrament*: I presented the *Turcois Locket* & 16 *Diamonds* cum Symbolo &c.[3]

My *Sonn* now publish'd his version of *Rapinus Hortorum* &c dedicated to the Ear: of *Arlington:*[4]

7 I went to Councel in the morning; din'd at my L: *Treasurers*,[5] where dined also my L: *Chancellor:*[6] 8: ☆ went first from Court to *Berkeley house* whither I conducted her, after she had obtained a favourable dismission from their Majesties.[7] Thence to the R: *Society:* 9 Dined at L: *Berkeleys* where ☆ was to reside some time. 10: To *Parsons-Greene* to visite my L: *Mordaunt:* return'd that Evening with my

---

[a] MS. *3.*

---

[1] The pentacle (above, iii. 628 n.) is now used as a symbol for Margaret Blagge.

[2] Richard Colebrande, *c.* 1614–74; D.D. 1661; sub-dean of the chapel 1672–4: Venn.

[3] The present was to Margaret Blagge.

[4] *Of Gardens. Four Books. First written in Latine Verse by Renatus Rapinus, And now made English By J. E.,* ... 1672 (1673). The dedication is signed 'J. Evelyn'. The book is advertised in the *Term Catalogues,* 7 Feb. (ed. Arber, i. 127). For Rapin see *Nouvelle biog. gén.*; the original work, *Hortorum libri quatuor,* was first published in 1665. Keynes, p. 283.

[5] Clifford; he had taken office as lord high treasurer on 30 Nov. 1672.

[6] Shaftesbury; he had received the seals as lord chancellor on 17 Nov. 1672.

[7] *Life,* pp. 32–4.

Lord & Lady *Cornbery*[1] to Lond: 12 Dr. *Bredox*[a][2] deane of *Salisbury* preached on 2. *Luke* 49, concerning Christs obedience (See your *notes*) Then *coram rege* the Sub-deane[3] on
   Psal: Thy Word is a lantern &c: and I dined at the *Duke* of *Lauderdalls*.[4] 14: Visited ✰ & dind at *Berkley-house*, Thence to Council, & next day home:

19 A stranger on: 17: *Mat:* 4. a Curious discourse on our Saviours *Transfiguration*: 20: *Lond:*

21 Dine'd at my L: *Berkeleys* with Mrs. *Blagg*, thence to *Council*: 23 dined with the *Maids* of honor, thence to *Council*. 24 I dind with the Gent: of the *Bed-Chamber*[5] & spake with his *Majestie* & the *Duke*:

25 home: 26 A stranger on 5. *Matt:* 3. shewing how rich, & greate persons might be poore in Spirit: 28 To *Lond:* about buisinesse, din'd at Bar: house,[6] & after dinner visited *Dom Francisco de Melos*[7] *Portugal* Ambassador, who used me extreamely civily, shewed me his curious collection both of Books & Pictures; he was a person of good parts & a Vertuous man. 29 I din'd at my L: *Treasurers*, where was the Duke of Ormond, L: Chancelor & others.

30 The *Bishop* of *Chester*[8] preached *coram rege* on the Latekings *Anniversarie*: I supp'd with my L: *Ossorie* &c:

Feb: 2. A stranger at W:hall on 2: *Luke*: 34, being purification, The holy Sacrament follow'd &c: In the aftersermon[b]

---

[a] Or *Bredoy*.   [b] Altered from *afterno-*.

---

[1] Flower, 1641–1700, daughter of Sir John Backhouse, K.B.; married previously to William Bishop and (1662) to Sir William Backhouse, bart.; married Lord Cornbury 1670 as his second wife: Constance Russell (Lady Russell), *Swallowfield and its owners*, 1901, pp. 131–85.

[2] Ralph Brideoake, 1613–78; D.D. 1660; dean of Salisbury 1667; chaplain in ordinary *c.* 1663–75; bishop of Chichester 1675: *D.N.B.*

[3] Colebrande: see p. 1, n. 2. His text is Psalms cxix. 105, from the Prayer Book.

[4] Lauderdale had been created duke of Lauderdale (Scotland) on 26 May 1672.

[5] See above, iii. 366 n.

[6] i.e. Berkeley House.

[7] Dom Francisco de Mello (Manuel da Camara): above, iii. 481. He had come here for his second term as ambassador in 1671, and died here in 1678.

[8] John Pearson: above, iii. 15, &c. He had been elected bishop on 23 Dec. 1672 and was consecrated on 9 February of this year: *Cal. S.P., Dom., 1672–3*, p. 305.

Dr. *Pierce*[1] (Deane of *Sarum*) coram rege, on 21. *Matt:* 31, The *Parable* of the Husbandmen, excellently: 4: visited ☆ din'd at *Bark: house*, & in the afternoone went with my *Lady*[2] to see Pictures at *Remeès:*[3] 5. I went to waite on my L: *Treasurer:*

6 To *Council* about reforming an abuse of the *diers* with *Saunders* & other false drogues, exam⟨in⟩ing divers of that trade &c:[4] 7: I return'd home. 9. A stranger preach'd on 2. *Rom* 7. I stayed at home all this Weeke. 16. Mr.   Preached on 2. *Cor:* 6. 3. 4. *Gospel* of the day,[5] shewing how afflictions perfected the Saints. 17. To *Lond:* 18 Visited ☆ & dined with her, thence to *Council.* 19 Dr. *Castillion*[6] preached on *be Carefull for nothing* &c. and

21. Dr. *Bathurst*[7] (*Deane* of Wells) coram rege on   *my burden is light*, incomparably.

23 (It being now *Lent time*) Dr. *LLoyd*[8] (my L: Tressurers *Chaplaine*) on *Acts*   : *But now God commands all men to repent* &c: on which he made a profitable discourse: he had ben formerly Curate of our Parish at *Deptford*: & coram rege the Bish: of *Chichester*[9] on 2. *Coloss:* 14. 15. admirably well,

---

[1] Thomas Pierce: above, iii. 183, &c. He did not become dean of Salisbury until 1675. The text is wrong; the Parable of the Husbandmen begins at verse 33.

[2] Christian, 1639–98; daughter of Sir Andrew Riccard, sometime governor of the East India Company; married first John Gayer; secondly Henry Rich, styled Lord Kensington; thirdly, between 1659 and 1662, Lord Berkeley: G.E.C.

[3] Remigius van Leemput, 1607–75, artist and collector; commonly called Remée or Remy: *D.N.B.*; Thieme, *Lexikon.*

[4] Andrews, p. 146. Saunders or sanders is sandalwood: *O.E.D.* For the present business see *Cal. S.P., Colonial, 1669–74*, no. 973.

[5] The first Sunday in Lent; the text forms part of the Epistle.

[6] John Castillion: above, iii. 8;

he was a chaplain in ordinary from *c.* 1663 to *c.* 1685. This was one of the Lenten sermons at court; it should have been preached by Dr. Pierce: list in *London Gazette*, 30 Jan. The text is Philippians iv. 6.

[7] Bathurst was dean of Wells from 1670 until his death in 1704. His text is St. Matthew xi. 30. Lenten sermon at court.

[8] The nonjuror. I have found no other notice of him as Clifford's chaplain. For the latter's conversion and reception into the Roman Catholic church see above, iii. 577; below, p. 14 n. Lloyd's text is Acts xvii. 30. Ash Wednesday had fallen on 12 February. This was the service for the royal household.

[9] Dr. Peter Gunning: above, iii. 190, &c. Lenten sermon at court.

as he can do nothing but well: 25. To *Council,* thence to visite ✡:

26 Dr. *Cradock*[1] *coram rege* 3. *Rom:* 24. Justified by free Grace: incomparably well:

28 Dr. *Stradling*[2] on   *James   Every man is Tempted when* &c: exceedingly well, and practicaly:

Mar: 2: Dr. *Smallwood*[3] at *W:hall* on   *Let us come with boldnesse to the throne of grace* &c: The *Communion* follow'd: *Coram Rege: Bish:* of *Oxon:*[4]   Matt   *Yea rather blessed are they who heare the word & keepe it* &c. I din'd at Mr. *V: Chamb:* 4: *Council,* visited ✡: 5: our New *Viccar Mr.*[a] *Holden*[5] in the Kings Chapell at *White-hall* before the household on   *Let your light so shine before men*: ⟨7⟩[b]: Deane of Sarum[6] on. 1. *Apoc.* 5.6. I returned home:

9 Our new *Minister* Mr. *Holden* preached 4: *Psal:* 6.7. shewing the difference of the Choice which the men of the world make, different from that of the Saints: This Gent: a

---

a Altered from *D'*:   b MS. *6.*

[1] Zachary Cradock, *c.* 1633–95; D.D. 1666; chaplain in ordinary *c.* 1665–95; provost of Eton 1681: *D.N.B.* Lenten sermon at court.

[2] Above, iii. 305; he was now dean of Chichester. His text is James i. 14. Lenten sermon at court; the preacher should have been the dean of Canterbury (Tillotson: above, iii. 517).

[3] Presumably Matthew Smalwood, *c.* 1615–83; D.D. 1660; chaplain in ordinary *c.* 1663–83; dean of Lichfield 1671: Foster. His text is Hebrews iv. 16 misquoted. The service for the household.

[4] Nathaniel Crew, 1633–1721; D.C.L. 1664; bishop of Oxford 1671; of Durham 1674; third Baron Crew of Stene 1697: *D.N.B.*; G.E.C. His text is St. Luke xi. 28. Lenten sermon at court.

[5] Richard Holden, *c.* 1627–1702. Son of William Holden, vicar of Whaplode, Lincs. Matriculated at Cambridge 1642 (Emmanuel; migrated to St. John's 1645); B.A. 1646; M.A. 1649; fellow of St. John's 1650; rector of Casterton Magna cum Pickworth, Rutland, 1653 (intruded 1650)–86; rector of Deptford 1673–1702 (admitted 27 Feb. 1673); rector of St. Dunstan's in the East 1686–98; author of *The Improvement of Navigation,* 1680 (Trinity House sermon): Venn; H. I. Longden, *Northamptonshire and Rutland clergy,* 1938–43; Newcourt, *Repertorium,* i. 334; Drake's Hasted, p. 30. The text is St. Matthew v. 16. The accuracy of the present notice is questionable; there was apparently only one sermon at court on Wednesdays in Lent; the preacher listed is Stillingfleet (above, iii. 407).

[6] Dr. Brideoake: above, p. 2. Lenten sermon at court.

very excellent & universal Scholar, a good & a wise man, but
he had not the popular way of preaching, nor in any measure
fit for our plain & vulgar auditorie, as had ⟨been⟩ his predecessor; though there were no comparison 'twixt their parts
for profound learning &c: but time, & experience, may forme
him to a more practical way, than that I find he now is in
of university lectures, & erudition, which is now universaly
left off, for a much more profitable:[1] *Pomeridiano* one Mr.
Holland[2] on. 4. *Coloss:* 1: shewing how Masters were the Lords
servants. 12: Dr. *Littleton*[3] preached at Lond: W:hall: on
  Aske and ye shall have &c *seeke & ye shall find* &c. very
excellently: ⟨14⟩ *Coram rege* Dr. *Thomas*[4] on 13. *Luke:* 3.
Except ye repent &c. 15. I heard the Speech made to the *Lords*
in their house by Sir *Sam: Tuke*, in behalfe of the *Papists*,
to take off the *Penal Laws*;[5] and then dined at Coll: *Nor-
woods*[6] with severall Lords &c: 16 Dr. Littleton to the family,
on   that Love the *L: Jesus in sincerity* &c a pathetical discourse:[7] Then *coram Rege* Dr. *Pierson* Bish: of *Chester*[8] on
9: Heb: how much more shall the bloud of Christ &c, a

---

[1] With this passage compare
Mitchell, *English pulpit oratory*, pp.
359–60; he refers to Evelyn's criticism of an earlier sermon, above, iii.
185–6.

[2] Described as curate of Deptford, below, p. 11; not further
identifiable.

[3] Adam Littleton, 1627–94; D.D.
1670; chaplain in ordinary *c.* 1672–
94; lexicographer: *D.N.B.* His text
is St. Matthew vii. 7; sermon
printed in his *Sixty one Sermons*,
1680, ii. 48–62. Lenten sermon at
court.

[4] William Thomas, 1614–89;
D.D. 1660; dean of Worcester from
1665 to 1683; bishop of St. David's
1677; of Worcester 1683: *D.N.B.*
Lenten sermon at court.

[5] The Test Act (see below, p. 7)
was before the lords in committee
this day. There appears to be no
other reference to Tuke's making a
speech on this occasion. The notice

may be incorrect: cf. above, iii. 249–
50.

[6] Henry Norwood, d. 1689; of
Leckhampton,   Gloucestershire;
royalist; an esquire of the body in
ordinary *c.* 1663–*c.* 1682; served in
various regiments 1661–*c.* 1669;
deputy-governor of Dunkirk 1662;
lieutenant - governor of Tangier
1666–*c.* 1669; commissioner for
Tangier 1673; M.P. for Gloucester
1675: S. Rudder, *New history of
Gloucestershire*, 1779, p. 521; P.R.O.,
S.P., Dom., Charles II, vol. 76, no.
67; Chamberlayne; Dalton, *English
army lists*, vol. i; Routh, *Tangier*;
&c. He was presumably the author
of 'A voyage to Virginia' in [A. and
T. Churchill], *Collection of Voyages*,
1704–32, vi. 143–70.

[7] The text is Ephesians vi. 24.
The family is the royal household.

[8] Pearson. Lenten sermon at
court.

most imcomparable sermon, from the most learned Divine of
our Nation. I dind at my L: *Arlingtons* with the *Duke*, &
Dutchesse of *Monmoth*[1] who is certainely one of the wisest &
craftiest of her sex; she has much witt: here was likewise the
learned *Isaac Vossius*.[2] 17: At *Council* about the *Barbados*
buisinesse: 18 home: 23: our *Viccar* on. 1. *Cor:* 6. 20:
Pomerid: the Curat. 1. *Cor:* 11. 28. 24 To *Lond:* to solemniz
the Passion-Weeke & heare the excellent Preaching which
there constantly is by the most eminent Bish: & Divines of
the Nation, during lent &c:

26 I was sworn a Younger-brother of the *Trinity Company*
with my most worthy & long acquainted noble friend My
Lord Ossorie Eldest sonn to the Duke of *Ormond*: Sir *Richard
Browne* my F. in *Law*, being now Master of that Society;
after which there was a greate Collation &c:

28 Preached *coram rege* the *Bish: of Rochester*[3] on 23. *Luke*.
34. being *Good-friday*, in a most passionat & pathe⟨t⟩ic discourse, according to his usual way:

29 I carried my Sonn to the *Bishop* of *Chichester* that
learned & pious man, Dr. *Peter Gunning*, to be instructed by
him before he received the holy *Sacrament*, when he gave him
most excellent advise, which I pray to God may influence, and
remaine with him as long as he lives;[4] and ô that I had ben so
blessed, and instructed, when first I was admitted to that
Sacred Ordinance! 30: Easter-day preached in the Morning

[1] Anne Scott, 1651–1732; succeeded as countess of Buccleuch
(Scotland) *suo jure* 1661; married
Monmouth 1663, he being then
created duke of Buccleuch (Scotland); a further grant, 1666, made
them duke and duchess of Buccleuch (Scotland) conjunctly and
severally, &c. The Scottish dignity
not being affected by Monmouth's
attainder by the English parliament
in 1685, she retained the dukedom
until her death (she is, however,
generally called the duchess of
Monmouth despite the attainder).
She married secondly, in 1688,
Charles Cornwallis, third Baron

Cornwallis of Eye (below, 6 Sept.
1680): G.E.C. 'Elle était pleine
d'*Agrémens*, & son Esprit avoit tous
ceux qui manquoient au *beau
Montmouth*': Hamilton, *Mémoires
de Grammont*, 1713, p. 389 (c. xi).
[2] Isaac Vossius (Vos), 1618–89;
D.C.L. 1670; divine and scholar:
D.N.B. For Evelyn's opinion of
him see also his letter to Pepys,
23 Sept. 1685 (Bohn, iii. 278).
[3] Dolben, preaching as dean of
Westminster. Lenten sermon at
court.
[4] Evelyn's son was now eighteen
years old. For his own confirmation see above, ii. 23.

one Mr. *Field*[1] . . . a Resurrection sermon with much eloquence: The Blessed *Communion* followd, at which both my
selfe, & my Sonne received, it being his first time, & with
that whole weekes more extraordinary preparation, I besech
God make him a sincere good Christian, whilst I endeavor
to instill into him the feare & love of God, & discharge the
Duty of a Father: The Sermon *Coram Rege* this day, was by
Dr. *Sparrow*[2] Bishop of *Excester*; but he spake so very low,
& the crowde so greate, that I could not heare him: however
I staied to see whither (according to custome[a]) the *Duke of
York* did Receive the Communion, with the *King*, but he did
not, to the amazement of every body; This being the second
yeare he had forborn & put it off,[3] & this being within a day
of the *Parliaments* sitting, who had Lately made so severe an
Act against the increase of *Poperie*,[4] gave exceeding griefe &
scandal to the whole Nation; That the heyre of it, & the sonn
of a Martyr for the *Protestant Religion*, should apostatize:
What[b] the Consequence of this will be God onely knows, &
Wise men dread: 31 I went home.

---

[a] Altered from *costome*.   [b] Altered from *G-*.

[1] Probably Robert Feild, *c.* 1638–
80; D.D. 9 July of this year; sub-
dean of York 1670–80: Foster.

[2] Anthony Sparrow, 1612–85;
D.D. 1661; bishop of Exeter 1667;
of Norwich 1676; author of *A
Rationale upon the Book of Common
Prayer*: *D.N.B.* The sermon should
have been preached by the lord
almoner, Henchman.

[3] James had spent the preceding
Easter at sea: *Cal. S.P., Dom.,
1671–2*, pp. 287, 291, 296, 304. On
5 June 1672, N.S., Colbert de Croissy,
the French ambassador, writes of
'les indices ou plutôt les preuves
manifestes que le duc d'York a
données de sa conversion': Mignet,
*Négociations relatives à la succession
d'Espagne*, iv. 42; but this perhaps
reflects the apprehensions of the
participants in the Secret Treaty of
Dover. The date of James's reception into the Roman Catholic
Church is not known. No formal
acknowledgement of his conversion
was published during Charles II's
reign.

[4] Parliament had adjourned on
29 March; on that day the king had
given his assent to the Test Act
(25 Car. II, c. 2), which required all
office-holders, civil, military, or
naval, to receive the sacrament according to the usage of the Church
of England, to take the Oaths of
Supremacy and Allegiance, and to
make a declaration against the doctrine of Transubstantiation, before
18 June (1 August for persons outside London, &c.); persons appointed
to office henceforward were to
qualify in the same way within a
stated period. The act was repealed,
so far as it concerned Protestant
nonconformists, in 1828, and so far
as it concerned Roman Catholics, in
1829.

Aprill: 6 There being no Communion at our Church, I went to *Greenewich* where a Chaplain of my L: *Ossories* preached on 4. *Hosea*. 14 in a pious discourse of Gods forbearance to correct incorrigible sinners any more: The Communion follow'd: *Pomerid*: our Curate on 1. *Cor*: 5.8. &c: 7 to Lond: to visite Mrs. *Blagg* at my *Lord Berkeleys*. 10 To Council, and thenc to thank Mr. Secretary,[1] for a kindnesse[a] don my *Lady Tuke*: 11 I dined with the *Plenepotentiaries* Designed for the Treaty of *Nimegen*,[2] where was a greate feast, & thence home: ⟨13⟩[b] Our *Minister* on 12 *Rom*: 17: Not to render Evil for Evil &c: *Pomerid*: our *Curate* on 2. *Jam*: 19: That some men were worse than even the *Devils* themselves, who never blasphem'd, that we reade of 'til the *Incarnation*, as hoping (likely) that Christ, would have rather taken the nature of *Angels* than of *Man*, which when he found he did not, he rag'd & blasphem'd &c:

14 I went to *Lond*: with my Wife. 15 We both visited Mrs. Blagg, & 17th: I carried my *Lady Tuke* to visite, & thank the Countesse of *Arlington*, for speaking to his *Majestie* in her behalfe about being one of the *Queene Consorts* Women:[3] she carried us up into her new dressing roome at Goring house,[4] where was a bed, 2 glasses, silver jarrs & Vasas, Cabinets & other so rich furniture, as I had seldom seene the like; to this excesse of superfluity were we now ariv'd, & that not onely

---

[a] Or *kendnesse*.   [b] MS. *12*.

---

[1] Arlington; for Lady Tuke's appointment see below.
[2] Negotiations for a general peace began at Cologne in June; the English plenipotentiaries were Sir Joseph Williamson, Sir Leoline Jenkins (above, iii. 499), and Sunderland; the latter, who was ambassador at Paris, did not attend. The negotiations were broken off in April 1674; meanwhile, on 9/19 February England had made a separate peace with the United Provinces, by the Treaty of Westminster. New negotiations for a general peace began at Nimeguen in January 1676 and resulted in August 1678 in a treaty between France and the United Provinces; other treaties were made between the various belligerents in the following months.

[3] Warrants for the payment of £300 per annum as salary and £60 per annum as board wages (in lieu of diet) to Lady Tuke as a dresser in ordinary to the queen were issued on 22 May: *Cal. S.P., Dom., 1673*, p. 283.

[4] It is Lady Arlington's dressing-room.

at Court, but almost universaly, even to wantonesse, & profusion:

19 I went to *Parsons Greene* to visite the Vicountesse Mordant, that virtuous Creature, & our long & intimate acquaintance abroad:[1]

20 Dr. *Stillingfleete*[2] made an incomparable sermon on 6: Matt: 33. before the family: *Coram rege* Dr. *Compton*[3] (bro: to the E: of *Northampton*) on: 1. *Cor:* 11.16. shewing the churches powers in ordaining things Indifferent: This worthy Persons Talent is not preaching; but he is like to make a grave & serious good man:

This Evening Mrs. *Thornhill*,[4] sister to the Earle of Bath, & a relation of ours, shewed my Wife and me her Majesties rich *Toylet* in her Dressing roome, which being all of Massie Gold, & presented her by the King, was valued at 4000 pounds.

22 I visited my *Lord Tressurer* (who had lately ben my bro: Commissioner for the sick & Wounded) who was ever more than ordinarily kind to me, even to intimacy & friendship:

23 I dind at my L: *Arlingtons*; Thence to Council, where there was a Cause pleaded before us:

24 I was sent by his Majestie into the *Citty* to borrow ten-thousand Pounds, upon the third quarter Tax, *per*[a] advance for the Sick & Wounded & Prisoners at War: &c.[5]

---

[a] MS. *pr*.

---

[1] Evelyn mentions meeting Lady Mordaunt first in 1655, after his return to England.

[2] Above, iii. 407.

[3] Above, iii. 533; his brother, iii. 228.

[4] Joanna, 1635–1709 (1708?), daughter of Sir Bevil Grenville (1596–1643: *D.N.B.*) and sister of John Grenville, first earl of Bath (below, p. 95); married, 1653, as his second wife, Col. Richard Thornhill, *c.* 1614–*c.* 1657, of Olanteigh, Wye, Kent; one of the queen's dressers from at least 1669 to 1676 or later; living in France 1675–9. Her only traceable relationship to

Evelyn is through her husband, whose first wife was Frances, daughter of Evelyn's 'nearest kinsman' Gregory Cole (above, iii. 470): R. Granville, *Hist. of the Granville family*, 1895; *Life of . . . Dennis Granville*, 1902, pp. 155–205; W. S. Morris, *Hist. . . . of Wye*, 1842, pp. 68–9; C. S. Orwin and S. Williams, *Hist. of Wye Church*, &c., n.d. [1913?], p. 58; Vivian, *Visitations of Devon*, p. 215; Chamberlayne; Foster, *Alumni Oxon*.

[5] The sum of £1,238,750, granted to Charles by parliament on 29 March, was to be raised in six quarterly instalments.

25 I returned home to entertaine the Resident of *Hambrow*:[1] 27: To Lond: to Council:[2]

⟨27⟩[a] Dr. *Compton* pr: at W.hall to the household on: 10: *Luke* 42, Thence at St. *Martines* the *Minister* on 1. *Cor:* 11. 29 the holy *Sacrament* following: which I partooke of upon Obligation of the Late *Act* of *Parliament*,[3] injoyning every body in Office Civil or Militarie, under penalty of 500 pounds, to receive the holy Sacrament within one moneth, before two authentique Wittnesses: so as I had besides Dr. *Lamplughs*[4] the Viccars hand, the two *Church-Wardens* also ingrossed in parchment to be afterwards producd in the Court of *Chancery* or some other Court of Record: which I did at the *Chancery* barr, as being one of the *Council* of *Plantations* & *Trade*, [*May* 3][b] taking then also the *Oath* of *Allegiance* & *Supremacy*, signing the clause in the said Act against *Transubstantiation*. Dined at Mr. *Herveys*[5] the Queens Tressurer with Mr. *Sid: Godolphin*.[6] 4 A stranger at *White hall*, first sermon on 10: *Heb:* 21 & *Coram Rege* Dr. *Fell* Deane of Christ-Church *Oxford*: on 1. Cor: 13. ult. when I also received the *B: Sacrament*: it being the first Sonday in the Moneth: 6: I dined with Mrs. *Blagg* at *Berkeley* house: 7: At *Council*, my L: Chancelor being our President, being present: 8: Ascension—pr: at St. *Martines* Dr. *Lam⟨p⟩lugh* on 1. *Heb:* 13: The holy Comm: follow'd, & so home to my house: 11: I had a greate swelling in my face, & could not go to Church: 13: Buisinesse caled me to Lond: where I stayed til the 16: 18 Mr. *Plume* at

---

a MS. *26*.   b Marginal date.

---

[1] Presumably Vinzent Garmers: above, iii. 288, 585.

[2] The date is presumably wrong.

[3] The Test Act, passed on 29 March: above, p. 7. Besides forfeiting £500, persons who continued to exercise their offices without qualifying were to be deprived of important civil rights. For the time allowed see p. 7 n.

[4] Thomas Lamplugh, *c.* 1618–91; D.D. 1660; chaplain in ordinary *c.* 1665–76; vicar of St. Martin in the

Fields 1670–6; dean of Rochester 1673; bishop of Exeter 1676; archbishop of York 1688: *D.N.B.*

[5] John Hervey: above, iii. 165.

[6] Sidney Godolphin, 1645–1712; created Baron Godolphin of Rialton 1684; earl of Godolphin 1706; the statesman: *D.N.B.* At this time he was one of the grooms of the bedchamber. In 1675 he married Margaret Blagge and became a friend of Evelyn. Further notices below.

Greenewich (there being no Communion at our Church) on: 2: *Acts*: 1.2. a very choice discourse (*opus diei*)[1] the Bl: Sacr: followed: *Pomerid*: our Curate on 16. Joh: 8. of the Conviction of sin &c: Gods *Justice* in punishing it &c: ⟨19⟩[a] I went to *Lond:* with Mr. *Bernard Greenevill*[2] bro: to the *Earle* of *Bath* & one of the *Groomes* of his *Majesties Bed-chamber*: who with his Lady, & Lady Catharin *Morley*,[3] Mrs. *Howard*,[4] one of the *Maids* of honour, came to dine with us: 20: I visited ☆ & returned home: 21: Came to see us[b] & Dine with me, my Lord Jo: *Berkeley*[5] and his Lady, my deare Friends Mrs. Blagg, Mr. *Sidny Godolphin* (a *grome* of the Bedchamber) Sir Robert Morray, Mr. *Lucie Gore*,[6] & Sir *Elis Leighton*[7] &c:

25 Our Viccar on 19 *Psal:* 13. of the Danger of presumptuous sinns: *Pomerid*: the *Curate* Mr. *Holland*[8] on 16 St. Joh: 8. as the Sonday before: 26: Trinity Moneday The *Bishop* of *Rochester* at our church: before the *Trinity Comp:* on 107: *Psal:* 23.24 of usefull matter: My F: in Law Sir *Rich: Bro:*

---

[a] MS. *29*.   [b] Altered from *me*.

[1] The day is Whit-Sunday (Pentecost); the text forms part of the passage 'For the Epistle' of that day.

[2] Bernard Granville (Grenville, &c.), 1631–1701; brother of Mrs. Thornhill (above, p. 9); M.P. for Liskeard 1661; Launceston (or Saltash) 1678/9; Saltash 1681; Plymouth 1685; Saltash in the Convention; Launceston 1690; and Lostwithiel 1695. A groom of the bedchamber 1672–85. Envoy extraordinary to Savoy and Genoa 1675–6. His wife was Anne, daughter of Cuthbert Morley of Hawnby, Yorkshire, N.R. They were the parents of George Granville, Lord Lansdowne (*D.N.B.*): Granville, *Granville family*, pp. 404–6, &c.; *V.C.H.*, *Yorkshire, N.R.*, ii. 33; Chamberlayne; *Cal. S.P., Dom.*; see also *Life of Mrs. Godolphin*, p. 66. Granville's marriage licence (1664) gives his wife as Anne, daughter of James Morley of St. Martin in the Fields: *London marriage licences*; this is presumably an error.

[3] Catherine, d. 1693; daughter of Sir Francis Leeke, first earl of Scarsdale; wife of Cuthbert Morley of Hawnby; mother of Mrs. Granville: (*Westminster Abbey registers*), p. 231.

[4] Dorothy Howard: above, iii. 529.

[5] Lord Berkeley of Stratton: above, iii. 445, &c.; his lady, iv. 3.

[6] Presumably the name is a phonetic spelling of Leveson Gower; and the person, William Gower, d. 1691; assumed the additional name Leveson c. 1668; succeeded as fourth baronet 1689: G.E.C., *Baronetage*, i. 147.

[7] Above, iii. 516.

[8] Above, p. 5.

being *Master*, Sir *Jer: Smith*[1] (one of the Commissioners of the Navy & a stout sea-man, who had interposed & saved the Duke from perishing by a fireship in the late Warr) succeeding: My Sonn, was now sworn a Younger brother, there was a mighty feast: 28. I carried one *Withers* an ingenious *Shipwright*, to the *King*, to shew his Majestie some new method of building &c: 29: preached Mr. *Woodruffe*[2] *coram rege*, it being his Majesties Birthday, on 126. *Psal:* 1.

I saw the *Italian* Comedie[3] act at the Court this afternoone.[a]

June 1: At St. *Martines* a stranger on ⟨⟩ *In the last*[b] *days perilous times shall come &c: men shall be lovers of Pleasures* &c.[4] Shewing the danger of self-love: The holy communion follow'd: 3. I dined with my deare friend at *B: house*: 5. I went to my *L: Tressurer* for Mony, & then to Says-Court: 8: Both *Viccar* & *Curate* preached on their former Text. 10 To *Lond:* return'd the next day: 12 Came to Visite and dine with me, my Lord V: Count Cornbery & his Lady, My Lady *Francis Hyde*[5] Sister to the *Duchesse* of *York*, Mrs. *Dorothy*

---

[a] Followed by *& so went home* deleted. [b] Followed by *times* deleted.

[1] Jeremiah Smith, d. 1675; knighted 1665; admiral: *D.N.B.*; *Mariner's Mirror*, xii (1926), 258–9. He was comptroller of victualling from 1669 to 1675. The deed to which Evelyn refers took place during the Battle of Lowestoft, 3 June 1665 (see above, iii. 410), when Smith brought his own ship, the *Mary*, between the duke of York's ship and an attacking Dutch man-of-war, the *Orange*: James II, *Life*, ed. Clarke, i. 413; Pepys, 8 June 1665.

[2] Presumably Benjamin Woodroffe, 1638–1711; D.D. 14 Jan. 1673; at this time chaplain to the duke of York as lord high admiral; chaplain in ordinary *c.* 1682–*c.* 1688: *D.N.B.*; Chamberlayne.

[3] A troupe of Italian players was here from April to September under the leadership of 'Scaramouche', i.e. Tiberio Fiorilli, 1608–94, who adopted the name of his principal

characterization: Boswell, *Restoration court stage*, pp. 118–19 (the citation there from *Letters to Sir Joseph Williamson* establishes the identification); A. Constantini, *Birth . . . of Scaramouche* (1695), trans. C. W. Beaumont, 1924, preface, pp. xxxiii–xxxvii. For Fiorilli see *Encic. italiana*; L. Rasi, *I Comici italiani*, 1897–1905. Further notice below, p. 75.

[4] 2 Timothy iii. 1, &c.

[5] Francis, 1658–1726; Clarendon's youngest daughter and sister of Cornbury as well as of the first duchess of York (who had died in 1671); married, 1675, Thomas Keightley, 1650?–1719, son of Evelyn's cousin William Keightley (above, ii. 149, &c.). Keightley was an Irish official; Lady Francis appears to have been a source of anxiety to him and to her brothers: *D.N.B.*, art. Keightley, and sources there indicated; &c.

Howard Mayd of *Honour*: We all went after dinner to see the formal, & formidable Camp, on Black-heath, raised to invade Holland, or as others suspected for another designe &c[1]—: Thence to the *Italian Glasse-house* at *Greenewich*, where was Glasse blowne of finer mettal, than that of *Muran* &c:—[2]

13 Came to visite us my *Lady Carr*[3] (sister to my *L: Chamb:* & Wife to the *Chancelor* of the *Dutchy*) Lady *Scroope*,[4] Lady *Stanhop*,[5] Mrs. *Baron*, & Mrs. *Sidly*,[6] daughter to Sir *Charles*, who was none of the most virtuous, but a Witt &c: 15 our *Viccar* on: 11: *Matt* 30. describing the ease of Christian *Professors*: *Pomerid*: Curat: on: 1. *Pet:* 5.9. 16 To *Lond:* to our *Council*. 17 Din'd with Mrs. *Blagg*, at *B: house*, thence to Mr. *Dicksons*[a][7] the Painters, to whom she sate the first time for her picture, which I desired her to give me: 19 I din'd at my Bro: *Evelyns*, Visited my *Sister*; Con-

---

[1] Charles arranged to hold a general review of all his forces on Blackheath on 14 June; it was estimated that there would be 12,000 foot present. They had been sent elsewhere by 14 July: *Cal. S.P., Dom.*, *1673*, pp. 287, 293, 353, 431, 437. The suspected other design is that mentioned by Marvell: 'The dark hovering of that Army so long at *Black-Hearth*, might not improbably seem the gatherings of a Storm to fall upon *London* . . .': *Account of the Growth of Popery*, 1677, p. 46.

[2] Buckingham is said to have had a glasshouse here from at least 1663, but no documents are cited: W. A. Thorpe, *Hist. of English and Irish Glass*, 1929, i. 101 (citing A. Hartshorne, *Old English glasses*, 1897, p. 225). For Buckingham's factory at Lambeth see below, pp. 98–9.

[3] Above, iii. 358, 372. Her brother, Arlington, did not become lord chamberlain until 1674; Sir Robert Carr was appointed chancellor of the duchy in 1672. A letter from Mrs. Evelyn to Lady Carr, 26 March 1672, shows their relations: Bohn, iv. 32–3.

[4] Above, iii. 275. She was a sister-in-law of Lady Carr.

[5] Dorothy, c. 1621–86; daughter of Sir John Livingstone; wife of Charles Stanhope, second Baron Stanhope of Harrington: G.E.C.

[6] Catharine Sedley, 1657–1717; mistress of James II c. 1677 to 1685 or 1686; created countess of Dorchester 1686; married 1696 Sir David Colyear (d. 1730), created Lord Portmore (Scotland) 1699; earl of Portmore (Scotland), 1703. Her father was Sir Charles Sedley, 1639–1701, the dramatist: for both see *D.N.B.*; V. de Sola Pinto, *Sir Charles Sedley*, 1927.

[7] Identifiable as Matthew Dixon, d. 1710, active from 1671: C. H. Collins Baker, *Lely*, &c.; very few works by him are known. The present picture is the portrait of Margaret Blagge with the urn, now at Wotton; reproduction in the *Life of Mrs. Godolphin*. For the attitude and accessories see the *Life*, p. 71.

gratulated the new Lord Tressurer Sir Tho: *Osborn*, a Gent: whom I had ben intimately acquainted with at *Paris*, & who was every day at my F in *Laws* house & Table there; on which account I was too Confident of succeeding in his favour, as I had don in his Predecessors; but such a friend never shall I find, & I neglected my time, far from believing that my *Lord Clifford* would have so rashly laied down his staffe as he did, to the amazement of all the World; when it came to the Test of his receiving the Communion; which I am confident he forbore, more for some promise he had entered into, to gratifie the *Duke*, than for any prejudice to the *Protestant* Religion, though I found him wavering of a prety while:[1] 20 I returned home, where I found my *Nephew Geo:*[2] & his *Lady*. 22: our *Viccar* as above. 23. To *Lond*, to accompanie our Council, who went in body to congratulate the new L: *Treasurer*, no friend to it, because promoted by my L: *Arlington* whom he hated:[3] 24: Dind with Mrs. Blagg: 25. her Picture was finished &c: 25 Visited my L: *Clifford* late Lord Tressurer: returned home. 26: Came my *Bro: Evelyn*, my *Sister* of *Woodcott*, my *Niepce Montague* & severall persons of quality from Court, to dine with me, and

---

[1] Osborne (above, iii. 21, &c.) was at present Viscount Oseburne of Dunblane (Scotland); and was created Viscount Latimer of Danby on 15 August. Clifford, who had not complied with the Test Act (above, p. 7), had this morning surrendered his white staff as lord high treasurer to Charles II, who had thereupon delivered it to Osborne: *London Gazette*, 23 June. The duke of York had resigned his offices on 15 June; Clifford's resignation was due not to any intention of standing by him but to his own sincerity in religious matters. His conversion to Roman Catholicism was a slow process; the Test Act perhaps forced him to make up his mind. His reception into the Roman Catholic Church perhaps took place on 17 May: Hartmann, *Clifford*, pp.

270–84. Evelyn was dependent on the lord high treasurer for supplies for the sick and wounded; he had also a private interest, the satisfaction of Sir Richard Browne's claims as ambassador in France during the Civil War and the period of exile: see below, p. 20.

[2] Above, ii. 97, &c. His wife was Catherine, daughter of Robert Gore of Chelsea, a merchant; he had married her in 1667: Foljambe, p. 74; *London marriage licences.*

[3] Arlington appears to be an error for Shaftesbury, the chief promoter of the council and from 9 November of this year the declared enemy of the court party. Evelyn probably alludes to the abolition of the council on 21 Dec. 1674; for the reasons for it see below, p. 50.

see the army,[a] still remaining Encamp'd on Black-heath:[1] next day came & din'd with me my *Lady Blount*,[2] her sonn, & two Daughters: together with my Lord *Manchester*:[3] 29: our *Viccar* preach'd on 8: *Matt:* 30: In the afternoone our *Curate* on[b] the Gospel of the day, &c:

July to *Lond* about buisinesse, supped with Mrs. *Blagg*: 6: Dr. *Durell*[4] (*Deane* of *Winsor*) preached on 7: *Joh:* 37.38, shewing the sweete invitations of the Spirit: The 2d Serm: *Coram rege* by Dr. Parry[5] on   *Except your righteousnesse exceede* &c: This evening I went to the funerall of my deare & excellent friend, that good Man & accomplish'd Gent: *Sir Rob: Moray*, Secretary of Scotland: he was buried by his Majestie in *Westminster* Abby:[6] 7: I went to Council:

8 To visite ✩, and in the afternoone with my *Lady Berkeley* in the Dutchesse of *Albemarls* Coach,[7] to *Twicknam* to see Mrs. *Talbot*,[8] the next day I returned home:

---

[a] Substituted for *Camp*.   [b] Followed by *8 Matt:* deleted.

---

[1] See above, p. 13.

[2] Perhaps Hester, daughter of Christopher Wase of Islington; married first Sir William Mainwaring; secondly (before 1649) Sir Henry Blount (above, iii. 233); she was probably a first cousin of Sir Samuel Tuke and of Christopher Wase the poet: G.E.C., *Baronetage*, iv. 113; see also *Notes and Queries*, clxi (1931), 345–6. For other possible identifications see G.E.C., *Baronetage*, ii. 202–3.

[3] Robert Montagu, 1634–83; third earl of Manchester 1671: *D.N.B.*, art. Montagu, Edward, second earl.

[4] Durel was not appointed dean of Windsor until 1677 (he died on 8 June 1683); he was a chaplain in ordinary from *c.* 1672 until his death.

[5] Probably Benjamin Parry, 1634–78; D.D. 1670; bishop of Ossory 1678; at this time a prebendary of York; otherwise his brother, John Parry, d. 1677; D.D.

1662; bishop of Ossory 1672: for both men see *D.N.B.* The text is St. Matthew v. 20.

[6] He had died suddenly on the Friday: see also *Letters . . . to Sir Joseph Williamson*, i. 94 (Camden Soc., new ser., vol. viii, 1874). He had acted as deputy-secretary for Lauderdale, the secretary for Scotland, at various times between 1663 and 1670: Robertson, *Life of Moray*, pp. 115–43.

[7] Elizabeth, 1654–1734; daughter of Henry Cavendish, second duke of Newcastle; married 1669, Christopher Monck, 1653–88, second duke of Albemarle 1670; married secondly in 1692, when insane, Ralph Montagu, earl and later duke of Montagu (below, p. 90): *D.N.B.*, arts. Monck, Montagu; E. F. Ward, *Christopher Monck, duke of Albemarle*, 1915.

[8] Identifiable as Katherine, d. 1678, daughter of Col. Matthew Boynton; maid of honour to the queen 1662–9; married 1669 Col.

13 Our *Viccar* as formerly, of the Constancy of the Saints: *Pomerid*. Curate on 39. *Psal:* 5. concerning preparation to Death: The minister himselfe so weake, that I was expecting when he himselfe should faint away. 14 To *Lond:* to sp⟨e⟩ake with my L. *Arlington*, and returned: ⟨20⟩[a] our *Viccar* as before: *Pomerid*: the Curate of *Greenewich* there, on: 118 *Psal* 18.

⟨21⟩[b] To *Lond:* Council: 21 I spake with his *Majestie* about the sick & Wounded & returned home.

25 I went to *Tunbridge* Wells, to visite my *Lord Clifford*, Late *L: Tressurer*, who was ther to divert his mind, more than body, that he had so engag'd himselfe to the Duke (as was believed) that rather than take the *Test*, without which he could[c] be capable of no office, he would resigne that greate & honorable station; This, I am confident grieved him to the heart, & at last broke it; for though he carried with him musique & people to divert him, & when I came to see him, Lodged ⟨me⟩[d] in his owne appartmen⟨t⟩, & would not let me go from him, I found he was struggling in his mind, & being of a rough & ambitios nature, could not long brooke the necessitie he had brought on himselfe of submission to this conjuncture; besides that he saw the *Dutch-Warr*,[e] which was made much by his advise, as well as the shutting up of the Exchequer, very unprosperous: These things his high spirit could not support.[1] 26. I went to the *Wells* with my Lord,

---

a MS. *19*. b MS. *20*. c Followed by *kepe no of-* deleted.
d MS. *in*. e Followed by *to which* deleted.

Richard Talbot (below, p. 23): P. W. Sergeant, *Little Jennings and fighting Dick Talbot*, 1913, pp. 164 n., 205–6, 266, &c. For Talbot's occupying a house in Twickenham in 1674 see Sergeant, p. 257.

[1] Clifford's health apparently began to break down as early as 1670; he visited Bath in 1672; his illness appears to have been strangury or the stone: Hartmann, *Clifford*, pp. 240–1, 297–8; for a regimen for him at this time see ibid., pp. 285–6. While the chief responsibility for

the third Dutch War rests with Charles II, Clifford was his principal minister and adviser in the negotiations leading to it (in July 1668 he is reported as saying, in reference to the good reception of the Triple Alliance by parliament, 'Well, for all this noise, we must yet have another war with the Dutch before it be long': Sir W. Temple, *Works*, 1770, i. 463). For his conduct as regards the Test Act see above, p. 14 n.; for his share in the Stop of the Exchequer, iii. 607 n.

& visited my *Lady Henrietta Hyde*:[1] 27: Sunday, was no [pub:][a] prayers in the morning:[2] but in the afternoone I heard Prayers at my Lady *Henriettas*: so having staied here two or 3 daies I obtain'd leave of my Lord, that I might returne, by the way I saw my Lord of *Dorsets house* at *Knowle* neere *Sevenock* a greate old fashiond house &c.[3]

30 To *Lond:* to Council, where the buisinesse of Transporting Wooll was brought before us: I dined at the *Countesse* of *Suffolcks*[4] in her Lodging, groome of the *stole* to her Majestie, who used me with greate respect. 31 I went home, turning in, as I went through Cheape side to see the Pictures of all the Judges & Eminent men of the Long robe newly painted by Mr. *Write*, & set up in *Guild-hall* costing the Citty 1000 pounds: most of them are very like the Persons they are made to represent, though I never tooke *Write* to be any considerable artist.[5]

Aug: 3 our *Viccar* on 1. *Sam:* 3. 18. That God does not immediately punish sinn, & that it was a warning to *Eli*: I received the holy Sacrament:

6 To *Lond:* to the Commissioners of the *Admiralty*[6] about buisinesse & returned:

---

a Interlined.

---

[1] Above, iii. 446.

[2] Tunbridge Wells had as yet no church: see above, iii. 295 n.

[3] Knole; the house dates mainly from the sixteenth century or earlier. For it see V. Sackville-West, *Knole and the Sackvilles*, 1922. The present owner was Richard Sackville, 1622–77, fifth earl of Dorset 1652: *D.N.B.*, art. Sackville, Sir Edward.

[4] Barbara, 1622–81, daughter of Sir Edward Villiers; married 1651 ?, as her third husband, James Howard, 1620–89, third earl of Suffolk 1640; groom of the stole, mistress of the robes, and keeper of the privy purse to the queen 1662–81: G.E.C.; P. W. Sergeant, *My Lady Castlemaine*, 1912, p. 57.

[5] By an act of parliament, 18 and 19 Car. II, c. 7, the judges of the king's bench and common pleas and the barons of the exchequer were appointed to decide all disputes between landlords and tenants relating to buildings burnt or demolished during the Fire of London. Wright painted in all twenty-two full-length portraits; they are still preserved in the Guildhall. He is said to have received £60 apiece for them: H. Walpole, *Anecdotes of painting in England*, ed. Wornum, 1862, ii. 473.

[6] The Admiralty had been put into commission on 9 July, following the duke of York's resignation on 15 June.

10 Our *Viccar* as before; Pomerid, at *Grenewich* the *Curate* on 5. *Mat:* 4 upon one of the beatitudes &c: 13 I rid to *Durdens* where I dined at my L: *Berkeleys* of *Berkely Castle* my old & noble friend; it being his Wedding *Anniversarie* where at a mighty feast,[1] I found the Dutchesse of Albemarle, my Sister Evelyn, N: Montague & much companie, & so return'd home that evening late:

15[a] Came to visite me my Lord Chancelor the Earle of Shaftsbery. Then I went to *Lond:* having buisinesse both at the Admiralty, & L: Treasurer: and so home: 17 Our *Viccar* on 2. Pet: 1. 16. of the veracity of the Gospel, & its wonderfull propagation: *Pomerid*, a stranger on 5. *Matt:* 16. a pious discourse of exemplarie walking &c:

18 To Lond: to speak with his Majestie: My *Lord Clifford* being about this time returned from *Tunbridge* where I left him, & now preparing for Devonshire, I went to take my Leave of him at Wallingford house,[2] where he was packing up of Pictures, most of which were of hunting wild beasts, & vast pieces of bull-baiting, beare baiting &c:[3] with other furniture: I found him in his study, & restored to him several papers of state, & other importances, which he had furnished me with, upon ingaging me to write the historie of the Holland War; with other private letters of his acknowledgements to my L: *Arlington*, who of a private Gent: of a very noble family, but inconsiderable fortune, had advanc'd him from almost nothing:[4] The first thing was his being a Parlia-

---

[a] Reading doubtful.

---

[1] Lady Berkeley was Elizabeth, d. 1708, daughter of John Massingberd, treasurer of the East India Company; the marriage took place on 11 Aug. 1646: G.E.C.

[2] Above, iii. 490. Clifford had occupied it at least since December 1672: *Cal. Treasury Books, 1672–5*, p. 23. It was afterwards occupied by his successor, Danby.

[3] None of these pictures survives:

see Hartmann, p. 289.

[4] On Clifford's early relations with Arlington see also Povy's statement, in Pepys, 24 June 1667. Evelyn told Pepys that Clifford's income when he first entered political life was 'about seven-score pounds a year': ibid., 26 April 1667. He belonged to a younger branch of the Westmorland family of Clifford.

ment man,[1] then knighted, then made one of the *Commissioners* of the Sick & Wounded,[a] upon which occasion we sate long together:[2] then on the death of Hugh Pollard,[3] he was made Comptroller of the Household & Privy Counselor, yet still my bro: Commissioner: after the death of my *L: Fitzharding*[4] *Treasurer* of the Houshold, which (by letters of his my L: Arlington has shew'd me) he beging of his Lordship to obtaine for him as the very height of his ambition, with such submissions, & professions of his patronage, & being totaly his creature,[b] as I had never seene more accknowledging: The Earle of *Southampton* then dying,[5] & he with others made one of the Commissioners of the *Treasury*, his Majestie inclining to put it into one hand, my L: *Clifford*[c] under pretence of making all his Interest for his Patron my L: *Arlington*, cutt the Grasse under his feete & procur'd it for himselfe, assuring the King, that my L:A: did not desire it, & indeede my Lord A: has himselfe protested to me, that his Confidence in my L: *Clifford*, made him so remisse, & his affection to him so particular that was absolutely minded to devolve it on my L: Clifford, that was his Creature, all the world knowing how himselfe affected Ease & quiet, now growing into Yeares, but yet little thinking of go-by:[6] This was the onely greate

---

[a] Followed by *in which* deleted.
[b] Followed by & deleted.
[c] Followed by *pretend pre-* deleted.

---

[1] M.P. for Totnes in the Convention Parliament and again in 1661. According to Wood he was 'a frequent and forward Speaker, especially in behalf of the Kings Prerogative': *Fasti*, in *Athenæ*, 1691–2, ii. 772.

[2] The commissioners were appointed in October 1664: above, iii. 387–8. Clifford was not knighted until 1665.

[3] Above, iii. 344; Clifford's appointment (28 Nov. 1666), pp. 469–70. He was appointed a privy councillor on 5 Dec. 1666.

[4] Above, iii. 251. He died on 12 June 1668; the warrant for Clifford's appointment as treasurer of the household was issued on 14 June: *Cal. S.P., Dom., 1667–8*, p. 436; see also *London Gazette*, 15 June 1668.

[5] He died on 16 May 1667; Clifford was one of the commissioners appointed on 24 May following.

[6] Clifford's promotion (28 Nov. 1672) was due to his being, in view of Charles's policy at the time, the most suitable man for the post. Arlington complained to Colbert de Croissy about his behaviour; while Clifford opposed the conferring of any further dignities or honours on Arlington: Barbour, *Arlington*, pp. 205–6.

ingratitude which my L: *Clifford* shew'd, keeping my Lord
Ar: in ignorance, whom he ⟨continualy⟩ᵃ assurd, he was pursuing his Interest, which was the *Duke*,ᵇ intoᵇ whose greate
favour *Clifford* was now gotten, but which did certainely cost
him the losse of all; namely his going so irrevocably far in his
Interest: &c:¹ For the rest my Lord *Clifford* was a valiant,
uncorrupt gent: ambitious, not Covetous, generous, Passionate, and a most constantᶜ sincere friend to me in particular;
so as when he lay'd downe his office, I was at the end of all
my hopes, and endeavors; which were not for high matters,
but to obtaine what his *Majestie* was realy indebted to my
F. in law, which was the uttmost of my ambition, and which
I had undoubtedly don, if this friend had stood; he who succeeded him, Sir *Thomas Osborn*, though much more obliged
to my F in Law & his family, & my long & old acquaintance;
being of a more haughty & far lesse obliging nature, & from'
which I could hope for little; a man of excellent natural
parts, but nothing generous or gratefull:² Well, thus taking
Leave of my L: *Clifford*, wringing me by the hand, & earnestly
looking onᵈ me, he bid me *god buy*,ᵉ adding, Mr. E: I shall
never see thee more; no ⟨said⟩ᶠ I my L: whats the meaning
of this? I hope I shall see you often, and as greate a person
againe; No Mr. E: do not expect it, I will never see this
Place, this Citty or Court againe, or words of this sound: In
this manner, not without mutual tears almost Iᵍ parted from
him: nor long was it after, but the newes was, that he was
dead; and as I have heard from some that I believe knew,

ᵃ MS. *continuely*. ᵇ⁻ᵇ Or *Dukes into*. ᶜ Altered from *constantly*.
ᵈ Altered from *one*. ᵉ Followed by *Mr* deleted. ᶠ MS. *saided*.
ᵍ Substituted for *he*.

---

¹ For Evelyn's views on Clifford's
fall and on his relations with the
duke of York see above, p. 14. The
account given in James II, *Life*, ed.
Clarke, i. 481–2, of their relations at
the time of Clifford's appointment as
lord high treasurer does not occur in
Carte's extracts from James's original memoranda, in James Macpherson, ed., *Original papers*, 1775,
i. 67.
² Whatever Osborne's defects
may have been, he was a good business man; during the greater part
of his period of office strict economy
was necessary.

made himselfe a way, after an extraordinary Melancholy:[1]
This is not confidently affirm'd; but a servant who lived in
the house, & afterward with Sir *Ro: Clayton*[2] L: Mayor,[a] did
report it, as well as others; & when I hinted some such thing
to Mr. *Prideaux*[3] one of his *Trustees*, he was not willing to
enter into that discourse: but tis reported with these particulars, That causing his Servant to leave him one morning
unusualy, locking himselfe in, he strangled himselfe with his
Cravett, upon the bed *Tester*: His Servant not liking his manner of dissmissing, & looking through the *key hole* (as I remember) & seeing his Master hanging, brake in before he was quite
dead, & taking him downe, vomiting out a greate deale of
bloud, was heard to utter these words; Well, let men say what
they will, there is a God, a just God above, after which he
spake no more &c: This if true, is dismal, and realy, he was
the chiefe occasion of the *Dutch Warr*, & of all that bloud
which was lost at *Bergen*, in attaquing the Smyrna fleete, &
that whole quarell &c:[4] which leads me to the calling to mind,
what my Lord Chancellor affirm'd not to me onely, but to all
my brethren (the Councel of forraine *Plantations*) when not

---

[1] Clifford died on 13 October.
The only other known contemporary
allusion to his supposed suicide
occurs in the pseudo-Marvellian 'An
Historicall Poem' (*c.* 1680):
  'Clifford and Hide before had lost
      the day,
  One hang'd himself, the other
      fled away.'
(Reprinted in Marvell, *Poems*, &c.,
ed. Margoliouth, i. 204.) There is
no known authentic account of
Clifford's death; it was almost
certainly due to natural causes and
the details of the story given by
Evelyn are clearly suspicious; but
there remains a possibility that in
the course of his sufferings Clifford
did something that hastened his
end. For a refutation of Evelyn's
story see G. Oliver, *Cliffordiana*,

[*c.* 1828], pp. 30–3; see also Hartmann, p. 300.
[2] Above, iii. 625. He was lord
mayor of London in 1679–80.
[3] No person of this name is said
to appear 'in the lists of his Lordship's Trustees': Oliver, *Cliffordiana*, p. 33. Evelyn perhaps
means Richard Prowse, Clifford's
cousin and agent for his private
affairs: for him see Hartmann,
p. 125, &c.
[4] The Dutch War is the third one;
for Clifford's share in the policy
leading to it see above, p. 16. For
the attack on the Dutch fleet at
Bergen (1665) see above, iii. 562,
618; for that on the Smyrna fleet,
pp. 605–6. 'That whole quarrel' is
redundant.

long after, this accident being mention⟨ed⟩, as we were one
day sitting in Council; his Lordship told us this remarkeable
passage; That being one day discoursing with him, when he
was onely Sir Tho: *Clifford* and a Parliament man:[a] speaking
of mens advancement to greate Charges in the Nation: Well
says he, my *Lord*: I shall be one of the greatest men in England; don't impute what I say, either to fansy, or vanity;
I am certaine that I shall be a mighty man, but it will not
last long, I shall not hold it, but dye a bloudy death: What
says my L: your *horoscop*[b] tells you so: 'tis no matter for that,
it will be as I tell you: Well says my L: Chancelor *Shaftsbery*,
if I were of that opinion, I either would be no greate man, but
decline preferrment, or prevent[c] my danger &c: This my
Lord, affirmed in my hearing, before severall Gent: & noble
men sitting in Council together at *Whitehall*: And I the rather
am confident of it; remembring what Sir Ed: Walker *Gartyr*
K. at *Armes*, had likewise affirmed to me[d] long time before,
even when he was first made Lord: Sir Ed: told me, that
carrying to him his Pedegreè,[1] & finding him buisy, he bid
him go into his study, & divert himselfe there, till he was at
Leasure, to discourse with him about some things relating to
his family: There lay says Sir Ed: on his Table, his *Horoscope*
& *Nativity* calculated, with some writing under it, where he
read, That he should be advanc'd to the highest degree in
the state could be conferred upon him, but that he should
not long Enjoy it, but should Die, or[e] expressions to that
sense, & I think (but cannot confidently say) a bloudy death:[2]

---

a Followed by *he to* deleted.　　b Followed by *is* deleted.　　c Followed
by *that* deleted.　　d Followed by *some time before* deleted.　　e Followed
by *worse* deleted.

---

[1] Clifford had been created a
baron on 22 April 1672; the grant
of supporters for his coat of arms
is dated 20 May of that year; his
illuminated pedigree was apparently
completed only in May 1673: Hartmann, p. 224.

[2] A copy of Clifford's horoscope,
cast by John Gadbury (*D.N.B.*) in
1670, is preserved in Bodleian

Library, Ashmole MS. 179, ff. 1–25
(the original is at Ugbrooke: Hartmann, p. 9 n.). He is twice to rise
to eminence, the first time suffering
a temporary eclipse in 1673; the
second time about 1681/2, with a
crisis in his fortune about 1692.
There is no word of his attaining
the 'highest degree in the state' or
of his death. Two other horoscopes

This Sir Edw: affirmed both to me and Sir *Rich: Browne*: nor could I forbere to note this extraordinary passage in these memoires: &c:

19 I dined with my L: *Arlington*, & then went with him to see some Pictures in Lond: & returned home: 24: A *stranger* on 22: *Matt:* 39, not *quantitively*, but *qualitatis*, not so much on⟨e⟩s friend, or neighbour as thyselfe, or another; but all men whatsoever *Christians*, with as true & sincere love: our Viccar in the afternoone as formerly: 2. Pet: 1. 16.

26 I went to *Twicknam* Park[1] with my deare friend Mrs. *Blagg.* 27: We dined at *Coll:* Talbots,[2] & next day I returned home: 31. Our viccar as above: & Curat on 118 Psal: 18. A thanks giving to God, for restoring him after a long indisposition: & it was a usefull sermon:[3]

September Came my deare friend ✰ to visite & dined with us. 6 I was to attend the Lords *Commissioners* of the Admiralty about the sick & wounded: & so returned: 7: our *Minister* preached on 13. *Luke* 24 the difficultys of the way to blisse, from the corruption of our Natures: &c: I received the holy *Sacrament.* Afternoone an excellent serm: by a young man, on 6. Rom: 21, of the bitter fruits of sinn, in respect of the little & short satisfaction they yeilded &c: & punishment attending:

13 To *Lond:* 14 Dr. *Crighton* son to the late eloquent *Bish: of Bath & Wells* to the household on 59 Isa: 8.[a] on the perverse wayes of the wicked &c: See your notes: To the king

---

a Altered from *18*.

(Ashmole MSS. 243, f. 131; 436, f. 58) give few or no accidents, but state that Clifford bled to death.
[1] On the boundary between Twickenham and Isleworth; it belonged to Lord Berkeley of Stratton and his family from 1668 to 1685. The house was pulled down *c.* 1817 and the park has been largely built over: R. S. Cobbett, *Memorials of Twickenham*, 1872, pp. 224–35.

[2] Richard Talbot, *c.* 1630–91; created earl of Tyrconnel (Ireland), 1685; duke of Tyrconnel (Ireland), by James II, 19(30) March 1689: *D.N.B.*; Sergeant, *Little Jennings*, &c. For his two wives see above, p. 15; below, p. 79.
[3] Apparently the curate of Deptford (Mr. Holland?): see above, p. 16. The curate of Greenwich had preached on this text on 20 July.

Dr. *Stradling* on   *I came not to send peace but the sword*:¹
&c:

15 I procurd 4000 pounds of the^a Lords^a of the *Tress:* & rectified divers matters, about the sick & wounded:² 16 Visited my ✰, thence to *Council*, about choosing a new Secretary &c:³ 17: I went with some friends to visite Mr. Bernard *Grinvill* at *Abs-Court*⁴ in *Surrey*, an old house in a pretty parke, & next day home:

20 To the *Admiralty* about the *Hospitals*,⁵ return'd. 21 our *Viccar* on his former, of the narownesse of the way, & streitnesse of the gate &c: *Pomerid*, a Young man on 8 *Matt:* 1.2.3. our B: Saviours benignity & continualy doing good:

23 To *Lond*; dining with Mrs. Bl: we went to see *Paradise*,⁶ a roome in *Hatton Garden* furnished with the representations of all sorts of animals, handsomely painted on boards or cloth, & so cut out & made to stand & move,^b fly, crawll, roare & make their severall cries, as was not unpretty: though in it selfe a meere bauble, whilst the man who shew'd, made us Laugh heartily at his formal *poetrie*. 24 I went home. 27 To *Lond:* to the Admiralty &c: return'd: 28^c our Curate did very well on 4. *Eph:* 3. That *immorality* was not so greate

---

^{a-a} Altered from *my L^d: Tress^r*.
^c Followed by *one* deleted.

^b Followed by *with* deleted.

---

¹ St. Matthew x. 34.
² Evelyn's alteration (see critical note) is wrong; the office of lord high treasurer was not in commission but was held by Osborne: see above, p. 14. He was now Viscount Latimer of Danby. Business was done by him with the chancellor of the exchequer (Duncombe) generally, the surveyor-general of crown lands (Sir C. Harbord) frequently, and other persons sometimes, present.
³ See below, p. 25.
⁴ Apps (Apse, Aps) Court at Walton-on-Thames: Manning and Bray, ii. 765–7; *V.C.H., Surrey*, iii. 472–3. Dobson quotes Pope, 'Imitations of Horace', Ep. ii, bk. ii, l. 232.

Granville (above, p. 11) does not appear to have owned the property.
⁵ Hospital accommodation was required probably as a result of the battle of the Texel on 11 August. The Savoy was requisitioned on 26 August: *Cal. S.P., Dom., 1673*, p. 514.
⁶ An exhibition of this character is advertised in *City Mercury*, no. 7, 23 Dec. 1675 (repeated in no. 23). A description of a similar exhibition, or of the same exhibition at an earlier period, by 'I. H., gent.', was published in 1661 as *Paradise transplanted and restored . . . shown at Christopher Whiteheads . . . in Shooe-Lane*.

a sinn, as *Incharity*: & how long the Church though divided in Opinion, were yet united in Communion: &c: *Pomerid*, our Viccar proceeded on his former. 30 To Lond. 31 Visited my ✩, returned:

Octob: 5 Our *Viccar* as before: The holy Communion follow'd: Pomerid. Mr. *Holland* on 1. *Cor:* 11. 30, of the Danger of unworthy communicating: &c. 12 To Lond: returned: ⟨12⟩.[a] our *Viccar* as before, & so the Curate. 14. To *Lond:* visited & din'd with Mrs. *Blagge* at *Barkeley* house.

15 Council, & sware Mr. *Lock* Secretary, Dr. *Worsley* being deceased:[1] 16 I went home. My Lord *Brounker*, L: *Cornbery*, Mr. *Harvey*[2] & Mr. *Newport*[3] came to visite me. *Anniversary*, I writ to a friend:[4] 19 Mr. *Mills*[5] preached on 14 Joh: 21 of the Love of God: &c.

21 To *Lond:* 23: home: 26: Mr. *Bohune* late Tutor to my sonn, preached on. 1. *Cor:* 22.23 very excellently well: *Pomerid*: a stranger on 7: *Matt:* 21. 27. To Lond *Council*, about sending succours to recover *New-York*; & then we read the Commission & Instructions to the new Governor of *Barbados* Sir *Jonathan Atkins*.[6]

28 I dined at My L: Berkeleys with ✩, & then to visite a poore sick person.

30 I sat with the Commissioners of Sewers in *Southwark*,[7] & returned home:

---

[a] MS. *13*.

---

[1] Worsley did not die until 1677. He apparently resigned his office as a nonconformist unable to take the oaths prescribed by the Test Act (above, p. 7): Brown, *Shaftesbury*, p. 147.

[2] Possibly John Hervey: above, iii. 165, &c. Like Brouncker and Cornbury, he belonged to the queen's household.

[3] Possibly Andrew Newport: below, p. 103. He was a friend of Laurence Hyde: *Corr. of Henry Hyde, earl of Clarendon*, ed. S. W.

Singer, 1828, i. 92.

[4] See above, iii. 628.

[5] Above, iii. 622.

[6] Andrews, p. 147. New York was at present occupied by the Dutch; for the project for its recapture see *Cal. S.P., Colonial, 1669–74*, no. 1145 (see also no. 1157). Atkins (above, iii. 619) was governor from 1674 to 1680.

[7] The Surrey and Kent Commission: above, iii. 151 n. Its records at this date are not accessible.

31 Was my birth-day *Anniversarie*, now the 53d: it being also a preparation day for the blessed Sacrament.

November 2 Our *Viccar* on 10. *Heb:* 25 of the antiquitie of Church Assemblies, in opposition to sectaries & separatists &c: The holy Communion followd: *Afternoone* Mr. *Holland* on: 11. *Ecclesiast:* 1.2. concerning Charity, & good Works:[a] &c: 3. To Lond: to Council. 4: To visite[b] ✩, fainting at Pr: reviv'd: 5. Dr. *Stillingfleete* on 7: *Matt.* 15 of the hypocrisie of the Popish Emissaries, preach'd before the house of Commons at St. *Margarits*[1] (See your notes): This night the youths of the Citty burnt the *Pope* in *Effigie* after they had made procession with it in greate triumph; displeased at the D: for altering his Religion, & now marrying an *Italian Lady* &c:[2]

6 I returned home: 9: our *Viccar* as before: 10 To Lond: buisinesse: 11: Dind with ✩, went home: 16 our *Viccar* as above: shewing that the first born had a double portion,[3] because he was the Priest of the family, & to be at Expense of the Offerings, That *Caine* & *Abel* brought their Oblations to *Adam* their father, who sacrific'd it for them: &c: *Pomerid*: the *Curate* on 2: Joel: 12. about fasting & mortification.

---

[a] Or *Worke*.   [b] Altered from *visited*.

---

[1] On 27 October the commons ordered that Stillingfleet should be requested to preach this day; parliament was prorogued on 4 November; on 15 Jan. 1674, in the next session, the commons ordered him to be thanked: *C.J.*, ix. 282, 286, 294. The present sermon was published in 1674 (three editions) and reprinted in Stillingfleet's *Ten Sermons* (*Sermons*, vol. ii), 1697, pp. 59–120. The text is verses 15, 16.

[2] A description of the celebration was published, *The burning of the Whore of Babylon, as it was acted, with great applause, in the Poultrey*, 1673. 'There was more bonfires from Charingcrosse to Whitechapple then had beene in 30 yeares before. The young fry made the effigies of popes, carried them in procession, and there burnt them.' 'Should shee [the new duchess of York] arrive to-night [5 Nov.], that madnes has a lycence, shee would certainely bee martyr'd, for the comon people here and even those of quallyty in the country beleeve shee is the Pope's eldest daughter': *Letters to Sir Joseph Williamson*, ii. 67, 63 (Camden Soc., new ser., vol. ix, 1874). The duke had been married at Modena by proxy on 20/30 September; for the new duchess see below.

[3] This presumably refers to Deuteronomy xxi. 17, a text not mentioned here.

17 To Lond: Council: 18 Din'd with Mrs. *Blagg*: 19 returned. 23 Our *Viccar* on 1. *Cor:* 13 ult. *Pomer:* a stranger on 59 *Isa:* 1.2. 24 To Lond: to *Council* of *Trade & Plantations*, & Commission for S: & Wounded, dind at *Berkeley house*. 28 *jejun:*[1] 29 Supped with ✩: 30 Communicated with — at a sick persons in Covent Garden, Mr. *Benson*[2] sonn to the *Deane* of *Hereford* officiating. This morning *Coram rege* preached a stranger on   *God shall send them strong delusions to believe a Lie*[3] &c an excellent Discourse against the *Popes* pretence to *Infallibillity*, then prayed with ♎,[4] dind with the Vice *Chamberlaine:*

It being St. *Andrews* day I saw first the new *Dutchesse* of *York*,[5] and the *Dutchesse* of *Modena*[6] her mother, newly come over & married &c:

December 1 In the morning to the *Council* of *Plant:* & thence to *Gressham Coll:* whither the Citty had invited the *Royal Society*, by severall of their chiefe Aldermen & Magistrates and gave us a Collation, to wellcome us to our first place of Assembly, from whence we had ben driven to give place to the Citty to make it their Exchange upon the dreadfull Conflagration, 'til their new exchange was now finished:

---

[1] i.e. *jejunium*, a fast-day; presumably as being the Friday preceding a Sunday on which Evelyn communicated: cf. above, p. 26 (31 Oct.).

[2] Presumably Samuel Benson, b. c. 1647; M.A. 1671; archdeacon of Hereford 1684; deprived as a nonjuror 1690: Foster. For his father see above, iii. 629.

[3] 2 Thessalonians ii. 11.

[4] This symbol, which is that for the sign of the zodiac Libra, the scales, here stands for Margaret Blagge; the identification is made certain by its occurrence in a notice below, p. 45. Miss Sampson points out that it represents the period from 23 September to *c.* 23 October, and suggests that it may be intended to commemorate the vows before the Altar of Friendship on 16

October: *Life of Mrs. Godolphin*, p. 211.

[5] Mary Beatrice Anne Margaret Isabel, 1658–1718; daughter of Alfonso IV d'Este, duke of Modena: *D.N.B.*; 'Martin Haile', *Queen Mary of Modena*, 1905. She had arrived in London on 26 November and had taken up residence at St. James's Palace: *London Gazette*, 27 Nov.

[6] Laura Martinozzi, 1635–87; daughter of Margherita Mazzarino, a sister of Cardinal Mazarin; married, 1655, Alfonso d'Este, 1634–62, succeeded 1658 as Alfonso IV, duke of Modena; regent of Modena 1662–74: *Encic. italiana*. She came with her daughter; and left London, apparently on 31 December: *Hollandtze Mercurius*, vol. for 1674, p. 18.

the *Society* having til now ben entertaind & met at *Arundel* house: This day we also Chose Officers, St. *Andrews* day being on the Sonday & day before:[1]

2 I dined with ☱ & visited the sick, thence to an Almeshouse, where was prayers, & reliefe, some very sick & miserable: returning prayers,[a] and it was one of the best daies I ever spent in my life: There was this day at Dinner my Lo: *Lockart*[2] design'd Ambassador for France, a gallant & a sober person &c: 3. To the Council of Plant: & so home. 4: To Lond: & next morning to the L: of the *Tress:* soliciting for monies;[3] Thence to our *Council* about this yeares *Accompts*: Thence home:

7: Our *Viccar* on his former text: The Communion follow'd, at which my Sonn & I participated: *Pomerid*: *Curate* on 8 Nehem: 1 of Pub: Assembling to Worship God &c:

8 I went to the Lords of the Council, & stayed all this Weeke in Towne about severall affaires with the Lords Commissioners of the *Tress:* 9: ☱: pr: & dined with the *Maids of honour*.

9 I saw againe the two *Italian* Dutchesse⟨s⟩ & her bro: the Prince *Reynaldo*,[4] supped [11][b] at Berkley house with Mrs. *Blagg*. 14: pre: Dr. *Lamplugh* coram rege on 1. *Cor:* 6. 11 very practicaly, according to his manner: Din'd at the V.

---

a MS. *pr:*   b Marginal date.

---

[1] For the removal of the Society to Arundel House see above, iii. 472; for the return to Gresham College, Birch, iii. 93, 100–1, 107–8. The new Royal Exchange had been opened on 28 Sept. 1669: *London Gazette*, 30 Sept.

[2] William Lockhart, 1621–75, of Lee, Lanarkshire; knighted (Scotland?) *c.* 1672 (he had been knighted by Cromwell 1656 and summoned to his 'other house' 1657). He was appointed ambassador to France on 20 October and took leave of the king on 20 December (he had been envoy extraordinary to France from May to October of this year).

It is presumably as being ambassador that he is here styled 'Lord'. Article in *D.N.B.* is unreliable; MS. Life by A. Robertson, *c.* 1914, in National Library of Scotland.

[3] The lords of the treasury here and below is wrong: see above, p. 24.

[4] Rinaldo d'Este, 1655–1737; brother of Alfonso IV (see p. 27, n. 6); cardinal 1686; laid down his cardinalate and succeeded his nephew as duke of Modena 1694; married 1696 Charlotte Felicitas of the house of Hanover, a first cousin of George I: J. H. Zedler, (*Lexikon*), vol. xxx, 1741, pp. 688–97.

Cham: 16: Dined and supp'd with ⇌ pr: & next day returned
home: 19 To *Lond:* to the Lords of the *Admiralty*, and to
signe things at our Council.

20 I had some discourse with certaine strangers, not un-
learned, who had ben born not far from the old *Niniveh*:
They assur'd me the ruines being still extant, & vast,
wonderfull was the buildings, Vaults, Pillars, & magnificent
fragments now buried, & remaining: but little could they say
of the Toure of *Babel* that satisfied me: but the description
of the amœnitie & fragrancy of the Country for health, &
cherefullnesse, did almost ravish me; so sensibly the⟨y⟩ spake
of the excellent aire & climat, in respect of our cloudy &
splenetic Country:[1]

21 Dr. *Patrick* preached the first serm: to the Houshold
at W:hall on 4. *Phil:* 4 most patheticaly seting forth the Love
of God; & the obligation[a] we had to rejoice in it: &c: Before
the *King*, a Stranger on 5. *Gall:* 11, of the Liberty of the
Christian Religion preferrable to the *Jewish* Ceremonies &c.
22. To Council:—dind, ⇌ Pr: Went to see a poore Creature
had poyson'd herselfe by accident, but recovered: Made Court
at St. *James's* to see the new *Dutchesse*. 24. *Christmas*
Eve, *jejun*, returning home visited some prisoners at *Ludgate*,
taking order about the releasing of some &c: for ⇌ &c:[2] 25.
our *Minister* on 1. *Heb:* 1, apposite to the festivity: when
I received the bl: ⸱Sacrament: 26. Invited some *Neighbours
more solito*:

28 our *Viccar* on his former: 30, I gave Almighty God
thanks for his infinite goodnesse to me the yeare past: &c:

1674 *January*: 1 Beseeching Gods mercy & protection for
the yeare following: severall neighbours dined with me. 2. To
Lond: on buisinesse: 4: A chaplaine, in the morning on 5:
Matt. 22. of the danger of causelesse anger: The holy Sacrament followed: blessed be God: *Coram Rege* Dr. *Bredoy*[3] on

---

[a] Altered from or to *occasion*.

---

[1] For what were believed to be
the ruins of Nineveh and of the
Tower of Babel see J. B. Tavernier,
Les six voyages, 1676, i. 175, 213–14.

[2] Ludgate was a debtor's prison;
for its history see Wheatley.

[3] i.e. Brideoake: above, p. 2.

17: *Joh:* 4, the necessity of finishing the work of an holy life &c: 5, I saw an *Italian Opera* in musique, the first that had ben in *England* of this kind:[1]

6 Came Mrs. *Blagge* to see us[a]—pr: I supp'd at my L: *Cornberies*, where at a Ball divers greate Ladys daunced: 7 I dind with my L: *Berkeley*: This night there was a greate Supper and Ball, at my L: *Chamberlaines*,[2] the *King*, *Duke*, *Dutchesses* &c:

8 Home: 9 Sent for next morning to *Lond:* by his Majestie to write some thing against the *Hollanders*, about the Duty of the flag & fisherie:[3] so returned with some papers. 11. our *Viccar* on 37: *Psal:* 37: 12 Sent for againe to Lond: 13 Din'd with ☆:

14 Din'd at L: *Arlingtons*, went to the Council of Pl: 18 Dr. Beaumont[4] at *W:hall*: on 10: *Matt* 29. 30. 31 Concerning the Providence of God: *Coram rege* 103. Psa: 14, 15. of his Mercies: *Mental Comm:*[5] ♎. 20 dined with ☆— Pr: 25 A stranger at *W. hall*: on   *I know how both to abound, & how to want*[6] &c. *Coram rege* Dr. *Turner*[7] on and because I will do this, prepare thyselfe &c: afterwards ment: Com: ♎:

27 Dined at *B: house* ☆. Pr: 28 To the Commiss: of

---

a Altered from or to *me*.

[1] 'Danceing and Operas were practissed' on several nights in January at the Whitehall theatre: Boswell, *Restoration court stage*, pp. 111, 252. It has been suggested that the performance seen by Evelyn was a rehearsal of *Ariane*, by P. Perrin; music by R. Cambert; it was performed at Drury Lane (King's Company) on 30 March: A. Loewenberg, *Annals of opera*, 1943, pp. 27–9. It is possible that there was some sort of musical performance in Italian specially arranged in honour of Mary of Modena, the new duchess of York.

[2] St. Albans, lord chamberlain from 1671 until 11 September of this year.

[3] See below, p. 41.

[4] Above, iii. 351.

[5] i.e. Mental Communion. For the form used by Evelyn see his *Devotionarie Book*, 1936, pp. 17–34; for the origin of the form and its use by Mrs. Blagge, ibid., pp. 13–15. There are frequent references to the practice below. See also *Life of Mrs. Godolphin*, p. 86.

[6] Philippians iv. 12, loosely rendered.

[7] Presumably Francis Turner: above, iii. 630. The text is Amos iv. 12, loosely rendered.

Sewers,[1] returned: 30 our Vicc: on the late Kings Martyrdom: 2. Chro: 35: 25. apposite to the occasion:

Feb: 1: Our *Viccar* on 3: *Heb:* 13, danger of resisting the
calls of the holy Spirit: That the day of grace & offers of
salvation, is not allwayes during our whole life; &c. The bl:
Sacrament followd: at which I received with my Wife &
sonn: Pomerid: on: 1. *Tim:* 4. 8. The advantages of Piety
above riches: 2:[a] To Lond: ☆ : pr: vis: Wid:[2] 4 Dr. *Meaws*[3]
on 11. *Hosea*: 8 Gods unwillingnesse to punish: *Coram rege*
Bish: of *Rochester* 3. Matt: 8: shewing the little fruite produc'd
after much culture: being a solemn fast; before the Lords in
Westminster *Abby*, on a solemn fast day, & time of greate
Calamitie:[4]

6 To my L: *Tres:* for the sick. 8: Dr. *Pierson*[5] on: 10: *Matt:*
17: of Piety in our Youth: *Coram rege* a stranger on: 1. *Sam:*
13. 1. Shewing how *Saule* reigned but one yeare, when he
had reigned above 40: reconciling the Texts, in as much as
he had reigned but one as he ought, & religiously, the rest
passing for nought in Gods account. 10: Visited ☆ & to
Council.

11 returned home. 15 our Viccar on 22: *Gen:* 2. of *Abrahams*
obedience &c. 16. To *Lond:*

17: To ♎ pr: 18 To Council:[6] 19 home: ⟨22⟩,[b] *Viccar* as
before: shewing that when we are to obey, we ought not
conferr with sense; for then we are lost, but immediately

---

[a] Altered from *3*.   [b] MS. *21.*

---

[1] See above, p. 25.

[2] i.e. 'prayers: visited Widow';
presumably the woman described in
Life of Mrs. Godolphin, p. 106.

[3] Mews, now bishop of Bath and
Wells: above, iii. 536. The words
coram rege belong with this sermon,
which was for the fast: see next
note.

[4] The fast was on account of the
calamities of the war and those
caused by popish recusants: Pro-

clamation, 16 January (Steele, no.
3587). The lords asked the bishops
of Rochester and Hereford (Crofts)
to preach before them in the Abbey
and thanked them both on 5
February: *L.J.*, xii. 610, 619, 627.

[5] Pearson. The text is apparently
wrong.

[6] The date should perhaps be
17 February: for the meeting that
day see Andrews, pp. 149–50.

duty: *Pomerid* a stranger on 9: *Heb:* 27: concerning death & Judgment:

22: To Lond: Council:[1] 23 din'd with ☆ pr: 25 returned home:

March: Viccar on his former Text; the reality of true faith, examp: *Abrahams* obedience: The holy Sacrament followed, receiving my Wife & sonn: *Pomerid*: 51 *Psal:* 6. of the sincerity of the heart. 7 To *Lond:* din'd with the *Bishop* of *Rochester*: 8: Bishop of *Salisbury*[2] *coram rege*, on 24: Act: 25: The Effects of Gods threatning: Feare & trembling nothing without reformation of life: In the morning a young man on 1. *Pet:* 5. 8. 8 din'd at Mr. *Grinvils*, thence to the Chancelors of the *Excheq:*[3] ♎ visited me —Pr: 10 I dind at B: house ☆ pr:

11 At Westminster *ægro:* cum ♎ *farræ*[a] *Synax:*[4] *postea* W:hall Dr. *Pierce* on 1. *Joh:* 5. 3:[5] din'd at Mrs. *Thornhills* one of the bedchamber women to the Queene & sister to the Earle of Bath:[6] *coram rege mane* Dr. *Frampton* on. 12. *Eccles:* 1 the perill of late Repentance:[7] 13 home:

15 *Viccar* on 1. *Cor:* 11. 23. 17: Lond: din'd with ☆: pr: 18 Dr. *Cradock cor: rege*, on 49 *Psa* 13.[5]

21 home: 22. our *Viccar* as before: *Pomer:* Curate 1 *Joh:* 2. 16. 24 Lond: dind with ☆. —pr:

---

a Or *turræ*, or *furræ*, or *tarræ*.

---

[1] The date is obviously wrong.

[2] Seth Ward. Lenten sermon at court: list in *London Gazette*, 2 Feb.

[3] Sir John Duncombe. He was chancellor of the exchequer from 1672 to 1676.

[4] 'Ægro:' is an abbreviation for *ægrotus* (or *ægrota*), a sick person; 'Synax:' for *synaxis*, the communion. The word here transcribed 'farræ' is perhaps a false rendering for, or misreading of, *farinæ*, of flour. Mrs. Blagge was in the habit of attending the administration of the Sacrament to the sick: *Life*, p. 86.

[5] Lenten sermon at court.

[6] Above, p. 9.

[7] Lenten sermon at court; Frampton preached as dean of Gloucester. The date should be 13 March; the following date, '13', is perhaps an error.

25 Dr. *Littleton*[1] *Cor: Rege* on 1. *Luke* 26. concerning *Angels,*
their *Nature, Office,* manner of Salutation of the B: *Virgin*
&c: I din'd at *Knightsbridge*[2] with the Bishops of *Salisbury,*
Chester & *Lincoln* my old friends:[3] 26 returned home:
28 Lond: ⟨29⟩ W:hall first sermon, on. 14 *Hosea*: 2. *Coram*
Rege Bishop of Chester on 1. *Cor*: 3. 18. incomparably.[4] 31
with ✶: —

Aprill: 1 Dr. *Patric coram Rege* on 6: *Heb:* 1; the deceite
of Repentance, if the foundation be not sure, all is to no purpose; how to examine it:[4] I return'd home this Evening:

5: Lond: W:hall: 1. ser: a stranger on 6. *Gal:* 1, how ready
we should be to pardon others, considering our owne faillings.
Coram Rege Dr. *Gunning* Bishop of *Chichester* on   *get thee*
behind me Satan &c Proving by many comparisons & deductions that our bl: Saviour did not speake that as meaning the
Dovil, but St. *Peter*, & signified *Adversarie* to his Passion, &
so to the salvation of man kind, by the[a] suggestion of *Satan*:[5]
I received the bl: Sacrament: din'd at a poore Widows[6] with

✶ —pr: 7: at L: Bark: with ☌—pr: 8. At W:hall
Dr. *Compton* on 1. *Reg*: 21. 29. concerning the hypocritical[b]
humiliation of *Ahab*: & the benefit of true repentanc:[4] I went
home:

12 Our *Curate* on *Palme* Sonday (our *Viccar* sick) on: 22.
Luke: 19. 20. [The Communion followed.][c] *Pomer*: 19 Luke
41. 42. of our B: S: weeping over the Citty: 13 To *Lond*. about
buisinesse: 14: din'd with ✶—pr:

---

[a] Followed by *ins-* deleted.   [b] Followed by *repe-* deleted.   [c] Interlined.

---

[1] Above, p. 5. Lenten sermon
at court. The day is the Annuncia-
tion. The sermon is printed in
Littleton's *Sixty one sermons,* [i].
1–23; the text should be verse 28.

[2] Presumably at Ward's house;
he died at his house here: Pope,
Life of (Ward), pp. 182, 184.

[3] Ward; Pearson; and William
Fuller, *c.* 1612–75; D.C.L. 1660;

bishop of Limerick 1664; of Lincoln, 1667: *D.N.B.* This is the first
occasion on which Evelyn mentions
Fuller.

[4] Lenten sermon at court.

[5] Lenten sermon at court. The
text is either St. Matthew xvi. 23
or St. Mark viii. 33.

[6] See above, p. 31.

15 Dr. *Stillingfleete Coram Rege* on 15. Luke: 17. on the Prodigal, incomparably:[1]

17 *Goodfriday*, I received the holy Sacrament at St. *Martines* Dr. *Lamplugh* on 1. *Threnæ* 12. *Pomerid*: at *White-hall Coram Rege Bish: of Rochester*[2] on the same Text most patheticaly describing the Passion: The *Duke of Yorke* was present:[3] I returned home.

19 our *Viccar Easter day* on: 3. *Coloss:* 1. 2. a Resurrection sermon, The *Com:* follow'd: the Lord make me ever mindfull of the comfort of this day: *Pomer:* 4. Act: 12 &c:

23 Came to see us my L: *Cornbury*, & his *Lady* & Lady *Mordaunt*, & din'd with us:

26 our *Viccar* as before: *Pomerid* the Curat of *Greenewich* on. 19 Job. 25. 26. 27: To *Lond:* This day came to visite me my Lady Berkely & my friend: 28: dind with ☌ —pr:

30 I return'd:

May: 3. our *Viccar* on his former: I received the bl: Comm: *Pomer*: *Curat* as before:

4 Came the Queenes Maids of honour & my friend to dine with us at Says-Court:

5 To Lond: din'd with ✶. 6 Carried my La: *Berkely* & Mrs. *Blagg* to see the *Repositary* of the *Royal Society*. 7: I visited my L: *Mordaunt* at *Parsons Greene* it being his *Wedding*-day & a greate feast with much Companie &c:[4] 8: To L: *Tressurer*: home that Evening: 10: our *Viccar* on 1. *Pet:* 11. 12.[5] against Temptation, That the Superior faculty as Governor, should Command obedience &c: *Pomerid*: Curate: on. 2. Coloss: 2. 13. 14. the Efficacy of Christs death: 11. To Lond: 12: dind with ✶—pr: I gave her the forme of a Will, as she requird: & went home 13th: 14:[a] dined at my [house my][b]

---

[a] Followed by *Lond.* deleted.   [b] Interlined.

---

[1] Lenten sermon at court.

[2] Dolben, preaching as dean of Westminster; Lenten sermon at court.

[3] James continued to attend at Anglican services until about March

1676: see below, p. 87.

[4] The marriage took place in 1657: above, iii. 194.

[5] Evidently 1 Peter ii. 11, 12; in the following text one '2' is redundant.

Lady *Cathr:* ⟨*Morley*⟩[a][1] with Mrs. *Howard,* & the 2 Maides of honor her daughters:[2] 16 To *Lond.* ⟨17⟩ at St. *Martines* a stranger on 12. *Eccles:* 1. I received the *B: Sacrament,* at *W:hall* Dr. *Killegrew*[3] on 22. *Matt:* 21. of Obedience to Kings, a Court sermon: 19 Din'd with ☆. 20 returned home leaving my little Daughter *Betty*[4] at my L: *Barkeleys* with Mrs. *Blagge.* 23: To *Lond:*

24 Rogation-Sonday[b] at St. *Martines* a stranger on 32. *Jer:* 19. the omnipresence of God: The holy *Sacrament* follow'd: dind at L: Berk: ☆ : *Pomerid:* a Young man at St. *James's* chap: on 48: *Isa:* 22: 26: I visited & din'd with my pious friend Dr. *Jasp: Needham.*

27 Council in the morning: *Jejun:* 28: St. *Martins* a stranger on 14. *Joh:* 16. 17. shewing how the *H: Spirit* was a Comforter; not a quality, perstringing the *Arians Sabellians Socinians*[5] &c: that he was a distinct person, & therefore to be adored & praied to: The ho: *Comm:* follow'd, it being *Ascention* day: Din'd at my *Brothers* & returned home: The Lord make me thankfull:

29 His *Majesties* Birthday & restauration Mr. *Sanders*[6] preached well on 2. Reg: 11. 12. apposite to the occasion: My Bro: *Evelin,* Mr. *Demelhoy,*[7] Mr. *Roger L'Estrange*[8] & severall of my friends came to dine with me: 31. our *Viccar* on: 1. *Pet:* 2. 11. of the danger of the smaler sinns, the force & power of the flesh: *Pomerid: Curate* on: 2. *Coloss:* 13. 14.

---

[a] MS. *Morleys.*   [b] Substituted for *Weeke.*

---

[1] Above, p. 11.

[2] The second daughter is Ann, a maid of honour from 1673 to 1677, and afterwards Lady Sylvius: above, iii. 529–30.

[3] Above, iii. 301, &c.

[4] Above, iii. 495. She was now six years old.

[5] For Evelyn's views on the tenets of these sects see *Hist. of Religion,* ii. 231, 235, 248–50.

[6] A Mr. Saunders preaches occasionally at Deptford between 1678 and 1683; he was presumably a curate there. This is perhaps the same man. He is not further identifiable.

[7] Presumably Thomas Dalmahoy, d. 1682, of the Friery, Guildford; of Scottish extraction; M.P. for Guildford 1664, 1678/9: [T. Falconer], *Family of Dalmahoy,* n.d. [*c.* 1870], pp. 8, 38–42; Paul, *Scots peerage,* iii. 130; Manning and Bray, i. 21.

[8] Above, iii. 167.

June: 2. *Lond:* to *Council*: 4: so also Council, about nominating Commissioners to go to *Syrenam.*[1] 5. returned home: 7: *Whitsonday Vicc:* as before. [the holy Communion followed:][a] *Curate.* 2. *Act:* 4.

11 To *Lond:* to see Mrs. Blagge, after Evening prayer I returned home: 14 *Lond: Trin: Sonday*: at St. *Martines*, a young man on   *Why will ye dye ye house of Israel?*[2] Gods readinesse to receive penitents, that his decrees are not irreversable &c: The holy communion follow'd. Din'd at Mrs. *Howards*: Pomerid: at St. James: Mr. *Leake*[3] *Dukes Chaplaine* on 20 *Matt:* 20. concerning the power of the Keys, & ministerial function for *Absolution,* recomending the use of more frequent Confession: then with ⟳ *Vidua paup:*[4]— pr: & went home on foote that Evening.

15 The *Bish:* of *Rochester* Dr. *Dolben* at *Deptford* on *Psal:*   *Blessed is he that provides for the poore & needy, the Lord shall*   :[5] A sermon to incite *Charity*, being the *Anniversary* of the meeting of the *Trinity* Companie: I dind with the Comp: at a mighty feast:

17 Lond: to visite ✶— pr: returnd: 21 A stranger on *The Lord searches the* heart & *reines*,[6] excellently against hypocrisie &c: *Pomerid*: *Curate* on: 13. *Hosea*: 9[7] That we may please God evangelicaly, though not[b] without infirmitie: I went this Evening to see ⟳ and visite a Sick Lady, &

---

a Interlined.   b Followed by *per*- deleted.

---

[1] Surinam was part of the modern Dutch Guiana. By article v of the Treaty of Westminster, 9/19 Feb. 1674, which had established peace with the Dutch, the king's subjects in Surinam were to remove elsewhere; the king was empowered to send commissioners there to superintend the removal. On 2 June the king ordered the Council of Trade, &c., to nominate two commissioners; the Council's reply is dated 8 June: *Cal. S.P., Colonial, 1669–74*, pp. 589–90. The business continued into 1675.

[2] Ezekiel xviii. 31 or xxxiii. 11.

[3] Edward Lake, 1642–1704; D.D. 1676; chaplain to the duke of York *c.* 1676, *c.* 1684; tutor to the princesses Mary and Anne: *D.N.B.* The text is perhaps an error for St. Matthew xvi. 19.

[4] See above, pp. 31, 33.

[5] Psalms xli. 1, from the Prayer Book, loosely rendered.

[6] The text may be Psalms vii. 10 (from the Prayer Book) or Jeremiah xvii. 10 or Revelation ii. 23, in any case loosely rendered.

[7] The text is apparently wrong.

returnd on Tuesday: 26: *Lond:* to Council: but no *quorum*, so return'd. 27: Mr. *Dryden*[1] the famous Poët, & now *Laureat* came to give me a Visite: It was the *Anniversarie* of my *Marriage*,[2] & the first day I went into my new little *Cell*, &[a] *Cabinet* which I built below towards the South Court, at East end of the Parlor:[3] 28: a stranger on 32. *Deut:* 19[4] of Gods Decrees, that he desires no mans Perdition, by several instances out of Scripture & Gods mercifull invitations: *Pomerid.* the Curate as before:

July 4. To *Lond: Council*, home: 5. one Mr. *Fletcher* a pathetical orator, on 32 *Deut:* the former Text:[5] the excellency of Consideration: The H. *Sacrament* followd: *Pomerid: Curat* on 7: *Matt:* 21. the inefficaccy of the most holy external duties, without good life & uprightnesse in our Callings: 7: *Lond: Council*, returnd the next. 9: To *Lond:* to pay Dr. *Jacomb*[6] 360 pounds for his sonn now of age: for his part of the purchase of the Mill & Land, I bought of the *Beechers* in Deptford: returned the 10: 12: The same preached on: 23. *Luke*: 24.[7] of forgiving injuries &c: *Pomer:* Curat as before:

16 To *Lond:* Sent for by ⁓, return'd that evening, not well pleas'd, upon an unjust report: 19.[b] Lond:[8] Mr. *Fletcher* againe on 7: *Heb:* 19, shewing the infirmities of the *ritual* Law; the easinesse & perfection of the Evangelical,[c] & how much more obliged to our B: *Saviour* for it: *Pomer: Curate* of *Greenewich* on 19. *Job*: 25 of the Resurrection & future Judgement:

---

a Followed by *stud-* deleted.   b Altered from *16*.   c Altered from *Ch-*.

[1] John Dryden, 1631–1700; poet laureate 1668–88: *D.N.B.*

[2] In 1647: above, ii. 536.

[3] It is probably the 'little *Cell*' mentioned in the *Life of Mrs. Godolphin*, p. 51.

[4] The text is perhaps a mistake for Deuteronomy xxxii. 29: see entry for 5 July.

[5] See preceding note. Fletcher preached again at Deptford on the next two Sundays and on 8 November of this year. He is not identifiable.

[6] Thomas Jacombe, 1622–87; D.D. 1661; nonconformist divine: *D.N.B.*; Matthews, *Calamy revised*; Drake's Hasted, p. 14. His son was named William; his connexion with the Beecher property is unknown. For the purchase of this property, which was made in 1668, see above, iii. 508.

[7] A slip for St. Luke xxiii. 34. The preacher is Fletcher.

[8] This is evidently an error; Fletcher was preaching at Deptford.

22 I went to *Winsore* with my Wife & sonn, to see my Daughter *Mary*[1] who was there with my *Lady Tuke*; & to do my Duty to his Majestie: next day to a greate entertainement at Sir *Robert Holmes's* at *Cranburne* Lodge[2] in the forest: There were his *Majestie, Queene, Duke, Dutchesse* & all the Court: I returned in the Evening with Sir Jos: *Wiliamson* now declared Secretary of state:[3] Sir *Jos:* was sonn of a meane Clergyman[a] some where in Cumberlandshire,[4] brought up at Queenes Coll: [Oxon]:[b] of which he came to be a fellow;[5] Then traveled with[c] . . . & returning when the King was restord, was[d] received as a Cleark under Mr. Secretary Nicholas:[e] Sir *Hen: Bennet* (now *L. Arlington*:) succeeding, *Williamson* is transferred to Sir Henry:[6] who loving[f] his ease more than buisinesse, (though sufficiently able had he applyed himselfe to it) remitted all to[g] his man *Williamson*, & in a short time let him so into the seacret of affaires, that (as his Lordship himselfe told me) there was a kind of necessity to advance him; & so by his subtilty, dexterity & insinuation, he got now to be principal Secretary; absolutely my

---

a Followed by *of* deleted.   b Interlined.   c Followed by *so-* deleted.
d Followed by *ma-* deleted.   e Followed by *my* deleted.   f Followed by *much* deleted.   g Followed by *Wi-* deleted.

---

[1] Above, iii. 421. She was now eight years old.
[2] Cranbourn Lodge. I have not found any other reference to Holmes's occupying it. The custody of the lodge appears to have belonged to Lord Cornbury: *Cal. S.P., Dom., 1660–1*, p. 368. It is perhaps identifiable with the New Lodge, for which see *Cal. Treasury Books, 1676–9, 1685–9*. Further notices below, 23 Oct. 1686, &c.
[3] Williamson was appointed secretary of state on 11 September of this year: *London Gazette*, 14 Sept. The forthcoming appointment is reported on 8 July in *Correspondence of the family of Hatton*, ed. E. Maunde Thompson (Camden Soc., new ser., vols. xxii–xxiii, 1878), i. 111.
[4] Williamson's father, Joseph Williamson, was vicar of Bridekirk, Cumberland, from 1625 to 1634. The annual value of the living was certified to the governors of Queen Anne's Bounty as £33, and in 1777 was nearly £60: J. Nicolson and R. Burn, *Hist. . . . of Westmorland and Cumberland*, 1777, ii. 99.
[5] He entered the college in 1650; B.A. 1654; fellow 1657. He travelled abroad from 1656 to 1658: letters to him in *Cal. S.P., Dom.*
[6] Williamson entered Nicholas's service in or before July 1660; Bennet (Arlington) succeeded Nicholas as secretary of state in 1662.

L: *Arlingtons* Creature, and ungratefull enough; for so it has ben the fate of this obliging favorite, to advance those who soone forgot their original:[1] Sir *Joseph* was a Musitian,[2] could play at *jëu de Goblets*,[3] exceeding formal; a severe Master to his Servants; but[a] so inward with my *Lord Obrian*, that after a few moneths of that Gent: death, he maried his *Widdow*, who being daughter & heire of the *Duke* of *Richmond*, brought him a noble fortune;[b] but, twas thought, they lived not so kindly after marriage as they did before: & she was infinitely censur'd for marrying so meanely, being herselfe alyed to the royal family:[4] 24 I came home. 26 The same person[5] preached mor: on[c] his former Text, & afterwards the Curate on 6. *Rom:* 11. 27: To *Lon:* returned 28:

Aug: 2: Our *Viccar* on 130 *Psal:* 3. 4 of Gods infinite mercy to sinners: The Comm: followed: *Pomer: Curate* on 23: *Exod:* 2. not to follow a multitude to do evil, applyed to those who left the Church assemblies for Conventicles: 6 I went to

---

a Substituted for *&*.   b Followed by *&* deleted.   c Substituted for *& afternoone of.*

---

[1] Williamson's rise was due primarily to his industry and ability. Some time in the winter 1672–3 Arlington had agreed with Williamson that the latter should on payment of £6,000 succeed him as secretary of state whenever he, Arlington, should become lord chamberlain; the king had agreed to this arrangement. But in March Arlington offered the succession to Sir William Temple, who refused it. Williamson immediately attached himself to the new lord treasurer, Danby; as Arlington regarded the latter as his rival he might consider that Williamson had deserted him: see *D.N.B.*; Temple, *Works*, 1770, iv. 25–6; *Essex papers*, i. 236, 242; Barbour, *Arlington*, p. 243. Evelyn also alludes to Clifford's supposed misconduct towards Arlington.

[2] So *Cal. S.P., Dom., 1660–1*, p. 312; cf. above, iii. 601.

[3] A *joueur de gobelets* means both a juggler and a cheat.

[4] Lord O'Brien is Henry O'Brien, d. 1678, also styled Lord Ibrackan, son of Henry O'Brien, sixth earl of Thomond (Ireland; above, iii. 555). He married in 1661 Katherine, 1640–1702, sister of Charles Stuart, duke of Richmond; on his death in 1672 she succeeded as Baroness Clifton (of Leighton Bromswold): G.E.C. She married Williamson in 1678 within three months of her first husband's death. The Stuarts of Aubigny, the family to which she belonged, were descended in the male line from the great-grandfather of Robert II, the first Stuart king of Scotland; they were also descended from James II of Scotland; genealogical table in Lady E. Cust (Lady Brownlow), *Some account of the Stuarts of Aubigny*, 1891.

[5] Presumably Fletcher.

Groomebridge to see my old friend Mr. *Packer,*[1] the house built within a Moate & in a woody Valy: The old house had ben the place of Confinement of that duke of *Orleance* taken by one *Waller* (whose house this then was) at the Bataile of *Agencourt*;[2] but now demolish'd, a new ⟨w⟩as built in its place; though a far better had ben on the south of the wood on a gracefull ascent: At some small distance is a large *Chapell* not long-since built by Mr. *Packers* father, upon a *Vowe* he made to do it, upon the Returne of *Charles* the first, out of Spaine 1625. & dedicated it to *St. Charles*: but what saint there was then of that name, I am to seeke; for being a Protestant, I conceive it was not *Borrhimeo*.[3] 7: I went to the Wells,[4] but did not drink the waters: 8 I went to see my farme at *Ripe*[5] in *Sussex* neere *Lewes*, return'd the same day:

9 Mr. *Pogton*,[6] preached at[a] a church neere *Chafford*[7] the seate of the *Rivers's* on   *My Yoake is easy* &c; in the after-noone at Mr. *Packers* Chapell, on: 3. *Apoc:* against hypocrisy, & did excellently well on both: I went to the Wells at *South-borrow*[8] to visite my deare friend Mrs. *Blagg*, then drinking

---

ᵃ Followed by *yᵉ Chap:* deleted.

---

[1] Above, ii. 547–8; Groombridge, iii. 72; for the new house see *Country Life,* xii (1902), 625–31, 657–60; xiv (1903), 400–5.

[2] According to the story current in Evelyn's time Richard Waller (*D.N.B.*) captured Charles, duke of Orleans (the poet), at Agincourt and kept him here in honourable cus-tody: T. Philipot, *Villare Cantia-num,* 1659, p. 320. But the duke was found in a pile of dead on the battlefield; although he remained a prisoner until 1440 he was never, so far as is known, in Waller's custody; the latter had charge for some time of his brother, John, count of Angoulême: P. Champion, *Vie de Charles d'Orléans,* 1911; above, iii. 72 n.

[3] For the chapel see above, iii.

72; it is dedicated to St. John the Baptist. For St. Charles Borromeo see above, ii. 496; he was canonized in 1610.

[4] Tunbridge Wells.

[5] Above, ii. 555 n.

[6] John Poeton, *c.* 1615–92; per-haps matriculated at Oxford 1637; minister of the chapel for thirty-six years: epitaph in J. Thorpe, *Regi-strum Roffense,* 1769, p. 810. His text is St. Matthew xi. 30.

[7] An estate in the parish of Penshurst; it belonged to the family of Rivers (baronets from 1621) from Henry VIII's time until *c.* 1734; the house was pulled down soon after that date: Hasted, *Kent,* i. 417–18.

[8] Southborough; above, iii. 68 n.

the Waters with my Lady *Berkeley*: 11 passing againe by the Wells, I went home:

16 our *Viccar* on 12: *Luke* 47: 48. first describing our Duty: Then shewing Gods Justice in proportioning the punishment to the Crime: *Pomerid Curate* on 23 *Pro:* &c: concerning the integrity of the heart, & to what perfection of moral virtues the heathen arived, without their being able to carry them to *Christ*: 18 To *Lond*, and next day to *Winsore* about buisinesse with my *Lord Tressurer*: next day his *Majestie* told me how exceedingly the *Dutch* were displeased, at my Treatise of *historie* of *Commerce*; That the *Holland Ambassador* had complained to him of what I had touch'd of the *flag*,[a] & *fishery* &c: & disired the booke might be caled in: whilst on the other side, he assur'd me he was exceedingly pleased with what I had don & gave me many thanks: However it being just upon conclusion of the *Treaty at Breda*,[b] (for indeed it was designed to be published some moneths before, & when we were at defyance) his Majestie told me, he must recall it formaly, but gave order that what Copies should be publiquely seiz'd to pacifie the Ambassador should immediatly be restord to the Printer, & that neither he nor the *Vendor* should be molested: The truth is, that which touch'd the *Hollander*, was much lesse, than what the *King himselfe* furnish'd me with, & oblig'd me to publish, having[c] caus'd it to be read to him 'ere it went to the presse: but the error was, it should have ben publish'd before the peace was proclaim'd: The noise of this books suppresion, made it be presently bought up, & turn'd much to the Stationer⟨'s⟩ advantage: Nor was it other, than the meere preface, prepard to be præfix'd to my Historie of the whole *Warr*; which I now pursu'd no farther.[1]

---

[a] Or *flags*.   [b] Followed by *his Ma^{te}:* deleted.   [c] Altered from *&*.

---

[1] This refers to *Navigation and Commerce, their original and progress. Containing a succinct Account of Traffick in General: its Benefits and Improvements: Of Discoveries, Wars and Conflicts at Sea, from the Original of Navigation to this Day: with special Regard to the English Nation; Their several Voyages and Expeditions, to the Beginning of our late Differences with Holland; In which His Majesties Title to the*

21 There was approches, & a formal seige,[a] against a Work with *Bastions*, Bullwarks, Ramparts, Palizads, ⟨Graft⟩,[b] hornworks, Conterscarps &c: in imitation of the[c] Citty of *Maestrict*, newly taken by the *French*: & this being artificialy design'd & cast up in one of the Meadows at the foote of the long *Terrace* below the Castle, was defended against the *Duke of Monmouth* (newly come from that real seige) who [with the Duke of York][d] attaqu'd it with a little army, to shew their skill in *Tactics*: so on Saturday night, They made their approches, opened trenches, raised batteries, [took][d] the Conterscarp, Ravelin,[e] after a stout Defence. Greate Gunns fir'd on both sides, Granados shot, mines Sprung, parties sent out, attempts of raising the seige, prisoners taken, Parlies, & in short all the Circumstances of a formal seige to appearance, & what is most strange, all without disorder, or ill accident, but to the greate satisfaction of a thousand spectators, when being night it made a formidable shew, & was realy very divertisant:[1] This mock seige being over, I went with *Mr.*

---

[a] Followed by *with* deleted.   [b] MS. *Groft*?   [c] Followed by *late* deleted.   [d] Interlined.   [e] Followed by *taken* deleted.

Dominion of the Sea is Asserted, against the Novel, and late Pretenders, 1674. For Evelyn's projected history of the Dutch war see above, iii. 523. The preface in its original form was submitted to Clifford on 31 Aug. 1672 (Bohn, iii. 230–1). It is not clear whether Evelyn made any alterations at the king's instance. The book is advertised in the *Term Catalogues*, 26 May; peace had been made with the Dutch by the treaty signed at Westminster on 9 February (the Treaty of Breda terminated the preceding war in 1667). On 12 August Charles ordered it to be called in: *Cal. S.P., Dom., 1673–5*, p. 332; it is clear, however, that he allowed its sale to continue. On 19 Sept. 1682 Evelyn sent Pepys his 'thoughts upon second meditation' about the subjects with which it dealt and controverted many of his former arguments (Bohn, iii. 267–72). The book is reprinted in *Misc. writings*, pp. 625–86, and elsewhere. Keynes, pp. 200–4.

[1] The siege of Maastricht by the French, with a small English auxiliary force commanded by Monmouth, began on 6 June 1673, N.S.; the town surrendered on 30 June, N.S.; Monmouth greatly distinguished himself. A fort about 200 feet square had been constructed at the entrance into the Park for the present display; attacks were made on 14, 15, and 18 August, and presumably on the following days: *A true description of the New-Erected Fort at Windsor . . . With the several Skirmishes and Stratagems . . . Being an heroick representation of the . . . siege of Maestritch*, 1674.

Pepys back to Lond: where we arived about 3 in the morning:
& at St. *Martines* heard a sermon [⟨23⟩]ᵃ on 26: *Matt:* 74
exaggerating the sinn of *Peter* in denying his Master with
Oathes; and how yet some greate & sad failings, sometimes
contribute to the amendment of Gods dearest Saints, to abate
their over Confidence, & rendering them more vigilant: The
very same sermon, by the same preacher, I happn'd to heare
againe at St. *Jamess*[1] this Afternoone: 25 I return'd home.
30: our *Viccar* as before: *Curate* on 12: *Luke*: 5: 31 our Vicc:
on: 2: *Luke*: 29: 30 at the funerall of Mr. *Uttart*[2] a neighbour
of mine: The Song of *Simeon*: That therefore he wished to
die for that having seene the *Lord*, there was no other object,
that he ever desired to see in this world: so St. *Paule* wished
to be disolv'd: that it was sometimes profitable to dwell
among the Tombs:

September 3. I went to Lond: about sealing writings in
Trust for Mrs. *Blagge*,[3] & then home. 6: our *Viccar* on 12:
Luke 47. 48. shewing the difference 'twixt sinns of Ignorance
& Knowledge: with this notion; that a presumptuous sinner
is at that instant of time, an *Atheist*; since it were impossible,
he should believe any such thing as a sin-revenging God, &
yet commit a deliberate sinn against God: That few or no
Christians could pretendᵇ invincible ignorance: *Christians* in
worse condition than heathens who livd disolutely: A general
Repentance sufficient, through Gods mercy, in sinns of *sub-
reption*,[4] daily incursion, & pure frailty: The holy Sacr:
follow'd. *Pomerid*: our Curate on 6: *Matt:* 15 on the meekenesse of *Christ*: Mutual forgivenesse, bearing,ᶜ pardoning injuries, & subduing passions, the principal parts of *Christian
Religion*: That the *Heathen* who went so farr in *Moral* Ver-

---

ᵃ Marginal date; MS. *24.*
ᶜ Followed by *&* deleted.

ᵇ Followed by *to sinns of* deleted.

---

[1] The palace. These services took
place on 23 August.
[2] Apparently John Uthwat (Uth-
warth), clerk of the survey at Deptford since 1657, who died on 28
August: *Cal. S.P., Dom.*; Drake's

Hasted, p. 32.
[3] See below, p. 44.
[4] A variant for surreption, sudden or surprise attack, of sins, &c.:
O.E.D.

tues, built on a wrong foundation, as being out of pride &
Contempt, not the true grace of humility: 8 To Council:
9 returnd:

11 Came to Visite me the *Bishop* of *Rochester*, Sir *Stephen
Fox*[1] &c:[a]

13 A stranger on 4: *Eph:* 1. the necessity of holy conversation, that it consisted in inward, & outward acts, beyond the
utt⟨m⟩ost exactnesse of the *Moral* Law, *Political*, Customarie,
or other inferior to the *Evangelical*: *Pomerid* Curate as before
&c:

15 To *Council*, about the fetching off the English left at
Syrenam &c since our reconciliation with *Holland*:[2] I visited
✮, gave her the deedes about the 500 pounds I had disposed
of for her &c. —pr: 16 I went to Congratulate our new
Secretary of state:[3] &c: 20: To Lond: Ember Weeke[4] Dr.
Lamplugh preaching on 119 *Psal:* 60, Against deferring repentance: The holy Comm: followed: I din'd at *White-hall*:
Pomerid: stranger at *Covent Garden* on 1. *Cor:* 15. ult: of the
infinite reward which the saints shall receive: I went home
on foote. 22: To *Lond*, dind with ♎ —pr: having ben at
Council: 23. I went to ⟨see⟩[b] the greate losse that my Lord
Arlington had received by fire, at *Goring-house*, now this
night consum'd to the ground, with exceeding losse of hang-
ings, plate, rare pictures and Cabinets, in a word, nothing
almost was saved, of the best & most princely furniture that
any subject had in England: My Lord & Lady being both
absent at the *Bathe*;[5] so returned home full of astonishment
at the uncertaintie of worldly enjoyments: 27 Our *Vicc:* on
40: *Isa*. 6. 7. concerning Gods Providence against *Atheists*
&c. *Pomerid*. *Curate* on 28 *Pro:* 13. The danger of concealing
sinn, or committing on⟨e⟩ sinn for anothe⟨r⟩: That 'twas not

---

[a] Followed by *then* deleted.   [b] MS. *seee.*

---

[1] Above, iii. 447.
[2] See above, p. 36.
[3] Williamson.
[4] The Ember days at this time of
the year are the Wednesday, Friday, and Saturday succeeding 14

September.
[5] Arlington had gone to Bath on
12 September and returned on 27
September: *Bulstrode papers*, i. 267–
8. Arlington rebuilt the house at
once.

impossible not to sinn; That true Repentance was a through
reformation of any known sinn &c: 29: To *Lond:* to *Council,*
passd the Evening with ☆ —pr: and returnd next day
home.

Octo: 1 To *Lond: Council*: return'd. 4 Viccar on the same
Text; the holy Comm: followed: Curate as before: 6 To
Lond: Council: dind with ☆ return'd: 8: Lord *Chief Barron
Turner,*[1] and *Serjeant Wild*[2] *Recorder* of Lond: came to visite
me: 11: our Doctor on his former, with farther explanations
of Gods generall providence, but more especialy particular
care of his church, & that as to particular persons, when good-
men suffer, and evil prosper; though we comprehend not the
reason of Gods so dealing; yet he dos, and so shall we one
day, & acknowledge, & glorifie him, & his justice: *Pomerid.*
Curate on 4. *Phil:* 11, of Contentment in all Conditions: That
there is no want to moderate desires; no Affection, or Virtuous inclination, but has ordain'd for it something to satisfie
& fill it: 13 To *Lond: Council*: spent the Evening with ♎—
pr: next day having buisinesse with Sir *Den: Gauden*[3] I,
din'd with him, & 15 home:

16 Anniversarie ♎ inviol: 18. *Viccar* as above: of the
danger of Curiosity: That Gods back-parts were his works;
Mose'ss desire to see his face, was his way of Government:
They placed *Sphynxes*[a] & ænigmatical figures before their
Temples to denote the invisibilitie of the Deity: The *Jewes*
say they slew *Jeremiah,* for affirming he saw God & lived:[4]
God sent the Prophets to predict future events, to prove him-
selfe to be God, since onely God can tell them: *Pomer:*

---

[a] Altered from *Sphinxes.*

---

[1] Sir Edward Turnor: above, iii.
400. He was lord chief baron of the
exchequer from 1671 to 1676.
[2] William Wilde, *c.* 1611–79;
knighted 1660; created a baronet
1660; serjeant-at-law 1661; recorder of London 1659–68; he was now
a judge of the king's bench: *D.N.B.*
[3] Above, iii. 510.

[4] I have not traced this account
of Jeremiah's death to any authority. He is said by some writers
to have been stoned to death:
e.g. pseudo-Epiphanius, *De vitis pro-
phetarum*; by the Jews as a requital
for his prophesying new woes: Zon-
aras, *Annales,* lib. iii, cap. i.

Curate of *Greenewich* on 19 *Job*: 26. That this expression in *Job*, did not concerne his[a] restauration to his former prosperous state in this world, as some interpreted; but the last Resurrection of the body &c: 20: *Lond:* Council, dind with ✪ at my L: *Berkeleys* where I had discourse with Sir *Tho: Modiford*,[1] Late *Governor* of *Jamaica*, & with *Coll: Morgan*[2] who undertooke that gallant exploit from *Nombre de Dios* to *Panamà* on the Continent of *America*: he told me 10000 men would easily conquer all the *Spanish Indies*, the⟨y⟩ were so secure: greate was the booty they tooke, & much, nay infinitly greater had it been, had they not ben betraied & so discovered before their approch, as they[3] had time to carry on board the vast Treasure, which they put off to sea, in sight of our Men, that had no boates to follow &c: They set fire of *Panamà*, and ravag'd the Country 60 miles about. The⟨y⟩[4] were so supine, & unexercis'd, that they were afraid to give fire to a greate gun &c: 22 To *Council*, return'd:

25 Our *Viccar* on the same &c: Afternoone Wett, had prayers at home: 27: To ✪ —pr: To *Council*, next day home: 31 My Birth-day 54th yeare Blessed be God: It was also now preparation day for the holy Sacrament on ⟨Sunday⟩. —I sent *Memoria Sard.*[b][5] ♎.

Nov 1 *Viccar* on 23. *Luke*. 31. why Afflictions constantly abide[6] the Godly: on which he perstringed our *English* rendittion of that Text, our *Saviou⟨r⟩s* Cursing the Fig-tree; for saying it was *not the time of Figs*;[7] whereas it should be, it was not a seasonable Yeare for *Figgs* in generall; & so it

---

[a] Followed by *resurrection* deleted. [b] Reading doubtful.

---

[1] Above, iii. 579–80.
[2] Above, iii. 583. He was in England from 1672 to 1675: Cruikshank, *Life*, pp. 218–26; and was knighted on 29 November of this year: *Bulstrode papers*, i. 272.
[3] The Spaniards. There was no betrayal of the English project; the Spaniards fled as Morgan advanced.
[4] The Spaniards. The statement

about the gun is untrue; but the Spaniards' resistance was ineffectual. It was they who set fire to the city.
[5] Presumably an engraved sardonyx.
[6] i.e. await; an obsolete use: *O.E.D.*
[7] St. Mark xi. 13. The suggested rendering is false.

had nothing on but leaves; aluding to the *Jewish* nation at that time, which was full of hypocrisie: The bl: *Communion* followed, at which I participated, imploring Gods protection for the yeare following, & confirming my resolutions of a more holy life, even upon the holy booke: The Lord assist, & be gracious to me. *Pomer*: *Curate* 1. *Pet:* 3. 15. proving the Verity of the *Christian Faith* by many arguments.

2 Was the annual meeting of the foefeès for the Poore, when our *Viccar* also preached on 12: *Heb:* 14. concerning peace & Unity. 3. Lond: Council, visited ☆. 5: Dr. *Littleton coram Rege* 13 Rom: 1. of Obedience to Magistrates:[1] dined with Mrs. *Howard*: 6 Council, The *Surenam* buisinesse: I visited my L: *Chamb*:[2] 7 returned home:

8 A Stranger Mr. Flet⟨c⟩her[3] preached on: 23: *Psal:* 4, patheticaly describing the terrors of Death to some men, & how differently religious men[a] entertain'd it: exhorting to prepare for it: That God seldome or never take⟨s⟩ those a way who realy turne from their sinns, 'til they have wrought out their Salvation: A comfortable Text for me: *Pomerid* Mr. *Mills*[4] on 14 *Pro:* 16. shewing who fooles, who Wise: The horrid nature of sinn by its Effects; how infinitly calamitous that must needes be to wiccked men, which was so intollerable to him, who sufferd for [ours][b] but imputatively: To Lond:

15 The *Anniversary* of my *Baptisme* I first heard that famous & Excellent Preacher *Dr. Burnet*[5] (Author of the

---

[a] Followed by *might* deleted.   [b] Interlined above *us*, which is not deleted.

---

[1] For Gunpowder Plot.
[2] Arlington, who had succeeded St. Albans about 11 September of this year: *London Gazette*, 14 Sept. He retained the office until his death.
[3] Evidently the man mentioned above, p. 37.
[4] Above, iii. 622; iv. 25.
[5] Gilbert Burnet, 1643–1715; D.D., Lambeth, 1680; bishop of Salisbury 1689; author of the *History of my own time*: *D.N.B.*; T. E. S. Clarke and H. C. Foxcroft,

Life, 1907. He had been professor of theology in Glasgow from 1669 to 1674 and is sometimes called 'Dr. Burnet' in 1675: *C.J.*, ix. 321; Grey, *Debates*, iii. 18, &c.; but elsewhere 'Mr. Burnet'. Although elected F.R.S. in 1664 (expelled 1685; again F.R.S. from 1689) he had settled in London only in July of this year. The first part of *The History of the Reformation* was published in 1679: below, 14 June 1680, n.

Burnet was 'the most celebrated

Historie of the *Reformation*) on: 3 Coloss: 10: explicating the
nature & Dignity of the human *Soule*, & new-man: how to be
made conformable to the Image of God; with such a floud
of Eloquence, & fullnesse of matter as shew'd him to be a
person of extraordinary parts: The B: Comm: followed: &
din'd with my friend Dr. *Needham*: This night being her
Majesties Birth-day: the Court was exceeding splendid, in
Clothes & Jewells to the height of excesse:

17 A Council in the morning, din'd with ☆, & Council also
in the afternoone still about the buisinesse of *Surenam*, where
the *Dutch* had detained some *English* in prison, ever since the
first War *1665*.

19 I heard that stupendious Violin Signor *Nicholao*[1] (with
other rare Musitians) whom certainly never mortal man Exceeded on that Instrument: he had a stroak so sweete, &
made it speake like the Voice of a man; & when he pleased,
like a Consort of severall Instruments: he did wonders upon
a note: was an excellent Composer also: here was also that
rare *Lutinist* Dr. *Wallgrave*:[2] but nothing approch'd the
Violin in *Nicholas* hand: he seem'd to be *spiritato'd*[3] & plaied
such ravishing things on a ground[4] as astonish'd us all: 20 I
went home after Council:

22 our *Viccar* on 1. *Cor:* 10. 12: That none can be certaine
of his state, & therefore should be allways fearing, & allways
working: *Curate* 1. *James*: 21.

23 *Lond: Council* & severall buisinesses with my *Lord
Treasurer*.

---

extempore preacher of his day':
Mitchell, *English pulpit oratory*, p.
341, where an account of his
characteristics as a preacher is
given; see also Clarke and Foxcroft,
p. 142.

[1] Nicola Matteis: *Grove's Dictionary of music*; R. North, *Memoirs
of musick*, ed. Rimbault, 1846, pp.
122–8.

[2] Identifiable from notice below
(28 Feb. 1684) as William Waldegrave, *c.* 1636–1701; M.D., Padua,

1659; a Roman Catholic; physician
to the duke of York *c.* 1684; to the
queen *c.* 1687; knighted 10 June
1688 on the birth of the Old Pretender: *D.N.B.*; I.H.R., *Bull.*, xvii
(1940), 49. North describes him
as 'a prodigy of an arch-lutanist':
Memoirs, p. 123; see also p. 127.

[3] The Italian word *spiritato* was
used in English in the seventeenth
century for a religious enthusiast:
O.E.D.

[4] See above, iii. 167.

26 With Mr. [Bap]ᵃ May¹ *Privy Purse to his Majestie* & Mrs. *Blagg* christned Mrs. *Wattsons* sonn, *Baptist*: Mr. *Leake*² officiated in its mothers Lodging *Kings-streete*:³

29 Dr. *Alestree Coram Rege* on   *shall he find faith on Earth?*⁴ shewing the wonderfull decay of piety, & cause of it: A stranger in the Morning on: 2. *Apoc:* 10. I din'd at the *Vice Chamb:*

30 Anniversarie of Electing Officers at the *R: Society*, we all din'd together a greate appearance of Noble men &c:

December 1 To Visite ♎. There was a *Council.* 2: heard Signor *Francisco*⁵ on the *Harpsichord*, esteem'd on⟨e⟩ of the most excellent masters in Europe on that Instrument: then came *Nicholao* with his *Violin* & struck all mute, but Mrs. *Knight*,⁶ who sungᵇ incomparably, & doubtlesse has the greatest reach of any English Woman: sheᶜ had lately ben roming in *Italy*: & was much improv'd in that quality: There was other Musique, & this Consort was at Mr. *Slingsbys* Master of the Mint, my worthy friend, & greate lover of Musique: 4 A *Council.* 5 home:

6 our *Viccar* & Curate on their former Texts: The holy Communion followed:

8 To *Lond* to *Council*: visited ☆ —pr: I spent this whole weeke in affaires chiefly with my L: *Tresurer*: 12 went home:

13 our *Viccar* proceedes: The *Curat* on 12. *Rom:* 16, of the danger of Selfe Conceit &c.

15 To *Lond:* to *Council*: Saw a Comedie⁷ at night, at Court,

---

ᵃ Interlined.   ᵇ Or *sang*.   ᶜ Altered from *The*.

¹ Baptist May, *c.* 1628–97; keeper of the privy purse 1665–85: *D.N.B.* (where he is confused with his cousin Hugh May the architect); Pote, *Windsor Castle*, pp. 391–2.
² Lake: above, p. 36.
³ There were streets of this name in Westminster and Covent Garden; that in St. James's was perhaps also built at this time.
⁴ St. Luke xviii. 8.
⁵ Presumably the performer mentioned below, 27 Jan. 1682; Fran-

cesco Corbetta, *c.* 1620–81, the guitar player (*Grove's Dict. of Music*) is unlikely.
⁶ Above, iii. 230.
⁷ The piece is identifiable as *Calisto: or, The Chaste Nymph*, by John Crowne (fl. 1665–1703: *D.N.B.*); he published his second version of it in 1675. Miss Boswell has questioned Evelyn's statements about this performance and that on 22 December on the ground of the bills for costumes, &c.; she regards

acted by the Ladys onely, viz: The Lady *Mary*[1] & *Ann*[2] his R: hignesses two Daughters, & my deare friend Mrs. *Blagg*, who having the principal part, perform'd it to admiration: They were all covered with *Jewels*:

17 Mrs. Blagg, with the two Maids of honor, Mrs. Howarde, & my Wife, came to house warming to my new Lodging:[3] 19 I went home: 20 *Viccar* on his former. The *Curate* on: 1. *Tim:* 3. ult. The Mysterie of the H: *Eucharist* &c:

22 *Lond:* to *Council*,[4] & for the poores mony: was at the

---

them as rehearsals. Crowne himself says that the piece was 'Rehearsed and Acted' twenty or thirty times, or 'near so often'; an audience might attend on any occasion: Epistle to the Reader. It is certain that in November the princesses and various members of the court were preparing 'for the great ball and comedy y^t is to be next month'. It is reported later that performances were to be given on 1 Jan. 1675 and Shrove Tuesday (16 February); there were probably one or more performances after Easter. The available evidence does not permit a positive statement. It seems unlikely that Evelyn did not attend a regular performance. He could have attended that on Shrove Tuesday as he was apparently in London on that and the following days. It is possible that in transcribing he transferred the episode of the lost jewel from some later date to 22 December and likewise that he omitted a later notice, or what remained of it after the transfer of this episode; but equally the notice of the performance on 22 December may be accurate as it stands; in that case it was a regular performance, but apparently not accompanied by a court entertainment. Evelyn gives a longer but vague account in the *Life of Mrs. Godolphin*, pp. 52–5.

For the production see Boswell, *Restoration court stage*, pp. 177–227, &c.; for the date, pp. 181–2; and Miss Sampson, appendix to *Life*, pp. 231–6, and the passages from *Bulstrode papers* there quoted.

The statement that the piece was acted by the ladies only applies to the play alone; Monmouth and five other courtiers took part in the dancing, and professionals of both sexes performed in the prologue and intermezzi.

[1] Mary, 1662–94; married William III, prince of Orange, 1677; queen of England as Mary II 1689.

[2] Anne, 1665–1714; married Prince George of Denmark 1683; queen of England 1702.

[3] Presumably in or near the palace of Whitehall.

[4] Andrews, p. 151; this was apparently its last meeting, Charles having revoked the commission for it on 21 December: ibid., p. 111. Andrews suggests as reasons for this action the fact that Shaftesbury, the president, was now in opposition to the court; the need for economy; and the inherent weakness of advisory and independent bodies, possessing no power to act for themselves. The work of the Council was given in February 1675 to a committee of the Privy Council known as the Lords of Trade.

repetition of the *Pastoral*, on[a] which [occasion][b] my friend Mrs. Blagg, had about her neere 20000 pounds worth of *Jewells*, of which one she lost, borrowed of the Countesse of Suffolck, worth about 80 pounds, which the *Duke* made good; & indeede the presse of people was so greate, that it was a wonder she lost no more:[1] 23 I visited ☌ —pr: 24 home:

25 *Christmas day* our *Viccar* on 24. *Num:* 17:[2] how & why God makes sometimes use of evil men & false prophets to convince the world, & preach to it: so the *Devels* confesse *Christ*: applied to the occasion: I received the blessed *Communion*:

26 I had divers *Naighbours* at Dinner. 27: our [Viccar &][b] *Curate* as before, a little amplified.

28 I invited Neighbours: 31 Gave almighty God thanks for his Mercys: the Yeare past.

167⅘ *January* 1 I implored Gods protection for the yeare following: & divers of my Neighbours came to dine with us:

3 Our *Viccar* as above. 5 To Lond: visited ☆ —pr: 6. return'd, din'd at a friends:

8 To Lond: returned that evening:

10 A stranger on 1. *Tim:* 4. 8, the unprofitablenesse of sensual injoyments &c: excellently: see your notes: *Pomerid*: Curate 10 Luke. 5. 6. in praise of the Gospel: That it was a religion of reconcilement, & to plant peace in the World &c:

11 To *Lond*, dind at *B: house*: 17: At St. *Martins* Dr. *Beaumont* on 2. *Phil:* 14 against murmuring: I received the holy *Sacrament*: Then a stranger on 16 *Luke*: 31, That the Gospel was sufficiently predicated &c: spent the evening with ☌ —pr: 19 I carried Mrs. *Blagg*, & other Ladys to heare the famous *Nicholaos* Violin at Mr. *Slingsbys*:

20 Visited ☆ —pr: & to see Mr. *Streeter* that excellent

---

[a] Altered from *in*.   [b] Interlined.

---

[1] Evelyn repeats this story in *Life of Mrs. Godolphin*, p. 55. The date, of course, is perhaps wrong: see note above. For Lady Suffolk see above, p. 17.
[2] The text is perhaps wrong.

Painter of Perspective &c: & *Landscip*, to comfort, & encourage him to be cut for[a] the stone, with which that honest man was exceedingly afflicted: 21 returned home:

24 Viccar on 2: *Revel:* 4. That the most righteous have failings; That *God* averts his judgement from true penitents, notwithstanding his severe threatnings: *Curate* on 3. *Pro:* 17, the incomparable pleasure of true Piety, compard with worldly delights:

29 All the Queenes Mayds of honor[1] came to dine with mee: 30 *Vicc:* on 2: Sam: 11. 9.[2] of the Sacrednesse of Kings, being K. Charles the firsts Martyrdome Anniversarie:

31 Our Viccar as before: *Curate* on: 1. *Jacob:* 15, exhortation to search the heart for our most bosome & darling sinn, & speedily to reforme it.

Feb: 3 To Lond: in the Evening to visite ☆ —pr: returned on the 6:

7 Our Viccar on his former: The Care we should have to avoid sin, danger of impenitence; *see your notes*: The holy Sacrament followed: *Pomerid*: *Curate* as before, shewing to what Deaths sinners were exposed, temporal, & eternal, exaggerated the terrors of both, but especialy the later: exhorting to serious repentance:

9 To *Lond* about severall affaires, but especialy to begin the Lent: 11. Dind at L: *Berkeleys* with Mrs. *Blagg*, returned next day. 14 *Lond:* Dr. *Duport* at W. hall preached on 14 *John*: 21, setting forth the exceeding love of *God*: To the King Dr. *Pierce* on　*Let him that standeth take heede* &c[3] excellently pursued: 15 I received the blessed Communion at a sick persons with ♎ Dr. *Leake*[4] officiating.

17 *Ashwednesday coram Rege* Bish: of *Chester*[5] 16 *Luke*: 19. The absolute necessity of setting some time a part for

---

[a] Substituted for *of*.

---

[1] There ought to have been six at this time: above, iii. 621.
[2] The text is perhaps wrong.
[3] 1 Corinthians x. 12.
[4] Lake.

[5] Pearson; the sermon should have been preached by the dean of the chapel, Blandford: list of Lenten sermons at court, *London Gazette*, 18 Jan.

the work of Recollection, & mortification extraordinorie, & that we were not to use Creature comforts without restraint, especialy on some occasions & seasons: [See your notes:]ᵃ

19 *Coram Rege*, Deane of S. *Paules* Dr. *Sancroft*¹ on 139. *Psal:* 18. The duty of Morning Private, as well as pub: devotion, how after *Davids* example we might be continualy praysing God &c: I returnd this evening:

21 Our *Viccar* on. 4: *Matt* 1 of the nature of Temptation: when God is said to Tempt, or be Tempted, when Satan tempts: That no person or place is free: Why our B: S. would be tempted ; namely to shew how we should behave our selves when we are tempted: why so soone after his baptisme: that having then newly entered his extraordinary Ministrie, he might have the greatest Conquest; & that after holy exercises, he is ever most buisy & importunate: That solitude is not the best security: That it was a question whither *Satan* (at our Saviours birth) knew him to be the Sonn of *God*: &c: *Pomer*: *Curate* on 16: *Matt:* 26. The value of our Soule above all Created things, & therefore the care we ought to take about it. &c: 22. To *Lond:*

24 Dr. *Stillingfleete coram Rege* on 3. *Heb:* 13 exhorting to serious Examination, on the danger of our hearts Deceitfull- nesse, & the subtile nature of sinn ; excellently pressed:² [see your notes]:ᵇ 26: Dr. *Tillotson*³ *Coram Rege* on 119 *Psal:* 59. The greate advantage as well as necessitie of Consideration: [*Se your notes.*]ᵃ I supped with ⟨Mrs.⟩ᶜ B: at B: house —pr: ⟨28⟩ᵈ Dr. *Glanvill*⁴ W. hall 1 serm: 17 *Act:* 31. The certainty

---

ᵃ Marginal note.   ᵇ Interlined.   ᶜ MS. *Mʳ:* altered from *S-*.
ᵈ MS. *29*.

---

¹ Above, iii. 432. Lenten sermon at court.

² Lenten sermon at court. The sermon was printed this year (two editions) ; reprinted in Stillingfleet, *Ten sermons*, 1697 (*Sermons*, 1696– 1701, vol. ii), pp. 121–73.

³ Above, iii. 517. Lenten sermon at court. The sermon was printed this year (reprinted in Tillotson, *Works*, 1752, i. 110–17).

⁴ No doctor of this name is trace- able at this time. Presumably Joseph Glanvill, 1636–80, the author of *Sadducismus triumphatus*: *D.N.B.* Aubrey calls him D.D. (*Brief lives*, i. 266) but is mistaken. He appears from the title-pages of his books to have been a chaplain in ordinary from 1676 until his death; his name does not occur in the lists in Chamberlayne. A sermon

of the final Judgement, Justice & terror of it to the Wicked;
Joy to the Godly: Then I heard a stranger at *Covent Garden*
Church   how shall they preach unlesse they be sent,[1]
excellently well perstringing the bold sectaries, exhorting to
an esteeme of the Lawfull Ministrie &c: To this succeeded
an Ordination of about 30 *Deacons* & *Priests* by Dr. *Pierson*
Bishop of *Chester*, very solemn & the B: Sacrament follow'd
of which I communicated with greate Comfort; Din'd at a
poore widdows with ♎.

Mar: 6. I return'd home.[2] 3. To *Lond:* Dr. *Pierce coram
Rege* on 12: *Heb:* 13, shewing the perill of dissobedience:[3] I
supped with ⛤ —pr: at B: house: 4 I went to the *R: Society*,
where was read a paper from Monsieur *Isa: Vossius* concerning an appearance in ☾, & *Archimedes's Speculum Usto-
rium*:[4] I supped at Mr. Secretarie Williamsons with severall
of our *Society*: among whom[a] Mr. *Sheeres*[b][5] Sonn of *Cap:
Sheres* of our *Parish*, who undertooke and best succeeded in
the Mole of *Tanger*, affirmed, that if a *Scorpion* were placed
within a Circle of fire, or so invirond with danger as no way
to escape, he would sting himselfe to death:[6] he spake of the
prodigious bignesse of *Locusts* in *Africa*: That all the Teeth

---

[a] MS. *wh*.   [b] Followed by *the same* deleted.

on the present text is printed in
his *Seasonable reflections and discourses*, 1676, pp. 163–212.

Glanvill had been elected F.R.S.
in 1664. On 24 June 1668 Evelyn
wrote to thank him for a copy of his
Plus ultra (Bohn, iii. 204).

[1] Romans x. 15.
[2] The date is presumably wrong.
[3] Lenten sermon at court. The
text may be wrong.
[4] Two discourses by Vossius
(above, p. 6) were read at this
day's meeting. The first dealt with
the spots on the moon's surface
(perhaps the paper on this subject
printed in his *Variarum observa-
tionum liber*, 1685, pp. 195–200); the
second with the legendary burning-

glass of Archimedes: Birch, iii. 192–
3. The word *ustorius* is not found
in classical Latin.

[5] Henry Sheeres, d. 1710;
knighted 1685; military engineer
and author: *D.N.B.* Of the father
nothing is known (but see below,
9 Sept. 1682); it is the son who
was engaged in building the Mole
at Tangier from 1676 to 1683, after
Sir Hugh Cholmley's failure: Routh,
Tangier, pp. 354–64. He was elected
F.R.S. in 1676.

[6] This habit is not mentioned by
E. Topsell in his account of the
scorpion in his *Hist. of serpents*,
1608, pp. 222–31. It is entirely
fictitious.

of *Elephants* grew downewards, & not as commonly painted:[1]
That the *Camelion* preied chiefly on *flys* by a violent *Suction*,
first so exhausting its owne body of breath & aire as to reduce
itselfe to as thin as the edge of a knife in appearance, & then
sudainly relaxing and violent suction of the aire, filling himselfe againe drew in with it, the flies that were within it⟨s⟩
Spheare & opposite to him:[2]

5. Dr. *LLoyd*[3] Deane of *Bangor* a pathetical discourse
Coram Rege on 6. *Rom:* 17, of the Slaverie of sinn: &c: 6.
I went home:

7 Both *Viccar* & *Curat* pr: on their old Text: shewing the
subtilty of the Tempter (*Vide Notes*) [The Sacrament followed:][a] *Curate* shewd the dignity, & therefore the Care we
ought have of our soules, comparing it to riches, pleasure,
honour &c so obnoxious to decay & vanity: 10: *Lond:* Dr.
Littleton on 4: *Eph:* 3 about reconciliation:[4] I visited my *L:
Mordaunt* at Parsons Greene supped with ☆ —pr:

12 The pious & eloquent Dr. Frampton at *W:hall* (his
Majestie absent at New *Market* Sports) on. 1. *Pet:* 4. 18.
shewing the certainty, but difficulty of Salvation: even to the
most righteous, and onely possibility to the converted &
reformed sinner:[5] I went home that Evening:

14 *Viccar* on his former: Speaking of the famine of *Samaria*,
where a *Cab* of *pigeons* dung was sold at so deare a rate, he
shewed, that it was not real *pigeons dung* but a certaine kind
of *pulse* so called, being a very meane & poore sort of ⟨foode⟩:[b6]

---

a Interlined.   b MS. *foote* or *foole*.

---

[1] The male elephant's tusks grow
downwards, the female's upwards:
Topsell, *Hist of foure-footed beastes*,
p. 193.
[2] Topsell is already aware that
the chameleon captures its prey by
means of its tongue but notices its
power of inflating its body: *Hist. of
serpents*, p. 114.
[3] The apocalyptic; he was dean
of Bangor from 1672 to 1680.
Lenten sermon at court.

[4] Lenten sermon at court.
[5] Lenten sermon at court. The
king was absent at Newmarket from
about 9 until 27 March: *Bulstrode
papers*, pp. 278, 281.
[6] 'And there was a great famine
in Samaria: and, behold, they besieged it, until an ass's head was
sold for fourscore pieces of silver,
and the fourth part of a cab of
dove's dung for five pieces of silver':
2 Kings vi. 25.

Curate as before, & but weakely perform'd: 16 To *Lond:*
Next day preached at *W:hall*: Dr. *Outram*[1] on 119 *Psal:* 59,
How serious consideration of the folly & consequences of
sinn, did most contribute to the reforming of our lives:
Example, *Soloman*, the Prodigal: &c: I sup'd with ☆. —pr:

18 I received the B: Sacrament at a poore dying christians with ♎ &c: din'd at my L: *Sunderlands*, suped with
Mr. Seccr: *Williamson.* 19 A stranger[2] at *W:hall* on 1. Pet:
2. 11. shewing the diference, strength, & danger of fleshly
lusts; delights of the soule in contemplation of spiritual
pleasures. &c:

20 I went home: 21 *Viccar* on his former, (*vide your notes*)
miracles of no use, but to do good: no good thing to be don
upon *Satans* instigation: because his Designe is to introduce
some sinn &c: *Pomerid:* To *Greenewich* Dr. *Plume* on 7:
Luke 47. Gods mercy to penetents: v: *Notes:*

22 To *Lond:* 24: A^a Stranger[3] W:hall^a on 26 *Matt:* 43: of
Vigilancy against tentation. I supped at Sir *William Pettys*,[4]
with The Bish: of *Salisbury*,[5] & divers honorable persons: we
had a noble entertainement, in a house gloriously furnished;
The *Master* & *Mistris* of it extraordinary Persons: Sir *Will:*
being the sonn of a meane man some where in *Sussex*, was
sent from Schole to *Oxon:* where he studied Philos: but was
most eminent in Mathematics & Mechanics, proceeded Doctor
of *Physick*,[6] & was^b growne famous as for his Learning, so for

---

a–a Substituted for *Our Viccar.*   b Followed by *the D^r:* deleted.

---

[1] William Owtram, 1626–79;
D.D. 1662: *D.N.B.* Lenten sermon
at court.
[2] The preacher for the day in the
list of Lenten preachers is Dr.
William Clarke, dean of Winchester:
above, iii. 605.
[3] The preacher for the day is
Dr. Cradock: above, p. 4.
[4] Above, iii. 304, &c. Evelyn
gives a similar notice of him in a
letter to W. Wotton, 12 Sept. 1703
(Bohn, iii. 393–5). Petty had
bought in 1673 a house at the corner

of Chip Street, now Sackville Street,
and Piccadilly: *The Petty–Southwell
correspondence*, ed. Lord Lansdowne, 1928, p. 147; he died in it
in 1687, and was presumably living
in it already.
[5] Seth Ward. For his friendship
with Petty see Aubrey, *Brief lives*,
ii. 141.
[6] Petty was the son of Anthony
Petty of Romsey, Hants, where he
was born in 1623. Leaving school,
he went to sea at the age of fifteen;
after spending some time abroad,

his recovering a poore wench that had ben hanged for felonie, the body being beged (as costome is) for the *Anatomie* lecture, he let bloud, put to bed to a warme woman, & with spirits & other meanes recovered her to life ; The Young Scholars joyn'd & made her a little portion, married her to[a] a Man who had severall children by her, living 15 yeares after, as I have ben assured:[1] He came from *Oxon:* to be ⟨pedagogue⟩[b] to a neighbour of mine ;[2] Thence when the Rebells were dividing their Conquests in Ireland, he was employed by them to measure & set out the Land, which he did upon an easy contract so much per *Acker*: which he effected so exactly, & so expeditiously, as not onely furnish'd him with a greate summ of mony, but enabled him to purchas an Estate worth 4000 pounds a yeare ;[3] he afterwards married the Daughter of Sir *Hardresse Waller*, she an extraordinary witt, as well as beauty, & a prudent Woman :[4] Sir *William* amongst other inventions

---

[a] Followed by *anoth-* deleted.   [b] MS. *pedagouge.*

---

partly studying at Caen and in the Netherlands, he came to Oxford about 1649; he was created D.Med. there on 7 March 1650.

[1] This refers to Anne Greene, *c.* 1628–59 ?, who on 14 Dec. 1650 was hanged for murdering her illegitimate child: *D.N.B.* For Petty's own account see *The Petty papers*, ed. Lord Lansdowne, 1927, i. 157–67 ; for the contemporary literature, Madan, *Oxford Books*, vol. iii, nos. 2151, 2153, 2158–62; see also Plot, *Oxford-shire*, pp. 197–9. Petty was at the time deputy for the professor of anatomy at Oxford.

[2] Although nothing is known of Petty's activities between his leaving Oxford early in 1651 and his arrival in Ireland on 10 Sept. 1652, he is not likely, in view of his status at Oxford and at Gresham College, where he was professor of music, to have taken a position as a tutor in a private house. In 1648 he had entered into partnership with John Holland of Deptford for the exploi-

tation of his inventions: Lord Edmond Fitzmaurice, *Life of Sir William Petty*, 1895, p. 13.

[3] This refers to the 'Down Survey' of forfeited lands in Ireland to be distributed among the officers and men of the Army; it was made by Petty in 1655–6; and to the further surveys made by him *c.* 1657 of lands there to be distributed to other persons. His charge for the work was very low; he appears to have been paid about £9,600 for it. In 1685 he considered his property in Ireland to be worth £4,800 per annum, but that was after various changes had taken place; by that date he also possessed a considerable amount of property in England. He estimated his total income in 1685 at about £11,300: Fitzmaurice, pp. 23–65, 125, 319–21.

[4] Elizabeth, d. *c.* 1708–10; married first, in 1653, Sir Maurice Fenton; secondly, in 1667, Petty; created Baroness Shelburne (Ireland) 31 Dec. 1688: G.E.C.; for her

author of the Double-bottom'd ship; which though it perishd,
& he censur'd for rashnesse; yet it was lost in the bay of
Biscay in a storme when, I think 15 more Vessels miss-
carried: The Vessell was flat-bottom'd, of exceeding use to
put into shallow Ports, & ride over small depths of water; It
consisted of two distinct *Keeles* crampt together with huge
timbers &c: so as a violent streame ran betweene: It bare a
monstrous broad saile; & he still persists it practicable & of
exceeding use, & has often told me he would adventure himselfe in such another, could he procure sailors, and his
Majesties Permission to make a second Experiment, which
name the King gave it at the Launching:[1] The Map of *Ireland*
made by Sir *William* is bilieved to be the most exact that ever
was yet made of any Country: he did promise to publish it:
& I am told it has cost him neere 1000 pounds to have it
ingrav'd at *Amsterdam*.[2] There is not a better Latine pöet
living, when he gives himselfe that Diversion;[3] nor is his
Excellency lesse in Counsil, & prudent matters of state: &c:
but is so extraordinary nice in scifting, & examining all possible contingences, that he adventures at nothing, which is
not Demonstration: There were not in the whole world his
equal for a superintendent of Manufacturs, & improvement
of Trade; or for to govern a Plantation: If I were a Prince,
I should make him my second Counselor at least:[4] There is

---

character see Aubrey, *Brief lives*,
ii. 142–3. Her father was Sir
Hardress Waller, 1604?–1666?, the
regicide: *D.N.B.*

[1] The *Experiment* was Petty's
second double bottom: above, iii.
69, 392.

[2] *Hiberniæ Delineatio quoàd hac-
tenus licuit, Perfectissima Studio
Guilielmi Petty Eq^{tis}: Aurati.* The
engraving of the maps was ap-
parently completed by 1672; the
date of publication was probably
1685; there have been various later
reprints. For it see Y. M. Goblet,
*La transformation de la géographie
politique de l'Irlande au xviie siècle*,
1930, ii. 125–45; *Term Catalogues*,

ii. 126. Goblet accepts Evelyn's
statement that the engraving was
done in Amsterdam: ii. 152–6.

[3] Specimens of his compositions
are given in *Petty papers*, ii. 243–
54 (no. 155 is a translation from
Dr. Walter Pope's 'The Old Man's
Wish'). See also below, p. 61.

[4] Charles II once said, 'That he
thought [Petty] one of the best
Commissioners of the Navy that
ever was; That [he] had vast knowledge in many things—"But" sayd
he "the man will not be contented
to be excellent, but is still Ayming
at Impossible Things"': *Petty–
Southwell corr.*, p. 281.

nothing difficult to him; besids he is Coragious,[a] on which
account I cannot but note a true storie óf him: That when
Sir *Aleyn Brodrick* sent him a Challenge, upon a difference
twixt them in *Ireland*: Sir Will: though, exceedingly *pur-
blind*, accepted the challenge, & it being his part to propound
the Weapon, defied his Antagonist, to meete him with an
hatchet or Axe in a darke Cellar; which he refusing, was
laught at, for challinging one whom every body knew was so
short sighted:[1] Sir William was[b] with all this facetious, & of
Easy Conversation, friendly, & Courteous &[c] had such a
faculty to imitate others, that he would take a Text, and
preach now like a grave orthodox Divine, then fall-into the
Presbyterian way, thence to the Phanatical, the Quaker, the
Moonk, & frier, the Popish Priest, with such[d] admirable
action, & alteration of voice & tone, as it was not possible
to abstaine from wonder, & one would sweare, to heare[a]
severall persons, or think he were not in good earnest an
Enthusiast & almost beside himselfe, when he would fall out
of it in to a serious discourse &c which was very divertisant:[2]
but it was very rarely he would be courted to oblige the company with this faculty, unlesse among most intimate friends:
My Lord *Duke* of *Ormond* once obtain'd it of him, & was
almost ravished with admiration of it; but by & by he fell
upon a serious reprimand of the faults & miscarriages of some
Princes & Governors, which though he named none, did so
sensibly touch my L: *Duke*, who was then *Lieutenant* of
Ireland;[3] that my Lord began to be very uneasy, & wish'd
the spirit alayed: for he was neither able to[e] indure[e] such truths,

---

[a] Followed by *the* deleted. [b] Followed by *one that* deleted.
[c] Followed by *when* or *where* deleted. [d] Followed by *natu-* deleted.
[e–e] MS. *to b indure*.

[1] Alan Broderick, *c.* 1623–80;
knighted 1660; surveyor-general of
Ireland 1660; M.P. for Orford 1660,
1661–78: Foster, *Alumni Oxon.* He
quarrelled with Petty, and Fitzmaurice accepts this story: pp. 151–
2; but Aubrey names Sir Jerome
Sankey as the challenger: *Brief
lives*, ii. 148 (see also p. 143, where
the name is left blank); for Petty's
quarrels with the latter see Fitzmaurice, pp. 69–93.
[2] See also Aubrey, *Brief lives*, ii.
143.
[3] Ormonde was lord lieutenant of
Ireland from 1662 to 1669 and from
1677 to 1685.

nor could he for his heart but be delighted; so at last he mealted his discourse to another more ridiculous subject & came done from the joyne stoole;[1] but my Lord, would heare him preach no more. He could never get to be favoured at Court; because he outwitted all the projecturs that came neere him:[2] In my life having never know⟨n⟩ such a Genius, I cannot but mention these particulers, among multitude of others, which I could produce: When I have ben in his splendid Palace, who knew him in meaner Circumstances, he would be in admiration himselfe how he ariv'd to it;[a] nor was it his value ⟨or⟩[b] inclination to splendid furnitur & the curiositie of the age: but his Elegant Lady, who could indure nothing meane, & that was not magnificent; whilst he was very negligent himselfe & of a Philosophic temper: Lord, would he say, what a deale of do is here; I can lie in straw with as much satisfaction: & was indeede rather negligent of his person &c: Sir *William* is the Author of the ingenious deductions from the bills of Mortality which go under the name of Mr. Graunt:[3] also of that usefull discourse of the manufactur of Wooll, &

---

[a] Followed by *nor But* deleted.   [b] MS. *for*.

---

[1] i.e. a joint-stool, a stool made by a joiner, as distinguished from a roughly made one: *O.E.D.*

[2] For his powers of criticism see two anecdotes in Aubrey, *Brief lives*, ii. 147.

[3] *Natural and Political Observations mentioned in a following index, and made upon the Bills of Mortality. By John Graunt, Citizen of London. With reference to the Government, Religion, Trade, Growth. Ayre, Diseases, and the several Changes of the said City*, 1662. A second edition was published in 1662; the third, with enlargements, and the fourth, in 1665; the fifth, with further enlargements, in 1676; a German translation appeared in 1702. The question of the authorship is discussed by C. H. Hull, *Economic writings of Sir William Petty*, 1899, introd., vol. i, pp.

xxxix–liv; he concludes that Graunt (1620–74; *D.N.B.*) was the author, but that he received suggestions and some assistance from Petty, who perhaps wrote the conclusion and the dedication to Moray. Further discussion by Lord Lansdowne, *Petty papers*, ii. 273–84; *Times Literary Supplement*, 1932, p. 624, &c. Evelyn's evidence is of little independent value for the discussion; it dates probably not from 1675 but from the period of transcription. The authorship was publicly claimed for Petty already in 1683: J. Houghton, *Collection of letters for the improvement of Husbandry and Trade*, i. 147*, cited in *Petty papers*, ii. 274; and early in 1683 Petty's *Observations upon the Dublin-Bills of Mortality* was published as 'By the Observator on the London Bills of Mortality'.

severall other, in our Register of the R: Society:[1] The Author of that Paraphrase on 104 Psal: in Latine Verse, which gos about in MSS: & is inimitable:[2] In a word, there is nothing impenetrable to him.

26: Dr. *Bredox*[3] Elect Bish: of *Chichester*, on the translation of Dr. *Gunning* to *Ely*, preached at W:hall on 73. *Psal: 27*, on repentance: I visited ≏ —pr. 27 home: 28 Our Vicc: as before with little addition: The holy Comm: followed: *Pomer*: Curate 1. *Cor:* 11. 27. Exhorting to frequent Communion: 28[a] To *Lond.*

⟨31⟩[b] Dr. *Alestree* on 6: *Rom:* 3: The necessitie of those who are Baptiz'd to die to sinn: a very excellent discourse, from an excellent Preacher:[4] Supped at B: house ⛤ —pr:

Aprill: 2: In the Morning Dr. *Lamplugh* at St. *Mart:* 5 Pet: 3. 18.[5] setting-forth the intollerable passion of *Christ*: The holy *Sacrament* follow'd, it being Good-friday: Afternoone *Coram Rege* L: *Almoner Bish:* of *Rochester*:[6] 22. *Luke* 42. our *B: Saviou⟨r⟩s* Submission, & exinanition: exhorting to imitation: the difficulty of the task, absolute necessity of it, for had not our *Saviour* don it (to whom yet it was irkesome as flesh & blood) we had all miserably perish'd: exaggerating his infinite love &c: I went home:

⟨4⟩[c] Our *Viccar* on 4 *Rom:* 25. how our *B: Sa:* Resurrection was our Justification; That Justification was not by one

---

a Reading doubtful. b MS. *30*. c MS. *3*.

---

1 A discourse, 'Of making cloth with sheep's wool', is printed in Birch, i. 55–65; another, on dyeing, in Sprat, pp. 284–306.

2 This part of the notice is premature, as Petty did not make, or at least complete, his translation until 1677, when he also made a greatly revised, or perhaps a new, version: *Petty–Southwell corr.*, pp. 17–27. A version was published in 1678 or 1679 (licence 31 Aug. 1678) with the title, *Colloquium Davidis cum anima sua*, (*accinente Paraphrasim in 104 Psalmum*) *De Magnalibus Dei*.

3 Brideoake: see above, p. 2, &c. Gunning had been elected bishop of Ely on 13 February and confirmed 4 March; Brideoake had been elected bishop of Chichester on 9 March; he was confirmed on 15 April and consecrated on 18 April. Lenten sermon at court.

4 Lenten sermon at court.

5 A slip for 1 Peter iii. 18.

6 The preacher is Dolben, the bishop of Rochester; he did not become lord almoner until October of this year. Lenten sermon at court. The lord almoner, Henchman, was listed to preach on Easter Day.

single act, but continual progresse: that had not *Christ* risen
from the Dead, all his Miracles, life & doctrine had ben to
no Effect: That so we must proceede in good life & works
&c: The bl: Sacrament follow'd: The *Curate*, (but a weake
preacher) as formerly, nothing extraordinary:

11 Our *Vicc:* & *Curate* both as before: This note yet
observable in the *Viccars*, That we never reade our *B: Saviour*
called the *Lord Jesus* 'til after his *Resurrection*, as being by
that made & constituted *Lord* of all to whome all power in
heaven & Earth was given &c: 12 To *Lond:* 16 dind with ✩
—pr:

⟨18⟩[a] A stranger at *W:hall*: on 73. *Psal:* 15. 16.[1] Asserting
Providence against *Atheists*: After I went to St. *Martines*,
wher also a stranger on 55 *Isa:* 6. The importance of heartily
seeking God: The holy Comm: followd: 24 Visited ✩ —pr:

25 Dr. *Barrow*[2] that excellent[b] pious & most learned man,
Divine, Mathematitian, Poet, *Traveller*, & most humble person, preached at W:hall, to the household on: 20 *Luke* 27:
Of Love & Charity to our Neighbour &c: Thence to St.
Martines, where our Bish: of *Rochester* on 15 *John*: 8 the
necessitie of a Christians producing fruite: Sacrament followed: 27 I was to visite ✩ —pr:

29 I read my first discourse of *Earth* & *Vegetation* before
the *Royal Society*, as a lecture in Course after Sir Rob:[c]
Southwell[3] had read his the weeke before on Water: I was
commanded to print it by our President & the Suffrage of the
Society:[4] returned home that Evening:

---

[1] Apparently cited from the
Prayer Book.
[2] Isaac Barrow, *c.* 1630–77; D.D.
1666; divine and scholar: *D.N.B.*
He had travelled as far afield as
Constantinople, and described an
incident of the journey in a Latin
poem. None of his poems (all in
Latin or Greek) was published
during his lifetime. He was a chaplain in ordinary from *c.* 1670 until
his death. The text is an error for
St. Luke x. 27.
[3] Robert Southwell, 1635–1702;
knighted 1665; member of the
Philosophical Society 7 May 1662;
F.R.S.; president 1690–5; diplomatist, &c.: *D.N.B.*; I.H.R., *Bull.*,
iii (1926), 67; xx (1947), 48–9.
[4] On 3 Dec. 1674 the council of

May: 1 Our *Viccar* on   keeping the unity of the Spirit in the bond of Peace:[1] Meeting of the foefeès for the poore, who dined together &c: 2: On: 12: *Heb:* 1: what the weights were that hindred our Christian Course: namely, Carnal reasoning, sensual Pleasure, Cares & anxieties for the things of this life: The holy Communion follow'd: *Curate* on: 2: Tim: 16. 17.[2] benefit of holy Scripture: 8 To *Lond:* 9: at[a] St. *Martines* the *Bish:* of *Oxon*[3] on 18 Joh: 36. of subjection to the higher powers &c: The Communion follow'd, 'twas Rogation Sonday, I dined at B: house with Mrs. *Blagg:* 13: A stranger (*Ascention* day) at St. *Mart:* on 24. Luke 51. 52. apposite to the solemnity & very well: The holy Sacrament follow'd, dind with ✩ at B: house:

15 I returned home, having ben all this weeke at *Lond:* about many affaires:

16. I had prayers at home in the Morning: *Pomerid Curate* on 4. John: 24.

This day was my deare friend Mrs. *Blagg* maried to Mr. *Sidny Godolphin*[4] Groome of the *Bed-Chamber* to his Majestie at the *Temple Church* by Mr. *Leake* Chap: to the *Duke:*

18 To *Lond:* invited by Mrs. *Blagg* to a Collation with my

---

[a] Followed by *Whitehall* deleted.

---

the Society decided that each member of the council should read an 'experimental discourse' to the Society during the ensuing year; on 10 December it was decided to invite some of the ordinary fellows also to do so: Birch, iii. 158, 160, 162. Southwell read his discourse on Water on 8 April; it is printed by Birch, iii. 196–216. Evelyn followed on the present day and on 13 May; on 17 June the council ordered it to be printed: ibid., pp. 218, 219, 222–3. It was published in 1676 as *A Philosophical Discourse of Earth, Relating to the Culture and Improvement of it for Vegetation, and the Propagation of Plants*: Keynes, pp. 206–11.

[1] Ephesians iv. 3.

[2] A slip presumably for 2 Timothy iii. 16, 17.

[3] Compton.

[4] Godolphin (above, p. 10) was a groom of the bedchamber from 1670 to 1678. Mrs. Godolphin did not announce the marriage to Evelyn until 26 April 1676: below, p. 89; the present notice is therefore an interpolation in the original notes for the Diary; his occasional use of her married name before the date of the announcement is also an indication of revision. For the circumstances of the marriage see *Life of Mrs. Godolphin*, pp. 56–7.

Lady *Yearbrow*,[1] Mrs. Howards,[a] my *Wife* & other friends;[b] & returned next day. 20: My pious friend Mrs. *Godolphin*, my Lady *Berkeley*, La: *Yarborow*, Mrs. *Howard*[c] came all downe to my house & return'd in the Evening. ☆ —pr: 23. A stranger on 8 *Rom:* 9. *Whitsondy*, The effects of the Spirit of Christ uniting the faithfull in him, not by a substantial Corporal union, but spiritual, shewed in an holy life, & conformity to his Doctrine: The blessed Communion follow'd: *Pomerid*: at Greenwich the *Curate* on *3. Joh: 8*: shewing the voluntary graces of Gods holy Spirit. I went then to visite one *Mr. Bathurst* a *Spanish Merchant* &c: a Neighbour:

27: *Ember-Weeke*, I went to *Lond:* 29: his Majesties Birth day at W:hall, By the Bish: of *Bath* & Wells[2] on: 2: *Hebb:*[d] 23. 30: Trinity *Sonday* a stranger on   *prove your selves whether ye be in the faith*[3] &c: Thence to St. *Martines*, where a Chaplain of the *Bish:* of *Caerliles*[4] on   *In this I exercise my selfe, to have a Conscience voide of offence* &c. The holy Communion followed: I went in the afternoone to visite my sick Lady *Vicountesse Mordaunt*.[5] 31. I went with my *L. Ossorie* to *Deptford* where we chose him Master of the *Trinity Companie*; our *Viccar* preaching on 4: *Eph:* 30 very excellently & appositely to the occasion: Thence by barge, to *Lond:* where at the Trinity house[6] we had a magnificent feast, & divers greate persons: I thence went with his Lordship to[e] his Lodging in White-hall:

---

[a] Or *Howarde*.   [b] Followed by *where I b-* deleted.   [c] Followed by *& al*; *al* deleted, *&* left standing.   [d] Or *Habb:*   [e] Followed by *my* deleted.

---

[1] Henrietta Maria Blagge, d. between 1709 and 1716; Mrs. Godolphin's eldest sister; married 1664 Sir Thomas Yarborough (below, 13 July 1683): Miss Sampson, in *Life of Mrs. Godolphin*, pp. 268–71.

[2] Mews. His text, whether in Habakkuk or Hebrews, does not exist.

[3] 2 Corinthians xiii. 5, misquoted.

[4] Rainbow: above, iii. 262. The text is Acts xxiv. 16.

[5] Lord Mordaunt died on 5 June of this year.

[6] The Trinity House had been rebuilt on its old site in Water Lane (above, iii. 314 n.), and was in use from 1670. It was burnt down in 1714 and again rebuilt on the same site: Barrett, *Trinity House*, pp. 101, 114.

June 1 I supped at Berkeley house with ⬠ —pr:

2 At a Conference of the Lords & Comm: in the painted Chamber upon a difference about imprisoning some of their Members I was present:[1] Din'd at the *Duke* of *Ormonds*, with the *Duke* of *Munmoth* & severall greate men. 3: I was at another Conference, where the Lords accused the Commons for their transcended misbehaviour, breach of Privelege, *Magna Charta*, Subversion of *Government*, & other high & provoking & diminishing Expressions; shewing what duties & subjections they owed to the Lords in Parliament by record *Hen:* 4th &c. which was like to create a notable disturbance:[2] I din'd at the Master of the *Mints*,[3] went to R: Society: The discourse being of Fountaines &c & so to my owne house:

6 our *Viccar* on 12: *Heb:* 1. what was ment by the sinn dos so easily beset us: viz. our most boosome sinn: The method of preventing it, by care, & firm resolution &c. There follow'd the blessed Sacrament. The Lord make me thankfull & vigilant. *Pomer: Stranger* on 9. *Heb:* 27: The Certainty of the last Judgement &c.

8 To *Lond:* about buisinesse, dined with ⬠ at B: house, where also din'd the young Prince of *Nieuburg*:[4] 10: I was upon an Evidence at *Guild-hall* & thence went home: 13 Our

---

[1] As a result of an appeal from chancery to the house of lords a member of the lower house was summoned to appear before the lords (*Shirley* v. *Fagg*). The commons treated this as a breach of privilege; the dispute between the two houses was worked up by the opposition in order to force the king to prorogue parliament. The present conference concerned a parallel but subsidiary case, *Stoughton* v. *Onslow*. The commons had sent their member, Sir John Fagg (above, iii. 238), to the Tower on 1 June for waiving his privilege by appearing before the lords; he was released on 3 June: *L.J.*; *C.J.*; Grey, *Debates*.

[2] The commons had imprisoned the counsel assigned by the lords to the appellant in a case before them in which one of the defendants was a member of the commons (*Crispe* v. *Lady Cranborne*, &c.). The lords in this conference denounced the commons' action.

[3] Henry Slingsby.

[4] Johann Wilhelm von Wittelsbach, of the Neuburg line, 1658–1716; prince of Neuburg; succeeded as Elector Palatine 1690; duke of Jülich and Berg: *Allgemeine Deutsche Biog.* He had arrived at Greenwich on 13 May and had received a degree at Oxford on 2 June: *London Gazette*, 20 May, 7 June.

Vicc: on his former & subject, little added: *Pomerid:* the *Curate* on: 4: John: 24, shewing the nature of *God* as a spirit &c:

14 Came divers *Ladys* to dine at my house, with whome I went to Lond:

15 Came Mrs. *Godolphin* to see me —pr: 18 home: 20: *Viccar* on 7: *Job:* 20. The necessity of Repentance & pungent sorrow for sinn:

This afternoone came Monsieur *Quierwill*[a] & his *Lady*[1] Parents to the famous beauty & . . . favorite at Court, to see Sir Rich: Bro: my F. in Law, with whom they were intimately acquainted in *Bretagne*, what time Sir Richard was sent[b] to *Brest*, to supervise his Majesties sea affaires during the later part of his Majesties banishment abroad:[2] This Gent: house being not a mile from *Brest*; Sir *Richard* made an acquaintance there, & being used very Civily, was oblig'd to returne it here, which we did in a Collation: after which they returned to Lond: He seem'd a souldierly person, & a good fellow, as the *Bretons* generaly are, his *Lady* had ben very handsom, & seem'd a shrew'd understanding woman: Conversing with him in our *Garden*, I found severall words of the *Breton* language[c] the same with our *Welch*: His daughter was now made *Dutchesse of Portsmouth*[3] and in the height of favour; but we never made any use of it: &c:

22 To *Lond:* stayed most of the weeke upon buisinesse:

27: At[d] *Ely-house* I went to the Consecration of my worthy friend the Learned *Dr. Barlow*, Warden of *Queenes Coll:*

---

a Or *Quieruvill.*   b Followed by *the* deleted.   c Spelling doubtful.
d Followed by *White-hall* deleted.

---

1 Guillame de Penancoët, comte de Kéroualle (Kerouazle), d. 1690; and his wife (married 1645) Marie-Anne de Plœuc de Timeur, d. 1709; de la Chenaye-Desbois and Badier, xv. 628–9. The château of Kéroualle is situated between Brest and Guilers: for it see Mrs. Colquhoun Grant, *Brittany to Whitehall*, 1909, pp. 21–4.

2 Browne was in Brittany, chiefly at Brest and Nantes, from 1652 to 1654, trying to obtain the king's dues on the prizes brought in by English royalists: correspondence in Evelyn, *Diary*, ed. Bohn, iv. 255–301.

3 She had been created duchess in 1673.

Oxon: now made Bishop of *Lincoln*,[a] Dr. *Hamilton*[1] preaching in that Chapell on   Tim: an excellent discourse of the *Episcopal* Office &c: after which succeeded a magnificent feast, where were the Duke of *Ormond*, E: of *Lauderdail*,[2] Lord *Tres: Keeper*[3] &c severall other Lords, & *Bishops*:

28 My F in Law had a Tryal before the *L: Chancelor*,[4] to advantage; but the Register prevaricated in the minutes, which is a shamefull abuse: & ought to be reform'd, by causing them to be read in Court: I visited Mrs. G — pr:

29 I went with Mrs. *Godolphin* to my house at Says-Court, where she staied a Weeke with us: *pr:*

July: 4: our *Viccar* on his former *Text* in *Job*: The holy Comm: follow'd which we all rec'd: In Afternoone at *Grenewich* the Curate on Eccles: 1[5] Remember thy Creator &c.

5 Came to dine with us Mr. *Sidny Godolphin*[6] to see his Lady, with the two *Howards Ma: of honour*, & returned that Evening: 6: I carried Mrs. *Godolphin* to *Lond:* & set her downe at my Lord *Sunderlands*.[7]

8 I went with Mrs. *Howard* & her two daughters towards *Northampton Assises* about a *Tryal* at *Law*,[8] in which I was Concerned for them as a *Trusteè*. We lay this night at *Henly* on the *Thames* at our *Attourney* Mr. ⟨*Stephens's*⟩[b] who entertain'd us very handsomely: Thenc next day dining at *Shotover* at Sir *Tim: Tyrills* a sweete place,[9] we lay at Oxford it being the *Act*:[10] when Mr. *Rob: Spencer*[11] Unkle to the *Earle* of *Sunderland* & my old acquaintance in *France*, entertain'd us at his appartment in *Christ-Church* (where he had hired one

---

[a] Comma supplied.   [b] MS. *Stephenss*.

---

[1] Perhaps a slip for Halton, i.e. Timothy Halton, *c.* 1633–1704; D.D. 1674; Barlow's successor as provost of Queen's College 1677: *D.N.B.*

[2] He had been created duke of Lauderdale (Scotland) in 1672.

[3] Heneage Finch: above, iii. 388. He had been appointed lord keeper in 1673 and became lord chancellor on 19 December of this year.

[4] Heneage Finch, still only lord keeper.

[5] Ecclesiastes xii. 1.

[6] Evelyn did not know of the marriage until 1676.

[7] Where Sunderland was living at this time is not known.

[8] See below, pp. 70–1.

[9] Above, iii. 383.

[10] See above, iii. 104.

[11] Above, iii. 37, &c.

of the Canons Lodgings,) entertain'd us all the while, with exceeding generosity: 10: The *Vice-Chancelor Dr. Bathurst*,[1] (who had formerly taken particular care of my Sonn) President of *Trinity*, invited me to Dinner, & did me greate honour all the time of my stay: The next day he also invited me & all my Company, though strangers to him, to a very noble Dinner: I was at all the *Academique* Exercises:[2] *Sondy*, at St. *Maries* preached a fellow of *Brasen nose* on 2: *Tit:* 15., not a little magnifying the dignity of Church-men: In the afternoone one of New Coll: but the heate and presse was so greate I could not hear &c: & was faine to go out:

We heard the Speeches & saw the Ceremonie of Creating Doctors[a] in Divinity, *Law, Physique* &c: I had in the morning early heard Dr. *Morison*[3] *Botanic Professor*, reade on divers Plants in the Physic Garden; & saw that rare Collection of natural Curiosities, of Dr. *Plots*[4] of *Magdalen* hall: *Author* of the Natural hist: of *Oxford-shire*; all of them collected in that shire, & indeede extraordinary, that in one County, there should be found such varietie of Plants, Shells, Stones, Minerals, Marcasites, foule, Insects, Models of works &c: Chrystals, Achates, Marbles: he was now intending to Visite *Staffordshire* & as he had of Oxfordshire to give us the *Natural, Topical, Political, Mechani⟨c⟩al* history: & pitty it is, more of this industrious mans genius were not employed so to describe every County of England, since it would be one of the

---

[a] Or *Doctor*.

---

[1] He was vice-chancellor from 1673 to 1676.

[2] Wood, *Life and times*, ii. 318–19.

[3] Robert Morison, 1620–83; M.D. 1648; professor of botany at Oxford 1669–83: *D.N.B.* For the Physick Garden see above, iii. 109, 386.

[4] Robert Plot, 1640–96; D.C.L. 1671; F.R.S. 1677; antiquary and scientist: *D.N.B.* It was not until 1677 that he published *The Natural History of Oxford-shire, being an Essay toward the Natural History of England.* In January 1681 he issued proposals for a similar work on Staffordshire: Wood, *Life and times*, ii. 511; it appeared in 1686, as *The Natural History of Stafford-shire.* Collections of natural objects made by him while preparing these two works were given by him to the Ashmolean Museum *c.* 1690: biographical notice prefixed to *Nat. hist. of Oxford-shire*, 2nd ed., 1705. Evelyn calls him 'my worthy Friend', 'my worthy and learned Friend' in *Numismata*, pp. 21, 84; see also p. 208.

most usefull & illustrious Workes that was ever produc'd in any age or nation: I visited also the *Bodlean* library & my old friend the Learned *Obadia Walker*[1] head of Universitie Coll: which he had now almost quite rebuilt or repair'd: So taking leave of the V: Chancelor, Dr. *Alestree* the Kings Professor in Divinity, Deane of *Christ Church* Dr. *Fell*, we proceeded to *Northampton* where we arived next day:

In this journey went part of the way Mr. *Ja: Grahame*[2] [Since *privy purse to the Duke*],[a] a Young Gent: exceedingly in love with Mrs. *Dorothy Howard* one of the *Mayds of honor* in our Company: I could not but pitty them both: The Mother not much favouring it: This Lady was not onely a greate beauty, but a most virtuous & excellent Creature, & worthy to have ben Wife to the best of men: My advice was required, & I spake to the advantage of the young gent: more out of pitty, than that I thought she deserv'd no better; for though he was a gent: of a good family, yet there was greate inequalitys &c:

14 I went to see my Lord *Sunderlands* seat at *Althorp*,[3] 4 miles from the ragged Towne of Northampton [Since burned

---

[a] Marginal note.

---

[1] Walker (above, ii. 550, &c.) did not become master of University until 1676; he continued as master until 1689. The greater part of the original quadrangle of the college was rebuilt between 1634 and 1666; the kitchen and library were rebuilt in 1668–70; the old east range was pulled down in 1669–74 and rebuilt by *c.* 1677: Wood, *Colleges*, pp. 56–7; W. Carr, *University College*, 1902, p. 217. Walker was generally in residence from 1660.

[2] James Graham, 1649–1730, soldier and politician: *D.N.B.* He was keeper of the privy purse to the duke of York from *c.* 1679 to 1685, and served him in the same capacity when he became king. For his marriage see below, p. 88 n. Further

notices below.

[3] Althorp was acquired by the Spencer family about 1512. The date when the house was built is unknown, but it appears to have been largely reconstructed by the parents of the present Lord Sunderland and by Sunderland himself. Cosimo III, visiting it in 1669, regarded it as 'the best planned and best arranged country-seat' in England. The house was greatly altered *c.* 1800; the old gate-house was removed about 1729–33: T. F. Dibdin, *Aedes Althorpianae*, 1822; Magalotti, *Travels of Cosmo III*, pp. 248–50 and plate; view by L. Knyff, *Nouveau theatre de la Grande Bretagne*, 1708, pl. 27.

& well rebuilt]:[a][1] tis placed in a pretty open bottome, very
finely watred & flanqued with stately woods & groves in a
Parke with a *Canale*, yet the water is not running, which is
a defect: The house a kind of modern building of Free stone:
within most nobly furnishe'd: The Apartments very commodious, a Gallerie & noble hall: but the *Kitching* for being
in the body of the house, & Chapell too small were defects:
There is an old, yet honorable Gate house standing a wry, &
out-housing meane, but design'd to be taken away: It was
Moated round after the old manner, but[b] it is now dry &
turf'd with a sweete Carpet:[2] above all are admirable & magnificent the severall ample Gardens furnish'd with the Choicest
fruite in England, & exquisitely kept: Great plenty of
Oranges, and other Curiosities: The Parke full of Fowle &
especialy Hernes, & from it a prospect to *Holmby* house,[3]
which being demolished in the late Civil Warre, shews like
a Roman ruine shaded by the trees about it, one of the most
pleasing sights that ever I saw, of state & solemne:

15 Our Cause was pleaded in behalfe of the Mother Mrs.
Howard & *Daughters* before baron *Thurland*,[4] who had formerly been Steward of Courte for me: We carried our Cause,
as there was reason; for here was an imprudent as well as
disobedient sonn, against his Mother by instigation doubtlesse of his Wife, one Mrs. *Ogle*, (an[c] antient Maid) whom he
had clandestinly married, & who brought him no fortune, he

---

a Marginal note.   b Followed by *th* deleted.   c Followed by *old*
deleted.

---

[1] On 20 September of this year
there broke out a fire which
destroyed 600 houses and the principal buildings here, probably more
than half of the town: *V.C.H.*,
Northants., iii. 31.
[2] Cf. the use of the word above,
iii. 555.
[3] Or Holdenby House, where
Charles I had been kept prisoner
from February to June 1647. It
had been built by Sir Christopher
Hatton, the lord chancellor, and
was acquired by James I in 1608.

It was sold in 1650 and shortly
afterwards the house was pulled
down. The estate reverted to
Charles II in 1660 and had recently
been acquired by Lord Duras
(below, p. 77): Baker, (*Northamptonshire*), i. 194–207. Two gates and
some other parts still exist.
[4] Sir Edward Thurland (above,
iii. 219, 509) was a baron of the
exchequer from 1673 to 1679. The
notice of the assizes shows that he
was to be at Northampton on this
day: *London Gazette*, 28 June.

heire aparent of the Earle of *Berkshire*.[1] After dinner we went toward *Lond:* Lay at *Brickhill* in *Bedfordshire* & came late next day to[a] our journeys end.

This was a journey of Adventure & knight errantry, one of the Ladys servants being as desperatly in love with Mrs. *Howards* Woman, who riding on horsback behind his *Rival*, the amorous & jealous Youth, having a little drink in his pate, had certainly here killed himselfe, had he not ben prevented; for alighting from his horse & drawing his sword, he endeavored to fall upon it twise or thrice, but was interrupted; ⟨by⟩[b] our Coach-man & a stranger that passed by, after which running to his rival, & snatching another sword from his side (for we had beaten his owne out of his hand) & on the suddaine pulling downe his Mistriss, would have run both of them through; but we parted them, though not without some blood: This miserable Creature Poyson'd himselfe for her not many daies after they came to Lond:

18 Came to visite me *Mrs. Godolphin* — pr. ⟨18⟩:[c] I received the B: *Sacrament* at St. *James* in the morning with ⌢: Thence to my *L: Tressurers* whose Chaplain preached at *Wallingford-house*[2] excellently well on 31 *Psal: 31*: The goodnesse and providence of God, over his Saints, who rely on him without solicitude: I dined at a poore Widdows with ⌢: *Pomerid*: Dr. *Leake* at St. *Jame's* on: 24. *Matt* 42. That we should watch & be ready for the comming of the Lord:

---

[a] Followed by *Lond* deleted.   [b] MS. *with* or *which*.   [c] MS. *19*.

---

[1] The son is Craven Howard, d. 1700; his wife, whom he had married in 1673, was Anne, d. 1682, daughter of Thomas Ogle of Pinchbeck, Lincs., and sometime maid of honour to the duchess of York: (*Westminster Abbey registers*), pp. 10, 205; A. R. Maddison, *Lincolnshire pedigrees*, ii. 731–2 (Harleian Soc., vol. li, 1903); Chamberlayne, 1669. Evelyn is wrong in calling Howard heir-apparent to the earl of Berkshire in 1675; he succeeded to this position in 1683 and his son by

his second wife succeeded to the title in 1706: Henry Howard, *Indication of memorials*, &c., pp. 59–60, 65; G.E.C. Evelyn was appointed a trustee by William Howard, Mrs. Howard's deceased husband: see below, pp. 105–6.
[2] Above, iii. 490; iv. 18. The chaplain is perhaps Henry Bagshaw, c. 1634–1709; D.D. 1671: *D.N.B.* He describes himself as chaplain to the lord treasurer in *A Sermon*, 1676. His text does not exist; perhaps a slip for verse 21 in the Prayer Book.

&c: 20 I returned home, where I had the un-wellcome newes of my sonns[a] being falln ill of the Small-pox: but *God* was mercifull to him in all his sicknesse.

25 St. Jam: day our *Viccar* absent, preached a stranger on 34. *Psal:* 14, of the vilenesse of Sinn, that therefore we should avoid it: Afternoone on the same, our obligation to Love & seeke Peace with all: 26 Lond: returned not till 29:

My Sonn recovers[b] blessed be God.

August 1 A stranger made a pathetical, & very tedious discourse on 13 *Jer:* ult. *When shall it once be?* Shewing Gods unwillingnesse that sinners should miscarry; by which & many other Texts he made out, that God had decreed none to ⟨irresistible⟩[c] destruction: The holy Comm: followed: *Pomerid*: another stranger on 73. Psa: 24. That the soules repose is onely in God &c:

4 To Lond: about affaires, returned next day: 8: Mr. *Hutcheson*[1] Minister of *Bow-Church*[2] on 3. *Joh:* 8: of the unconfin'dnesse of Gods holy Spirit: &c: that inspires where it lists: on some in Youth, some in riper yeares, some even[d] in their old age: exhorted to our giving ourselves up to his influences & motions, that he might no longer withhold his inbreathings; he illustrated its powerfull operations by the similitude of Wind, its inconspicuity, force & irresistible nature & purifying quality &c: *Pomerid*: our *Curate* ult. *Eph:* ult:

9 My Coach-house was broken open this night, & the Glasses & Damaske Cushions, Curtaines &c: taken away: Went to *Wimbledon* to see my Lord of *Bristoll* & return'd in the Evening: 10 To *Lond:* 11: Dind with my Lady *Sunderland* at my owne Lodging.[3] 12 Went to *Twicknam*[4] to visite Mrs.

---

[a] Or *sonne*.   [b] Or *recovering*.   [c] MS. *irreststable*.   [d] Altered from *in*.

---

[1] Identifiable as Thomas Hutchinson, M.A., appointed rector of All Hallows, Honey Lane, 1663, still living 1700; this church was not rebuilt after the Fire, the parish being united to St. Mary le Bow: Newcourt, *Repertorium*, i. 251–2.

[2] The present church, re-opened for service in 1673: A. W. Hutton, *Short hist. . . . of Bow Church, Cheapside*, 1908.

[3] Above, p. 50.

[4] Above, p. 23.

Godolphin, return'd: 15. our *Viccar* on his former Text in *Job*: The danger of changing one sinn for another: &c.

Pomerid: at Greenewich Dr. *Sprat*[1] prebend of *Westminster*, & Chap: to the *Duke* of *Buckingham* on *Epist: Jude* 3. shewing what the *Primitive Faith* was, how neere it & excellent that of the *Church* of *England*; the danger of departing from it &c: After sermon, I waited on our *Bishop*, whom I found at Cap: Cocks: 19 To *Lond:* return'd to dinner: 22: To *Lond:* and received[a] the B: *Communion* at *White-hall*, There was no preaching, The Court at *Windsor*:[2] *Pomerid*: at St. *Dunstans* in *Fleetestreet*[b][3] on 2: *Tit:* 13 an excellent discourse how lawfull & reasonable to expect a Reward, & how necessary the proposing it for incitement to Virtue: &c: I return'd home all the way on foote:

23 I went to *Bromeley*[4] to see the *Bish:* of *Rochester*: Dind at Sir *Phil: Warwicks* at *Frogpoole*.[c][5]

24 I went with my Wife to see my L: *Arch-bishop* of *Canterbery* where we dined & were exceeding kindly received: returned from *Croydon*[6] in the Evening:

29 our *Viccar* on his old beaten Text: Afternoone the *Curate* on 9: *Pro:* 8: of the benefit of reprofe: 30: To *Lond:* return'd next day; found Mrs. *Blagge* there,[d] she gave me a letter of *Attourney* about her Concernes[7] & return'd to

---

[a] There is here a wrong marginal date, *21*. [b] Or *fleetestreet*.
[c] Substituted for *Cray*. [d] Comma supplied.

---

[1] Above, iii. 533. He was a prebendary of Westminster from 1669 to 1683. The period during which he was chaplain to Buckingham is uncertain; it extended from at least 1663 to at least 1670: Wood, *Life and times*, i. 495–6; *D.N.B.*

[2] Charles went to Windsor on 7 July and returned to Whitehall on 11 September: *London Gazette*, 8 July, 13 Sept.

[3] St. Dunstan's in the West. It was a medieval building projecting into Fleet Street; the present church, occupying the north part of the

site, was built in 1831–3: Wheatley.

[4] For the bishop's palace here, see above, iii. 537.

[5] Above, iii. 253.

[6] The archbishops had a palace at Croydon from the Middle Ages until 1780: *V.C.H., Surrey*, iv. 206–15; C. G. Paget, *Croydon homes of the past*, 1937, pp. 6–15. Sheldon is buried at Croydon.

[7] Evelyn was to manage her affairs when she went to France with Lord Berkeley: below, pp. 76, 78–9; *Life of Mrs. Godolphin*, p. 60.

Twicknam that evening,[a] my Wife bringing her a good part
of the way:

September 2 I went to see *Dullwidge* Colledge,[1] being the
pious foundation of one *Allen* a famous *Comoedian* in K.
James's time: The Chapell is pretty; The rest of the *Hospital*
very ill contriv'd; it yet maintaines divers poore of both
sexes, 'tis in a melancholy part of *Camerwell* Parish; I came
back by certaine Medicinal *Spâ Waters* at a place called
Sydname[b] Wells[2] in *Lewisham* Parish; much frequented in
Summer time:

5 Our *Viccar* as formerly, of Gods care of man-kind; the
virtue & power of Conscience, & its accusations for profe of
a *Deity* & Judge: The holy Communion followed; & it was I
hope a blessed day to me.

9 I went to *Lond:* to see a sick [poore][c] person taken suddenly ill of a dumb Palsy.

10 I was Casualy shewed the *Dutchesse* of *Portsmouths*
splendid Appartment at *Whitehall*,[3] luxuriously furnished, &
with ten times the richnesse & glory beyond the *Queenes*, such
massy pieces of Plate, whole Tables, Stands &c: of incredible
value &c: 11 returned home: 12 our *Viccar* as before: *Curat*
on 1 *Joh:* 5: 7 concerning the *Mysterie* of the *Trinity*: My

---

[a] Comma supplied.   [b] Or *Sydnams*.   [c] Interlined.

---

[1] The College of God's Gift in
Dulwich had been founded by
Edward Alleyn the actor (1566–
1626: *D.N.B.*) in 1613–20; it was to
consist of a warden, four fellows,
twelve alms folk (six of either sex),
and twelve poor scholars; paying
pupils were also admitted. It was
of little importance until the modern
expansion of the school, which
began in 1841: *V.C.H., Surrey*, ii.
198–210.

[2] Sydenham Wells were discovered *c.* 1648; the water was similar in its properties to that of
Epsom. The spring was situated in
the present Wells Road and was destroyed in the late nineteenth cen-

tury: J. Peter, *A Treatise of Lewisham (But Vulgarly Miscalled Dulwich) Wells in Kent*, 1680; Sir W.
Besant, *London south of the Thames*,
1912, p. 296; see also B. Allen, *Nat.
hist. of the Chalybeat and Purging
Waters of England*, 1699, pp. 135–7.

[3] This apartment was situated at
the south end of the riverside range
of the palace. It had been extended
and altered for the duchess between
1672 and 1674, and there was a
further rebuilding about 1678. It
was destroyed in 1691 in the first
Whitehall fire: L.C.C., *Survey of
London*, xiii. 85–6. Further notices
below.

Lord *Brounchar* coming to visite me, interrupted my going this afternoone to church:

⟨14⟩[a] To *Lond:* din'd at B: house with Mrs. Bl:— pr: 19 *Ember* weeke & *Ordination* Sonday,[1] I receiv'd the bl: Comm: at St. *James's*, heard a serm: at W hall on the *Burden of Dumah*,[2] concerning Repentance: 21 Rec'd with ☆ at a poore sick persons. 22. returned home. 23: *Lond:* To visite my L: *Berkeley* falln ill. 26: Received the B: Sacrament at St. *Jamess*, Then *Coram Rege* at W:hall Dr. *Standish*[3] on: 2: *Cor:* 5. 20, of the Dignitie of the Ministerial function &c: *Pomer*: Dr.[b] Lake on 3. *Gen:* 13. of the *Womans* fall &c: 29: I went to *Parsons Greene* to visite my Lady *Mordaunt* with my Wife & Mrs. *Godolphin*: saw the Italian *Scaramucchio*[4] act before the King at *White-hall*; People giving monye to come in, which was very Scandalous, & never so before at Court Diversions:[5] having seene him act before in *Italy* many yeares past, I was not averse from seeing the most excellent of that kind of folly:

Octob: 1 I went home. 3: *Curate* as formerly: That the Father was God, how we his Children by *Adoption* & *Grace* &c: The holy Sacrament follow'd, with greate resolutions &c: God make me mindfull: *Pomerid*: a stranger on 3: *Matt* 8: what fruits were meete for Repentance &c: a very excellent sermon: 6 To *Lond:* dind at *Ber: house.* 7: At Sir *Step: Foxes.* 8. Supp'd at *Ber: house*: 9 home:

---

a MS. *24.*   b Altered from *Mr.*

---

[1] Ordination in the Church of England takes place on the Sundays following the four Ember Weeks: *Constitutions and Canons Ecclesiasticall*, 1604, no. 31.

[2] Isaiah xxi. 11.

[3] John Standish, 1634–86; chaplain in ordinary 1674–86; D.D. 1680: Venn. The sermon was published in 1676.

[4] A company of Italian comedians, presumably under the leadership of Tiberio Fiorilli (above, p. 12), was here from June to October: Boswell, *Restoration court stage*, pp. 121–2; see also Constantini, *Scaramouche*, trans. Beaumont, preface.

[5] 'Scaramuccio acting dayly in the Hall of *Whitehall*, and all Sorts of People flocking thither, and paying their Mony as at a common Playhouse; nay even a twelvepenny Gallery is builded for the convenience of his Majesty's poorer Subjects': Marvell to W. Popple, 24 July 1675, in *Poems*, &c., ed. Margoliouth, ii. 320.

10 *Viccar* on 12 *Pro:* 5, concerning care of our Thoughts: *Pomerid:* Curate on his former Text, proving the *Godhead* of the *Sonn:* &c:

11 To *Lond:* din'd at *B: house.* 14. Went on foote to *Kensington,* din'd with my old acquaintance Mr. *Henshaw,* newly returnd from *Denmark,* where he had ben left *Resident* in that *Court* after the Death of the *Duke* of Richmond who died there Ambassador:[1]

15 I got an extreame cold, such as was afterwards so epidemical, as not onely afflicted us in this Iland, but was rife over all Europe, & raged like a Plague; note that it was after an exceeding dry Summer & Autumn.[2] 16: *Anniver:* ≏ pr: when I settled affaires my sonn being to go into france with my Lord *Berkeley,* designed Ambassador Extraordinary for *France,* & Plenipotentiary for the gen: Treaty of Peace at *Nimegen:*[3]

17 Preached *coram Rege* Mr. *Barnes*[4] on 2. Pet. 3. 16: I received the holy Comm: the morning at St. *James's. Pomerid,* at my requeste preached at St. *Jamess* Mr. *Bohune* my sonns *Tutor* before the La: *Mary*[5] & an illustrious Auditorie excellently well on: 6: *Rom:* 12:

24 At St. *James'* I received the bl: *Sacrament,* then *Coram Rege* Dr. *Thisteltwhait*[6] on 1. *Gal:* 4. *Pomerid* at St. *James,* a

---

[1] The duke of Richmond (above, iii. 354) had been sent as ambassador to Denmark in 1671; he died there in December 1672; Henshaw, who had been his secretary, stayed on as envoy extraordinary until April 1674.

[2] For the epidemic in England see C. Creighton, *History of epidemics in Britain,* 1891–4, ii. 326–8.

[3] Berkeley's instructions are dated 28 July, his credentials 11 August, and his commission 17 October: Firth and Lomas, *Notes on the diplomatic relations of England and France,* p. 23; a commission to him, Sir William Temple, and Sir Leoline Jenkins (above, iii. 499), as ambassadors, &c., at Nimeguen, was issued on 13 December: W. Wynne, *The life of Sir Leoline Jenkins,* 1724, i. 349–51. Charles II had offered to act as a mediator between France and the United Provinces and their allies. The negotiations at Nimeguen made little progress until 1677; the treaty of peace with the United Provinces was signed in August 1678. For the earlier negotiations for a general peace see above, p. 8.

[4] Presumably Miles Barne or Barnes, d. c. 1709; matriculated at Cambridge 1657; D.D. 1682; fellow of Peterhouse 1662–89; chaplain in ordinary c. 1673–c. 1676: Venn.

[5] The princess: above, p. 50.

[6] Above, iii. 626.

stranger on 15. *Rom:* 4. din'd at L: *Chamberlains* with the
Holland Ambassador:[1] L: Duras[2] [since E: of *Faversham*][a]
nephew to the *Duke* of *Bullion* [Marshal Thuren][b] a Valiant
Gent: whom his Majestie made an Eng: Baron,[c] of a *Cadet*; &
gave his[d] seate of *Holmeby* in *Northampton* shire &c:

27 My Lord *Berkeley* now in precinct[3] for his departure
into France, coming to the *Council* fell downe in the Gallery
at *White*-hall of a fit of *Apoplexie*, & being carried into my
L: *Chamberlaines* Lodgings employed all that night severall
famous Doctors & with much adò was at last recovered to
some sense by applying hot fire-pans & Spirit of *Amber* to
his head, but nothing was found so effectual as cupping on
the shoulders: an almost miraculous restauration:[4] The next
day he was carried to *B: house*. This stopped for the present
his journey, & caused my stay in *Towne*, into whose hands he
had put all his Affaires & whole estate in *England* during his
absence, which though I was very unfit to undertake, in
reguard of ⟨many⟩[e] buisinesses then which tooke me up; yet
upon the greate importunity of my *Lady*, & Mrs. *Godolphin*
(to whom I could refuse nothing) I did; It seemes when he
was Deputy (not long before in Ireland)[5] he had ben much
wronged by one he left in trust with his affaires,[f] & therefore
wished for some unmercenary friend, who would take that
trouble on him; which was to receive his Rents, looke after

---

  a Marginal note.   b Interlined.   c Followed by & deleted.
d Followed by *Land* deleted.   e MS. *mony*.   f MS. has closing bracket;
comma supplied.

---

[1] Presumably Koenraad van
Beuningen, 1622?–93; ambassador
extraordinary here from 1674 to
1679: *Nieuw Nederlandsch biog.
woordenboek*. A second ambassador
was also here at this time.
  [2] Louis de Duras, *c.* 1638–1709;
son of Guy-Aldonce de Durfort,
marquis de Duras, by Elizabeth,
sister of the late duke of Bouillon
(above, ii. 382) and of Henri de
la Tour, vicomte de Turenne, 1611–
75, the general (*Nouvelle biog. gén.*);
naturalized 1665; created Baron

Duras of Holdenby 1673; succeeded
his father-in-law as second earl of
Feversham 1677: *D.N.B.*; G.E.C.;
de la Chenaye-Desbois and Badier,
vii. 122.
  [3] An error for procinct, from
procingere, to gird up: *O.E.D.*
Evelyn uses the incorrect phrase
again in a letter to Clifford, 16 June
1665 (Bohn, iii. 157).
  [4] Another account of the seizure
in *Life of Mrs. Godolphin*, p. 60.
  [5] He had been lord lieutenant
from 1670 to 1672.

his Houses & Tennants, solicite for Supplies from the *L: Tressurer* &c:[a] Correspond weekely with him, more than enough to employ any drudge in *England*: but what will not friendship & love make on⟨e⟩ do!

31 The *Anniversary* of my *Birthday* & 55th of my Age being Son-day likewise I received the holy Sacrament at St. *James's*: *Coram Rege* preached one Mr. *May* on 7: *Jer:* 4 shewing that all the Privileges of the Gospel, were nothing without an holy life, &c: I din'd at my *L: Chamb:* with my sonn; there were divers persons of quality, and the learned *Isa: Vossius & Spanhemius*[1] sonn of the famous man of *Heidelburg*, nor was this gent: lesse learned being a generall Schol: amongst other pieces, Author of that excellent Treatise concerning *Medails* &c: here were also the E: of *Northampton*[2] Constable of the *Towre* & the E: of *Westmorland*:[3] *Pomerid* at St. Jam: preached Dr. *Turner*[4] (sometime Tutor to my sonn at *Trinity Coll:* Oxon) on: 7: *Matt:* 14.

November 2 I went home: 7 our *Viccar* on: 7: *Matt:* 1. 2. of the danger of prejudging others, the holy Sacrament followd: *Curate* on 1. *Joh:* 5. 8, concerning the Unity of the holy Spirit with the *Godhead*: 8. To *Lond:* in order to my *Sonns* journey, & to provide bills of Exchange for Mrs. *Godolphin*, whose whole Concernes were still in my hands:

9 I din'd at *B: house*, & went late home: the next day being the time appointed for my *L: Ambassador* to set forth, [10][b] I met them with my *Coach* at *New-Crosse*:[5] There was with

---

[a] Followed by *among* deleted.   [b] Marginal date.

[1] Ezechiel Spanheim, 1629–1710, diplomatist and scholar; son of Friedrich Spanheim the elder, 1600–49, theologian: for both men see *Allgemeine Deutsche Biog.* The father is not closely associated with Heidelberg; Ezechiel and his brother Friedrich both held important posts there. Ezechiel was author of *Dissertatio de Praestantia et Usu Numismatum Antiquorum*, 1664; new ed. 1671 (later ed. 1717). He was now in England as envoy extra-ordinary from the Elector Palatine.

[2] Above, iii. 228, &c. He had been appointed constable of the Tower in July of this year.

[3] Charles Fane, 1634–91; third earl of Westmorland 1666: G.E.C.

[4] William Turner, *c.* 1647–85; B.A. 1666; M.A. 1668; B.D. 1676; D.D. not until 1683 (2 July): Foster.

[5] Where the principal road from Lower Deptford joined the Dover road.

him my Lady his Wife, & my deare friend *Mrs. Godolphin*
who, out of an extraordinary friendship, would needes accompany my Lady to *Paris* & stay with her some time, which was
the chiefe inducement of my permitting my *Sonn* to Travell;
but I knew him safe under her inspection, & in reguard my
Lord himselfe had so promis'd me to take him into his special
care, who had intrusted all he had to mine: Thus we set out
3 *Coaches*, 3 Wagons, and about 40 horse besides my *Coach*:
It being late and my Lord but *valetudinarie* yet, we got but
to *Dartford* the first day, & [11]ᵃ the next to *Citinburne*;¹
by the Way the *Major* of *Rochester Mr. Cony*,² who was then
an Officer of mine for the Sick & Wounded of that place &c,
entertain'd the Ladys with an handsome present of refresh-
ments, as we came by his house: 12 We came to *Canterbery*,
where next morning *Mrs. Godolphin* & I went to the *Cathedrall* to prayers, and thence to Dover: There was in my Lady
Ambassadors Company also my *Lady Hammilton*,³ a Spritefull
young Lady, who was much in the good-graces of that family,
& wife of that valiant & worthy Gent: *Geo: Hammilton* not
long after slaine in the Warrs; she had ben a *Maid* of Honor
to the *Dutchesse*, & now turn'd *Papist*:

13 At *Dover* Mrs. *Godolphin* delivered me her *Will*, which
her *Husband* had given her leave to make, & absolutely to
dispose of all her fortune, which was in value better than
4000 pounds: then after prayers, [14]ᵃ the next morning my

ᵃ Marginal date.

---

¹ Sittingbourne.
² John Conny, surgeon and mayor
of Rochester in 1676, 1696, and
1699: his son's epitaph in J. Thorpe,
Registrum Roffense, 1769, pp. 724–
5; F. F. Smith, *Hist. of Rochester*,
1928, p. 496.
³ Francis Jennings, *c.* 1649–
1731; sister of the future duchess of
Marlborough; maid of honour to
the duchess of York 1664?–6?;
married Sir George Hamilton 1666?
Hamilton, who was a Roman Catholic, was an elder brother of Anthony

Hamilton (born *c.* 1645), the author
of the *Mémoires*, and commanded
an Irish regiment in the French service; he was killed in battle on
1 June 1676, N.S. In 1676 Lady
Hamilton was to have been created
countess of Bantry, but no patent
passed; she married Col. Richard
Talbot (above, p. 23) *c.* 1680–1:
D.N.B.; G.E.C.; Sergeant, *Little
Jennings*, &c.; Clark, *Anthony
Hamilton*. She was apparently a
friend of Lady Berkeley: *Life of
Mrs. Godolphin*, p. 58.

Lord having delivered me before his Letters of Attourney, Keyes, Seale, & his Will, (it being *Sonday*-morning and a glorious day) We tooke solemn leave of one another upon the *Beach*, the Coaches[a] carrying them into the sea to the *Boats*, which delivered them to Cap: *Gunmans Yacht* the *Mary*:[1] & so I parted with my Lord, my sonn, & the person in the world whom I esteemed as my owne life Mrs. *Godolphin*; being under saile, the Castle gave them 17 Gunns, & Cap: *Gunman* answered with 11: Hence I went to Church to beg a blessing on their Voyage: The Ministers text was 1. Joh: 5. 4: That it was Faith onely, overcame the World: I dined at the *Majors*,[2] who was also an Officer of mine in this port: & lay that night at his house: 15. being the *Anniversary* of my *Baptisme* after prayers, I went back to *Canterbery* where I went to the *Cathedral* service:

16 To *Rochester*, lay at the *Majors*.[3] 17 returned home Blessed be God: 19 *Lond:* return'd:

21 our *Viccar* 7 *Matt.* 21. *Curate* 1. Gen: 1. the power of God in Creating, & consequently preserving:

22 Lond: buisinesse at the Doctor Commons for my *Lady Tuke*.[4] 28: *Coram Rege* Dr. *LLoyd*[5] on 53 *Psal:* 11 on the final Judgement &c: 28[b] Communion at St. Jame's Advent Sonday: 30 Royal Society *Anniversary* Ellection, the fellows all dining together *more solito*.

December 2 I visited my La: Mordaunt at P: Greene, my

---

[a] Followed by *deli-* deleted.　　[b] Altered from *3-*.

---

[1] Christopher Gunman, d. 1685: J. Charnock, *Biographia navalis*, 1794–8, i. 225–9; Clowes, *Royal Navy*, vol. ii; notice below, 26 March 1685. There is probably an error as regards the yacht. The *Mary* (above, iii. 296) was lost on 25 March of this year: *Cal. S.P., Dom., 1675–6*, pp. 43, 46–7. The name of the yacht provided for Berkeley is not given in a notice of his sailing: ibid., p. 402.

[2] John Bullack: J. B. Jones, *Annals of Dover*, 1916, pp. 308, 310.
[3] Conny: above, p. 79.
[4] Sir Samuel Tuke had died on 26 Jan. 1674. Doctors Commons was the society of doctors of civil law; in its building were held courts for all matters of ecclesiastical law, including testamentary cases.
[5] The apocalyptic. The text is apparently a slip for Psalms lviii. 11 in the Bible.

Lord her sonn[1] being sick: After dinner this pious woman delivered me 100 pounds to bestow as I thought fit for the release of poore Prisoners, & other Charitable Uses: I returned home:

5 Our *Viccar* on his former Text: the B: Sacrament followed. *Curat* as before: describing the nature of *Angels*: 12 *Viccar* on: 1 *Luke* 74.[a] 75. the Effect of Christs purchase: *Pomerid*: a stranger at *Greenewich* 12 *Jer:* 1. That the Wicked prosper but for a time.

16 *Lond:* about releasing Prisoners with the Charities given me by my L: *Mordant*: din'd at Sir R: *Claytons*. 19 Dr. *Outram*[2] on 130 *Psal:* 3. 4: of Gods infinite mercy to *Pinetents*: That though in the ritual-law there was no expiations for presumptuous sinners; Yet God did forgive them, as in *David*, *Manasses* &c: So willfull sinns after *Baptisme* remissable, & that the tirrible Text: 10: *Heb:* 26. ⟨27.⟩[b] 28: was clearely ment of *Apostates*, & the Lapsed *Jewes* that had once ben *Christians* as not onely that *chap:* but *Epistle* proved: That the Sinn against the *H: Ghost* was want of Faith, or Infidelity, Dispaire, & neglect of repenting, which want of faith made them do. 20[3] I received the holy Comm: at St. *Jamess* Ember Weeke & Ordination Sonday:[4] 21 Visited my *Lady Mordaunt* at Par: Gr: where I found the *Bish:* of *Winchester* whom I had long knowne in *France*: he invited me to his house at *Chelsey*.[5] I returned home: 23 To Lond: return'd: My *Lady Sunderland* gave me ten *Ginnies*, to bestow in Charities: 25 our *Viccar* on 2: *Heb:* 17: apposite to the day: The holy *Commun:* followed: 26: A stranger on 37: *Psal:* 4. of the pleasures of holinesse &c: 31 I gave God thanks for his mercys the yeare past:

---

[a] Altered from 77.   [b] MS. *22*.

---

[1] Charles Mordaunt, 1658–1735; second Viscount Mordaunt of Avalon 5 June of this year; created earl of Monmouth 1689; succeeded his uncle as third earl of Peterborough 1697; the general, &c.: *D.N.B.*
[2] Above, p. 56.
[3] This date is presumably in-

correctly inserted.
[4] See above, p. 75 n.
[5] The bishops of Winchester had a palace in Chelsea from 1664 until 1828, when it was pulled down; Oakley Street now occupies the site: Faulkner, *Chelsea*, i. 282–97; L.C.C., *Survey of London*, ii. 65–6.

1676 *Jan:* 1 Imploring the blessing of God for the ensuing yeare. 2: *Viccar* on 2: *Heb:* 17 enlarged his former discourse thro all the passages of our Saviours exinanition &c: That in all things he might be like to us (save sinn) & all objections prevented of his being truely man, he would be born an Infant & go through all the periods & infirmities of that age, obnoxious to the weaknesses of human nature, hunger, thirst, lassitude, nay even to Temptation from without: That *as man alone* he knew not many things, til after his Resurrection, as the End of the World &c: but as God, All things. The holy Sacrament follow'd: 3 we had divers Neighbours to dinner. 6 I was invited to one. 9 *Viccar* as above, proceeding That Christ was real man, that he might be capable of suffering death, & compassionate our infirmities: &c. *Pomer: Curate* on 1. Gen: 1. of the Creation of Man & his dignitie: To *London.*

11 Supped at the Co: of *Sunderlands:* 12 home: 16 our *Viccar* on 8 *Matt* 34 upon the Inhospitality of the *Gadareens,* a ⟨heathen⟩[a] people; our Saviours perilous journey to them, converted onely two poore *Demoniacs,* &c: The rest preferred their *Swine* before their Eternal Salvation: so do many *Christians: Curate* as above.

18 To *Lond:* was by accident at a Musique meeting, &[b] Voices before his *Majestie.*

19 Din'd with the Groomes of the *Bedchamber:* Visited Lo: *Arlington,* & *Shaftsbery:*[1]

20 Home: 23 A stranger on 1. *Pet:* 1. 11:[2] Holy Conversation[c] extended to all our actions, thoughts, Words, Prayers, hearing, Communicating &c: 27: To *London.*

30 A stranger at W:hall 5 *Ephes:* 6: *Coram Rege* on 37: *Psal:* 28. 31 on the Martyrdom of our Late King,[3] Dr. *Killegrew* on 1. *Sam:* 12. 25.

---

[a] MS. *heothen.*   [b] Substituted for *the.*   [c] Followed by *si-* deleted.

---

[1] Shaftesbury, now the leader of the opposition, was still at Exeter House in February: Christie, *Shaftesbury,* ii. 220–1.

[2] Probably a slip for 1 Peter 1. 15.
[3] For the postponement of the fast see above, iii. 542.

Febr: 6: Dr. *Pierce.* 1. *Tim:* 2. 2 Admirably: *Cor: Rege* Dr. *Duport* 119 *Psal:* 175. The holy Sacrament follow'd: 9 *Ashwednesday Bish:* of *Lond*[1] on 10 *Matt* 16. 13 Dr. *Pierson*[2] first Sonday in Lent: on 2. *Pet:* 3. 9. admirably on the certainty of pardon to sincere Penetents &c: I received this morning at St. *James's Chapell* &c: 15 home: 18 Dr. *Sancroft*[3] D: of S. *Paules* Friday *Coram Rege.* 2. *Act:* 40. How few should be saved &c: 19 At the R: *Society* Experiments to prove that the force of gun-powder was from the compression of aire in the Cornes.[4] 20 Dr. *Gunning*[5] Bish: of *Elie* (*Coram Rege*) 20 *Joh:* 21. 22. 23. Chiefly against an *Anonymous Booke* called *Naked Truth*, a famous & popular Treatise against the Corruption in the Cleargie, but not sound as to its quotations; supposed to have ben the Bish: Herefords: & was answered by Dr. *Turner*: it endeavoring to prove an Equality of Order of *Bish:* & *Presbyter*: That they were but one,[a] from different Commissions: Dr. *Gunning* asserted the difference of their functions, as divine & absolutely necessarie; implying that their antagonists were Sismatics: I received the B: Com: at St. *Jamess* in the morning. 21. I went home.

---

[a] Followed by *under* deleted.

[1] Compton, translated to London in December 1675. He was preaching as dean of the chapel, to which post he had been appointed in July 1675. Lenten sermon at court; list of preachers in *London Gazette*, 20 Jan. 1676.

[2] Lenten sermon at court.

[3] Presumably a lenten sermon at court; the preacher in the list is Dr. Thomas Pierce.

[4] The date should be 17 February: Birch, iii. 305.

[5] He had been translated to Ely in February 1675. Lenten sermon at court.

Dr. Herbert Croft, bishop of Hereford (above, iii. 524), had printed for circulation to members of parliament in 1675 (probably about April) a pamphlet, *The Naked Truth. Or, the True State of the Primitive Church. By an Humble Moderator.* At least two new editions were printed in the same year. It provoked a notable controversy. Dr. Francis Turner (above, iii. 630) published this year *Animadversions upon a Late Pamphlet Entituled The Naked Truth* (licence 23 Feb.; new ed., 1676). Gunning's sermon also provoked discussion and it was expected that it would be printed; the anonymous *Lex Talionis: or, the Author of Naked Truth stript naked*, 1676, was apparently attributed to him, but probably incorrectly: Marvell, *Mr. Smirke*, 1676, pp. 75–6 (this work is a reply to Turner). Bibliography of the controversy in *The Naked Truth*, ed. H. H. Henson, 1919: P. Legouis, *André Marvell*, 1928, pp. 461–3; see also Wood, *Athenæ*, iv. 312–14.

23. To *Lond:* 25 Dr. *Tillotson*[1] at *Whitehall* on 1. Joh: 3. 10.
shewing who were the true Children of God, & that without
those numerous signes, & marks that the *Presbyterians* require,
one may know; namely [by][a] an holy life & sincerity of heart
which every man might himselfe know without other Charac-
ters:[b] I received the B: Sacrament at a sick persons: 27:
Bish: of *Glocester* Dr. *Pritchard*[2] at *Whall*: on 5 *Isa:* 5 Very
Alegoricaly (according to his manner) yet very gravely a
wittily: That the Christian Church was a Vineyard, how in
particular God had planted & cultivated that of England;
how the true & generous Vine was to be known; with the
danger of not answering the Cost & paines of the dresser or
Vigneroon,[3] applied to the wickednesse of the age: I tooke
leave of my young *Lo: Mordaunt*[4] going into France, & sent
a recommendatary[c] letter to Mrs. *Godolphin*, to have some
eye over him: 29 I dind with Mr. *Povie*[5] on⟨e⟩ of the Masters
of *Requests*, a nice contriver of all Elegancies, & exceedingly
formall: supped at Sir *Jos: Williamsons*, where were of our
Society, Mr. *Rob: Boile*, Sir *Chr: Wren*,[6] Sir *W: Petty*, Dr.
Holder[7] (Subdeane of his Majesties Chapell), Sir *James
Shaen*,[8] Dr. *Whistler*[9] and our Secretary Mr. *Oldenburg*:[10]

---

[a] Interlined.   [b] Or *Character*.   [c] Altered from *recommendation*.

[1] He had been appointed dean of
Canterbury in 1672. Presumably
a lenten sermon at court; the
preacher in the list is Dr. William
Clarke, dean of Winchester (above,
iii. 605). The sermon was printed
this year (reprinted, *Works*, 1752, i.
125–35).

[2] John Pri(t)chett, *c.* 1605–81;
D.D. 1664; bishop of Gloucester
1672: Foster; Wood, *Athenæ*, iv.
862–3. Lenten sermon at court.
For his style of preaching see also
below, p. 166, where Evelyn compares it to that of Lancelot
Andrewes.

[3] i.e. vigneron, wine-grower.
Evelyn uses the word again in its
correct form in *The French Gardiner*,
1658, p. 273; *The English Vineyard*

Vindicated, 1666, p. 13.
[4] Above, p. 81.
[5] He was appointed a master of
requests (at this time a sinecure) in
1675: *London Gazette*, 1 April 1675.
[6] He had been knighted in 1673.
[7] William Holder, 1616–98; D.D.
1661; sub-dean of the chapel 1674–
89; member of the Philosophical
Society 16 Jan. 1661; F.R.S. 1663;
Wren's brother-in-law: *D.N.B.*; &c.
[8] d. 1695; knighted in or before
1660; created a baronet 1663; member of the Philosophical Society
17 Sept. 1662; F.R.S. 1663 (expelled 1685): G.E.C., *Baronetage*,
iii. 323.
[9] Above, iii. 341.
[10] Above, iii. 491.

Mar: 1 At *White-hall* Dr. *Megot*[1] incomparably on
Psal: Thou thoughtest me such a one as thy selfe but
— &c: shewing that God is most angery when most silent, &
is long in chastising: &c: 3: Dr. *Lamplugh*[2] Deane of *Roches-*
ter, on 1. *Sam:* 15. 2. 3. of Gods revenge on *Amalech* 400
yeares after their cruelty: shewing the danger of provoking
God, because patient &c: 4 I din'd at Sir *Tho: Linches*[3] late
Governor of *Jamaica*, with the Countesse of *Sunderland* &
Mordaunt. 5: Dr. *Smallwood*[4] on: 4. Job: 31. 32. on the Effects
of repentance, an ordinary Sermon: The holy Communion
follow'd: *Coram Rege* Dr. *Bredox*[5] B: of *Chichester* 22 Job:
26. 27. the joy & felicity of Good-men in this life; That of all
others they had least cause of Melancholy; a very meane discourse for a *Bishop*: I visited my La: *Mordaunt* at Parsons
Greene. 6: returned home:

9 To *Lond:* about Accompts: 10: *Coram Rege* Dr. *Framp-*
ton[6] Deane of Glocester on 25 *Psal:* 11. That no sinn was so
greate but *God* for *Christs* sake did pardon: & therefore exhorting earnestly to Repentance: That it was a greater King
than any on Earth who thus humbled himselfe to death; &
therefore no shame for the greatest potentate on Earth to
Repent & beg pardon: applying to us all & especialy to ——
12: Dr. *Littleton* on 51 *Psal:* 9: shewed the difference of *Gods*
hiding his face; one in Anger at our sinns, when we repent
not, another in Love from our sinns, when we do repent:
which is as much as the blotting out of our sinns & ⟨cancel-
ling⟩[a] them, erased, made white as Snow, from as red &
bloudy as Scarlet: A sermon of greate encouragement:

---

[a] MS. *conceling*.

---

[1] Dr. Richard Meggot: above, iii.
443. Lenten sermon at court. The
text is Psalms l. 21.
[2] He was dean of Rochester from
1673 to October of this year.
Lenten sermon at court.
[3] Above, iii. 574, 628. He had
returned to England by November
1675: *Cal. S.P., Dom., 1675–6*,

p. 394.
[4] Above, p. 4. The text is probably a slip for Job xxxiv. 31, 32.
[5] Brideoake. Lenten sermon at
court.
[6] He was dean of Gloucester from
1673 to 1681. Lenten sermon at
court.

Coram Rege, Dr. *Fleetewood*[1] *Bish:* of *Worcester* on 26 *Matt:* 38 of the Sorrows of Christ, a deadly sorrow, caused by our sinns: how much more should sinners sorrow: This *Bish:* no greate preacher &c: 13 I went to see *Coll: Talbot*[2] & Lady at *Twicnam* where I dined, afterwards Mrs. *Davis*[3] sister to my *L:* Ambassador *Berkeley*, Then to *Twicknam-Parke* my Lords Country seate, to examine how the *Baylife*[a] & Servants ordered matters &c: return'd to *Lond:* 15 Dr. *James*[4] on 4: *Heb:* 11. The danger of Infidelitie: it deprives of heavenly rest. 16 my Lady the Countesse of *Sunderland* & I went by water to *Parsons Greene* to Visite my Lady Vic: *Mordaunt:* & to consult with her about my Lords *Monument:*[5] we return'd by Coach: 17 Dr. *Ashley*[b][6] De: of *Norwich* on 27: Matt: 46. perstringing *Beza* & *Calvine* for saying our B: Sa: despaird on the Crosse; but that he was as far press'd, as could consist with the dignitie of his nature, united as it was to the Deity; & that therefore we must think of nothing unbecoming it: shew'd what our sinns brought him to, & misery we had ben in forever without him. His lamentable cry the same in all Translations, to shew that no propriety of Language can expresse it: 19 Dr. *Lloyd*[7] [now *Bish.* of *Landaf*][c] (late *Curate*

---

[a] Or *Baylifs*.   [b] Altered from *Ac-*.   [c] Marginal note.

[1] James Fleetwood, 1603–83; D.D. 1642; bishop of Worcester 1675: *D.N.B.* Lenten sermon at court.

[2] Above, p. 23. His lady is his first wife, Katherine Boynton: above, p. 15.

[3] No sister or sister-in-law of Berkeley's of this name is known. Possibly Mary Davies, *c.* 1664–1730, the heiress of the manor of Ebury, who was at this time under contract to marry Berkeley's elder son, Charles, 1662–82, who succeeded as second Baron Berkeley of Stratton in 1678 (he was succeeded as third Baron by his brother John); she married Sir Thomas Grosvenor, bart., in 1677: C. T. Gatty, *Mary Davies*, &c., 1921, i. 201–2, 221; ii. 189–90; G.E.C., *Baronetage*, i. 190.

[4] Henry James, d. 1717; admitted at Cambridge 1660; D.D. 1679; president of Queens' College 1675–1717; chaplain in ordinary *c.* 1676–*c.* 1687, *c.* 1700–17; Regius professor of divinity 1699–1717: Venn; *Cal. S.P., Dom., 1678*, p. 345. Lenten sermon at court.

[5] The monument, by John Bushnell (*D.N.B.*), is still preserved in Fulham parish church: Fèret, *Fulham*, i. 258–61.

[6] Herbert Astley, *c.* 1618–81; LL.D., Cambridge, (?); dean of Norwich 1670: Venn; Blomefield, (*Norfolk*), iii. 625. Lenten sermon at court.

[7] William Lloyd, the nonjuror. He was bishop of Llandaff from 1675 to 1679. Lenten sermon at court.

at *Deptford*), *Coram Rege* on 1 *Cor:* 15. 57. That though sin
subjects us to death; yet through *Christ* we ⟨be⟩come his
conquerers: I din'd at the *Bish: of Rochesters*: I received the
B: Sacrament.

⟨20 ?⟩[a] Dining at my *La: Sunderlands*, I saw a fellow swallow a knife, & divers greate pibble stones, which shaking his
stomach, would make a plaine rattling one against another:
The Knife was in a sheath of horne to bend in: 22: Dr. *Ironside*[1] on 14. *Proverbs*: 10, of the interiour griefe of heart for
outward concernes, how to turne it to a more advantagious
sorrow for sinn: 24 *Goodfriday* St. *Martines* Dr. *Doughty*[2]
(the *Dukes Chap:*) 1. *Pet.* 2. 21. incomparably describing the
incomparable sorrows of our Saviours; his demeanor to be
meekenesse, patience, Love, affable Carriage &c: Exhorting
imitation: The bl: Sacrament followd: *Pomerid: Coram Rege*:
W:hall: Dr. *North*,[3] sonn to my Lord *North*, a very young,
but learned, & excellent person on 53 *Isa:* 57: setting also
forth our Saviours Passion, appl⟨y⟩ing all to Comfort, &
excite gratitude: Note, this was the first time the *Duke*
appeared no more in the Chappell, to the infinite griefe and
threatned ruine of this poore Nation:[4] I went to *Says-Court*.

26 *Easter-day* our *Viccar* on 3 *Exod:* 3. shewing how the
burning bush was a Type of our Bl: Saviours resurrection, &

---

[a] MS. *30*.

---

[1] Gilbert Ironside the younger, 1632–1701; D.D. 1666; warden of Wadham College 1665–89; chaplain in ordinary *c.* 1672–89; bishop of Bristol 1689; of Hereford 1691: *D.N.B.* Lenten sermon at court.

[2] Thomas Doughty, *c.* 1638–1701; D.D. 1671; chaplain to the duke of York *c.* 1669–*c.* 1684; chaplain in ordinary *c.* 1687–*c.* 1692; canon of Windsor 1673–1701: Venn.

[3] John North, 1645–83; son of Dudley North, 1602–77, fourth Lord North 1666 (*D.N.B.*), and brother of Sir Francis North, Lord Guilford; master of Trinity College, Cambridge, 1677–83: *D.N.B.* The date of his doctorate is not recorded; he is called doctor in May 1677: *Cal. S.P., Dom., 1677–8*, p. 113. He was a chaplain in ordinary *c.* 1677; for his alleged clerkship of the closet see below, p. 97 n. Lenten sermon at court.

[4] On 23 March or shortly before James had resolved that he would no longer accompany the king to services in chapel; the king consented unwillingly: Campana de Cavelli, i. 166–7; see also Christie, *Shaftesbury*, ii. 222.

emergency out of trouble of all Gods people: That it was not (as some affirme) a Created *Angel*, but *Christ* the *Angel* of the *Covenant*: who thus appeared to *Moses*, & so did most times in the *Old Testament*; though Papists & Socinians dissent; The *one* because they would establish their errors of *worshiping Angels*, (as in the old Test: appeares): which they never would have don, if it had not ben realy God that appeared: & the other, namely the *Socinians*, who indeede acknowledge *Christ* to have so appeared, but that he was not God, though worshiping: The holy *Commun:* followd: *Pomerid: Curate* on 1. *Tim:* 2. 5. The efficacy of our B: Saviours Mediatorship: I went againe to *London* this Evening to speake to my L: Tressurer: returned on the 28:

Aprill 2: *Viccar*, as before, & so the *Curate* with much repetition: The blessed Communion followed. 4 I went to Lond: Visited my L: *Marshall*,[1] Lord *Shaftsbery*[2] where I found the *Earle* of *Burlington*:[3] I had now notice that *Mrs. Godolphin* was returning from *Paris* & landing the 3d at *Dover*; so I din'd with my L: *Sunderland* expecting her:

6 Came my dearest Friend to my greate joy; whom after I had welcom'd,[4] I gave accompt to of her buisinesse, & return'd home. 9: our *Viccar* on his former Text: (Se your *notes:*) Pomerid: a stranger on 33 *Luke:* 34[5] Against vindic⟨a⟩tion of Injuries:

10 To *Lond* about buisinesse & see my friend: return'd: 13 Came Mrs. *Godolphin*, Countesse of *Sunderland*, Mrs. *Graham*,[6] Mrs. *Howard* one of the Q: Maids of honor to see & dine with us: I went back to Lond: with them.

14 I supped with Mrs. *Godolphin* at my Lady *Sunderlands*

---

[1] Henry Howard: above, iii. 595–6 n.

[2] For Lord and Lady Shaftesbury at this time see T. Stringer to Locke, 6 April, in Christie, *Shaftesbury*, ii. 221–2.

[3] Richard Boyle, second earl of Cork (Ireland), created earl of Burlington 1664: above, iii. 242.

[4] This visit perhaps took place on 7 April: *Life of Mrs. Godolphin*, p. 67.

[5] A slip for St. Luke xxiii. 34. Vindication is used in the obsolete sense, revenging: *O.E.D.*

[6] The former Dorothy Howard; her licence to marry Graham (above, p. 69) was dated for 22 Nov. 1675: *London marriage licences*. Mrs. Howard is her sister Anne.

[returned.]ᵃ ⟨16⟩ᵇ A stranger on 4 *Matt:* 17. That true repentance, was a true reformation; that feare & love, the best motives, & the present dåy, the true season: *Pomer*: *Greenewich* Dr. *Plume*, 6: *Rom:* 8. 9. 10. A *Resurrection* sermon, That the natural body of *Christ* abode in the Grave, whilst his soule was in *Paradise*, as other holy soules enter; & not in local *Hell*; but in power & efficacy; that all other opinions are but pious conjectures:

17 To *Lond:* 23 St. *Geo:* day *W:hall* first ser: Dr. *Stillingfleete* 112 *Psal:* 7 of the assurance & holy *Confidence* of holy persons in all Circumstances:

26 Din'd with ⛤, discovered her Marriageᶜ by her sister:¹

27ᵈ My Wife entertaind her Majestie at *Deptford*, for which the *Queene* gave ⟨me⟩ᵉ thanks in the Withdrawing roome at White-hall.

28 The University of *Oxford* presented me with the *Marmora Oxon: Arundell:*² the *Bish:* of *Oxford*³ writing to me, that I would introduce Mr. *Prideaux* the *Editor* (a most learned young man in *Antiquities*) to the *Duke* of *Norfolck*,⁴ to present another, dedicated to his *Grace*, which I did, & we both din'd with the Duke at *Arundel* house: & supped at the *Bish:* of *Rochesters* with *Isa: Vossius*.

30 *Rogation Sonday*, a Young man, *W:hall* 12 *Joh:* 43, of the danger of Popularity & vaine glory: *Coram Rege*, a *Chaplaine* of my L: *Manchesters*⁵ on 20 *Joh:* 29 on the unreasonablenesse of incredulity: I returned to Says-Court.

ᵃ Interlined.   ᵇ MS. *15*.   ᶜ Word altered, spelling uncertain.
ᵈ Altered from *28*.   ᵉ MS. *in*.

---

¹ Presumably Lady Yarburgh: above, p. 64.

² *Marmora Oxoniensia, ex Arundellianis, Seldenianis, aliisque conflata. Recensuit, & Perpetuo Commentario explicavit, Humphridus Prideaux Ædis Christi Alumnus*, Oxford (e Theatro Sheldoniano), 1676. The book is dedicated to Henry Howard as earl of Norwich, Earl Marshal, &c. Prideaux, 1648–1724; D.D. 1686;

dean of Norwich 1702: *D.N.B.*

³ Fell, consecrated on 6 February of this year.

⁴ See note above; Howard did not succeed as duke of Norfolk until 1677.

⁵ Robert Montagu, 1634–83; succeeded as third earl of Manchester 1671: *D.N.B.*, art. Montagu, Edward, second earl.

May: 1 The meeting for the *Trustees* of the poore, we din'd together. 2: To *Lond:*

3 Visited Mrs. *Godolphin* éxpostulated with her about the concealement, & was satisfied, it was not her intention:[1] 4: *Ascention day* [com: at landladys[2] then][a] At St. *Martines* a stranger on 68: *Psal:* 18: of our Saviours Triumphant Ascension, & the blessed Gifts bestowed at his *Exaltation*: The bl: Comm: followed. 6[b] Returned home with my Wife: 7 our *Viccar* on 5. *Psal:* 8. shewing what were the ways of *God*: the Communion followed; *Curate* on. 1. *Tim:* 2. 5. 9: To *Lond* to visite ✩ : — pr: I spake to the *Duke* of *Yorke* about my L: *Berkeleys* going to *Nimegen* &c:[3] Thence to the *Queenes* Council at *Somerset house*[4] about my friend Mrs. G: lease of *Spalding* in *Lincolnshire*.[5] 11. I din'd with Mr. *Charleton*;[6] went to see Mr. *Montagues* new Palace neere *Bloomesbery*, built by Mr. *Hooke* of our Society, after the French manner:[7] Spake with my Lord *Treasurer* about Mony &c.

---

[a] Interlined.   [b] Followed by *There* or *Then* deleted.

[1] See *Life of Mrs. Godolphin*, pp. 67–8.

[2] Mrs. Godolphin was at present staying at '*Mrs. Warners in Covent Garden*, who was a Relation of hers': ibid., p. 67. Her husband was Edward Warner, b. 1612; M.D., Padua, 1638: ibid., pp. 267–8.

[3] A house was to be taken for Berkeley at Nimeguen about the end of this month, but he did not arrive until November: Wynne, *Life of Jenkins*, i. 418, 503.

[4] Somerset House had been granted to the queen on the death of Henrietta Maria as her official residence: *Cal. S.P., Dom., 1668–9*, p. 511. She apparently continued to live at Whitehall. For her council see Chamberlayne, 1676, i. 193.

[5] See *Life*, p. 68 and note.

[6] Presumably William Charleton, otherwise Courten, the collector: below, 16 Dec. 1686.

[7] Mr. Montague is Ralph Montagu, 1638–1709; third Baron Montagu of Boughton 1684; created earl of Montagu 1689; duke of Montagu 1705: *D.N.B.* In 1675 he bought the site for his house from William Russell (above, iii. 551 n.), the son-in-law of Lord Southampton (above, iii. 175). He began to build the house immediately; the roof of the main block was now under construction; the building appears to have been practically completed in 1678. It was burnt down in 1686 and rebuilt; the new house was bought by the nation in 1753 for the British Museum, which still occupies the site: *London topog. record*, xvii (1936), 59–62, 129–31; Walpole Soc., xxv (1937), 93–6. The only known view of this house is that in Ogilby and Morgan's plan of London, 1682; the French influence is to be seen especially in the pavilions with their characteristic roofs (cf. below, p. 184). For foreign influence in Hooke's work see Walpole Soc., xxv. 87–8.

12 Dind with my L: *Arlington.* 13 returned home, & found my sonn returned out of *France,* praised be God; for my deare friend Mrs. *Godolphin* coming thence I had no desire he should stay there any longer for many reason⟨s⟩:

14 *Viccar* as before: It was *Whitsonday* & the holy Sacrament,ᵃ I received: *Pomerid*: a stranger on 6. *Rom:* 23, describing the Joyes of heaven &c:

21 *Trinity Sonday* our *Viccar* as before, of Gods protecting providence guiding us in his way: &c: *Pomerid*: a stranger on 2. *Cor:* 5. 10. of the certainty & tirriblenisse of the final *Judgement.* &c: 22. *Trinity Monday* preached a Chaplaine of my L: *Ossories,* after which we tooke barge to *Trinity* house in Lond, where was a greate feast, Mr. *Pepys* (Secretary of the Admiralty) chosen *Master,* & succeeding my *Lord.*[1]

27 I visited Mrs. *Godolphin.* 28 at St. *Martins* a Chap: of the *Earle of Kents*[2] on 23 *Luke:* 42: of the wonderfull Conversion of the good *Thiefe:* The Communion follow'd: *Pomer:* a young man on 4. *Gal:* 18, of the Effects of prudent zeale, compar'd it to fire, which was allways burning; therefore 'tis said in the Text (*allways*): &c:

29 His Majesties Birth & Anniversarie returne, Bish: of *Rochester* on 118 Psal: 22. 23. 24. of his Majesties miraculous Restauration: How *Christ* & *Kings* were head stones, & especialy ours, as rejected, & yet set on the top, for the union of the whole building:

30 I dind at my L: *Chamberlains* with the Dutch *Ambassador*[3] & divers Lords &c. Visited ☆ — pr:

June: 2ᵇ I went with my L: *Chamberlaine* to see a Garden at *Enfield* towne;[4] Thence to Mr. *Secretary Coventries*[5] Lodge

---

ᵃ Comma supplied.   ᵇ Followed by *To Lond* deleted.

---

[1] For Ossory's mastership see above, p. 64. Pepys was secretary of the Admiralty from 1673 to 1679, and again later.

[2] Above, iii. 372.

[3] Presumably van Beuningen: above, p. 77 n.

[4] The garden of Robert Uvedale has been suggested: G. H. Hodson and E. Ford, *Hist. of Enfield*, 1873, p. 49. For Uvedale see *D.N.B.* and authorities there given.

[5] Henry Coventry, *c.* 1618–86; secretary of state 1672–80: *D.N.B.* He was a brother of Sir William Coventry.

in the *Chace*,[1] which is a very prety place, the house commodious, the Gardens handsome, & our entertainement very free; there being none but my Lord & my selfe: That which most I admir'd at, was, that in the compasse of 25 Miles (yet within 14 of Lond) there is never an house, barne, Church, or building, besides three Lodges: To this Lodge are 3 greate ponds, & some few inclosures, the rest a solitarie desert, yet stored with no lesse than 3000 deare &c: These are pretty retreates for Gent: especialy that were studious & a lover of privacy: We return'd in the Evening by Hamsted, where we diverted to see my Lord Wottons house & Garden;[2] built with vast expense by Mr. *Oneale* an *Irish* Gent: who married his Mother, the Lady Stanhop: The furniture is very particular for Indian Cabinets, Porcelane,[a] & other solid & noble moveables, The Gallery very fine: The Gardens very large, but ill kept; yet Woody & chargeable; the mould a cold weeping clay, not answering the expense:

4 Dr. *Gregory*[3] on 4. Heb: 7: at W:hall, concerning the

---

[a] Or *Porcelans*.

---

[1] Enfield Chase was a woodland tract between Enfield and Potter's Bar; it measured about four or five miles from north to south and from east to west; its area is given in 1650 as 7,900 acres and in 1777 as 8,349 acres. It was royal property from 1399 and was disafforested in 1777. Coventry occupied the West Bailey or Dighton's Lodge: William Robinson, *Hist. . . . of Enfield*, 1823, i. 175–230.

[2] For Wotton see above, iii. 555. His mother was Catherine, d. 1667, daughter of Thomas Wotton, second Baron Wotton of Marley; she married (1) Henry Stanhope, styled Lord Stanhope, d. 1634, by whom she was mother of the second earl of Chesterfield; (2) in 1641 John Polyander à Kerckhoven (Kirkhoven), lord of Heenvliet, d. 1660, by whom she was mother of Lord Wotton; (3) Daniel O'Neill (O'Neale),

c. 1612–64, the royalist (*D.N.B.*); in 1660 she was created countess of Chesterfield for life: *D.N.B.* She was generally known as Lady Stanhope until 1660. Wotton's house is Belsize House, which had been granted to O'Neill c. 1660. It was used as a place of amusement from 1720 to c. 1745 and was pulled down some time later. Belsize Avenue, &c., now occupy the site: J. J. Park, *Topog. . . . of Hampstead*, 1818, pp. 136–59; T. J. Barratt, *Annals of Hampstead*, 1912, i. 74–101, &c.; W. Wroth, *London pleasure gardens*, pp. 189–93; for the garden see also Pepys, 17 Aug. 1668.

[3] Francis Gregory, d. 1707; matriculated at Cambridge 1642; D.D. 1661; supernumerary chaplain in ordinary c. 1674–c. 1676: *D.N.B.*; *Term catalogues*, i. 183, 234, 367. His text is probably a slip for Hebrews ii. 7.

dignitie of man. The Sacrament followd: *Coram Rege*, a Young doctor on 7: *Mar:* 13. About Tradition: I dind at the L: *Treasurers*: 5 I din'd at L: ⟨*Arlingtons*⟩,[a] where among divers greate persons, was[b] *Monte Cuculli*,[1] Nephew to the Emperors Generall: 8 I visited Mrs. Blagg: 9 Din'd at Sec: *Williamsons*, return'd home: 11 our *Viccar* on 4: *Gal:* 18 on the assiduitie of our devotions & service of God:

12 I went to Sir *Tho: Bonds*[2] new & fine house by *Pecham*, the place is on a flat, yet has a fine Garden, & prospect thro the meadows towards *Lond:* 13 To *Lond:* about Mrs. *Godolphins* Lease at the Queenes Council:[3] 14 Visited ≏ —pr: 16 home: 18 *Viccar* as formerly, how we might be *zealous* in prosecution of holy things, how indifferent in *rebus medijs*, how neither, in evil things: *Curat* as before,[4] The priveledges of *Adoption*; and that faith that workes by Love is the onely justifying faith: 20 To *Lond:* to the *Council* at Somerset house againe: 21. To the *Duke* about the sick & Wounded under my inspection:[5]

23 din'd at Mr. Sec: *Williamsons*, 24. Return'd home. 25 *Vicc:* as formerly: That our Zeale must be according to knowledge, not to revenge our selves, or blind,[c] as the *Pharise's* & *Saules* was &c: but in charity: 26: To *Lond:*

---

a MS. *Arligntons*.   b Followed by *the Nephew of* deleted.   c Altered from *blindly*.

---

[1] The imperial general is Raimondo Montecuccoli, 1609–80: *Allgemeine Deutsche Biog.* No nephews are traceable; the family came from Modena, and a lady belonging to it (Maria Vittoria Davia) was in the duchess of York's service: T. Sandonnini, *Il generale Raimondo Montecuccoli e la sua famiglia*, 1911, especially pp. 195–6.

[2] Thomas Bond, d. 1685; created a baronet 1658: G.E.C., *Baronetage*, iii. 20. He bought the manor of Camerwell, otherwise called Peckham; his house was built *c.* 1672. He and his son were Roman Catholics; the latter fled abroad at the Revolution, when the house was sacked by the mob. The garden was admired by Defoe. The house was pulled down in 1797 and the property was built over soon afterwards: Manning and Bray, iii. 410–11; Blanch, *Parish of Camerwell*, pp. 30–1.

[3] See above, p. 90.

[4] His last text was 1 Timothy ii. 5: above, p. 90; it scarcely fits the note here.

[5] Evelyn's accounts as a commissioner during the last Dutch War continue to 28 June 1675; they were not declared until 1703: P.R.O., Declared Accounts, Navy, 1821/ 487–8.

27 My Marriage *Anniversarie*, I din'd with Mrs. *Godolphin*[a] at *Berkeley*-house, being the first day of her house-keeping since her Marriage & returne into *England*.[1]

July 2: Dr. *Castillion*[2] prebend of *Canterbery* on 15 *Joh:* 22 at W:hall: *Cor: Rege* a stranger on 15 *Psal:* 1: That all religion consisted in holinesse & integrity: &c: 3 din'd with my *Lo: Chamberlaine*, & sealed the Deedes of Mortgage for security of 1000 pounds lent by my friend Mrs. *Godolphin* to my Lord *Sunderland*. 4 I dind at B. house with ✡: 6 at Sir *Stephen Foxes*: 7: Went to *Parsons Greene*, dind with the *Vicountesse Mordaunt*: 8: with my Wife at L: *Chamberl:* where was the *Duke* of *Monmoth*, *Lord Ossorie*, *Dut⟨c⟩h Ambassador*,[3] and returned home that evening: 9 a stranger on 1. *Luke* 77, of the nature of sinn, repentance & pardon &c. 11. To *Lond* dind with ✡: Afternoone went to visite L: *Mordaunt*:

12 Dind at L: *Chamb:* with my Wife: 16 Received the holy Sacrament at St. *Jamess*, at W:hall, *coram Rege* preach'd Dr. *Megot* on 1. *Joh:* 3. 20, din'd at Mr. *Slingsbys*. 17 Supped with Mrs. *Godolphin*:

19 dind at L: *Chamb:* Went to Sir *William Sandersons* funerall (husband to the Mother of the Maides, & author of two large, but meane Histories of KK. *James* & *Charles* the first):[b] he was buried at *Westminster*:[4] 20. returned home:

---

a Substituted for *Blagge*.   b Closing bracket supplied.

[1] She now first received visits as a married woman: *Life of Mrs. Godolphin*, p. 68.
[2] He was instituted dean of Rochester on 13 November of this year.
[3] Presumably van Beuningen: above, pp. 77, 91.
[4] William Sanderson, born 1586?; knighted 1625; his wife was Bridget, c. 1592–1682, daughter of Sir Edward Tyrrell, bart., of Thornton, Bucks.: *D.N.B.* She was mother of the maids, i.e. of the queen's maids of honour, from 1669 to her death: Chamberlayne; and possibly held the post from 1662 (she had also been laundress to Queen Henrietta Maria). Sanderson's two histories are *A Compleat History of the Lives and Reigns of Mary Queen of Scotland, and of Her Son and Successor, James*, &c., 1656; and *A Compleat History of the Life and Raigne of King Charles from his Cradle to his Grave*, 1658. Evelyn made some use of the latter in the De vita propria: see notes there.

The Abbey register gives 18 July for the date of the funeral.

23 A stranger on 23: *Pro:* 23, the preciousnesse of Truth:
Pomerid, the *Curat* on his former Text: 25 To *Lond:* dind with
✡:

28 Went to the Navy Office about my Accompt: Supp'd
with L: *Chamberlaine*: 29 went to *Par: Greene* to visite my
Lady V.C. *Mordaunt,* where was Mrs. *Godolphin,* & after
dinner we went to *Wimbledon* to see the Countesse of *Bristoll.*[1]
30: I received the bl: *Communion* in the morning at St.
James: To the household at *Whitehall* preached a stranger on
3. *Matt* 8. of the fruits of Righteousnesse,[2] dind at L. *Chamb:*
Aug: 1. I din'd with Mrs. *Godolphin*: In the afternoone after
prayers at St. *Jame's Chapell* was christned a Daughter of
Dr. *Leakes,* the Dukes Chaplaine: Godmothers were *Lady
Mary,* daughter of the *Duke* of *Yorke*; *Dutchesse* of *Monmoth,* Godfather the *Earle of Bathe*:[3] I went home this Evening: 6: our *Viccar* on 6: *Heb:* 19: 20. of the nature of divine
Hope, how little it differ'd from faith, rising from a life of
holynesse, how at last it arives to assurance &c: The B:
Sacrament follow'd: *Pomerid: Curate* on 5 *Ephes:* 15. The
necessitie of accurate walking &c: 8: To *Lond:* dind with ✡:

Next day my L:V: *Countesse Mordaunt* and Mrs. *Godolphin*
called me to go to my house, where we dined, & I waited on
them to *Lond* againe: 13. I received at St. *Jame's,* in the
morning: Din'd at *Cap: Grahams,*[4] Serm: *Coram Rege* on
8 *Joh:* 9: by the *Bish:* of *Ossory,*[5] of the Conviction of Conscience &c: Supp'd at L: *Chamberlaines* with the *Portugal
Ambassador,*[6] & Earle of Ossorie &c: 14 din'd with ≏ — pr:
returned home. &c: Came the *Bishop* of *Rochester* to visite me:

---

[1] Anne, d. 1697, daughter of
Francis Russell, fourth earl of Bedford; married, by 1635, George
Digby, Lord Digby, who became
earl of Bristol in 1653. She was
an Anglican and mother of Lady
Sunderland.

[2] Possibly a slip for repentance.

[3] John Grenville, 1628–1701;
created earl of Bath 1661: *D.N.B.*
He was son of Sir Bevil Grenville,
the royalist commander.

[4] Above, p. 69. He was com-
missioned a captain in the Cold-
stream Guards on 30 Oct. 1675:
Dalton, *English army lists,* i. 184.

[5] Presumably Dr. John Parry,
bishop of Ossory from 1672 to 1677:
above, p. 15 n.

[6] Dom Francisco de Mello (Manuel
da Camara): above, iii. 481; iv. 2.

15 Came to visite & dine with me my *Lord Halifax*, Sir Tho: *Meeres*,[1] one of the *Commissioners* of the *Admiralty*: Sir *John Clayton*;[2] Mr. *Slingsby* (Master of the Mint), Mr. *Henshew*, & Mr. *Bridgeman*[3] &c: 17: I tooke preventing *Physick*: 20: A stranger on 4. *Philip:* 11. about contentment: *Pomerid* at *Greenewich* on 90 *Psal:* 10: the same person. 21 Came my Lady *Tuke* to visite us: I went to *Lond:* with her: 22: Dind with ≏ — pr:

25 Din'd with Sir *Jo: Banks's*[4] at his house in *Lincolns Inn* fields: upon recommending Mr. *Upman* to be Tutor to his sonn going into France: This Sir Jo: *Bankes* was a Merchant, of small beginnings, but by usurie &c: amass'd an Estate of 100000 pounds &c.

26 I din'd at the Admiralty, with Sec: *Pepys*: Supp'd at L: Chamberlaines, here was Cap: *Baker*,[5] who had ben lately on the attempt of the Nor-west passage: he reported prodigious depth of yce, blew as a *Saphire* & as transparant: That the thick mists was their chiefe impediment, & cause of returne: [I went home.][a] 27: A stranger preach'd on 17: *Act:* 30, concerning Repentance &c: (See your notes) 29 To Lond: dind with ≏ pr—

September 2 I paied 1700 pounds, to the *Marquis* de *Sissac*,[6] which he had lent to my L: *Berkeley* &c: which I heard the *Marqu⟨i⟩s* lost at play ⟨within⟩[b] a night or two:

---

[a] Interlined.   [b] MS. *withing.*

---

[1] Thomas Meres, 1634–1715; knighted 1660: *D.N.B.*, art. Francis Meres; Venn. He did not become a commissioner of the admiralty until 1679, retaining office until 1684.

[2] John Clayton; brother-in-law of Sir Robert Paston (Lord Yarmouth); admitted at Inner Temple 1649; barrister 1656; perhaps M.P. for Lostwithiel 1659, 1660; member of the Philosophical Society 9 Oct. 1661; F.R.S. (Original Fellow) until 1668; knighted 1664; of Parson's Green: Le Neve, *Pedigrees*, pp. 186–7; Fèret, *Fulham*, ii. 158; &c.

[3] Presumably William Bridgeman: below, p. 197.

[4] John Bankes (Banks), *c.* 1627–99; created a baronet 1661: G.E.C., *Baronetage*, iii. 228. I have not identified his house.

[5] The only expedition traceable about this time is that under Captain Zachary Gillam, which had returned in September 1675: *Cal. S.P., Dom., 1675–6*, p. 319.

[6] De Sessac: Forneron, *Louise de Kéroualle*, pp. 120, 121; see also *Cal. Treasury Books, 1676–9*.

3. The *Deane* of *Chichester*[1] preached coram Dom[a][2] on 24. *Act:* 16. shewing what Conscience was. The holy *Sacrament* follow'd: Din'd at *Cap: Grahams*, where I came acquainted with Doctor *Compton*[3] (bro: to the Earle of Northampton) now *Bishop* of *London*, & Mr. *North*,[4] sonn to the Lord *North* ; bro: to the L.C. *Justice*: & clerke of the Closet, a most hopefull young man: The Bishop had once ben a *Souldier*, had also traveld *Italy*, & became a most sober, grave and excellent *Prelate*: The 2d sermon (*Coram rege*) Dr. *Crighton* on 90 *Psal:* 12. of wisely numbering our daies & well employing the time &c: 5. dind with ≏ — pr: 6. Supp'd at L: *Chamberlains*, where also supped the famous beauty & errant Lady, the *Dutchesse* of *Mazarine*[5] (all the world knows her storie) the Duke of *Monmouth*, Countesse of Sussex,[6] both natural Children of the Kings, by that infamous Adulteresse the Dut: of *Cleaveland*: & the Countesse of *Derby*[7] a vertuous Lady,

---

[a] Substituted for *Rege*.

[1] Dr. George Stradling, dean of Chichester from 1672 to 1688.

[2] An abbreviation presumably of *domesticis*.

[3] Above, iii. 533. In 1661 he was a cornet in Oxford's regiment of horse-guards: Dalton, *English army lists*, i. 4 ; he appears also to have claimed that he had served in the royalist cause. He is perhaps the Henry Compton who signed the Padua visitors' album on 2 May 1665: H. F. Brown, no. 624 ; see also *Cal. S.P., Dom., 1663–4*, p. 494 ; *1665–6*, p. 286.

[4] Above, p. 87 ; his holding the position of clerk of the closet is also mentioned by Roger North, *The life of . . . Sir Dudley North*, &c., 1744, p. 255, and by Wood, *Fasti*, ii. 311 ; see also *Cal. S.P., Dom., 1673–5*, p. 359 ; it does not appear in the roll of the lord chamberlain's branch of the household: *Notes and Queries*, clxxiii (1937), 8–9 ; or in Chamberlayne. For his brother Sir Francis see above, iii. 613 ; he was lord chief justice of the common pleas from 1675 to 1683.

[5] Hortense Mancini, 1646–99, niece of Cardinal Mazarin ; married, 1661, Armand de la Porte, marquis de la Meilleraye, created Duc Mazarin 1661: *Nouvelle biog. gén.* ; C. H. Hartmann, *The Vagabond Duchess*, 1926. Having failed to marry Charles II in 1659–60, she appears now to have become one of his mistresses (she had arrived here at the end of 1675). She published her *Memoires* in 1675, giving an account of her unhappy marriage ; an English translation was licensed on 22 February of this year.

[6] Above, iii. 592 n. Monmouth was a half-brother ; the duke of Grafton, Arlington's son-in-law, was a full brother. For Lady Sussex's attachment to the Duchesse Mazarin at this time see Forneron, *Louise de Kéroualle*, pp. 118–30.

[7] Elizabeth Butler, c. 1660–1717 ; married William George Richard Stanley, c. 1655–1702, ninth earl of Derby 1672: G.E.C. She was a niece of Lady Arlington.

daughter to my best friend, the Earle of *Ossorie*: I returned next day:

10 our *Viccar* as before on 6: *Heb:* 19. 20. The signes of a comfortable Hope, Sincerity, and obedience. *Pomerid. Curate* 5 Ephes: 15. 16. Vigilancy against Temptations: 12 To *Lond:* to take order about the building of an house, or rather an appartment, which had all the conveniences of an house; for my deare friend Mr. Godolphin & Lady: which I undertooke to Contrive, & Survey, & employ workmen in, til it shold be quite finished: It being just over against his Majesties *Wood-yard*, by the *Thames* side, leading to Scotland yard:[1] I din'd with ♎ pr: [returned.]ᵃ 17: *Viccar* on 3. *Joh:* 16. Our Invaluable redemption: &c: There dined with me Mr *Flamested*[2] the learned *Astrologer & Mathematitian*, whom now his Majestie had established in the new *Observatorie* in *Greenewich* Park, and furnish'd with the choicest Instruments:[3] an honest, sincere man &c: *Pomerid: Curate*, as before: 18 To *Lond*, to survey my Workemen, dind with ♎ —pr: and [19]ᵇ then with Mrs. *Godolphin* to *Lambeth*, to that rare magazine of Marble, to take order for chimny-pieces &c: The Owner of the workes, had built him a pretty dwelling: This *Dutchman*, had contracted with the *Genoezes* for all their Marble &c: We also saw the *Duke* of *Bouckingams Glasse worke*,ᶜ where they made huge *Vasas* of mettal as cleare & pondrous & thick as Chrystal, also *Looking-*

ᵃ Interlined.   ᵇ Marginal date.   ᶜ Or *works*.

[1] The statement and the other available materials do not permit a precise identification of the position of the house. The Wood Yard lay to the east of Scotland Yard, and was connected with the river by a passage; the house perhaps consisted of the upper stories of part of the riverside range of buildings, such as the Cofferer's Office or the Great Bakehouse: see the Whitehall plan of 1670; L.C.C., *Survey of London*, xvi. 165, 192. There were many private lodgings in this part of the palace: ibid., p. 163.

[2] John Flamsteed, 1646–1719; 'astronomical observator' (Astronomer Royal) 1675–1719: *D.N.B.*
[3] Greenwich Observatory was founded by Charles II in order to obtain accurate observations of the stars for navigators. The foundation-stone was laid on 10 Aug. 1675; Flamsteed entered into residence on 10 July 1676: Drake's Hasted, p. 66 n.; E. W. Maunder, *The Royal Observatory, Greenwich*, 1900; W. D. Caröe, '*Tom Tower*', 1923, pp. 58–63, with reproductions of contemporary engravings.

glasses far larger & better than any that come from *Venice:*[1]
I dined with Mr. *Godolphin* & his Wife:

20: I went to visite also ♌ — pr: 21 home: 24: *Viccar* as
above; shewing that *Christ* died for all-men, even for those
who miscarry, & not for any particular person, or people
onely; The inference, that we should love all men, even
enemies, to pray for, & assist them &c: The *Curate* as before,
with small addition:

27 I went to *Twicknam* to see how the *Bailife* & housekeeper looked after their charge, that house & land, &c being
wholy under my care for my L: *Berkeley* &c: upon the importunity of my friend:

28 Came Mrs. *Godolphin* to visite & stay with us some time:[2]

October 1 Our *Viccar* as before, The holy Communion
follow'd, of which we all received: I went to *Lond:* to looke
after the workmen, with my friend, & [3][a] came back. 8:
Viccar as above.

9 I went with Mrs. *Godolphin* & my Wife to *Black-wall* to
see some *Indian* Curiosities, & as I was walking thro a streete,
the way being s⟨l⟩ipperie & misty, I fell against a piece of
Timber, with such violence, as quite beate the breath out of
my body, so as being taken up, I could not speake, nor fetch
any breath,[b] for some space, & then with greate difficulty,
coming to my sense, after some applications, being carried
into an house, & let bloud: I was carried to the water side,
[c]& so home, where after a daies rest, I recovered, though my
bruse was not quite healed: This being one of the greatest
deliverances that ever I had, The *Lord Jesus* make me ever
mindfull, & thankfull: 11 I went to *Lond:* with Mrs. G: 13:
supped with ✩:

---

[a] Marginal date; it should perhaps precede *I went*.   [b] Followed by
but deleted.   [c] There is a hand pointing to this passage in the margin of
the MS.

---

[1] Buckingham held patents for
the manufacture of crystal from
1660 to 1674; and owned a glasshouse in Vauxhall in 1676: Thorpe,
Hist. of English and Irish glass, i.

101–5, 141.

[2] Until 19 October, while Godolphin was with the king at New-
market: *Life*, p. 69.

15 Mindfull of Gods infinite mercy to me, I received at St. *James's* in the morning with ☌: A stranger preaching at *W-hall* on *Jude.* v. 3. I dind with ✮:—16 *Anniver* ☌ pr:

17 I din'd with my Wife at *B:house* & carried Mrs. *Godolphin* to our house that Evening: where she staied till 19. when I waited on her to Lond: 22: In the Morning *Comm:* at St. *James's*. At *White-hall* Dr. *Dove*[1] (*coram rege*) on 7: *John*: 16 *concerning Curiositie* &c: 24: Dind with ✮: return'd home:

29 A stranger on 23: *Pro: 26.* shew'd how the *heart* was *Gods* by *Creation*, & should be his by donation, & dedication: That many infirmities of the *Saints* were passed over, where the heart was sincere, as in *David* &c: but where was never so much zeale, & external profession, with an unsound heart, all was nothing: by the Example of *Jehu* &c: how happy a thing to dedicate our youth to God. *Pomeridiano* our *Viccar* on 6. *Rom: 23.* how death entred by sinne &c: 30 To *Lond:* about the building; Mrs. *Ann Howard* Mayd of honor to the *Queene*, whom I went to Visite, related to me the strang⟨e⟩ *Vision* she saw: which was thus: One of her maides being lately dead & one whom I well knew, had in her life time told her *Mistris*, that when she died she would certainly appeare to her: This Wench, being deeply in love with a young man, dying, a little while after appeared to her Mistris, as she lay in ⟨bed⟩,[a] drawing the Curtaine, siting downe by her, & beckning to her; her Mistris being broad awake, & sitting up at the affright, called alow'd for her maid to come to her, but no body came; The[b] *Vision*, now going from her, she[c] still continued to call her Maid, who lying in another chamber next to her, rose & came at last to her Mistris: begging her pardon that she did not come at her first

---

[a] MS. *bead*.   [b] Followed by *viss-* deleted.   [c] Followed by *calld* deleted.

---

call; for said shee, I have ben in a most deadly fright, & durst
not stirr for Mistress *Maundy* (for so was her name) who has
appear'd to me, and looked so wistly[1] on me, at the foote of
my bed, that I had not the power to rise or answer: These
two, Mistris *Howard* & her *Woman Davis*, affirming it so
positively, & happning to see it, neere the same time, & in
severall chambers, is a most remarkable thing: & I know not
well how to discredit it, Mrs. *Howard* being so extraordinary
a virtuous & religious *Lady*.

31 Being my Birth-day, & 56 yeare, I spent the morning in
Devotion, surveying my accompts & imploring Gods protection, with solemn thanksgiving for all his signal mercys to
me, especialy for that escape which concern'd me this Moneth
at *Blackwall*: I din'd with *Mrs. Godolphin* & return'd home
the Evening, thro a prodigious & dangerous Mist &c:

November Beging the blessing of *God*, for the ensuing yeare,
I went to Church, when [1][a] our *Viccar* preached on his former
subject, yet introducing something apposite to the [5][a]
solemnity,[b][2] shewing how signal judgements & mischiefes,
over-tooke signal wickednesse: That therefore sinners were
hereafter punish'd for ever; because if they lived, they would
sinn ever. The blessed *Sacrament* follow'd: The L. *Jesus*
assist my resolutions &c: *Pomerid, Curat* on 9. *Heb:* 27. 28.
The obligation we had in this *Kingdome* especialy, to thanke
God for this delivrance of his Church &c: 7: To *Lond:* dined
with ☆. 8: at my L: *Chamb:* 9: I sealed & finished the
Lease of *Spalding* for Mrs. *Godolphin* at her Majesties *Council*
at *Somerset* house. 10 returned home: 12 Our *Vicc:* on 1. *Joh:*
5. 3. of the pleasure & ease of a pious life: &c: *Curate* on.
12: *Heb:* 14, The necessity of peace & unity, for the enjoyment of God: 14. To *Lond:* dind with ☆. 15 Saw the famous
Ball, daunced at Court on her Majesties *Birth-day* &c:[3]

---

^a Marginal date.   ^b Followed by (*it being the day of the feofeès for the
poore meeting* deleted.

---

[1] With close attention, intently:
O.E.D.
[2] Gunpowder Plot. Evelyn has
apparently omitted a notice of the

feoffees' meeting on 1 November:
see critical notes.
[3] For the dresses see *Hist. MSS.
Comm., Rutland MSS.*, ii. 32.

16 My *sonn* & I dining at my *Lo: Chamberlaines*,[1] he shewed us, amongst others that incomparable piece of *Raphaels*, being a *Minister* of *state* dictating to *Guicciardine*, the earnestnesse of the Secretary looking up in expectation of what he was next to write, is so to the life, & so naturall, as I esteeme it for one of the choices⟨t⟩ pieces of that admirable Artist:[2] There was an other womans head of *Leonardo da Vinci*;[3] a Madona of old *Palma*,[4] & two of *Van-Dykes*, of which one was his owne picture at *length* when young, in a leaning posture,[5] the other an *Eunuch* singing;[6] but rare pieces indeede: 17: I returned: 19 Our *Viccar* as before, with little addition &c: 21. To *Lond*, returned next day:

23 Came to dine with me my Lord *Chamberlaine Earle of Arlington*, the Earle *of Derby*,[7] and their Countesses, The *Dutchesse* of *Grafton*,[8] *Countesse* of *Ossory*,[9] *Mademoiselle Beverward*;[10] & Sir *Gabriel Sylvius*,[11] & return'd to Lond: in the Evening:

26 A *stranger* preach'd on: 19: *Levit:* 30, shewing the necessity, duty, & reason of keeping the seaventh day holy, as *Moral* & indispensable &c: an excellent discourse. [(*See notes*)].[a] *Pomerid*: *Curate* on his ⟨former⟩;[b] Explaining what was meant by the *holy* that *should see God*:[c] That Seeing *God*,

---

[a] Marginal note.   [b] MS. *forner*.   [c] Followed by *&c* deleted.

[1] The pictures here mentioned descended from Arlington to the dukes of Grafton and were, with one exception, included in the Grafton sale at Christie's, 13 July 1923.

[2] The picture is by Sebastiano del Piombo and represents Cardinal Ferry Carondelet and his secretary; the ascription to Raphael was apparently first denied by J. D. Passavant; see also Venturi, *Storia dell' arte italiana*, vol. ix, pt. v, pp. 26–8. For Francesco Guicciardini, 1482–1540, the historian, see *Nouvelle biog. gén.*

[3] Not in sale catalogue.

[4] Sale catalogue no. 146.

[5] Sale catalogue no. 143; in 1931 in the possession of Mr. Jules S.

Bache of New York: G. Glück, *Van Dyck* ('Klassiker der Kunst'), 1931, pl. 122 and n.

[6] Sale catalogue no. 144. The picture represents Henri Liberti, organist of Antwerp Cathedral.

[7] For him and his countess see above, p. 97 and n.

[8] Arlington's daughter: above, iii. 622.

[9] Amelia (Emilia), d. 1688, a sister of Lady Arlington (above, iii. 622); married Ossory 1659.

[10] Another of the five daughters of Louis of Nassau, lord of Beverweerd, and so a sister of Lady Arlington and Lady Ossory. For one of them see below, p. 222.

[11] Above, iii. 471.

was that blisse the Saints should onely be capable of: & that blisse to consist in those inexpressible communications & emanations of such favours, as should render them consummately happy; That our natures should then be changed & fortified to see the glorious & beautifull face of *Christ*, that should ravish the very heart &c:

27 I went to *Lond:* 28 dind with ✰. 30: Was our *Anniversarie* Elections at the *R: Society*, where I was againe chosen of the Council: having in the morning before ben to visite & Com: with a poore sick person:

December 3 *Advent Sonday* Dr. *Patric* to the household excellently on 13 *Rom:* 12 insisting chiefly against Uncleanesse &c: as shewing how ill such works of darknesse became our expectations of Christs appearing: The holy *Sacrament* follow'd, the *Bishop* of Lon: Officiating. Coram Rege Dr. *Doughty*[1] on 7: *Matt:* 6 against Swearing, & prophaning the holy name of God: I din'd at Sir *Steph: Foxes*. 4. I saw the greate *Ball* daunced by all the *Gallants* and *Ladys* at the *Dut⟨c⟩hesse* of *Yorks*. 5. Supped with ⇌ pr: 6: I visited my L: *Vic: Mordaunt*[2] at P: Greene with my Wife, & returned to *Says-Court* next day:

10 Fell so deepe *a Snow*, as hindred us from Church &c:[3] 12: To *Lond:* in so greate a snow, as I remember not to have ever seene the like: supped with Mrs. *Godolphin*:

13 Din'd with Lo: *Chamber:* & Duke of *Ormond*: supp'd at L: *Ossories* &c: 15 at ✰: 16 Went againe to my La: *Mordaunt* about buisinesse: dind with Lo: *Clarendon*,[4] Lady *Henrietta Hyde*,[5] Mr. *Andr: Newport*,[6] & with much a doe got home through the snow:

---

[1] Above, p. 87.
[2] Lady Mordaunt is meant, not her son: see below.
[3] Cf. *Hist. MSS. Comm., Rutland MSS.*, ii. 33. The Thames was apparently frozen over at London towards the end of the year: T. T., *Modest observations on the present extraordinary frost*, 1684, p. 3.

[4] Henry Hyde, the former Lord Cornbury; he had succeeded his father in 1674.
[5] Above, iii. 446; iv. 17. Clarendon's sister-in-law.
[6] Andrew Newport, 1623–99, royalist: *D.N.B.* Further notice below, p. 188.

17 More Snow falling, I was not able to get to church &c: 19: To *Lond* about buisinesse: dind at Mrs. *Godolphins*; fell ill of a feavorish distemper &c: which confin'd me to bed two daies: 23 I returned home: 24. The extreame cold kept me within:

25 *Christmas day* our *Viccar* on 1. *Tim:* 3. 16, of the stupendious *Mysterie* of the *Incarnation*: The bl: *Sacrament* follow'd; giving God thanks for my recovery &c:

26 I had neighbours dine'd with me, & so also the 29: 31. our *Viccar* on his former, shewing the benefit of *Christs Incarnation*; that as God he might merit for us, & as man suffer: *Pomerid*: a stranger on: 8: *Matt:* 13:[1] Concerning Repentance. Blessed be God for all his mercifull preservations of me this yeare past; which were many & extraordinary:

1677 January I implor'd Gods protection & blessing for the yeare following: had divers Neighbours dined with me:

7 Our *Viccar* preached on his former subject: of the wonderfull expedient God the Father found out for our Redemption: *Amor ardens cogit ad impossibile.* Thus Gods love, did things beyond all wonder: The holy *Comm:* followed: &c. *Pomerid*, a Young man on. 2. *Luke:* 11 of the *Glad-tidings* on the[a] birth of *Christ*:

10 To *Lond*: dind with ☆: returned next day: 14: A *stranger* on: 1. *Heb:* 1. 2. shewing how truely & essentialy *Christ* was *God* & accomplish'd our Salvation according to the Scriptures, & by all such arguments as used to be urg'd to convince a rational man of matter of fact &c:

16: To *Lond:* dind at Mrs. *Godolphins*: 19: dind at my L:V: *Brounchars*. 21. Dr. *Lamplugh*[2] preached on: 11: *Rom:* 36. That *Afflictions* & even evil things come from God, but to evil-men onely for evill, & therefore we should mark the event of sufferings &c.

---

[a] Altered from *this*.

[1] Perhaps an error for St. Matthew ix. 13.

[2] He had been consecrated bishop of Exeter in 1676.

25 I return'd home, not very well disposed; yet din'd at Mr. *Gaudens*,[1] & then kept in.

30 Our *Viccar* on 13: *Rom:* 2: on which this observation on the original ἀντιτασσομενος signifying not onely a disobedience; but as if the *Apostle* had seene before hand that which those wicked *Rebells* would alledge in defence of their taking armes against their King: using that *very word*, prohibiting it in expresse termes: He also proved that κρῖμα imported Eternal damnation; & that the Kings person could not be separated from his right & power, as not obnoxious to any tribunal but Gods, to answer for what he dos amisse: 31. I went to *Lond:*

Feb: I supped with ☆: 4: Dr. *Craddock* to the house[2] on:

26: *Matt:* 41. shewing the necessitie of Watchfullnesse; *Satan* & our owne infirmities being so buisy to betray us: The power & efficacy of Prayer in faith with endevor:[a] The H: Comm: followed: *Cor: Reg:* by Dr. *Pierce* on 1. *Pet:* 2. 11. shewing the danger of sensual lusts. 5 I din'd at the Holl: *Ambassadors* Mr.[b] *Beverning*[3] with my Lady *Ossory, Arlington, Derby* & La: Mary *Cavendish*[4] daughter to the *Duke* of *Ormond*.

6 Din'd with ☆—7: with my Lo: *Ossory* at my Lord *Brounckers*: 8 Went to *Rohampton*[5] with my Lady *Dutchesse* of *Ormond*: The Garden & perspective is pretty, the Prospect most agreable, I went home that Evening: 11: our *Viccar* as above &c: I went this evening to *Lond*, to passe a fine early next day in Westminster at the *Comm: Pleas* barr about my Trust for Mr. William Howard, sonn to the Earle of

---

^a Altered from *endurance*.   ^b *M*^o: apparently altered to *Mr*.

---

[1] Not identifiable; presumably a son of Dr. John Gauden the bishop, or of his brother Sir Denis Gauden.

[2] i.e. the household.

[3] A slip for van Beuningen: above, p. 77, &c.

[4] Lady Mary Butler, 1646–1710; married, 1662, William Cavendish, at this time styled Lord Cavendish, who became in 1684 fourth earl and in 1694 duke of Devonshire (above, iii. 65).

[5] Roehampton House was the former Putney Park: above, iii. 329. It now belonged to the third earl of Devonshire.

Berkshire, which concerned his Daughters the two Maids of honor &c: dind with Sec: Williamson.

13 dind with Mr. *Godolphin*. 14 Supp'd at my *L: Chamberlain*: 16 home: 18 our *Viccar* as before of the infinite mercy of God to the penetent &c. Curate on 5 *Matt: 7*. 20 Lond. dind with ♎ pr: 25 In the morning at St. *James' Synax:* *W:hall* (*Cor: Rege*) Dr. *Durell* deane of *Winsore*, on. 2 Joel 2. to excite to repentance: I din'd at Sir St: Foxes: 28 Ashwed: the B: of *Lond*¹ on 2. *Zeph:* 1. 2. ⟨March⟩ 2 first friday lent: Dr. *Sancroft* D: of S. *Paules*, 2: *Jam:* 10, that to persist in any one sinn, breakes all the Commandments.² 4. 1 Sonday in Lent. Dr. *Littleton*: 1. *Joh:* 2. 1. 2, how *Christ* is our propitiation: The holy *Sacrament* followd, the *Bish:* of *Lond* officiating: *Cor: Rege* preached the *Bish:* of *Oxon:*³ on 19 *Pro:* 21, in his eloquent style, shewing the Vanity of the devices of mens hearts: &c. 6: dind with ☆. 7: Dr. *Tenison*⁴ excellently, as allways he dos on 1. *Cor:* 3. 3. against strife & devision: In the Evening I sealed writings concerning my Trust for Mrs. Howards &c.

8 Din'd at L. *Chamb:* 9: Dr. *Stradling* on 8 *Rom:* 22. shewing how even the Creatureᵃ should enjoy a manumission, & as much felicity as their nature is capable of, when at the last day they shall no longer grone for their servitude to sinfull man:² I returned to *Says Court*:

11 *Viccar* on 4: *Pro:* 23. of watchfullnesse over the heart: *Curate* on: 5. *Matt:* 10. 12 To *Lond:* 13 dind with Mrs. *Godol:* ⟨14⟩ Dr. *Littleton* on   against divisions in the Church &c:²

ᵃ Or *Creaturs*.

---

¹ Compton, preaching as dean of the chapel. Lenten sermon at court; list of preachers in *London Gazette*, 11 Jan. 1677.

² Lenten sermon at court.

³ Fell. Lenten sermon at court.

⁴ Thomas Tenison, 1636–1715; D.D. 1680; chaplain in ordinary 1676–91; vicar of St. Martin's in the Fields 1680–92; rector of St. James's, Piccadilly, 1686–92; arch-deacon of London 1689–91; bishop of Lincoln 1691; archbishop of Canterbury 1694: *D.N.B.* He was at this time minister of St. Peter Mancroft, Norwich (1671–8). Lenten sermon at court (the name misprinted as 'Dr. Jennison'). The notice obviously contains an accretion to the original text. Evelyn and Tenison later became close friends.

15 I spake to my L: Tressurer for supplies for my Lo: Ambassador of France[1] &c: 16 Dr. *Frampton*[2]—

18 At St. *Jam: Synax:* at *W:hall* B: of *Chester* (*C: rege*) on 17: *Psal:* ult:[3] 20: dind with ☆:

21 home:[4] 21 Dr. *Stillingflete* on: 13. *Luke*. 24, the difficulty of entring; some coming to seeke & strive remissly; some too late; that nothing will save but a ⟨constant⟩[a] & solemne course of holy living, not allowing our selves the least sinfull indulgence:[2] home: 25 Viccar on his former text: *Curate* on 3. *Matt:* 2. 27: Lond: dind at Ber: house with Mrs. *Godolphin*.

28: Sup'd at L: *Ossories:* 30: Dr. *Tillotson*[5] on 19 *Psal:* 12. incomparably of the greate care not to fall into sin: 31 Mrs. *Godolphin* remov'd to the Buildings I had finished in *W:hall* from *Berkeley house*:

Aprill: 1 at *White-hall Synaxis*: din'd at Mrs. *G:* at her *new* lodging: 2: at Sir St: *Foxes*.

3 with Mrs. *Godolphin* dined: 7 returned home: 8 *Palme Sonday* our *Viccar* as before, the bl: Comm: follow'd: *Curate* on 25 *Psal:* 16. 17: 10: Lond, dind with ☆: being holy Weeke.

11 Dr. *North* on 6. *Mark*: 12. necessity of repentance &c:[2] Supp'd with ☆: 12: din'd with ☆:

13 *Goodfriday* at St. *Martins* Dr. *LLoyd*[6] D: of *Bangor*, on: 10. *Joh:* 11. how our B: Saviour, was the good shepherd &c: (See your *notes*) the holy Comm: follow'd: I returned in the Evening:

---

a MS. *constand*.

1 Berkeley.
2 Lenten sermon at court.
3 Lenten sermon at court; but the preacher listed for this day is the bishop of Chichester (Brideoake), Pearson being listed for 11 March.
4 This word is presumably added wrongly; Evelyn appears to have remained in town until the evening.

5 Lenten sermon at court. The sermon is printed in Tillotson, *Works*, 1752, i. 40–7. The text is here cited from the Prayer Book.
6 Lloyd (the apocalyptic) had been instituted vicar of St. Martin's in the Fields on 6 Dec. 1676, and held the living and his deanery simultaneously.

15 our *Viccar* on 8 *Rom:* 24¹ a Resurrection discourse: the B: Sacrament follow'd being *Easter-day*:

22 our *Viccar* as before: In the afternoone to *Greenewich*. The *Curat* on 2. *Tit:* 13. the tirriblenesse of *Christs* appearing to the Wicked, & blessed hope of the righteous &c:

24 To Lond: din'd with ☆. 28 Din'd at the D: of *Ormonds*, returned: 29: Mr. *Bohune* (my sonns *Tutor*) on 2 *Tim:* 3. 5. of the danger of superstition & hypocrisie excellently: *Pomeridiano*, a stranger on 2. *Cor:* 5. 10, describing the final Judgement, danger of late repentance &c:

May: 1. Meeting of the *Foefees* for the poore: our *Viccar* on 12ᵃ *Luke* 21 against *Covetousnesse* &c. I din'd with the Foefees & did Parish buisinesse: 6: at *Grenewich* Dr. *Plume* on: 5: *Joh:* 14 on the duty of Gratitude: That the restored man went immediately to the Temple: reproved those who made any excuses to abstaine from the publique worship, & that frequently take Physick² on the Lords day: recommended above all publique & Congregational worship, as most acceptable, the danger of *Schismatical* meetings where the publique was protected & incourag'd: The holy Sacrament followd: *Pomerid* a young preacher on 2: *Apoc:* 5 exhortatory to Repentance &c:

8 I went to Lond: dined with Mrs. *Godolphin*, visited the Countesse of *Hammilton*,³ supp'd at Lord *Chamberlaines*. 10 Dined at my Lady Tukes with the *Dutchesse* of *Grafton*: Supped at the Earle of *Derbies*. 12 returned home: put 100 fish into the pond &c:

13 our *Viccar* as above 8: *Rom:* 33. 34. *Curate* on: 11: *Heb:* 6. the necessity of Faith &c.

15 Came the E: of *Peterbrough* to desire me to be a Trustee for my L: V: Mordaunt, & his *Countesse* for the sale of

---

ᵃ Altered from *21*?

---

¹ A slip for verse 34: see below.
² Here a strong purge; a common use of the word at this time.
³ Probably Lady Francis Hamilton: above, p. 79; a warrant had been issued on 7 July 1676 for

granting her the dignity of a countess of Ireland as countess of Bantry: *Cal. S.P., Dom., 1676–7*, p. 210; *1677–8*, pp. 200, 254; cf. p. 236. No patent passed the seal.

certaine lands, set out by Act of *Parliament* to pay debts &c:[1]
20: our *Viccar* on 7: *Mat:* 21. that God accounted not of any
outward profession, without the inward & operative effect in
our lives & conversations &c. *Curate* as above, in rather a
Philosophical lecture than sermon: ⟨22⟩:[a] To Lond, din'd with
✡: 24: Dr. *Lloyd* at St. *Martines* on: 4: *Ephes:* 8. 9. 10.
11. 12. an *Ascention* sermon (see your *notes*): holy Comm:
followd: ⟨27⟩:[b] *W:hall:* Dr. *Sudbury*[2] Deane of *Durrham*, on
6 *Gal:* 4. of proving, & examining our workes by the Conscience, whither sincere, and to the Glory of God; If that
justified us, then had we whereof to glory & rejoice &c:
I went afterwards to St. *Martines* to heare the remainder of
his[3] former discourse, it being *Ascention*: See your notes:
29 His Majesties Birth-day, buisinesse hindred me from the
sermon—I din'd with Mrs. *Godolphin*. 30 I return'd home:
next day againe to *Lond*, with the V. C: *Mordaunt*,[4] & Mrs.
Howards who came to visite my Wife: returned.

June 3. *Whitsonday* our *Curate* on: 2 Act. 1–5, weakely
enough: but the holy Sacrament follow'd: Afternoon a young
stranger on 1. *Joh:* 4. 16. shewing the Spirit of God to be love
&c:

6 I went to *Lond*, about my Lady Tukes processe, return'd
that evening. *Trinity Sonday*[5] our *Viccar* 7: *Matt* 21, not to
deferr repentance: *Curate* as before: 11: *Heb:* 6. My *Wifes*
Aunt *Hungerford* came to visite us:

---

[a] MS. *27*.   [b] MS. *22*; preceded by *at* deleted.

---

[1] This is not very clear. Peterborough (above, iii. 305), in accordance with a settlement made in
1649, had in 1668 appointed his
daughter Lady Mary Mordaunt
(below, p. 112) owner of Blechingley, subject to his life interest. This
year (29 Charles II), when she was
eighteen years old, he obtained a
private act of parliament (royal
assent 16 April) vesting Blechingley and other lands in Surrey in four
trustees for sale; Evelyn was one of
the trustees: Lambert, *Blechingley*,

i. 274; *Hist. MSS. Comm., 9th rep.*,
app., ii. 92. Viscount Mordaunt
(above, p. 81) was not concerned.
[2] John Sudbury, 1604–84; D.D.
(date unknown); dean of Durham
1661; chaplain in ordinary *c.* 1663–
84: Venn.
[3] Lloyd's.
[4] Presumably Lady Mordaunt.
[5] 10 June. The vicar had
preached on the present text on
20 May; it does not suit Evelyn's
note on this sermon.

12 I went to *Lond:* to give the L: *Ambassador Berkeley*[1] (now return'd from the Treaty at *Nimegen*) an accompt of the greate Trust repos'd in me during his absence, I having received & transmitted to him no lesse than 20000 pounds: to my no small trouble, & losse of time, that during his absence, & when the *Lord Tressurer* was no greate friend, I yet procurd him greate Summs, very often soliciting his Majestie in his behalfe, looking after the rest of his Estate & concernes intirely; without once so much as accepting any kind of acknowledgement, purely upon the request of my deare friend Mrs. *Godolphin.*

13 I din'd with Mrs. *Godolphin* & return'd, with aboundance of thanks & professions [16][a] from my Lord *Berkeley* & *Lady* &c: 17: *Viccar* as before & so the Curate.

24 My Lord *Berkeleys* troublesome buisinesses being now at an end & I delivered from that intollerable servitude & Correspondence; I had leasure to be somewhat more at home, & to myselfe: Our *Viccar* preached on his former, with little addition: Dr.[b] *Trumbal*[2] Doctor of Laws, & a Learn'd Gent: Chancellor to the B: of *Rochester* &c: din'd with me:

July 1 our *Curate* (the *Viccar* being absent) on 6: *Rom:* 21, of the cursed effects of sinn: The holy Communion follow'd: *Pomerid*, a stranger on 21. *Job*: 7. 2: To *Lond:* & 3d: Visited ☆ & dind: I sealed the deedes of Sale of the Mannor of *Blechinglee* to Sir *Rob: Clayton*, for payments of my Lord *Peterborows* debts, according to the trust by Act of Parlia-

---

a Marginal date.   b Altered from *M*[r].

---

[1] Berkeley left Nimeguen on 7 June/28 May: Wynne, *Life of Jenkins*, ii. 117. He was allowed £100 a week for his ordinary expenses; he had also been granted a pension of £1,200 per annum: *Cal. Treasury Books, 1672–5*, p. 801; *1676–9*, p. 807. His claims for extraordinary expenses, &c., were also in part settled before his return to England: ibid., pp. 264, 283, 573.

Evelyn presumably also remitted part of his private income to him: above, pp. 77–8, &c.

[2] William Trumbull, 1639–1716; D.C.L. 1667; knighted 1684; secretary of state 1695–7: *D.N.B.* He was chancellor of the diocese of Rochester already in 1672: *Hist. MSS. Comm., Downshire MSS.*, i. 7. How long he held the office is unknown.

ment:[1] Then visited ⌒—pr:[2] & so home: 8: A stranger preached on 2: *Ephes:* 8. That the grace which saved us, was the Love of *Christ* &c: *Curat* as above, a weake preacher: 12: I went to Cap: *Johnsons* funerall, Dr. *Mills* preaching on 25 *Matt.* 21, describing the joys of heaven &c:

15 Our *Curate* on 10. *Luke.* 25. 26. 27.—*Pomerid*, a stranger on 3. *Coloss:* 12. on the benefit of the grace of humility: Humility obtaines that which Pride seekes, namely, honour, & love &c: 16 I went to *Wotton* to see my deare Brother. 22: Mr. *Evans*[3] *Curate* at *Abinger*, preach'd an excellent sermon on 5. *Matt:* 12. In the Afternoone Mr. *Higham* at *Wotton* Catechiz'd: 23. I went to see *Albury*, a sweete Villa of the *Duke* of *Norfolcks*,[4] the plot of which Garden & *Crypta* through the mountaine, I had first design'd &c:

26 I din'd at Dr. *Duncombs*[5] at *Sheere* whose house stands inviron'd with very sweete & quick[a] streames: 29 Mr. *Bohune* my sonns late Tutor at *Abinger*[6] on 4: *Phil:* 8 very elegantly, & practicaly: 30 I returned home: next day to *Lond:* to speake to my Lo: Duke of *Ormond*,[7] now passing through Oxfor'd (where he was Chancelor) towards *Ireland*, to make

---

[a] Or *quiete.*

---

[1] The Claytons retained the manor until 1799, and some lands in the parish until later. They are buried in Blechingley, and frequently sat for the borough in parliament; but they lived at Marden in the adjoining parish of Godstone (below, p. 121), Peterborough having pulled down Blechingley manor-house: Lambert, *Blechingley*, pp. 275–6, 280, &c.

[2] Perhaps an accidental repetition of the notice of the earlier visit this day.

[3] Identifiable as John Evans, rector of St. Ethelburga 12 Dec. 1677–85: below, pp. 127, 173.

[4] Henry Howard, at present earl of Norwich and Earl Marshal, did not become duke of Norfolk until about December of this year.

[5] Thomas Duncomb(e), *c.* 1631–1714; D.D., Oxford, 1671; rector of Shere 1659–1714: Foster; Manning and Bray, i. 524, 528. He was a first cousin of George Evelyn's first wife. His house is presumably the old rectory near the Tillingbourne, 'encompass'd about with a large and deep Mote, which is full of Fish': Aubrey, *Surrey*, iv. 42; *V.C.H., Surrey*, iii. 111–12.

[6] Bohun had no regular connexion with Abinger.

[7] Ormonde set out for Ireland on 4 August and was at Oxford from that day to 6 August: *London Gazette*, 6 Aug.; Wood, *Life and times*, ii. 385–7. He was chancellor of the university from 1669 until his death.

Mr. *Cary*[1] a *Doctor* &c: supp'd at my La: *Ossories*, my Lord
having ben to visite me, as he tooke shipping for *Holland*.[2]
Aug: 2: I return'd home:

August 5 *Viccar* on 7: *Jer:* 12. shewing how often God
punishes lesser faults, & spares the gre⟨a⟩ter for terror &
amendment; for causes best known to himselfe, & which the
greate day will justifie him in &c: (see *notes*). The holy
Sacrament follow'd: *Curate* on: 10: *Mark*: 7. I went this
Evening to visite my Lo: *Brounker* now taking the waters at
Dullage.[3]

7 I came to *Lond:* to excuse my not accompanying the
Portugal Ambassador[4] to *Euston*, as I promised, but it did not
comply with my buisinesse: I supp'd at my Lady *Ossories*:
&c:

9 Dined at the Earle of *Peterborows*, the day after the
Marriage of my Lord of Arundell, to my Lady Mary Mordaunt,[a] [5] daughter to the E: of P: & so return'd home:

12 *Viccar* as before: *Pomerid*: a stranger on 27: *Psal:* 4.
of the delight of the Saints in the Service of God: a pious
discourse: 16 I went to visite my La: V. C. *Mordaunt* &
return'd:

19 Our *Viccar* as above adding little: *Curate* on 4: Eph: 14.
21. To *Lond*, to meete with one about a proposal of a Match
for my Sonn:[6] 24. home: 26: our *Viccar* as above, of the long-

---

[a] Followed by *his* deleted.

---

[1] No man of this name is traceable as being created a doctor at
this time, or as a likely candidate for
a doctorate.

[2] Ossory, on his way to join the
prince of Orange, was in Brussels
on 27 July/6 August: *London
Gazette*, 6 Aug.

[3] Sydenham Wells, near Dulwich: above, p. 74.

[4] Dom Francisco de Mello (Manuel
da Camara).

[5] Mary, *c.* 1659–1705; styled
Lady Mary Mordaunt; succeeded as
Baroness Mordaunt in her own right

1697; married on 8 August Henry
Howard, styled in the licence earl of
Norwich (presumably incorrectly);
he was styled earl of Arundel from
about December of this year, when
his father succeeded to the dukedom
of Norfolk, until 1684. He was
separated from her in 1685 on
account of her misconduct and
divorced her in 1700; in 1701 she
married Sir John Germaine: G.E.C.;
further notices below.

[6] He was now twenty-two years
old.

suffering of God. *Curate* on 4: *Eph:* 29, against Idle words, & evil Communication &c:

27 To *Lon:* designing to Visite my *Lord Chamberlaine* in *Suffolck*: 28 whither I came on *Tuesday*, his *Lordship* sending his Coach & 6 horses, to meete me at, & bring me from St. *Edmondsbury* to *Euston*:[1] 29, We went a hunting in the Park, & killed a very fat *Buck*: 31 I went a *Hauking*:

September 2: Preached one Mr. *Clegett*[2] on 6. *John*: 44, proving there was no such thing as irresistable Grace, & compulsorie; but a disposition; That there would otherwise ⟨be⟩ no Faith, or neede of Obedience [Se notes][a] &c: There din'd this day at my Lords, one Sir Jo: *Gaudy*[b][3] a very handsome person, but quite *dumb*: yet very intelligent by signes, & a very fine Painter; so civil, & well bred he was, as it was not possible to discerne any imperfection by him; his Lady & children were also there, & he was at church in the morning with us: 4: I went to visite my Lord *Crofts*,[4] now dying at St. *Edmonsbery*, and tooke this opportunity to see this antient Towne, & the remaines of that famous *Monasterie* & Abby;[5] There is little standing intire save the *Gate-house*, which shews it to have ben a vast & magnificent Gotique structure, & of greate extent: The Gates are Wood, but quite plated over with jron: There are also two stately Churches, one especialy.[6] 5. I went to *Thetford* the *Borrogh Towne*,

---

[a] Interlined.　　[b] Followed by *a Ge-* deleted.

[1] About ten miles.

[2] Presumably William Clagett, 1646–88; D.D. 1683; at this time preacher at Bury St. Edmunds: *D.N.B.*; his brother Nicholas (*c.* 1654–1727: *D.N.B.*), at this time rector of Great Ellingham, Norfolk, is less likely.

[3] John Gawdy, 1639–1709; second baronet 1669; of West Harling, Norfolk: *D.N.B.*; G.E.C., *Baronetage*, iii. 280. He is said to have studied painting under Lely; a letter from Lely probably relating to him (B.M., Harleian MS. 4713, ff. 23, 24) is printed in Collins Baker,

Lely, ii. 132. For his wife and children see *D.N.B.*

[4] Above, ii. 562. He died on the eleventh of this month; his house was at Little Saxham, about four miles west of Bury.

[5] 'The reliques that this *Abbey* still shews, are far more majestick, then the ruins of other *houses* of its kind'; R. Blome, *Britannia*, 1673, p. 210. The gatehouse is the Abbey Gate; the gates are not mentioned by other writers and were probably modern.

[6] Blome describes them as 'fair and spacious *Structures*'.

where stands likewise the ruines of another religious house;[1]
& there is a round mountaine artificialy raised,[2] either for
some Castle or Monument, which makes a pretty *Landscape*:
As we went & return'd a *Tumbler*[3] shew'd his extraordinary
addresse in the Warren: I also saw the Decoy,[4] much pleased
with the stratagem &c: 9: A stranger preach'd at *Euston*
Church on 1. *Thess:* 5. 21. Prove all things, that is examine
your faith, your life, your actions, & that of others, to imitate
the best; & then fell into an handsome *Panegyric* on my Lords
new building the Church,[5] which indeede for its Elegance and
cherefullnesse is absolutely the prettiest Country Church in
England: My Lord told me that his heart smote him, after
he had bestow'd so much on his magnificent Palace there
he should see Gods-house in the ruine it lay; he has also
rebuilt the Parsonage house all of stone, very neately &
ample:

10 My *Lord*: to divert me, would needes carry me to see
Ipswich, where[a] we dined at one Mr. *Manns*[6] by the way,
Recorder of the Towne: There was in our Company my Lord
Huntingtore,[7] sonn to the *Dutchesse* of *Lauderdail*, Sir *Ed*:

---

[a] Substituted for *so by the way*.

---

[1] Thetford is four miles north-west of Euston. For the remains of the Priory see T. Martin, *Hist. of . . . Thetford*, 1779.

[2] The mound is about 100 feet high and 338 feet in diameter at the base: Martin, p. 10. Its origin appears to be unknown.

[3] The tumbler was a dog trained for catching rabbits: for an account of it see Dr. J. Caius, *Of Englishe Dogges*, 1576, pp. 11–12.

[4] See above, ii. 59.

[5] A foundation-stone was laid by Arlington's daughter, the duchess of Grafton, on 21 April 1676: A. Page, *Supplement to the Suffolk Traveller*, 1844, p. 776.

[6] There is an error here; the present recorder was Thomas Edgar: J. Wodderspoon, *Memorials of . . .*

Ipswich, 1850, p. 124. For an Ipswich family named Mann, see Muskett, *Suffolk manorial families*, iii. 76–80 E. The present deputy-recorder was Christopher Milton, the poet's brother.

[7] Lionel Tollemache, 1649–1727, son of Elizabeth Murray, c. 1628–98, countess of Dysart (Scotland) in her own right from c. 1654, by her first husband, Sir Lionel Tollemache (Talmash), of Helmingham, Suffolk. He was styled Lord Huntingtower from 1651 to 1698, when he succeeded his mother as earl of Dysart; he had succeeded his father as fourth baronet in 1669; he was at this time M.P. for Suffolk. His mother married in 1672 as her second husband John Maitland, duke of Lauderdale: G.E.C., &c.

Bacon,[1] a learned Gent, of the family of the greate Chancellor
Verulame, & Sir Jo: *Felton*[2] with some other knights & Gent:
After dinner came the *Baylifs*, & *Magistrates* in their formali-
tie⟨s⟩ & Maces, to Complement my Lord, & invite him to the
Towne-house, where they presented us a noble Collation of
dried Sweetemeates & Wine, the Bells ringing &c: Then we
went to see the Towne,[3] & first the *L: Vicount Herefords*
house[4] which stands in a Park neere the Towne, like that at
Bruxelles in *Flanders*:[5] The house[a] not greate, yet pretty,
especialy the Hall: & the stewes of fish succeeding one
anoth⟨e⟩r & feeding one the other, all paved at bottome:
There is a good Picture of the B: *Virgin* in one of the parlours,
seeming to be of *Holbein*, or some good Masters.[6] Then we
saw the Haven, 7 miles from *Harwich*:[7] There is no River,
but it dies at the Towne running out every day with the tide;
but the bedding being soft mudd, it is safe for ships, & a
station: The Trade of *Ipswich* is for most part, *New-Castle
Coales* which they supply *London* with; but was formerly
Cloathing:[8] There is not any beggar dos aske any Almes in

---

[a] Followed by *meane* deleted.

---

[1] Either Edmund Bacon of Red-
grave, d. 1685, succeeded as fourth
baronet 1655; or his second cousin
Edmund Bacon of Gillingham, *c.*
1650–83, succeeded as second baronet 1666; both men were great-
great-nephews of Francis Bacon,
the lord chancellor: G.E.C.,
Baronetage, i. 2; iii. 242; *Visitation
of Norfolk, 1664* (Harleian Soc.),
i. 10.

[2] No knight or baronet of this
name is traceable. Presumably a
slip for Henry Felton, d. 1690, succeeded as second baronet 1624; his
wife was an aunt of Lord Huntingtower: G.E.C., *Baronetage*, i. 155.

[3] Evelyn had already visited
Ipswich in 1656: above, iii. 178–9.
There were two bailiffs: Wodder-
spoon, *Memorials*, p. 90.

[4] For the house (Christ Church),
see above, iii. 178. Its present owner

was an infant, Leicester Devereux,
c. 1673–83, succeeded as seventh
Viscount Hereford 1676: G.E.C.

[5] Above, ii. 71–2. It was inside
the walls of Brussels, whereas Christ
Church was outside those of Ipswich.

[6] For a possible later notice see
Moore Smith, *Family of Withypoll*,
p. 96. The picture is now lost.

[7] Harwich is about twelve miles
distant. Ipswich is situated at the
point where the Gipping expands
into the Orwell. A station is a port
for ships: O.E.D. Ipswich was the
most important place for the sick
and wounded in Sir William Doy-
ley's district in the war of 1664–7.

[8] Blome states that the Newcastle
trade is the most important part of
the town's trade; cloth manufacture
had given place to shipbuilding:
Britannia, p. 2c9.

the whole Towne; a thing very extraordinary; so ordered by
the prudence of the Magistrates: It has in it 14 or 15 very
beautifull Churches,[1] in a word 'tis for building, cleanesse &
good order, one of the sweetest Townes in England: *Cardinal
Wolsey*[2] was a butchers sonne of this Towne, but there is
little of that magnificent Prælates foundation here besides a
Schole, &, I think a *Library*: which I did not see; but his
intentions were to build some greate thing &c: Thus we
return'd late to *Euston*, having travelled above 50 miles this
day:[3]

Since first I was at this place,[4] seated in a bottome betweene two gracefull swellings, I found things exceedingly
improvd: The maine building being now made in the figure
of a Greeke Π with 4 pavilions two at each corner & a breake
in the front, rail'd & balustred at the top, where I caused
huge jarrs of Earth[5] to be plac'd full of Earth to keepe them
steady ⟨on⟩[a] their ⟨Piedestalls⟩,[b] betweene the statues, which
make as good a shew, as if they were of stone; and though
the building be of brick & but two stories, besides Cellars &
Garrets, covered with blew Slate, yet there is roome enough
for a full Court, the Offices & out-houses being so ample &
well disposed: The Kings appartment is both painted a fresca,
& magnificently furnish'd: There are many excellent Pictures
in the roomes of the greate Masters: The Gallery is a pleasant
noble roome, & in the breake or middle, a *Billiard* Table;[6]
but the Wainscot being of firr, & painted dos not please me

---

[a] MS. *non*.   [b] MS. *Piededestalls*.

---

[1] Camden says fourteen churches;
Blome twelve churches, besides
a chapel, &c.
[2] See above, iii. 179. The statement that he was a butcher's son is
found in Camden. Blome mentions
the '*Free-School*' and 'an excellent
Library' here: p. 209. For the
former see *V.C.H.*, *Suffolk*, ii. 325–
38; Wolsey appears to have enlarged an older school. The latter
was founded in 1578: Clarke, *Hist.
. . . of Ipswich*, p. 280.

[3] The distance from Euston to
Ipswich is about twenty-nine miles.
[4] For Evelyn's earlier notice of
Euston see above, iii. 591–2. There
is a good notice of it in 1698 in Celia
Fiennes, *Journeys*, ed. C. Morris,
1947, pp. 150–1.
[5] Presumably terra-cotta.
[6] Billiard tables appear to have
been fairly common at this time in
England: C. Cotton, *Compleat Game-
ster*, 1674, p 23. Celia Fiennes also
mentions this table.

so well as Spanish Oake without painting:[1] The Chapell is
pretty, & Porch descending to the Gardens: The Orange-
Garden is very fine, & leads into the Greene-house, at the end
whereoff is a sall[2] to eate in, & the Conservatory very long
(some hundred feete) adorn'd with Mapps, as the other side
is with the heads of *Cæsars*[3] ill cut in alabaster: over head are
severall appartments for my Lord, Lady, & Dutchesse, with
Kitchins & other offices below in a lesser volume, with lodgings for servants, all distinct, for them to retire to when they
please, & that he would be in private & have no communication with the Palace, which he tells me he will wholly resigne to his Sonn in Law,[4] & Daughter, that Wise, & charming
young Creature: The *Canale* running under my Ladys dressing chamber window, is full of Carps, & fowle, which come
& are fed there with greate diversion: The Cascade at end of
the Canale turnes a Corne-mill which finds the family, &
raises water for the fountaines & offices: To passe this
Chanal into the opposite Meadows, Sir *Sam: Moreland* has
invented a Skrew Bridge, which being turned with a Key
land⟨s⟩ you 50 foote distant, at entrance of an ascending
Walke of trees for a mile in length: as tis also on the front into
the Park, of 4 rows of Ashes & reaches to the Parke Pale
which is 9 miles in Compas, & the best for riding & meeting
the game that ever I saw, There were now of red & fallow
deere almost a thousand, with good Covert, but the soile
barren & flying sand in which nothing will grow kindly: The
Tufts of Firr & much of the other wood were planted by my
direction some yeares before:[5] In a word, this seate is admirably placed for field sports, hauking, hunting, racing:
The mutton small, but sweete: The stables are capable of
30 horses & 4 Coaches: The out offices make two large quad-
rangles, so as never servants liv'd with more ease & convenience, never Master more Civil; strangers are attended &

---

[1] Cf. *Sylva*, 1679, p. 26 (Norway
oak, but not Spanish, is mentioned
already in ed. 1670, p. 24).

[2] Presumably *salle* anglicized;
but there is also an English word
'sale': *O.E.D.*

[3] For what appears to be the
later history of some of them see
A. L. Hunt, (*Thetford*), 1870, pp.
154–5.

[4] The duke of Grafton.

[5] See above, iii. 591.

accomodated as at their home in pretty apartments furnish'd
with all manner of Conveniences & privacy: There are bathing roomes, Elaboratorie, Dispensatorie, what not: Decoy
& places to keepe & fat foule &c: He had now in his new
Church (neere the Garden) built a Dormitory or Vault with
severall repositories to burie in for his family:[1] In the expense
of this pious structure, I meane the church, exceedingly laudable, most of the houses of God in this Country resembling
rather stables & thatched Cottages than Temples to serve
God in: He has also built a Lodge in the Park for the Keeper,
which is a neate & sweete dwelling, & might become any
gentleman of quality, the same has he don for the Parson,[2]
little deserving it, for his murmuring that my Lord put him
for some time out of his wretched hovell, whilst it was
building: he has also built a faire Inn at some distance from
his Palace, a bridge of stone over a River neere it, and repaired all the Tennants houses, so as there is nothing but
neatenesse, and accomodations about his estate, which yet
I think is not above 1500 pounds a yeare: I believe he had
now in his family 100 domestic servants. His Lady (being
one of the *Bredrodes* daughters; grandchild to a natural sonn
of Henry Fred: Prince of Orange) is a good natured, &
obliging woman. They love fine things, & to live easily,
pompously, but very hospitable; but with so vast expense as
plunges my Lord into debt exceedingly; My Lord himselfe is
given to no expensive vise but building & to have all things
rich, polite, & Princely: he never plays, but reades much,
having both the Latine, French & Spanish tongues in perfection: has traveled much, & is absolutely the best bred &
Courtly person his Majestie has about him; so as the publique Ministers more frequent him than any of the rest of the
nobility:[3] Whilst he was secretary of state & prime Minister[4]

---

[1] Arlington is buried in the south
chapel of the church.

[2] Robert Mathew(s), *c.* 1615–82;
M.A., Cambridge, 1640; rector of
Euston 1655–82: Venn.

[3] Arlington's manners were in-
variably admired and praised: see

especially Clarendon, in Clarendon,
State papers, 1767–86, vol. iii, supp.,
p. lxxxi; G. Leti, *Del teatro Brittanico*, 1683, ii. 550–1.

[4] This is a very early use of the
term, especially in connexion with
England: see *O.E.D.* Neither the

he had gotten vastly, but spent it as hastily, even before he
had established a funds to maintaine his greatenesse, & now
beginning to decline in favour (the Duke[1] being no greate
friend of his) he knows not how to retrench: He was the sonn
of a Doctor of Laws[2] whom I have seene, & being sent from
Westminster Schole to *Oxon:* with intention to be a divine,
and parson of *Arlington*[3] a Village neere *Brainford*, when
Master of Arts, the Rebellion falling out, he followd the
Kings Army, & receiving an honorable wound in the face,[4]
grew into favour & was advanc'd from a meane fortune at
his Majesties restauration, to an Earle, & knight of the Garter: L: Chamb: of the Household,[5] & first favorite for a long
time, during which the King married his Natural Sonn the
Duke of Grafton, to his onely Daughter & heiresse:[6] worthy
for her beauty & vertue of the greatest Prince in Christen-
dom: My Lord is besids all this a prudent & understanding
person, in buisinesse, speakes very well: Unfortunate yet in
those he has advanc'd, proving ungratefull most of them:[7]

---

law nor such constitutional conventions as existed recognized any
predominating minister and Clarendon in 1667 repudiated the charge
of 'the credit and power of being
chief   minister':   Continuation,
§ 1197; he describes the term 'first
minister' as 'newly translated out
of French into English': ibid.,
§ 89. Arlington, although a leading
minister from 1667 to 1674, never
occupied such a position as Clarendon or Danby. He was secretary of
state from 1662 to 1674. Evelyn
later uses a variant, premier
minister: below, 23 Feb. 1686. See
also *Notes and Queries*, cxc (1946),
78, 284.

[1] Of York. He and Arlington
had generally been on bad terms.

[2] John Bennet, *c.* 1589–1658;
B.A., Oxford, 1608; knighted 1616:
Foster; Barbour, *Arlington*, pp. 3–
4, 46. He is not traceable as a doc-
tor of law; his father, also Sir John
Bennet (*D.N.B.*), was created D.C.L.

in 1589.

[3] Harlington, about five miles
west of Brentford. He was admitted at Christ Church 1635;
student 1636; B.A. 1639; M.A.
1642. Evelyn is the sole authority for
his education at Westminster. For
his intending to take holy orders see
J. Sheffield, duke of Buckinghamshire, *Works*, 1729, ii. 86.

[4] Arlington received a cut on the
nose in a fight at Andover, 1644;
his active service appears to have
been limited to the one campaign:
Barbour, pp. 11–12. He retained a
scar throughout his life; his portraits show him as wearing a patch.

[5] He was created earl of Arlington
on 22 April 1672 and was elected
K.G. on 15 June of the same year
(installed 22 June). He was lord
chamberlain of the household from
1674 until his death.

[6] See above, iii. 622.

[7] This refers to Clifford and Sir
Joseph Williamson.

The many obligations & civilities I have to this noble gent:
exacts from me this Character, and I am sorry he is in no
better Circumstances. Having now pass'd neere three weekes
at Euston, to my greate Satisfaction, with much difficulty he
sufferd me to looke homewards; being very earnest with me
to stay longer, & to engage me, would himselfe have[a] carried
& accompanied me to *Lynn regis*,[1] a Towne of important
Trafique about 20 miles beyond, which I had never seene, as
also the *Travelling Sands*,[2] about 10 miles wide of *Euston*,
that have so damaged the Country, rouling from place to
place, & like the Sands[b] in the desarts[c] of *Lybia*, quite over-
whelmed some gentlemens whole Estates, as the relation
extant in print, and brought to our Society describes at large:

The 13 of *September* my Lords-Coach conveyed me to
Berry:[3] & thence baiting at *New Market*, stepping in at Aud-
ly end,[4] to see that house againe, I lay at *Bishops Stratford*,[5]
& the next day home, accompanied in my Jorney with one
Major *Fairfax*[6] of a Younger house of the Lord Fairfax, a
Souldier, a Traveller, an excellent Musitian, good natured,
well bred gent:

16 Our *Viccar* preach'd on 5. *Matt:* 20, describing the hypocrisie of the *Scribes* & Pharesie⟨s⟩: &c: See notes:—Curat on
4: *Eph:* 29, concerning care in our discourse: I preferred Mr.
Philips[7] to the service of my L. Chamb: who wanted a *scholar*

---

[a] Followed by *gone* deleted.　　[b] Or *Sande*.　　[c] Or *desarte*.

---

[1] King's Lynn. The distance is
about thirty-four miles.
[2] At Downham, on the Ouse between Thetford and Brandon. Contemporary account in *Philosophical
transactions*, [vol. iii], no. 37 (1668),
pp. 722–5; modern account in
V.C.H., Suffolk, i. 21.
[3] Bury St. Edmunds.
[4] Above, iii. 140–1, 556.
[5] Bishop's Stortford.
[6] Thomas Fairfax, 1633–1712
(1710), second son of Sir William
Fairfax of Steeton, a third cousin of
the general. At this time he was a
captain in the first Foot Guards; in

September 1678 he was lieutenant-
colonel in Sir H. Goodrick's regiment. He was colonel of the Fifth
Foot (now the Northumberland
Fusiliers) from 1694 to 1703, and
was a major-general and governor
of Limerick at the time of his death:
Herald and genealogist, vi. (1871),
614; Dalton, *English army lists*, i.
192, 219, 244; iii. 74.
[7] Above, iii. 364, &c. He appears
to have taught the duchess of Grafton and a nephew of Arlington:
Wood, *Athenæ*, iv. 760. He dedicated to the duchess the fourth edition
(1678) of his *New World of Words*.

to reade to & entertaine him some times: My Lord has a library at *Euston* full of excellent bookes: 18 To Lond: dind with Mrs. *Godolphin*. 20 with my *Lord Treasurer*. 23: I received the holy Comm: at St. *James's*, heard Dr. *Burnet*[1] on 2. Titus 13. on Christs infinite condescention: visited ☌ — pr: 24 home.

30 Doctor as before with small addition, I dind at *Cap: Cocks* at Greenewich: *Pomerid* the *Curate* there on 1. *Psal:* 3 of the fruite of the Tree, that the waters signified *Christ* &c.

Octob: 3 To Lond: returned next day: 7: *Viccar* on his former subject (se your *notes*) the holy Communion follow'd: *Curat* on 22: *Pro:* 6, a profitable discourse concerning the Education of Children &c: 11. To Lond: 12 With Sir *Robert Clayton* to *Marden*,[2] an estate he had lately bought of my *kindsman* Sir *John Evelyn*[3] of *Godstone* in Surry: which from a despicable farme house Sir Robert had erected into a Seate with extraordinary expense: Tis seated in such a solitude among hills, as being not above 16 miles from Lond, seemes almost incredible, the ways also to it so winding & intricate: The Gardens are large & walled nobly, & the husbandry part made so convenient, & perfectly understood, as the like I had not seene: The barnes, the stacks of Corne, the Stalls for Cattell, Pidgeon house, &c of most laudable example: Innumerable are his plantations of Trees, espe⟨c⟩ialy Wallnuts,[4] the Orangerie & Gardens very curious; large & noble roomes in the house. He & his Lady[5] (very curious in Distilling &c) entertain'd me 3 or 4 dayes very freely: I earnestly

---

[1] Gilbert Burnet: above, p. 47; he did not obtain his doctorate until 1680. The text is perhaps wrong.

[2] Marden is about two miles north of Lee Place (above, ii. 557 n.), towards the north end of the parish of Godstone. The estate descended from Clayton to his nephew, and remained in the family's possession until 1911. The house built by Clayton was burnt down in 1879; the stables still exist: Lambert, *Godstone*, pp. 286–9, and views.

[3] John Evelyn, 1633–71; created

a baronet 1660; a son of Evelyn's first cousin, Sir John of Godstone (above, ii. 554 n., &c.): Foljambe, p. 57. Clayton bought Marden from his heir, Mary Gittings: Lambert, *Godstone*, pp. 277–80.

[4] Evelyn mentions them in *Sylva*, 1679, p. 49.

[5] Martha, *c.* 1643–1705, daughter of Perient Trott; married Clayton *c.* 1659; epitaph in Manning and Bray, ii. 310; for her father see H. Wilkinson, *The Adventurers of Bermuda*, 1933.

suggested to him, the repairing of an old desolate delapi-
dated Church,[1] standing on the hill above the house, which
I left him in good disposition to do, & endow it better, there
not being above 4 or 5 inhabitants in the Parish besids this
prodigious rich Scrivenor: This place is exceeding sharp in
Winter, by reason of the serpenting of the hills, & wants
running water, but the solitude exceedingly pleased me: all
the ground is so full of wild Time, Majoram & other sweete
plants, as is not to be overStock'd with Bees, so as I think
he had neere 40 hives of that industrious Insect: 14. I went
to Church at *Godstone*, where on 30 *Psal.* 4 the *Minister* made
a good sermon, concerning the Extent of Gods love &c: After
sermon I went to see old Sir Jo: Evelyns Dormitory, joyning
to the Church, pav'd with Marble, where he & his Lady lie
on a very stately Monument at length, in Armor &c: white
Marble: The *Inscription* (being onely an account of his particular branch of our family) is on black Marble.[2]

15 I went back with my Lady to *Lond:* leaving Sir Robert
behind: This Evening I saw the Prince of Orange,[3] & supp'd
with my Lord Ossory.

16 I dind with Mr. *Godolphin* it being Anniver &c: 17 at my
L: Chamberlaines, went home in the Evening. 21 our Viccar
pursues his former subje⟨c⟩t (see *notes*).

23 To *Lond:* dind with ☆. I saw againe the Prince of
Orange: his Marriage with the Lady Mary (eldest Daughter
to the Duke by Mrs. Hyde the late Dutchesse) was now
declared.[4] 24 dind with ☆. 25 at L: *Chamber:* returned.
at night:

28 Our *Viccar* as above little added: Curate as before also:

---

[1] Woldingham. Clayton did not rebuild the church.

[2] This Sir John is Evelyn's first cousin. He had died in 1664. For the inscription on his tomb see Foljambe, p. 27.

[3] Above, iii. 563. He had arrived at Harwich on 9 October and had come from Newmarket with the court to Whitehall on 13 October:

London Gazette, 11, 15 Oct.

[4] The match was announced to the council on 22 October: Privy Council register. It was immediately made public: Hooke; newsletter, 23 Oct., in *Hist. MSS. Comm., Le Fleming MSS.*, p. 141. A notice in *London Gazette*, 25 Oct., gives a wrong date for the council meeting.

31 Being my Birth day & 57th yeare, I blessed God for his protection &c:

November 1. Beging the favour of God for the yeare entering, I went to Church, where our *Viccar* preached on 12 *Luke* 21, the Text of the former yeare:[1] Then dined with the Foefees of the Poore according to Costome.

3 To Lond: visited Mrs. Godolphin.　4: Dr. LLoyd[a][2] at Wh:Hall: the holy Sacrament follow'd: I dind at ✶: & 5: at my Lady *Tukes* &c: 6 at ✶:

11 I received at St. *Jamess, Coram Rege* Dr. *Glanvill*[3] on Acts, *Felix trembled* &c, shewing the power of Gods Word, & accusation of Conscience even to a meere Heathen, from a poore & despicable Minister: *Felix* a proud & hauty person: I was all this Weeke in composing matters betweene old Mrs. *Howard*, and Sir *Gabriel Sylvius*, upon his long & earnest addresses to Mrs. Ann, her second daughter Mayd of Honor: my friend *Mrs. Godolphin* (who exceedingly loved the young Lady)[b] was most industrious in it, out of pitty to the languishing Knight; so as (though there were greate difference in Yeares)[4] it was at last effected, & they married on the 13. in Hen: 7th Chapell, by the Bish: of Rochester, there being besides my wife & Mrs. Graham her sister with Mrs. *Godolphin* very few more: We din'd at the old Ladys, & supp'd at Mr. Grahame's at St. *James's*:[5] I likewise dined there the next day, & supp'd at Sir Jos: Williamsons among severall of our Society.[6]

15 The *Queenes* birth-day, & of my *Baptisme*; a greate Ball

---

[a] Followed by *at St. Martines* deleted.　　[b] Closing bracket supplied.

---

[1] This is wrong; it was the vicar's text for the feoffees' sermon on 1 May of this year: above, p. 108.

[2] Presumably the apocalyptic.

[3] Presumably Joseph Glanvill: above, p. 53. His text is Acts xxiv. 25.

[4] Sylvius was about forty years old, Anne Howard about twenty-one.

[5] He would have an apartment in St. James's Palace as keeper of the privy purse to the duke of York.

[6] The Royal Society. For this gathering see Hooke, *Diary*; and below, p. 125 n.

at *Court*, where the Prince of *Orange* & his new *Princes* daunc'd:[1] I dind with ☆.

17 I din'd with Mr. *Godolphin* & his Wife, at which time he sealed the Deedes of settlement on his Lady, in which I was a Trustee: &c: 18. Dr. *Alestree* on 17: *Psal*:[2] Then shall I be satisfied, when thy Glory dos appeare &c: I received the *B: Sacrament* at *St. Jamess*, dind at Sir St: *Foxes*.

19 The *Prince & Princesse* of *Orange* went away,[3] and I saw embarqued my *Lady Sylvius* who went now also into *Holland* with her *Husband*, made *Hoffmaester* to the *Prince* a considerable Charge:[4] We parted with greate sorrow, for the greate respect and honour I bore to the Lady, a most pious and virtuous creature &c: I dind with my *Lord Berkely* at his house.

20 At Mrs. *Godolphins*, then visited Mr. *Rob: Boyle*, where I met *Dr. Burnet*[5] & severall *Scots* Gent: Mr. *Boyle* now shewing us his new Laboratorie:[6]

21 I din'd at my L: *Chamb:* Supp'd at Sec: *Williamsons* with Sir *Chr: Wren*, Dr. *Holder*[7] *Subdeane* of his Majesties *Chapell*, Sir *Jo: Lowther*,[8] Dr. *Grew*[9] &c:

---

[1] William and Mary had been married on 4 November: *London Gazette*, 8 Nov.

[2] The text is a paraphrase from verse 15, the Bible version.

[3] *London Gazette*, 22 Nov.

[4] *Hofmeester, maître d'hôtel*, steward. Sylvius is mentioned in this capacity in *Oprecht verhael . . . de reyse van . . . den . . . Prince van Orangien na Engelandt*, 1677, p. 33.

[5] Gilbert Burnet, not yet a doctor.

[6] Boyle was living with his sister Lady Ranelagh (below, 18 June 1690) in Pall Mall. Hooke (above, iii. 356, &c.) was planning alterations to her house in the summer of 1676; they were carried out in 1677, and included a laboratory for Boyle: *Diary*, 28 Aug. 1676, &c.; especially 18 and 24 Aug. 1677.

[7] Above, p. 84.

[8] Identifiable as John Lowther of Whitehaven, 1642–1706, second baronet 1644; F.R.S. 1664: *D.N.B.* John Lowther of Lowther, 1655–1700, second baronet 1675; created Viscount Lonsdale 1696; F.R.S. 1699 (*D.N.B.*, art. Lowther, Sir John), is also possible, but unlikely, as the party had almost certainly been invited in order to discuss Royal Society business. See note below.

[9] Nehemiah Grew, 1641–1712; M.D. 1671; F.R.S. 1671; curator to the Society 'for the Anatomy of Plants' 1672; secretary 1677–82; author of *Musæum Regalis Societatis*, 1681 (above, iii. 433); *præfectus* of the Society's museum 1682: *D.N.B.*

A notice for Sunday 25 November presumably fell out when Evelyn was transcribing the diary. The next notice starts a new page.

27: I dind at *Lo: Tress:* with *Prince Rupert,* Vicount *Falkenberg,*[1] Earle of *Bath,* Lo: *O Brian*[2] &c: & went home in the Evening. 29 To *Lond:* din'd at Sir *Rob: Claytons.* 30: To the R: Society, it being our Anniversary Election day, where we chose Sir *Joseph Williamson* (now prin: Secretary of state) *President* for the next yeare, after my Lord Vicount *Brounchar* had possessed the Chaire now 16 yeares successively: & therefore now thought fit to change &c: that prescription might not prejudice &c:[3] we had a greate Entertainment this night.[4]

December 2: A *stranger* at *White-hall* on 2: *Cor:* 5. 15, shewing the dreadfull Accompt to be given at the last day:[5] The holy Comm: follow'd, Bish: of *Lond:* Officiating: *Coram Rege* Dr. *Ball*[6] on. 5. Eph: 20. That we were to praise God, for all things, allwayes, yea for evil things & adverse &c: 4: Dind with ☆, having in the morning ben with our new *President,* as one of the *Council* to administer his *Oath,*[7] & this being the first day of his taking the chaire, he gave us a magnificent supper.[8] 8 home:

9 Our *Viccar* on 7: *Gen:* 1, shewing how Children were blessed for their Fathers sake &c: (See your *notes*) *Curate* on 1. *Eccles:* 14. The vanity of all earthly enjoyments:

12 To *Lond:* to a special Council about carrying on the

---

[1] Thomas Belasyse, 1628–1700; second Viscount Fauconberg of Henknowle 1653; created earl of Fauconberg 1689; husband of Cromwell's daughter Mary: G.E.C.; R. W. Ramsey, *Studies in Cromwell's family circle,* 1930, pp. 35–117.

[2] Above, p. 39.

[3] Birch, iii. 352–3. According to Hooke the elections of the officers and of the members of the council were unfairly conducted in 1675 and 1676, and a number of fellows decided to put forward a new candidate for the presidency. They tried various men; eventually Williamson was adopted at the gathering held at his house on 14 November (see above, p. 123); the supper at his house on 21 November was

apparently also part of the campaign (Hooke remarks that he himself was absent). Feeling ran very high: Hooke, *passim,* especially 8 June; 8–11, 18, 19, 27 Oct.; 8, 19 Nov.

[4] This was held at the Crown, in Threadneedle Street, on part of the site of the Bank of England; the Society had dined there on each St. Andrew's Day meeting from 1674: notices in Hooke; ibid., p. 465.

[5] The text is perhaps wrong.

[6] Dr. Richard Ball: above, iii. 627.

[7] For the swearing in see Hooke. Evelyn was not re-elected to the council.

[8] This belongs to 6 December: Birch, iii. 358–61. Hooke mentions the supper.

affaires of the Society &c:¹ supp'd with our President. 13: Din'd with *Lo: Chamb:* & so home: 16 our *Viccar* on his former (see notes) concerning the Sacrament of Baptisme, succeding Circumcision:² *Curat* as before; shewing the vexation of earthly things, unlesse sanctified &c:

20 To *Lond:* din'd at *Lo: Chamb:* Carried my *Lord Treasurer* an account of the *Earle* of *Bristols Librarie* at *Wimbleton*, which my Lord thought of purchasing, til I acquainted him, it was a very broken Collection, consisting much in books of Judicial Astrologie, Romances & trifles &c:³ Thence to our *Society*, where were experiments of the incumbency & gravitation of the Aire on ☿ for the *Barometer*. Peper wormes were first shewed us in the Microscope &c:⁴ 21 I return'd home:

23 Our *Viccar* as before (see notes). *Pomerid*: a stranger on 26: *Matt:* 26. a logical dry discourse, not at all fit for our Congregation:

I gave my *Sonn* an *Office*,⁵ with Instructions how to govern his Youth, I pray God give him the Grace to make a right use of it &c: 25 our *Viccar* on 3: Gen: 15 concerning *Gods* first promise to, & Covenant with Man-kind: The holy Sacrament follow'd: I entertain'd our neighbours this Weeke according to ⟨Custome⟩.ª 30: our *Viccar* as above, nothing extraordinary, nor the Curate: who preached in the afternoone on 20: Cor: 5: 10:⁶ of Christ⟨s⟩ last appearance &c:

ª MS. *Custame.*

---

¹ **The** meeting is not mentioned by Birch. It was presumably an informal gathering. See notices in Hooke, 12, 13, 19 Dec.

² His last text, which may be wrong, does not seem to apply here.

³ For Wimbledon House see above, iii. 315–6, &c. Bristol (above, iii. 295) had died on 20 March of this year; Danby was now purchasing the house. The library had been partly collected by Sir Kenelm Digby; it was sold by auction with another library on 19 April 1680: sale catalogue entitled *Bibliotheca Digbeiana* (the two libraries are not distinguished).

⁴ Birch, iii. 366–8; Hooke. The worms were those found in 'pepperwater'; see also Hooke, 10, 15, 22 Nov.

⁵ Properly an authorized form of divine service; here evidently a book containing forms of prayer, &c. Thus Evelyn mentions 'some devotionarie little paper Books of prayers, offices and Meditations which I drew up for Mrs. Blag': *Memoires for my Grand-son*, 1926, p. 64. The Instructions were presumably similar in form to the *Memoires*. Evelyn's son was nearly twenty-three years old.

⁶ A slip for 2 Corinthians v. 10.

31 Blessed be *God* for his mercys & protection &c:

1678. *January* 1. Imploring the blessing of Almighty God for the yeare following: divers Neighbours din'd with me.

4 My Lord *Ossory* going now Into *Holland*, sent his Barge to bring me to his *Yacht*, now under saile; I went with him a good part of the way towards Gravesend, & after dinner returned with my *Lord*, it beginning to be stormie &c:[1] 6: our *Viccar* on his former Text: shewing how Christ bruised the Serpents head, who had brused his heele by Tempting him, & persecuting him and his &c: (*See notes*) The holy *Sacrament* follow'd: *Pomeridiano* a stranger on 1. *Tim:* 2: 5, concerning the existence of a Deity &c: 7: To *Lond:* waited on the Bish: of Lond, to give him Thankes for bestowing *St. Helens* on *Mr. Evans*[2] upon my sole recomendation: I din'd with my Lo: *Chamb:* 8 with Mrs. *Godolphin*: return'd home next day: 11 My L: of *Ossorie* pursuing his Voyage, sent againe his barge for me &c: so having conducted him as before I return'd:[3] 13 A stranger preach'd on 5. *Eph:* 14. The danger of sleeping in sinn, especialy if long &c: (*see notes*) an excellent discourse. 20 Also a stranger on 4: *Phil:* 14:[4] The reason that Christians had to be allways rejoicing, that the glory of God was its object, and how it differd from worldly joy &c: *Pomer:* Curat, as before, of the place, & universality of Christs last appearance &c: 21. To *Lond:* about severall affaires: Din'd 22 with Mrs. *Godolphin*, and next day with the *Duke* of *Norfolck*; being the first time I had

---

[1] Ossory served under the prince of Orange against the French in 1677 and 1678; he was now supposed to be going to make an agreement about a body of English soldiers which he had leave to levy. For it and his journey this day see *Hist. MSS. Comm., Ormonde MSS.*, new ser., iv. 391; see also *Cal. S.P., Dom., 1677–8*, p. 554.

[2] Identifiable as John Evans, M.A., presented to the rectory of

St. Ethelburga by Compton in December 1677; resigned 1685: Newcourt, *Repertorium*, i. 346. For two men of this name see Venn. He is evidently the former curate of Abinger: above, p. 111; below, p. 173.

[3] For Ossory's journey this day see *Cal. S.P., Dom., 1677–8*, pp. 568–9.

[4] Probably a slip for Philippians iv. 4.

seene him since the Death of his elder *Bro:*[1] who died at
Padoa in *Italy* where as being *lunatic*, he had ben kept above
30 yeares: The *Duke* had now newly declard his *Marriage* to
that infamous Woman[2] his Concubine, whom he promised me
he never would marry: I went with him to see the *Duke* of
Buckingam, thence to my Lord *Sunderlands* now *Secretary*
of State,[3] to shew him that rare piece of *Vostermans*[4] (sonn
of old *Vostermans*) which was a View or *Landscip* of my Lords
Palace &c: at Althorp in *Northampton*-shire.

24 I dind at my L: *Treasurers* with the *French Ambassador*
Monsieur *Barillon*[5] & severall other Lords &c: Thence to the
R: Society, where in absence of the President it was voted I
should take the Chaire, which I did: The experiments were
Microscopical, particularly the motions of certaine particles,
or rather *Animalculs* in *Milk*, & another in *Bloud* upon which
some excellent discourses: I Supped at one *Monsieur
Obloors*[6] a French Merchant with my Lord Obrian &c: next
day home; after Prayers, it being the feast of St. *Paule*:

27 Our *Viccar* as before (see *notes*): *Curate*: 9: *Acts* 6. By
the history of St. *Pauls* conversion, shewing that we were
not hastily to pronounce of any that follow wicked & evil
Courses, but to pray for them, since God many times recald
them &c:

30 A stranger preached on: 10: Eccles: 20. (being his Late
Majesties day of *Martyrdom*) shewing that if we may not

---

[1] Thomas Howard, b. 1627; succeeded as earl of Arundel 1652;
restored to the dukedom of Norfolk,
with rights of succession to the
heirs of his father, grandfather,
&c., 1660. He was incurably insane
from 1645 and died at Padua in
December 1677: G.E.C.

[2] Jane Bickerton; the marriage
had perhaps taken place a year
earlier: above, iii. 592.

[3] He was secretary of state from
1679 to 1681 and from 1683 to 1688.

[4] Identifiable as Johannes
Vorsterman(s), 1643?–99?, land-
scape painter and etcher: A. von
Wurzbach, *Niederländisches Künst-*

ler-Lexikon; Walpole, *Anecdotes*.
His father is said to have been
a portrait painter; but by
'old *Vostermans*' Evelyn probably
means Lukas Emile Vorsterman(s),
1595–1675, the engraver.

[5] Paul Barillon (Barrillon), *c*.
1630–91, seigneur d'Amoncourt,
marquis de Branges. He had come
here as ambassador in ordinary in
August 1677 and remained until his
expulsion in December 1688: *Grande
encyclopédie*; Leti, *Del teatro Brittanico*, ii. 293–300.

[6] The name is perhaps an error
for Houblon: see below, p. 162.

indullge an evil Thought against our King, much lesse may
we perpetrate a wicked action &c (see your *notes*).

31 To Lond:

Feb: Dr. *Cradock White-hall* on 4: *Joh:* 21: of the Love
of God, & that obedience was this love:[1] (Coram *Rege*) Dr.
Pierce on: 4: Eph: 30. what it was to grieve the holy Spirit;
not that God was obnoxious to our Passions, but that the
Consequence of our sinns if willfull or habitual, did by their
punishment inferr, as if God himselfe were realy concern'd,
& angery, whilst these are onely termes to expresse his displeasure, as we are capable to understand it; for as to any
passion like ours in him, that is true of Lucretius *Nec bene
pro meritis capitur, nec tangetur ira*:[2] he being allways serene
& sedate: he also shewed how Gods H. Spirit did even woe
& strive to retrive us &c: [& if long refused, retires from us:][a]
The holy Sacrament follow'd: B: of Lond Officiated:

5 Dind at ☆: 6. I had a private audience of the Duke[3]
in his Closet about my pretence to the Fee of *Sayes-Court*:
Being in some dispute with my Lord *Gerhard* of *Brandon*,[4]
concerning the Corporal presence of Christ in the holy Sacrament, & that I told him, the impossibility of it, for that his
body[b] as man was after his Ascension to be & remaine in
Heaven, my Lord desiring to see the Text: (we being both in
the little privat chapell at White-hall)[5] we went to the desk,
& asked *Dr. Pierce* who ⟨was⟩ then officiating to shew us the
words; he said, such a Text there was, but he could not
readily turne to it; upon which I opning the greate Bible at

---

a Interlined.   b Followed by *&* deleted.

---

[1] The text should be 1 John iv.
21.
[2] 'Nec bene promeritis capitur
neque tangitur ira': *De natura rerum*,
ii, 651 (in old editions the line is
repeated as i, 62).
[3] Presumably the duke of York.
Evelyn and Sir Richard Browne
were at present only lease-holders
of the two parts of the Sayes Court
property: see above, iii. 59 n.,

where also the term fee-farm is
explained.
[4] Above, iii. 37.
[5] The Private Oratory, between
the Privy Chamber and the Presence
Chamber; it was demolished in
1691: L.C.C., *Survey of London*, xiii.
68, 74. Pierce was in attendance as
part of his duty as a chaplain in
ordinary: above, iii. 347.

adventure put my finger exactly on 3. *Acts*: 21: which[a] did both exceedingly astonish[a] & satisfie my Lord: 8: Supping at my Lord Chamberlaines I had a long discourse with the *Conde de Castel Melior*,[1] lately the prime Minister in Portugal, who taking part with his Master *King Alphonso*, was banished by his Brother *Dom Pedro* now Regent; but had behav'd himselfe so uncorruptly in all his ministrie, that though he was acquitted & his estate restored, yet would they not suffer him to returne: he is doubtlesse a very intelligent, & worthy Gentleman.

9 I returned home. 10 *Viccar* on. 6. *Matt:* 14. 15. the danger of Wroth, & incharity &c: *Curate* on: 9. Act: 6:

13 *Ashwednesday* to *Lond*, to begin the solemnity of Lent: *B: of Lond*[2] preached W:hall on. 13 *Luke* 3: it was the best sermon I ever heard him make: *Except ye repent, ye shall all likewise perish.*

17 I received the B: Sacrament at St. *James* in the morning, afterwards at Wh:hall, preached the B: of *Excester*[3] for the Bish: of *Sarum* on 24. *Act:* 16, a little to critical about Words at first, the rest very well: I din'd with ☆.

18 My *Lord Treasurer* sent to me that I would accompanie him to Wimbledon which he had lately purchased of the Earle of Bristoll,[4] so breaking fast with him privately in his Chamber (at what time was very like to be choaked in drinking too hastily) I accompanied him, with two of his

---

a–a MS. *which did exceedingly both exceedingly astonish.*

---

[1] Luis de Vasconcellos e Sousa, conde de Castelmelhor, 1636–1720; chief minister of Dom Affonso VI from 1662 to 1667, when Affonso was deposed by his brother Dom Pedro, who ruled as regent until Affonso's death in 1683 and then as king until his own death in 1706. Castelmelhor was in exile from 1667 to 1685, in this country from September 1677 until his return to Portugal: works by F. Palha, 1883; E. Prestage, 1917; *Revista de historia*, v (1916), 193–232. Affonso VI and

Pedro II were brothers of Queen Catherine.

[2] Compton, preaching as dean of the chapel. Lenten sermon at court: list of preachers in *London Gazette*, 10 Jan.

[3] Lamplugh. Lenten sermon at court; the bishop of Salisbury (Seth Ward) is named in the list.

[4] Danby bought the house from Lady Bristol (above, p. 95). It is described as a recent purchase on 7 Aug. 1677: *Cal. S.P., Dom., 1677–8*, p. 295.

daughters,[1] my L: Conway,[2] & Sir *Bernard Gas⟨c⟩ogne* & having surveied his Gardens & alterations, returned late at night:

20 Dr. Sprat preached on 3. *Coloss:* 2: excellently, *Set your Affections on things above* &c.[3] I supped at the Countesse of *Ossories:* 21 Din'd at La: *Sylvius,* sup'd at L: *Chamberlain.*

22 Dr. *Pierce* on 2. *Thessal:* 3. 6. Against our late Schismatics in a very rational discours but a little over sharp, & not at all proper for the Auditory at White-hall:[3]

I had a private *Audience* of his *Majestie* in his *Bed-chamber* &c. went home:

23 I was at the Funerall of my kind neighbour *Cap: Tinker,*[4] our *Viccar* preaching on 1. *Phil:* 23 the preference of being with Christ &c:

24 Mr. *Saunders*[5] on. 2. *Phil.* 12. shewing how we were to work out our salvation with feare &c: Feare of God, for his Majestie & power, 2. feare of sinn, because of its destructive nature, 3 feare of our selves, least we fall into it: That those who stood never so fast were to feare falling; since it was spoken to them onely; since those who were already downe, could fall no farther: *Pomerid.* on 11. Eccl: 9. in a most pathetical discourse the dreadfull accompt to be given at the last day, after all our enjoyments here, upon that Ironical Text. 26 To Lond: 27: Dr. *Megot Coram Rege* on 2. *Tim:* 3. 4.[3] shewing how dangerous, & degenerous[6] *Christians* were now become, by being Lovers of Pleasures, a most admirable Converting discourse:

March 1 Dr. *Tillotson* on 5. *Gal.* 22. of the fruite of the Spirit: excellently:[3] 2: I went to P: greene to visite my Lady *Mordaunt* now indisposed:[a] returned in the Evening: 3: Dr.

---

[a] Colon supplied.

---

[1] Danby had apparently at least five daughters now living.

[2] Edward Conway, *c.* 1623–83; third Viscount Conway of Conway Castle 1655; created earl of Conway 1679; secretary of state 1681–3: G.E.C.

[3] Lenten sermon at court.

[4] Captain John Tinker, master-attendant at Portsmouth dockyard, *c.* 1666–9; at Deptford dockyard 1669–78: *Cal. S.P., Dom., 1665–6,* p. 257; *1668–9*; &c.; (*Catalogue of Pepysian MSS.*), iv. 590.

[5] Not identifiable. Further notices below; cf. Mr. Sanders, above, p. 35.

[6] Degenerate: *O.E.D.*

Littleton on 1. Cor: 11. 28, Examine your selves &c: The Communion follow'd. *Coram Rege* Bish of *Oxford*[1] on: 2: *Rom:* 4 how the goodnesse of God Leads to Repentance: 6: Dr. *Craddock*: on 26 *Matt:* 41. Watch & pray &c: applying it to the Lenten Abstinence.[2] 8 Dr. *Standish*[3] 11 *Joh:* 35 *Jesus Wept* &c. 10: *Bish:* of *Rochester*[4] for the B: of *Chichester* on 11 *Luke* 24. 25. 26. shewing the deplorable estate of a man Repenting, & returning to the same fault: The holy Sacrament followed. 11: I went home.

17 our *Viccar* on 6. *Matt:* 14, concerning Charity, & forgivenesse of Enemies: *Pomeridiano* a stranger on 24 Josh: The brave resolution of that religious Captaine for himselfe & household:[5] 19, I went to Lond: Dine'd at Mr. *Gores*,[6] return'd:

22 I went to *Graves-end* about a Pay & Accompt, for the quarte⟨r⟩s of men, during the late Warr, where to my extraordinary affliction, I found my Agent[7] there had missbehaved himselfe; I returned home next day: 24. our Viccar on his former: The holy Sacrament follow'd; Now was our Comm: Table placed Altar wise,[8] The Church Steeple, Clock & other reparations finish'd: *Curate* on. 21. *Mat.* ⟨8. 9.⟩[a] Rhetoricaly describing our B. Saviours Triumphal entrie into *Jerusalem*, previous to his passion. 25 To Lond: 26 dind with Mrs. *Godolphin.* 27: Dr. *Alestree* on 2. *Cor.* 2. 6. That there is a period, & day set for the conversion of sinners, beyond which,

---

[a] MS. *89.*

---

[1] Fell. Lenten sermon at court.

[2] Lenten sermon at court.

[3] Above, p. 75. Presumably a lenten sermon at court; the preacher in the list is North.

[4] Evidently a lenten sermon at court; but the preacher in the list is the bishop of Chester (Pearson), not Chichester (Brideoake).

[5] Joshua xxiv. 15.

[6] Perhaps a relation of the wife of Evelyn's nephew George Evelyn: below, 4 Oct. 1699.

[7] Robert Birstall or Burstall, searcher at Gravesend: P.R.O., Declared Accounts, Navy, 1821/ 488; *Cal. Treasury Books, 1676–9*, p. 839, &c.; *1679–80*, pp. 263–4.

[8] Evelyn states that this was ordered already in 1662: above, iii. 317; no charges relating to it appear in the accounts of expenditure as printed: Drake's Hasted, p. 34. The repairs of the clock, &c., appear in them; Evelyn is one of the signatories of the accounts.

God will not accept them &c:[1] 29 I received the B: Sacrament
at *St. Martines* in the Morning: *Coram Rege* Dr. *South* (for
the Lord *Almoner* the B: of Rochester)[a] on   A Wounded
spirit who can beare? an incomparable discourse:[2] I supped
with Mrs. *Godolphin,* & next day home:

31 *Easter-day* our *Viccar* on 22. *Matt.* 29. 30: shewing the
mistake of the *Sadduces* of certaine places of Scripture &c:
The holy Communion follow'd: *Pomerid*: the *Curate* on 26:
Act: 8: the possibility of the Resurrection: &c:

Aprill 4 Came to dine with me Sir *Will: Godolphin,*[3] his
Bro: *Sidny,* his *Lady* (my deare friend,) and their Sisters:[4]
7: Mr. *Bohune* on 33. Isa: 14. shewing the deplorable estate
of ungodly men: &c: 10 To *Lond:* Dr. *Pettus*[5] at W:hall on
14. *Rom:* 10: I received in the morning at St. *Jamess*:

16 I went to shew Dom: *Emanuel de Lyra*[6] (Portugal
Ambassador) & the *Count de Castel Mellor*[7] the Repository
of the R: Society, & Coledge of *Physitians*:[8] 18 I went to see

---

[a] Closing bracket supplied.

---

[1] Lenten sermon at court. The
text should perhaps be 2 Corinthians vi. 2. A sermon on that text,
probably the present one, is printed
in Allestree's *Forty Sermons,* 1684,
[ii]. 201–14.

[2] Lenten sermon at court; the
preacher in the list is the dean of
Westminster, it being his duty *ex
officio* to preach the sermon on this
day; the present dean was Dolben,
who was also bishop of Rochester
and lord almoner; in the latter
capacity it was his duty to preach
the sermon on Easter Day, and as
almoner he is named in the list for
it. South's text is Proverbs xviii.
14.

[3] William Godolphin, *c.* 1640–
1710; created a baronet 1661:
G.E.C., *Baronetage,* iii. 188; Marsh,
The Godolphins, pp. 8–9.

[4] There were at least four sisters
now living besides Jael, wife of

Edward Boscawen (below, p. 147):
Marsh, pp. 9–13.

[5] Thomas Pittis, 1636–87; D.D.
1670; chaplain in ordinary *c.* 1677–
87: *D.N.B.* The date for this entry
should presumably be 14 April.

[6] Don Manuel Francisco de Lira y
Castillo, Spanish diplomatist, at this
time envoy extraordinary to the
United Provinces; he had perhaps
come here on a mission in 1674:
Enciclopedia universal ilustrada. If
his being named here is correct, his
visit to England was presumably
private. The Portuguese ambassador
here was Dom Francisco de Mello:
above, iii. 481, &c.

[7] Above, p. 130.

[8] Above, iii. 337. For the present
building, designed by Robert Hooke,
see Walpole Soc., xxv (1937), 89–
90, and plates; it was now practically completed.

New *Bedlam* Hospital,[1] magnificently built, & most sweetely placed in *Morefields*, since the dreadfull fire of *Lond:* dind with ✡: 20: Din'd at Lo: *Treasurers.* 21 Dr. *Stillingfleete*[2] (*Deane of St. Paules*) on 6. *Gal:* 14. admirably: To the *King*: Dr. *Tillotson* (Deane of *Canterbery*) on 16 *Luke* ult, That there needes neither Miracle, nor Tradition to Confirme the faith, having the written word of God: &c:[3] I received the holy Sacrament at St. *Martines* after the Court sermons were don: 28: Synax. at St. *James's*: Then at *W:hall* (*Coram Rege*) The Deane of St. *Paules* on 16 *Joh:* 33. The Comfortablenesse of a Christians life under whatever suffering he lay: I never heard him do better: 30 I dind at my Lord *Berkeleys*:

May 1 Dind at *Mrs. Godolphins*: 3 went home: 5 ⟨*Rogation*⟩[a] Sunday our *Viccar* on 22. Matt: 29. 30 of the nature of *Angels* & Saints, how they shall be like *Angels* (see your *notes*) the bl: Sacrament follow'd: Blessed be God: *Pomer*: Curate on. 12. *Heb:* 1. shewing how like a race the christian Profession &c: never to be at rest, but still proceeding, & therefore to cast away all impediments, pursuing with patience for the Crowne &c: 8 To *Lond:* 9. *Deane of Bangor*[4] at St. *Martines* on 24 *Luke.* 50. 51 Ascension: I received the B: Comm: Dind with ✡: 12 a stranger at *Court* on 33 *Ezek:* 15. 16. concerning the duty of Restitution, whither of Goods or fame: *Coram rege* another stranger on 16. *Luke.* 31. Dind with Mrs. *Godolphin*:

13 I went home:

16 Being the Wedding *Anniversarie* of my excellent friend Mrs. *Godolphin*,[5] she, with my Lady *Sylvius* & her sister

---

[a] MS. *Rogatian.*

[1] For the old hospital see above, iii. 191; it was not affected by the Fire. The present building, which was designed by Hooke, was built in 1675–6; it accommodated about 120 patients. The hospital was moved to St. George's Fields in 1815: Walpole Soc., as above, pp. 91–3 and plate; *Notes and Queries*, clxxvii (1939), 362.

[2] He had been installed dean of St. Paul's on 19 January of this year.
[3] Presumably the sermon printed in Tillotson, *Works*, 1752, ii. 485–[91].
[4] Lloyd the apocalyptic, at this time vicar of St. Martin's.
[5] Married in 1675: above, p. 63.

Grahame came to visite, & dine with me; returning in the
ªEvening, & was the last time, that blessed Creature ever
came to my house, now being also greate with Child, & seldome stirring abroad:

19 Our *Viccar* on. 1. *Thess:* 5. 19. *Whitsonday*: shewing
what the spirit was, what praying with it, & that it might
be as well in set formes: The abuse of it by those who fancie
the exuberance of Words & Expressions to denote it, spring-
ing from heate of phancy, when it indeede consists in Understanding what we pray, & in the effects of it after prayer &c:
The holy *Sacrament* followd: *Pomer*: *Curate* on 16: *John.*
13 describing the coming of the H: *Ghost* historicaly onely:
23. To *Lond:* 26: At St. *Jam: Synax*, being *Trinity Sonday*:
Coram Rege at *W:hall*ᵇ Dr. *Hayward*¹ on 1. 13 *Cor:* 12:
blaming the too much temerity in some in defining the
Mysterie of the sacred *Trinity*, & that have not that tremen-
dous reverence we ought to thatᶜ glorious Deity &c: I dind
with ⛤: 27: At L. *Chamb:* 28 At Mrs. *Godolphins* & went
home. 29: *Anniversary* of his Majesties Birth &c. our *Viccar*
on 8: *Pro:* 15 shewing by very learned & excellent readings,
The reasons of the preference of *Monarchical* above all other
formes of Government: & that from *Adam* (to whom God had
given the *Empire* of all things & Persons) that it seemed to be
not onely of divine, but most natural Institution: how it was
at first, in the Eldest of each Family, where the first borne
was King & Priest, & therefore had a double portion above
his breathren to sustaine the Charge of sacrifices & the pub:
worship: The weaknesse of all other Constitutions; concluding in an Exhortation to be obedient, & thankfull &c:

June 2: Our *Viccar* on 1. *Thess:* 5. 19. what the Spirit was,
& how many-ways quenched, by water, & cold entertaine-

ª Hand in margin here.   ᵇ Followed by *Dr. Hall son to the late pious
Bish: of Norwich* deleted (the word *pious* is doubtful).   ᶜ Followed by
sacred deleted.

---

¹ Roger Hayward, *c.* 1639–80;   Venn. For Bishop Hall in the de-
D.D. 1674; chaplain in ordinary *c.*   leted passage see above, iii. 222;
1679–80 (supernumerary *c.* 1673):   none of his sons were now living.

ments; by wind, (i) our impetuous passions & temptation; by substracting oyle & nourishment, (i) not cherishing his Graces &c: The Monethly *Communion* followd: *Pomer*: *Curate* on 19 *Matt:* 21. That we are many times, too confident of our state &c. 6 Came my Lady Hungerford,¹ & her Mother in Law (my wifes *Aunt*) to visite us: 9 our *Viccar* as above: *Pomer*: The exceeding raine hindred my going to church.

11 To *Lond.* 16 *Synax* St. *Jamess Cor: rege* a Chaplaine on 16 *Num:* 24 against the sinn of Murmuring: I din'd at my Bro: & returned home:

19 Lond: Dr. *Patrick* Co: Garden on. 1. *Tim:* 1. 17, The reverence, love & honour we owe to God, & his Ministers:² I dind with Mrs. *Godolphin.* 22. returned home:

23 A stranger on 4. Heb: 7: To take heede we deferr not Repentance: Pomer: *Curat*, on 5. *Hosea*: 15 &c. 26: To Lond: 27: Dind with my L: *Ossory*, at the Vico: *Brounkar*:

28 I went to *Windsor* with my *Lord Chamberlain* (the Castle now new repairing with exceeding Cost &c) to see the rare Worke of *Virrio*, & incomparable Carving of *Gibbons*:³ 29 returned with my Lord &c: by *Hownslow* heath where we saw the new raised *Army* encamp'd, designed against France, in pretence at least, but gave umbrage to the Parliament: his Majestie & a world of Company in the field, & the whole Army in Batallia, a very glorious sight:⁴ now were brought

---

¹ Frances, d. 1715, half-sister of Francis Seymour and Charles Seymour (*D.N.B.*), dukes of Somerset; wife of George Hungerford, d. 1714, knight (Foster, *Alumni Oxon.*): Hoare, *Hungerfordiana*, pp. 23, 54–7; her mother-in-law is Susanna Prettyman, Mrs. Edward Hungerford of Cadenham.

² I cannot trace a regular Wednesday service here at this date, but Patrick was an advocate of daily public worship, and more especially of prayer and fasting on Wednesdays and Fridays: *Works*, 1858, iv. 591–8, 744–52; viii. 562–5.

³ Between 1675 and 1677 the building later known as the Star

building had been completed; it was now being decorated: Hope, *Windsor Castle*, i. 324. For the work here of Verrio and Gibbons at this time see ibid., pp. 316–17.

⁴ The Country party distrusted Charles so greatly as to attach absurd conditions to the votes of supply for the war against France, and some of its leaders were receiving bribes from Louis XIV to hold them to this policy; on the other hand, Charles does not appear to have wanted to participate in the war. For the review this day see *Hist. MSS. Comm., Ormonde MSS.*, new ser., iv. 158.

into service a new sort of souldier called *Granadiers*, who were dextrous to fling hand granados, every one having a pouch full, & had furr'd Capps with coped crownes like Janizaries, which made them looke very fierce, & some had long hoods hanging down behind[a] as we picture fooles: their clothing being likewise py bald yellow & red:[1] so we returned to Lond:

30 A stranger at W:hall: on: 10: *Luke:* 30 of Gods Universal Providence, for the Safty of his Saints especialy:[b2] Thence to St. *Martins* where Dr. *Lloyd* preached on 3. *Rom:* 20. shewing by the imperfection of Legal Justification, the onely effectual to be *Christs*.

July 1 I return'd home to *Says-Court*. 7: Our *Viccar* on 1. *Thess:* 5. 19: That the sinn against the *H. Ghost* was the Contempt & Blasphemy of the malicious *Jewes* &c, against the Evidence of their owne senses: *See notes*: the holy *Comm:* followd:

8 Came to dine with me my Lord *Longford*[3] Tressurer of *Ireland*, & nephew to that learned gent, my *L: Angier*, with whom I was long since acquainted &c: also the Lady *Stidolph*[4] & other Company:

10[c] Came to take his leave of me the *Earle* of *Ossory*, going into *Holland* to Command the English forces &c:[5]

---

[a] Followed by *like* deleted.   [b] Followed by *Po-* deleted.   [c] Date altered from *9*; reading doubtful.

---

[1] On 28 March of this year orders were issued for the raising of eight companies of grenadiers, to be attached one to each of the eight senior regiments already raised or now raising. They wore caps instead of the usual broad-brimmed hats: Sir F. W. Hamilton, (*Grenadier Guards*), 1874, i. 209; Sir John Fortescue, *Hist. of the British Army*, 1910–30, i. 324–5. Yellow and red together in costume was regarded in France as 'ridiculous': Sir J. Reresby, *Memoirs*, 1936, Oct. 1659. They were the Spanish colours.

[2] The text may be wrong.

[3] Francis Aungier, d. 1700; succeeded his uncle (above, iii. 142) as third Baron Aungier of Longford (Ireland) 1655; created Viscount Longford (Ireland) 1675; earl of Longford (Ireland) 1677; vice-treasurer of Ireland 1670–3: G.E.C.; *Notes and Queries*, cxlvi (1924), 205–8.

[4] Elizabeth, c. 1626–1703, sister of Sir John Stonhouse (below, p. 189); married first Sir Richard Stiddolph (Stydolph), bart., d. 1677, son of Sir Francis Stydolph of Mickleham (above, iii. 157); secondly, in 1685, William Byron, Lord Byron: G.E.C., *Baronetage*, iii. 145.

[5] He arrived at Middelburg a few days before 22 July, o.s.: *Cal. S.P., Dom., 1678*, p. 307.

17 I went to *Lond:* 18 To visite L: *Mordaunt,* returned to *Lond:*

20 I went to the *Tower* to try a Mettal at the Say-Masters,[1] which onely proved *Sulphur*: then saw *Monsieur Rotiere*[2] that incomparable Graver belonging to the Mint, who emulates even the Antients in both mettal & stone; he was now moulding of an Horse for the *Kings statue* to be cast in silver of a Yard high: I dined with Mr. *Slingsby* Master of the Mint. Visite⟨d⟩ L: *Brouncker*:

21 *Synax:* at *St. James's. Coram Rege* Dr. *Megot* on 16 Luke: 30. 31. 32.[3] on the rich *Epulo,* That since we had the holy *Scriptures,* it were unreasonable to expect Miracles; since when they were so frequent, they did not the more readily believe or reforme; That it were now to Tempt *God,* who owed us no such convictions as to alter the course of nature for our phancies, after what he had already don & suffered:

23[a] Return'd, having ben[b] to see Mr. *Elias Ashmoles*[4] Library & Curiosities at *Lambeth,* he has divers *MSS,* but most of them *Astrological,* to which study he is addicted, though I believe not learned; but very Industrious, as his history of the Order of the Gartir shews, he shewed me a Toade included in Amber: The prospect from a Turret is

---

[a] Reading doubtful; *25* is also possible.　　[b] Substituted for *gon.*

---

[1] The assay-master, one of the officers of the Mint; the office was held from 1668 until his death in 1692 by John Brattle, who was knighted in 1682: *Cal. S.P., Dom., 1668-9,* p. 124; *Cal. Treasury Books, 1689-92,* p. 1917; notices in Chamberlayne.

[2] Presumably John Roettiers (Rotier), 1631-1703, the medallist: *D.N.B.*; L. Forrer, *Biog. dict. of Medallists,* 1904-16. He worked at the Mint from 1662 to 1697; other members of his family were also employed there. Nothing is known of the present statuette. Evelyn mentions him and his family in *Numismata,* pp. 22, 27-8, 239.

[3] The citation should be verses 30, 31; there is no verse 32.

[4] Above, iii. 159, 199. He occupied a house in South Lambeth next door to that formerly occupied by Tradescant (see next note): Gunther, *Early Science in Oxford,* iii. 289-91. Ashmole's library came to Oxford about 1692 and was transferred to the Bodleian Library in 1858-60; the manuscripts, about 850 in number, are largely heraldic, genealogical, and astrological: Wood, *Life and times,* iv. 83; Macray, *Annals of the Bodleian,* pp. 364-5. Ashmole's work here mentioned is *The Institution, Laws & Ceremonies of the most Noble Order of the Garter,* 1672, fol.

very fine, it being so neere Lond: & yet not discovering any house about the Country. The famous *John Tradescant*, bequeath'd his Repositary to this Gent: who has given them to the University of Oxford, & erected a[a] Lecture on them &c: over the Laboratorie, in imitation of the *R: Society*:[1] My deare friend *Mrs. Godolphin*[2] & my Wife were with us: I think it was the last of her going abroad:

25 I went to *Lond:* to the wedding of my Bro: in Law Glandvills Niepce, married to *Cap: Fowler*[3] &c: Thence to R: *Society*: supp'd[b] with Mrs. *Godolphin* whose husband was now made Master of the Robes to the *King*.[4]

There was now sent me 70 pounds from some ⟨one⟩ whom I knew not to be by me distributed among poore people at my discretion; I came afterwards to find it was from that heavenly creature my deare friend: who had frequently given me large Summs to bestow on Charities &c:[5]

28 A *stranger* on 6: *Rom:* 11 Shewing the necessitie of dying to sinn, by the Type of Baptisme: See your *notes*: *Pomerid*: 32 Psal. 6.[6] the benefit of Confession, & our obligation to it: Se your notes:

---

[a] Followed by *Pr-* deleted.   [b] Followed by *at* ✭ ; *at* left standing, ✭ deleted.

---

[1] For Tradescant and his collections see above, iii. 198–9. Ashmole had already offered the latter to Oxford; the building to house them, now the Old Ashmolean, was erected in 1679–82; they were installed in it in 1683; for it see Chamberlayne, *Angliæ Notitia*, pt. ii, edns. 1684, &c. The Royal Society had proposed erecting a similar building in 1667–8: above, iii. 505. The use of the word lecture in the present sense, a lecture-room, is not recorded in *O.E.D.*

[2] Evelyn describes this visit rather differently and with some additional matter in his *Life of Mrs. Godolphin*, pp. 72–3 (the passage does not occur in Wilberforce's text of the *Life*).

[3] The bride was Anne Cowse of Deptford, presumably a daughter of James Cows of All Hallows, Barking, who in 1654 married Jane Glanville in the presence of William Glanville, Evelyn's brother-in-law; the bridegroom was Thomas Fowler of Greenwich, *c.* 1648–1685/8, traceable as a naval officer from 1670 onwards: Foster, *London marriage licences*; Glanville-Richards, *Records of . . . Glanville*, p. 154; (*Catalogue of Pepysian MSS.*), i. 352.

[4] Godolphin bought the office about 21 July: *Hist. MSS. Comm., Rutland MSS.*, ii. 52.

[5] Evelyn mentions this gift again in *Life of Mrs. Godolphin*, p. 71. For her charity in general see pp. 105–9.

[6] Cited from the Prayer Book.

August 2 To *Lond:* 4: Dr. *Offley*[1] at *W:hall*, on 7: *Joh:* 37, an honest pious, discourse: *Coram Rege*, a young Chaplain on 22. *Psal:* 6.[2] Admonishing unquiet spirits to peace & unity in Church matters &c. I din'd with Mrs. *Godolphin* & La: *Mordaunt*:[3]

6 My Wife & I dind againe with the Master of the *Robes*[4] & my deare Friend, and returned home. 11 A young man preached on 98 *Psal:* 1. Shewing for how many favours & graces we were obliged to serve & blesse God: Pomerid: the Minister of *Roderith*[5] on 6. *Rom:* 23: The gaine we obtaine by Christ over the Condemnation, & deadlinesse of sinn: &c:

16 I went to my La: *Mordaunts*, who put 100 pounds into my hands, to dispose ⟨of⟩[a] for pious uses, reliefe of Prisoners &c: poore &c: & many a summ had she sent me on the same occasion; for a blessed Creature she was, one that feared & loved God exemplarily:[b][6] ⟨18⟩[c] *Synax* St. Jamess: home: &c a stranger: 3 *Jude*:

23 Upon Sir *Rob: Readings*[7] importunity, I went to Visite the *Duke of Norfolck* at his new Palace by *Way bridge*;[8] where he has laied out in building neere 10000 pounds, on a Copyhold, & in a miserable barren sandy place by the streete side, never in my daies had I seene such expense to so small purpose: The roomes are Wainscoted, & some of them richly

---

[a] MS. *af.*　　[b] Followed by *20 I returned home* deleted.　　[c] MS. *19.*

---

[1] Dr. Gabriel Offley. He was a chaplain in ordinary.

[2] Probably a slip for Psalms cxxii. 6.

[3] This notice is probably wrong: in the *Life* of Mrs. Godolphin it is Mrs. Evelyn who dines with her and Lady Mordaunt on this day: p. 73.

[4] Godolphin: see above.

[5] Rotherhithe. The rector from 1675 to 1681 was George Stoodley, B.A.: Manning and Bray, i. 237. For a man of this name, but with no degree, see Foster.

[6] For her piety see her *Private Diarie*; it is a collection of prayers, meditations, &c.

[7] Robert Reading, d. 1689; F.R.S. 1671; created a baronet (Ireland) 1675: G.E.C., *Baronetage*, iv. 208. He was concerned with Evelyn in negotiating the transfer of the Arundel library to the Royal Society: Birch, iii. 430-1; Hooke, 22 Aug.; below, p. 144 n.

[8] Norfolk had acquired a house near the confluence of the Wey and the Thames through his second wife Jane Bickerton; after his death it was sold to Catherine Sedley (above, p. 13); it was pulled down *c*. 1830: Manning and Bray, ii. 788-9, with short description; Brayley, *Surrey*, ii. 398-9; *V.C.H., Surrey*, iii. 476.

parquetted with *Cedar, Yew,* Cypresse &c. There are some good Pictures, especialy, that ⟨incomparable⟩[a] painting of *Holbens* where The Duke of Norfolck, Charles Brandon, & Hen: the 8: are dauncing with the three Ladys, such amorous countenances, & spritefull motion did I never see expressed:[1] 'Tis a thousand pitties (as I told my Lord of Arundel his sonn) that Jewell should be given away to the present broode, & not be fixed to the incontaminate issue:[2]

24 I went to see my L: ⟨St. *Albans's*⟩[b] house at *Byfleete,*[3] an old large building; and thence to the *Paper-mills,*[4] where I found them making a Course white paper: First they cull the raggs (which are linnen for White paper, Wollen for browne) then they stamp them in troughs to a papp, with pestles or hammers like the powder mills: Then put it in a Vessel of Water, in which they dip a frame closely wyred, with wyer as small as an haire, & as cloose as a Weavers reede: upon this take up the papp, the superfluous water draining from it thro the wyres: This they dextrously turning shake out like a thin *pan-cake* on a smoth board, betweene two pieces of flannell; Then presse it, betweene a greate presse, the ⟨flannel⟩[c] sucking out the moisture, then taking it out ply & dry it on strings, as they dry linnen in the Laundry, then dip it in allume water, lastly polish, & make it up in

---

a MS. *in comparable.* b MS. *St. Albons's.* c MS. *flanner.*

---

[1] The picture, which is not by Holbein and does not represent the persons named in the text, is said to have been bought in 1701 from a member of the duke of Norfolk's family by an ancestor of its present owner, Col. Sotheby of Ecton Hall, Northants: *Exhibition of the royal house of Tudor,* New Gallery, 1890, no. 145 (pp. 49–50); Vertue, *Note books* (Walpole Soc.), v. 10–11, where the identifications of the men are accepted, the three women identified, and the occasion for the picture suggested.

[2] Norfolk's eldest son Henry was styled earl of Arundel from his father's succession to the dukedom

in 1677 until his own in 1684. The reference is to the present duke's children by his second duchess, Jane Bickerton (above, iii. 592; iv. 128); there were seven of them: Collins, *Peerage,* ed. Brydges, i. 135.

[3] The Manor House; part of it still exists, much altered. Both it and the palace of Oatlands in Weybridge had belonged to Henrietta Maria and had been leased to St. Albans: Manning and Bray, iii. 183–4; *V.C.H., Surrey,* iii. 401–2, 478.

[4] A paper-mill was working here c. 1691: *Hist. MSS. Comm., House of Lords MSS., 1690–1,* pp. 435–7.

quires: &c: note that the⟨y⟩ put some gumm in the water, in which they macerate the raggs into a pap: note[a] that the marks we find in the sheetes is formed in the wyres.[a]

25 The *Minister* preached on 19. *Gen:* 26, shewing by the example of *Lots* Wife, the danger of the Love of Pleasure, & disobedience to the least of Gods commands even against small sinns, as we may account them: After Evening prayer[b] Visited *Mr. Sheldon*[1] (Nephew to the late *Archbish:* of *Cant:* where I found the Bish: of *Rochester*)[2] and his pretty melancholy Garden, I tooke notice of the largest *Arbor Thuyæ*[3] I had ever seene: The place is finely water'd, & there are many curiosities of India which we were shew'd in the house: There was at *Way-bridge* the Dutchesse of *Norfolck*, My Lord *Thomas* Howard[4] (a worthy & virtuous gent, with whom my sonn, was sometime bred up in Arundel house) who was newly come from *Rome* where he had ben some time; also one of the Dukes Daughters by his first Lady:[5] My Lord leading me about the house, made no scruple of shewing me all the *Latebræ* & hiding places for the popish Priests, & where they said Masse, for he was no bigoted *Papist*: He told me he never trusted them with any seacret; & used *Protestants* onely in all buisinesses of importance: I went with my *L. Duke* this evening to *Windsore*, where was a magnificent Court, it being the first time of his Majesties removing thither, since it was repaired:[6] 26: I din'd with Mr. *Secretary Coventrie*,[7] & then returned with the Duke of *Norfolck*. 27: I tooke leave of him, & dined at Mr. *Hen: Brounchers*[c][8] at the Abby of

---

[a-a] Inserted after next notice was written. [b] Followed by *having* deleted. [c] Altered from *Brounchars*.

[1] Daniel Sheldon of Ham Court, a barrister: Le Neve, *Pedigrees*, p. 209.

[2] He was Sheldon's brother-in-law: below, p. 257.

[3] The thuya was rare in England at this time: *Sylva*, 1679, p. 129.

[4] Norfolk's second son by his first wife, so styled since Norfolk's succession to the dukedom: above, iii. 329, &c. He is perhaps the 'Thomas Horward' who signed the Padua visitors' album on 4 July 1677: H. F. Brown, no. 710.

[5] There were two surviving daughters by the first marriage: Collins, *Peerage*, ed. Brydges, i. 135.

[6] Charles II was at Windsor from 14 August to about 25 September: *Hist. MSS. Comm., Ormonde MSS.*, new ser., iv. 181, 200.

[7] Above, p. 91.

[8] Above, iii. 578.

Sheene[1] formerly a *Monastery* of *Carthusians*, there yet remaining one of their solitary Cells with a Crosse: within this ample inclosure are severall pretty Villas, and fine Gardens of the most excellent fruites, Especialy Sir William *Temples*,[2] lately Ambassador into Holland, & the *Lord LIles*[a] sonn to the Earle of Licester,[3] who has divers rare Pictures, above ⟨all⟩ that of Sir *Brian Tukes* of *Holbein*:[4] After dinner I walked to *Ham*, to see the House & Garden of the *Duke* of *Laderdaile*,[5] which is indeede inferiour to few of the best

---

[a] Altered from L*s*-.

[1] Sheen is the old name for Richmond. The Carthusian priory at West Sheen was founded by Henry V in 1414 and is referred to in Shakespeare's *Henry V*; it was suppressed in 1539, refounded in 1557, and finally suppressed in 1559. The history of the site at this time is not clear. The ownership had reverted to the crown in 1660. A lease of part or the whole of it was granted in that year to Philip Sidney, Lord Lisle (above, iii. 164), who parted with it in 1662, but who appears to have lived here some time longer. In 1675 a lease was granted to trustees for Brouncker and Sir William Temple (see next note); Brouncker appears to have occupied Lisle's house. The site came into royal possession in the eighteenth century. The last remains of the priory were removed in 1769: Lysons, *Environs*, i. 451; Manning and Bray, i. 422; *V.C.H., Surrey*, ii. 89–94; iii. 537–8; see also below.

[2] William Temple, 1628–99; created a baronet 1666; the diplomatist and author: *D.N.B.*; H. E. Woodbridge, *Sir William Temple*, 1940. He was ambassador at The Hague from 1668 to 1670, from 1674 to 1676, and again from July of this year until March 1679. He bought a house at Sheen in 1665 and lived there (perhaps in more than one house), when his duties allowed it, until 1686: Manning and

Bray, i. 422. For a description of his garden in 1691, after he had left it, see *Archaeologia*, xii (1796), 184–5.

[3] Robert Sidney, 1649–1702; styled Lord Lisle from 1677; called to the house of lords as Baron Sydney of Penshurst 1689; fourth earl of Leicester 1698: G.E.C. For his father see above, iii. 164; the reference here is perhaps to him rather than to the present Lord Lisle: see note above.

[4] There appear to be at least five versions extant of Holbein's portrait of Sir Brian Tuke (d. 1545; secretary to Henry VIII: *D.N.B.*). The present picture is not the Munich version, but is not further identifiable: Chamberlain, *Hans Holbein the younger*, i. 331–3.

[5] Ham House. The manors of Petersham and Ham had been granted to William Murray, afterwards earl of Dysart; they were sequestered and in 1672 were granted to Lauderdale in right of his wife, daughter of William Murray and countess of Dysart in her own right. The house was built *c.* 1610; was enlarged by the duchess; and again in the eighteenth century. It still belongs to the earl of Dysart, a descendant of the duchess by her first husband: *V.C.H., Surrey*, iii. 525–9, 530–1; Mrs. C. Roundell, *Ham House*, 1904.

Villas in Italy itselfe, The House furnishd like a greate
Princes; The Parterrs, flo: Gardens, Orangeries, Groves,
Avenues, Courts, Statues, Perspectives, fountaines, Aviaries,
and all this at the banks of the sweetest rivcr in the World,
must needes be surprizing &c: Thence I went ⟨to⟩ my worthy
friends Sir *Hen: Capels*[1] (bro: to the Earle of *Essex*) it is an
old timber house, but his Garden has certainely the Choicest
fruite of any plantation in England, as he is the most industrious, & understanding in it: from hence To Lond: & [28][a]
next day to Says-Court; after a most pleasant & divertisant
Excursion, the weather bright & temperate:

29 I was cald againe to *London* to waite againe on the
Duke of Norfolck who having at my request onely, bestow'd
[b]the *Aru⟨n⟩delian Library* on the *Royal Society*, sent to me to
take charge of the Bookes & remove them;[2] onely that I
would suffer the *Heraulds* Chiefe Officer Sir W: *Dugdale*[3] to
have such of them as concernd Herauldry & Martials Office
As bokes of Armorie & Geneologies; the *Duke* being Earle
Marishal of England: I procured for our Society besides
Printed bookes, neere 700 MSS:[4] some in Greeke of greate
concernement; The Printed books being of the oldest Impressions, are not the lesse valuable; I esteeme them almost

---

a Marginal note.   b Hand in margin here.

---

[1] Above, iii. 482. He had acquired
his house here through his wife.
It was occupied by members of the
royal family from *c.* 1730, George
III living here frequently as a youth
and in later life, and was pulled
down in 1802. It occupied a site
near the existing Kew Palace,
originally a secondary building:
V.C.H., Surrey, iii. 482-4; description of the garden in 1691 in
Archaeologia, xii (1796), 185. Evelyn
presumably followed the old road,
Love Lane, from West Sheen to
Kew: for it see W. J. Bean, *Royal
Botanic Gardens, Kew*, 1908, p. 7.

[2] See above, iii. 472. Sir Robert
Reading (above, p. 140) had
announced to the Society on 22

August the duke's permission for
the collection to be removed to
Gresham College: Hooke, 22 Aug.;
Birch, iii. 430. The original gift
had been made in 1667.

[3] Above, iii. 171, &c. Norfolk's
gift consisted of manuscripts numbered 1-54 and includes chronicles
and other historical manuscripts
as well as specifically heraldic
manuscripts, &c.; Dugdale tried
to obtain twenty-three other miscellaneous historical manuscripts:
[W. H. Black], *Catalogue of the
Arundel manuscripts in the library
of the College of Arms*, 1829.

[4] There were probably 562
volumes of manuscripts and about
4,000 printed books: above, iii. 472.

equal with MSS: Most of the Fathers printed at *Basil* &c: before the *Jesuites*, abused them with their Expurgatorie *Indexes*:[1] There is a noble MSS: of *Vitruvius*:[2] Many of these Bookes had ben presented by Popes, Cardinals & greate Persons to the Earles of Arundell & Dukes of Norfolck;[3] & the late magnificent Tho: E: of *Arundel* bought a noble Library in Germanie,[4] which is in this Collection; nor should I for the honour I beare the family, have perswaded the Duke to part with these, had I not seene how negligent he was of them, in suffering the Priests, & every body to carry away & dispose of what they pleased: so as aboundance of rare things are gon, & irrecoverable:

Having taken Order here, I went to the *R: Society*,[5] to give them an *account* of what I had procured, that they might call a Council, & appoint a day to waite on the *Duke* to thank him for this munificent gift:

There were this afternoone also severall Experiments shewn, and divers learned & curious discourses: as first, Concerning a Woman that in *Lions* had ben 24 yeares with Child, which had ben dead 7 yeares before the Mother, who lived to 60: Also that this Child was found out of the Womb: Also of another Conceiv'd out of the Womb, lying in the hollow of the body, during which the Mother conceiv'd &

---

[1] An 'Index expurgatorius' is a list of passages to be corrected, &c., in works otherwise fit for general circulation; several indexes of this kind were published between 1571 and 1607 (their compilers do not appear to have been Jesuits). Thomas James (*D.N.B.*), the principal assailant in England of these indexes, associated with them alleged falsifications in the editions of the Fathers published at Rome in the later sixteenth century. The texts in these editions differ from those in the earlier editions published at Basel and elsewhere; how far the differences are tendentious is controversial: James, *A Treatise of the Corruption of Scripture, Councels, and Fathers*, 1611 (1612;

new eds. 1688, 1843); F. H. Reusch, *Der Index der verbotenen Bücher*, 1883–5, i. 549–59; &c. Evelyn was probably influenced by James's book. Early Basel editions of several of the Fathers are included in *Bibliotheca Norfolciana*.

[2] Now British Museum, Arundel MS. 122. It dates from the fifteenth century and is well written, and illuminated, but is without textual importance.

[3] This statement appears to be false or greatly exaggerated.

[4] That of Bilibald Pirckheimer, 1470–1530, the humanist: *Allgemeine deutsche Biog*.

[5] Birch, iii. 430–2; Evelyn's notice is much fuller.

brought forth another Child; the first coming forth by piece-
meale, bones, & putrid flesh, through severall ulcers in
severall parts below: This was in *England*: An other (abroad)
who went divers yeares with an *Embrio* in her body, at last
brought forth, a Child whose head and limbs were halfe
petrified: Divers learned *Physitians* now present held, that
these *extra-Utrine* Conceptions happn'd through the Eggs
passing out of the *Ovarium* or *Fallopian Tubes*, by some
occult *meatus*, besides that into the womb: There being a discourse of *Iseland*; It was affirm'd, that the bodys of men when
dead, are piled up for severall monethes without corruption,
frozen as hard as marble; till the Thaws come, & then buried:
the ground being 'til then too hard to dig: The same is sayd
of *Muscovy*, & that they commonly remaine so expos'd til
about mid-*May*: Dr. *Croone*[1] affirmed that *Freezing* is not by
any ⟨gradual⟩[a] conjelation of the Water, but an instantaneous
action or operation, so as listning attentively, one may heare
a kind of obscure sharp frizling noise when it shoots the[b] Icy
skin or first *Epidermis* which is swift as thought: This he
tried by a glasse of Water. Also ⟨that⟩[c] all water shoots into
the shape of branches infinitely multiplied at right angles, &
resembling the veines in the Leafe of a Vegetable: That
Snow by accression[2] did grow when falling, & shot like a tree,
at right angles also, besides the Stellifying of every individual
atome of it ✳. It was by some there also assured us, that
the *Greeneland* Whale when struck hastens to the shore, a
Vast fish in Thicknesse with a huge head & jawes:[3] That the
Bermudas is longer & more slender, with a sharp snout, & he

---

[a] MS. *gratual*.   [b] Followed by *Isy* deleted.   [c] MS. *tall*?

---

[1] Above, iii. 475.
[2] The word is not given in *O.E.D.*
It is apparently formed from accress
(*O.E.D.*, s.v. Accresce), and has the
same meaning as accretion.
[3] The Greenland Whale is the
Right Whale: for it see F. Martens,
*Spitzbergische oder Groenlandische
Reise Beschreibung*, 1675, pp. 98–

125 (this is the book that led to the
present discussion). The Bermuda
Whale is identifiable as the Hump-
back Whale: A. E. Verrill, *Bermuda
Islands*, vol. i, 1907, pp. 270–8. For
the fishery there see Wilkinson,
The Adventurers of Bermuda, pp.
322–4, &c.

being smitten contrarie to the other, hastens out to sea, for they find them at a certaine season, among the rocks neerer the Iland; & being gotten out no rope is long enough to fasten to their harping Irons; so as it was so difficult to kill them, that the trade (which is very Considerable) had certainly failed there, had not an halfe drunken fellow, after he had[a] flung his speare & wounded a Whale, desperately hoped out of his boate upon the fishes back, where he so hacked him, as killed him before he could get to sea; & this is now familiarly practised by those of the Bermudas ever since. This story was affirmed me for a certaine truth by Sir *Rob: Clayton* who has one of the most considerable Plantations in that fertil Iland:[1] I returned home this evening:

September 1. Our *Viccar* preached on 4: *Heb:* 1, describing the infinite glory of the Saints in heaven: The blessed Sacrament follow'd: *Pomerid: Curate* on 5 *Hosea*: 15 &c.

3 I went to *Lond:* to dine at Mrs. *Godolphins* according to my custome every Tuesday, and found her in Labour; & staye'd 'til they brought me word the infant was borne, a lovely boy,[2] the Mother exceeding well laied to all appearance, Mr. G: (the *Father*) being at *Windsore* with the Court:[3] 5 It was christned, The *Susceptors* being Sir Will: *Godolphin*[4] (head of the family) Mr. Jo: *Hervey*[5] Tresurer to the Queene, & Mrs. *Boscawen*[6] (sister to Sir William & the Father);[b] and named after the Gra⟨n⟩dfathers name *Francis*:[7] *It was baptiz'd* in the Chamber where it was borne, in the mothers presence, at *White-hall*, by the Chaplaine who used to officiate in her pretty family; so I returned this evening home with

---

a Followed by *was* deleted.   b Closing bracket supplied.

[1] Clayton was not a fellow of the Society. He had obtained some land in Bermuda from his father-in-law: Wilkinson, *Adventurers*, p. 363.

[2] Francis, d. 1766; second earl of Godolphin 1712: *D.N.B.*

[3] See above, p. 142.

[4] Above, p. 133. A similar notice of the baptism occurs in the *Life of Mrs. Godolphin*, p. 75.

[5] Above, iii. 165; and see Miss

Sampson's note to *Life*, p. 75.

[6] Jael Godolphin, 1647–1730; married 1665 Edward Boscawen (below, p. 189): Miss Sampson, notes to *Life of Mrs. Godolphin*, p. 247. Her daughter Anne married Evelyn's grandson John Evelyn in 1705.

[7] Francis Godolphin, 1605–67; K.B. 1661: Marsh, *The Godolphins*, p. 8.

my Wife, who was also come up to see her & congratulate.
8: our Curate (in absence of the *Viccar*) preaching on his
former Text, whilst I was at Church this morning, came a
Letter from Mr. *Godolphin* (who had ben sent for from *Winsore* the night before) to give me notice that my deare friend,
his Lady, was[a] exceedingly ill, & desiring my Prayers &
assistance, his affliction being so extreme: so my Wife and I
tooke boate immediately, & went to *White-hall*, where to
mine unexpressable sorrow I found she had ben atacqu'd with
the new feavor then reigning, this excessive hot *Autumne*,
which being of a most malignant nature, & prevailing on her
now weakned & tender body, eluded all the skill & help of the
most eminent Physitians;[1] and ⟨surprizing⟩[b] her head, so as
she fell into *deliriums*, & that so vilontly & frequent, that
unlesse some (almost mira⟨c⟩ulous) remedy were applied, it
was impossible she should hold out; nor did the *Doctors* dare
prescribe such remedies as might have ben proper in other
cases, by reason of her condition, then so lately brought to
bed; so as the *paroxysmes* increasing to greater height, it was
now despair'd that she should last many houres, nor did she
continue many minutes, without repeated fitts, with much
paine & agonie, which carried her off [9][c] the next day, being
moneday, betweene the houres of one & two in the afternoone,
in the 26t yeare of her Age:[2] to the unexpressable affliction
of her deare Husband, & all her Relations; but of none in
this world, more than my selfe, who lost the most excellent,
& most estimable Friend, that ever liv'd: I cannot but say,
my very Soule was united to hers, & that this stroake did
pierce me to the utmost depth: for never was there a more
virtuous, & inviolable friendship, never a more religious, discreete, & admirable creature; beloved of all, admir'd of all,
for all the possible perfections of her sex: But she is gon, to

---

[a] Substituted for *being*.   [b] MS. *surprizind*.   [c] Marginal date.

---

[1] The hot autumn is also mentioned in the *Life*, p. 76. Mrs.
Evelyn attributed the illness to the
midwife's lack of skill or care. The
account of it in the *Life* is far longer
and better than that given here:
pp. 76-8. The death was due to
puerperal sepsis.

[2] She was born on 2 Aug. 1652.

receave the reward of her signal Charity, & all other her Christian graces, too blessed a Creature to converse with mortals,
fitted (as she was) by a most holy Life, to be receiv'd into the
mansions above: But it is not here, that I pretend to give
her *Character*, who have design'd, to consecrate[a] her worthy
life to posterity:[1] I must yet say, she was for witt, beauty,
good-nature, fidelitie, discretion and all accomplishments, the
most choice & agreable person, that ever I was acquainted
with: & a losse to be more sensibly deplord by me, as she had
more particularly honord me with a friendship of the most
religious bands, & such, as she has often protested she would
even die for with cherefullnesse: The small services I was
able to do her in some of her secular concernes, was immensly
recompenc'd with her acceptance onely;[b] but how! ah how!
shall I ever repay my obligations to her for the infinite good
offices she did my soule, by so o'ft ingaging me to make religion the termes & tie of the friendship which was betweene
us: She was certainely the best *Wife*, the best *Mother*, the best
Mistris, the best *friend* that ever *Husband, Child, Servant*,[c]
friend [or][d] that ever[e] any creature had,[f] nor am I able to
enumerate her vertues: Her *husband* fell downe flat like a
dead man, struck with unspeakeable affliction, all her Relations partooke of the losse; The King himselfe & all the Court
express'd their sorrow, & to the poore and most miserable it
was irreparable; for there was no degree, but had some obligation to her memorie: So virtuous & sweete a life she lead, that
in all her fitts, (even those which tooke away her discernement); she never was heard to utter any syllable unbecoming
a Christian, or uninnocent, which is extraordinary in *delirious*

---

[a] Substituted for *recomend*.   [b] Evelyn has retouched the following
passage; the exclamation-marks are altered from commas.   [c] Followed
by *or* deleted.   [d] Interlined.   [e] Followed by *yet* deleted.
[f] Substituted for *was*.

---

[1] This refers to Evelyn's *Life of
Mrs. Godolphin*. The date of composition is uncertain, but, as Miss
Sampson shows, he was probably
writing it between November 1682
and July 1684: pp. 116–20; see also
p. 185 (note to pp. 18–19). This
part of the Kalendarium was copied
not before 1680, and more probably three or four years later.

persons: So carefull, & provident she was to prepare for all possible accidents, that (as if she fore-saw her end), she received the heavenly *Viaticum* but the *Sunday* before, after a most solemn recollection; & putting all her domestic Concerns in the exactest order, left a Letter directed to her Husband (to be opened in case she died in Child-bed) in which, with the most pathetic and indearing[a] expressions of a most loyal & virtuous wife, she begs his[b] kindnesse to her Memorie, might be continu'd; by his care and esteeme of those she left behind, even to her very domestic servants, to the meanest of which she left considerable Legac⟨i⟩es, desiring she might be buried in the Dormitorie of his family neere 300 miles from all her other friends;[1] And as she made use of me to convey innumerable & greate Charities all her lifetime, so I paied 100 pounds to her chiefe woman, 100 to a kindswoman in declining circumstances: To her sister the value of 1000 pounds: In *diamond* rings to other of her friends, 500 pounds: & to severall poore people, widows, fatherlesse, Prisoners & indigents, *pensions* to continue:[2] ô the passionate, humble, mealting disposition of this blessed Friend; how am I afflicted for thee! my heavenly friend: It was now seaven yeares since she was maid of *Honor* to the *Queene* that she reguarded me as a *Father*, a *Brother*, & (what is more) a *Friend*:[3] we often prayed, visited the sick & miserable, received, read, discoursed & communicated in all holy Offices together without reproch: She was most deare to my *Wife*, affectionate to my *Children*, intrested in my Concernes, in a word, we were but one Soule, as aboundance of her profes-

---

a Followed by *instances* deleted.   b Followed by *continu'd* deleted.

---

[1] At Breage in Cornwall, 282 miles from London: *Life*, pp. 82, 111. Godolphin is buried in Westminster Abbey.

[2] Mrs. Godolphin did not make a will; she asked her husband in the letter mentioned above to make these gifts as legacies from her. The letter is printed in the *Life*, pp. 79–81. Evelyn's statements about the

gifts in this passage represent what was given; but 'her sister' should probably be 'her sisters': cf. *Life*, p. 82. See Miss Sampson's notes to the former passage.

[3] She was a maid of honour to the queen from 31 March 1671, or shortly after, until about 8 Jan. 1673. Her compact with Evelyn was made on 16 Oct. 1672.

sions & letters in my hands testifie: But she is gon, & the
absence so afflicting to me, as I shall carry the sense of it to
the last: This onely is my Comfort, that she is happy, & I
hope in Christ, I shall shortly behold her againe in the boosome of our deare Saviour, where she is in blisse, & whence we
shall never part:

The excessive affliction of this losse did so exceedingly
affect her husband, and other neere Relations, that knowing
in what[a] profession of a most signal Friendship, she ever
own'd me; The Fees to the *Physitians*, The intire Care of her
funeral, was wholy comitted to me; so as having closed[b] the
Eyes, &[c] drop'd a teare upon the Cheeke of my blessed Saint,
Lovely in death, & like an Angel; I caused her Corps to
be embaulmed, & wrap'd in Lead, with a plate of Brasse
sothered on it, with an *Inscription* & other Circumstanc⟨e⟩s
due to her worth, with as much dilligence &[d] care as my
grieved heart would permitt me;[e] being so full of sorrow, &
tir'd with it, that retiring home for two daies, I spent it in
solitude, & sad reflections:

15 our *Viccar* preach'd on 4: *Heb:* 1, describing the glory
of that Rest; The Covenant on Gods part, & ours, the possibility of loosing our right to it; with an exhortation to holinesse of life &c: *Pomerid: Curate* 11. *Eccles:* 1. *Cast thy bread
upon the Water* &c, exhorting to charity &c:

16 I went to *Lond:* in order to the funeral of my deare
Friend: so as on the 17th in an *herse* with 6 horses, & two
other *Coaches* of as many, & with about 30 people of her
relations & servants, we as privately, & without the least
pomp (as expressly required by her) proceeded towards the
place, where she would be buried: There accompanied her
hearse her husbands Bro: Sir Will. & two more of his Bro:
& 3 Sisters:[1] Mr. G: her husband, so surcharg'd with griefe,

---

a Followed by *relation* deleted.   b Followed by *her* deleted.
c Followed by *Wept up-* deleted.   d Substituted for *as*.   e Followed
by *and thus prepard, she was on the 13th* deleted, except for the last two
words, which are altered into *being*.

---

1 For the various brothers and sisters see Marsh, *The Godolphins*, pp. 9–14.

that he was wholy unfitt to Travell so long a journey 'til he should be more composed, & for this reason, after I had waited on the companie as far as *Hounslow* heath, with a sad heart, I was oblig'd to returne, upon some indispensable affaires: The Corps was ordred to be taken out of the *hearse* & decently placed in the house, with tapers about it, & her servants attending, every night during all the way to the foote of Cornewell, neere 300 miles, & then as honorably interred in the Parish Church of *Godolphin*.¹ This funerall, as private as it was, costing her deare husband not much lesse than 1000 pounds; and ô that ten thousand more might have redeemed her life! Returning back, I caled in to visite & Condole with my *Lady Berkeley*, my *Lord*, being also newly dead, which repeated sorrowes:²

18 I spent most of the afternoone with disconsolate Mr. *Godolphin*, in looking over & sorting his Ladys Papers, most of which consisted of Prayers, meditations, Sermon-notes, Discourses & Collections on severall religious subjects, & many of her owne happy Composing, & so pertinently digested, as if she had ben all her life a student in *Divinity*: There we found a Diarie of her solemn resolutions, all of them tending to Institution of life, & practical virtue; with some letters from select friends &c all of them put into exact method; so as it even astonish⟨ed⟩ us to consider what she had read, & written, her youth considered, few *Divines* having taken halfe that paines, or to better purpose; for what she read, or writt, she liv'd, full of Charity, and Good works which she did.³ 19 I return'd home to my house:

22: Our *Viccar* & Curate, on their former Texts: My Family being also this crazy season, much discomposed with sicknesse.

23 I went to waite on my L: *Arch Bish.* of *Canterbery* Dr. *Sancroft*⁴ late *Deane* of *Paules*, who was exceedingly civil to me, There din'd with us the *Bishops* of *Lond:* & *Rochester*:

---

¹ For her epitaph see *Life*, p. 114.
² He had died on 28 August.
³ See *Life of Mrs. Godolphin*, pp. 11–17, 83, 93–4, 95, 107.

⁴ Sancroft (above, iii. 432) had been consecrated archbishop on 27 January of this year. He was dean of St. Paul's from 1664 to 1678.

I went back: 26: To *Bromely* to Visite the *Bishop* of *Rochester*, but found him not at home:

29 our *Viccar* on 22. *Revel:* 9, of the civil respect due to men, & what to *Angels & Saints*, to none of them religious worship; how vainely contended for by the Ch: of *Rome*. *Pomerid*: The Minister of *Roderith*[1] on: 2. *Tit:* 11. 12. That the Gospel was promulg'd that men might live holily & magnifie the grace of God: That to none was it ever more signaly declar'd than to us of this Nation; to reinforce our gratitude, & obligation to live as become⟨s⟩ us for such extraordinary blessings:

My family continued very sickly, especialy a Laquay, whose life God was yet pleas'd to spare: My Daughter *Mary*, was this day 13 yeares old:[2]

Octob: 1 I went with my *Wife* to *Lond:* The Parliament being now alarm'd with the whole Nation, about a conspiracy [a]of some Eminent Papists, for the destruction of the King, & introducing Popery;[3] discovered by one *Oates*[4] and Dr.

---

[a] Hand in margin here.

---

[1] Rotherhithe; for the minister see above, p. 140.

[2] Evelyn states that she was born on 1 Oct. 1665: above, iii. 421.

[3] This is the Popish Plot, the alleged conspiracy of the Roman Catholics against Charles II. The first 'revelations' were presented to the king on 13 August; a further attempt to launch the plot, on 31 August, failed; but on 28 September Oates (see following note) appeared before the Privy Council and swore to the truth of his allegations. The whole subject is controversial; the plot as described by Oates was fictitious, although some of his statements were true or partly true; it received apparent confirmation from Coleman's correspondence and the violent death of Sir E. B. God-frey (see notes below). For the bibliography see *A compleat catalogue of all the stitch'd books* . . .

printed since the first discovery of the Popish Plot, 1680, and its two *Continuations*; Sir J. Pollock, *The Popish Plot*, 1903 (reissue 1944); the letters from the English court to Ormond, in *Hist. MSS. Comm.*, *Ormonde MSS.*, new ser., vol. iv, are extremely important. Hooke 'heard of Popish Plot Discovered' on 29 September: *Diary*; this was about when it first became public. Parliament had been prorogued from 29 August to this day and was now prorogued to 21 October.

[4] Titus Oates, 1649–1705, styled Dr. Oates from his claim to be D.D. of Salamanca; the perjurer: *D.N.B.* (unreliable); an apology for him in Sir E. Parry, *The Bloody Assize*, 1929. He had professed reconciliation to the Roman Church in April 1677 and had spent some time in the English Jesuit colleges at Valladolid and St. Omer; he was expelled from

Tongue,[1] which last, I knew, being the Translator of the *Jesuites Morals*:[a] I[a] went to see & converse with him, now being at *White-hall*, with Mr. *Oates*, one that was lately an *Apostate* to the Church of Rome, & now return'd againe with this discovery: he seem'd to be a bold man, & in my thoughts furiously indiscreete; but everybody believed what he said; & it quite chang'd the genius & motions of the Parliament, growing now corrupt & intrested with long sitting, & Court practises; but with all this Poperie would not go downe:[2] This discovery turn'd them all as one man against it, & nothing was don but in order to finding out the depth of this &c: *Oates* was encourag'd, & every thing he affirm'd ⟨taken⟩[b] for Gospel: The truth is, The *Roman* Chath: were Exceeding bold, & busy every where, since the D: forbore to go any longer to the Chapell &c:[3] 2: I went to *Parsons Greene* to visite my *Lady Mordaunt*, & condole with her for my Deare Mrs. G: 4: I returned home:

⟨6⟩[c] Our *Viccar* on his former Text: The blessed Communion follow'd: *Curate* as before:

---

a–a Or *Morals 2 I.*   b MS. *taten.*   c MS. *5.*

---

both of them. Evelyn presumably formed the view of him here set down at this time; Burnet also claims that he understood his worth from his first meeting with him, also about this time: *Own time*, ed. Airy, ii. 162. Official opinion was apparently sceptical until the discovery of Coleman's correspondence (see below): *Hist. MSS. Comm., Ormonde MSS.*, new ser., iv. 207, 454–7.

[1] Ezereel (Israel) Tonge (Tongue), 1621–80; D.D. 1656: *D.N.B.* The book here mentioned is probably *The Jesuits Morals. Collected by a Doctor of the Colledge of Sorbon . . . exactly Translated into English,* 1670; what appears to have been a new edition, with Tonge's name, was published this autumn: *Term catalogues*, i. 335. The original work, by N. Perrault, introd. by A. Varet,

was published in 1667.

[2] This parliament had first met in 1661; the active members were divided about equally between the Court and Country parties; they were almost all opposed to Roman Catholicism. Cf. Luttrell, *Brief relation*, i. 3, passage 'Here it is worth noting . . . speech of the king' (this passage appears to be an original composition of Luttrell's, written in 1681 or later).

[3] James had ceased to attend Anglican services in 1676: above, p. 87. The general apprehension of the apparent progress of Roman Catholicism is shown in Marvell's *Account of the Growth of Popery,* 1677, and in the commons' debates in the early part of this year; see also *Hist. MSS. Comm., Ormonde MSS.*, new ser., iv. 207, 457.

13 our *Viccar* proceedes: & *Curate* on 14. *Luke*: 16: ad: 20. shewing that no sinner but has his Excuse, but that no Excuse will serve sinn; no, not from our first parents, *Eve* 'til the end of the world: 17: I went to Lond: to make up *Accompts* with Mr. *Godolphin*, as on the 16,[1] I was constantly wont to do with his Lady, when she lived: He then requested me to continue the trust she reposed in me, in behalfe of his little sonne, & would by no meanes alter anything; conjuring me to transferr the kindnesse & friendship I had for his deare wife, on him & his:

20 Dr. Ball[2] preached (*Coram Rege*) on   *Seacret things belong to God, things revealed to us & our Children*: The danger of too much curiosity, especialy into the decrees of God; but to practise the plaine duties discove⟨re⟩d in the Scriptures: I din'd with Sir *Gab: Sylvius* & his *Lady* at St. *James's.*

21 The barbarous murder of Sir *Edmund*ᵃ *Bery-Godfry*,[3] found strangled about this time, as was manifest by the Papists, (he being a Justice of the Peace. and one who knew much of their practises, as conversant with *Coleman*,[4] a Servant of the . . . now accus'd) put the whole nation in a new fermentation against them:—I din'd with my *Lady Tuke*.

ᵃ MS. *Ed*ᵈ*:*

---

[1] The anniversary of the pact of friendship.
[2] Dr. Richard Ball: above, iii. 627; iv. 125.
[3] Edmund Berry Godfrey, born 1621; knighted 1666: *D.N.B.* He left home on 12 October and was found dead on 17 October; according to the inquest (18 and 19 October) he had been strangled and, after death, transfixed with his own sword; proclamations for the discovery of his murderers were issued on 20 and 24 October; it was said at court that he had been strangled: *Hist. MSS. Comm., Ormonde MSS.*, new ser., iv. 219. It was assumed that he had been murdered by some Roman Catholics and eventually three men were hanged for his murder; a few years later an attempt was made to prove that he had committed suicide; it is now generally assumed that he was murdered. The various conjectures as to the identity of the murderers, &c., are discussed by J. D. Carr, *The murder of Sir Edmund Godfrey*, 1936. No solution is satisfactory.
[4] Edward Coleman, sometime secretary to the duke and duchess of York; probably matriculated at Cambridge 1651: *D.N.B.*; Venn.; I.H.R., *Bull.*, vii. 122. He had surrendered himself on 30 September: Pollock, p. 79.

22 At the Countesse of *Sunderlands*. 23 Supp'd at my L: *Chamberlaines*. 24: Din'd at Mrs. *Boscawens*. 25 went home: 27 Our *Viccar* as above (see your notes). 31. Being the 58th of my age, requir'd my humble addresses to Almighty God, & that he would take off his heavy hand still on my family, and restore comforts to us, after the losse of my Excellent friend: I also now review'd & new made my Will:

November 1 Imploring Gods mercy for the Yeare entering, I went to Church, where our *Viccar* proceeded on his former yeares *Anniversa⟨r⟩y* Text, concerning works of Charity:[1] I din'd with the foefees: 3: *Vicc:* on 1. *Pet:* 5. 7. That we ought to rely on the Providence of God, discovering the wonderfullnesse of it from the Creation, & Government of the World: The holy *Sacrament* follow'd: *Pomerid*: Sir Tho: *Clutterbooks* Chaplaine[2] made a pious & eloquent discourse on: 1. *Tim:* 2: 8: concerning the stated houres of Prayer, how antient; the necessity & advantages of it: That the sacrifices of old, were ever accompanied with prayer: That when sacrifices themselves, however rich & aboundant, were of no force (as in case of presumptuous sinns, *Murder*, *Adultry* &c) yet Prayer was heard & prevail'd, as in the Case of *David*, *Manasses* &c. That persons at ease & leasure were most obliged to frequent prayer & much devotion; That poore & labouring men prayed in *Working* in their Calling: *Laborare est Orare*: & none yet so oppressed with buisinesse, but was oblig'd to pray, especialy Mor: & Evenings, as an indispensible homage due to the sovraine Lord:

4 To *Lond:* 5. Dr. *Tillotson* before the house of *Commons* at St. *Margarits*: 'Tis since Printed:[3] 'Twas now he sayed, the *Papists* were ariv'd to that impudence, as to deny there was ever any such thing as the Gun-powder Conspiresy: To this he affirm'd, he had himselfe severall letters written by

---

[1] See above, p. 123.
[2] Thomas Clutterbuck, *c.* 1627–83; sometime merchant and consul at Leghorn; knighted 1669; of Blakesware, Herts.: Clutterbuck, (*Hertfordshire*), iii. 299, 302, 303, 312; Le Neve, *Pedigrees*, p. 225. The chaplain is not identifiable.
[3] The sermon was printed by 6 December: *Term catalogues*, i. 326 (reprinted, *Works*, 1752, i. 158–66).

Sir *Everard Digby*[1] (one of the *Traytors*) in which he glories
that he was to suffer for it; & that it was so contriv'd, that
of the *Papists*, not above 2 or 3 should have ben blown-up,
& they such, as were not worth the saving:

10 I went to St. *Jamess* in the morning *Synax*: *Cor: Rege*
at *W:hall* Dr. *Butler*[2] on 5. *Gal:* 1, shewing by way of Paralell,
the Case of the *Protestants*, wavering betweene us & the
Papists: he spake very home to his *Majestie*, exhorting to
stedfastnesse in the Faith, & Liberty, in which Christ had
made us free in this Land especialy, reckning up the heavy
Yoake of *Popish* bondage &c.

13 Was an Universal Fast;[3] That God would avert his
Judgements, & bring to naught the Conspirators against the
K: & Government: In the morning preach'd to The *Lords*,
the A:*Bishop* of Cant:[4] in the *Abby* on 57: *Psal:* 1. shewing
how safe the Church & People of God were in the midst of
the most iminent dangers, under the wings of the Almighty:
This was also Printed.

15 The *Queenes* birthday &c: I never saw the Court more
brave, nor the nation in more apprehension, & Consternation
&c: It was also my *Baptismal Anniversary*:

17 Dr. *LLoyd* at *Whitehall* on 10: Heb: 24. Exhorting to
Religious Conversations and Friendship, for the doing good
to our brethren, & encouraging others by our example, re-
proofes, Instruction & holy Offices; that it was incumbent on
every Christian to do some good to others; nothing else likely
to reforme the World in this declining age: *Cor: Rege*: Dr.
Allestry on   *Luke*   shewing how much wiser the Children
of this world were, as to the end they pursued, than the
Children of Light &c:[5] 18 I returned home: 23 To *Lond:*

---

[1] 1578–1606; father of Sir
Kenelm Digby: *D.N.B.* The letters
here mentioned are printed, with a
preface signed 'J. T.' (presumably
Tillotson), as an appendix to *The
Gunpowder-Treason*, new ed., 1679.

[2] John Butler, d. 1682; D.D.,
Cambridge, 1669; canon of Windsor
1668; chaplain in ordinary, *c.* 1672–

82: Wood, *Fasti*, ii. 71 n.; Venn.

[3] The Proclamation for it is dated
25 October and was published in
London Gazette, 31 Oct.

[4] The sermon was preached to the
house of lords. It was printed by
16 Feb. 1679: *Term catalogues*, i.
339.

[5] The text is St. Luke xvi. 8.

24: Dr. *Allestry W:hall*, on 26 Isa: 20:[1] Elegantly shewing, the greate benefit, & privileges of Private Prayer: Retirement, & Meditation. *Coram Rege* the Deane of Bangor Dr. *Lloyd*:[2] on 2: *Act*: 46 That the Essentials & Character of the[a] true *Christian* Religion was comprehended in the Text &c:[b] Concerning the Sacrament, & Prayer, without any of the *Romans* late *Additions*: That the name & Terme of *Catholique* was wholy *Greeke*, not *Roman* in the least, nor belonging to them, who were onely Usurpers of it; nor were they ever understood by it, more than other Christians: So as to say a *Roman Catholick* is a ridiculous Contradiction.

Now had *Coleman*[3] ben try'd, & one *Staly*,[4] both Condemn'd & Executed: *Oates* on this grew so presumptuous as to accuse the *Queene* for intending to Poyson the *King*;[5] which certainly that pious & vertuous Lady abhorred the thought off, & *Oates* his Circumstances, made it utterly unlikely in my opinion: 'Tis likely he thought to gratifie some, who would have ben glad his Majestie should have married a more fruitfull Lady:[6] but the King was too[c] kind an husband to let any of these make impression on him. However, Divers of the Popish Peres sent to the *Toure*, as accused by Oates,[7] all the

---

^a Perhaps deleted.   ^b Followed by *See your notes* deleted.
^c Followed by *much* deleted.

A sermon on this text, probably the present one, is printed in Allestree's *Forty sermons*, [ii]. 230–46.

[1] A sermon on this text, probably the present one, is printed ibid., [ii]. 107–17.

[2] The apocalyptic. The text should be Acts ii. 42. The sermon was printed in 1679.

[3] Coleman was tried on 27 November, sentenced on 28 November, and executed on 3 December: *London Gazette*, 28 Nov., 2, 5 Dec.

[4] William Staley the younger: *D.N.B.* He was tried on 21 November for treasonable words and was executed on 26 November: *London Gazette*, 25, 28 Nov. Oates did not take part in the trial.

[5] Oates denounced the queen to the king on Sunday 24 November and was examined next morning by the Privy Council: *Hist. MSS. Comm., Ormonde MSS.*, new ser., iv. 480–1; *L.J.*, xiii. 389–91. He repeated the accusation before the house of commons on 28 November and before the house of lords on 29 November.

[6] Cf. the Imperial ambassador, 22/12 Nov., in O. Klopp, *Der Fall des Hauses Stuart*, 1875–88, ii. 463–4. Charles believed that Oates had been 'tampered' with: *Hist. MSS. Comm., Ormonde MSS.*, new ser., iv. 481.

[7] In consequence of Oates's informations against them William

Ro: Cath: Lords were by a new Act, for ever Excluded the
Parliament:[1] which was a mighty blow: The *Kings, Queenes
& Dukes* servants banished,[2] & a *Test* to be taken by every
body, who pretended to enjoy any Office of publique Trust,
or not be suspected of Popery:[3] This was so Worded That
severall good Protestants scrupuled; & I went with Sir W:
Godolphin (a Member of the Commons house) to *Bish:* of *Ely*
(Dr. *Pet: Gunning*) to be resolved, whether *Masse* were
Idolatry, as the *Test* expressed it: for Sir *William* (though a
most *learned Gent:* & excellent *Divine* himselfe) made some
doubt of it: but the *Bishops* opinion was he might take it, &
that the *Papists* could not excuse themselves from Idolatry;
though he wished it had ben otherwise worded in the Test:[4]

Herbert, earl of Powis (*D.N.B.*),
Viscount Stafford (above, iii. 550),
Lord Petre (below, p. 169), Lord
Belasyse (above, iii. 351), and Lord
Arundell of Wardour (above, iii.
62), had surrendered themselves
between 25 and 31 October and had
been imprisoned in the Tower.
Lord Castlemaine, who was an Irish
peer, was also sent there.

[1] The parliamentary test act
(30 Car. II, st. ii, c. 1), excluding
Roman Catholics (with the exception of the duke of York) from sitting in either house of parliament,
passed by the king on 30 November
(notice in *London Gazette*, 2 Dec.).
They were already practically excluded from the commons by the
obligation to take the Oath of
Supremacy and individual Roman
Catholics were expelled: *C.J.*, ix.
393, 501. The present act was
repealed in 1829.

[2] A proclamation of 30 October
ordered all Roman Catholic recusants to withdraw by 7 November
from the royal palaces of Whitehall,
Somerset House, and St. James's,
the cities of London and Westminster, and places ten miles about;
permanent residents engaged in
trade were excepted: *London Gazette*,
4 Nov. A later order of 6 December

shows that 'Her Majesties allowed
Servants' were also excepted; they
were permitted to attend services
in her chapel: ibid., 23 Dec.

[3] This apparently refers to the
Test Act of 1673 (above, p. 7);
but in addition the justices of the
peace could require all persons to
take the Oath of Allegiance (7 Jac.
I, c. 6). By a proclamation of
10 November (Steele, no. 3662)
recusants were ordered to return
to and to keep within five miles of
their abodes or settlements, and the
oaths were to be tendered to sus-
pects. The commons also concerned themselves in this: *C.J.*, ix.
536–8.

[4] Godolphin was member for
Helston in Cornwall. The passage
questioned occurs in the parliamentary test act (1678) and runs:
'I . . . doe . . . declare That I doe
believe . . . that the Invocation or
Adoration of the Virgin Mary or
any other Saint, and the Sacrifice of
the Masse as they are now used in
the Church of Rome are superstitious and idolatrous.' Gunning,
with Sancroft and Dolben, is reported to have voted against the
bill on account of this or a similarly
worded clause: *Hist. MSS. Comm.*,
Ormonde MSS., new ser., iv. 473.

30 Dining at *Gressham* Coll. (being the *Anniversary* for Elections at the R: Society) I returned home:

December 1 Dr. *Patric* at Whitehall preached to the family on *God forbid that I should glory save-in the Crosse*[1] &c which according to his manner he handled most profitably: *Coram Rege* Dr. *Owtram* on 6 *Matt:* 11, that by the tenor of our lives & dispositions, our *Love* to God might easily be known:[2] 5 I din'd at my L: *Chamb:* & returned to my house.

8 I tooke *Physick* being indisposed, & stirr'd not out all this weeke:

15 Preach'd Mr. *Saunders*[3] on 5. Eccles: Shewing the reverence due to the house of God, by the expression of *keeping the foote* &c a *Synechdoche*, for the intire man: & this by considering, that the Church is Gods house, dedicated to him, where his special presence is, by the example of all holy persons; from the offices there perform'd, especialy prayer, by which it was more properly cal'd than by that of Preaching: That we ought to pray standing, or kneeling, uncovered; Dilligently repaire to it at the houres appointed, assist in it: The benefit of publique prayer & formes &c: a seasonable discourse there being some in our Congregation not so reverent at prayers, as they should be.

16 To *Lond:* the nation exceedingly disturb'd at the publique commotions: for now was also the Lo: Treasurer *Danby* impeach'd &c:[4] 21 I return'd:

22 Our *Viccar* pr: on. 1. *Pet:* 5. 7. Upon the care & providence of God over his Creatures, Especialy his owne Servants, & how profitable it was to observe it, what on our part to be don, prudently, yet chiefely to relie on God, for Events, without anxiety.

25 *Viccar* on 1. *John*: 4. 2. 3. shewing what was ment by

---

[1] Galatians vi. 14.

[2] The text is apparently wrong. It should perhaps be St. Matthew, vi. 21; a sermon on this text is printed in Owtram's *Twenty sermons*, 1697, pp. 436–63.

[3] Above, p. 131.

[4] Proceedings against Danby began only on 19 December, when two letters of his were read in the house of commons, and he was ordered to be impeached. The articles of impeachment were read on 21 December and sent up to the house of lords on 23 December.

trial of *spirits*, against those who either denied, or did not rightly understand & confesse the Incarnation of *Christ*: whose name & office he explain'd, with the historie of his nativity, & the use we were to make of it in order to holinesse, & the participation of the bl: Sacrament, which followed:

29 Being very ill of Gripings I was faine to keepe my bed: Divers of my Neighbours invited &c: according to Costome: 31 I gave God thanks for his goodnesse to me the yeare past, &[a] begg'd that I might make a sanctified use of those Afflictions I had pass'd thro for the losse of a deare friend.

1679. *Jan:* 1 I implord Gods blessing for the Yeare now entred: 5. our *Viccar* as before what was ment by Confessing *Christ* &c namely the *Christian* doctrine &c: (See your *notes*) The holy Comm: followed: *Pomerid: Curate* on 21 *Luke* 27: 28: concerning *Christ* coming to Judgement: 12: *Viccar* on his former; When so strange a Clowd of darknesse came over, & especialy, the Citty of *London*, that they were faine to give-over the publique service for some time, being about 11 in the forenoone, which affrited many, who consider'd not the cause, (it being a greate Snow, & very sharp weather,) which was an huge cloud of *Snow*, supposed to be frozen together, & descending lower than ordinary, the Eastern wind, driving it forwards:[1]

13 I went to *Lond:* on foote: 14 Din'd with Mr. *Godolphin* now newly return'd from the funeral of his deare Wife, which he follow'd after some daies of its setting forth from *London*, he being then not able to ⟨have⟩ accompanied ⟨it⟩ on the way, for very griefe:[2]

15. I went with my ⟨*Lady*⟩[b] *Sunderland* to *Chelsey* & din'd with the *Countesse* of *Bristòl*, in the greate house formerly Duke[c] of *Buckinghams*,[3] a spacious & excellent place for the

---

[a] Followed by *that* deleted. [b] MS. *Lody*. [c] Followed by *Hamiltons* deleted.

[1] 'The black Sunday . . . when it grew so dark on a sudden, about eleven in the morning, that ministers could not read their notes in their pulpits, without the help of candles': E. Calamy, *Hist. account*

of my own life, ed. J. T. Rutt, 1829, i. 83.

[2] See above, pp. 151–2.

[3] The house originally built by Sir Thomas More and enlarged or rebuilt *c.* 1595–7. It appears to have

Extent of Ground & situation, in a most sweete aire; The house large, but ill contriv'd, though my L: of *Bristol*, who purchased it after he sold *Wimbledon* to my Lord *Tressurer*, expended much mony on it:[1] There were divers pictures of *Titian* & *V:Dyke* and some of *Bassano* very excellent: Especialy an *Adonis & Venus*,[2] a *Duke* of Venice, a Butcher in his Shambles, selling Meate to a Swisse: &c: and of *V:* Dykes My Lord of *Bristols* picture with the Earle of *Bedfords* at length in the same table.[3] There was in the Garden a rare collection of *Orange trees*, of which she was pleased to bestow some upon me: 16 To the R: *Society*, Mr. *Sec: Williamson* president, the Exper: of the *Lamp*, describ'd in Mr. *Hooks Lampas*; a letter from Germany read, of a *Menstrue* to preserve dead bodys:[4] I supp'd this night with Mr. *Secretary*[5] at one Monsieur *Houblons*[6] a french Merchant, who had his

been occupied by George Villiers, first duke of Buckingham, in 1626 and was granted to him in 1627; after his death it was occupied by his widow; it was sequestrated but was recovered by the second duke in 1660. He sold it to Bristol in 1674. The countess sold it in 1681 to Henry Somerset, marquis of Worcester and later duke of Beaufort (above, iii. 94), from whom it acquired the name Beaufort House. It later belonged to Sir Hans Sloane (below, 16 April 1691) and was pulled down in 1739–40. Beaufort Street now traverses the site: L.C.C., *Survey of London*, iv. 17–27; R. Davies, *The Greatest House at Chelsey*, 1914.

[1] Wimbledon was not sold to Danby until after Bristol's death: above, p. 130 n.

[2] The picture afterwards at Althorp; acquired by Mr. J. P. Widener of Philadelphia 1925. It is one of several versions of this composition and is now considered a school-piece or a derivative work: *Münchner Jahrbuch der bildenden Kunst*, 1925, pp. 274–9.

[3] The picture is dated 1633; the earl of Bedford is William Russell, who succeeded to the title in 1641, Bristol's brother-in-law: above, iii. 512. It now belongs to Earl Spencer at Althorp.

[4] Birch, iii. 454–7. Williamson had been elected president in 1677: above, p. 125; and retained the office until 1680. Hooke's *Lampas: or, Descriptions of some Mechanical Improvements of Lamps & Waterpoises* was published in 1677; for the present experiment see p. 7. The letter from Germany is not mentioned by Birch.

[5] Williamson; he was superseded on 9 February of this year.

[6] Identifiable as James Houblon, *c.* 1629?–1700; grandson of a Protestant refugee from Lille; alderman, London, 1691; knighted 1691; a director of the Bank of England 1694–1700; M.P. for London 1698–1700; his brother, Sir John, was first governor (1694–7) of the Bank of England. He was a friend of Pepys. His house was situated in (Great) Winchester Street: *D.N.B.*, art. Houblon, Sir

house furnish'd *en Prince* & gave us a splendid entertainement. 17: I din'd[a] at Lo: *Chamb:* & went home:

19 Our *Viccar* on his former, of the danger of *Hypocrisy*: *See notes*: *Curate* as before, the impossibility of Escaping the final Judgement:

25 Was the Long *Parliament* (which now had sate eversince his Majesties restauration) disolv'd by perswasion of the *L: Tressurer*: though divers of them were believed to be his Pensioners; at which all the polititians were at a stand: they being very eager in pursuite of the late plot of the *Papists*:[1]

26 Our *Viccar* as before, (See your *notes*) *Curat* as before: The infinite mercy of God: That *Christ* who wore, & knew our nature best, & infirmities should come to be our *Judge*, & not a stranger, or Enemy to it: 29 To *Lond:* 30. *Cor: Rege* his late *Majesties Anniversary*, Dr. *Cudworth*[2] on. 2. *Tim:* 3. 5. reckoning up the perils of the last times, in which amongst other wickednesse *Treasons* should be one of the greatest, applying it to the occasion, as committed under a forme of Reformation & Godlinesse; concluding that the prophecy did intend more particularly the present age, as one of the last times, the sinns there innumerated more aboundantly reigning than ever &c:

---

[a] Followed by *neere y[e] E* deleted.

John; Lady A. Archer Houblon, *The Houblon family*, 1907, vol. i. Further notices below; see also above, p. 128, M. 'Obloor'.

[1] The parliament, known as the Long Parliament of the Restoration, the Cavalier Parliament, or the Pensionary Parliament, was dissolved on 24 January: proclamation of this date, printed, as news item dated 25 January, in *London Gazette*, 27 Jan. Danby was trying to prevent further proceedings against himself and was believed to have advised the dissolution: Barillon, 31 Jan., o.s., in Christie, *Shaftesbury*, ii. 306 (paraphrase); Reresby, 24 Jan. 1679; Burnet, *Own time*, ed. Airy, ii. 187–8. For the alleged corruption of members see *A Seasonable Argument to Perswade all the Grand Juries in England, to Petition for a New Parliament*, 1677 (Feb. 1678; attributed to Marvell); *A List of one unanimous Club of Voters in his Majesties Long Parliament, dissolved in '78*, n.d. (summer?, 1679). A politician here is 'One that understands the Art of Governing, or judges of it according to the Parts he has acquired': E. Phillips, *New world of words*, 5th ed., 1696. The word was also used in a bad sense, a schemer, &c.

[2] Ralph Cudworth, 1617–88; D.D. 1651; the Cambridge Platonist: *D.N.B.*

Feb: *White-hall, Candlemas day*[1] Dr. *Durell* D: of Winsore preach'd to the household on: 1: Cor: 16. 22. Of our obligation to Love the L. *Jesus*, not to do it, an ingratitude so unreasonable as the *Apostle* thinkes such a one worthy the bitterest of Curses, not onely the *Anathema* to be abandond of all, & exposed to temporal punishment; but to *Maranatha*, the Judgement & indignation of God to eternity: This being the forme of the greater Excommunication amongst the Jewes: &c: The Doctor read the whole sermon out of his notes, which I had never seene *Frenchman* (he being of *Jersey*, & altogether bred at Paris &c) do before.[2] The holy *Communion* follow'd. *Coram Rege* Dr. *Pierce* D: of *Salisbury* on 1. *John*: 4: 1. *Try the Spirite*—there being so many delusorie ones gon forth of late into the world, he inveied against the pernicious doctrines of Mr. *Hobbs*:[3] see your *notes*:

5 I dind with the *Dutch* Ambassador,[4] where were divers publique ministers. 6 To the R: *Society*. 8 went home: 9: Our *Viccar* on 11: *Deut*: 12. on Gods peculiar care of his owne Children:

11 To *Lond*: 16 W:hall a *stranger* on 5. *Eph*: 6. of the deceivers gon out into the *World* &c: *Coram Rege* Dr. *Pierce*, 12: *Luke*: 4. 5 of the Courage a true *Christian* ought to have to go thro his profession &c: 23: Dr. *Cradock Coram Rege*: 3. *Matt*: 8: shewing how altogether ⟨necessary⟩ fruite was, to the outward profession of the faith: I received the holy *Sacrament* in the Morning at St. *Jamess*: ⟨25?⟩[a] Went home: My *Bro*: *Evelyn* of *Wotton* was now chosen knight for the County of *Surrey*, carying it against my Lord *Longford* and

---

[a] MS. *15*.

---

[1] Sunday, 2 February. For the meaning of Anathema Maranatha see above, iii. 337.

[2] The supposed French author of *A Character of England* remarks that the Presbyterians 'for the most part' read their sermons 'out of a book': p. 14 (*Misc. writings*, p. 152). English sermons were now generally either 'extemporary' (with or without notes) or memo-

rized: Mitchell, *English pulpit oratory*, pp. 22–7. Evelyn remarks on the reading of sermons on several occasions below.

[3] Pierce printed the sermon in his *A Decad of Caveats to the People of England*, 1679. In it he attacks certain passages in *Leviathan*.

[4] Koenraad van Beuningen: above, p. 77.

Sir *Adame Browne* of *Bechworth* Castle; The Country coming-
in to give their suffrages for my bro: were so many, that I
believe they eate & dranke him out neere 2000 pounds by a
most abominable costome:[1]

Mar: ⟨2⟩[a] Mr. *Bohune* late *Tutor* to my sonn preachd on
17: *Act.* 30. 31: a most learned discourse exhorting to repentance, (see your *notes:*) The holy Comm: follow'd. *Pomer.*
Curate on: 2: *Cor:* 6. 2 of Gods infinite mercy in affording
sinners such opportunities of Grace &c: 6: To *Lond:*

7 Dr. *Stillingfleete* on 10: *Matt:* 16. *Wise as serpents* &c:
shewing sincerity to be liveliest Character of a true *Christian*
&c:[2] 9: *Cor: Rege,* the Bish: of Chester[3] 58 *Isa:* 5. *Is this
the fast I have chosen?* That the true way of mortification
& abstinence, did best appeare by our abstinence from
sinn, by doing works of mercy & charity. 14: Dr. *Pierce*
2. *Tim:* 1. 12.[4]

16 St. *Jamess Synax: Coram Rege Bishop* of *Ely*[5] on 18
Joh: 36. 37: That *Christ* came not to exercise a temporal
power like the *Pope*: &c: 19: Dr. *Cradock* on 3. *Heb:* 12. The
danger of unbeliefe:[4] 21. A *stranger* for Dr. *Frampton* on 6:
Gal: 4, The method of selfe examination, and necessity of it.[4]
23 I dind with the *Bish:* of *Rochester.* 24 returned home:

30 Our *Viccar* on 2. *Sam:* 24: 14. Why David was bid

---

[a] MS. *3.*

---

[1] Arthur Onslow (above, iii. 540)
and George Evelyn were returned
for Surrey on 28 February; their
opponents were Lord Longford
(above, p. 137) and Sir Adam
Browne (below, 8 April 1685; Longford had sat for Arundel from 1661
to 1678; Browne for Surrey from
1661 to 1678; he sat for the county
again in 1685). Evelyn was invited
to stand 'by the country, for that
my Lord say they went too much
with the Court'; Longford was believed to have spent £1,500 or
£2,000 on the election: *Hist. MSS.
Comm., Ormonde MSS.,* new ser.,
iv. 317, 341. The *Domestick Intelligence,* giving an account of the next

election, when Onslow and Evelyn
were again returned, rather
pointedly remarks that they were
not put to any charge: 29 Aug.
On election expenses at this time
see *English hist. review,* xxviii
(1913), 79–83.

[2] Lenten sermon at court: list of
preachers in *London Gazette,* 16
Jan. Printed in 1679 (reprinted in
Stillingfleet, *Ten sermons,* pp. 238–
301).

[3] Pearson. Lenten sermon at
court.

[4] Lenten sermon at court.

[5] Gunning. Lenten sermon at
court.

choose *one* of *Three* for his punishment: & why God sent such a Plague on the people; namely because when he numbred the people, he did not pay the head mony which the Law required, as an offering to God, which he was obliged to do, & also for his pride, & dependance on his owne power: *Pomerid*: The *Lecturer* of *Lee*[1] of charity, love & friendship: on 2. *Phill*[a] 1.

My friend Mr. *Godolphin* was now made one of the *Lords Commissioners* of the *Treasury*, and of the *Privy Council*:[2]

Aprill 1. To *Lond.* 2: Dr. *Megot* on. 1. *Joh:* 3. 15,[3] the danger of Loving the world, excellently: ⟨4⟩ *Cor: Rege* Dr. *Tillotson* on 1. Joh: 4: 3. *Believe not every Spirit* &c:[4] ⟨6⟩[b] Dr. *Stillingfleete*, on 2. *Phil:* 13. of *Working out Salvation*, the difficul⟨t⟩y & paines to be taken in it &c.[5] *Coram Rege* the *Bish:* of *Glocester*[6] on 95 *Psal:* 13. *Come let us Worship*: This *Bishops* preching, is very like *Bish: Andrew's* way, full of divisions, & Scholastical, & that with much quicknesse: The holy Comm: follow'd: 9: Dr. *Littleton* 4: Rom: 25, *Obser:* That the *Skinns* which coverd the nuditie of our first Parents, but which their owne Figleaves could not do, was probably of the sacrific⟨e⟩d Beasts, slaine & offered for their sinn, an Embleme of the righteousnesse of Christ, who was to be a Sacrifice for us:[7] 10. home: ⟨11⟩[c]: Was the solemn pub: Fast:[8] our *Viccar* on

---

[a] Spelling doubtful.   [b] MS. *4*.   [c] MS. *17*.

---

[1] Presumably John Jackson: below, p. 206.

[2] Danby having been dismissed, the Treasury was put into commission on 26 March: *London Gazette*, 27 March (notice dated 26 March). Godolphin did not become a privy councillor until 1680.

[3] A slip for 1 John ii. 15. Lenten sermon at court.

[4] Lenten sermon at court. Evelyn has wrongly treated it as if Meggot's and it had been delivered on the same day to the household and before the king. The text should be 1 John iv. 1; the sermon was printed this year (reprinted in *Works*, 1752, i. 176–86).

[5] Sermon to the household. The text should be Philippians ii. 12.

[6] Prichett: above, p. 84, where Evelyn also remarks on his style of preaching. 'Bish: Andrew' is Lancelot Andrewes: above, iii. 139. His *XCVI. Sermons*, first published 1629, all show the characteristics here noted. Lenten sermon at court.

[7] Lenten sermon at court.

[8] On account of the Popish Plot: proclamation, 28 March, in *London Gazette*, 31 March.

2: *Sam:* 24 pursuing his former subject. 13 *Curate Palme Sonday* on 21 *Matt:* 8. 9. 15 To *Lond:*

16 *White hall*, Dr. *Sprat* 7: *Matt*ᵃ 21: That all Religion consisted in practical obedience, not in verbal profession, eloquently & excellently:[1] after which the Bishop of *Lond:* Confirm'd many Children & others, & amongst them my *Daughter Mary*, now about 14 yeares old:[2]

18 Dr. *LLoyd* at St. *Martines* on 1. *Cor:* 5 & 7. shewing the meaning of putting away *leaven* before the *passover* could be eaten, see your *notes*: The holy *Sacrament* followed: & went home in the evening, having heard the B: of *Bath & Wells*[3] on 19 *John*: 30 *Coram Rege* upon our B: Saviours last Words, It is *finishd*:

20 *Easter-day* our Viccar exceeding well on the same Text as Dr. *LLoyd*: The holy Communion followd; at which I & my Daughter *Received* for the first time: The holy *Jesus* continue his grace to her, & improve this beginning:

Afternoone the *Curate* on 1. *Cor:* 15. 19. &c: very indiferently, as he used to do:

24 To *Lond:* 27: A stranger at *W:hall* on 1. *John*: 3. 3. & *Cor: Rege* Dr. *Pettus*[4] on 1. *Phil:* 27. I dined at my *Lord Gerards* of *Brandon*[5] &c.

His Royal highnesseᵇ the *Duke*, *Voted* against by the *Commons* for his Reouoancy, went over into *Flanders*,[6] which made much discourse among the Politicians: &c:

May: 4. A *stranger* at *W.hall* on 5. Eph: 6. The holy Sacrament follow'd: B: of *Lond:* officiating: & *Coram Rege*, Dr. *Sudbery*[7] Deane of *Duresme* on 7: *Matt* 21. 22. 23. I din'd at my L: *Arlingtons*. 7: went home: 11: Mr. *Bohune* excellently

---

ᵃ Followed by *8. 9.* deleted.   ᵇ MS. *higse*

[1] Lenten sermon at court.
[2] She was born on 1 Oct. 1665.
[3] Mews.   He was probably preaching as a substitute for Dolben who, as dean of Westminster and as lord almoner, was listed to preach on Good Friday and on Easter Day.
[4] Pittis: above, p. 133.

[5] He was created earl of Macclesfield on 21 July of this year.
[6] He and the duchess had embarked for the United Provinces on 3 March; they arrived in Brussels on 17/27 March: *London Gazette*, 6, 24 March.
[7] John Sudbury: above, p. 109.

on. 1. *Cor:* 11. 1. recounting the sinns & defects of most of the old Testament, Patriarchs, Kings &c with many of the *new*, he exhorted us to imitate that onely which was best, and most perfect in them, according to the *Apostles* advice,[1] & no farther *him*, nor the best of mortal men, than they follow'd *Christ*, the perfection of whose Religion he described: *Pomerid*: *Curate* of *Roderith*[2] on 11: *Matt:* 30, a plaine discourse:

⟨18⟩[a] To Lond: at St. *Jamess Synax*, at St. Martines[b] a stranger on 24. *Matt.* 21. describing the Calamities of the Jews[c] for their rejection of Christ &c: applied to our publique confusions: I din'd at my Bro: *Pomerid*: the *Bish:* of *Rochester* in *Covent Garden* on 16 *Matt:* 3 signes of the weather discern'd by the Clowds, and not the signes of the Times? applying it to the Nation &c:

16 I went to chelsey, & din'd with the *Countesse* of *Bristoll*. 25 Dr. *Onely*[3] at *White-hall* on: 2: *Cor:* 5. 20. How Ministers were *Gods Ambassadors* & his infinite Condescention in sending them: Then went with my Lord the Earle of *Ossory* to the *French church*, where one preached on 16 *John*: 7. 8. shewing the Necessity, & benefit of our B: Saviours absence from his Disciples: I din'd with my *Bro:* & heard the B: of *Exon*[d][4] at *Co: Garden* on 19 John: 41. 42. on Christs Weeping over the Citty *Jerusalem*, comparing our time of Visitation, with a pathetical discourse: &c:

29 *Ascention* & his Majesties *Birth-day*, Dr. *Pettus* at St. *Mart:* on 2 *Sam:* 14. 19,[e] of Obedience to Princes &c: with a short application, or rather *Transition*, as to the *Ascention* of our Lord: &c: 31 Dining at L: Chamberlains I returned home:

June: 1. Our *Viccar* on 2: *Tim:* 3. 16. what Scripture was, & why given &c: The ho: Sacrament followed. *Curate* on 42:

---

^a MS. *15*.   ^b Altered from *Margarets*.   ^c Altered from *Jewish*.
^d Substituted for *Rochester*.   ^e Reading doubtful.

---

[1] 1 Thessalonians v. 21, the source of Evelyn's motto.
[2] Rotherhithe.
[3] Nicholas Onley, *c.* 1640–1724; D.D. 1671; chaplain in ordinary 1669–*c.* 1688; canon of Westminster 1672: Venn.
[4] Lamplugh. His text should be St. Luke xix. 41, 42.

Gen: 21 by Example of the *Patriarchs*, their Conscience accusing them for their ill usage of *Joseph*; shews the state of guilt, & danger of sinn:

4. To *Lond:* Din'd with Mr. *Pepys* at the *Tower*, whither he was committed by the house of Commons, for misdemeanors in the *Admiralty*, where he was Secretary; but I believe unjustly:[1] Here I saluted my *Lord Stafford* & *Peters*[2] who were also committed for the *Popish* Plot: 7: I saw the magnificent Cavalcade and Entery of the Portugal Ambassador:[3] din'd at L: Chamberlaines: 7: *went home.*

8: *Whitsonday* our *Viccar* on his former: Not all things true which even the holiest prophets said; but what they receiv'd immediately from God &c: *See your notes*: *Curate* on. 16 *Joh:* 13. The assurances of the *B: Spirits* being come; how he guid⟨e⟩s us into all Truth, all Truth coming from him alone: I received the B: Sacrament this morning:

14 To *Lond:* 15 Being *Trinity-Sonday* at St. *Martins* Dr. *LLoyd*, on 2: *Cor:* 13. 14. All the Persons of the holy Trinity being mentiond in that Text, he made an excelent sermon, with divers arguments against the *Socinians* exhorting us to an humble faith in such *Mysteries* as exceed our narrow Understanding & therefore to avoid pride & singularitie, the father of many heretics &c: the holy Communion followed.

17 I was *Godfather* to a *Sonn*[4] of Sir *Chr: Wren* Surveyor of his Majesties building⟨s⟩, that most learned & excellent per-

---

[1] A committee had been appointed by the house of commons on 28 April; in view of its report Pepys was committed to the Tower on 20 May: *C.J.* (see also 22 May); Grey, *Debates*, vii. 303–12. He was transferred to the Marshalsea on 20 June and released on bail on 9 July; and was finally discharged on 28 June 1680: A. Bryant, *Samuel Pepys*, vol. ii, *The years of peril*, 1935. The attack on Pepys was malicious and fraudulent.

[2] William Petre, *c.* 1626–84; fourth Baron Petre 1638: *D.N.B.* For his and Stafford's imprisonment see above, p. 158 n.

[3] The ambassador is Henrique de Sousa Tavares, 1626–1706, created Marquez d'Arronches 1674; ambassador here 1679–81: M. de Sousa Moreyra, *Theatro hist. . . . casa de Sousa*, 1694, pp. 859–968; A. C. de Sousa, *Mem. . . . dos Grandes de Portugal*, 2nd ed., 1755, pp. 4–5; *Revista de historia*, v (1916), 202–7; Leti, *Del teatro brittanico*, ii. 307–10. Notice of his entry in *London Gazette*, 9 June.

[4] William, d. 1738: *D.N.B.*, art. Wren, Sir Christopher.

son; with Sir William *Fermor*[1] & my Lady *Vicountesse Newport*[2] wife of the Treasurer of the household: Thence to Chelsey with Sir *Step: Fox* and my *Lady*,[3] in order to his purchas of the Co: of Bristols house ther, which she desired me to procure a Chapman for: 19 I din'd at Sir *R: Claytons* & Sir *Rob: Viner*[4] (the greate *Banquers*): thence to our *Society*,[5] where was read Dr. *Grews* discours on the *Salts* of severall *Waters* about the Citty, Extracted, and produc'd before us, & examin'd:[6] Then our *Curator* M: *Hooke* shew'd us his *Weather Clock* describing the winds, Weather & severall other curious motions, by night and day: &c:[7] 21 I return'd hom⟨e⟩ in my New Coach: 22: Our *Viccar* as before: No neede of more Miracles, the Scriptures sufficient: That *Tradition* continued onely 'til *Moses*, for that *Abraham* might have spoken with *Methusalem*:[8] That the Verity of the *Christian Religion*, had as greate, & better proofe as any matter of fact could have &c: The *Curate* on 16: Psal: 12.[9] of the felicity of being in the presence of God, as the Saints are: There were now divers *Jesuites* executed about the Plot;[10] & a Rebellion[a] in

---

[a] Altered from *Rebelling*.

---

[1] William Fermor, 1648–1711; second baronet 1661; created Baron Leominster 1692; connoisseur: *D.N.B.*; G.E.C. Wren built part of his house at Easton Neston.

[2] Diana, *c.* 1623–95, daughter of Francis Russell, fourth earl of Bedford, and sister of Lady Bristol; married 1642 Francis Newport, Lord Newport (above, iii. 526). Newport was treasurer of the household from 1672 to 1687 and again from 1689 to 1708.

[3] Elizabeth Whittle, d. 1696, married Fox *c.* 1654. For the negotiation with Lady Bristol see also below, p. 185.

[4] Robert Viner, 1631–88; knighted 1665; created a baronet 1666; banker: *D.N.B.*; Dorothy K. Clark, in *Essays . . . in honor of Wilbur Cortez Abbott*, 1941, pp.

3–47.

[5] Birch, iii. 490. Clayton and Viner both attended the meeting.

[6] This paper is not mentioned by Birch in this day's proceedings. Grew had read a paper on the subject on 5 June.

[7] This instrument recorded the weather: Birch, iii. 487–8; see also Hooke, *Diary*, 17, 29 May.

[8] Methuselah, a common corruption. He died about 300 years before the birth of Abraham; the latter is perhaps a mistake for Adam.

[9] Cited from the Prayer Book.

[10] Five Jesuits (Father T. Whitbread, &c.) were convicted for the Plot on 13 June and were executed on 20 June: *London Gazette*, 16, 26 June.

Scotland of the Phanatics there;[1] so as there was a sad prospect of publique affaires: 14 To *Lond:* returned next day to meete the new Commissioners of the Admiralty,[2] who came to Visite me, viz: Sir *Hen: Capel* bro: to the Earle of *Essex,* Mr. *Finch*[3] eldest sonn to the L: Chancelor, Sir Humphry *Winch,*[4] Sir Tho: *Meeres*;[5] Mr. *Hales*;[6] with some of the Commissioners of the *Navy.* I went with them to *Lond:* 29:*Whitehall* a young Chaplaine on 6: *Matt:* 18. 19[7] St. *Peters* day, concerning his Supremacy, confuted very well by the ordinary arguments: After this his Majestie Offered:[8] I din'd at the Master of the Mints.[9] 30 Went to take leave of my L: *Chamberlaine,* now removing with the Court to *Winsore*:[10]

July 1 I din'd at Sir *William Godolphins,* & with that most learned Gent: to take the aire in *Hyde-park*; where was a glorious *Cortege*:[11] 3. Sending a piece of *Venison* to Mr. *Pepys* Sec: of the Admiralty, still a *Prisoner,* I went & dined with him;[12] Thence to the *R: Society,* where was both a discourse, & experiment of innumerable wormes or Insects in the *Sperme* of an *horse* by the *Microscope*: And also of a Liquor, in which flesh, or fish being boiled, the bones were rendred as soft as marrow, yet neither over boiled, or ill relished, all by the Contrivance of a Digestorie, with very inconsiderable

---

[1] The rising of the Covenanters described in *Old Mortality*; it was preceded by the murder of Archbishop James Sharp on 3 May and was suppressed by Monmouth at Bothwell Bridge on 22 June: *London Gazette,* 12 May, 12–30 June.

[2] A new commission, consisting of seven members, was announced on 22 April: *London Gazette,* 24 April.

[3] Daniel Finch, 1647–1730; second earl of Nottingham 1682; sixth earl of Winchilsea 1729: *D.N.B.*

[4] Above, iii. 392–3, &c.

[5] Above, p. 96.

[6] Edward Hales, *c.* 1645–95; third baronet *c.* 1683; created by James II earl of Tenterden 1692; the Jacobite: *D.N.B.*; *Notes and Queries,* clxx (1936), 164. For his father see above, iii. 153.

[7] A slip for St. Matthew xvi. 18, 19.

[8] See Chamberlayne, *Angliæ Notitia* (ed. 1676, i. 139–41). St. Peter's was not one of the normal days for the king's offering; presumably the ceremony had this year been transferred from St. John Baptist's day, 24 June.

[9] Slingsby.

[10] Charles left for Windsor on 30 June, the queen on 1 July: *London Gazette,* 3 July.

[11] Evelyn apparently uses the French word; no other occurrence is recorded in *O.E.D.* until 1816; cf. corteggio, above, iii. 256.

[12] He was now in the Marshalsea: above, p. 169 n.

expense as to fire: This by Dr. *Papin*[1] of our *Society*: I went home in the Evening. 5: Sir *Denis* Gauden[2] & his sonn dined with me:

6: our *Viccar* as before; The holy *Comm:* follow'd: *Pomerid.* a Fellow of *Trinity* Coll: *Camtab:* on 15 *John*: 4. 5. That the grace of Perseverance was from *Christ* onely. Now were there Papers, Speeches, Libels, publiquely cried in the streetes against the *Duke* of *York*, & Lauderdail &c obnoxious to the Parliament, with too much, & indeede too shamefull a liberty; but the People & Parliament had gotten head, by reason of the vices of the greate ones:[3]

There was now brought up to *Lond.* a Child[4] (sonn of one Mr. *Wotton* formerly *Amanuensis* to Dr. *Andrews* Bish: of *Winton*) who both read & perfectly understood Heb: Gr: Latine, Arab: Syriac, & most of the Modern Languages; disputed in Divinity, Law, all the Sciences, was skillfull in Historie both Ecclesiastical & Prophane, in Politic &c, in a word so universaly & solidly learned at 11 yeares of age, as he was looked on as a Miracle: Dr. *LLoyd*[5] (one of the most deepe learned Divines of the nation, in all sorts of literature)[a] with Dr. *Burnet* who had severely Examin'd him, came away

---

[a] Closing bracket supplied; MS. has comma.

---

[1] Denis Papin, 1647–1712?: *D.N.B.* He was this day appointed an under-secretary to the Society: Birch, iii. 491, 514; he appears as F.R.S. from 1682 in the annual *Lists* of the Society. For his digester see below, pp. 278–9.

[2] Above, iii. 510. His son is presumably Benjamin Gauden, sometime a victualler of the Navy.

[3] The Licensing Act of 1662, after two short renewals, had been prolonged by an act of 1665 to the end of the first session of the succeeding parliament, which occurred on 27 May. The first number of *Domestick Intelligence* is dated 7 July; two unsuccessful newspapers also started in this month. For the great outburst of pamphlets see *A compleat catalogue* (above, p. 153 n.) and its two continuations.

[4] William Wotton, 1666 (13 Aug.)–1727; D.D. 1707; F.R.S. 1687; the scholar: *D.N.B.* His father, Henry Wotton, rector of Wrentham 1664–96, had matriculated at Cambridge in 1644; no association with Bishop Andrewes, who died in 1626, is traceable. The son had matriculated at Cambridge on 20 April 1676; for his knowledge at the age of six see Henry Wotton, *An Essay on the Education of Children*, 1753. He later became a friend of Evelyn's, and several letters between them have been published (Bohn, iii. 346, &c.).

[5] The apocalyptic.

astonish'd and told me, they did not believe there had the
like appeared in the world since *Adame* to this time: He had
onely ben instructed by his Father, who being himselfe a
learned person, confessed that he knew all that he knew to
a tittle: but what was more admirable was not so much his
vast memorie, but his judgement & invention, he being tried
with divers hard questions which required maturity of
thought & experience: he was also dextrous in Chronologie,
Antiquities, in the Mathematics &c: in summ a⟨n⟩ Intellectus
Universalis beyond all that we reade of Picus Mirandula[1] &
other precoce witts: &c: with all this a very humble Child:
10 To *Lond:* dind at *Sir Ro: Claytons*, went home on friday
evening: 13 A stranger on :14:[a] *Joh:* 6 & In the Afternoone
Mr. *Evans*[2] whom I had holpen to a Competent living in
Lond, having casualy heard him preach in an obscure place
in Surry, where he was but *Curate*: his Text was 139[b] *Psal:*
7 shewing Gods *omnipresence*, knowledge of all our *Actions,
motions* & thoughts, which ought to be the most powerfull
restra⟨i⟩nt to preserve us from sinn: &c: My buisinesse called
me this Evening to Lond: 14: To see how things stood at
Parsons Greene, my *Lady V. Countesse Mordaunt* (now sick
in Paris, whither she went for health)[3] having made me a
Trustee for her Children, an office I could not refuse this most
excellent, pious & virtuous Lady, my very long acquaintance &c:

15 I dind with Mr. *Sid: Godolphin* now one of the Lords
Commissioners of the Treasury: 17 I din'd with my Wife at
Sir R: *Claytons* where dined also the Marquis of *Winchester*:[4]

18 I went early to the *old-Baily* Sessions-house to the
famous Trial of Sir *Geo: Wakeman*[5] (one of the *Queenes*

---

a Altered from *19*.   b Or *129*.

---

[1] See the life of Pico by G. F.
Pico della Mirandola prefixed to
various editions of Pico's works.
[2] Above, pp. 111, 127.
[3] She had apparently died in
Paris on 5 April (N.S. ?); she was
buried at Fulham on 1 May; her
will was proved on 20 May: G.E.C.

[4] Above, iii. 529, as Lord St. John.
[5] George Wakeman, of Beckford,
Glos.; created a baronet 1661;
except in connexion with his trial
very little is known about him:
D.N.B. One of the three monks
tried with him was James (Maurus)
Corker: *D.N.B.*; below, p. 175 n.

Physitians) & 3 *Benedictine Monkes*; The first (whom I was well acquainted with, & take to be a worthy gent: abhorring such a fact) for intending to poyson the King: The other as complices to carry on the Plott, to subvert the Government, & introduce *Poperie*: The Bench was crowded with the Judges, Lo: Major, Justices, & innumerable spectators: The chiefe Accusers Dr. *Oates* (as he called himselfe) ⟨and⟩ one *Bedlow*,[1] a man of inferior note; but their testimony were not so pregnant, & I feare much of it from *heare-say*, but sworne positively to some particulars, which drew suspicion upon their truth; nor did Circumstances so agree, as to give either the bench or Jurie so intire satisfaction as was expected: After therefore a long & tedious tryal of 9 houres, the Jury brought them in not guilty to the extraordinary triumph of the *Papists*, & not without sufficient disadvantage & reflections on the Witnesses, especialy *Oates* & *Bedlow*: And this was an happy day for the *Lords* in the *Tower*, who expecting their Triall (had this[a] gon against the Prisoners at the barr) would all of them ⟨have⟩ ben in uttmost hazard: For my part, I do looke on *Oates* as a vaine, insolent man, puff'd up, with[b] the favour of the Commons, for having discovered something realy true; as more especialy[c] detecting the dangerous intrigue of Coleman, proved out of his owne letters: & of a generall designe, which the *Jesuited* party of the Papists, ever had, & still have to ruine the Church of England; but that he was trusted with those greate seacrets he pretended, or had any solid ground for what he accused divers noble men of, I have many reasons to induce my contrary beliefe; That amongst so many Commissions as he affirm'd he delivered to them from *P: Oliva*[2] & the *Pope*, he who made no scruple of opening all other Papers, letters & seacrets, should not onely, not open any of those pretended Commissions, but not so much as take any Copy, or Witnesse, of any one

---

[a] Followed by *pro-* deleted.   [b] Followed by *wh-* deleted.
[c] Followed by *the* deleted.

[1] William Bedloe, 1650 (or 1651)–80: *D.N.B.*; *I.H.R.*, *Bull.*, viii. 188.
[2] Giovanni Paolo Oliva, 1600–81; general of the Society of Jesus 1664–81: *Encic. univ. ilustrada*; *Catholic encyc.*

of them, is^a ⟨almost⟩^b miraculous: But the Commons (some leading persons I meane of them) had so exalted him, that they tooke for Gospell all^c he said, & without more ado, ruin'd all whom he nam'd to be Conspirators, nor did he spare whomsoever came in his way; But indeede the Murder of Sir *Ed: Godferie* (suspected to have ben compassed by the *Jesuite* party, for his intimacy with *Coleman* (a buisy person whom I also knew) & the feare they had he was able to have discovered some thing to their prejudice)^d did so exasperate, not onely the *Commons*, but all the nation; That much of these sharpnesses against^e even the more honest *Ro: Catholicks* who lived peaceably, is to be imputed to that horrid fact:[1] The *Sessions* ended I dined, or rather indeede supped, (so late it was) with the Judges, in the large ⟨roome⟩^f annexed to the^g Place,[2] & so returned to my house: And though it was not my ⟨Custome⟩^h or delight, to beⁱ often present at any *Capital Trials*, we having them commonly, so exactly published, by those who take them in short hand;[3] Yet I was inclined to be

---

a Followed by *also* deleted. b MS. *almast*. c Altered from *as*.
d Closing bracket supplied; MS. has colon. e Followed by *th* deleted.
f MS. *raame* or *raome*. g Followed by *S*- deleted. h MS. *Castome*.
i Followed by *much* deleted.

---

[1] The general reflections in this passage date probably from about 1684, when the trials for the plot were well past; it was certainly written before the trials of Oates for perjury in 1685.

[2] 'Over the Court Room is a stately Dining Room, sustained by ten Stone Pillars': Strype's Stow, iii. 281. The sessions house had been rebuilt after the Great Fire and was destroyed in the Gordon Riots in 1780.

[3] The accuracy of the published reports of the Popish Plot trials has been questioned by various writers, and notably by J. G. Muddiman, in *State Trials: the need for a new and revised edition of "State Trials"*, 1930, principally following [Father J. M. Corker], *Some of the most material Errors and Omissions in the late Printed Tryals of the Romish Priests . . . Jan. 17. 1679*, 1680. The reports vary considerably in character. Some are ostensibly verbatim reports, while others are clearly not more than summary reports set out in a form similar to that of the verbatim reports. No critical investigation of the whole group has as yet been published. So far, however, no adequate evidence has been produced to prove serious and deliberate falsification in the better reports; statements made in the course of the trials suggest that they were accepted as reliable by Sir William Scroggs and Sir George Jeffreys, although for technical reasons they could not be used in court.

at this signal one, that by the occular view of the carriages, & other Circumstances of the Manegers & parties concerned I might informe my selfe, and regulate my opinion of a Cause that had so alarm'd the whole Nation, & filled it with such expectations:

20: A stranger on: 16: Luke 25. on the parable of *Dives*: *Pomerid*: 17: Luke: 32. *Remember Lots wife*, both plaine & ordinary discourses; insisting on the necessity of reflection on things past, & how dangerous to set our hearts on temporall & perishing things; yet shewing how riches may be safely enjoyed by good men:

21 To Lond: 22 Dind at *Clappham* at Sir *D: Gauden*,[1] went thence with him to *Winsore*, to assist him in a buisinesse with his Majestie. I lay that night at Eaton Coll: in the Provosts Lodging (Dr. Craddock[2]) where I was courteously entertained: 23. To Court, after dinner I visited that excellent Painter *Verrio* whose worke in *Fresca*, the Kings Palace at *Winsor*, will celebrate as long as those walls last:[3] Signor *Verrio* shewed us his pretty Garden, choice flowers & curiosities, he himselfe being a skillfull Gardner;[a][4] after an herty Collation with him, I went to *Clifden*[5] that stupendious natural Rock, Wood, & Prospect of the Duke of *Buckinghams*,

---

[a] Followed by *The* deleted.

---

[1] Gauden is said to have built the house, which was on the north side of Clapham Common. He later sold it to William Hewer (below, 25 July 1692), and Evelyn came to it to visit Pepys. It was pulled down *c.* 1762; the present Victoria Road covers the site: J. W. Grover, *Old Clapham*, 1887, pp. 34–7; W. H. Whitear, *More Pepysiana*, 1927, pp. 99–100.

[2] Cradock did not become provost until 1681. He was at this time a fellow, the provost being Allestree.

[3] For Verrio's work in 1678–9 see Hope, *Windsor Castle*, i. 317, 320. The present notice is perhaps influenced by Evelyn's visit in 1683.

[4] Payments of rent for a house taken at Windsor for Verrio in the summer of 1681 are traceable until June 1686: *Cal. Treasury Books, 1681–5*, pp. 301, 750; *1685–9*, pp. 123, 1107. For him as a gardener see also below, pp. 208, &c.

[5] Buckingham had acquired Cliveden Park in Taplow at some unknown date. He is mentioned as building a house here in 1677 and 1680; it was completed some time after his death; it was burnt down in 1795. A new house having also been burnt down, the existing house was built in 1851: *V.C.H., Bucks.*, iii. 241; *Cal. S.P., Dom., 1677–8*, p. 205; Steinman, (*Mrs. Myddelton*), p. 36.

& building of extraordinary Expense: The Grotts in the Chalky rock are pretty, 'tis a romantic object, & the[a] place alltogether answers the most poetical description that can be made of a solitude, precipice, prospects & whatever can contribute to a thing so very like their imaginations: The ⟨house⟩ stands[b] somewhat like *Frascati*[1] as to its front, & on the platforme is a circular View to the uttmost verge of the Horison, which with the serpenting of the *Thames* is admirably surprising: The Staire Case, is for its materials, singular: The *Cloisters*, Descents, Gardens, & avenue through the wood august & stately: but the land all about wretchedly barren, producing nothing but ferne: & indeede, as I told his Majestie that evening, (asking me how I liked *Clifden*?) without flattery: that it did not please me yet so well as Windsore, for the Prospect & the Park, which is without compare; There being but one onely opening, & that but narrow, which let[c] one to any Variety, where as That of Winsore is every where greate & unconfin'd:

Returning I called in at my Co: Evelyns,[2] who has a very pretty seate in the Forest, 2 miles behether[3] Cliffden, on a flat, with sweete Gardens, exquisitly kept though large, the house a stanch good old building; & what was singular some of the roomes floor'd Dove-tailed wise without a naile; so exactly cloose, as I was exceedingly pleas'd with the manner of it, one of the Closets being parquetted, with plaine deale

set in Diamond thus exceeding stanch & pretty:

but my Kindsman & Lady being from home, I went back to Winsor, & next morning followed the King to *Hampton*

---

a Substituted for *an.*   b Or *stande.*   c Followed by *you* deleted.

---

[1] The Villa Aldobrandini: above, ii. 392–3.

[2] George Evelyn, 1630–99, a grandson of Evelyn's half-uncle, Thomas Evelyn of Long Ditton; married, 1664, a widow, Elizabeth Walsham (d. 1686): Foljambe, p. 56. His father had acquired the manor of Burnham *alias* Hunter-combe between 1649 and 1657; Huntercombe Manor House, a building of various dates, still exists: *V.C.H.*, *Bucks.*, iii. 169, 171.

[3] Correctly behither, on this side of. The latest occurrence quoted in *O.E.D.* is dated 1711, but the word perhaps survives in some dialects.

Court, where was a *Council*, at which I had affaires: thence dining at *Kingstone* I returned that night to Says-Court: not at all displeased at the journey: 27: our *Curate* on 16 *Psal:* 12,[1] Describing the Joyes of Heaven, by earthly similitudes & metaphors, agreable to our weake Conceptions: *Pomerid*: a Stranger on: 55 *Esay*: 7: Gods infinit mercy in pardoning Penitents:

31 To *Lond:* Din'd with Sir *William Godolphin*, went with him to the *R: Society*,[2] & so home:

Aug: 1.[a] I went on board his Majesties Yach't, his Majestie saling towards *Portsmouth*,[3] Mr. *Henry Thynn*[4] & Mr. *Brisbane*,[5] the one Secretary to *Mr. Coventry* Sec: of state, & the other, to the Admiralty, dining with me: afterwards to *Lond:* to see my deare friend, Mr. *Godolphins*[b] little sonn, who was sick, & with my Wife came back at night.

3 A stranger on 90: Psal: 12. shewing the shortnesse of our time here, & losse of it, through all the periods of Infancy, Childhood, Youth, Man-hood, & age: The goodnesse of God to

---

[a] Followed by *To Lond:* deleted.   [b] Followed by *&* deleted.

[1] See above, p. 170 n.

[2] Godolphin had been elected F.R.S. in 1664.

[3] Charles was at Deptford on 30 July and wrote a letter from the *Charlotte* yacht (Anderson, no. 579) on 31 July: *Cal. S.P., Dom., 1679–80*, p. 211. For his journey to Portsmouth see *Domestick Intelligence*, 5 Aug.

[4] Henry Frederick Thynne, d. 1705; nephew of Henry Coventry (above, p. 91); with his brother James keepers of the king's library 1677–89; a commissioner of the treasury 1684–5; grandfather of Thomas Thynne, second Viscount Weymouth: Collins, *Peerage*, ed. Brydges, ii. 508; British Museum, *Catalogue of Western MSS. in the old Royal and King's Collections*, 1921, by Sir G. F. Warner and J. P. Gilson, 1921, vol. i, introd., pp. xxv–vi. Henry Coventry was secretary of state from 1672 to 1680.

[5] John Brisbane, c. 1638–84; graduated at Edinburgh 1652; held various civilian offices in the Navy, including judge-advocate, and minor diplomatic appointments 1677–8; secretary to the lords commissioners of the Admiralty 1680 (28 Jan.)–4; appointed envoy extraordinary to Portugal at the time of his death. He married c. 1676 Margaret Napier, d. 1706, who succeeded as Baroness Napier of Merchiston (Scotland) in 1686. He was highly gifted; Miss Foxcroft conjectures that he suggested to Burnet the composition of the *History of my own time*: Paul, *Scots peerage*, vi. 427–8; E. Ashmole, *Antiquities of Berkshire*, 1719, iii. 185; Pepys, *Diary*; Sir J. Lauder of Fountainhall, *Historical observes*, 1840, (Bannatyne Club, 1838), p. 136; Clarke and Foxcroft, *Burnet*, p. 187, &c. Further notices below.

those yet who wrought but at the E⟨l⟩eaventh houre, exhortatory to take hold of the remainder: The blessed Sacrament follow'd: *Pomerid: Curate* on 11: *Matt.* 28. 29. but nothing of much note: 6: Came Sir *William Godolphin* & other Company to dine with me, his Sisters bringing with them that deare child, now almost a yeare old, & next day to be weaned:

7. To *Lond:* Dined at the *Sherifs*, when the Company of Drapers & their Wives being invited, there was a sumptuous entertainement according to the formes of the Citty, with Musique &c: comparable to any Princes service in Europ:[1]

8 I went this morning to shew My L: Chamberlaine, his Lady, & the Dutchesse of Grafton, the incomparable work of Mr. *Gibbons* the *Carver* whom I first recommended to his Majestie, his house being furnish'd like a Cabinet, not onely with his owne work, but divers excellent Paintings of the best hands:[2] Thence to Sir *St: Foxes* where I dined with my Lord, & all our Company,[3] & so home:

10 Our *Viccar* (of late absent, at his living in Rutlandshire)[4] return'd, preached on: 11: *Matt:* 30 of the Easinesse of an holy & good life, according to the Christian Institution: *Curate* on 5. *Luke* 5, of the reward of Industry in a lawfull Calling, with patience & obedience:

12 To *Lond:* about buisinesse, & return'd not 'til the 15th: 17: Mr. *Bohune*[5] preached at *Lee* (whither I went this morning) on 1. *Phil:* 27, shewing very usefully, what Graces of holinesse & humility it became *Christians* to walke in. *Curate* on: 1. *Jam:* 27 against the *Atheisme* of the times: 24. our Vicc: as before, with small addition, nor more the *Curate*:

---

[1] I cannot trace any reason for this feast. The sheriffs for the coming year had presumably been elected on 24 June, but were not sworn in until 30 September. None of the existing sheriffs and the sheriffs elect, or the lord mayor, had any connexion with the Drapers' Company. Nor can I find anything to suggest that the Company feasted on this day.

[2] Gibbons appears to have been living in 1682 at the King's Arms in Bow Street, Covent Garden: Tipping, *Grinling Gibbons*, p. 47; his name occurs in the Covent Garden parish register from 1678 onwards.

[3] Presumably at Fox's house in Whitehall, by Scotland Dock, near the east end of Scotland Yard: L.C.C., *Survey of London*, xvi. 205.

[4] Great Casterton with Pickworth: above, p. 4 n.

[5] For his connexion with Lee see below.

Dr. *Needham* came to see my Sonn, now indispos'd, & next day was sent for to *Windsore* the King being sick, & he one of his *Physitians* in Ordinarie:[1]

25 I went to meete the Countesse of *Sunderland* at *Parsons Greene* to see the children.[2] Thence to *Chelsey* the *Countesse of Bristols* (her mother) thence to Lond: 27 I dined with Sir Ro: *Clayton* having buisinesse: 29 home: 31. *Viccar* as before: In the afternoone to *Lee*, & after evening service, to see a neighbour one Mr. *Bohune*[3] (related to my sonns late Tutor of that name) who being a rich Spanish Merchant, lives in a most prety place, which he has adorn'd with all maner of curiosities, especialy Carvings of Mr. Gibbons,[a] & a Cabinet of his *Wives* (a most ingenious Lady) furnished with many rarities, some paintings of Mr. *Streeters* &c & so home:

September 6 To *Lond:* 7: Mr. *Blagrave*[4] at White-hall 1 *Jam:* 14. 15. The danger of Tempting our Selves, & laying our faults on God: The bl: Comm: follow'd: In the afternoone Dr. *Meriton*,[5] at a temporary Chapell, (caled the Tabernacle) whilst *St. Albans* Church was building:[6] on: 11 *John*: 9, concerning the working out of our Salvation: a tedious Preacher: 11[b] I returned home: 13: To *Lond:* thence to Winsore to

---

[a] Or *Gibbins*; altered from *Gibson*.   [b] Altered either from or to *12*.

---

[1] Needham was not one of the four physicians in ordinary who regularly waited at court, but must have been one of the additional physicians in ordinary. Charles was taken ill on 22 August: Foxcroft, *Halifax*, i. 186.

[2] Presumably Lady Mordaunt's children.

[3] Christopher Boone, d. 1686; a committee (member of the governing body) of the East India Company from 1660 to at least 1676; married to Mary Brewer, d. 1721; their house was Lee Place, a short distance to the east of the existing Boone's Chapel; it was demolished in 1825: Drake's Hasted, p. 222, &c.; Lewisham Antiq. Soc., *Register of . . . St. Margaret, Lee*, 1888; *Cal.*

Court Minutes . . . East India Company. Further notices below.

[4] Possibly Jonathan Blagrave, c. 1652–98; canon of Worcester 1690; D.D., Lambeth, 1693; chaplain in ordinary c. 1692–8: Foster.

[5] John Meriton, c. 1636–1704; D.D. 1669; rector of St. Michael's Cornhill 1664–1704; lecturer at St. Martin's in the Fields c. 1660–1704? Venn; notices below. The text is apparently wrong.

[6] St. Alban's, Wood Street, which was rebuilt in 1682–7; a 'tabernacle' to serve the parish was erected c. 1670: *Archaeologia*, lxvi (1915), 2–3, 21; Bell, *Great Fire*, p. 306. The word tabernacle in this sense first occurs apparently in 1669: ibid., p. 304; see also *O.E.D.*

congratulate his Majesties recovery; I also kissed the *Dukes* hand, now lately returned from *Flanders* to visite his Brother the King, of which there were various, & bold & foolish discourses, the *Duke* of *Monmoth* being sent away.[1]

14 Dr. *Stradling* (*Deane* of *Chichester*) preached to the household excellently on 1. *Thess:* 22[2] That it became Christians not onely to live innocently, but free of all appearance of evil: *Coram rege,* Dr. *Crighton* on 7: *Matt:* 16, shewing by what fruites a True Christian was to be known: much perstringing the *Jesuites:* My *Lord Sunderland* (one of the principle Secretarys of State)[3] invited me to dinner, where was the Earle of *Shrewsbery,*[4] Earle of *Essex,* E: of *Mulgrave,*[5] & (the Kings natural sonn) the E: of *Plymoth:*[6] Mr. *Hyde,*[7] Mr. *Godolphin* &c: After dinner, I went to Prayers at *Eaton,* & visited Mr. *Hen: Godolphin*[8] fellow there, & Dr. *Cradock:* 15 Dined with my *Lady Tuke* (one of the *Women* of the Queenes *Chamber,* & my relation). The Lord Major, & Aldermen came this morning to congratulate his Majesties recovery;[9] I return'd with them to Lond: & next day home: ⟨21⟩:[a] A *stranger* on 36: Ezek: 26. shewing how by the fall, our hearts were hardned, that *God* could onely soften it, &

---

[a] MS. *31.*

---

[1] The king had recovered from his illness by about the end of August. James arrived at Windsor on 2 September: *London Gazette,* 4 Sept. Monmouth was deprived of his commission as captain-general about 12 September: ibid., 15 Sept.; at the same time the king required him to go abroad: letter from Sunderland in Sidney, *Diary,* i. 127. For the explanation of these events see Foxcroft, *Halifax,* i. 186–91.

[2] A slip for 1 Thessalonians v. 22.

[3] Sunderland was appointed secretary of state on 9 February of this year.

[4] Charles Talbot, 1660–1718; twelfth earl of Shrewsbury 1668; created duke of Shrewsbury 1694;

the statesman: *D.N.B.* For his mother see above, iii. 596.

[5] Above, iii. 626.

[6] Charles FitzCharles, c. 1657–80; created earl of Plymouth 1675; his mother was Catherine Pegge: *D.N.B.*

[7] Presumably Laurence Hyde, the future earl of Rochester: below, p. 188.

[8] Henry Godolphin, 1648–1733; brother of Sidney Godolphin; D.D. 1685; fellow of Eton 1677; provost 1695–1733: *D.N.B.*

[9] Notice in *London Gazette,* 18 Sept. The lord mayor is James Edwards, d. 1691; alderman 1669; knighted 1670: Beaven, *Aldermen,* ii. 104.

fit it for his impression: (See your *notes*:) *Pomeridiano Curate* as before 1 *Jam:* 27.

25 Came to visite & dine with me Mr. *Slingsby* Master of the *Mint* & Signor *Verrio* the famous *Painter*, to whom I gave China[a] oranges of my owne trees, as good as were ever eaten I think, to Signor Verrios no small admiration: 28 our *Viccar* on 8: *John*: 36 That Christian Liberty did not qualifie any to Rebell against Magistrates: excellen⟨t⟩ (*see your notes*). The *Curate* on 4: *Phil:* 11 of Contentednesse in our present estate:

Octob: 1 To *Lond:* 3. Dined at Sir *Rob: Claytons*, now *Lord Major Elect*:[1] Thence to the R: Society:[2] 5. I went with the *L: Major*[3] to dine with the Bish: of *London* at *Fullham*,[4] where also I met Dr. *Stillingfleete*: I called at Parsons *Greene*, visited the Countesse of *Bristoll* at *Chelsey*, & so to Lond:

5[b] Dr. *Bell*[5] (of *St. Sepulchres*) preach'd at W:Hall on 1. Tim: 2: 1. of the necessity & excellency of Prayer: The holy *Sacrament* followed: *Bish:* of *Lond:* officiating: din'd at Mr. *Slingsbys*.

6 I return'd home, a very wett, & sickly season:

12 our *Viccar* as before, & so the Curate: 16 to *Lond:* made up my first Accompts with Mr. *Godolphin*, as intrusted for his little *sonn* &c: 19 A stranger at *W:hall* to the household on: 5: *Matt:* 34. ad 38,[6] against the horrid Vice & habite of swearing vainely: *Coram rege*, one of his *Chap:* on: 2: *Tim:* 1. 13. Excellently asserting the *Christian* Doctrine, as professed in the Church of England: 23: I din'd with my L:

---

a Altered from *Cha-*. The word is interlined.   b Date altered, apparently from 9 to 6, and then to 5.

---

[1] The election had been held on 29 September.

[2] There were at this time only informal meetings on Thursday afternoons: Birch, iii. 503. The date of the present notice is presumably wrong, 3 October being a Friday.

[3] Sir James Edwards; but Evelyn perhaps means Clayton. The date of this notice is probably wrong, 5 October being a Sunday.

[4] See below, p. 258.

[5] William Bell, 1626–83; D.D. 1668; vicar of St. Sepulchre's 1662–83; chaplain in ordinary *c.* 1665–83: *D.N.B.*

[6] Probably a slip for St. Matthew v. 34–7.

Chamb: the King being now newly return'd from his *New-market* recreations:[1]   24 I went home:

26 Our *Viccar* on 73: *Psal:* 25.[2] shewing the transitorinesse of worldly delights, the blessednesse of being in the favour of God; & that but to prepare for that glorious & happy state with him, no good man ought to wish for a long life here on Earth: *Pomerid: Curate* 1. John: 5. 3. of the Easinesse of the Christian yoake, & service of God, compared to the difficulties of other Religions: &c: & most pleasures of sinn:

31 My *Birth* day: & 59th of my age, I spent in recollection of my life, especialy of the yeare past, & prepare for the Communion the following moneth, beseeching Almighty God to be gracious to me the Yeare entering, & giving him thanks for the past:

November 1 I met with the *foefees* of the poore about their buisinesse, our *Viccar* (according to *Costome*)[3] preaching on 51 *Psal:* 19, by way of *Paraphrase* &c: That God would be gracious to the Publique, Spiritual & temporal Concernes &c:

2 Being the first *Sunday* the *Viccar* prosecuted his former text, describing the Vanity of Riches &c: The holy *Communion* followed; of which almost all my familie participated: blessed be God:

4. To Lond: din'd at *Lo: Majors*,[4] & in the Evening went to the funerall of my pious, deare & antient learned friend *Dr. Jasper Needham;*[5] he was buried at St. *Brides Church;* he was a true & holy Christian, & one who loved me with greate affection: Dr. *Dove*[6] preached on   *Psal,* with an Elogie due to his memorie: I lost in this person one of my dearest remaining sincere friends.

---

[1] The king and queen had gone to Newmarket on 26 September and had returned on the 13th of this month: *London Gazette,* 29 Sept., 16 Oct.

[2] Presumably according to the Prayer Book enumeration of the verses; but that of the Bible is also possible.

[3] This refers to the sermons in general, not to the text for this day's sermon.

[4] Clayton, who had been sworn in on 29 October.

[5] He had died on 31 October: epitaph in *Survey of London,* xxxv. 68. A notice of his death occurs in *Domestick Intelligence,* 4 Nov.

[6] Above, p. 100. He was vicar of St. Bride's from 1674 to 1695.

5 I was invited to dine at my *Lord Tividales*[1] (a Scotch Earle of my acquaintance, a learned & knowing noble man) we afterwards went to see *Mr. Montagues* new Palace neere Blomesbery,[2] built by our *Curator* Mr. Hook, somewhat after the French; it was most nobly furnished, & a fine, but too much exposed Garden:

6 Dind at the Co: of *Sunderlands*, & was this evening at the remarriage of the *Dutchesse* of *Grafton* to the *Duke* (his Majesties natural son) she being now 12 yeares old:[3] The Ceremonie was perform'd in my *Lord Chamberlaines* (her fathers Lodgings) at *Whitehall* below,[4] by the Bish: of *Rochester*, his Majestie Present: a suddaine, & unexpected thing (when every body believed[a] the first marriage, would have come to nothing:)[5] But the thing being Determined, I was privately invited by my *Lady* her mother, to be present: but I confesse I could give her little joy, & so I plainely told[b] her; but she told me, the *King* would have it so, & there was no going back: & this sweetest, hopfullest, most beautifull child, & most vertuous too, was Sacrific'd to a boy, that had ben rudely bred, without any thing to encourage them, but his Majesties pleasure: I pray God the sweete Child find it to her advantage; who if my augurie deceave me not, will in few yeares be such a paragon, as were fit to make the Wife of the greatest Prince in Europe: I *staied Supper*, where his Majestie sate betweene the *Dutchesse of Cleaveland* (the incontinent mother of the Duke of *Grafton*) & the sweete *Dutchesse* the

---

a Followed by *it would ha-* deleted.   b Followed by *him* deleted.

[1] i.e. Tweeddale: above, iii. 370.
[2] Above, p. 90. Hooke had been elected curator (of experiments) to the Royal Society in perpetuity on 11 Jan. 1665: Birch, ii. 4.
[3] For the first marriage, on 1 Aug. 1672, see above, iii. 622. A report in *Domestick Intelligence*, 11 Nov., also states that it was Dolben who married the couple. Another writer does not mention his presence: *Cal. S.P., Dom., 1679–80*, p. 277.
[4] As lord chamberlain Arlington had lodgings in the Privy Gallery wing of the palace, apparently on both the ground and first floors: L.C.C., *Survey of London*, xiii. 100.
[5] The duchess had tried in 1678 to marry Grafton to Lady Elizabeth Percy (below, p. 260), daughter of the earl of Northumberland: *Hist. MSS. Comm., 6th rep.*, App., p. 386 b. Another rumour said one of Louis XIV's natural daughters: *Cal. S.P., Dom., 1678*, p. 244.

Bride, with severall greate Persons & Ladies, without Pomp; my Love to my Lord *Arlingtons* family, & the sweete Child made me behold all this with regret: Though as the *Duke* of *Grafton* affects the *Sea*, to which I find his father intends to use him; he may emerge a plaine, usefull, robust officer; & were he polish'd, aᵃ tollerable person, for he is exceedingly handsome, by far surpassing any of the Kings other naturall Issue:[1] 7: I dind at my *Lady Sylvius*.

8 At Sir *St: Foxes*, & was agreeing for the Countesse of Bristols house at Chelsey, within 500 pounds.[2] 9: Dr. Smith[3] to the household on: 2: Coloss: 13. very Well: To the *King* a Chaplain, on 13 *Jer:* 16. not to deferr repentance:

16 At. St. *Jams's Synax*: At *Whitehall coram rege* the Provost of Eaton Dr. *Alestree* on 24: *Act:* 16,[4] shewing how nice we should be in the scrutining[5] of our Conscience.

18 I dined at my *Lo: Majors*,[6] being desired by the *Countesse* of *Sunderland* to carry her thither on a Solemn Day, that she might see the pomp & ceremonie of this Prince of Citizens, there never having ben any, who for the statlinesse of his Palace, prodigious feasting & magnificence exceeded him: This *Lord Majors* acquaintance had ben from the time of his being Apprentice to one Mr. *Abbot* (his Unkle) who

---

ᵃ Followed by *fine* deleted.

[1] Grafton had already spent some months at sea on the *Happy Return*: H. Teonge, *Diary*, ed. Manwaring, 1927, 24, 28 Jan., 14 Feb., 1679; *London Gazette*, 24 July; *Domestick Intelligence*, 8 Aug., 4 Nov.; the ship's movements are traceable in the *London Gazette*. He was again sent to sea for a year on 21 Feb. 1680: *Cal. S.P., Dom., 1679–80*, p. 397. He is Othniel in *Absalom and Achitophel*, pt. ii.

[2] The negotiation failed; Lord Worcester bought Lady Bristol's house in 1681 (above, p. 162 n.), while Fox built himself a house at Chiswick: below, p. 294.

[3] Perhaps Dr. Smith of Christ Church: below, p. 240.

[4] An undated sermon by Allestree on the present text is printed in his *Forty sermons*, 1684, [ii]. 65–78.

[5] For this form see *O.E.D.*

[6] The lord mayor's 'Table is . . . such, that it is not only open all the year to all comers, strangers and others, that are of any quality, but so well furnished, that it is always fit to receive the greatest Subject of *England*, or of other Potentate': Chamberlayne, *Angliæ Notitia*. For a dinner on a 'private day' see below, p. 187. For Clayton's house in Old Jewry see above, iii. 625. There is a reference to Lady Sunderland's conversation with Clayton in Sidney, *Diary*, i. 191.

being a Scrivenor, & an honnest worthy man, (one who was condemn'd to die [(but escaped)]ᵃ at the beginning of the Troubles 40 years past, as concerned in the Commission of Aray, for K. Char: 1:)¹ I often used his assistance in mony matters: Rob: Clayton (now *Major*) his Nephew, then a boy, became after his Unkle *Abbotts* death, so prodigiously rich & opulent, that he was reckoned on⟨e⟩ of the welthiest Citizens: he married a freehearted Woman,² who also became his hospitable disposition, & having no Children, with the accession of his Partner & fellow Apprentice,³ who also left him his Estate; he grew Excessively rich, was a discreete Magistrate, & though, envied, I thinke without much cause: some believ'd him gilty of hard-dealing, especialy with the Duke of *Buckingham*, much of whose estate he had swallow'd:⁴ but I never sawᵇ any ill by him, considering the trade he was off: The reputation, & known integrity of his Unkle Abbot, brought all the Royal party toᶜ him, by which he got not onely greate credite, but vast riches; so as he passed this Office with infinite magnificence & honor:

20 I dind at the Master of the Mints with my Wife, invited to heare Musique which was most exquisitely performed by 4 the most renouned Masters, *Du Prue*ᵈ⁵ a *French-man* on the *Lute*: Signor *Batholomeo*⁶ Ital: on the *Harpsichord*: & *Nicolao*⁷

ᵃ Interlined.   ᵇ Followed by *him* deleted.   ᶜ Followed by *deale* deleted.   ᵈ Or *Du Prie* or *Du Pree*.

---

¹ Robert Abbot, d. 1658; scrivener in Cornhill, 'dives et probus': Richard Smyth, *Obituary* (Camden Soc., vol. xliv, 1849), p. 47; *Cal. Committee for Compounding*, p. 893. He was concerned in Waller's plot (above, ii. 478), being one of the council of war appointed to raise troops in London by Charles I's commission of array, 16 March 1643: *A Brief Narrative of the late Treacherous and Horrid Designe*, 1643.

² Above, p. 121; her only son died in infancy.

³ John Morris, d. 1682; elected alderman 1669; M.P. for Blechingley 1679: Beaven, *Aldermen*, ii. 104.

⁴ Clayton, Sprat, and a third man (John Wildman), were appointed trustees for some part of Buckingham's estates in 1675: *Hist. MSS. Comm., House of Lords MSS., 1678-88*, p. 306; *1689-90*, p. 218.

⁵ Presumably the 'Du Pre' of *Numismata*, p. 285.

⁶ A harpsichord player named Bartleme or Bartholomew appears to have performed in *Calisto*: De Lafontaine, *King's Musick*, pp. 281, 290.

⁷ Presumably Nicola Matteis: above, p. 48.

on the Violin; but above all for its swetenesse & novelty the *Viol d'Amore*[1] of 5 wyre-strings, plaied on with a bow, being but an ordinary *Violin*, play'd on *Lyra* way by a *German*, than which I never heard a sweeter Instrument or more surprizing: There was also a *Flute douce*[2] now in much request for accompanying the Voice: *Mr. Slingsby* Master of the house (whose Sonn & Daughter[3] played skillfully) being exceedingly delighted with this diversion, had these meetings frequently in his house: 21 I din'd at my *Lord Majors*, to accompany my worthiest & generous Friend, the *Earle* of *Ossorie*; it was on a *Friday*, a private day;[4] but the feast & entertainement, might have become a *King*: such an hospitable costome, & splendid Magistrature, dos no Citty I believe in the world shew. 23:[a] Dr. *Allestree* before the household on: 11: Luke: 2: shewing how in all things we should submitt our Wills to that of Gods, as our best choice: *Coram Rege, Dr. LLoyd* on 28 *Matt:* 20: shewing with how little reason the *Papists* applied those words of our B: *Saviors* to maintaine the pretended Infallibility they boast of: I never heard a more Christian & excellent discourse: Yet were some offended that he seemed to say, the Church of *Rome* was a *true Church*; but 'twas Captiously mistaken; for he never affirmed any thing that could be more to their reproch: His Instances were, That a Man may be a *true man*, though full of sores, & botches, yea of a mortal plague; & an house a *true house*, though infected & *leaprous*; and that such was the present Church of *Rome*; shewing at large how frequently, and desperately it had erred; as by adopting false & doubtfull Articles into the *Creede*, to be believed on paine of *Damnation*, by which meanes the *Council* of *Trent* exclude all possible reconciliation &c: But men were now very angery with the *papists*, & violently transported, by reason of the late plot,

---

[a] Followed by *Coram Rege* deleted.

---

[1] For this passage see *Grove's Dict. of Music*, 3rd ed., art. Viol.

[2] The *flûte douce* is the recorder; it is also called the English flute: ibid., art. Fipple flute.

[3] Slingsby had two sons and a daughter: Sir H. Slingsby, *Diary*, ed. Parsons, p. 404.

[4] Friday was a fast-day.

& especialy the *Murder* of Sir E: *Godfery*,[1] which so exasperated, that they would endure nothing which was not carried with the uttmost Violence against all persons of that church: but here was in this Sermon, not so much as any shadow for censure, no person of all the Cleargy, having testified greater zeale against the errors of the[a] Papists, than this pious & most learned person:[2]—I din'd at the *Bish:* of *Rochesters*, & then went to heare that greate *Wit* Dr. *Sprat*, now newly succeding Dr. *Outram* in the *Cure* of St. *Margarits*,[3] who preached an incomparable sermon on: 1. *Thess:* 4: 11: Exhorting to Unity, & not to be so buisy & curious in others affaires, as the world was now too much, to the Danger of the publique peace: Dr. *Sprats* talent was, a greate memorie, never making use of notes, a readinesse of Expression, in [a][b] most pure and plaine style, for words & full of matter, easily delivered:[4]

26 I met the *Earle* of *Clarendon* with the rest of my fellow Executors of the Will of my late Lady *Vicountesse Mordaunt*,[5] namely[c] with Mr. *Laurence Hyde*[6] one of the Lords Commissioners of The *Treasury*, & lately *Plenepotentiary Ambassador* at *Nimegen*; also *Andrew Newport*,[7] & Sir *Charles*

---

a Altered from *that*.   b Interlined.   c Altered from *&*.

---

[1] Godfrey: above, p. 155. This was the time of the Meal-tub plot. The first great Pope-burning had taken place on 17 November (Queen Elizabeth's birthday); and on 25 November Thomas Knox and John Lane were convicted of conspiring to defame Oates.

[2] Lloyd had published several books against Roman Catholicism: list in *D.N.B.*

[3] He had been appointed curate and lecturer on 29 September. Owtram had held the living from 1664 (or 1670?) until his death on 23 August of this year.

[4] The preacher's using no notes was still apparently a novelty: Mitchell, *English pulpit oratory*, pp. 22–3. For Sprat's preaching style

see ibid., pp. 331–3.

[5] For her death see above, p. 173 n. She had befriended the elder Clarendon in his second exile: Continuation, §§ 1237, 1239.

[6] Laurence Hyde, 1642–1711, the elder Clarendon's second son; created Viscount Hyde of Kenilworth 1681; earl of Rochester 1682;. 'Lory' of the lampoons: *D.N.B.* He had been sent to Nimeguen by Charles II in 1677 as a mediator; he had been appointed a commissioner of the treasury on 26 March of this year (first lord 19 November) and remained in office until 1684.

[7] Above, p. 103. He had been concerned with Mordaunt in preparing a rising in July 1659.

Wheeler;[1] for the Examining, Auditing, & Disposing of this yeares Accompt, of the Estate of this Excellent Lady, according to the directions of her Will &c:—I din'd at Mr. *Boscawen*:[2] [a]27: I went to see Sir *John Stonehouse*,[3] with whom I was treating a Marriage, betweene my Sonn, & his Daughter in Law:[4] & dined with Sir *James Shaen*,[5] & thence to the *R: Society*, where there was excellent Conversation. 28: Came over the *Duke of Munmoth* from *Holland* unexpectedly to his Majestie whilst the *D: of Yorke* was on his Journey to Scotland, whither the *King* sent him to *preside*, & governe &c: The Bells & Bone-fires of the Citty at this arival of D:M: publishing their joy to the no small regret of some at Court; This Duke (whom for distinction they cal'd the *Protestant Duke*, though the sonn of an[b] abandoned[b] woman) the people made their *Idol* of:[6] I returned home: 30: *Viccar*: on 73: *Psal*: 25 as before: &c:

December 1. Being the day after St. *Andrews*, was the *Anniversarie* of choosing Officers at the R: *Society*, when

---

[a] Hand in margin here.   [b-b] Substituted for *wretched*.

---

[1] Above, iii. 586.

[2] Presumably Edward Boscawen, 1628–c. 1686; of Worthevall, Cornwall; M.P. for Truro in all parliaments 1660–81; married, c. 1665, Jael, sister of Sidney Godolphin: Vivian, *Visitations of Cornwall*, pp. 47, 185.

[3] John Stonehouse, c. 1639–c. 1700; of Radley, Berks.; second baronet 1675; M.P. for Abingdon in all parliaments from 1675 to 1690; married, 1668, Martha, c. 1642–c. 1705, daughter of Robert Brigges (a younger son of a Shropshire baronet) and widow of Richard Spencer, a London merchant: G.E.C., *Baronetage*, iv. 47.

[4] Martha, c. 1661–1726; daughter of Lady Stonhouse by her first husband Richard Spencer: Foljambe, p. 75. For the marriage see below, p. 194.

[5] Above, p. 84.

[6] Monmouth returned to London about midnight 27/28 November; there were bonfires, bell-ringing, &c., from the early morning until night on 28 November: *Mercurius Anglicus*, 29 Nov.; *Domestick Intelligence*, 2 Dec.; *True Domestick Intelligence*, 2 Dec. He had returned without the king's permission. James had left London on 27 October and arrived in Edinburgh on 24 November: *London Gazette*, 30 Oct., 4 Dec. Monmouth was hailed by the crowds as 'the Protestant Duke' when on his progress in Somerset and Devon in August and September 1680: *A true narrative of the Duke of Monmouth's late journey into the West*, 1680; the author of the pamphlet also uses the appellation. I have not found notices of its earlier use, but it was no doubt a popular cry already in 1679.

continuing our former President, I was chosen & sworn of the *Council*: for this yeare: After Elections were over, we (as, usual) din'd together, his Majestie having sent us in two *Does*: &c:

4 I dined (together with my *L: Ossorie* & E: of Chesterfild) at[a] the *Portugal* Ambassadors[1] now newly come, at Cleaveland house:[2] a noble Palace, too good for that infamous——: The Staire Case is sumptuous & Gallerie: with the Garden: but above all the costly furniture belonging to the *Ambassador*, especialy the rich ⟨*Japan*⟩[b] *Cabinets*[3] of which I think there were a dosen; & a *Billiard* table with as many more hazards as ours commonly have: the game being onely to prosecute the ball til hazarded, without passing the port or touching the pin: If one misse hitting the ball every time, the game is lost, or if hazarded: & 'tis more difficult to hazard a ball though so many, than in our Tables, by reason the board is made so exactly Even, & the Edges not stuff'd: The balls also bigger, & they for the most part use the sharp & small end of the billiard-stick, which is shod with brasse or silver:[4] The Entertainement was exceeding Civile, but besids a good *olio*, the dishes were trifling, hash'd & Condited[5] after their way, not at all fit for an English stomac, which is for solid meate: There was yet good fowle, but roasted to Coale; nor were the sweetemeates good: I had much discourse with the Secretary, who seem'd an understanding person.[6]

5 I din'd with my L: *Major*: 7: To the house—preached at *W:hall*, Dr. *Patrick* on 1. *Tim:* 6. 3. shewing what was to be understood by Godlinesse, viz, all the Duties of religion: The

---

[a] Substituted for *with*.   [b] MS. *Jopon*.

---

[1] The Marquez d'Arronches, who had arrived on 7 June: above, p. 169.

[2] The former Berkshire House: above, iii. 470, 573.

[3] See above, iii. 324 n.

[4] The game here described appears to be that called 'French billiards' in the eighteenth century; in the English (and French) game in the seventeenth century there were set on the table a small arch of ivory called the port and a peg called the king; it was played with broad-ended masts or maces: J. Bennett, *Billiards*, ed. Cavendish, 1873, pp. 3–6, and works there cited.

[5] Seasoned; the word is more frequently used for preserved with salt, sugar, &c.: *O.E.D.*

[6] For the ambassador's suite see *O Instituto*, xcviii (1941), 225–6.

B: Sacrament follow'd: (*Cor: Rege*) Dr. *Leake* on 119 *Psal:* 34 of the understanding Godes Law. I din'd at the *Earle* of *Ossories* who had before invited all the Company who dined with him at the *Portugal* Ambassadors, that is, the *Ambassador* himselfe, a *Portugal* knight, the Secretary, Duke of *Grafton*, Earle of *Chesterfield*, Earle of Bath, Lo: *Cavendish*, son to the Earle of *Devonshire*: & severall other noble persons.

10 I was summond to meete at a Council of the R: *Society* at Sir Jos: Williamsons, for the reforming divers things out of order, & carrying on the Experiments to be prosecuted this following yeare,[1] after which we had a noble supper:

11 I introduc'd the *Conde de Castell Melior*[2] (late prime Minister & favorite to the King of Portugal) & a Portugal Gent: with him, into our Society: where he saw severall experiments: &c:

12 I supped with the Countesse of Sunderland at Whitehall[3] & next day got home.

14 Our *Viccar* on 23. *Luke*: 31, shewing by the afflictions of our bl: Saviour, who was so innocent, what the ungodly may expect; by comparing the greene, & dry tree: pursuing the metaphor, of mans being compared to a tree: I was ill this afternoone:

18 To Lond: to our Society: 19 Din'd with[a] the E: of ⟨*Ossorie*⟩[b] and[c] the Earle[d] of Clarendon: at my *Lord Majors*: 21. A stranger preach'd at *W:hall* on 1. *Pet:* 4: 18. *Coram Rege*. Dr. *Sprat* on: 3: *Jam*: 13. That true Wisdome consisted in divine & sanctified knowledge.

24 I returned home, & [25][e] on Christmas day our *Viccar* on: 1. Heb: 1. after which the holy Sacrament &c: The [three following][f] days after divers of my neighbours dined with mee according to Costome:

28 Mr. *Bohune* preached on: 1: *Luke* 31, of the danger of

---

[a] Substituted for *at*.   [b] MS. *Ossories*.   [c] Substituted for *with*.
[d] Altered from *D—*.   [e] Marginal date.   [f] Interlined.

---

[1] Birch, iii. 514–16.
[2] Castelmelhor: above, p. 130.
[3] As secretary of state (above, p. 181) Sunderland had lodgings in the palace, and he and his family would as a rule live there.

Infidelity, excellently:[1] In the afternoone, a stranger on: 2: *Tim:* 3. 5. of the perill of hypocrisie &c.

30 I went to Lond, to meete Sir *John Stonehouse,* and give him a particular of the settlement on my Sonn, who now made his addresses to the Young Lady his Daughter in Law; & so returned home:

31 Recollecting the passages of the Yeare, I gave thanks to Almighty God &c:

1680. Jan: 1 Imploring the blessing of God on me & mine [&c]:[a] Divers Neighbours din'd with us.

4 our *Viccar* preached on his former text, shewing how the Gentiles were enlightned by the comming of *Christ* &c: (*see your notes*) the Com: follow'd: some friends dind with us; *Pomerid*: one Mr. *Burton*[b] on 3: *John*   That *Christ* in the flesh was perfect God, as well as man:

11[c] I tooke *Physick* my face & eye swelled by a Cold: 13 Came to Visite me Sir *W: Godolphin*: *La: Sylvius* &c: 18 The Minister of Lee[2] on: 133: *Psal.* 3. recomending Unity: I went in the afternoone to *Lond:* about special buisinesse, heard evening prayer at *W:hall.* 23. Supp'd at La: *Sylvius* with Mr. *Laurence* Hyde & Lady,[3] Sid: *Godolphin* &c.

25 Dr. *Cave*[4] (Author of *Primitive Christianity,* a learned & pious man) at W:hall to the household on 3: *Jam:* 17: Concerning the duty & grace of charity: *Coram Rege* Dr. *Pellin,*[5] 49 Isa: 23. a Prerogative discourse, but very honestly shewing what obedience is due from Subjects to their Princes; it being in a Conjuncture when there was a very ill understanding 'twixt the Court & Countrie upon his Majesties

---

a Interlined.   b Or *Barton.*   c Altered from *12.*

---

[1] The text is questionable.
[2] John Jackson: below, p. 206.
[3] Lady Henrietta Hyde: above, iii. 446.
[4] William Cave, 1637–1713; D.D. 1672; chaplain in ordinary 1674–c. 1688: *D.N.B.* The work here mentioned is *Primitive Christianity: or, the Religion of the Ancient Christians*

in the first Ages of the Gospel, first published 1673; new editions 1675, 1676, 1682 (there are also more recent editions).
[5] Presumably Edward Pelling, d. 1718; he was not created D.D. until 1690: *D.N.B.* He was a chaplain in ordinary from c. 1689 until his death.

unwillingnesse to let the *Parliament* sit. &c:[1] 26 I went to Counsel[a] for the settling my Estate on my Sonn, now in treaty about a marriage, with my Lady *Stonehouse's* Daughter:

30 Being the *Anniversarie* fast of K: *Charles* the 1. his *Martyrdom*, the B: of *Rochester* preached very patheticaly, as his costome ⟨was⟩,[b] on 27: *Matt:*   noting that that lesson (describing the suffering of our *B: Saviour*) was the proper lesson for the day of old apointed;[2] & paralelling[c] his sufferings in a very pertinent manner:

I supp'd at Sir *Steph: Foxes*, now made one of the Lords Commissioners of the Treasury:[3] &c:

Feb: 1 Dr. *Cradock* to the house at *W:hall* on 15 *John:* 10, concerning our Love to God, & of the benefit of Teares & true remorse, in an incomparable discourse: The blessed Sacrament follow'd: *B: of Lond:* Officiating: *Cor: Rege:*[d] Dr. *Pierce* on 45. *Jer:* 5, That[e] in time of publique calamity, we should not seeke greate things for our selves:[4]

⟨5⟩[f] Din'd at my Lord *Majors*, thence to the R: Society, returned hom:

8 Our *Viccar* on 73. *Psal:* ult: on what our Love, & Confi-

---

a Altered from *Council.*   b MS. *way.*   c Or *paralalling.*   d MS. has marginal date 5 in line with these words.   e MS. has marginal date 6 in line with this word.   f MS. 7.

---

[1] Parliament had been summoned to meet on 17 Oct. 1679; on that day it was prorogued to 26 January of this year, but on 11 December a proclamation announced that it would be further prorogued until 11 November; another proclamation, issued on 12 December, forbade tumultuous petitions. This did not prevent a number of petitions being signed and presented to the king: notices in *Domestick Intelligence*, 23 Dec.–27 Jan.; *True Domestick Intelligence*, 19 Dec.–10 Feb.; *London Gazette*, 15–26 Jan., 12, 23 Feb., 8 April, 6 May; *Cal. S.P., Dom., 1679–80*, pp. 307, 364, 376–7. Parliament eventually met on 21 Oct. 1680, after seven prorogations in all.

[2] It was appointed as the second lesson at Morning Prayer in the Book of Common Prayer from when it was first published until the revised tables of lessons were issued in 1871. When Juxon read the chapter to him on the morning of his execution Charles I asked whether he had chosen it for the occasion: Herbert, *Memoirs*, p. 131.

[3] Fox was one of the commissioners appointed on 21 Nov. 1679.

[4] A sermon on this text was printed by Pierce in *The law and equity of the Gospel*, 1686. See also below, p. 197.

dence of God ou⟨gh⟩t to be grounded &c. *Curate*, on 4: *Eph:* 30: I had some Neighbours dined with me.

9 To *Lond* about my sonns *Marriage*. 15 Dr. *Durell* D: of *Winsore* to the household on 1. *Eph:* 7: of our Redemption by the blood of *Christ*. &c. *Cor: Rege*, Dr. *Thisteltwhait* on 16: *Matt:* 27. of the Certainty, Glory, & Terrors of the final Coming of *Christ* to Judgment: Afternoone at St. *Jame's* Dr. *Leake* on 84. *Psal:* 10, The pleasures of Gods publique service:

19 Were the Writings for the Settling Joynture, & other Contracts of Marriage of my Sonn finish'd and sealed[a] &c: at *White-hall* Mr. *Thursby*[1] & *Melldecot*[2] being our Counsel, Sir *John Stonehouse* & *Nephew Glanvill* being *Trustees*: The Lady was to bring 5000 pounds in consideration of a settlement of 500 pounds a yeare present maintenance,—Which was likewise to be her joynture, & 500 pounds, after myne & my Wifes decease: though with Gods blessing it will be at the least 1000 pounds a yeare more in few yeares; I pray God make him worthy of it, and a Comfort to his excellent Mother, who deserves much from him: 20: I dined at a Servant of my Wifes, with the Earle of Ossory, whose servant had married her, & so home: 22: *Viccar* on 5. *Eph:* 15 of exact & Circumspect Conversation: I went in the Evening againe to Lond:

[b]24 It being *Shrove tuesday* was my *Sonne Married* to Mrs. *Martha Spencer* Daughter to my Lady *Stonehouse* by a former Gent: at St. *Andrews* in *Holborn* by our *Viccar*, (borrowing the Church of Dr. *Stillingfleete* Deane of St. *Paules* who was the present incumbent)[3] & afterward dined ⟨at⟩[c] an House in *Holborn*; & after the solemnity & Dauncing was don, They were beded at Sir *Jo: Stonehouses* Lodging in *Bow streete* Covent garden: I would very faine have had the marriage deferr'd til after the Lent; but severall accidents

---

a Followed by *with* deleted.   b Hand in margin here.   c MS. *an*.

---

[1] Presumably William Thursby, 1629–1701, of the Middle Temple; barrister 1656: Venn.

[2] Presumably Thomas Medlicott, 1629–1716, of the Middle Temple;

barrister 1653: Venn.

[3] Stillingfleet was rector from 1665 to 1689; and dean of St. Paul's from January 1678 to 1689.

requiring it now, it was left to the disposall of her friends, & their convenience:

25 *Ashwednesday Coram Rege* preach'd the B: of *Lond*[1] on 119 *Psal:* 71. shewing us the benefit of Afflictions: 26: To the *R: Society*, where I met an *Irish Bishop*[2] with his Lady, who was Daughter to my worthy & pious friend Dr. *Jer: Taylor* late Bish: of *Downe* & *Conner*, they came to see the *Repositorie*; she seemed to be a knowing Woman beyond the ordinary talent of her sex: 27: first friday in Lent. *Coram Rege*, D: of S. *Paules*[3] preached: a buisinesse of Charity keeping me from all but a fragment of his sermon: 29 Dr. *Tailor*[4] before the household on 6. *Gal:* 10, concerning the extent of our Charity, though chiefely to those of the faithfull &c: *Co: Rege* the *Bish:* of *Excester* (Dr. *Lamplugh*)[5] incomparably on 39: *Psal:* Shewing the Vanity of man within & without &c: exhorting to humility & sanctity: I din'd with Sir *Jo: Stonehouse* (my Sonns-Wifes Father in Law) at his Lodging: Afternoone heard a stranger at Co: Garden Church on 23.[a] *Luke*: 43, concerning the Immortality of the Soule, from what our B: Saviour promised the Penetent Theife of his being that day with him in Paradise: that the soules of the blessed, or Wicked had not their consummation and rewarde[b] 'til after Judgement; nor likely in Heaven or Hell, but in a mansion of repose, or dreadfull expectation:

Mar 3 Preached Dr. *Tenison*[5] *Coram Rege*, on 119 *Psal:* 106, of the absolute necessitie, and admirable Use of Resolution & performance of it: I dind at L: *Majors* in order to the meeting my *Lady Beckford*, whose Daughter (a rich heyresse) I had recommended to my Bro: of *Wotton* for his onely sonn:

---

a Altered from *33*.   b Or *rewards*.

---

[1] Compton, preaching as dean of the chapel. Lenten sermon at court; list of preachers in *London Gazette*, 29 Dec. 1679.

[2] Francis Marsh, 1627–93; bishop of Limerick, &c., 1667; of Kilmore, &c., 1673; archbishop of Dublin 1682; husband of Mary, younger daughter of Jeremy Taylor (above, iii. 94, &c.) by his first wife: *D.N.B.*

[3] Stillingfleet. Lenten sermon at court.

[4] Possibly Thomas Taylor, b. *c.* 1645; D.C.L. 1674: Foster; but it is not clear whether he was ordained.

[5] Lenten sermon at court.

she being the daughter of this Lady by *Mr. Ersfield* a *Sussex Gent.*[1]

4 I went home, to receive my new *Daughter* in *Law* & her husband my sonn, with his Wifes Relations, who all dined with us, & returning to *Lond:* in the Evening, left my Daughter in Law with us for altogether.

7 Our *Viccar* on 1. Pet: 5. 8. shewing the sinn of all manner of Intemperance, especialy lust, & drunknesse, & the abuse, instead of the Use of *Gods* creatures: The H: Sacrament follow'd: *Pomer: Curat,* on 16 *Matt* 26. of the vanity of worldly things and infinite losse of the soule for the short pleasures of this life &c:

14 The sermons of both *Viccar* & *Curate*[a] on former texts, a little amplified:

16 To *Lond:* to receive 3000 pounds of my Daughter in Laws Portion, which was paied in Gold: 17: Dr. *Cradock* at *W:hall* on 2: *Phil:* 13, shewing, that though to will, and to *do*, were of Gods good pleasure, yet he expected & received our Coöperation with that *Grace* through the abilities he had given us; & that it was not sufficient to pray for, but endeavor to live a life of Grace, & to worke-out our owne salvation &c: an excellent discourse, as his allways are, pious & cleare & very sound divinity.[2]

18 At the *Ro: Society*[3] was a letter from *Surenam* of a certaine small *Eele* that being taken with hooke & line at 100

---

a Followed by *alike* deleted.

---

[1] This refers to John Evelyn, 1653-91, George Evelyn's only surviving son by his second wife, Lady Cotton (George, his son by his first wife, was still living); the proposed wife is Katherine, d. before 1699, daughter of John Eversfield of Denne, in Horsham, by Mary Thomas, b. 1646, d. before 1732, who married secondly Thomas Beckford, d. 1685, knighted 1677, sheriff of London 1677-8, and two further husbands: Foljambe, p. 74; Comber, *Sussex genealogies,* *Horsham,* pp. 94-5; Le Neve, *Pedigrees,* p. 322; Beaven, *Aldermen,* ii. 107. For the marriage see below, p. 238.

[2] Lenten sermon at court.

[3] Birch, iv. 26-9, where the letter (from Flamsteed reporting information which he had received; dated from Greenwich, 10 March 1680) is printed. It refers to the electric eel of the Orinoco and the Amazon; the method of taking it here described is not traceable elsewhere.

foote length, did so benumb, & stupifie the limbs of the
Fisher, that had not the line suddainly beene cutt, by one of
the Iland (who was acquainted with its effects) the poore man
had immediately died: There is a certaine wood growing in
the Country, which put into a *Waire*[1] or *Eele-pot*, dos as much
intoxicate the[a] fish as *Nux Vomica* dos other fish, by which
this *mortiferous Torpedo* is not onely caught, but becomes
both harmelesse, & excellent meate: I this day introduc'd
Mr. *Bridgeman*[2] (Secretary to the E: of *Sunderland* now Pr: Sec:
of *state*) to be a member of the R: *Society*, he being a very
ingenious Person: 19 Dr. *Megot*[3] on 12: Rom: 17: 20 Din'd
with my L: *Chamb:* & so went home: 21. our *Viccar* on his
former, & *Curat* on 9: *Matt* 15. concerning the observance of
the *Lenten* abstinence, &c:

26 To *Lond:* the D: of *Sarum*[4] on a Text he entred on 5.
Feb: viz: 45 *Jer:* 5. Not to seeke greate things to our selves,
Gods counsel to *Baruc*, in the time of distresse: In which he
assembled so many Instances out of heathen histories, &
greate persons, who had quitted the Splendor & opulence of
their births, fortunes, & grandures, that he seemed for an
houre & halfe to do nothing else but reade *Common-places*,
without any thing of Scripture almost in his whole sermon,
which was not well: I went home next day:

28 Our *Vicc:* & *Curate* both on their former Texts, concerning Vigilancy & Temperance.

31 To Lond: A stranger at W:hall on 5: *Matt:* 8.[5]

---

^a Altered from or to *that*.

[1] Weir, but perhaps used in the special sense, a weel or fish-trap: *O.E.D.*

[2] William Bridgeman, *c.* 1646–99; matriculated at Oxford 1662 (Queen's College); a clerk in the secretary of state's office from 1669; a clerk of the council 1685–8 and 1692–9; M.P. for Bramber 1685; in the secretary of state's office 1692–7; secretary of the Admiralty 1694–5, joint secretary 1695–8: Foster; *Cal. S.P., Dom.*; &c. He had been elected F.R.S. on 18 December.

[3] Lenten sermon at court.

[4] Pierce: see above, p. 193; the date 5 February is an error for 1 February. Lenten sermon at court. On Pierce's preaching—'more like a Grecian orator than a Christian preacher for three parts of each sermon'—see Mrs. Evelyn, letter to Bohun, Jan. 1673 (Bohn, iv. 35).

[5] Sprat is listed for this day's sermon.

Aprill: 1 Din'd at *L. Majors*, thence to the R: *Society*: 2: Dr. *Tillotson* on 24 Josh: 15, shewing upon occasion of speaking of the *Israelites* worshiping false Gods, both before, and after Abrahams time; that the objections made[a] to us of the *Papists*, concerning the novelty of the Reformation, lay as much against all the people of God, in all times of their Reformation: The whole discourse was incomparable,[1] (*see your larger notes*) I return'd home this Evening:

4 our *Viccar* on 4: *Rom:* 25 shewing in what capacity *God* might be saied to suffer, as well as Man in *Christ*; & that it was not *Christ* as man which merited expiation of our sinns; but as *God*; the dignitie of that one person, giving that inestimable value to the other: (see the *rest in your notes*). *Pomerid*: Curate: 24: *Luke* 25: 26. upon the Suffering, & Resurrection of our *Lord* &c:

7 Being holy *Weeke*, I went to *Lond:* Dr. *Littleton* on 10: *Heb:* 5 (*Coram*[b] *rege*) shewing the necessitie of *Christs* assuming a real body, & being made man, that it might be possible for him to Suffer for us: The invalidity of the ritual Sacrifices; how they all vanished as soone as this body was offered &c:[2]

9: Being *Goodfriday* at St. *James*, where the *Dukes* Chap:[3] on 12: *Joh:* 27: shewing that the very Soule of our Deare Lord was afflicted, as well as his body; being man had not else Suffered; since it is the soule that denominates[c] mankind: *See your Notes*: the holy Communion follow'd: *Pomerid*: Dr. *Goodman*,[4] an excellent *Divine*, on: 13. *Heb* 11. 12 of the reason of the legal sacrifices of Expiation, how to be burnt without the Camp, to intimate our B: Saviours Suffering without the Citty, & that therefore we should not be asham'd to suffer for him &c: I return'd home this Evening:

---

a Followed by *against the* deleted. *the* deleted.   b MS. *Cor̃:*   c Followed by

---

[1] Lenten sermon at court. The sermon was printed this year as *The Protestant Religion vindicated, from the charge of singularity & novelty* (reprinted, *Works*, 1752, i. 246–53).

[2] Lenten sermon at court.

[3] Lists of the duke's Anglican chaplains (above, iii. 624 n.) are given by Chamberlayne. The present preacher cannot be identified.

[4] John Goodman, c. 1626–90; D.D. 1673; chaplain in ordinary c. 1682–90: Venn.

11 *Easter-day* our *Viccar* on 4: *Rom: ult:*[1] That the nature
& meaning of *Justification* was the Clearing & acquitting of
the accused & gilty &c: see your *notes*: The bl: *Sacrament*
follow'd, of which I participated with my family: *Pomer*:
Curate on 24: *Luke*: 45. 46. with usual application &c:

17 I went to Lond. and the next day, upon the earnest
invitation of the *Earle* of *Essex* went with him to his house of
Cassioberie[2] in Hartford-shire: It was on *Sunday*, but going
early from[a] his Lordships house in the Square of St. *Jamess*[3]
we ariv'd by ten a clock; but my Lord, thinking it too late
to go to Church, we had prayers in his Chapell: The House
is new, a plaine fabric, built by my friend Mr. *Hugh-May*;
there are in it divers faire & good roomes, excellent Carving
of *Gibbonss*, especialy the chimny ⟨piece⟩[b] of his Library:[4]
There is likewise a painting in the porch or Enterance of
Signor *Virrios*, *Apollo* & the *Illiberal* Arts:[5] One roome parquetted with yew which I liked well: The Chimny mantles
are some of them of a certaine *Irish Marble* (which his *Lordship* brought[c] with him when he was *Lieutennant* of Ireland
not long before)[6] not much inferior to *Italian*: The *Tym-*

---

a Followed by *Lo-* deleted.   b MS. *piecie*.   c Altered from *g-*

---

[1] i.e. Romans iv. 25, as above.

[2] Cassiobury Park forms part of
Watford. It had come to Essex's
father, Lord Capel, by marriage;
it was forfeited in the Civil War
and in 1645 was granted to Robert
Devereux, earl of Essex; it was
restored to Essex in 1660. There was
an old house of which one wing was
left unaltered by May; Essex's principal addition was the series of rooms
of state. The house was much altered
about 1800 by James Wyatt, who
gave it a Gothic exterior; it belonged to the earls of Essex until it
was sold in 1922; it is now demolished. For it see J. Britton,
Hist. . . . of Cassiobury Park, 1837,
with plates; *V.C.H., Herts.* ii. 453–
4; Tipping, *Grinling Gibbons*, pp.
68–79. View by Knyff in *Nouveau
Theatre de la Grande Bretagne*.

[3] Essex occupied the corner house
on the south side of King Street,
afterwards Cleveland House (no.
19), from 1677 until his death:
A. I. Dasent, *Hist. of St. James's
Square*, 1895, p. 242, &c.

[4] Figured by Tipping, p. 75.

[5] The mechanical or useful arts,
the handicrafts: *O.E.D.*; especially
M. Fotherby, *Atheomastix*, 1622, pp.
353–62. Verrio's picture survived
until the destruction of the house;
according to Britton 'the subject'
was 'composed chiefly of allegorical
figures of Painting, Sculpture,
Music, and War': p. 27.

[6] He was lord lieutenant of Ireland from 1672 to 1677. These
mantelpieces were removed probably in the early nineteenth
century.

panum or Gabel at the front is a *Bass-relievo* of *Diana* hunting cut in Portland stone handsomely enough:[1] The middle
Dores being round I did not approve of: but when the Hall
is finishd as his Lordship designs it, being an Oval *Cupol'd*,
together with the other wing, it will be a very noble Palace:
The Library is large, & very nobly furnish'd, & all the books
richly bound & gilded: No *Manuscripts*, except of the *Parliament Rolls*, and Journals, which his Lordship assured me cost
him 500 pounds transcribing & binding: No man has ben
more industrious than this noble Lord in Planting about his
seate, adorn'd with Walkes, Ponds, & other rural Elegancies;
but the soile is stonie, churlish & uneven, nor is the Water
neere enough to the house, though a very swift & cleare
streame run within a flight-shot from[a] it in the vally, which
may fitly be cald cold-brook,[2] it being indeede excessive
Cold, yet producing faire Troutes: In a word, 'tis pitty the
house was not situated to more advantage; but it seemes it
was built just where the old one was, & which I believe he
onely meant to repaire at first, which leads men into irre-
mediable errors, & saves but little: The Land about it is
exceedingly addicted to Wood, but the coldnesse of the place
hinder⟨s⟩ their growth: onely *Black-Cherry* trees[3] prosper
even to Considerable Timber, some being 80 foote long:
The⟨y⟩ make also very handsome avenues: There is a pretty
Oval at the end of a faire Walke, set about with treble rows
of Spanish firr-trees: The Gardens are likewise very rare, &
cannot be otherwise, having so skillfull an Artist to governe
them as *Mr. Cooke*,[4] who is as to the *Mechanic* part not
ignorant in Mathematics, & pretends to *Astrologie*: Here is
an incomparable Collection of the choicest fruits:[b] As for my

---

a Followed by *her* deleted.   b Or *fruite*.

---

[1] For this see Collins Baker, *Lely*,
&c., ii. 133.
[2] This is not traceable as a local
name.
[3] Service trees.
[4] Moses Cook, author of *The
Manner of Raising, Ordering, and
Improving Forrest-Trees*, 1676 (new

issue 1679; new editions 1717,
1724); he was still living in 1715:
Britton, p. 17. Evelyn mentions
him in *Sylva*, 1679, pp. 59, 66, 79,
239–40; and Cook mentions Evelyn
fairly frequently in his book. The
latter is dedicated to Essex.

Lord, he is a sober, wise, judicious & pondering person, not illiterate[1] beyond the rate of most noble-men in this age, very well Versed in our English Histories & Affaires, Industrious, frugal, Methodical, & every way accomplished: His Lady[2] (being sister to the late Earle of *Northumberland*) is a wise [yet somewhat][a] melancholy woman, setting her heart too much upon the little *Lady*[3] her daughter, of whom she is over fond: They have a hopefull sonn, at the *Academie*:[4] My Lord was now not long since come over from his *Lieutenancy* of *Ireland*, where he shew'd his abillities in Administration & government there; as well as prudence in considerably augmenting his Estate, without reproch:[5] He had also ben Ambassador Extraord: in *Denmark*;[6] & in a word, such a person as becomes the sonn of that worthy *Hero* his Father, the late *Lord Capel*, who lost his life for K: *Charles* the first: We spent our time in the mornings in Walking or riding about the Grounds & Contriving; The Afternoones in the Library among the Books; so as I passed my time for 3 or 4 daies with much satisfaction: He was pleased also during this Conversation, to impart to me divers particulars of state relating to the present times; but being no great friend to the D——[7] was now laied aside; his integritie & abillities

---

[a] Interlined.

---

[1] 'Learning is become so easy of access by the late industry of some who have removed the bar language put to the illiterate, and make women pretenders to judge of Alexander's valour and conduct': Mrs. Evelyn to Bohun, January 1673 (Bohn, iv. 34). This use also occurs in the eighteenth century.

[2] Lady Elizabeth Percy, 1636–1718, married Essex (as Lord Capel) 1653; half-sister of Joceline Percy, eleventh earl of Northumberland (above, iii. 481).

[3] Anne, c. 1675–1752; married 1688 Charles Howard, 1669–1738, third earl of Carlisle 1692: G.E.C.

[4] Algernon Capel, 1670–1710; styled Viscount Malden until 1683,

when he succeeded his father as second earl of Essex: G.E.C. In view of the boy's age the academy can scarcely be Foubert's (below, p, 257).

[5] For Essex's conduct as lord lieutenant see *D.N.B.*

[6] He was ambassador extraordinary to Denmark in May–July 1670.

[7] The duke of York. Essex was first commissioner of the treasury from 26 March 1679 to 16 November, when he resigned; a privy councillor from 1672 to 24 Jan. 1681, when his name was struck out; and a member of the first 'triumvirate', which lasted from about May 1679 to about December.

being not so sutable in this Conjuncture: 21 I came back in my Lords Coach with him to *Lond:*

22 I din'd at my L: *Arlingtons,* & thence to the R: *Society,* where was read a letter out of *Germanie,* with some *haire* inclos'd, that had ben taken from a *Corps* long buried, that was totaly covered with it, of an Inch in length, exceeding thick, and somewhat harsh & reddish: It seem'd to grow on the skinn like *Mosse* upon a *Tree,* the rest of the *Cadaver* being totaly consum'd. Then a *Physitian* present, shew'd us a *Tooth,* or rather a *trebble Grinder,* with its roote, which he affirmed to have ben found in the *Testicle* of a *Woman* whom he Discected:

23 I went home, it being St. *Georges* day: 25 our *Viccar* on his former Text, of the necessitie of fortifying our assur-ance of our Justification, by an holy life: (*Se your notes*) *Curate* 12: *Joh:* 21 The *Greekes* asking *Philip*: Sir, we would see *Jesus*: noting their civil request, & Curiositie as Prose-lytes &c: but that this Corporeal sight was of little advan-tage: To see him indeede, was to looke into his Word, his Sacraments &c. 29 Came downe to dine with us the *Coun-tesse* of *Sunderland,* Sir *William Godolphin, Lady Sylvius* & others:

30 To *Lond:* about buisinesse, to meete the *Earle* of *Peter-borow,* E: of *Clarendon,* Mr. *Laur: Hyde* (his brother), Mr. *Newport* to take & adjust this halfe-yeares Accompts of my Lady V: *Countesse Mordaunts* Estate as *Executors,* & to con-sider of the Sale of *Parsons Greene,* &c: being in treaty with Mr. *Loftus*: Then returned home:

May: 1. Was a meeting of the *Foefees* for the Poore of our Parish, our Doctor (according to *Costome*)[a] preach'd on Let your Conversation be without Covetousnesse &c.[1] I this yeare would stand one of the Collectors[b] of their rents; to give Example to others: My *Sonne* was also now added to the *Foefees* &c:

---

[a] Closing bracket supplied.   [b] Followed by *for* deleted.

---

[1] Hebrews xiii. 5. It is the preaching, not the text, that was customary.

There came to visite me this *Afternoone* Sir *Edw: Deering*[1] of *Surrenden* in *Kent*, one of the Lords of the *Treasury*, with his daughter, married to my worthy friend Sir *Rob: Southwell*, Cleark of the Council; now extraordinarie Envoyè to the Duke of *Brandenburg* & other Princes in *Germanie*, as before he had into *Portugal*;[2] being a *sober, wise* & virtuous Gent:

2 Our *Viccar* preach'd on 3: Revel: 20, excellently shewing the greate Condescention of *Christ*, inciting, & waiting our Conversion; The earnestnesse he shews of being admitted into our hearts; That if we continue to refuse, he gos at last away, and leaves us, as unkind, & ungratefull, & that a miserable state: That we should therefore be watchfull, & readily open at his Call. &c: The bl: *Sacrament* follow'd: *Pomeridiano*, our *Curate* on the same Text, as before: 3: Buisinesse with the LL Commiss: of the Treasury cald me to *Lond:* but returned that Evening: 9: our *Viccar* as before: noting, That many righteous might be saved by *Noah's* preaching, especialy during those 40 daies that the *Floud* was in rising to its height, when they saw the likliehod of what *Noah* had told them would certainely come to passe, whilst they formerly derided him for building such a *Vessell*, in a place perhaps so far distant from any Water able to set it a floate. 13: I was at the funerall of old Mr. *Shish*[3] Master[a] *Shipwrite* of the *Kings Yard* here in this Parish, an honest and remarkable man, & his death a publique losse, for his excellent successe in building Ships, (though illiterate altogether) & for the breeding up so many of his Children to be able Artists:[4] I held up the

---

[a] MS. *M^r:*

---

[1] Edward Dering, 1625–84; second baronet 1627; of Surrenden Dering in Pluckley, near Ashford; a commissioner of the treasury 1679–84: G.E.C., *Baronetage*, ii. 6–7.

[2] See above, p. 62. His wife is Elizabeth Dering, *c.* 1649–82; she married him in 1665. He was a clerk of the council from 1665 (or 1664) to 1679; envoy to Portugal 1666–8; envoy extraordinary to Portugal 1668–9; abroad as envoy extra-ordinary to the Elector of Brandenburg, and on an abortive mission to Saxony, from March to November of this year; he was also sent on missions to Spain (1666) and the Spanish Netherlands (1671–2). His character is amply revealed in his letters to Ormond.

[3] For him and his family see above, iii. 506. He had died on 7 May: Drake's Hasted, p. 32.

[4] Here persons skilled in the useful arts.

Pall, with three *knights* who did him that honour, & he was worthy of it: our *Viccar* preaching on a Text of the goodmans choice out of 12 *Isa:* 2. shewing his Trust, and faith in God, & thankfullnesse for his mercies: It was the Costome of this good man, to rise in the night, and to pray kneeling in his owne Cofin; which many yeares he had lying by him: he was borne that famous yeare of the *Gunpowder Plot 1605:*

16 The morning wet stayed us at home: Afternoone *Curate* on his former Text: shewing the miserie of the best of men, if no Resurrection, and happinesse for its undoubted Certainty. &c:

18 To *Lond:* 20ᵃ *Ascention* day, a stranger at St. *Mart:* on 8. *Rom:* 12 how we are all debtors to God &c: There was no *Communion,* as I thought there might have ben: return'd: 23: Mr. *Bohune* on 2: *Rom:* 15, shewing the Effects of natural Conscience, & how even the Heathens themselves did convince & torment them for their seacret wickednesse; how much *Christians* abuse their knowledge, when they sinn against it:

Pomerid: Curate on 11: *Matt:* 28, The blessed effect of faith & repentance, to ease the oppressed sinner:

29 His Majesties Birth & returne; but there was so thin a Congregation, that our Viccar who came prepar'd to Preach, omitted it: so soone do we slight & forget Gods benefits:ᵇ

30 *Whitsonday Viccar* on 2: *Act:* 2. 3. 4. Describing the Mission of the *H: Ghost,* manner, time, place, Effect: &c: *See your notes:* the holy *Sacrament* followed: The excessive raine in the afternoone confin'd me to home, whereᶜ we used the Office of the Day &c:

June 3: To *Lond:* Society: 4: Supped with *La: Sylvius.* 6: White-hall Dr. *Turner*¹ pr: on 3. *Luke* 8. The efficacy of Repentance for the pardon of the greatest sinners: The severity of it in the Primitive times; that the same reasons hold at present: The holy Sacrament follo⟨w⟩ed: I din'd at

---

ᵃ Altered from *21.* ᵇ Followed by *Pomerid: Curate on* deleted.
ᶜ Followed by (*as* deleted.

---

¹ Probably Dr. Francis Turner: above, iii. 630.

my Bro: *Evelyns*: Pomerid: Co: Garden a stranger: 7: *Joh:*
39: That the *Spirit* was so plentifully poured forth at first,
to Convert the *Jewes* & Gentiles, to encourage and animate
the *Apostles* against their Persecutors; its effect eminent in
St. *Peter*, who so little before denied his Master, & was now
become so bold: The Effects of Gods *H: Spirit* to encourage
& up-hold the faithfull:

8 I returned home. 13: *Viccar* on his former; proving the
Godhead of the third person, see your notes: *Pomerid*: Curate
on 2: *Sam:* 12. 7. on the Message of *Nathan* to *David*: That
Gods Ministers are to speake his Message to the greatest King.

14 Came to Dine with us the *Countesse* of *Clarendon*,[1] Dr.
Lloyd[2] *Deane* of *Bangor* [since Bish: of St. *Asaph*.][a] and Dr.
Burnet[3] author of the Hist: of *Reformation*, & my old friend
Mr. *Henshaw*. After dinner we all went to see the Observatory
& Mr. *Flamsted*; where he shewed us divers rare Instruments,
especialy, the greate *Quadrant*:[4]

20 Our *Viccar* pr: on his former Text in the *Apocalypse*:
See your notes: *Curat* as above:

24 To *Lond:* R: Society, a Council summon'd to meete at
the presidents next day, which [25][b] we did; & made an order,
that the next experiments to be examin'd, should be my L:
Verulams, & an account to be given of them to the publique
from yeare to yeare 'til we had gon through them:[5]

---

[a] Marginal note.   [b] Marginal date.

[1] Above, p. 2, &c.
[2] The apocalyptic. He was consecrated bishop of St. Asaph on
3 October of this year (warrant for
congé d'élire 1 July).
[3] Gilbert Burnet: above, p. 47,
&c. He was created D.D. of Lambeth on 29 September of this year:
Gentleman's magazine, 1864, i. 636;
for his being called 'Dr. Burnet' at
an earlier date see above. The first
part of *The History of the Reformation of the Church of England* had
been published in 1679 (licensed
23 May); the second part followed
in 1681; the third not until 1714.

[4] For Greenwich Observatory
and Flamsteed see above, p. 98. The
notice is in part premature: the large
quadrant was constructed in 1681–3:
F. Baily, *An account of the Revd. John
Flamsteed*, 1835, pp. 51–2, 54.
[5] This meeting is not mentioned
in Birch. On 24 June Williamson,
the president, had given the Society
a copy of Bacon's *Sylva Sylvarum*;
an excerpt was read and discussed
on 8 July; it is not mentioned again
by name. The *Philosophical Transactions*, the Society's publication,
had stopped in 1678 (vol. xii, no.
142); *Philosophical Collections*, no.

26 I din'd with Mr. *Pepyss* at my La: *Mordaunts,*¹ where was Sir W: Portman² &c: thence home. 27 our *Viccar* absent, Chap: of my Lo: *Berkeleys*³ on 127: *Psal: 2.* That all our care & fore-cast comes to nothing, with Gods blessing & assistance:

July: 4 our *Viccar* on: 1: *Sam:* 3: 8.⁴ shewing after what sort God dos usualy chastize the faults of men in their posterity,ᵃ & the way to prevent it, Repentance, & resignation: See your *notes*: The holy Com: followed: *Pomerid*: *Curate* went on with his parable, The benefit of honest⟨l⟩y accknowledging our fault; by which *David* obtained a speedy remission: See *Notes*:

6 To *Lond:* 8. To our *Society* on the first Exp: of my L: *Bacon*: 9 home:

11 A stranger on 9: *Mar:* 43. 44. The advantage of parting with the greatest pleasure to secure Eternal life: He spake of the Death they put Malefactors to in *Egypt*,⁵ the cutting them asunder, & ⟨setting⟩ᵇ the upper halfe of the body on a hot plate: the suffering mans paine expressed in weeping teares, & gnashing of teeth, which he applyed to the paine of Hell-fire. *Pomerid*: Mr. *Jackson*⁶ Minister of *Lee* on: 1. *Sam:* 3. 18. The Text our *Viccar* preached on the Weeke before; That the way to aleviate Gods anger in Chastising, is humble

---

ᵃ Altered from *prosperity*; spelling doubtful.　　ᵇ MS. *set thing*.

1, had appeared in 1679; nos. 2 and 3 were published in 1681 and nos. 4–7 in 1682; they do not differ in character from the *Philosophical Transactions*. The latter was revived in 1683 and still continues.
¹ Elizabeth, *c.* 1645–87, daughter of Nicholas Johnson of London and niece of Sir William Turner, lord mayor 1668–9; married first, 1663, Sir Charles Mordaunt, bart., d. 1665; secondly Francis Godolphin of Coulston, Wilts.: G.E.C., *Baronetage*, i. 62. Pepys had long been acquainted with her: *Diary*, 11 Dec. 1666 (where he gives her maiden name wrong), 1 Feb., 9 March 1669.
² William Portman, *c.* 1644–90; sixth baronet 1645; K.B. 1661;

F.R.S. 1664: *D.N.B.*; *C.J.*, iv. 276; v. 592.
³ The earl (above, iii. 166, &c.). His chaplain is identifiable as John Rogers: below, p. 248 n. The text may be taken either from the Bible or from the Prayer Book; in the latter case 'with' is probably a slip for 'without'.
⁴ A slip for 1 Samuel iii. 18: see notice for 11 July.
⁵ Sandys states that a similar form of capital punishment had formerly been in use in Turkey: pp. 62–3.
⁶ John Jackson, rector of Lee 1672–1701: Drake's Hasted, p. 229. Not further identifiable. Further notices below.

submission under his hand: The excessive heate made me extreame sleepy:

13 To *Lond:* about severall afaires: 18: At St. *James's Synax*: At *White-hall* preached Mr. *Crispin*[1] (the *Confessor*, & also one of the *Quire*) on: 13: *Luke* 24; very excellently well on the greate difficulty of entering the straite gate, our duty of striving, & infinite importance of continual dilligence: *Pomerid*: Dr. *Sprat* at St. *Margarites* on: 1. *Sam:* 15. 22. of the Preference of Obedience to all outward Ceremonies, admirably handled:

24 Sir *Will: Godolphin* lending me his six-horses, I went with my Wife & Daughter[a][2] to *Winsore*, to see that stately Court, now neere finished:[3] there was now erected in the Court, the *King* on Horseback lately cast in Coper, & set upon a rich Piedestal of white Marble, the worke of Mr. *Gibbons* &c:[4] at the expense of *Toby Rustat*,[5] a *Page* of the *Back stayres*, who by his wonderfull frugality had arived to a greate Estate in Mony, & did many works of Charity; as well as this of gratitude to his Master; which cost him 1000 pounds: he is a very simple, ignorant, but honest & loyal creature: We all dined at the *Countesse* of *Sunderlands*,[6] afterwards to see

---

[a] Or *Daughters*.

[1] Stephen Crespion, *c.* 1649–1711; a gentleman of the chapel royal 1673; confessor to the royal household 1675 (for the duties see Chamberlayne); prebendary of Bristol 1683: (*Westminster Abbey registers*), p. 273.

[2] Evidently Mary, now aged fourteen.

[3] This presumably refers to the rebuilding and reconstruction of the state apartments (the Star Building); the principal parts remaining to be finished were St. George's Hall and the king's chapel; most of the windows in the Upper Ward were remodelled in this period: Hope, *Windsor Castle*, i. 312–35.

[4] The statue was cast by Josias

Jbach, who is not otherwise known; the sculptor was a German; his name is not known. The pedestal did not form part of Rustat's gift; it has been reconstructed but the reliefs by Gibbons still ornament it; and the whole monument has been moved to a different position in the court: Hope, ii. 551–2, 555; Wren, in Caröe, '*Tom Tower*', p. 33.

[5] Tobias Rustat, *c.* 1606–94; yeoman of the robes 1660–85: *D.N.B.* He is not mentioned elsewhere as a page of the backstairs, and may have held the post under Charles I.

[6] The king resided at Windsor from 1 May to 9 September; the court was there at least during the later part of his stay: *London Gazette*, 3 May, 9 Sept.

Signor *Virios* garden; thence to *Eaton* Coll to salute the
Provost,[1] & heard a Latine Speech of one of the *Alumni* (it
being at the Election)[2] were invited to supper, but tooke our
leaves, and got to *Lond:* that night in good time: 25 A stranger
at *W:Hall* on 9: *Eccl:* 11. on the vicissitude of earthly things;
& that what is called chance by *Solomon*, is onely so in respect
of our narrow reach, whilst all is by the Providence of God:
　[a]26[3] my most noble & illustrious friend, the *Earle of Ossorie*
espying me this morning after sermon,[4] in the Privy-Gallerie,
calling to me, told me he was now going his journey;[b] (meaning to *Tangier*, whither he was designed Governor, & Generall
of the *Forces*,[5] to regaine the losses we had lately suffer'd[c]
from the *Moores*, when *Inchequeene* was *Governor*):[6] I asked
his *Lordship* if he would not call at my house (as he allways
did when ever he went out of *England* on any exploit) I feare
I shall not said his *Lordship*, for I foresee I must embarque
at Portsmouth; wherefore I pray, let you & I dine together
to day, I am quite alone, and have something to impart to
you: I am not well, & have taken a little Physick this morning; & so shall be private, & I desire your Company: Being
retird to his Lodgings[7] & sat downe on the Couch, he sent to
his *secretary*[8] for the Copy of a Letter, which he had written

---

a Hand in margin here.　　　　b Followed by *but says he* deleted.
c Altered from ⟨*su*⟩*stain'd*; spelling doubtful.

---

[1] Allestree.
[2] The election of scholars to
King's College, Cambridge.
[3] The date of this notice is a week
out: the king supped at Fishmon-
gers' Hall on 20 July: below, p. 210 n.
Other notices (*Cal. S.P., Dom.,
1679–80*, p. 568; *Hist. MSS. Comm.,
Ormonde MSS.*, new ser., v. 352)
confirm this as the approximate
date of the beginning of the illness.
[4] Presumably a slip for after
prayers.
[5] He was appointed governor of
Tangier on 23 June: *Cal. S.P.,
Dom., 1679–80*, p. 527.
[6] William O'Brien, *c.* 1640–92;
second earl of Inchiquin (Ireland),

1674: *D.N.B.* (for his father see
above, iii. 26). He had been appointed governor of Tangier in
1675 and proved negligent; the
Moors became united in 1676 and
steady hostilities began in 1678; a
regular siege of Tangier began on
25 March of this year: Routh,
Tangier, pp. 146–69. Charles refused to allow Inchiquin to kiss his
hand on his return in July: *Hist.
MSS. Comm., Ormonde MSS.*, new
ser., v. 346.
[7] Ossory presumably occupied
Ormond's lodgings: above, iii. 284.
[8] Ossory's usual secretary was
Richard Mulys: letters, &c., in
Ormonde MSS.

to my Lo: *Sunderland* (secretary of state) wishing me to reade
it; and it was to take notice, how ill he resented it, That he
should tell the *King* before my L: *Ossories* face, That *Tangier*
was not to be kept, but would certainly be lost; & yet added,
that twas fit, my L: *Ossorie* should be sent, that they might
give some account of it to the world, meaning (as supposed,)
the next *Parliament*, when all such miscarriages would probably be examin'd,[1] This my L: O: tooke very ill of my L:
S. & not kindly of his *Majestie*, who resolving[a] to send him
with an incompetent force, seem'd (as his *Lordship* tooke it)
to be willing to cast him away upon not onely an hazardous
Adventure, but, in most mens opinions[b] Impossible;[b] seing
there was not to be above 3 or 400 horse & 4000 foote, for
the *Garison* & all, both to defend the Towne, forme a Camp,
repulse the Enemie, & fortifie what ground they should get
in:[2] This touch'd my Lord[c] deepely, that he should be so
little consider'd, as to put him on a[d] buisinesse, in which he
should probably, not onely loose his reputation, but be
charg'd with all the miscarriages & ill successe; where as at
the first they promis'd him 6000 *foote* & 600 *horse effective*: My
Lord, being an exceeding brave & valiant person, & that had
so approv'd himselfe in divers signal batailes, both at Sea, &
Land; so beloved, so esteem'd by the people, as one they
depended on upon all occasions worthy such a Captaine;
looked on this as too greate an indifference in his Majestie
after all his services (& the merits[e] of his father the Duke of
Ormond) & a designe of some who envied his Virtue; And[f] it[f]
certainly, tooke so deepe roote in his mind, that he who was
the most voide of feare in the world (and assur'd me he would

---

[a] Substituted for *promising*; perhaps altered from *resolved*.   [b-b] Or
opinion, Impossible.   [c] Followed by *so* deleted.   [d] Altered from
an.   [e] Or *merite.*   [f-f] Substituted for *this*, which had already been
substituted for *as.*

---

[1] Ossory's letter to Sunderland is
not available. A letter from him to
Ormond describes a conversation
between him, the king, and Sunderland, on 5 July, probably the same
as that here noticed : *Ormonde MSS.*,
new ser., v. 344.

[2] The total forces were to be 600
horse and 4,080 foot; the order was
given on 30 June: Routh, *Tangier*,
p. 317 n.

go to *Tangier* with ten men, if his Majestie Commanded him)
could not beare up against this unkindnesse: Having dis-
burdned himselfe of this to me after dinner, he went with his
Majestie to The *Sherifs*, at a greate supper in Fishmongres
Hall;¹ but my Lord, finding himselfe ill, tooke his leave
immediately of his Majestie & came back to his Lodging,
without staying at all at the *Sherifs*: Not resting well this
night, he was perswaded to remove to *Arlington* house for
better accommodation; where being no longer able to sustaine
his indisposition, it manifestly turn'd to a *Malignant* feavor;
which increasing to violence, after all that six of the most
able *Physitians* could do to save him, beginning now and then
to be somewhat delirious, at other times with intervalls of
better sense: Dr. *LLoyd*, (now Bish: of St. *Asaph*) adminis-
tring then to him the holy *Sacrament*,² (ofᵃ which I also
participated) he died the friday after, about 7 in the Evening,
being the 30th of *July*, to the universal griefe of all that either
knew, or ever heard of his greate worth: nor had any a greater
losse than my selfe, he being so much my friend; Oft would
he say I was the oldest acquaintance he had in England
(when,ᵇ his Father was in Ireland) it being now of above 30
yeares, contracted abroad, when he rid at the *Academie* in
Paris, & that we were seldome asunder:³ Surely his Majestie
never lost a worthier Subject; nor Father, a better, & more
dutifull sonn, a loving, goodnatured, generous and perfectly
obliging friend, & one who had don innumerable kindnesses
to severall persons, before they so much as kn⟨e⟩w it; nor
advanc'd he any but such as were worthy; None more brave,
more modest, none more humble, sober, & every way virtuous: Ô unhapy *England*! in this illustrious persons losse:
Universal was the Mourning for him, the Elogies on him, nor
can I sufficiently deplore him: I staied night & day by his
bed-side to his last gasp to close his deare Eyes: ô sad Father,
Mother, Wife & Children! What shall I add? he deserved all

ᵃ Opening bracket supplied.   ᵇ Followed by *as now* deleted.

¹ This supper took place on 20
July: *London Gazette*, 22 July.
² Ossory received the sacrament
on 29 July: *Ormonde MSS.*, new
ser., v. 361.
³ See above, iii. 2, &c.

that a sincere friend, a brave Souldier, a Virtuous Courtier,
a Loyal Subject,[a] an honest man, a bountifull Master, & good
Christian could merit of his Prince & Country:[1] One thing
more let me note, That he often expressed to me, the abhor-
rance he had,[b] of that base & unworthy action, which he was
put upon, of Engaging the *Smyrna* fleete in time of Peace,[c][2]
which, though he behaved himselfe like a greate Captaine;
yet he told me[d] was the onely blot of his life, & troubled
him Exceedingly: for though he was commanded, & niver
examin'd it farther,[e] when he was so: yet allways spake of
it with regret, & detestation:

30 I went home very sad: & then write his *Countesse*[f][3] a
letter giving her an Account of what pass'd in his sicknesse,
she being then at her Daughters the Countesse of *Derby*, at
his seate almost 200 miles off:

Aug: 1 A *stranger* on 23: *Psal:* 4, of the use of Afflictions:
The holy Sacrament follow'd: *Curate* on 30: *Pro:* 8: indifferently: 5 Sir Jo: *Stonehouse*, his *Lady*, and other Company
came from *Lond.* to dine with us. 8 our *Curate* as before, with
the usual *Common places*: *Pomerid*: Mr. *Jackson*[4] on 11.
Eccles: 9. That *Solomon* spake by *Ironie*; & describ'd the
dreadfullnesse of the last Judgement:

15 *Viccar* on 1. *Reg:* 18. 21, the danger of Inconstancy in
R⟨e⟩ligion:

17 Went to *Bromely* to visit the Bish: of *Rochest⟨e⟩r* wher
I met Dr. *Alestrie* provost of Eaton, who having lately
received a fall, appeared to me, as if he would not[g] overcome,
the indis⟨pos⟩ition it put him into:[5]

---

a Followed by *&* deleted.   b Followed by ⟨*& repentance* deleted.
c Followed by *in* deleted.   d Followed by *it* deleted.   e Followed by
than deleted.   f Altered from *Council*.   g Followed by *lo-* deleted.

---

[1] The letters of condolence in *Ormonde MSS.*, new ser. v. 357–81, are sufficient evidence of the general regard for Ossory. Elegies were published by Thomas Flatman (*D.N.B.*) and one or two other writers.

[2] See above, iii. 605–6.

[3] Lady Ossory (above, p. 102)

was in Ireland at this time: *Ormonde MSS.*, pp. 345, 371, 385. Lady Derby (above, p. 97) was presumably at her husband's seat at Knowsley, Lancs.

[4] Presumably the rector of Lee: above, p. 206.

[5] He died of dropsy on 28 Jan. 1681.

22 Our Viccar inlarg'd somewhat his former discourse: A⟨f⟩ternoone a stranger on 8: *Rom:* 13: Shewing the greate mistake of many concerning the sinns of the flesh, as imagining it to signifie, acts of Uncleanesse onely, whereas it comprehended all inordinate Affections to any Earthly thing whatsoever &c: see your notes:

24 Came Mr. ⟨*Boscauen*⟩[a] & his Lady, & my sweete Child Godolphin, to dine with us:

27 To *Lond:* return'd that Evening: 29 *Viccar* as before, against the sinn of Scandal, &c: see your notes: 30: Lond:[b] I went to visite a French Stranger, one Monsieur *Jardine*[1] [since Knighted by his Majestie & made Denison of *England*][c] who having ben thrice at the *East Indias, Persia* & other remote Countries, came hither in our returne ships from those parts;[2] and it being reported he was a very curious man, & knowing, I was desir'd by the *Ro: Society*[d] in their name, to salute him, & to let him know how glad they should be to receive him, if he pleased to do them that honour: &c.[3] There were appointed to accompanie me Sir *Jo: Hoskins*[4] & Sir *Chr: Wren* &c. We found him at his lodging, in his Eastern habite, a very handsom person, extreamely affable, not inclin'd to talke Wonders, but exceedingly modest, & a[e] well bred man: It seemes he traveld in search of *Jewels*, & was

---

[a] MS. *Roscauen.*   [b] Interlined above *pr:*?   [c] Marginal note.
[d] Followed by *to* deleted.   [e] Altered from *w.*

---

[1] John Chardin, 1643–1712; knighted 1681; endenizened 1682; F.R.S. 1682; naturalized 1685; the traveller: *D.N.B.*; W. A. Shaw, ed., *Letters of denization*, (&c.), *1603–1700* (Huguenot Soc., vol. xviii, 1911), pp. 132, 171; for his works see his *Voyages*, ed. Langlès, 1811 (the edition here cited), preface, &c.; *Travels in Persia*, ed. Penzer, 1927, preface; below, 23 Feb. 1684.

[2] Chardin made only two journeys to the East; on the second he left Persia in 1677 and was at Surat in 1678; he returned to Europe by the Cape: *Voyages*, vol. i, pp. xv,

xxviii; ix. 264; Leti, *Del teatro brittanico*, ii. 789.

[3] There is perhaps an allusion to Chardin in the society's minutes for 8 July: Birch, iv. 44. There is no other notice relating to him and the date of the present passage may be wrong. The society held no ordinary meetings after 29 July until 4 November.

[4] John Hoskins, 1634–1705; knighted 1676; succeeded as second baronet on 10 February of this year; member of the Philosophical Society 4 Dec. 1661; F.R.S. (Original Fellow); president 1682–3: *D.N.B.*

become extreamely rich: He spake *Latine,* understood the
Greeke, Arabic'& Persian by 11 yeares Conversation in those
Parts, yet seem'd he not to be above 36 years of age: After
the usual Civilities, we told him, we much desired an account
of the extraordinary things he must have seene; having (as
we understood) trav⟨e⟩ld over land, those places, where few,
if any *northern Europeans* used to go, as about the Black &
Caspian Sea, *Mingrelia,*[1] *Bagdat, Ninive,* ⟨*Persepolis*⟩[a] &c:
He told us the things most worthy of our sight, would be, the
draughts he had caused to be made of some noble ruines &c:
for that (besides his little talent that way) he had carried two
very good Painters along with him, to draw Landskips,
Measure, and designe the remainders of the *Palace* which
Alexander burnt in his frolique at *Persepolis,* with divers
Temples, Columns, Relievos, & statues, yet extant, which he
affirm'd were Sculptures far exceeding, any thing he had
observ'd either at *Rome,* [Greece][b] or any other part of the
World, where Magnificence was in estimation:[2] That there
was there an Inscription, of Letters not intelligible, though
exceedingly intire; but was extreamely sorry he could not
gratifie the Curiosity of the *Society,* at present, his things,
not being yet out of the ship; but would take the first opportunity to waite on us with them, at his returne from Paris,
whither he was hastning the very next morning, but with
intention, to be suddenly back againe, & stay longer in our
Country, the persecution in *France*[c] not suffering *Protestants,*
& such he was, to be quiet:[3] so we failed of seeing his Papers;
but it was told us by others, that he durst indeede not open
or shew them, 'til he had first shew'd them to the French
King; though of this he himselfe said notthing: On farther

---

[a] MS. *Persepalis.*   [b] Interlined.   [c] Followed by *of y-* deleted.

---

[1] The ancient Colchis, part of the
modern Georgia.

[2] For Chardin's account of Persepolis see *Voyages,* viii. 242–410.
One of his artists was unsatisfactory: viii. 242; the other was
Guillaume Joseph Grelot, who pro-

vided all the drawings: vol. i, p.
xliii and note; for Grelot see
Thieme, *Lexikon.*
[3] For the present position of the
Huguenots see Lavisse, *Hist. de
France,* VII. ii. 57–70. The dragonnades had already begun.

discourse, he told us that *Nineveh* was a vast Citty, all now
buried in her ruines, and the Inhabitants building on the
subterranean Vaults, which were (as appeared) the first
stories of the old Cittie; That there were frequently ⟨found⟩,[a]
huge Vasas of fine Earth, *Columns*, & other Antiquities &c:[1]
That the straw which the Egyptian *Pharoah* so tyrannicaly
requir'd of the *Israelites*, was not to burne, or Cover their
rowes of brick, as we use; but being chopp'd small, to mingle
with the *Clay*, which drying in the Sunn (for they bake not
in the furnaces)[b] would else cleave asunder: That in *Persia*
are yet a race of *Igniculi*,[2] that still Worship the Sunn, & the
fire as Gods: That the Women of *Georgia* & *Mingrelia* were
Universaly, & without any compare, the most beautifull
Creatures for shape, features, & figure in the whole world,
& that therefore The *Grand Signor*, & *Bashaws* &c had thence
most of their Wives & Concubines:[3] That there had within
these 100 yeares ben *Amazons* amongst them (that is) a sort
or race of Valiant Women, given to Warr:[4] That *Persia* was
infinitely fertile.[5] He spake also of Japon, & China,[6] & of
the many greate errours of our late Geographers &c: as we
suggested occasion to discourse; & so we tooke our leaves, &
made report to our *Society*: & I returned home:

　　September 2: I went to *Lond:* because of an Opportunity I
had of his Majesties being yet at *Winsor*,[7] to see his private
Library at *Whitehall*,[8] which I now did at my full Ease; and

---

[a] MS. *faund*.　　　[b] Followed by *the* deleted.

---

[1] Chardin does not mention
Nineveh in his *Voyages*.

[2] The word *igniculi* means
sparks; Chardin uses the word
ignicoles. For his description of the
Guèbres (*gabrs*), the Persian Zoroas-
trians, see *Voyages*, viii. 355–82.

[3] For the beauty of the Min-
grelian women see *Voyages*, i. 169–
70; of the Georgian, ii. 40. Chardin
does not mention the Turks taking
them as wives.

[4] Chardin gives some reports of
a nation of Amazons supposed to
exist in his time to the north of the

Caucasus: *Voyages*, ii. 32–6.

[5] Chardin declares that the soil
is fertile, but barren owing to lack
of moisture: *Voyages*, iii. 268, 288–
93.

[6] Chardin prints some documents
relating to the Europeans and
Japan: *Voyages*, ix. 268–323; he
appears not to have visited the
Far East.

[7] The king stayed at Windsor
until 9 September: above, p. 207 n.

[8] There appears to have been a
library at Whitehall from when it
became a royal palace; it was sepa-

went with expectation of finding some Curiosities: But tho
there were about a thousand Volumes, there were few of any
greate importance, or which I had not perused before; they
consisting chiefely of such books as had from time to time
ben dedicated, or presented him: Few Histories, some
Traveles, & french bookes, Aboundance of *Mapps* & Sea-
⟨Charts⟩:[a] Entertainements, & Pomps; buildings, & Pieces
relating to the Navy: some *Mathematical* Instruments &c:
But what was most rare were 3 or 4 Romish *Breviaries* with
a greate deale of *Miniature* & Monkish Painting & Gilding;
one of which is most exquisitely don, both as to the figures,
Grotescs & Compartiments, to the uttmost of that curious art:[1]
There's another in which I find written by the hand of *Henry*
the 7th, his giving it to his deare Daughter *Margarite*, afterwards *Queene* of *Scots* ([Greate][b] mother of our K. *James*, &
greate greate Grandmother to the successive Kings, uniting
the two Kingdomes) in which he desires her to pray for his
soule, subscribing his Name at length:[2] There is also the
Processe of the Philosophe⟨r⟩s greate *Elixir*, represented in
divers pieces of incomparable miniature; but the Discourse
is in high-Dut⟨c⟩h & a MSS: Also another MS. in quarto of
above 300 yeares old in *French*, being an *Institution* of *Physic*,
& in the *Botanical* part, the Plants are curiously painted in

---

[a] MS. *Chards*.   [b] Interlined.

---

rate from the main royal library at
St. James's Palace, but at this time
the one librarian had charge of
both collections, and transference
of books may have occurred. The
greater part of the present collection was destroyed in the White-
hall fire of 1698: B.M., *Catalogue of
Western MSS. in the old Royal and
King's Collections*, by Warner and
Gilson, vol. i, introd., especially pp.
xxv–xxvi, where this passage is discussed. The room was probably in
the building between the Privy
Stairs and the old Volary Garden,
a short distance to the south:
L.C.C., *Survey of London*, xiii.
74–6.

[1] Warner and Gilson suggest that
this may be Queen Mary's Psalter,
now in the British Museum, Royal
MS. 2 B vii: p. xxv n.

[2] Warner and Gilson suggest that
this is a manuscript now belonging
to the duke of Devonshire: ibid.
Henry's daughter is Margaret,
1489–1541; married first, 1503,
James IV of Scotland, who was
killed at Flodden in 1513; secondly,
1514, Archibald Douglas, sixth earl
of Angus (Scotland), 1489?–1557.
She was great-grandmother of
James VI and I, by her first marriage on his mother's, by her second
on his father's side.

Miniature: There is likewise a *Folio Manu-script* of a good thicknesse, being the severall exercises, as *Theames, Orationes, Translations* &c: of K. *Edward* the *sixt*, all written[a] & subscrib'd by his owne hand, & with his name very legibly, & divers of the Greeke, interlin'd, & corrected, after the manner of Schole-boys exercises, & that exceedingly well & proper, with some Epistles to his *Præceptor* &c,[1] which shews that Young Prince to have ben extraordinarily advanc'd in learning, & as *Cardan*[2] that greate Wit &c (who had ben in Englan'd) affirmed, stupendiously knowing for his age: There is likewise his Journal,[3] no lesse testif⟨y⟩ing his earely ripenesse & care about the affaires of state: [Dr. *Burnet* has transcribd many remarks out of this in his *Hist* of the *Reformation*.][b]

There are besides many other pompous Volumes, some emboss'd with Gold, & Intaglios on *Achats, Medailes* &c: I spent 3 or 4 intire daies locked up, & alone amongst these bookes &c: There is in the rest of the Private Lodgings contiguous to this,[4] divers of the best pictures of the greate *Masters, Raphael, Titian* &c (& in my esteeme) above all the *Noli me tangere* of our *B: Saviour* to M: *Magdalen*, after his *Resurrection*, of *Hans Holbeins*,[5] than which, in my life,

---

a Followed by *with* deleted. b Marginal note.

---

[1] Several of Edward's exercise-books survive. Warner and Gilson note a similar manuscript, B.M., Add. MS. 4724, but the identification has not been established.

[2] Girolamo Cardano (Cardan), 1501–76, doctor, philosopher, mathematician, &c.: *Nouvelle biog. gén.* His account of Edward VI appears in his 'Geniturarum exempla' appended to his commentary on Ptolemy's *Quadripartitum* (ed. 1554, pp. 403–13); the principal passages are reprinted and translated by Burnet in his *History of the Reformation*, vol. ii, 1681, [ii]. 89–90; [i]. 2–3.

[3] Edward VI's journal was in the Cotton Library, as MS. Nero C. x,

by 1654, but was in the King's Library when shown to Bishop Montague before 1616. It may have been lent for exhibition at Whitehall; but equally the notice may be a wrong addition to Evelyn's original notes. The journal is now in the British Museum: Warner and Gilson, p. xxv n. Burnet printed it, with some other passages from the same volume, and some other writings of Edward VI, in *Hist. of the Reformation*, ii. [ii]. 3–88.

[4] The king's lodgings, to the south of the Privy Stairs.

[5] The picture now at Hampton Court.

I never saw so much reverence & kind of Heavenly astonishment, expressed in Picture: There are also divers Curious *Clocks, Watches & Penduls* of exquisite work, and other Curiosities: An antient Woman, who made these lodgings Cleane, & had all the Keyes, let me in at pleasure, for a small reward, by the meanes of a friend:

5 I found our late affected fantastical *Curate* Mr. Al——[1] preaching in the Chapel at *W:hall* on 119 Psal: 175 ver: that mens soules were certainely immortal, distinct from the animal life &c: It was not ⟨possible⟩[a] to heare him without astonishment at his Confidence & formalitie: He was a boy of our *Parish*, that from a poore grammar schole, turn'd Preacher; & at last got the degree of Batchelor of Art, by a Mandamus, at *Cambridge*, where he had ben 2 or 3 daies, in his whole life: when he came back, that people might take notice of his degree, he ware his lamb-skin not onely two[b] whole Sundays in the Church, but[c] going all over the Towne, and Every streete, with a wonderfull traine of boys & girles running after him, (as they do when the Beares are led about) came to give me a visite in his formalities, at which I could not ⟨possibly⟩[d] containe my Countenance: This yet I must say of Mr. A. . . . that he has together with a vast stock of Confidence, a prodigious Memorie, & strong lungs, & some are taken with his Preachment, that know not the man out of the Pulpet: In a word he is a most singular person, & exceedingly conceited of his abillities: The blessed Sacrament follow'd: *Pomerid*: Co: *Garden* the Lecturer, on. 1. Joh: 2. 23.[2] an heavenly discourse concerning the love we owe our brethren:

6 I din'd with Sir *St: Fox*,[3] now one of the Lords Commis-

---

[a] MS. *possibly*. *came to give* deleted.   [b] Substituted for *one* or *ane*.   [c] Followed by [d] MS. *possible*.

---

[1] Identifiable as Samuel Alderson, d. 1696; described as B.A. of Emmanuel when ordained deacon 1668; M.A. by royal letters 1673; rector of St. James, Garlickhithe, 1685–96: Venn; *Cal. S.P., Dom., 1672–3*, p. 459.

[2] Apparently a slip for 1 John iii. 23.

[3] The principal authority for Fox's life is the *Memoirs*, 1717 (apparently by William Pittis; later reprints); Evelyn adds some new circumstances.

sioners of the *Treasury*: This Gent: came first a poore boy
from the Quire of Salisbury, then was taken notice of by
Bish: *Duppa*,[1] & afterwards waited on my Lord Percy[2] (bro:
to *Algernon* E: of Northumberland) who procured for him an
inferior place amongst the Clearks of the *Kitchin* & *Greene-
Cloth* side: Where he was found so humble, dilligent, industrious, & prudently to behave himselfe, that his Majestie
being in Exile, & Mr. Fox waiting, both the *King* & Lords
about him, frequently Employed him about their affaires,
trusted him both with receiving and paying the little mony,
they had:[3] Returning with his *Majestie* into England after
greate Wants, & greate sufferings: his Majestie[a] . . . so honest
& industrious, & withall so capable & ready; that being
advanced, from Cl: of the *Kitchin* to that of the Greene-
Cloth &c:[4] he procured to be pay-Master to the Whole Army,[5]
& by his dexterity, & punctual dealing ⟨obtained⟩ such credit
amongst the Banquers, that he was in short time, able to
borrow vast summs of them, upon any exigence; The con-
tinud[b] Turning thus of mony, & the souldiers moderate
allowance to him, for his keeping touch[6] with them, did so

---

[a] End of page; break in construction.   [b] Or *continual*.

---

[1] Brian Duppa, 1589–1662; bishop of Chichester 1638; of Salisbury 1641; of Winchester 1660:
D.N.B. Fox was born in 1627.
[2] Henry Percy, *c.* 1604–59;
created Baron Percy of Alnwick
1643: *D.N.B.*
[3] Percy was appointed chamberlain of the household in 1653; when
Charles II left Paris in 1654 Fox,
who had been 'bred under' his
'severe discipline', was given charge
of the expenditure of the household:
Clarendon, *Hist.*, bk. xiv, § 89,
where there is a short character of
Fox.
[4] Fox was never apparently clerk
of the kitchen; he was appointed
younger clerk comptroller in 1660;
younger clerk of the green cloth
1661; elder clerk of the green cloth

c. 1673; he retained the latter office
until *c.* 1688: Firebrace, *Honest
Harry*, pp. 210–11; notices in
Chamberlayne.
[5] Fox was paymaster of the forces
from 1660 to 1676 (the office appears
to have been regularized in this
period).
[6] The phrase usually meant to
keep faith, to act faithfully: *O.E.D.*
Fox described his work to Pepys:
'They give him 12*d.* per pound
quite through the Army, with condition to be paid weekly. This he
undertakes upon his own private
credit, and to be paid by the King
at the end of every four months. If
the King pay him not at the end of
the four months, then, for all the
time he stays longer, my Lord
Treasurer, by agreement, allows

inrich him; that he is believed to be worth at the least
200000 pounds honestly ⟨gotten⟩,[a] & unenvied, which is
next to Miracle, & that with all this he still continues as
humble, & ready to do a Courtesie, as ever he was; nay he is
generous, & lives very honorably, of a sweete nature, well
spoken, & well bred, & so very highly in his Majesties
Esteeme, & usefull, that being long-since made a Knight,[1]
he is also advanc'd to be one of the Lords[b] Commissioners[b]
of the *Treasury*:[2] & has the reversion of the Coferers place
after Harry Brounckar:[3] He has married his Eldest Daughter[4]
to my Lord Cornwallis, & gave her 12000 pounds & restored
that intangled family besides: Match'd his Eldest Sonn[5] to
Mrs. *Trallop* who brings with her (besides a greate summ)
neere, if not altogether 2000 pounds per annum: Sir Stephens
Lady[6] (an excellent Woman) is sister to Mr. *Whittle* one of the
Kings Chirurgions: In a word, never was man more fortunate
than Sir Stephen; & with all this he is an handsom person,
Vertuous & very religious, & for whom I have an extraordinary esteeme:

7 I visited my L: *Major*: & went home:

9 Solemnly remembred a deare deceased Friend, whose
memory is never by me to be forgotten on this day:

11 I went with my *Wife* to see my deare *Bro:* at *Wotton.*

---

[a] MS. *gooten.*   [b–b] MS. *Lords of Commissioners; Commissioners*
altered from *the.*

---

him eight per cent. per annum for
the forbearance': *Diary,* 16 Jan.
1667; see also *Papers illustrative of
the origin and early hist. of the Royal
Hospital at Chelsea,* ed. G. Hutt,
1872, p. 127.

[1] In 1665.

[2] See above, p. 193.

[3] Brouncker was cofferer (also a
member of the Board of Green
Cloth) from 1679 to 1685: *Cal. S.P.,
Dom., 1679–80,* p. 307; *Cal. Treasury
Books.*

[4] Elizabeth, *c.* 1655–81; married
1673 Charles Cornwallis, 1655–98,
third Baron Cornwallis of Eye

1673 (he afterwards married the
widowed duchess of Buccleugh:
above, p. 6 n.): G.E.C.

[5] Charles Fox, 1659–1713; pay-
master-general 1682–5; M.P. for
Eye 1679; for Cricklade 1685, 1689–
98; for Salisbury 1698–1700, 1701–
13; married 1679 Elizabeth, d.
1704, daughter of Sir William
Trollop, bart.: Collins's *Peerage,* ed.
Brydges, iv. 537–8; &c.

[6] Above, p. 170. Her brother,
Sackvile Whittle, appears to have
been married to a niece of Sir
Stephen: ibid., iv. 530.

12: one Mr. *Wye*[1] the *Curat* of *Abinger* preach'd[a] at[a] Wotton, on 1. Sam: 3. 18. Exhorting to submissivenesse to the will of God in all distresses, we being not onely his Creatures, but of right his Vassals: *Pomerid*: were Prayers at my Brothers:

13 My Lord the Earle of *Chesterfield* now *Justice in Iyre*;[2] sent me a fat Buck out of *New-Park*,[3] which I presented to my Bro: & we eate among severall good friends & gent: of the neighbourhood:

17 I returned home: 19 *Viccar* on: 4: *Phil:* 11. shewing the Duty, Ease & benefit of Contentation in all Conditions: the sinn of Covetousnesse, and Excesse; immoderate riches, love of Pleasure, & the danger of them. *Pomer: Curate* of *Roderith*[4] on 23. *Jer:* 10, of the greate sinn of rash & vaine swearing on trivial occasions: See your *notes*:

23 Came to my house some German strangers, & *Signor Pietro*[5] a famous *Musitian*, who had ben long in *Sweden*[b] in *Queene Christinas*[6] Court: he sung *admirably* to a *Guitarr* & has a perfect good tenor & base &c: & had set to *Italian* composure, many of *Abraham Cowleys* Pieces which shew'd extreamely well: He told me the heate [some part][c] in summer was as excessive as the Cold in winter in Sweden; so cold he affirm'd, that the streetes of all the townes are desolate, no creature stirring in them for many moneths, all the in-

---

a-a MS. *preach'd on at.*   b Followed by *with* deleted.   c Interlined.

---

[1] Roger Wye, d. 1701; matriculated Cambridge 1669; fellow of Trinity 1674; M.A. 1676; traceable as curate of Abinger 1675?; vicar of Ware 1682–99; rector of Wotton 1699–1701 (presented by Mary Crosse): Venn; Abinger, *Parish registers*, p. 18; Manning and Bray, ii. 158.

[2] He was chief justice in eyre of all the royal forests south of Trent from 1679 to 1685.

[3] This was the former name of the present Richmond Park, which was enclosed in 1634–7: *V.C.H., Surrey,* iii. 536. The present ranger was the duke of Lauderdale: ibid., p. 537.

Chesterfield's connexion with it, apart from his chief justiceship, is not apparent.

[4] Rotherhithe.

[5] Pietro Reggio, d. 1685: R. Eitner, *Quellen-Lexikon*; with a list of his works. About thirty poems by Cowley are set to music in his *Songs*, which were published this year (advertisement in *London Gazette*, 11 March). Further notices below.

[6] Christina, 1626–89, queen of Sweden from 1632 until her abdication in 1654; in 1655 she received the additional names Maria Alexandra.

habitans retiring to their stoves: He spake high things of
that romantic *Queene,* her Learning, skill in Languages, the
Majestie of her behaviour, her Exceeding Wit, & that the
Histories she had read of other Counteries, especialy of *Italy*
& *Rome* made her despize her owne: That the real occasion
of her resignation of the Crowne to her *Cousin,*¹ was the
Noblemens importuning her to Marie, and the Promise which
the Pope had made her of procuring her to be *Queene* of
Naples,² which also caused her to change her Religion, but
she was cheated by his crafty holinesse, working on her
ambition: That the reason of her *Killing* her secretarie at
*Fontain Beleaw,*ᵃ was his revealing that Intrigue with the
Pope:³ But after all this, I rather believe it was her mad
prodigality & extreame Vanity, which had Consum'd all those
vast treasures, the greate *Adolphus* (her father) had brought
out of Germany, during his enterance there, & wonderfull
successes; & that if she had not voluntarily resign'd (as forseeing the Event) the States of her Kingdome would have
compell'd her.

26 A stranger on 1. *Jobe*ᵇ 20:⁴ That the most righteous are
sinners: *Jobe* himselfe, yet a man of Integrity: *Pomer:* on
12: *Heb:* ult:,⁵ concerning the true Worship of God:

ᵃ Spelling uncertain.   ᵇ Substituted for *John.*

---

¹ Charles X Gustavus: above, ii.
521; he was Christina's first cousin.
Her abdication was due to her
desire to enter the Roman Catholic
Church, which dated back to 1651;
when she learnt that a secret
conversion was impossible she determined to abdicate. Her unwillingness to marry Charles Gustavus or
anyone else was a contributory
inducement: Baron de Bildt, *Christine de Suède et le Cardinal Azzolino,*
1899, pp. 22–7.

² The project of making herself
queen of Naples, by taking it from
the Spaniards, was formed apparently by Christina herself in
1656; it dropped in 1658; the pope,

Alexander VII, when he heard of it,
proved hostile: Bildt, pp. 60–91;
Count F. U. Wrangel, *Première
visite de Christine . . . à . . . France,*
1930, pp. 11–13, 248–50.

³ This refers to the assassination
at Christina's command of her
equerry the Marquis Gian Rinaldo
Monaldesco in the Galerie des Cerfs
at Fontainebleau in 1657; he is
believed to have betrayed to the
Spaniards Christina's and Mazarin's negotiations for an attack on
Naples (see preceding note): Bildt,
pp. 73–9; C. Weibull, *Drottning
Christina och Monaldesco,* 1936.

⁴ The text is perhaps wrong.

⁵ Presumably a slip for verse 28.

October 3 our *Viccar* on 12 *Luke* 47: 48: shewing, how being all Gods servants in this World, our Accompts would be exacted: see your notes: The holy Sacrament follow'd: *Pomer*: a stranger on. 4. Psal: of the infinite benefit of daily Examination; Comparing to a Merchant, keeping his books, to see whither he thrived, or went backward; & how it would facilitate our reckonings, & what a Comfort on our death bed: That the fittest time for it was the Evening, & that even the very Heathens practiz'd it, & no good *Christian* might neglect it. 6 To Lond.

9 I was *Godfather*, with the Earle of *Fevershame*[1] Monsieur Duras (of the family of *Turen*;) Lord Chamberlaine to the Queene, together with the *Dutchesse* of *Grafton* & *Mademoiselle* de *Beverward*[2] to *Signor Del Campos Twinns*, a Boy & a Girle; Christend at *White-hall*: *Del Campo*,[3] was one of the Pages of the back-stayres to her *Majestie*. 10: Dr. *Goodman*[4] pre: on 119 *Psal:* 96 That there was in this life nothing perfect or satisfactorie, that all fell short of expectation; nothing fills & satisfies but God, & Religion. *Coram Rege*: Dr. *Bell*[5] on: 1: *Eccles:* 16, Against unmercifullnesse & too much severity: *Pomeridiano* to St. *Martines*, where I saw Christned, by the Bish: of St. *Asaph*[6] a *Jewesse* of quality come out of *Holland*, her *Susceptors* were Sir *Lionel Jenkins*[7] pr: *Secretary* of state, The Countesses of *Thannet*[8] & *Clarendon*. 16 I returned home:

---

[1] Above, p. 77. He was lord chamberlain to Queen Catherine from 1680 until her death.

[2] Presumably Charlotta Philibert, 1649–1702, youngest daughter of Louis van Nassau, lord of Beverweerd, and sister of Lady Ossory and Lady Arlington; traceable as a lady of the bedchamber to Princess Anne 1692–1702: *De Nederlandsche Heraut*, vii (1892), 168; Chamberlayne.

[3] Giovanni Battista Del Campo, traceable as a page 'of the *Bed-Chamber* attending at the *Back-Stairs*' to Queen Catherine 1682–

94: Chamberlayne.

[4] Above, p. 198.

[5] Above, p. 182. The text is presumably wrong.

[6] Lloyd, the apocalyptic. He had been consecrated bishop on 3 October.

[7] Jenkins (above, iii. 499) had been appointed secretary of state on 26 April of this year and held office until 1684.

[8] Elizabeth, d. 1725, daughter of Richard Boyle, first earl of Burlington; married 1664 Nicholas Tufton, 1631–79, third earl of Thanet 1664: G.E.C.

17 Our *Viccar* as before, against Presumptuous & habitual sinners &c: *Pomerid*: a young man on 22: *Matt:* 12, of the extraordinarie Scrutinie at the greate Day & Tribunal; & therefore how infinitely it concern'd us to make ready our Accompts in this life: 24 I was wonderfully indispos'd by a Cold, so as I could not stirr out:

ᵃ30 I went to *Lond:* [to be private:]ᵇ My Birth-day being the next; & I now arived to the sixtieth yeare of Age; [31]ᶜ upon which, I began a more solemn survey of my whole Life, in order to the making, and confirming my peace with *God*, by an accurate Scrutinie of all my actions past, as far as I was able to call them to min'd: And oh, how difficult, & uncertaine, yet most necessarie worke; The Lord be mercifull to me & accept me. Who can tell how oft he offendeth? Teach me therefore so to Number my daies, that I may apply my heart to wisdome, make my calling & election sure: *Amen Lord Jesus*: I spent this whole day in Exercise &c: A *stranger* preaching at *White-hall* on 16 *Luke* 30. 31: That if *God* should do Miracles never so often, or even send one from the *dead*; People would not believe, but looke on them as Impostures: &c: & that we neede onely *Moses* & the Prophets to Convince us of a future state &c: I thence went to St. *Martines*, where the Bish: of *St. Asaph* preach'd on 1. *Pet:* 3. 15. How necessary it was every *Christian* should be able to render an account of their Faith & Religion, applying it to the present Conjuncture:¹ The holy *Communion* follow'd, at which I participated, humbly imploring Gods Assistance in the greate Work I was entering into. *Pomerid*: I heard Dr. *Sprat* at St. *Margarites* on 17: Act: 11, shewing how Religion & Holinesse, & Dexterity in the Scriptures dos truely enoble,ᵈ from the Example of the *Bereans* &c:

November 1. I began, and spent this whole Weeke in examining my life, beging pardon for my faults, Assistance

---

ᵃ Hand in margin here.   ᵇ Interlined.   ᶜ Marginal date.
ᵈ Altered from *inable*.

---

¹ Parliament had met on 21 October; the passing of the second Exclusion Bill in the commons and its defeat in the lords on 15 November form the crisis of the Popish Plot ferment.

& blessing for the future, that I might in some sort be prepared for the time that now drew neere, & not have the greate worke to begin, when one can worke no longer: The Lord *Jesus* help[a] & assist me: I therefore stirred little abroad til the 5t, when I heard Dr. *Tenison*[1] the now *Viccar* of St. Martines (Dr. *LLoyd,* the former incumbent, being made Bishop of St. Asaph):[b] his Text was on   They will thinke they do God good service, whosoever killeth you, applied to the solemnity of the day, which was the *Papists* Conspiracy: On the

7 Dr. *Patrick* at *Covent Garden* on 1: *Phil:* 9, excellently setting-forth the Love we ought to have to our fellow *Christians,* & to all man-kind: after which succeded the blessed *Communion,* at which I participated finishing, & confirming my Resolutions, of giving my-selfe up more intirely to God, to whom I had now most solemnly devoted the rest of my poore remainder of life in this World; The *Lord* inabling me, who am an unprofitable servant, a miserable sinner, yet depending on his infinite goodnesse & mercy, accepting my endeavors: I dind at my Bro: now come up to the Parliament, being Knight of the Shire for *Surrey*:[2] In the afternoone a stranger on 1. *Eccles:* 2. against Vanity, & on the 12, returned to my house, finding my Daught⟨e⟩r *Mary* (whom I left very ill) well recovered, for which Almighty God be praised. 15 Came to Visite & dine with us Sir Ri: *Anderson,*[3] his Lady, Sonn & Wife sister to my Daughter in Law:

21 our *Viccar* on 13 *Luke:* 6 *ad* 9. on the Parable of the fruitlesse fig-tree, & how it imports greate sinners, & unprofitable livers to redeeme the time, & not provock the

---

a Spelling uncertain.   b Closing bracket supplied.

[1] He was appointed vicar on 8 October of this year. His text is St. John xvi. 2.

[2] He had been returned on 20 Aug. 1679.

[3] Richard Anderson of Penley, Herts., *c.* 1635–99, second baronet 1653; his wife Elizabeth, d. 1698, daughter of Sir William Hewett, bart.; his son Richard, d. 1695; the latter's wife, Elizabeth, *c.* 1657–1724, daughter of Richard Spencer (above, p. 189 n.); she married secondly, as his second wife, Simon Harcourt, first Viscount Harcourt (below, 2 March 1701): G.E.C., *Baronetage,* ii. 211; T. Wotton, *English Baronetage,* 1741, ii. 386–7; &c.

patience, & expectance of God. *Pomerid*: a stranger, on 17:
Act: 30. 31. St. Paules Argument to induce sinners to amend,
by the certaintie of a future Judgement:

28 Our *Viccar* on his former without much addition: The
Curate on 12. *Heb:* 1, concerning the darling sinn, the difficulty, but absolute necessitie of abandoning it, by the example
of St. *Augustine* & other saints:

30 The Anniversary Elections at the R: Society brought
me to Lond: where was chosen Præsident, that excellent person, & greate Philosopher Mr. *Robert Boyle* who indeed, ought
to have ben the very first; but neither his infirmitie, nor
modestie could now any longer excuse him:[1] I desir'd I might
for this yeare be left out of the *Council*, by reason my dwelling
was in the Country;[2] The *Society*, according to Costome, din'd
together: This signal day, began the *Trial* of my Lord
Vicount Stafford for conspiring the Death of the King, and
was likewise his *Birth-day*.[3]

December 2. I was curious to see & heare the famous
Triale of my *L: Stafford* [second][a] sonn to my Lord *Thomas*

---

[a] Interlined.

---

[1] Birch, iv. 58. Boyle refused to serve as president; Wren was elected in his place and was sworn in on 12 Jan. 1681.

[2] Evelyn was a member of council in 1679–80 and again in 1681–2 and 1682–3.

[3] Evelyn's account of Stafford's trial is wrong in its chronology; he apparently relied on his own notes, but probably made some use of *The Tryal of William Viscount Stafford*, 1681 (the authorized report), in his description of the arrangement of Westminster Hall. His comments apparently reflect contemporary discussions; for the latter see especially *Hist. MSS. Comm., Ormonde MSS.*, new ser., v. 511–22. For contemporary opinions of the trial see John Smith, *No Faith or Credit to be given to Papists . . . the Perjury of Will. Viscount Stafford*, 1681; [J. M. Corker], *Stafford's*

Memoires, 1681. Modern comment in Sir J. F. Stephen, *Hist. of the Criminal Law*, 1883, i. 392–6; Pollock, *Popish Plot*, pp. 362–9. S.N.D., *Sir William Howard Viscount Stafford*, 1929, gives the modern Roman Catholic view.

Stafford was selected for trial from the five Roman Catholic peers probably on account of the statements made by Edward Turberville (below, p. 228) before the house of commons on 9 November; the impeachment was voted on 10 November: see Grey, *Debates*, vii. 439–45; Turberville, *Information*, 1680. The usual view, that Stafford was selected on account of his age (he was born in 1614) and weakness, is given by Reresby, 29 Nov., and R. North, *Examen*, 1740, pp. 217–18. The Exclusion Bill was rejected by the lords on 15 November.

Howard, Earle of *Arundel* & Surry, *Earle Marishall* of England, & Grandfather to the present Duke of Norfolck, whom I so well knew, & from which excellent person, I received so many favours:[1] The Trial was in *Westminster Hall*, before the *King, Lords* & *Commons*,[2] just in the same manner as just 40 yeares past, the greate & wise Earle of Strafford (there being but one letter differing their names) received his Tryal[3] (for pretended ill government in Ireland) in that famous *Parliament* [and same place]:[a] This Lord *Staffords*[b] Father being High-Steward &c: Onely the Place of sitting was now exhalted some considerable height from the Paved flore of the Hall, with a stage of boards, His Majesties Throne or state, the *Woolsacks*[c] for the Judges, long formes for the Peeres, Chaire[d] of the Lord Steward *pro tempore*,[4] exactly ranged as in the house of Lords:[5] All the sides on both hands Scaffolded to the very roofe, for the Members of the H: of Commons: At the upper end, & right side of the *Kings* state, was a box for his *Majestie*,[6] others for the Greate Ladys on the left hand; and over head a gallerie for Ambassadors & Pub: *Ministers*: At the lower-end or Enterance was a Barr, & place for the Prisoner, The *Lieutennant* of the *Toure* of *London*,[7] the *Axe-bearer* & Guards, My Lord *Staffords* two

---

[a] Interlined.   [b] Altered from *Straffords*.   [c] Or *Woolpacks*; word altered.   [d] Substituted for *seate*.

[1] Arundel was created earl marshal for life in 1621. Stafford was his fifth son, but the second to reach manhood.

[2] Charles was present only as a spectator; the lords, the lord steward presiding, were the judges; the commons, apart from the managers, took no collective part in the immediate proceedings, and attended not as the house but as a committee: *C.J.*, ix. 668; and see *Hist. MSS. Comm., Ormonde MSS.*, new ser., v. 511.

[3] See above, ii. 27.

[4] Heneage Finch, the lord chancellor and future earl of Nottingham.

[5] For the arrangement of the hall see the *Tryal*, pp. 1–2, and pictures of Strafford's and later impeachments, by Hollar, &c. (there is a small view of the present trial in Richard Burton, *Hist. Remarques . . . of London*, 1681, ii. 114). The south end of the hall was occupied by the court of king's bench and the chancellor's court; the unoccupied throne was placed immediately to the north of these; the lord steward sat with his back to the throne and the court extended northwards.

[6] At the right hand of the imaginary occupant of the throne; the east side.

[7] Thomas Cheke, *c*. 1638–88; of Pyrgo, Essex; ensign, king's regi-

Daughters,[1] the Marchionesse of Winchester being one. There was likewise a Box for my Lord to retire into ;[2] At the right hand in another box some what higher, stood the *Witnesses*, at the left, the *Manegers*, who were to produce & manege[a] the Evidence & whole processe in the name of the *Commons* of *England* :[3] viz: Serjeant *Maynard*,[4] (the greate lawyer, the same who prosecuted the Cause against the Earle of Strafford 40 yeares before in the same place, being now neere 80 yeares of age)[b] Sir *William Jones*,[5] (late Attourney Gen:) Sir *Fran: Winnington*[6] (a famous Pleader) & Mr. *Treby*[7] (now Recorder of Lond:) not appearing in their gownes as Lawyers, but in their cloakes & swords, as representing the Commons of *England*. To these were joyn'd *Mr. Hamden*,[8] *Mr. Sechevarell*,[9] *Mr. Poule*,[10] *Coll: Titus*,[11] *Sir Tho: Lee*[12] all Gentlemen

---

a Spelling uncertain.   b There are deleted closing brackets after *lawyer* and *place*.

---

ment of foot guards, 1664; captain 1665; lieutenant of the Tower 1679–87: Morant, *Essex*, i. 61; *London marriage licences*; Dalton, *English army lists*, i. 37, 52, 53, 260; *Cal. S.P., Dom., 1679–80*, pp. 131–2; &c.

[1] The one daughter is Isabella, d. *c.* 1702, third wife of John Paulet (Powlett), fifth marquis of Winchester ('the loyal marquis': above, ii. 546); the other is presumably Anastasia, *c.* 1646–1719, who married *c.* 1687 George Holman of Warkworth: J. Gillow, (*Bibliog. dict. of the English Catholics*), 1885–1903, art. Holman. Three more daughters were nuns.

[2] See *Tryal*, p. 69.

[3] The managers appear to have been some members of the committee appointed to consider the evidence against the Roman Catholic peers: *C.J.*, ix. 643, 650, 652, 667. No appointment of managers for this particular trial is mentioned.

[4] John Maynard, 1602–90; serjeant-at-law 1654–8, 1660–90; knighted 1660: *D.N.B.*

[5] Above, iii. 580; he was attorney-general from 1675 to 1679.

[6] Francis Winnington, 1634–1700; knighted 1672; solicitor-general 1674–9: *D.N.B.*

[7] George Treby, *c.* 1644–1700; recorder of London, appointed 2 December of this year, dismissed 1683; again 1688–92; knighted 1681; judge, &c.: *D.N.B.*

[8] Richard Hampden, 1631–95; son of John Hampden; chancellor of the exchequer 1690–4: *D.N.B.*

[9] William Sacheverell, 1638–91: *D.N.B.* He is not mentioned in the *Tryal* as taking much part in the proceedings.

[10] Henry Powle, 1630–92; member of the Philosophical Society 3 July 1661; F.R.S., Original Fellow (expelled 1685); speaker of the Convention Parliament 1689–90: *D.N.B.*

[11] Titus (above, iii. 526, &c.) is not mentioned in the *Tryal* as taking part in the proceedings.

[12] Thomas Lee, 1635–91; created a baronet 1660: G.E.C., *Baronetage*, iii. 111; *D.N.B.*, art. Lee, Sir William.

of Qualitie & noted Parliament men: The two first dayes (in^a which was read, the *Commission*, & Impeacchment) was but a very tedious enterance^b into Matter of fact, the Charge, at which I was little present:¹ But on *Thursday* being commodiously seated amongst the *Commons*, when the wittnesses were sworn, & deposed, of which the principle were Mr. *Oates*² (who cal'd himselfe *Doctor*) Mr. *Dugdale*³ & *Turberville*:⁴ *Oates* tooke his *Oath*, that he delivered a Commission to V. Count *Stafford* from the *Pope*, to be *Pay-Master Generall*, to an Army intended to be raised &c:⁵ *Dugdale*, that being at my Lord *Astons*, the ⟨*Prisoner*⟩^c dealt with him plainely to Murder his *Majestie*,⁶ & *Turbervile*, that at *Paris* also he proposed the same to him &c.⁷

3 *Friday* was spent in Depositions of my *Lords* Wittnesses, to invalidate the Testimonie of the *Kings Witnesses*, which being very^d slight persons, though many, viz, 15 or 16: tooke up all that day: and in truth they rather did my Lord injurie than service, & made but little for him.⁸ 4: *Saturday* came other Witnesses of the Commons, to corroborate^e the *Kings*, of which some were *Peeres*, & some *Commons*, with other of

---

a Altered from or to *on*.   b Altered from *entertainement*.   c MS. *Prisoners*.   d Followed by *many, and* deleted.   e Followed (at beginning of new line) by 5 *Preached to the* deleted.

---

¹ On the first day, Tuesday, 30 November, the articles of impeachment were read and, after speeches by three of the managers, evidence was given for the general existence of a plot (Finch's commission as lord high steward was read in the house of lords); on the second day, Wednesday, 1 December, the evidence against Stafford was given—this Evelyn wrongly places on the third day, Thursday, 2 December. On that day most of Stafford's witnesses were heard.

² Stafford questioned Oates's doctorate: *Tryal*, p. 123.

³ Stephen Dugdale, *c.* 1640-83; perjurer: *D.N.B.*

⁴ Edward Turberville, *c.* 1648-81; perjurer: *D.N.B.*

⁵ *Tryal*, pp. 46-7.

⁶ *Tryal*, pp. 41-3. Aston is Walter Aston, 1633-1714, third Lord Aston of Forfar (Scotland) 1678 (23 April): G.E.C. His house was at Tixall, Staffs.

⁷ *Tryal*, pp. 49-50.

⁸ This was on Thursday, 2 December: Stafford called more than twenty witnesses on this day, and two more on Friday. They included three peers and three knights or baronets, but were mainly servants, &c. See the remarks in *Hist. MSS. Comm., Ormonde MSS.*, new ser., v. 514. Their business was to disparage Dugdale, Oates, and Turberville. Stafford called three more witnesses on Saturday, one of them a peer.

good qualitie, who tooke off all the former days objections, & set the Kings *Witnesses recti in Curia*,[1] & then adjourn'd 'til *moneday*:

5 Preach'd to the Household at *White-hall* Dr. *Calamie*[2] (sonn to the famous *Presbyterian*, but of quite other Principles) on 5: *Matt* 24. Against taking Gods sacred-name in vaine; an excellent discourse & highly seasonable, the people of all degrees being ariv'd to a most dredfull excesse of that prophanatie, in such oathes & execrrations, as would make a *Christian* tremble to recite or heare: Also of the Lawfullnesse of *Oathes* in Judicial cases: &c: The holy Sacrament follow'd: *Coram Rege* preached Dr. *Patric*[3] *Deane* of *Peterborow* on: 2: *Pet:* 3. 16, asserting the right & duty of the Common people to reade the Scriptures, & be conversant in them; & that notwithstanding those places which the Apostle mentions to be more difficult in St. *Paules Epistles*; in which Cases, they were to consult their Spiritual Guides, set in the church, whose lips were to preserve knowledge; proving that *Schismes* chiefly sprung from peoples not duly reading the Word of God, & from mens ignorance in it: For that both *Women* & even *Children*, were both before, & since *Christ* very expert in them: I din'd at my Bro: After dinner[a] I heard prayers, & a good sermon at *Co: Garden* church on 5. *Luke* 25. 26.

6 *Moneday*, being the 6 of December I went againe to the Trial,[4] where I heard the Evidences summ'd up by Sir

---

[a] Substituted for *prayers*.

[1] This was on Friday, 3 December. The managers called twenty-seven witnesses, including three peers. Their business was to disparage Stafford's witnesses.

[2] Benjamin Calamy, 1642–86; D.D. 1680; chaplain in ordinary (supernumerary) 1679–86; son of Edmund Calamy the elder, 1600–66, one of the authors of 'Smectymnuus': for both men see *D.N.B.* The text probably should be St. Matthew v. 34.

[3] Patrick had been appointed dean of Peterborough in 1679; he continued to hold the rectory of St. Paul's, Covent Garden, until 1689.

[4] The proceedings here reported belong to Saturday, 4 December, but are given in wrong order. Stafford first called some more witnesses, then summed up the evidence in his defence; then Jones summed up for the managers, followed by Powle and Maynard; then Stafford raised various points of law; his counsel appeared and the judges gave their ruling.

William Jones, which was very large; and when he had don,
& said all he could to exaggerate[1] the charge succeeded all
the rest of the *Lawyers* Manegers; Then began Mr. *Hen:
Poule* in a vehement Oration, as to the profes of the *Jesuitical*
doctrine, of holding it not onely *lawfull*, but meritorious to
Murder an Heretic King; which my Lord, had in his plea
denyed:[2] After this my *Lord* (as upon all occasions, & very
often he did during the whole Trial) spake in his owne
defence, denying the Charge altogether; that he[a] never in his
life saw either *Turbervile* or *Oates* at the time, and manner
affirmed; & in truth their Testimonie did little weigh with
me; *Dugdales* onely seemed to presse hardest: To which my
Lord spake a greate while, but without any method, & con-
fus'dly: One thing my Lord said, which I confesse did exceedingly affect me, as to *Titus Oates*, That a Person, who,
during his[b] depositions, should so vauntingly as he did, brag
that[c] though he went over to the Church of Rome, yet he was
never a Papist, nor[d] of their Religion, all the time that he
seem'd to *Apostatize* from the Protestant; but onely as a spie;
Though he confess'd he tooke their Sacraments, Worship'd
Images, went through all the Oathes & discipline of their
Proselytes, swearing seacrecy, & to be faithfull, but with
intention to come over againe & betray them: That such an
Hypocrite, that had so deepely prevaricated,[e] as to turne
even Idolater, (for so we of the *Church* of *England* esteem'd
it) attesting God so solemnly, that he was intirely theirs, &
devoted to their interests, & consequently (as he pretended)
trusted; I say that the Witnesse of such a proflygate wretch
should be admitted, against the life of a Pere; This my Lord,
looked upon as a monstrous thing, & such as must needes
redown'd to the dishonor both of our Religion & Nation: And
verily, I am of his *Lordships* opinion; Such a mans Testimonie

---

a Followed by *was* deleted.   b Substituted for *their*.   c Followed
by *he* deleted.   d Followed by *all* deleted.   e Followed by *&* deleted.

---

[1] To make much of; not necessarily, as now, to exceed the limits
of the truth: above, ii. 512, &c.
[2] Stafford had spoken on this
subject on Wednesday, 1 December:
Tryal, pp. 53–4; Powle's remarks,
pp. 188–9.

should not be taken against the life of a Dog:[1] 'Tis true,
many Protestants had defected, & return'd againe; but we
know of none, (nor if any, can approve them) who when they
turned *Papists*, did not heartily believe they were in the
right, 'til they were convinc'd to the Contrary: But this is
not *Oates* his case, he went thro all the mysteries of their
Religion, thro all their Oat⟨h⟩es, Execrations on himselfe,
Sacraments &c, whilst by his owne Confession, he disembl'd
all; This he affirmed & I know not on what occasion it
escaped from him, no lesse impiously: than foolishly:[2] From
this moment foreward, I had quite lost my opinion of Mr.
Oates. But the merite[a] & service of something material which
he discovered against *Coleman*[3] at first, put him in such
esteeme with the Parliament &c: that now I fancy, he stooke
at nothing, & thought every body was to take what he said
for *Gospel* afterwards: The Consideration of this, and some
other Circumstances began to stagger me; particularly, how
'twas possible, that one who went amongst the *Papists* with
such a designe, & pretended to[b] be intrusted with so many
letters, & Commissions from the *Pope* & *party*, nay & delivered them to so many greate Persons, should not reserve
one of them to shew, or produce, nor so much as one Copie of
any Commission; which he who had such dexterity in opening

---

a Or *merits*.   b Followed by *de-* deleted.

---

[1] For the principal part of
Stafford's speech see *Tryal*, pp.
163–6. About Oates's pretended
conversion he said, 'If I were a
Judge, I would not hang a Dog upon
such Evidence.' He had already
attacked Oates on this ground on
Friday, 3 December: *Tryal*, pp. 128–
9. Jones for the managers confused
the issue as best he could: p. 179.
[2] The opening of this passage
reflects a passage in Jones's speech:
Tryal, p. 179; the last part is perhaps an accretion to Evelyn's
original notice. Oates acknowledged (or claimed) from the
beginning of his revelations that his
conversion to Roman Catholicism
had been fraudulent: when he was
examined by the Privy Council on
28 Sept. 1678: *Hist. MSS. Comm.*,
Ormonde MSS., new ser., iv. 455;
a few days later to Burnet: *Own
time*, ed. Airy, ii. 162; again in this
trial: p. 123.
[3] See above, pp. 155, 158.
Oates's evidence against Coleman
was perjured; but Coleman's papers,
which were genuine, silenced doubts
as to its truth; Godfrey's violent
death had a similar effect. For
Oates's conduct at this time see
Reresby, 26 Dec. 1680.

letters &c, might[a] certainely have don, to the undenyable
Conviction of those whom he accus'd:[1] But, as I said, he
gained Credit upon *Coleman*, but as to others whom he so
madly flew upon, I am little inclined to believe his testimonie; he being so slight a person, so passionate,[2] ill-bred,
& [of][b] impudent behaviour: nor is it at all likely, such piercing
politicians as the *Jesuites* should trust him with so high, &
so dangerous seacrets. [7][c] On *Tuesday* I was againe at the
Trial,[3] when Judgement was demanded, and after my Lord
had spoken what he could in denying of the fact &c: The
Manegers answering the objections &c: The Peeres adjourned
to their House, & within two houres, return'd againe: There
was in the meane time this farther question put, whither
there being but one witnesse to[d] any single Crime or act, it
could amount to convict a man;[e] upon this, the Judges being
cald on to give their opinion, unanimously declar'd, that in
case of *Treason* they all were overt acts; for though no man
should be condemn'd by one witnesse for any one act, yet for
severall acts to the same intent, it was valid, which was my
Lord Staffords Case; for one sware he practised him to Kill
his Majestie at *Paris*, another at my L: *Astons*, a Third that
he delivered him a Commission from *Rome*, but to neither of
these were ⟨there⟩[f] above one Witnesse, so it was overruled:
This being past, and The Peres in their seates againe, my *Lord*
[Chancelor][b] *Finch* (who was this day *High Steward*) removing to the *Wool-sack* next his Majesties state, after summoning the *Lieutennant* of the *Tower* to bring forth his Prisoner,
and Proclamation made for silence;[4] demanded of every

---

a Substituted for *would*.   b Interlined.   c Marginal date.
d Followed by *every* deleted.   e Followed by *of Treason* deleted.
f MS. *their*.

---

[1] Stafford called attention to this
point: *Tryal*, pp. 126-7.

[2] See *Tryal*, pp. 129-30, 179-80.

[3] The proceedings here reported
belong to several days. Stafford
made a further speech in defence
on Monday, 6 December, and the
managers replied to it; the verdict
and the sentence were given on

Tuesday, 7 December; the judges'
opinions were taken on Saturday,
4 December: *Tryal*, pp. 195-7.

[4] 'The *Lords* being sat, Proclamation was made for silence;
and the *Lord High Steward* being
seated on the Woolpack . . . took
the Votes of the Peers upon the
Evidence . . . the Lord *Stafford* being

Peere (who were in all 86) whither William *Lord Vicount Stafford* were Guilty of the Treason Laied to his Charge, or not Guilty: Then the Peere (spoken to) standing up, & laying his right hand upon his breast, sayed *Guilty*, or *Not Guilty* Upon his honour; & then sate downe: & so another 'til all were asked: the L: *Steward* noting their severall Suffrages as they[a] answered upon a paper: When all had don, the number of not Guilties being but 31, the Guiltys 55, after *Proclamation* for silence againe; The *Steward* directing his speech to the Prisoner[1] (against whom the Axe was turn'd edge ways towards him, & not before)[2] in aggravation of his Crime, he being enobled by his *Majesties Father*, & since received many favours & graces from his present Majestie: That came of such a stock, & noble family, had appeared in his defence in time of the late rebellion &c: & all that could signifie to the charge of his ingratitude & disloyalty: Then inlarged on the honor & justice of their Proceedings against him[3] with a *Christian* exhortation to Repentance, & Confession, deploring first his owne unhapinisse, that he who never Condemned any man before, should now be necessitated to begin with him, &c: & then Pronounced Sentence of Death, by *Hanging, Drawing* & *Quartering* (according to forme) with greate solemnity, and dreadfull gravity; last of all, after a short pause; Told the *Prisoner*, That he believed the *Lords* would interceede with his *Majestie* that some Circumstances of his sentence, might be omitted, beheading onely excepted & then breaking his White-staff, the Court disolved. My *Lord Stafford* during all this later part spake very little, & onely Gave their Lordships thanks, after the sentence was pro-

---

[a] Followed by *spak* deleted.

(as the Law requires) absent': *Tryal*, p. 209. This was the beginning of Tuesday's proceedings. Finch was lord high steward for the whole trial and sat on the woolsack throughout.

[1] Evelyn omits the summoning of Stafford to hear the verdict, his speech for arrest of judgement, and the adjournment and reassembling of the court.

[2] The changed position of the axe is noticed in the *Tryal* only when Stafford was being led from the court after the delivery of the sentence: p. 215.

[3] This does not appear in the speech as reported in the *Tryal*.

nounc'd; & indeede behav'd himselfe modestly, and as became him: 'Twas observ'd, that all his owne Relations, &
of his Name & family Condemn'd him, excepting onely his
Nephew the *Earle* of *Arundel*:[1] sonn to the D: of *Norfolck*:
and it must be acknowledg'd that the whole Trial was carried
on from first to last, with exceeding gravity, & so stately and
august appearance I had never seene; for besides[a] innumerable spectators of Gent: & forraine Ministers &c: who saw &
heard all the proceedings, the Prisoner had the Consciences
of all the Commons of England for his Accusers, and all the
Peeres to be his *Judges* & *Jury*: He had likewise the assistance of what Counsel he would to direct him in his plea, that
stood by him:[2] And yet I can hardly think, a person of his
age & experience, should engage men, whom he never saw
before, (& one of them that came to visite him as a stranger,
at *Paris*), *point blanque* to Murder the *King*: God onely, who
searches hearts, can discover the Truth, & to him it must be
left: My Lord *Stafford*, was not a man belov'd, Especialy of
his owne family,[3] & had ben suspected, & in danger to by
it, of a Vice in Germanie, which neede not be nam'd,[4] and[b]
I doubt not but he had seriously repented.

11 I returned home:

---

[a] Followed by *the* deleted.　　　　[b] Followed by *perhaps* deleted.

---

[1] Henry Howard, the future
seventh duke of Norfolk, summoned to the house of lords in 1678
as Baron Mowbray; he was Stafford's great-nephew. The other
Howard peers voting were the
earls of Suffolk, Berkshire, and
Carlisle, and Lord Howard of
Escrick.

[2] Stafford had counsel in court
throughout, but they could speak
only on points of law; this was the
law at the time. On the second day
(1 December) the managers objected to his counsel standing near
Stafford, lest they should prompt
him on matters of fact: *Tryal*, p.
40. They raised the point of law
noticed by Evelyn above on Satur-

day, 4 December: pp. 167-8,
189-95.

[3] Stafford had had lawsuits with
his nephews Henry Howard (Evelyn's friend) and Charles Howard of
Greystoke (above, iii. 154, &c.) after
his mother's death in 1654: S.N.D.,
Stafford, pp. 41-7; see also Burnet,
ii. 269.

[4] Stafford was in prison at
Heidelberg in October 1652, and
apparently remained there until
about November 1653, when he
was released without trial: *Nicholas
papers*, vol. i (Camden Soc., new
ser., vol. xl, 1886), pp. 311-13; *Cal.
Clarendon S.P.*, ii. 222, 263, 276.
Burnet also gives the general
charge: *Own time*, ed. Airy, ii. 269.

12 Our *Viccar* & *Curate* proceeded on their former Texts: This Evening looking out of my Chamber Window towards the West, [a]I first saw a Meteor, (or what ever other *Phæno-menon* it was) of an obscure bright Colour (if so I may call it without a solecisme) resembling the brightnesse of the *Moone* when under a thin Clow'd, very much in shape like the blade of a sword, whose point to the starre[b] in appearance, bending Northwards towards London, not seeming at the *Horizon* to be above a yard in bredth, & so pyramidal, the rest of the skie, very serene & cleere; The Moone new, but not appearing, the Weather exceeding sharp, hard frost with some snow falling 2 daies before: What this may Portend (for it was very extraordinarie) God onely knows; but such another *Phæno-men⟨on⟩* I remember I saw, which went from *North to South*, & was much brighter, & larger, but not so *Ensiforme* in the yeare *1640*, about the Triall of the greate Earle of *Strafford*, præceeding our bloudy Rebellion: I pray God avert his Judgements; we have had of late severall *Comets*, which though I believe appeare from natural Causes, & of them-selves operate not, yet I cannot despise them; They may be warnings from God, as they commonly are for-runners of his Annimadversions: After some daies this plainly appeared to be headed with a small hazy-starr distant from *Venus* 23°–'58 & the bright st: of *Aquila*[c] 28–15–$\frac{1}{2}$–5°–09 *Latitude*-9°–44 South, the taile or point extending to the middle of Sagitta above a *degree* broad, & was 35 *deg:* long.[1]

17 This day being friday, at exactly halfe an ⟨houre⟩[d] after one at noone, was my Daughter in Law brought to bed of a *Sonn*,[2] a very fine babe; for which I gave God Thanks:

[a]18 Came the *Duke of Norfolck* to visite me, and lay this

---

[a] Hand in margin here.　　　[b] Or *starrs*.　　　[c] Altered from *Aquara*.
[d] MS. *haure*.

---

[1] For this comet see Carl, *Reper-torium der Cometen-Astronomie*, pp. 80–5. Evelyn's statement about its position agrees with that given by Flamsteed for the evening of Sun-day, 12 December: *Hist. coelestis Britannica*, vol. i, 1725, p. 104

(Flamsteed gives no measurements for the breadth and length of the tail). The phenomenon to which he compares it is presumably that which he saw on 10 March 1643: above, ii. 80.

[2] Richard, d. 6 Sept. 1681.

Night at my house, being the next day going towards *Dover* & Embark for Flanders: he did not seeme to be at all Concern'd for his Unkle Stafford: but We were discoursing & talking of other matters 'til it was neere one a Clock at night: After his Grace was gon, who kept me from church all the Morning, [19]ᵃ being the last Sonday of Advent ; was Christned my little Grandsonn, by the name of *Richard*: his Grandfather *Sir Rich: Browne* & my Bro: *Geo: Evelyn* being Susceptors with my *Lady Stonehouse* mother of my Daughter in Law:

22 Was the solemn Publique Fast thro out England,¹ that God would prevent all popish plotts, avert his Judgements, & give a blessing to the proceedings of the *Parliament* now assembled, & which struck at the *Succession* of the *Duke of York* &c: our *Viccar* preached on 122 *Psal:* 7 pray for the peace of *Jerusalem. 25 Chr:mas day*, on 1 *Tim* 1. 15: This is a true saying, that *Christ* came into the World, to Save sinners. The holy Sacrament follow'd. 26: on the same Text: I had neighbours dined with us. 29, was the unhappy ViCount *Stafford* beheaded on *Tower* hill.² 31 After recollection &c: I humbly gave thanks to God, for his mercies to me this past Yeare:

1681. *Jan:* 1, I beged the blessing of Almighty God upon me & mine the yeare now entered:

2 Our *Viccar* as before, insisting on the faithfullnesse of Gods promises, upon supposition of our obedience. *That Christ came into the world to save sinners* meaning, repenting sinners, noting that Gods promises were ever attended with an *If*: The holy Communion follow'd: *Pomerid: Curate* on 4: *Phil:* 4. The greate Cause good men have of rejoicing. 9: our *Vicc:* as above: That it was onely want of Faith, made

---

ᵃ Marginal date.

---

¹ Proclamation 2 December, printed in *London Gazette*, 6 Dec. The more especial object of the fast was to implore God's blessing on the king and the present parliament, 'that Our Consultations and Endeavours may produce Honour, Safety and Prosperity to Our Self and Our People'. The Exclusion Bill had been rejected on 15 November, more than a month previously. The vicar's text is a slip for verse 6.

² The sentence had been commuted. Notice of the execution in *London Gazette*, 30 Dec.

men sinn: *The foole hath said in his heart, there is no God*;
then it follows—They are Corrupt, & become abominable in
their doings; so as their Corruption proceedes from their
Atheisme, & want of Faith: *Curate* on his former also,
describing the joys of the other life:

After many daies & nights of Snow, Clowdy & dark weather, the *Comet* was gotten as far as the head of *Andromeda*
& not above 23 deg: long, much wasted:[1]

12 I went to *Lond:* about buisinesse, returned the 15. 16
our *Viccar* sick, a stranger, on 50 *Psal:* 15, of the Effect of
Prayer, rightly directed & qualified: This day was my
Daughter in Law *Churched*: *Pomerid.* on 16: Matt: 26. The
ill bargaine, of loosing the soule for the world: 17: I went to
Lond, return'd immediatcly:

23 Our *Viccar* on his former, pressing the necessity of
Faith, with no greate addition: *Pomerid*: a *stranger* on 85
Psal: 10: 30 *Viccar* on. 24. *Act*: 16, Concerning Conscience,
what it was? its effects; when not allways bound to follow
its dictates &c: see your *notes*: *Curat* on his former, nothing
very observable. 31 To *Lond:* Dr. *Turner*[2] *Coram Rege*,
(being the *Anniversarie* of his fathers *Martyrdom*) on 4:
Threnæ 20. describing the Tretcherie of his Enemies, & in
what sense a good Prince & Governor, is the life of his
People &c:

Feb: ⟨6⟩:[a] Dr. *Patrick* at *Co: Gard:* 10 *Heb:* 38: how the
Just live by Faith, by the example of all holy persons mention'd in that Chap: That they came not into the promis'd
land 'til after much patience: That *Abraham* & *Patriarches*
obtained not the full promise, but waited for them, & therefore we were not to make hast, but believe, & attend his
providence & motion &c: The holy Sacrament follow'd:
I dind at my Bro: & afternoone heard the *Curate* on 23 Pro:
17. That nothing, so Effectual to keepe us steady in duty, as
the Constant feare of God &c:

---

a MS. 7.

---

[1] For the position this night see
Flamsteed, *Hist. coelestis*, i. 106.
[2] **Dr. Francis Turner.** The sermon, on vv. 19–21, was printed this
year. For the transference of the
fast see above, iii. 542; iv. 82.

10 I was at the Wedding & Marriage of my Nephew *Jo:
Evelyn* of Wotton, married by my L: *Bish:* of *Rochester* at
Westminster (in *Hen: 7th Chapell*) to the daughter & heyre
of Mr. *Erskin* of *Sussex*, her portion 8000 pounds: I wish it
may ⟨prove⟩ᵃ happy to him, & the familie, having first proposed it to my Bro: & that she is like to be a proper beautifull
young Lady, & of an honourable familie: The solemnity was
kept with a few select friends only, at Myᵇ *Lady Beckfords*
mother of the Lady:¹ ⟨13⟩:ᶜ Dr. *Thistletwhait coram Rege*, on
8 Eccl: 11. How wiccked men abuse the goodnesse of God,
because final Sentence is not immediately executed: I din'd
with my Bro: *Pomerid*: Dr. *Sprat* at St. *Margarits* on 2: *Tit:*
14. The necessity of purity in this life. 18: Dr. *Stillingfleete*
excellently on 18 *Luke* 13 on the parable of the penitent
Publican; how far hearty contrition, exceedes formal repent-
ings:² (See your *notes*:) 19 I returned home: ⟨20⟩ᵈ our *Viccar*
on (24ᵉ Act: 16 his former Text) the necessity of a sincere
Conscience, of a doubting, an erroneous conscience (&c: see
your *notes*). *Curate* on 19: Luke: 41. our B: *Saviours* teares
proofe of his humanitie & sweete & tender nature; his sorrow
for our obstinacy:

27 Our *Viccar* proceedes on the nature of Conscience, how
ignorance excuses not (Se your notes at large). *Pomerid*:
Curate on 18 *Ezek: 27*:

Mar: 6: Viccarᶠ & Curate as before, most of it repetition:
The holy *Communion* follow'd:

7 To *Lond:* din'd at the *Earle* of *Sunderlands*. ᵍ8 Visited,
& din'd at the *Earle* of *Essexes*,³ with whom I spent most of
the Afternoone alone in his study: Thence to Visite my (yet
living) *Godmother* & kindswoman Mrs. Keightly⁴ (Sister to

ᵃ MS. *provee* (altered from *proves* ?). ᵇ Substituted for *the*. ᶜ MS.
14. ᵈ MS. *22.* ᵉ Altered from *20*. ᶠ Altered from *Dʳ*:
ᵍ Hand in margin here.

---

¹ See above, pp. 195–6. Erskin is
a mistake for Eversfield ('Ersfield').
² Lenten sermon at court (first
Friday in Lent): list of preachers in
London Gazette, 6 Jan.

³ For his house in St. James's
Square see above, p. 199.
⁴ For her see above, ii. 5; she
was baptized on 12 Sept. 1596. For
her brother see V.

Sir *Tho:* Evelyn & niepce to my Father,) being now 86 yeares
of age, a spritfull woman & in perfect health, her Eyes yet
serving her as well as ever, & she of a Countenance very
Comely, one would not take her to be above 50 at most:

9 Dr. *Young*[1] *Coram Rege* on 5: *Matt* 3. excellently; I din'd
at my L: Chamb: & so home:

13 A stranger on 51 *Psal* 9. & *Pomerid* on 23 Matt: 37. both
extreamely well, concerning the necessity & effects of Repentance &c: 20 *Viccar* persues[a] his former Text, but with little
addition, concluding with an exhortation to more frequent
Communion. In the Afternoone a stranger on 5 *Rom.* 12.
How death pass'd on all, for sinn &c:

27 Our Viccar on his former Text, shewing by Instances,
that God did not punishe so severely for the greatenesse of
the thing we did, as our Contempt of his Command: as in that
of *Adame*, for tasting a little fruite, He that gathered sticks
on the Sabbath,[2] Saules sparing Amalec &c: (See your notes
at large) That men deceive them-selves[b] by making Conscience onely of committing some enormous actions &c:
holy Sacrament followed: *Pomerid*: *Curate* on 1. *Cor*: 2. 2.
upon the preference of our knowledge of the Gospell, & Crosse
of Christ, (which is his Religion & Institution) before all
other learning &c. The *Parliament* now conven'd at *Oxford*:[3]
Greate expectation of his *Royal Highnesses* Case, as to Succession, against which the house was set:

An extraordinary sharp, cold Spring, not yet a leafe on the
trees, frost & snow lying: whilst the whole nation was in a

---

a Altered from or to *pursues*.   b *Them* altered from *their*?

---

[1] Identifiable as Edward Young,
c. 1642–1705; B.C.L. 1668; sometime chaplain to Lord Ossory;
canon of Salisbury 1682; chaplain
in ordinary *c.* 1692–1705; dean of
Salisbury 1702; father of the poet:
Foster. Ossory styles him 'Dr.
Young' in 1679: *Hist. MSS. Comm.*,
Ormonde MSS., new ser., v. 219,
263. Lenten sermon at court.

[2] Numbers xv. 32–6.

[3] Parliament had met at Oxford
on 21 March; on 26 March the third
Exclusion Bill was ordered to be
brought in; and parliament was
dissolved on 28 March, the proxi-
mate cause being a quarrel between
the two houses, also beginning on
26 March, relating to a proposed
impeachment: Sidney, *Diary*, ii.
184, 186.

greate ferment. 30 To *Lond:* in order to preparation against Easter:

Aprill 1.[1] At. St. *Martines Dr. Tenison* on 2: *Tit:* 14: our B: *Lord* giving himselfe for us, did it not for the fallen Angels; but for every individual person receiving him, on the easy & happy termes of the Gospel; our part being onely to seeke purity, & holinesse, Love & Charity, to fit us for the heavenly place & society there hereafter, & Gods holy presence here, the holy Comm: follow'd. *Pomerid* Dr. *Smith*[2] of Chr: *Church Oxon (coram rege)*[3] on 2. *Heb:* 17. shewing how our B: Saviour was made like us, that he might be passible,[4] & also compassionate, inferring how little it would conduce to our benefit, but rather condemnation, unlesse we also endeavor to belike[5] Christ in holinesse & obedience to God &c. I supp'd at my L: Chamberlains. 2 went home: 3 *Easter-day* a stranger on 24 *Luke* 34 asserting the truth of the *Resurrection*: The holy *Sacrament* follow'd: I received with my family: *Pomer: Curate* on: 1. *Cor:* 15. 20. on the same subject: 9: To *Lond:* 10: Dr. *Stillingfleete* first serm: on 1. *Jam:* 12. The reward of not yeilding to Tentation: (*Coram Rege*) Dr. *Tillotson* on 13 *Jer:* 23. The exceeding difficulty of reforming habitual sinns & making it next to impossible, from that of the *Ethiops* changing his skin, ⟨*Leopard*⟩[a] his spotts: (*See your notes:*) like the Camels going through the needles Eye, which our *B: Saviour* makes onely possible with God; to expresse the Rich-mans difficulty &c: It was a tirrible & severe discourse, shewing how it concerned sinners to serious repentance:[6] 11 I went to Visite the Bish: of *Rochester*, & tooke my leave of Dr. *Lloyd* now Bish: of St. *Asaph*, at his

---

[a] MS. *Leopord.*

---

[1] Good Friday.
[2] Henry Smith, d. 1702; matriculated at Oxford 1656; D.D. 1674; canon of Christ Church 1675; perhaps a chaplain in ordinary *c.* 1679– *c.* 1688: Foster.
[3] Charles had returned to London on 29 March: *London Gazette,*

31 March.
[4] Capable of suffering: *O.E.D.*
[5] Probably only a slip for 'be like', but possibly a survival of the old verb.
[6] Evidently the sermon printed in Tillotson, *Works*, 1752, i. 263–70.

house in Licester fields,[1] now going to reside in his Diocesse: 12 I din'd at Mr. Brisbans[2] Secretary to the Admiralty, a learned & industrious person: whither came Dr. *Burnet* to thank me for some Papers I had contributed towards his excellent *Historie* of the *Reformation*:[3] Thence to the R: *Society*,[4] next day home: 17: Our *Viccar* on his former *Text*,

---

[1] Leicester Fields was called Leicester Square already in 1678 in an act of parliament, but the older name persisted into the eighteenth century: Kingsford, *Piccadilly*, pp. 55–6.

[2] Above, p. 178.

[3] Burnet printed two documents, both relating to Mary, queen of Scots, 'given me by that most ingenious and vertuous Gentleman, Mr. *Evelyn*, who is not satisfied to have advanced the knowledg of this Age, by his own most useful and successful Labours, about Planting, and divers other ways, but is ready to contribute every thing in his Power to perfect other Mens Endeavours': *Hist. of the Reformation*, vol. ii, 1681, [i]. 417; the two documents, ibid., [ii]. 369–77. The originals are now in the Pepysian Library at Magdalene College: *Hist. MSS. Comm., Pepys MSS.*, pp. 166–70, 170–2.

Evelyn later believed that through this loan he had lost some part of his collection of manuscripts. On 10 Nov. 1699 he wrote to Archdeacon William Nicolson (below, 15 June 1702): 'Those letters & papers of the Q. of Scots, originals & written with her own hand to Q. Eliz. & Earle of Leycester, before & during her imprisonment, which I furnish'd to Dr. Burnet (now B. of Salisb.) some of which being printed in his History of the Reformation, those, & others with them, are pretended to have ben lost at the presse, which has bin a quarell betweene me & his Lp, who lays the fault on Chiswell [the

publisher]' (Bohn, iii. 380–1; quoted from 2nd ed., ii. 291). The accusation is questionable. On 5 or 6 December of the present year Evelyn sent Pepys a collection of manuscripts and papers; from a memorandum made by or for Pepys it appears that a postscript (not now extant) to the covering letter mentioned some papers lent to Burnet; these were not in the package received by Pepys: Pepys, *Private corr.*, i. 20–1. Some of the documents listed in the covering letter (ibid., pp. 14–20; draft in Bohn, iii. 260–3) are now in the Pepysian Library. Either the two letters printed by Burnet had been or were later returned to Evelyn and forwarded to Pepys, or were sent direct by Burnet or his agent to Pepys. I have found in Burnet no traces of other letters coming from Evelyn's collection. In any case no great loss of Queen Mary's letters through this loan is to be inferred. Evelyn described item no. 70 of his collection of manuscripts as including letters from 'Q. Eliz. Mary Q. of Scots, &c. which I have given to Sam. Pepys Esq.': Bernard, *Catalogi librorum manuscriptorum*, vol. ii, pt. i, p. 95. It now contains one letter of Elizabeth's and two of Mary's: *Hist. MSS. Comm., Pepys MSS.*, pp. 96–7, 177, 182. By his own confession, in the letter to Nicolson, Evelyn was a bad guardian of the manuscripts which he had inherited.

[4] Presumably the meeting on 13 April: Birch, iv. 80; there was no meeting on 12 April.

of the benefit of selfe Examination, & that every night, even from the Example of very heathen, *Seneca, Pythagoras* &c. *Curate* on 3 *Zech:* 2 of Obedience to *Magistrates*, not much to the Text:[1] 22: To Lond about my Accompts: 24. at *W:hall*: Dr. *Pettus* on 1. *Pet:* 48,[2] concerning the grace & virtue of Charity, excellently: (*Cor: Rege*) Dr. Hall[3] on Iniquity shall not be your ruine: shewing how sinn was the ruine & destruction of all Kingdomes & states, as well as of private persons: *Pomerid*: B: of St. *Asaph*, at the *Tabernacle* (neere St. *Martines*)[4] on 1. *Pet:* 3. 6 against slanders and uncharitable Censurers:

26 I dined at *Dom Piedro Ronquillos*[5] the Spanish *Ambassador* at *Wild house*,[6] used me with extraordinarie Civility: [a]After dinner (which was plentifull, halfe after the Spanish, & halfe after the English way) he led me into his Bed-chamber, where we both fell into a long discourse about *Religion*; in which, though he was a learned man in Politiques,[b] & an Advocate; I found him very ignorant, & unable to defend any point of Controversy, blindly recurring at every foote, to the Churches *Infallibility*, & *Tradition*—he was however

---

[a] Hand in margin here.   [b] Or *Politique*; termination abbreviated.

---

[1] The subject has no apparent relation to the text.

[2] A slip for 1 Peter iv. 8.

[3] Presumably John Hall: above, iii. 534 n. He was a chaplain in ordinary from *c.* 1677 to *c.* 1682, and from 1689 to 1691. His text is Ezekiel xviii. 30.

[4] Presumably the chapel of ease in Oxenden Street, built by Richard Baxter in 1676, but soon afterwards let to the parish of St. Martin's; it was still known as the Tabernacle *c.* 1720: Kingsford, *Piccadilly*, pp. 85–6; Strype's Stow, vi. 68; for the word tabernacle as here used see above, p. 180. The text is apparently a slip for verse 16.

[5] Don Pedro Ronquillo, d. 1691; envoy extraordinary to the emperor 1673–4; to England 1675–6; other diplomatic appointments; ambassador to England from 1680 until his death; for his character see Leti, *Del teatro brittanico*, ii. 300–7.

[6] Wild House was situated on the east side of Wild Street, which runs out of Great Queen Street; it takes its name from Humphrey Weld, who acquired most of the east side of the street *c.* 1640–9, and who constructed on part of it in 1657 a residence suitable for an ambassador, with a private chapel. It was occupied by the Portuguese ambassador *c.* 1659–*c.* 1665, apparently by the French in 1673, and by the Spanish *c.* 1675–*c.* 1694; it was pulled down soon after and Wild Court occupies the site: L.C.C., *Survey of London*, v. 93–7.

far from being fierce; onely at parting earnestly wishing that
I would humbly apply my selfe to the *Blessed Virgin* to direct
me, & that he had know⟨n⟩ divers that had ben averse from
the *Roman Catholique* religion, be wonderfully inlightned &
convinced by her Intercession. This was a pretty *Postulatum*;
he would have one be a *papist*, that he might be a *Papist*:
They have not a weaker tenet in all their Religion, than this
error of Invocation of Saints & Adoration: so I tooke leave
of the *Ambassador*, who importun'd me to come & visite him
offten:

27 To the *R: Society*, where many were assembled.

29 I gave in my grand Accompt to the Lords *Commissioners*
of the Treasury,[1] & so home, but one showre of raine all this
Moneth, the whole yeare dry &c:[2]

May 1 *Viccar* on 11 *Heb:* 17. By the Example of *Abraham*,
to rely on God for deliverance in all Tentations & straites:
The ho: sacrament followed &c: *Curate Pomerid*: on: 2:
Phil. 1. 7.[3] of Charity & Union &c, it being Mr. Smith our
Curates valedictory Sermon, now going to a living in the
Country: a good man, but had not the talent of Preaching:

2 The Foefees of the poore mett according to Costome:

5 Came to visite & dine with me Sir *William Fermor*,[4] of
N:hamptonshire, & Sir *Chr: Wren*, his Majesties *Architect* &
Surveyor, now building the Cathedrall of St. Paules,[5] & the
Columne in memorie of the Cities Conflagration,[6] & was in
hand with the building of 50 Parish Churches:[7] a ⟨wonderfull⟩[a]
genius had this incomparable Person:

---

[a] MS. *wonder full.*

---

[1] The account was apparently
that relating to the sick and
wounded in the last war; the commissioners' treasurer had recently
submitted the general account and
now the separate accounts were required: *Cal. Treasury Books, 1681–
5*, pp. 89, 119.

[2] For the abnormally dry weather in April, May, and June of this
year compare Wood, *Life and times*,
ii. 538.

[3] Apparently a slip for Philippians ii. 1–7.

[4] Above, p. 170.

[5] Rebuilding began in 1675.

[6] The Monument had been begun
in 1671 and finished in 1677. An
addition to the inscription, attributing the Fire to the Roman
Catholics, was made this year:
Welch, *Hist. of the Monument*, pp.
19–21, 33, 36–41.

[7] By an act passed in 1670 parlia-

8 our *Viccar* as before, shewing the certaine reward of Faith and waiting upon God: *Pomerid*: our new Curate (Mr. *Dolby*)[a][1] on 6. *Mich*: 6. 7. 8. describing the 3 chiefe things which God requires of man: Justice, Mercy, humility.

9 To *Lond*: about my *Accompt* with the *Auditor* of the Exchequer.[2] ⟨12⟩[b] *Ascention* day, a stranger at St. *Martins* on 3 *Jonah*: 4. of Gods mercy & forbearance, upon repentance of the *Ninevites* sparing them 100 yeares after, as by history is made out.[3] The holy com: followed: 15 At the Abby church, Dr. *Brevall*[4] a *French* Proselyte (now a prebend there) on 14 *John* 16. 17: upon the mission of the *H. Ghost* in the absence of our Lord (See your notes).

I dined at Sir *James Shaens*,[5] who had married my Lady *Frances*, daughter to the Earle of[c] *Killdare* a relation of ours, where was also her sister, the Countesse of *Clancarne*, virtuous & most religious Ladys, *Niepces* to *Boyle* Earle of *Corke & Burlington* &c: *Pomerid*: we all went to St. *Margarites* where Dr. *Tillotson*; shewing the danger of deferring Repentance 'til old age, how hard for habitual sinners to convert (see your notes) it was an excellent discourse: That God damns none previously, nor saves any against their wills: of the virtuous heathen, whither any saved, if any, none but by Christ, & for his sake: &c:

---

a Altered from *Dolben*.   b MS. *14*.   c Followed by *Clanc-* deleted.

ment had provided for the rebuilding of fifty-one churches in the City of London: *Statutes of the Realm*, v. 677. Work was proceeding in about twenty-eight of them at this time. Wren also built three London churches outside the City.

[1] Perhaps Thomas Dolby, b. *c.* 1660, M.A., Oxford, 1681: Foster. Other identifications are possible.

[2] This presumably refers to the account presented on 29 April: above, p. 243.

[3] According to Archbishop Ussher Jonah lived during the reign of Joash, A.M. 3163–79, while Nineveh fell in A.M. 3378: *Annales Veteris Testamenti*, 1650, pp. 74–8, 114–15.

[4] Above, iii. 602; he was appointed a prebendary of Westminster in 1675.

[5] Above, p. 84. His wife, Frances, whom he married in 1650, was fifth daughter of George FitzGerald, sixteenth earl of Kildare (above, iii. 169; his connexion with the Brownes, ibid., n.). Her sister Elizabeth, d. *c.* 1698, married first Callaghan Maccarty, d. 1676, third earl of Clancarty (Ireland) 1666; secondly, 1682, Sir William Davis, d. 1687, chief justice of the king's bench, Ireland, 1681–7: G.E.C. For their uncle, Lord Burlington, see above, iii. 242.

ᵃ16 Came my Lady the *Countesse* of *Sunderland*, to desire
me, that I would propose a Match to Sir *Stephen Fox*, for her
sonn, my *Lord Spencer*,¹ to Marry Mrs. *Jane*² Sir *Stephens*
daughter: I excused it all I was able; for the truth is, I was
afraid he would prove an extravagant man; for though a
youth of extraordinary parts, & that had all the Education
imaginable to render him a worthy man; yet his early
inclinations to vice made me apprehensive I should not serve
Sir *St: Fox* in it, like a friend: This being his now onely
Daughter,³ so well bred, &ᵇ whoᶜ was like to receive a large
share of her fathers kindnesse, as far as opulence & mony
could expresse it: For Sir *Stephen* is my Friend, & for whom
I have much esteeme; & I consider'd that My Lord *Sunderland*, being much sunke in his Estate, by Gaming & other
prodigalities,⁴ it could not at this time answer Sir *Stephens*
expectations; for my *Lord*, was now no longer secretary of
state, but was falln in displeasure with the King, for his
siding with the Commons &c: about the Succession;⁵ but
which, I am very well assured he did not do, out of his owne
inclination, or for the preservation of the *Protestant* religion;
but by mistaking a party, which he believed would have
carried it, & perhaps had good reason to think so:⁶ For other-

---

ᵃ Hand in margin here.   ᵇ Followed by *to* deleted.   ᶜ Altered
from *whome*.

---

¹ Robert Spencer, 1666–88; styled Lord Spencer from birth; he died unmarried: *D.N.B.*, art. Spencer, Robert, earl of Sunderland.
² Jane, d. 1721; married 1686, as his first wife, George Compton, 1664–1727, fourth earl of Northampton 1681: G.E.C.
³ Lady Cornwallis (above, p. 219) had died on 28 February of this year; the date of death of the other daughter, Margaret, is unknown.
⁴ Sunderland was an habitual gambler: Bonrepaux, 1687, in Macaulay, *Hist. of England*, ed. C. H. Firth, 1913–15, p. 722 n.; Dartmouth, in Burnet, ed. Airy, ii. 23 n. In May 1680 and again in

August his countess complains of his excesses: Sidney, *Diary*, ii. 55, 100; see also i. 279.
⁵ Sunderland had been deprived of the secretaryship on 31 January of this year. It was usual for a newly appointed secretary to make a considerable payment to his predecessor (Sunderland had paid Sir Joseph Williamson £6,000); the king refused to allow such a payment in the present case: Sidney, *Diary*, ii. 165. Sunderland had voted for the second Exclusion Bill and had joined in the protest when it was rejected; he had also voted Stafford guilty.
⁶ Sunderland joined the Exclu-

wise Sir *Stephen* did not stand so much upon a rich fortune
for his Favorite daughter, but was willing to marry her to a
noble familie, both to fortifie his interests, & better his ally-
ance: However so earnest & importunate was the *Countesse*
that I would use my interest, & breake it to him; that I was
over come, and did accordingly promise it: so next day, I
tooke an opportunitie to introduce the proposal: Sir *Stephen*
(who knew nothing of the young gallants inclinations, but
that he was as to appearance, one of the loveliest & spiritous
Youths in England) professed to me, that no man in England's recomendations should be sooner receiv'd than mine;
but told me That it was too greate an honour to him, that his
Daughter was very Young, as well as my Lord, & he was fully
resolv'd never to marry her, without the parties mutual
liking, which she could not judge of 'til more advanc'd in age,
with other difficulties and objections that I neither could, nor
would contradict: I told him how I was ingag'd, & that I
would serve them both, if he thought good to proceede, and
take what measures he should give me in this matter; I onely
told him that I was my Lady *Sunderlands* friend, one that
she trusted with many ⟨of⟩[a] her concernes, & did Confesse
their condition as to *Estate* was impair'd; but that I verily
believ'd, that if it were set-free, they would husband things
better for the future, & that he would do an act of greate
Generositie, & as already he had, (by marrying his Eldest
Daughter with a vast Portion,) redeem'd my Lord *Cornwallis's* intangled estate,[1] (& who proved a very worthy gent:)
so it would be his glory to set up the Earle of Sunderlands
family againe; with how greate an obligation it would be to
those who sought his Alyance: This did a little worke upon
Sir Stephens good nature, who I am sure might have had his

---

[a] MS. *af.*

---

sionists, apparently thinking it
wiser to be on what he believed
would be the winning side; he seems
to have let it be understood that he
regarded surrender as necessary for
the good of the country; it would
unite king and parliament: letters
in Sidney, *Diary*, ii. 135, 137.

[1] For Cornwallis as gambler see
Hamilton, *Mémoires de Grammont*,
c. ix.

choice in any of the best families in England: However he desired me to write to the Countesse, & to expresse the greate sence he had of the honour don him; that his Daughter & her sonn were too Young, that he would do nothing without her liking, which he did not think her[a] capable of expressing judiciously, 'til she should arive to the age of 16 or 17: of which she now wanted 4 yeares; & in short, that I would put it off as civily as I could for the present; which indeede I did: But my Lady, (now that I had broken the ice,[b]) continues to conjure my assistance, & that I would not leave it in this posture:

20 I went home. 22: our *Viccar* on *Whitsonday* pr: on: 4: Eph: 30. shewing in what manner the holy Spirit was said to be grieved, not that the Godhead could suffer any such passion; but in relation to our ingratitude & neglect, & so after many unkind repulses, deserting him as grieved: ending with a perswasion of entertaining his motions: The Bl: Sacrament followed: *Pomerid*: the new *Curate*, a pretty hopefull young man, yet somewhat raw, & newly come from the Colledge, full of latine sentences &c: which in time will weare off: He read prayers very well, & preached on 6: *Matt*. 33 of the preference of Heaven before Earthly fruitions; &c:

There had scarce fallen yet any raine since *Christmas*:

25 There came to visite me Sir *William Walter*[1] & Sir *Jo: Eloues*:[2] 26: and next day the Earle of Kildare,[3] (a young gent related to my Wife) and other company to dinner: 29 His Majesties Birthday &c. & *Trinity Sonday*, our *Viccar* on 13: Rom: 1. of the duty of subjects, very well &c: *Curate* on 11: *Matt:* 28 the infinite inviting mercy of Christ to burdened sinners.

30 *Trinity* Monday, (a festival day with the *Society* in our

---

[a] Followed by *able to* deleted. [b] MS. *jce*.

---

[1] *c*. 1635–94; nephew of David Walter (above, iii. 56); second baronet 1675: G.E.C., *Baronetage*, ii. 142.

[2] John Elwes, 1635–1702; brother of Sir Gervase Elwes (above, iii. 31, &c.); knighted 1665: J. E.

Cussans, *Hist. of Hertfordshire*, 1870–81, Edwinstree hundred, p. 110; Fèret, *Fulham*, iii. 279–82.

[3] John FitzGerald, 1661–1707; eighteenth earl of Kildare (Ireland) 1664; he was a nephew of Lady Shaen and Lady Clancarty: G.E.C.

Parish, where the Elections are made by Graunt from H: 8:)¹ my *Lord Berkeley* being chosen *Master*, his Chaplaine² preach'd on 1. *Jonah* 6: shewing the greate reason sea-men (of all others,) have of being well prepared for death, & most exposed to danger &c: I went up to Lond, with my Lord, & din'd at the *Trinity* house:

June: 1 Din'd at Sir R: *Claytons*,³ thence᷃to the R: *Society*. 2: To *Hampton-Court* where the Surry Gentlemen presented their Addresses to his Majestie⁴ whose hand I kissed, introduc'd by the *Duke* of *Albemarle*:⁵ but my chiefe affaire was with some of the privy Council about my greate accompt:⁶ I tooke likewise another occasion of discoursing with Sir *Steph: Fox* about his daughter, & to revive that buisinesse, & at last brought it to this, That in case the young people liked one the other, after 4 yeares, (he first desiring to see a particular of my Lords present estate, if I could transmitt it to him privately, ᵃ& not 'til then acquaint them with what now past betweene us) he would ᵇ make her Portion 14000ᶜ pounds: though to all appearance, he may likely make it 50000 pounds as easily: his Eldest son,⁷ having no child, & growing very fatt: &c: So I went back to Lond: & the 4th home:

5 Mr. *Bohune* preached on 12. *Rom* 21. of the greate duty of Charity & christian union, *Pomer*: *Curate* on 13 *Joh:* 34.

ᵃ MS. has here a second opening bracket. deleted.   ᶜ Altered from *12000*.

ᵇ Followed by *grante* deleted.

---

¹ Henry VIII's charter (1514) permitted the establishment of Trinity House as a guild in Deptford parish church; it did not prescribe the place for elections: printed in Barrett, *Trinity House*, pp. 3–5.

² John Rogers, *c.* 1647–1715; M.A., Oxford, 1673; F.R.S. 1681; rector of Seagrave, Leics., 1682–1715; archdeacon of Leicester 1703: Foster. He printed the present sermon this year.

³ No longer lord mayor.

⁴ The address is printed in *London Gazette*, 6 June; see also *Cal. S.P., Dom., 1680–1*, p. 357. Charles was residing at Windsor at this time.

⁵ Christopher Monck, 1653–88; second duke of Albemarle 1670: *D.N.B.*; Ward, *Christopher Monck, duke of Albemarle*. He had no connexion with Surrey, and was presumably officiating on account of either his rank or his office as a gentleman of the bedchamber.

⁶ See above, pp. 243, 244.

⁷ Charles Fox: above, p. 219.

on the same subject: 6: To Lond: returned the 8:[a] also the 9th, returned the 11. about severall buisinesse:

12 Our *Viccar* on 4 *Eph:* as before, shewing the various acceptations of *Spirit* in *Scriptures*: *See your notes*: *Curate* on 5. *Matt:* 3. The blessednesse of humility, & poverty of Spirit: My exceeding drowsinesse hindred my attention, which I feare proceeded from Eating too much, or the drinesse of the season & heate, it still continuing so greate a drowth, as was never knowne in Eng: & was said to be universal: 13 To *Lond:* 14: about my Accompt with the Lords Commiss: of the *Tres:*

16 returned home: 19 our *Viccar* proceeded, against grieving Gods H: Spirit: &c: That the irremissible sinn against him, was obstinate & Pharisaical malice, & final impenetency: (See your notes) The *Curate* also went on: The dry weather had now withered every thing, & threatned some universal dirth &c:

21 To *Lond:* againe about my Accompts, return'd next day:

24 Came to dine with us the Earle of *Kildare*, Countesse of *Clancartie*, and some other persons of qualitie: I went to *Lond* with them returned next day.

26 our *Viccar* on 18 *Luke* 9 on the Parable of the *Pharisee* & *Publican*: *See your notes*. *Curate* on 5 *Matt:* 4. The benefit of penetential teares: the Mourning here expressed, importing godly sorrow & contrition. Some raine now fell:[1]

July To *Lond*, about my Accompts: was very ill of gripings, & went home:

3 our *Viccar* absent; the Minister of *Roderith*[2] supplied 5: Judg: 8. part of the storie of *Debora*; shewing how Idolatry, & defection from the true religion weakned a Nation: The holy Commu: followed: *Curate* on 2: *Act:* 37 of the deplorable condition of sinners, by the almost despaire of them in the *Text*: &c:

---

[a] Altered from 9.

---

[1] So also Wood, *Life and times*, ii. 538.

[2] Presumably George Stoodley: above, p. 140 n.

6 To *Lond:* to the R: *Society*, an Exper: of the effect & reason of impressed force, by the appulses of severall magnitudes: There were present two *Italian* Gent: recomended by Signor *Malphigi* of *Boulogna*:¹ 8 I returned home:

10 Mr. *Saunders*² on 73. *Psal:* 25 shewing how neere *God Almighty* is to his servants in distresse, & that 'tis meere want of Faith & Patience which produces that distresse & anxiety in his Children &c: *Pomeridiano* on 19 *Luke* 42 The sad condition of a People, when no warning reformes them; from Example of the *Jewes*: & that there's a time when God will visite no longer, but leave them to themselves; That such shall wish in vaine for opportunities now neglected: Perstring'd the wanton temper of the Nation, the *schisme* & sedition in Church & state: &c: 11 To *Lond:* returnd that evening. 17: our *Curate*ᵃ on 4: *Pro: 23* of the difficulty in keeping the heart, in reguard of the many tentations: importance of vigilancy over it: *Pomerid*: a young *Scotch-man* on 1. *Eph: 7, Christs* infinite love & condescention in the *Incarnation*, & Passion: & what an obligation is incombent on us to obedience & love:ᵇ 20 To *Lond*, returned that evening.

21 My *Wife* & *Daughter* Mary &c: went to *Tunbridge* to drinke the Waters: &c:

24 A stranger preached on 5: *Eph:* 1. shewing how we might & should be imitators of *Christ* in all things, except his incommunicable qualities; but in *Mercy, justice, Love, humility* &c: *Pomer*: Curate onᶜ his former subject very well, and in good Method, of which the former Curate had none: 31. The *Minister* of *Roderith* on 21 *Isa:* 11, The Calamities of an impenitent Nation &c:³ *Curate* on 19 *Luke*: 41. 42. on our B:S: teares over Jerusalem, upbraided for their Ingratitude, which ever fore-runs destruction &c:

Aug: 4. To *Lond:* about severall affaires: Went to the

ᵃ Altered from *V-*. ᵇ Followed by *The holy Sacrament followed* deleted. ᶜ Followed by *5. Eph: 1.* deleted.

---

¹ There was no regular meeting, but an Italian gentleman recommended by Malpighi (above, iii. 524) was entertained: Birch, iv. 94.

² Above, pp. 131, 160. The text is probably cited from the Prayer Book.

³ The text may be wrong.

R: Society[1] where was produced by Dr. *Slaer*[2] (one of the Members) an extraordinary Experiment: He prepared a matter, which without exposure to the Sunn, or light, (as other *Phosphorus's* were)[a] shoone as bright as the flame of a Candle: It was a substance of the Colour of mouth glew;[3] had an urinous smell; with this he wrote on a sheete of paper, ⟨nothing⟩[b] in the least appearing, but being put into a dark place, shoone forth in a bright & delicate stroke these two words *Vivat Rex Carolus*, which remain'd above halfe an hour, & longer than we were willing to stay: A beame of the Sunn was not more perspicuous, it did not flame up, but remained close to the paper, in a neate stroake about the bignesse ⟨of⟩ Text letters, so as to give a pretty light about it; The very motion of drawing it on a paper, (as one would write with a black-lead pen) seting it on[c] this lambent fire: & when[d] it was almost quite spent, rubbing it a little with ones hand or finger, it would rekindle, yet without taking hold of, or leaving any track on the paper, when exposed to the day againe: Many *Phosphorus* had I seene, as that famous *Lapis illuminabilis* of *Boulogna*,[4] which I went there to see being in *Italy* many years since; but never did I see any comparable to this:[e] Washing my hands & face with it, I appeared in the darke like the face of the moone, or rather like some spirit, or strange apparition; so as I cannot but attribute it to the greate providence of God, that it was not first found out by the *Papists*; for had they the *seacret* onely, what a miracle might[f] they make it, supposing them either to rub the Consecrated Wafer with it, or washing the Priests face & hands with

---

a Closing bracket supplied.   b MS. *nathing*.   c Altered from *in*.
d Followed by *you* deleted.   e Colon supplied.   f Substituted for *would*.

---

[1] Birch records no meetings between 27 July and 5 October; the present meeting was presumably informal.

[2] Frederick Slare (Slear), *c.* 1647-1727; M.D. 1680; F.R.S. 1680: *D.N.B.* An account by him of the present substance and its properties is printed in *Philosophical Collections*, no. 3, 1681, pp. 48–50. For the discovery of phosphorus see F. Hoefer, *Hist. de la chimie*, 2nd ed., 1866–9, ii. 174–5, 193–8.

[3] A compound of glue and sugar, which can be used by moistening it: *O.E.D.*

[4] Above, ii. 423.

it, & doing the feate in some darke Church or Cloyster, pro-
claime it to the Neighbour hood; I am confident the Imposture
would bring thousands to them, & do an infinity of mischiefe,
to the establishing of the common error about Transubstantiation; all the world would ring at the miracle &c: This
matter being rubbed very hard on paper or board, set it in a
devowring flame, which I never saw any *Phosphorus* do but
this, & it being of a nature to spend it selfe, or if a little
warmed either by the fire or the Sunn, would flame out right,
& burne most fiercely, but being kept continualy in a glasse
of water, lasted without impaire: He affirm'd it to be *chymi-
caly* & with extraordinary preparation, composed of Urine &
humane bloud: which gives greate light to Dr. *Willis*[1] &c[a]
notions of the *flamula Vitalis* which animates the bloud, & is,
for ought we know, the animal life it selfe of all things living:
It is certainely a most noble Experiment; first excogitated
& hinted (as this Doctor Confessed) by Mr. *Boyle,*[2] with whom
this industrious young Physitian, some time wrought in his[b]
Laboratory: He tooke a small portion, not bigger than a small
peper Corne, layed it on a dry piece of fir board, & with the
flatt of a knife bruised it, as one would spread a *Plaister*, &
it immediately rose up in a fierce flame, & consum'd the
board: Then he had a *Phiol* of *Liquor*, which he said was
made of a disolution of this, which dropping into a beere glasse
of *Ale*, conceived a flame, so soone as it touched & mingled
with the *Ale*: of this I drank, & seem'd to me to be of an
agreable amber scent, with very little altering the tast of
the *Ale*: The Doctor pretends to bring it into a usefull &

---

a Followed by *opin-* deleted. b Substituted for *the.*

---

[1] Thomas Willis, 1621–75; M.D.
1660; member of the Philosophical
Society 13 Nov. 1661; F.R.S. 1663:
D.N.B. The reference is to his 'De
Sanguinis Accensione', printed with
his *Affectionum . . . histericæ &
hypochondriacæ pathologia,* &c.,
1670. The *flammula vitae* was discussed at the Royal Society on
8 Feb. 1682: Birch, iv. 125.

[2] Boyle's account of his method
of making phosphorus, dated 30
Sept. 1680, was published in 1693
after his death: *Philosophical Transactions,* vol. xvii, no. 196, pp. 583–
4. A material resembling that produced by Slare is described already
in 1677: ibid., vol. xii, no. 135,
p. 867.

precious *Medicine* or *Panaceam*: This liquor was *red*: This noble Experiment, exceeded all that ever I had seene of this nature, unlesse that which my learned Friend, & fellow Traveler *Mr. Hensheaw* & I accidentaly beheld a certaine *Mountebank* at *Rome* in the *Piazza Navona* (formerly Circus Maximus) now the Market place;[a] here, whilst the other *Charlatans*, invited people to their stages, by Monkies, Jackpuddings & *Pantomimes*; This Fellow onely tooke from his finger a *Ring* (w⟨h⟩ither gold, brasse or silver, I could not examine, nor did I[b] mind) which seem'd to have a lump of a blackish wax upon it, about the bignesse & of the shape, of those we call *Toade stones*, (which are indeede, but the grinders of the shark-fish). This he no sooner touched with the tip of his finger, which he seemed to wet with spittle at his mouth onely (though perhaps dip'd in some oyle or other *menstrue*[1] before) but it immediately rose into a flame, as big & bright as any Wax light; This we saw him two or three times blow out, & accend[2] againe, with the least touch of his finger, & then put the ring on his finger,[c] & having by this surprizing trick, gotten Company about him, he fell to prating for the vending of his pretended Remedies &c:[3] But a thousand times have we deplored, that whatever it Cost, we had not purchased this rare receit; Tis mention'd how to make the like both in Wecker[4] & *Jo: Bap: Porta*[5] &c: but on many tryals, it did not succeede: & what stupidity should seaze &[d] possesse us, that all the time we were in *Rome*, we should never think of this, 'til some yeares after we were nearer home,[e] We have both admir'd: The matter of fact is true, & I wish

---

[a] Followed by *where* or *when* deleted.   [b] Followed by *thinke* deleted. There is a drawing of the ring in the margin here.   [c] Followed by *& fell* deleted.   [d] Substituted for *us*.   [e] Followed by *I* deleted.

---

[1] An alternative form for *menstruum*, a solvent: *O.E.D.* Evelyn uses the word in *Sylva*, 1670, p. 6; and several times in *A philosophical discourse of earth* (*Terra*).
[2] Kindle, set alight: *O.E.D.*
[3] For this man see above, ii. 397–8.

[4] Johann Jacob Wecker, 1528–86: *Allgemeine deutsche Biog.* The reference is to *De Secretis libri xvii*, 1582, pp. 61–3, 640–2 (see also English translation, *Eighteen Books of the Secrets of Art & Nature*, 1660, pp. 15–16, 247–8).
[5] Above, ii. 398 and n.

I[a] knew how to make the like for a greate summ of mony; since, ⟨if⟩[b] it could be made without exceeding Cost, it would be an expeditious way to kindle any fire, light a Candle, & use upon a thousand occasions, abroad or at home:

4. I din'd at the E: of *Sunderlands*, the Countesse of Bristol, & Mr. *Sidney*,[1] sonn to the Earle of *Licester* who had ben Ambassador in Holland: & returned home in the Evening:

7 A stranger preached on 3: *Lam:* 26. That we should waite on God in the method of his proceedings, with *Faith, Hope & Patience*, & ⟨not⟩ be over curious in diving into the causes of his actings &c: (*See your notes*) The holy Communion follow'd: &c: Afternoone the *Curate* on his former subject, with little addition of moment: 14: Our *Viccar* still indisposed, the Curate preached on 3: Apocalyps. 19. That all Chastizements come from God, that this was for encouragement even to the luke-warm *Laodiceans*, against despaire: & a toaken of his Love, & desire of their repentance, who stood yet indifferent. No *Sermon* this afternoone, which I think did not happen twice in this *parish* these 30 yeares; so gracious had God ben to it, & indeede to the whole Nation: God Grant, we abuse not this greate privelegdge: either by our wantonesse, schismes, or Unfruitfullnesse under such meanes, as he has not favoured any nation with under heaven besides:

16 To Lond: din'd next day at the Earle of Arlingtons: returned the 18:

21 Our *Viccar*, pursued his former subject on 18 *Luke* 9. The Parable of the *Pharisee*, concerning the posture & demean⟨o⟩ur at Prayer: &c: (*See notes*) The *Curate* as before &c:

23 I went to visite my deare Bro: at *Wotton*, the place of my birth: & Country:

---

a Followed by *had it* deleted.   b MS. *it*.

---

[1] Henry Sidney, 1641–1704; brother of the present earl of Leicester (above, iii. 164) and uncle of Sunderland; created Viscount Sydney of Sheppey 1689; earl of Romney 1694: *D.N.B.* He was envoy extraordinary at The Hague from August 1679 until June of this year. He was the author of the *Diary*.

24 I was invited to Mr. *Denzil Onslows*[1] at his seate at *Pur-ford*,[a][2] where was much company, & such an extraordinary feast, as I had hardly ever seene at any[b] Country Gent: table in my whole life; but what made it more[c] remarkeable was, that there was not any thing, save what his Estate about it did not afford; as Venison, Rabb⟨i⟩ts, hairs, Pheasants, Partridge, [pigeons,][d] Quaile, Poultrie, all sorts of fowle in season (from his owne Decoy[3] neere his house) all sorts of fresh fish: so Industrious is this worthy Gent: After dinner we went to see sport at the decoy, I never saw so many herons &c. The seate stands on a flat, the ground pastures, rarely watred, & exceedingly improved; since Mr. Onslow bought it of Sir *Rob: Parkhurst*,[4] who spent a faire Estate &c: The house is Timber, but commodious, & with one ample dining roome, & the hale adorned with paintings of fowle, & huntings &c: the work of Mr. *Barlow*,[5] who is excellent in this kind from the life: It stands neere part of Guildford river, within 12 or 14 miles of Lond:[6] we returned to Wotton in the Evening:

28 A stranger preached at Wotton on 4: Eph: 4. on *Christian Unity*: no Sermon after noone:

30 I went to visite *Mr. Hussey*[7] a neere neighbour of my Bro: who has a very pretty seate, delicately watred, & he cer-

---

a Altered from or to *Purflet*.   b Followed by *pri*- deleted.
c Followed by *extr*- deleted.   d Interlined.

---

[1] *c.* 1635–1721; younger brother of Sir Arthur Onslow (above, iii. 540); M.P. for Haslemere 1679; 1689–95; for Surrey 1695–8; for Guildford 1701–13, 1714–17; for Surrey 1717–21: Manning and Bray, i. 157; iii. 54; &c.

[2] Pyrford, seven miles northeast of Guildford. Onslow bought the manor in 1677; the house, which was Elizabethan, was pulled down *c.* 1776: *V.C.H., Surrey*, iii. 432–3; Aubrey, *Surrey*, iii. 197.

[3] For it see Aubrey, iii. 198; *V.C.H., Surrey*, iii. 431. It is now disused.

[4] Robert Parkhurst, d. 1674; admitted Cambridge 1647; M.P. for Guildford in Richard Cromwell's parliament; knighted 1660: Venn.

[5] Above, iii. 166. Pyrford descended to the earls of Onslow and the present Lord Onslow owns (at Clandon) six pictures by Barlow representing birds, hounds, &c., four of them important for their size; one is dated 1667 and another apparently belongs to 1671 or earlier: Sparrow, *British sporting artists*, pp. 29–31.

[6] It is on the Wey, which runs through Guildford, and is twenty-three miles from London.

[7] Identifiable as Peter Hussey of Sutton in Shere: above, iii. 561.

tainely the neatest husband for curious ordering his Domestic
& field Accomodations, & what pertaines to husbandry, that
in my life I have ever seene, as to his severall Graneries,
Tackling, Tooles & Utensils, Ploughs, Carts, Stables, Wood-
piles, Woork house, even to the hen rosts & hog troughs: so as
mithought I saw old *Cato or Varro*[1] in him: all substantial, all
in exact order, which exceedingly delighted me: The sole
inconvenience he lies under, is the greate quantities of sand,
which his streames bring along with them, which fills his
chanales & receptacles of fish too soone: The rest of my time
of stay at *Wotton* was spent in walking about the grounds &
goodly Woods, where I have in my Youth entertained my
solitude &c: & so on the 2d of *September* I returned to my
home, being two daies after my Wife &c was returned from
Tunbridge, where they had ben, I blesse God, with good successe, now neere five weekes:[2]

4 Our *Viccar* preach'd on his former Text concerning the
humility of the *publican*: unsincerity of the *Pharisee*, shewing
how far an hypocrite may go with shew of religion, & after
all his paines, be rejected; whilst others with lesse outward
shew may be accepted: That it was the costome in St. *Augus-
tines* time for the *People* at Confession, to beate their brests
in the church, as being the seate of the heart; where all our
Affections are lodged &c: The holy *Communion* follows;
Pomer: a *Stranger* on 1. *Coloss:* 2. That all things were sanctified to us by the Grace of God.

6. Died my pretty Grand-child at Nurse of the gripes.[3]
8. My good neighbour Mr. *Turner*[4] was buried, our *Viccar*
preached on 126. *Psal.* 7:[5] when ⟨likewise⟩[a] was interred our
little Child: 9: I sadly remembred the losse of another deare

---

[a] MS. *likewas*.

---

[1] Marcus Porcius Cato, Cato the
Elder, 234–149 B.C., general; author
of *De agri cultura*; Marcus Terentius
Varro (Reatinus), 116–27 B.C.,
miscellaneous author; author of
Rerum rusticarum libri III. The two
works were first printed in 1472,
together.
[2] See above, p. 250.
[3] Richard Evelyn: see above,
pp. 235, 236.
[4] Thomas Turner: above, iii. 622 n.
[5] From the Prayer Book.

friend:[1] This afternoone came the Bish: of *Rochester* & his Lady[2] to visite us:

11 our *Viccar* as formerly; & *Curate* likewise, shewing the advantage of Chastizement, with this difference from that of Earthly parents; that they punish their Children, whom they for their faults do not love; God *Almighty* those whom he dos, but 'tis only for trial, & ⟨to⟩ better them: Parents often of their owne froward & peevish nature, &c. 12 Came my *La: Sylvius* & other Ladys to Visite us, with whom I went to Lond: that evening: 14. Din'd with Sir *Step: Fox*: Who proposed to me the purchasing of *Chelsey Coll*; which his Majestie had some time since given to our *Society*, & would now purchase it of us againe, to build an *Hospital* [Infirmary][a] for Souldiers there; in which he desired my assistance as one of the Council of the R: Society:[3] 15 I had another opportunity of perusing his Majesties private Library at Whitehall:[4] I dined at Mr. *Chichleyes*: thence to see Sir *Sam: Morelands* house, & Mechanics: supp'd at L: *Syl*: 17: I went with Monsieur *Faubert*[5] about the taking of the *Countesse* of

---

[a] Interlined.

---

[1] Mrs. Godolphin.

[2] Catherine Sheldon, *c.* 1621–1706, niece of the archbishop and sister of Daniel Sheldon of Ham Court (above, p. 142); married Dolben *c.* 1657 (so *D.N.B.*; presumably 14 Jan. 1658: below, p. 266).

[3] For Chelsea College see above, iii. 397, &c. It is doubtful whether it was used to house prisoners of war in the last Dutch war; since then the Society had made various attempts to let it: notices in Birch. For the proposed Hospital see below, pp. 269–70, &c. Evelyn was not a member of the Council of the Royal Society at this time: above, p. 225; on 5 October he and Wren were appointed to negotiate with Fox: Birch, iv. 97.

[4] Above, pp. 214–16.

[5] Solomon Foubert, d. 1696. He is described in 1668 as 'écuyer du roi tenant academie Royale au Faubourg St Germaine'. As a result of the closing of the Protestant academies in France he came to England about July 1679 with his wife, his son Henri, and other members of his family. He settled at the corner of Sherwood (Sherard) and Brewer Streets, and, with the help of grants from Charles II, James II, and William III, conducted an academy there; among his pupils were Robert Harley and Count Philipp Christoph von Königsmarck (below, p. 274 n.). Henri Foubert (d. 1743), who served in the English army and became a major, apparently tried to carry on the academy; later he moved to Swallow Street, where he established a riding-school; Foubert's Place, Regent Street, commemorates it:

Bristols house &c: for an *Academie*, he being lately come from *Paris*, for his Religion, & resolving to settle here: I dind at Sir *Bernard Gas⟨c⟩oynes*, & home in the Evening: ⟨18⟩[a] *Viccar* & Curat as above, with the usual applications:

23 I went to see Sir *Tho: Bonds fine house & Garden* at *Peccham*:[1] 25 our *Viccar* on 3. *Jam:* 18. of the good of peace & righteousnesse, & its fruits: Curat as before:

Octob: 2 As above: That Righteousnesse was onely our obedience & conformity to the Law of God: The holy Sacrament followd: (See your *notes.*) *Pomeridiano* I went to *Camerwell* where that good man Dr. *Par*[2] (late Chapl: to the Primate of Ireland *Bishop Usher*) preached on 16 *Act:* 30 on the Conversion of the *Goaler*: See your notes: 4: To *Lond:* about severall affaires &c:

9 Dr. *Tenison* at St. *Martines* on 46 *Isa:* 8: That the dignitie of mankind above all other Creatures, should prompt him to do nothing unworthy himselfe, & unbecoming his Character &c: Se your *notes:*—I din'd at Mr. *Brisbanes*: *Pomerid*: a stranger at St. *Margarits* 5 *Matt:* 20 of the danger of *Hypocrisie*; & necessity of exceeding formal christians:

11 I went to *Fullham* to visite the *Bish:* of *Lond:*[3] in whose Garden I first saw the *Sedum arborescens* in flowre, which was exceeding beautifull: I called in at *Parsons Greene* to see our Charge, my L: Vic: *Mordaunts* Children: 13. I went to visite my worthy friend Mr. *Boyle*:

16 *Cor: Rege* preached Dr. *Ball* on 13 *John*: 17. concerning the necessity of Practising what we know; That the *Christian*

---

[a] MS. *12*.

W. H. Manchée, in Huguenot Soc., *Proceedings*, xvi (1941), 77–97; see also Leti, *Del teatro brittanico*, ii. 795–6; notices in contemporary correspondence show the high social standing of the academy. Late in 1679 Foubert was negotiating with the Royal Society for a lease of Chelsea College, but failed to come to terms: Birch, iii. 505–6; iv. 2.

[1] Above, p. 93.

[2] Above, iii. 603.

[3] The bishops of London had owned the manor of Fulham from 691; the earliest existing part of their palace was built in the early sixteenth century. Compton is especially associated with the planting of the grounds: Fèret, *Fulham*, iii. 94–146, especially pp. 129–37. Ray identifies the *Sedum majus arborescens* as the Tree houseleek: *Hist. Plantarum*, 1686–1704, i. 687.

World was sufficiently instructed: That knowledge was pernicious without doing, in as much as the *Devils* know more
than men; no man happy or better for his knowledge without
Grace acctualy to apply it. 18 My *Coach-house* was robbed,
they ript off the Velvet &c: There was this day a meeting
with the rest of the *Trustees*,[1] upon my Young *Lord Vicount
Mordaunts* offer to procure 20000 pounds for the payment of[a]
his Bro: & sisters portions, in consideration that we would
possesse him of *Parsons Greene*, & the *Coale-farme*,[2] which
were worth 3000 per Annum: This tooke up long debates with
our Council, who were for us Sir *William Jones*[3] late *Attourney*
Gen: and Mr. *Keck*:[4] There were with me the *Earle* of *Clarendon*, Mr. *Newport*, & Mr. *Herbert*: but nothing concluded.
19 I dind at *Somerset-house* with my L. *Clarendon*;[5] thence
to The *R: Society*,[6] where in absence of our *President*, I was
faine to take the Chaire: There was much Company, it being
the first day of meeting after our summers accostom'd
Recesse:

21 Dr. *Tenison* Cat⟨e⟩chiz'd at St. *Martines*,[7] very profitably on that[b] article of the *Creede*: *I believe the forgivenesse
of sinns* &c shewing what sinn was, the Kinds of it: None so
greate (*Apostacy* and malice excepted) but were remissable
even after *Baptisme*, (against the *Heresy* of *Novatus*:[8]) if it
had ben otherwise, our *B: Lord* would not have taught us
to pray daily for the forgivenesse of our Trespasses: That it
was attainable only by Confession to God, amendment, &

---

[1] See above, pp. 188–9.

[2] There was an export duty of 4s.
per chaldron on coal, and it was
collected through a farm: *Cal. Treasury Books, 1679–80*, p. 259; *1685–
9*, pp. 230–1. There is nothing to
show that Mordaunt was in any
way connected with it.

[3] Above, iii. 580; iv. 227.

[4] Presumably Anthony Keck,
1630–95; knighted 1689; commissioner of the great seal 1689–90:
D.N.B.

[5] Clarendon was appointed
keeper of Somerset House in 1679:
Cal. S.P., Dom., 1679–80, p. 299;
and was treasurer to the queen
from 1680 to 1685.

[6] Birch, iv. 97–8.

[7] This day was a Friday; cf.
below, p. 269.

[8] Novatus is an error for Nova-
tian, the third-century schismatic.
It is presumably due to Evelyn, as
it occurs again in *Hist. of religion*, ii.
230.

Faith in the blood of Christ: I supp'd with my L. *Chamberlaine*, 21 returned home:

23 *Viccar* on his former: See your *notes*: Curate on 3: *Apoc:* 19 That nothing can recover greate sinners, but greate repentance, industrious obedience: 30: *Viccar* as before: *Pomerid*: a *stranger* on 2: *Heb:* 3: The danger of neglecting the meanes. &c. 31ᵃ Being my Birth-day and 61 yeares of my age, I spent in recollection of the yeare past, giving God thankes for his many signal mercys, & imploring his blessing on the yeare now entering:

November 1 Met the foefoès for the poore, the *Viccar* (as usualy¹) on 73 *Psal:* 1. 2. Concerning the Providential care of God over his Creatures &c: &c: 3 To *Lond:* 5. *Coram Rege* preached Dr. *Hooper*² on 12. *Mar:* 16. 17. of the Usurpations of the *Chur⟨c⟩h* of Rome: this is one of the first rank of pulpet men in the Nation.

6 To the household a *stranger* on 1. *Jam.* 27. Concerning the Grace of Charity: The B: *Sacrament* follow'd: Bish: of *Lond:* officiating: *Coram Rege* Dr. *Jane*³ 2: Tim: 3. 2. of the prodigious defecction & vices of the last times, an excellent discourse:ᵇ 13 A chaplain on 23 *Pro* 17. 18 of holinesse & patience, & waiting the providence of God:

ᶜ15 I went to Visite, & dined with the *Earle* of *Essex*, who after dinner in his study sitting alone with him by the fire, related to me how much he had ben scandaliz'd & injur'd in the report of his being privy to the Marriage of his Ladys Niepce, the rich young Widdow of my late Lord *Oagle*, sole daughter of the Earle of *Northumberland* ;⁴ shewing me a letter

---

ᵃ Altered from *33*. ᵇ Followed by *23* deleted. ᶜ Hand in margin here.

---

¹ i.e. preaching, not the particular text; cf. above, p. 183, &c.
² George Hooper, 1640–1727; D.D. 1677; rector of Lambeth 1675–1703; chaplain in ordinary *c.* 1684–1703; dean of Canterbury 1691; bishop of St. Asaph 1703; of Bath and Wells 1704: *D.N.B.* The sermon was printed in 1682, the text St. Matthew xxii. 21, the paral-

lel to that given by Evelyn.
³ William Jane, 1645–1707; D.D. 1679; Regius professor of divinity at Oxford 1680–1707; chaplain in ordinary *c.* 1682–1707; dean of Gloucester 1685: *D.N.B.*
⁴ Lady Elizabeth, 1667–1722, only surviving daughter and heiress of Joceline Percy, eleventh earl of Northumberland (above, iii. 481),

of *Mr.*[a] *Thinns* excusing himselfe for his not communicating his Marriage to his Lordship; acquainting me also with the whole storie of that unfortunate Ladys being betraied by her Grandmother the Countesse of *N-humb:*[1] & Coll: *Bret*[2] for mony; and that though upon the importunitie of the *Duke* of *Monmoth,*[3] he had delivered [to the Grandmother][b] a particular of the Joynture, which *Mr. Thynn* pretended he would settle on the Lady; yet he totaly discourag'd the proceeding, as by no meanes a competent Match, for one that both by her birth, & fortune might have pretended to the greatest Prince in Christendome: That he also proposed the Earle of *Kingston*[4] (a kinds man of mine) or the Lord *Cranborn*;[5] but was by no meanes for Mr. *Thynn:*

---

[a] Followed by *Tinns* deleted.   [b] Interlined.

who was a half-brother of Lady Essex; married first, in 1679, Henry Cavendish, 1663–80, styled Lord Ogle from 1676, son of Henry Cavendish, second duke of Newcastle; secondly, in 1681, Thomas Thynne, 1648–82, of Longleat, 'Tom of Ten Thousand' (*D.N.B.*; his murder, below, p. 274 n.); thirdly, on 30 May 1682, Charles Seymour, 1662–1748, sixth duke of Somerset 1678 ('the proud duke'): *D.N.B.*, art. Seymour; G. Brenan, *Hist. of the house of Percy*, 1902, ii. 373–418, &c.; G.E.C. On 7 November, apparently very soon after her marriage with Thynne, and before it was consummated, she fled to Holland. Thynne was said to have been under a pre-contract to marry a woman whom he was believed to have seduced. Notices relating to the marriage in *Hist. MSS. Comm., Rutland MSS.*, vol. ii; *Buccleugh MSS. at Montague House*, i. 334–5; *Ormonde MSS.*, new ser., vol. vi; *Hatton corr.* (Camden Soc.), vol. ii; *Cal. S.P., Dom., 1682*, pp. 48–50; Sidney, *Diary*, ii. 224, Reresby, 2 Jan., 12 Feb. 1682.

[1] Lady Elizabeth Howard, widow of Algernon Percy, the tenth earl:

above, iii. 264; she was stepmother of Lady Essex. By Earl Joceline's will she was to become guardian of his daughter in the event of his widow's remarriage: Brenan, ii. 316; the latter had remarried in 1673: below, p. 344.

[2] Identifiable as Richard Brett, husband of Lady Catherine Boyle, *c.* 1653–81, a daughter of Lord Orrery (above, iii. 405) and through her mother a first cousin once removed of Lady Ogle: J. Lodge, *Peerage of Ireland*, ed. M. Archdall, 1789, i. 192–3; &c. He was said to have been paid £10,000 for the marriage: *Hist. MSS., Comm., Ormonde MSS.*, new ser., vi. 107; *R. R. Hastings MSS.* ii. 173. For Lady Ogle's opinion of him see her letter in *Cal. S.P., Dom., 1682*, p. 50.

[3] Thynne was a violent Exclusionist.

[4] Robert Pierrepont, *c.* 1660–82; third earl 1680: G.E.C.; for his relationship to Evelyn see V, 31 Oct. 1620.

[5] James Cecil, 1666–94, styled Lord Cranborne from 1668 until 1683, when he succeeded as fourth earl of Salisbury: *D.N.B.*

19 I din'd with & visited my worthy friend Mr. *Aerskin*[1] Master of the *Charterhouse*, a Wise & learned *Gent:* ⟨fitter⟩[a] to have ben a Privy Councelor & Minister of state than laied aside: he is likewise Unkle to the *Dutchesse* of *Monmoth.*

20 D⟨r⟩. *Jane*[b] on *Heb:* concerning the infinite value of *Christs* Sacrifice: *Cor: Rege* Dr. *Smith*[2] on 112. *Psal:* 7. of the Security & Confidence of a Christian, through faith and obedience. 23 To the *R: Society.* 24. I was at the Audience of the *Russia Ambassador*[3] which was befor both their Majesties in the Banqueting-house: The presents were carried before them, held up by his followers standing in two rankes towards the Kings state, & consisted of Tapissry (one suit[4] of which was doubtlesse brought from France as being of that fabric, this *Ambassador* having passed through that *Kingdom* as he came out of *Spaine*) a large *Persian* Carpet, Furrs of *Sable* & *Ermine* &c: [c]but nothing was so splendid & exotick, as the *Ambassador* Who came soone after his Majesties restauration:[5] This present *Ambassador* was exceedingly offended that his Coach was not permitted to come into the Court; [6]til being told that no *Kings* Ambassadors did, he was pacified, yet requiring an attestation of it under Sir *Ch: Cotterells*[7] the Master of the Ceremonies hand; being it seemes

---

[a] MS. *fitteer.*   [b] Altered from *Viccar.*   [c] Hand in margin here.

---

[1] William Erskine (commonly written Aerskine), d. 1685; son of John Erskine, second earl of Mar (Scotland); cupbearer to Charles I; member of the Philosophical Society 11 Sept. 1661; F.R.S. (Original Fellow) 1663; master of the Charterhouse 1677–85: Paul, *Scots peerage*, v. 622; [R. Smythe], *Historical account of Charter-House*, 1808, p. 238. His eldest sister was maternal grandmother of the duchess of Monmouth: *Scots peerage*, ii. 236, vii. 299.

[2] Presumably Dr. Smith of Christ Church: above, p. 240.

[3] Prince Peter Potemkin; his mission was to confirm the existing friendly relations between Charles

II and the Tsar (Theodore II): Lubimenko, *Relations de l'Angleterre avec la Russie*, p. 251. Notice of the audience, but as taking place on 23 November, in *London Gazette*, 28 Nov.; as taking place apparently on 24 November, in *True Protestant Mercury*, 26 Nov.; the latter is presumably correct. The ambassador stayed here until 25/15 Feb. 1682. He had been in Paris in May and in Madrid in August.

[4] A series: *O.E.D.* Leti also notes the French tapestries: *Del teatro brittanico*, ii. 348.

[5] In 1662: above, iii. 344, 349.

[6] Cf. Leti, ii. 347.

[7] Above, iii. 515.

afraid he should offend his Master if he omitted the least
puntillo: 'Twas reported he condemn'd his sonn to loose his
head, for shaving off his beard, & putting himselfe in the
French mode at *Paris*, & that he had executed it, had not the
french *King* interceeded: of this *quære*:

27 At W:hall, Dr. *Smith*[1] on 12: *Heb:* 1 of the necessitie of
subduing our darling sinns,[a] *Cor: Rege:* Dr. Jane: 2. Reg: 7.[b]
1. 2. Gods extraordinary Providence, in bringing about
wonderfull & unexpected[c] Events: full of Instances &
Encouragements to rely on God, & most excellently discoursed: *Pomerid:* St. *Margarits* where Dr. *Lamb:*[2] preached
on   The haires of your head are numbred.

28 Several Fellows of our *Society* met at diner in the Citty,
to consult about Electing a fit Secretarie, & to regulate some
other defects:[3] This Evening I got Dr. *Slaer*[4] to shew my
Lord Chamberlaine, the Duke & Dutchesse of Grafton, the
Earle of Chesterfild, *Conde de Castel Melior*[5] & severall others,
that admirable and stupendious experiment of[d] both the
liquid & drie *Phosphorus*, at which they were all astonish'd:
30 Being *St. Andrews* day, we continued Sir *Chr: Wrenn* our
President, elected a new Council according to the Statute,
of which I was one; & chose *Mr. Austine* secretary with Dr.
Plott, the ingenious Author of the Natural *Hist.* of Oxford-
shire: There was a most illustrious appearance:[6]

December 1 I went home to my house, after neere a Moneths

---

a Or *sinne*.   b Followed by *12* deleted.   c Followed by *effects*
deleted.   d Followed by *the* deleted.

---

[1] Presumably Dr. Smith of
Christ Church.
[2] No Dr. Lamb is traceable at
this date. Presumably John Lambe,
c. 1649–1708; M.A. 1672; D.D.
1693 (*c.* 1682?); chaplain in
ordinary *c.* 1676–1708; dean of Ely
1693: Venn.
[3] The present secretaries (there
were always two) were Hooke and
Dr. Thomas Gale (below, p. 300,
&c.). The latter was now replaced
by Aston (see below).

[4] Slare; for him and the phosphorus see above, pp. 251–4.
[5] Castelmelhor: above, p. 130.
[6] Birch, iv. 105–6. Wren had
been elected president in 1680 in
place of Boyle: above, p. 225 n.
Austine is Francis Aston, d. *c.* 1715;
F.R.S. 1678; secretary 1681–5:
Weld, *Hist. of the Royal Society*, i.
302–3, 305, 428. Plot (above, p.
68) was not elected secretary until
30 Nov. 1682 (he continued in office
until 1684).

absence upon buisinesse with Sir *Denis Gauden*, & Commissioners of the Navy:[1] 4: our *Viccar* on 8: Joh: 36. of the bondage of the ceremonial law, & freedome by Christ & his law: *Pomer*: a stranger, on: 2: *Phil:* 13. That all our Graces spring from the good pleasure of God, cultivated by our endeavors & coöperation with it: which likewise is his ⟨gift⟩.[a] 11: our *Viccar* as before: shewing how we had no liberty to sinn, by being freed from the Law; but that Pardon onely did free us &c: Curate on : 6: *Rom:* 21 of the bitter and shamefull fruites of sinn; Their pleasure short, staine perpetual; & though remitted through repentance, yet leaving a scarr; opposing the fruits of Righteousnesse to it which were permanent & lasting: 11. To Council of the R: So: about letting a lease of some Lands belonging to the Society:[2] Din'd at Mr. *Ben: Bathursts*.[3] 15 The *Duke* of *Grafton* invited me to a magnificent Feast at the Trinity house:[4] 17. home:

18 Mr. *Bohune* preached on 25 *Matt* 25.[5] perstringing *Pharesaical* Hypocrisie of the present age: That Religion consisted not in the *minutiæ*, but greater[b] lines[b] of *Christian* duty, *Faith, Love, Justice* &c: not in refusing to receive indifferent Ceremonies of Ornament, Edification & Order, in the poure of the Magistrate to impose, so long as there was nothing repugnant or unagreable to the life of the Gospel:

---

[1] This business is not traceable. The accounts of the commission for sick and wounded were not yet wound up.

[2] The date is obviously wrong. The Council met on 14 December and discussed the lease of some lands attached to Chelsea College; Evelyn is not recorded as attending; Birch, iv. 111–12. There was perhaps an informal meeting earlier in the week.

[3] Benjamin Bathurst, *c.* 1638–1704; brother of Dr. Ralph Bathurst; deputy governor of the Royal African Company 1681–2; knighted 1682 (17 Jan.); alderman, Cripplegate ward, 1683–6; M.P. for Beeralston 1685; governor of the East India Company 1688–90; cofferer to Queen Anne 1702–4; M.P. for New Romney 1702–4; D.C.L. 1702; married, 1682, Frances Apsley, *c.* 1653–1727, a friend from their childhood of both Queen Mary and Queen Anne; father of the first Earl Bathurst: Baker, (*Northamptonshire*), ii. 203, 207; B. Bathurst, *Letters of two queens*, [1924], pp. 144–6; &c.

[4] There is a notice of the feast in *London Gazette*, 19 Dec.

[5] Presumably an error for St. Matthew xxiii. 25.

such as the Crosse in Baptisme, Surplice &c: at which precise people are scandalized without cause: *Pomer*: a stranger, on: 11: *Psal:* 11¹ of the Sovraine Good, the felicity of entertaining our thoughts with the Contemplation of the beatifical Vision.

21ª To *Lond:* to a Council of the Society:² 22 return'd home:

25 *Christmas day* our *Viccar* on 2. *Heb:* 17 apposite to the day: The holy Comm: followed. See your Notes: *Pomer*: *Curate* 2: *Luke* 14, on the same subject, the Incarnation &c: 31 I gave thanks to God for the past yeares protection, & his gracious dealing with me:

1682. *Jan:* 1 Our *Viccar* preached on his former subject 2. *Heb:* 27.³ *See your notes*: why God passed by the Angels that fell, & was thus gracious to Man-kind &c: The holy Sacrament *followd*, at which I implored the blessing of Almighty God for the yeare now entering:

Some Neighbours dined with us according to Costome: *Pomerid*: Curate on 6: *Rom:* 21: with no greate addition, it being on his former Text:⁴ 8: our *Viccar* as above see your *Notes*: & so the *Curate*, of the cursed *fruite*ᵇ of sinn & vice:

ᶜ11 To Lond: Saw the *Audience* of the *Morroco Ambassador*:⁵ his retinue not numerous, was receivd in the Banqueting-house both their Majesties present: he came up to the Throne without making any sort of Reverence, bowing so much as his head or body: he spake by a *Renegado English* man,⁶ for whose safe returne there was a promise: They were

---

ᵃ Altered from *20*. ᵇ Or *fruits*. ᶜ Hand in margin here.

---

¹ This text does not exist; perhaps an error for Psalms xvi. 11.
² Birch does not mention the Council's meeting this day, but gives an ordinary meeting: iv. 113–15.
³ A slip for verse 17: see above, 25 December.
⁴ Above, p. 264.
⁵ Ahmed Hadu (Mohammed Ohadu): for his embassy see Routh, *Tangier*, pp. 220–31; Defontin-Maxange, *Le grand Ismail*, 1929, p. 151; notice of this audience in *London Gazette*, 12 Jan. (reprinted

in Routh). Further notice of the ambassador in F. Pidou de St. Olon, *Estat present de . . . Maroc*, 1694, pp. 123–5; see also *Hist. MSS. Comm., Le Fleming MSS.*, pp. 186–7; engraved portrait by R. White. His mother is said to have been French or English. He remained here until July.
⁶ Hamet Lucas; he was not English, but had twice deserted from Tangier: Routh, pp. 211–13, 222, 229–32; see also *London Gazette*, 24 July 1682.

all Clad in the *Moorish* habite Cassocks of Colourd Cloth or silk with buttons & loopes, over this an *Alhaga*[1] or white wollan mantle, so large as to wrap both head & body, a shash[2] or small *Turban*, naked leg'd & arm'd, but with lether socks like the *Turks*, rich *Symeters*, large Calico sleev'd shirts &c: The Ambassador had[a] a string of Pearls odly woven in his Turbant; I fancy the old Roman habite was little different as to the Mantle & naked limbs: The Ambassador was an handsom person, well featur'd, & of a wise looke, subtile, and extreamely Civile: Their Presents were *Lions* & *Estridges* &c:[3] Their Errant, about a Peace at Tangire &c:[4] But the Concourse & Tumult of the People was intollerable, so as the Officers could keepe no order;[5] which they were astonish'd at at first; There being nothing so regular exact & perform'd with such silence &c, as [in][b] all these publique occasions of their Country, & indeede over all the Turkish dominions: 12 I din'd at Sir *Gab: Sylvius* with the Countesses of *Bristol* & *Sunderland* & supped at the Earle of *Arlingtons*. 13 din'd At Sir St: *Foxes*. 14 At the *Bish:* of *Rochesters*[6] at the *Abby* it being his Marriage day after 24 yeares: He related to me after dinner, how he had ben treated by Sir *William Temple* for-

---

a Followed by *som-* deleted. b Interlined.

---

[1] Properly haik: see *O.E.D.* An 'Alheick of lile grogram', defined as 'a long loose garment much like an Irish mantle', is mentioned in *Late Newes out of Barbary*, 1613, sig. B3v.; the same form is used by L. Addison, *West Barbary*, 1671, pp. 184, 185, 203. Further description in Pidou de St. Olon, pp. 94, 96.

[2] i.e. sash; the older form of the word; originally the strip of material forming the turban: *O.E.D.* Evelyn has already used the word in its modern sense: above, iii. 465.

[3] Two lions and thirty ostriches, 'which his Majesty laughed at, saying he knew nothing fitter to return for them then a flock of gheese': Reresby, 11/12 Jan. The former had been sent to the Tower; the latter

were to be sent to St. James's Park: *Domestick Intelligence*, 9 Jan. Charles appears to have given the ostriches to any of the courtiers who would accept them: Routh, p. 224.

[4] The objects of the embassy were the revision of a treaty relating to Tangier made in 1681 and the negotiation of a treaty for peace at sea: Routh, p. 220.

[5] There appears to have been no disorder in the Banqueting House; but the gates of Whitehall had to be shut against the crowd: *Loyal Protestant, and True Domestick Intelligence*, 12 Jan.

[6] Dolben was also dean of Westminster. For Mrs. Dolben see above, p. 257.

seeing he might be a Delegate[1] in the Concerne of my Lady *Ogle*, now likely to come in Controversy, upon her Marriage with *Thynn*:[2] Also how earnestly the late *E: of Danby* L: Tressurer sought his frie⟨n⟩dship, and what plaine & sincere Advice he gave him from time to time about his miscarriages & Partialities;[a] particularly, his outing Sir *Jo: Duncomb*[3] from being *Chancelor* of the Exchequer, & Sir *St: Fox* above all from Pay-Master to the Armie:[4] The *Treasurers* excuse & reason was that *Foxes* Credit was so over-greate with the *Bankers* & monied men, that he could procure none, but by his meanes: For that reason (replied the Bishop) I would have made him my Friend: Sir *Steph⟨en⟩* being a person both honest & of credit: he told him likewise of his statlinesse, & difficulty of Accesse & severall other miscarriages, & which indeede made him hated &c:[5] & so I returned home: 15 *Vicc: & Cur:* as before, & so on the 22d:

24 To *Lond:* where at the Council of the *R: Soc:*[6] we passed a new Law, for the more accurate consideration of *Candidates* before admission, as whither they would realy be Usefull: & also concerning Honorarie Members, that none should be admitted but *per diploma*: An exper: for the describing any *Parabola line* whatsoever. This Evening I was at the Entertainement of the *Morroco* ⟨*Ambassador*⟩[b] at the Dut: of

---

a Followed by *the* deleted.   b MS. *Ambassadors*.

---

[1] The Court of Delegates was the court of appeal for ecclesiastical cases; the members were specially appointed for each case: notices in Chamberlayne.

[2] Above, p. 260 n. Lady Temple had joined Henry Sidney in helping Lady Ogle to escape to Holland: *Hist. MSS. Comm., Ormonde MSS.*, new ser., vi. 223.

[3] See above, iii. 442. He was superseded about April 1676: *Cal. S.P., Dom., 1676–7*, p. 91.

[4] Fox was superseded early in 1676: *Cal. Treasury Books, 1676–9*, pp. 126, 128, 145. The present

statement about the reason for his removal is worthless.

[5] Evelyn himself accuses Danby of pride: above, p. 20; letter of 6 Dec. 1681, in Pepys, *Private corr.*, i. 16; so also Shaftesbury, in Christie, *Shaftesbury*, ii. 312; a satirist in the 'Chequer Inn', printed in Marvell, *Poems*, &c., ed. Margoliouth, i. 313. Danby's unpopularity was largely due to his efficiency in conducting an unpopular policy.

[6] The council and the subsequent meeting were held on 25 January: Birch, iv. 120–2.

Portsmouths glorious Appartment at W.hall,[1] where was a greate banquet of *Sweetemeates*, & *Musique* &c but at which both the *Ambassador* & *Retinue* behaved themselves with extraordinary Moderation & modestie, though placed about a long Table a Lady betweene two Moores: viz: a Moore, then a Woman, then a Moore &c: and most of these were the Kings natural Children, viz: the Lady Lichfield,[2] Sussex,[a][3] DD of *Portsmouth, Nelly*[4] &c: Concubines, & catell of that sort, as splendid as Jewells, and Excesse of bravery could make them: The *Moores* neither admiring or seeming to reguard any thing, furniture[b] or the like with any earnestnesse; and but decently tasting of the banquet: They dranke a little Milk & Water, but not a drop of Wine, also they drank of a sorbett & Jacolatte:[c][5] did not looke about nor stare on the Ladys, or expresse the least of surprize, but with a Courtly negligence in pace, Countenance, & whole behaviour, answering onely to such questions as were asked, with a greate deale of Wit & Gallantrie, & so gravely tooke leave, with this Compliment That *God* would blesse the D: of P: and the Prince her sonn, meaning the little Duke of Richmon'd:[6] The *King* came in at the latter end, just as the Ambassador was going away: In this manner was this Slave (for he was no more at home)[d] entertained by most of the Nobility in Towne;[7] & went often to *Hide-Park* on *horse back*, where he and his retinue shewed their extraordinary activity in

---

a Followed by *his* deleted.   b Followed by *of* deleted.   c Or *Jacolatt*.   d Followed by *was* redundant.

---

[1] For the duchess's apartment see above, p. 74. According to the *Loyal Protestant . . . Intelligence*, 26 Jan., it was the Russian ambassador who supped with her on 24 January. But the paper is probably wrong, as the Moroccan ambassador was certainly there: cf. *Cal. S.P., Dom., 1682*, p. 43. For his enjoyment of the party see Leti, ii. 351.

[2] Charlotte Fitzroy, 1664–1718, daughter of Charles II by the duchess of Cleveland; married 1677 Edward Henry Lee (of Ditchley),

1663–1716, fifth baronet 1667, created earl of the City of Lichfield 1674: G.E.C.

[3] Above, iii. 592; iv. 97.

[4] Nell Gwyn: above, iii. 573.

[5] Chocolate; Pepys uses the form 'jocolatte': 24 Nov. 1664.

[6] Charles Lennox, 1672–1723; created duke of Richmond 1675; and of Lennox (Scotland) 1675: *D.N.B.*

[7] Various notices are collected in Ward, *Christopher Monck*, pp. 134–47.

Horsmanship, and the flinging & Catching their launces at full speede;[1] They rid very short, & could stand up right in full speede, managing their speares with incredible agility. He also went sometimes to our *Theaters*,[2] where when upon any foolish or fantastical action he could not forbeare laughing, he endeavored to hide it[a] with extraordinary modesty & gravity: In a word, the *Russian Ambassador*[3] still at Court behaved himselfe like a Clowne, compar'd to this Civil *Heathen*:

27 I went to heare Dr. *Tenison* at St. *Mart:* Expound on that part of the Church Catechisme, which relates to the Decalogue, particularly the Sabboth: how God created this aspectable[4] world in six periods &c. Se Your Notes:

This Evening Sir *St. Fox* acquainted me againe with his Majesties resolutions of proceeding in his Erection of a[b] *Royal Hospital* for Emerited Souldiers on that spot of ground The *Ro: Society* had sold his Majestie for 1300 pounds & that he would settle 5000 pounds per Annum on it, & build to the value of 20000 pounds for the reliefe & reception of 4 Companies, viz. 400 men, to be as in a Coledge or Monastrie:[5] I was therefore desired by Sir *Stephen* (who had not onely the

---

a Followed by *from* deleted.   b Altered from *an.*

[1] The ambassador and his suite gave exhibitions of their horsemanship in Hyde Park on 13 and 27 January: *Loyal Protestant . . . Intelligence,* 14 Jan.; *Impartial Protestant Mercury,* 31 Jan. He gave later exhibitions there and at Newmarket.

[2] He saw Shadwell's *Psyche* on 19 January; *The Tempest* (presumably Shadwell's opera) on 1 February; and *Macbeth* on 16 February; all at the Duke's Theatre: *Impartial Protestant Mercury,* 24 Jan.; *Loyal Protestant . . . Intelligence,* 2, 18 Feb. See also *Cal. S.P., Dom., 1682,* p. 28.

[3] Above, p. 262.

[4] Visible; Evelyn uses the word again in *Acetaria,* preface (*Misc.*

writings, p. 728). This was a Friday service.

[5] Fox was the chief mover in the project for Chelsea Hospital, and there seems little room for doubting that it was he who inspired Charles II to found it. It was he who had negotiated the purchase of Chelsea College, and who provided the money (£1,300) for the purchase. The project was now generally known. For its history to this time see Lord Ilchester, in *The Times,* 27 Feb. 1932, pp. 11–12; *Notes and Queries,* clxxv (1938), 273–5. Occupation began in 1689, and the principal buildings were completed by 1691: L.C.C., *Survey of London,* xi. 7–11.

whole menaging of this, but was (as I perceiv'd) himselfe to be a grand benefactor, as well it became him, who had gotten so vast an Estate by the Souldiers &c) to assist him & Consult what Method to Cast it in, as to the Government: So[a] in his Study,[1] we set downe the Governor, Chaplaine, Steward, Housekeeper, Chirurgion, Cooke, Butler, Gardner, Porter & other Officers, with their severall salaries & entertainements: I would needes have a Librarie, & mentioned severall books &c. since some souldiers might possibly be studious, when they were at this leasure to recolect: Thus we made the first Calculations, & set downe our thoughts to be considered & digested better to shew his *Majestie* & the *Archbishop*: He also engaged me to consider of what Laws & Orders were fit for the Government, which was to be in every respect as strickt as in any religious Convent &c: After supper, came in the famous Trebble *Mr. Abel*[2] newly return'd from *Italy*, & indeede I never heard a more excellent voice, one[b] would have sworne it had ben a Womans it was so high, & so well & skillfully manag'd:[c] being accompanied with Signor *Francesco*[3] on the *Harpsichord*:

[d]28 Mr. *Pepys* (late Sec: to the Admiralty[4]) ⟨shewed me⟩ a large folio containing the whole Mechanic part, & art of Building royal ships & Men of Warr; made by Sir *Anth: Deane*,[5] being so accurate a Piece, from the very keele to the lead block, rigging, Gunns, Victualing, Manning, even to every individual Pin & naile, in a Method so astonishing & curious; with the draughts both Geometrical, & in Perspective, & severall sections; That I do not think the Whole

---

[a] Altered from *T*.   [b] Altered from *as*.   [c] Followed by *Th-* deleted.   [d] Hand in margin here.

---

[1] For his house see above, p. 179 n.

[2] John Abell, 1660?–1716?: *D.N.B.*

[3] Presumably the performer mentioned above, p. 49.

[4] He had been secretary to the lords commissioners of the admiralty from 1673 to 1679. He was to be secretary to Charles II and James II as lords high admiral from 1684 to 1689.

[5] Anthony Deane, *c.* 1638–1721; master-shipwright at Harwich, &c.; commissioner of the navy 1686–8; knighted 1675; F.R.S. 1681; *D.N.B.* He was a protégé and friend of Pepys, and had been imprisoned in the Tower with him in 1679.

World can shew the like; I esteeme this one booke above any of the *Sybillas*, & it is an extraordinary Jewel: hence I returned home.

⟨29⟩ᵃ *Viccar* on 8: *Joh:* 26.¹ shewing that Christian liberty consisted in an Ingenuous, not servile or Jewish, & ritual worship & feare of God: &c: See *your notes*: *Curate* on 5: *Matt* 5. of *Meekenesse* &c: 31. To *Lond:* but tooke such a cold that the next day returning from our *Society* (where we had the *Phosphorus* experimented in *Vaccuo Boyliano* which greately surprized me) to my Lodging at *White-hall*,² I was attaq'd with a fit of an *Ague Tertian* for 3 fitts, which so exceedingly weakn'd me, that I was not able to stirr out til Sonday when

Feb: 5ᵇ I went to Chapell a Young Divine on 90. *Psal:* 12. of preparation for death: The blessed Sacrament followed: B: of *Lond:* officiating: *Cor: Rege* Dr. *Perce*³ out-doing him-selfe in an incomparable discourse on: 18 *Luke*: 8: when the Sonn of man cometh, shall he find faith on the Earth? Shew-ing by the deprav'dnesse of mankind, & especialy among Christians, particular⟨l⟩y England more than had ever ben known, the end of the world could not now be long, & that it would come surprizingly, none minding:

My fitts continuing with much violence I sent to my Wife to fetch me home in the Coach: There came & sent to Visite me my L: *Chamberlaine*, Dutchesse of *Grafton*, Countesse of *Bristol* & *Sunderland*, Sir William *Godolphin*, & severall of my friends almost daily:

7. I went home: My Daughter *Mary* now first began to learne Musick of Signor *Bartholomeo*,⁴ & Dauncing of Mon-sieur *Isaac*,⁵ both reputed the best Masters &c: I continu'd

---

ᵃ MS. *30*.   ᵇ Altered from *2*.

¹ A slip for St. John viii. 36. This and the succeeding sermon pre-sumably belong to the Sunday, 29 January; there should have been a further sermon on 30 January.
² See above, p. 50.
³ Pierce.
⁴ Above, p. 186.

⁵ Isaac emerges about this time as a fashionable dancing-master; in Queen Anne's reign he composed a number of dances, of which some were performed at court. He was perhaps the dancer of this name who took part in *Calisto*; and was perhaps still living in 1727, when

ill for 2 fitts after, and then bathing my leggs to the knees in *Milk* made as hott as I could endure it, & sitting so in it, in a deepe *Churn* or Vessell, Covered with blanquets & drinking *Carduus* posset,[1] then going to bed & sweating, I not onely missed that expected fit, but had no more; onely continued so weake that I could not go to church 'til *Ash-wednesday*, which I had not missed I think[a] so long in twenty yeares, so long had God ben gracious to me:

[b]After this Warning & admonition, I now began to looke-over & methodize all my *Writings, Accompts, Letters, Papers* &c: Inventoried the goods &c of the house, & to put things into the best order I could; & also new made my Will: That growing now in yeares, I might have none of these secular things & Concernes, to distract me, whensoever it should please Almighty *God* to call me from this transitorie life: And with this prepared me some special Meditations & devotions for the time of sicknesse: The Lord *Jesus* grant them Salutary for my poore Soule at that day, that I may obtaine Mercy & acceptance.

[b]*March* 1 Was my second Grand-child borne,[2] exactly at Sunn-rising; & Christned the next day by our *Viccar* at *Sayes-Court*, his Susceptors being My Selfe with my *Nephew* Jo: *Evelyn* of *Wotton*, by the Name of *John*: his God-mother was Mrs. *Anderson*,[3] sister to his Mother: I beseech God to blesse him.

⟨1⟩[c] *Ashwednesday* I went to our Church Office &c: 5: Our

---

a Followed by *in* deleted.　　b Hand in margin here.　　c MS. 2.

Soame Jenyns published *The Art of Dancing*. As early as 1653 a Monsieur Isac was one of the best dancing-teachers in Paris: Mauger, *True advancement of the French tongue*, p. 150; this must refer to another man, but suggests that the name was assumed and not personal: C. W. Beaumont, *Bibliography of dancing*, 1929, and works by J. Weaver, 1706, and E. Pemberton, 1711, there mentioned; Boswell, *Restoration court stage*, pp. 202,

222; *Loyal Garland*, 5th ed., 1686, song xxxv; *Hist. MSS. Comm., Rutland MSS.*, ii. 163; *Pepys, Private corr.*, ii. 300.

[1] A preparation of *carduus benedictus*, blessed thistle: O.E.D.

[2] John Evelyn, d. 1763; created a baronet 1713; Evelyn's heir and successor at Wotton and Sayes Court: G.E.C., *Baronetage*, v. 17; H. Evelyn, pp. 156–77. His baptism is entered in the parish register.

[3] Above, p. 224.

Viccar on   Pro: shewing what care and vigilancy was required for the keeping of the heart upright; how to manage & govern our ordinary thoughts; not indulging any idle imagination, or morose delight, in speculative lusts; with what danger of being rejected, when we procrastinate holy duties for secular respects, Impatience or the like, by the Example of *Felix*: the holy Comm: followd: on which I gave God thanks for his gracious dealing with me in my late sicknesse, & affording me this blessed opportunity of praising him in the Congregation, and receiving the Cup of Salvation, with new & serious resolutions:—The *Curate* on 73. *Psal:* 24[1] —shewing that there was no Comfort, no satisfaction, no dependence or security but in the Love & favour of God. 9: Came to see & congratulate my recovery Sir *John Lowther*,[2] Mr. *Herbert*,[3] Mr. *Pepys*, Sir *Anth: Deane*, & Mr. *Hill*,[4] which last gave me a hopefull account of the successe my Letter was like to have (which I lately sent to Mr. *Dan: Callwell*[5]) in behalfe of the *Royal Society*: See a *Copy* of the Letter in my book of Letters: 10: To *Lond:* to a Master of *Chancery*, about our Answer of the L: V: *Mordaunts* bill &c:[6] I return'd, having return'd my Visites to the L: *Chamberlain*, Sir *Ste: Fox* and other my kind friends: There was this day Executed *Coll: Vrats* & some of his Complices, for their Execrable Murder of Mr. *Thynn*, set on by the Principal *Koningsmarke* ⟨who⟩ went to Execution like an undaunted Hero, as one that had don a friendly office for that base Coward C. *Coningsmark*, who had hopes to marry his Widdow the rich Lady Ogle; & was quitted by a Corrupt Jury, & so got away:

---

[1] Probably from the Prayer Book.

[2] Above, p. 124; here almost certainly Sir John of Whitehaven, who was this year a member of the council of the Royal Society.

[3] Presumably John Herbert, F.R.S. 1677.

[4] Abraham Hill, 1635–1721; member of the Philosophical Society from 28 Nov. 1660; F.R.S., Original Fellow; treasurer of the Royal Society 1663–5 and again 1679–1700; secretary 1673–5: *D.N.B.*

[5] Daniel Colwall, d. 1690; member of the Philosophical Society 16 Jan. 1661; F.R.S., Original Fellow; treasurer of the Royal Society 1665–79: *D.N.B.* The present letter perhaps related to Evelyn's East India Company stock: below, p. 297.

[6] See above, p. 259.

Vrats told a friend of mine, who accompan⟨y⟩ing him to the Gallows & gave him some advice; That[a] dying he did not value a rush, & hoped & believed God would deale with him like a Gentleman; never man went so gallant, & so unconcern'd to his sad fate:[1]

12 Our *Viccar* on his former *Text*: with little addition: That the old Philosophers us'd to fancy them selves in the presence of a Grave *Cato*,[2] *Socretes* &c to preserve them from doing any unworthy action; how much more should a christian set *Christ* before him, the necessity of care over our thoughts & imaginations; all things being naked to the Eyes of *God*: The smal difference 'twixt evil thoughts & Actions, the *Adulterie* of the Eye &c: *Curate* 5. *Matt: 7*, The Beatitude

---

[a] Followed by *he* deleted.

---

[1] Tom Thynne (above, p. 261) was murdered on the evening of 12 February in Pall Mall near St. Alban's Street by Christopher Vratz, a Dutch or German (Pomeranian?) soldier of fortune, assisted by two accomplices; while Vratz stopped Thynne's coach one of the accomplices shot him (this is the scene represented on Thynne's monument in Westminster Abbey). Vratz declared that he had a personal quarrel with Thynne, but he had been connected with the Königsmark family since boyhood and had murdered Thynne in the interests, and perhaps at the instigation, of Count Karl Johann von Königsmark (1659–86: *Allgemeine deutsche Biog.*), who himself wanted to marry Lady Ogle (above, p. 260). Vratz and his two accomplices were tried for murder on 28 February, and Königsmark with them as an accessory before the fact; the jury was half English, half foreign. Königsmark's acquittal was probably due to his guilt not being positively established; but an attempt had been made (by Foubert; above, p. 257; see below) to corrupt Sir John Reresby, one of the examining magistrates; and the king wanted an acquittal in order to escape the political difficulties which would have arisen if Königsmark had been found guilty. Königsmark had been taken in disguise at Deptford when trying to escape to Sweden; he appears to have been a brave soldier and died during a campaign in the Morea. His brother Count Philipp Christoph (1665–94), the future lover of Sophia Dorothea of Hanover, was at this time at Foubert's Academy: *Tryal . . . of George Borosky*, &c., 1682; Reresby; Luttrell; *Hist. MSS. Comm., Ormonde MSS.*, new ser., vi. 328; for Vratz see W. F. Palmblad, *Aurora Königsmark och hennes slägt*, 1846–9, i. 116, &c. He and his accomplices were hanged on the site of the murder; they were attended by Burnet and Dr. Horneck (below, p. 306) who together published *The last confession, prayers and meditations of Lieuten. John Stern*. The former was probably Evelyn's informant; the phrase 'dying he did not value a rush' appears to be Evelyn's paraphrase.

[2] Cato the Elder: above, p. 256.

to the Mercifull; that it consisted not onely in pardoning our
Enemys, but in doing them kindnesse, by our B:S: example:
19 A *stranger* on 122: *Psal:* 6 How necessary in these distracted times to pray for the peace of the Church, in a most
excellent discourse: See your *notes*: The same in the After
noone: I was this day exceedingly paind in both my kidnies,
which gave me apprehension of some farther evil, which *God*
in mercy avert: 21, I went to *Lond*, to ⟨meete⟩ᵃ the rest of
the *Trustees*, viz. the *Earle* of *Clarendon*, Lo: *Hyde*,[1] Mr
Newport &c to my L: *Chancelor*,[2] where was severall of the
most learned Council on both sides, to consider what security
we might expect, in Case we relinquish'd our Trust for the payment of the Portions to my Lady V: C. *Mordaunts* Children,
& that my L: *Chan:* would settle it by decree &c. I dind at
the C: of *Sunderlands*. ᵇ22: I dined with severall of the *R:*
Society (as frequently we did on the meeting daies) & the
President being absent, I was voted into the *Chaire*: Severall
letters from abroad were red, & answers ordered to them:
There was shewed a live *Scorpion* found in an Oyle-shop in
Lond:[3] Also were presented divers faire pieces of *Amber* from
the *Duke* of *Brandenburg*,[4] in one of which was a large spider,
in another a gnat, both very intire & rare: The experiment
for the day, was the *Anatomical* demonstration of Dr. *Tysons*,[5]
of the *decussations*[6] of the *optic-nerves*, so as to cause the sight
to be single, & not double, from the paralelle fibers on the
Retina, exactly answering one-the other, which being by any
accident distorted, caused *Squinting*, & indirect Vision &c:
Then follow'd a discourse in *Latine*, endeavoring to shew how

---

ᵃ MS. *neete*.   ᵇ Hand in margin here.

---

[1] Laurence Hyde, who had been
created Viscount Hyde of Kenilworth on 24 April 1681; he was
created earl of Rochester on 29
November of this year.

[2] Heneage Finch, created earl of
Nottingham in 1681; lord chan-
cellor since 1675; he died on 18
December of this year.

[3] It was shown preserved in
spirit; it had been shown alive at
an earlier meeting.

[4] These were sent by Sir Robert
Southwell, who had recently been
envoy to the elector of Brandenburg, Frederick William, 1620–88,
succeeded 1640, the Great Elector.

[5] Edward Tyson, *c.* 1650–1708;
M.D. 1680; F.R.S. 1679: *D.N.B.*

[6] Intersections in form like the
letter X: *O.E.D.*

much wider the pores of *Gold* were than *Silver*; & affirm'd to be the occasion of the operation of *Aqua regalis* upon it, insinuating more easily;[1] which being reasoned upon, was rejected: Also there was a discourse of the tinging of *Glasse*, especialy with red, & the difficulty of finding[a] any red colour effectual, to penetrate glasse among the *glasse-painters*; That the most diaphanous as blew, yellow &c did not enter into the substance of what was ordinarily painted, but very shallowly, unlesse incorporated in the mettal itselfe, other redds & whites, not at all farther than to the superficies onely: &c:[2]

I went hence to see the Corps of that obstinate creature, Coll. *Vratz*[b] the *German*[c] murderer of Mr. *Thynn* (set on by the Principal Count *Koningsmark*) the King permitting his body should be transported to his owne Country, (being it seemes a person of a good family) it being one of the first, which was *embaulmed* by a particular art invented by one *Will: Russell* a Coffin Maker; which preser⟨v⟩ed the body without disboweling or using to any appearance any bituminous[d] matter; The flesh florid, soft & full, as if the person were onely sleeping: The *Cap:* having now ben dead neere 15 daies: He lay exposed in a very rich Coffin, lined with lead: &c to⟨o⟩ magnificently for so daring, & horrid a Murderer:[3] 23 I visited severall friends, dind at Sir *St: Foxes*: 23. 24: Both these daies were spent in a most anxious attendance of my *Lady Tukes* Cause, at the *Assizes* in *Southwark*:[4] I dined with the high *Sherif* & *Judges* &c where was a mighty

---

[a] Followed by *th-* deleted.   [b] Altered from *Vrats*.   [c] Substituted for *Polonian*.   [d] Altered from *bituminious*.

---

[1] This formed part of a letter from abroad.

[2] The passage appears to be badly reported. The only colour that glass can be 'stained' is yellow; all other colours must be produced either when making the glass or as enamels, a thin coating on one surface of the glass.

[3] William Russell, coffin-maker 'at the Sign of the Four Coffins in

Fleet-street', advertises his skill in embalming in *London Gazette* (e.g. 21 Aug., 10 Nov., 1684); see also *Hist. MSS. Comm., Portland MSS.*, iii. 458; below, 4 Oct. 1699 n.

[4] The assize for part of Surrey: *London Gazette*, 13 Feb. (list of the circuits). It was held presumably at the town-hall on St. Margaret's Hill: *V.C.H., Surrey*, iv. 130.

feast, & returned home on our Lady day. 26 Our *Viccar* on
57. *Isa:* 10 That Afflictions oftimes awaken us to *Repentance.*
Pomer: *Curate* on 9 *Eccles:* 10: inciting to a religious use of
the present opportunitie:

Apr⟨i⟩ll 2: Our *Viccar* on his former, much repetition: The
Curate on: 2: *Phil:* 8. of our *B: Saviours* infinite humiliation,
preparatory to the solemne time approching, for which reason
there was no Communion this Sonday (as there ought to have
ben) there being three to succeede the weeke following:

My Daughter in Law was Churched this day, after the
birth of my *Grandson* John, whom I pray God to blesse:

5: To Lond: our *Society*, where at a Council, was regulated
what *Collections* should be monethly published, as formerly
the *Transactions*, which had of late ben discontinued; but
were now much desired & called for by the Curious both from
abroad, & home:[1]

6 I supped with severall of our Society, at Sir Jos: *Williamson's*, where we had also Musick:

9 Preached Dr. *Stillingfleete* Deane of *S. Paules*, (*Palme
Sondy*) W.hall, to the household, on 8. *Act:* 15: learnedly
asserting that the Scriptures were not to be prohibited the
Laytie, both from Scrip: & the constant usage of the Church
in all the best ages &c:[2] See your notes: *Coram Rege* Dr.
⟨*Tillotson*⟩[a][3] (Deane of Cant) on 24: *Jo⟨s⟩h:* 15, of the Ease of
the Christian Yoake (see your *notes*) I dind with our *Bish: of
Rochester* at the Abby: after which I there heard a sermon on
4: *Rom:* 5. concerning Obedience to Magistrates:[4]

12 *Wednesday* (*passion*-weeke) *coram Rege* pre Dr. *Craddoc*[5]

---

a MS. *Tillotsan.*

---

[1] There is no mention of a
meeting of the council this day in
Birch. For the *Philosophical Collections* and *Philosophical Transactions*
see above, p. 205 n. The latter was
resumed in 1683.

[2] The text is presumably wrong.

[3] The preacher appointed for this
occasion was the archbishop of
Canterbury; Tillotson was to preach

on 7 April: list of lenten preachers
at court in *London Gazette*, 26 Dec.
1681. The present sermon is perhaps that printed in Tillotson's
Works, 1752, i. 254–63; but see
below, p. 371.

[4] The text is presumably wrong.

[5] Cradock had been instituted
provost of Eton in 1681. Lenten
sermon at court.

Provost of *Eaton* on 12: *Heb:* 2ª recomending the virtue & grace, as well as necessity of *Patience* from our B: Lords example, in a most excellent discourse, of which Consult your *Notes*:

ᵇI went this Afternoone to a Supper, with severall of the R: Society, which was all dressed (both fish & flesh) in Monsieur *Papins Digestorie*; by which the hardest bones of Biefe itselfe, & Mutton, were without water, or other liquor, & with lesse than 8ᶜ ounces of Coales made as soft as Cheeze, produc'd an incredible quantity of Gravie, & for close, a Gellie, made of the bones of biefe, the best for clearnesse & good relish, the most delicious that I had ever seene or tasted; so as I sent my Wife a glasse of it, to the reproch of all that the ladys ever made of the best Harts-horne &c: We Eate Pickᴵ & other fish with bones & all without any impediment: but nothing exceeded the Pigeons, which tasted just as if baked in a *pie*, all these being stewed in their owne juice, without any add⟨i⟩tion of water, save what swam about the ⟨digester⟩,ᵈ as in balneo: The natural juice of all these provisions, acting on theᵉ grosser substances, reduct the hardest bones to this tendernesse: but it is best described (with infinite more particulars for extracting tinctures, preserving & stewing fruite &c, & saving fuel) by Dr. *Papins* booke, published, & dedicated to our Society, of which he is a member, though since gon to *Venice* withᶠ Signor   late Resident for that State here, & a member also of our Society, who carried this excellent Mechanique Philos: & Physitian, to set up a Philos: meeting in that Citty: By this Experiment it is plaine, that the most obdurate bones are but the more compacted & closer parts of the same matter (by *juxtaposition*) which composes the tenderest flesh & Muscular parts; & reduces them to a friable, rather than glutinous substance, which disolves into gravy, or composes the Gelly: These bones then, breaking as it were into crumbs, one may strew on bread & eate without harme:

ᵃ Altered from 7.   ᵇ Hand in margin here.   ᶜ Or 6.
ᵈ MS. *digesterter*.   ᵉ Altered from *their*.   ᶠ Followed by *the* deleted.

ᴵ Pike.

This Philosophical Supper, raised much mirth amongst us,
& exceedingly pleased all the Companie:[1]

14 *Good Friday* (at St. *Martins*) preached Dr. *Tenison* on
1. *Threnæ* 12. a Passion Sermon, demonstrating that our Bl:
Saviours suffering was by many degrees, far exceeding the
suffering of any Creature, through his soules Agonie for us,
at apprehension of his Fathers wrath, due to us sinners, &
who onely truely understood, what it was to have the light
of his Countenance ecclipsed but for a moment: Then the
dignity of his person &c: see your notes, for an excellent discourse: The blessed Communion followed: I suppd at my
old & worthy friends Mr. P: Packers: This afternoone *Coram
Rege* preached Dr. Sherlock[2] on 1. Cor: 1. 22. 23: which I also
heard; historicaly displaying our bl: Lords passion, & what
influence the contemplation of it, ought to have on our lives
&c.

15 I returned home: 16 *our Viccar* (*Easter day*) on 28 *Matt:*
5. 6. That our bl: *Saviours Resurrection* was the maine foundation of the Truth of our Religion, with the ordinarie Topics
on this beaten text: &c: The holy Comm: followed, at which
I with my family participated: *Pomerid*: *Curate* on. 1. Cor:
15. 20. That *Christ* was the first ever raised himselfe, & must
then needes be able to raise & quicken others, he being the
first fruits & pledge of it. As now I grew in yeares, I becam

---

[1] Papin (above, p. 172) describes
his digester in *A New Digester or
Engine for softning bones*, 1681, the
book to which Evelyn refers. The
Venetian resident is Paolo Sarotti,
who was here from 1675 to 18/28
Feb. 1681; his son Giovanni An-
tonio Sarotti was elected F.R.S.
in 1679. An academy was established in their library in Venice:
'nelli Lunedì il doppo pranso vi
sogliono tener Accademia publica
di scienze filosofiche, e mate-
matiche': D. Martinelli, *Il ritratto
di Venezia*, 1684, pp. 604–5. Paolo
Sarotti returned here in 1686
(remaining until 1689) and his
academy was abandoned; the only

known account of it and its work
occurs in Papin, *A Continuation of
the New Digester of Bones*, 1687, pp.
84–123; see also L. de la Saussaye
and A. Péan, *La vie et les ouvrages
de Denis Papin*, vol. i (all published),
1869, pp. 111–14. He was abroad
already in February 1681 and returned to England by 2 April 1684:
Birch, iv. 72, 279. The Society was
experimenting with the digester in
March and May 1681.

[2] Presumably Dr. William Sherlock: below, 14 Nov. 1685; but
possibly Richard Sherlock, 1612–
89, D.D. 1660, rector of Winwick
1662: *D.N.B.*

much subject to sleepe in the Afternoones, which I formerly censured in some others, and believed impossible; I beseech God to pardon & help me: Seldome & rarely did I sleepe in the morning Exercises &c:

23 Our *Viccar* on his former upon the occasion of the Churches changing the *Jewish* Sabba⟨t⟩h to the *Lords day*, & necessity &c: See notes: *Curate* of *Greenewich* on 1. *Cor:* 15. 10, That all the[a] good receiv'd by the best of Saints, proceeded only from the free Grace of God: I stirr'd not forth this Weeke, but tooke *Physick*, the season un-usualy wet, with such stormes of Raine & Thunder, as did greate damage:[1]

⟨30⟩[b] Our *Viccar* Indisposed: The *Curat* pr: on 2: *Phil:* 9, on the exceeding exinnanition[c] & selfe debasement of our *B: Lord*, previous to his exaltation & Resurrection: & that it was to teach us how to attaine the same &c:

May: 6 I went to *Lond:* about buisenesse. 7: A stranger at *W:hall* on 1. *Pet.* 3. 18 describing Christs sufferings, & how cogent an argument of our love in returne: The holy Sacrament follow'd: 11 I returned home:

14 A stranger preached on 15 *John*: 12. earnestly exhorting to Christian Charity, as the onely Commandment of our blessed Saviours, the most Easy, sweete, profitable & delightfull; & who might have left us some more painefull and different; That this love of ours was not to be any wor⟨ld⟩ly affection, or voluptious love, but of a pious & indeared tendèr friend & brother: &c: *Pomerid*: The *Same*: on: 17: John: 20: upon *Christ⟨s⟩* heavenly prayer for his Disciples, & those that should believe & be converted by their preaching: &c:

19 To *Lond:* in order to a *Trial*, with the *Legatie⟨s⟩* of *Geo: Tuke*, in which I was a *Trustee*, but which was put off, 'til my *Lady Tuke*, could obtaine leave of her Majestie to come from Winsore, where the Court now was:[2]

---

[a] Altered from *our*.   [b] MS. *29*.   [c] Altered from *innanition* by interlining *ex*.

---

[1] cf. Wood, *Life and times*, iii. 13.
[2] For George Tuke see above, iii. 172, &c. The court was at Windsor from 22 April to about 20 June: *London Gazette*, 24 April, 26 June.

21 I received the blessed *Eucharist* at St. *James's* this morning. Afterwa⟨r⟩ds heard a *stranger* at *W:hall* on 19 *Luke* 41, of our B: Saviours weeping over the obstinate Citty, the very day of his Triumph, forseeing their future destruction, for their rejection of him, applied to the present ingratitude of this our Nation, & the dangers threatning: I din'd at Mr. *Packers*, then at St. *Margarits* pr: one *Dr. Lee*[1] on 1. *Coloss:* 27 of a Christians hope of the Glory to be revealed, if *Christ* be truely in us: which signifies not a meere local inbeing; but a spiritual & mysterious; namely by receiving him for our *Lord*, so as to obey him intirely, without which no hope of [the][a] glory:

25 *Dies Ascentionis*: I was desired by Sir St: *Fox*, & Sir Chr: *Wren*, his Majesties Surveior, and *Architect*, to accompanie them to *Lambeth*, with the plot, & designe of the College to be built at *Chelsey* for emerited Souldiers, to have the *Archbishops* approbation: It was a quadrangle of 200 foote square, after the dimensions of the larger quadrangle of *Christ Church* in *Oxon*[b] for the accommodation of 440 Persons with Governor & Officers:[2] This being fix'd, & agreed upon, we went to dinner, & then returned: 27: As a *Trustee* of *Geo: Tuke*, in behalfe of my Lady, we had a Trial before my L: Chancelor, against the Plaintifs, who being of the Kindred, expected[c] Legacies before the debts were paied, and that there were *assets*: After many yeares charge & trouble, the Accompts were referred to a Master to be examin'd, which was just, & what we desired: I din'd at Mr. *Sheldons*:[3] The *Duke* & *Dutchesse* of York were just now

---

[a] Interlined and perhaps deleted.   [b] MS. *Oxoñ*.   [c] Altered from *expecting*; preceded by *&* deleted.

---

[1] Apparently Richard Lee, *c.* 1612–84; D.D. 1664; rector of Hatfield 1660–84; father of the dramatist: *D.N.B.*, art. Lee, Nathaniel.

[2] Wren's drawings for the hospital are lost. At this time it was to consist of the three wings surrounding the principal court: Wren's description, *c.* 1682, in Wren Soc., xix. 64–5. The short side of the court is about 230 feet long, the other two sides 325 feet; Tom Quadrangle at Christ Church is about 270 feet square.

[3] Probably a near relation of Lady Tuke, whose maiden name was Sheldon: pedigree in Wood, *Life and times*, iii. 99–101.

come to *Lond:* after his Escape & shipwrack by sea, as he went for *Scotland.*[1] 28: Sonday, At the *Rolls*-Chapell[2] preached the famous Dr. *Burnet* on 2: *Pet: 1.* 10, excellently well describing what was meant by Election &c: viz, not the effect of any irreversable decree; but so cal'd, because they embraced the *Gospel* readily, by which they became *elect,* or precious to God &c: see your notes: It would be very needlesse to make our Calling & *Election* sure, were they irreversable: and what the rigid *Presbyterians* pretend: No neede of working out Salvation with feare & trembling, were there no danger of relapses &c:—I din'd at Sir *Tho: Beckfords*[3] to visite my Niepce Evelyn of Wotton, who had miscarried of a *sonn* in the Coach as she came up to lie-In at *Lond:* This afternoone I went to St. *Laurences*[4] where the *Minister* (naming his Text 18 *Ezek: 27)* spake so very low, & was so feeble an old man, that I could by no meanes hear[a] what he saied: The church is new & a cherefull pile: 29. I din'd [Sir S: Foxe][b] at the B: of *Rochesters*: congratulated his eldest sonns Marriage:[5] He is a good scholar & studying the Law, like to make a worthy & usefull gent: I gave notice to the Bish: what *Maimburg* had published, about the motives of the late Dutchesse of *Yorks* Perversion, in his *Historie* of *Calvenisme*;[6]

---

a Spelling doubtful.   b Interlined.

---

[1] The duke and duchess had gone to Scotland in October 1679; in March of this year James came to Newmarket and obtained the king's permission to return to court. The *Gloucester* frigate, on which he sailed to bring back the duchess, was wrecked off the Yorkshire coast with great loss of life on 6 May. Notice of the arrival of the duke and duchess in London in *London Gazette,* 29 May.

[2] Above, iii. 14. Burnet was minister here from 1675 to 1684.

[3] For him and his stepdaughter, Evelyn's niece by marriage, see above, p. 196 n.

[4] St. Lawrence Jewry. It was rebuilt in 1670–86. The present vicar was Benjamin Whichcote, 1609–83, D.D. 1649: *D.N.B.*

[5] Gilbert Dolben, *c.* 1658–1722; created a baronet 1704; judge; married Anne, *c.* 1661–1744, daughter of Tanfield Mulso of Finedon, Northants: *D.N.B.*

[6] Louis Maimbourg (1610–86; Jesuit: *Nouvelle biog. gén.*) appended to his *Histoire du Calvinisme* (published this year) a 'Declaration de Madame la Princesse d'Iork', containing the grounds for her conversion to Roman Catholicism.

& did my selfe write to the Bish: of *Winchester*[1] about it, who being concernd in it, I urged to set forth his *Vindication*: 30: The Kings *Anniversarie*,[2] I was hindred from going to the pub: Office: 31: To our *Society*, where the *Morocco Ambassador* being honorarily admitted, & subscribing his Name & Titles in *Arabic*, I was ⟨ordered⟩ by the *Council*, to go and complement him, &c.[3]

Jun 1. I din'd at my Lord *Sunderlands* with Mr. *Sidny*[4] & so home: 4: *Whitsonday* our *Viccar* on 4: *Heb:* 1. Text formerly begun, not much agreable to the festival:[5] The holy *Sacrament* followed: *Curate* on 2: *Act:* 1. against the *Dissenters* choosing barnes, & obscure places to meete in, rather than the Church; so as they were not together like the Assemblies of the *Apostles*, which was in a Conspicuous well known place & house, where so many of all nations came to heare them, & were all of one accord:

7 Came to visite & dine with me, the Countesses of *Bristol* & *Sunderland*. 11. Our Viccar as above 4: *Heb:* 1 of the failings that made men come short of the Rest there mention'd &c:[a] viz, want of perseverance: Continual Repentings, & continual sinning; which he call'd sinning, & sorrowing in a Circle: Then relyance on a Deathbed repentance, of which the danger, & many profitable Cautions: *Curate* on: 2: *Eph:* 8. 9. The reward & exhaltation of *Christs* humiliation; discussing that Question, whither our B: *Lord* by his sufferings merited for himselfe, which 'tis certaine he did not, & being

---

a Followed by *See your notes* deleted.

---

[1] Morley, who had been the duchess's spiritual adviser from 1660 to 1667. Evelyn wrote to him apparently on 1 June (Bohn, iii. 255–6, with false date 1 June 1681). Morley, who was further attacked by Thomas Jones in *Elymas the Sorcerer*, 1682, vindicated himself in the preface to his *Several Treatises*, 1683, and among them published his letter to the duchess, 24 Jan. 1670/1. Burnet, who had seen the duchess's letter before it was pub-

lished, had informed Morley about its contents: *Own time*, ed. Airy, i. 556–7.

[2] A mistake; it falls on 29 May.

[3] Birch, iv. 149; these proceedings are not mentioned. The ambassador had been entertained and admitted F.R.S. on 26 April: ibid., p. 144.

[4] Presumably Henry Sidney: above, p. 254.

[5] This is the vicar's first sermon on this text heard by Evelyn.

God, he could not suffer, or merit as sinfull man; but as he assum'd our Nature & infirmities, he merited for us in his unsinning Person, & also all that Glory which God advanc'd his humanity to, in which the Faithfull have an Interest, and are already, as in their head & chiefe, possessed of, and shall be consummat at his second appearing, when all the members shall be glorified with him.—15 Came my *Bro: Evelyn* & Company to dine with me:

18 Our *Viccar* (preaching before the *Lord Major* & Judges)[1] left a young man to supply, on 1. *John*: 5. 4: shewing in what sense our Faith over-came the World; & how to judge of our[a] Condition, by the progresses of our Victories &c: *Pomerid* on 19 *Psal*: 60. The advantages of Early Piety, & danger of Procrastination:

19 About buisinesse to *Lond.* 20[b] To our *Society*, where Mr. *Hook* read to us his ingenious *Hypothesis* of Memorie, which he made to be an Organ of sense, distinct from any of the five; placed somewhere in the braine, which tooke notice of all *Ideas* & reposited them; as the rest of the senses do of their peculiar objects:[2]

[c]The[d] *Bantame* or *East India* Ambassadors[3] (for we had at

---

a Followed by *Victorie* deleted.   b Altered from *10*?   c Hand in margin here.   d Preceded by a date *27* deleted.

---

[1] This was the first Sunday of Trinity term. It was apparently customary for the lord mayor, sheriffs, and aldermen, to attend service at St. Paul's on the first Sunday of each term: Strype's Stow, v. 170. Where the present service was held is not traceable. The lord mayor was Sir John Moore (*D.N.B.*).

[2] This meeting was held on 21 June: Birch, iv. 153. A paper on Memory is printed, as section vii of his Lectures on Light, in Hooke's *Posthumous works*, 1705, pp. 139–47.

[3] Bantam was a town near the north-west extremity of Java, at this time the capital of a considerable kingdom, and a fairly impor-

tant trading station; the East India Company had had a factory there since 1603. The purpose of the present embassy was to obtain heavy ordnance; from the Company's point of view it proved a failure as, owing to a local civil war, the Company was expelled from Bantam this year. The ambassadors made their entry into London on 9 May; had their first audience on 14 May; were knighted on or about 8 July; and left a few days later: full account of the embassy, with reproductions of portraits, in Foster, *John Company*, pp. 97–120; see also Leti, ii. 351–4. The Russian ambassador had left London in February.

this time in Lond together The *Russian, Morrocan, & Indian*
Ambassador) being invited to dine at my Lord Geo: Berekeleys
(now created Earle)[1] I went to the entertaincment, to Consider the exotic guests: They were both very hard favour'd,
& much resembling in Countenance to some sort of *Munkeys*:
We eate at two Tables, The Ambassador & Interpreter by
themselves: Their Garments were rich Indian silks flowred
with gold, viz, a Close *Wast-Coate* to their knees, Drawers,
Naked leggs; and on their heads Capps made just in fashion
like fruit baskets: They Ware poison'd Daggers at their
boosome, the haft carved with some ougly serpents or devils
head, exceeding keene, & of damasco mettal: they wore no
sword:[2] The second *Ambassador* (sent it seemes to succeede,
in case the first should die by the Way in so tedious a journey)[3] having ben at *Méca* (for they were *Mahumetans*) ware
a Turkish or rather *Arab Shash*, a little part of the linnen
hanging downe behind his neck, With some other diference
of habite; & was halfe a negro; bare legg'd & naked feete;
esteem'd[a] a very holy man: They sate Crosse-legd like Turks,
& sometimes in the postures of *Apes* & *Munkys*; Their nailes
& ⟨Teeth⟩[b] black as any jeat & shining, which being the effect
of perpetual chewing *betell*, to preserve them from the *Tooth-
atch* more raging in their Country, is esteem'd beautifull:[4]
The first *Ambassador* was of an Olive hue, had a flatter face
& narrow eyes, squat nose & morish lips, haire none appeared:
Wore severall rings of silver, gold, coper on their finger, which
was a toaken of Knighthood or nobility: They were of[c] *Java*

ᵃ Altered from *& deem'd?*   ᵇ MS. *Teete.*   ᶜ Followed by *M-*
deleted.

---

[1] He had been created earl of
Berkeley in 1679. He was connected with the East India Company through his wife (above, iii.
230) and was elected a committee
every year from 1660 to 1696: Sir
W. Foster, *The East India House*,
1924, p. 95. He took a prominent
part in the reception of the present
embassy. This entertainment took
place on 22 June; for it see the

Company's account in Koninklijk
Bataviaasch Genootschap van Kun-
sten en Wetenschapen, *Tijdschrift*,
vol. lxiv, pt. i (1924), p. 225.
[2] A full-length portrait of one
of the ambassadors is prefixed to
Glanius, *A New Voyage to the East-
Indies*, 1682.
[3] The journey had taken about
six months.
[4] On this see Glanius, pp. 92–3.

major, whose Princes have ben turn'd *Mahumetans* not above 50 yeares since, The Inhabitants stil *Pagans* & Idolaters:[1] They seem'd of a dul & heavy Constitution, not wondering at any thing they saw; but exceedingly astonish⟨ed⟩ to understand, how our *Law's* gave us propriety in our Estates, & so thinking we were all Kings; for they could not be made to Comprehend, how subjects could[a] possesse any thing but at the pleasure of their Prince, they being all slaves, but infinitly surprized at it, & pleased with the notion, & admiring our happinesse; They were very sober, & I believe subtile in their way: Their meate was cook'd, carried up, & they attended on, by severall[b] fat slaves, who had no Covering save drawes, their whole body from the girdle upward stark naked, as well as their leggs, which appeared very uncouth, & lothsom;[c] They eate their *pilaw* & other spoone-meate without spoones, taking up their pottage in the hollow of ⟨their⟩[d] fingers, & very dextrously flung it into their mouthes, without spilling a drop:

25 Preached at *W:hall*. Dr. *Comber*[2] on 7: *Joh:* 17. Serious reformation the onely signe of our being in the right way: *Pomerid*: at St. Margarets a stranger on 71[e] Psal: 12.[3] Prosperity fatal to the Wicced in the end:

28 home, having ben in the morning to heare *Dr. Tenison* on our Church Cat⟨e⟩chisme:[4]

July: 1 Sir Jo: Stonehouse & Lady &c dined with us:

2 Mr. *Fowler* preached on 6: *Jam:*[f] 10,[5] of the danger & possibilitie of falling from Grace, into even wasting, & habitual sinns: He distinguish'd twixt Venial, & deadly sinns, that all were Capital as to their owne nature, 'til repented of:

---

a Altered from or to *should*.   b Followed by *fl-* deleted.   c Followed by *&* deleted.   d MS. *thire*, altered from *there*.   e Reading doubtful; altered from 75.   f Badly written; reading uncertain.

---

[1] Java Major is the present Java. Bantam became Mohammedan about 1522–7.
[2] Thomas Comber, 1645–99; D.D. 1678; dean of Durham 1691; chaplain in ordinary *c.* 1694–9: *D.N.B.* He was a second cousin of Evelyn: Comber, *Sussex genealogies, Lewes*, pp. 65–70.
[3] The correct text is presumably Psalms lxxiii. 12.
[4] Wednesday service.
[5] The text does not exist.

though some effectualy of more danger: The *B: Sacrament* follow'd &c: 5. To *Lond:* Society,[1] where I met those two excellent persons *Monsieur Justell*,[2] & Monsieur *Azoule*[3] that greate Mathematician & Virtuoso: 6: Din'd at my L:ᵃ *Sunderlands*: 8 home.

9 Our *Viccar* on 53: *Psal:* 3. of the Saints ardent desire for the good of the church. The *hyperbolical* expressions which excesse of Charity, & the glory of God, made Moses, *St. Paule* & other Saints to use, rather than the Children of *Israel* & Gods people should be cut off from *Christ*: &c: See your notes. *Curate*: 1 *Cor:* 2. 2. The preference of the knowledge of *Christ*, above all other Sciences & Mysteries: 11 I went to *Lond:* to have seene againe the ⟨*Morocco*⟩ᵇ *Ambassador*, but he was gon to *New-hall*[4] invited by the *Duke* of *Albemarle*, so I return'd:

16 Our *Viccar* (absent at *Tunbridge*) The *Curate* on 1. *Cor:* 6: 20. shew'd by what ties of spiritual & temporal benefits, as well as our owne promises, we are obliged to glorify *God* both in body & spirit, they being both from God:

ᶜ17 Came to dine with me the *Duke* of *Grafton*, & young Earle of *Ossorie*,[5] sonn to my most deare deceased friend:

ᵃ Followed by *Chamberlain* deleted. in margin here.   ᵇ MS. *Moracco*.   ᶜ Hand

---

[1] Birch, iv. 154. The two Frenchmen are not mentioned as being present; they attended the meeting on 12 July when Evelyn was absent.

[2] Henri Justel, 1620–93; D.C.L., Oxford, 1675; Huguenot refugee 1681; F.R.S. 1681; chief inspector of the king's manuscripts at St. James's 1681; keeper of the royal library at St. James's 1689–93: *D.N.B.*; *Cal. S.P., Dom., 1680–1*, p. 601. Evelyn describes him as 'obliging and universally Learned'; 'whilst he lived my excellent Friend': *Numismata*, p. 247. See also Evelyn to Pepys, 12 Aug. 1689 (Bohn, iii. 305, 310). Further notices below.

[3] Adrien Auzout, 1630–91; F.R.S. 1666; noted for his improvement of a kind of astronomical micrometer: *Nouvelle biog. gén.*

[4] Above, iii. 179. Albemarle had inherited it from his father, who had bought it from Buckingham; he entertained James II here in 1686; it passed to his widow in 1688 and was sold in 1713. For the present visit see Ward, *Christopher Monck*, p. 146.

[5] James Butler, 1665–1745; called Lord James Butler until his father's death in 1680; then styled earl of Ossory until 1688, when he succeeded his grandfather as second duke of Ormond: *D.N.B.*

18: Came Sir St: Fox, his Lady, Sonn and Daughter¹ to Visite us: 22: Came Mr. *Onslow*² of Surrey, & Lady to Visite us:

23 A stranger: on 1. *Jam:* 22. of the necessity of practise,ᵃ and doing, as well as hearing: That in the Easter⟨n⟩, & *African* Churches was much preaching heretofore, but in no nation under heaven more than in ours, even to the nauseating of Prayers, & placing all religious duties in sermons &c:³ *See your notes*: The danger of our being given-up to barbarizme, as they were, for our neglect of practise. *Pomerid*: a stranger on 2. *Tit:* 2:⁴ Obloquie the reigning sinn of the times &c.

27 I went to *Bromely* to visite the Bish: of *Rochester*:

30 A stranger on the 5t of *Matt:* 20. the danger of Hypocrisie &c: *Pomerid* at *Lee* the Lecturer on: 1. *Pet:* 55,⁵ of the grace of humility, danger of traducing of this age: spiritual pride & prejudices among the *dissenters* &c:—We went after to visite our good neighbour Mr. *Bohune*,⁶ whose whole house is a Cabinet of all elegancies, especialy *Indian*, and the Contrivement of the ⟨*Japan*⟩ᵇ⁷ Skreenes instead of Wainscot in the *Hall*, where an excellent *Pendule*-Clock inclosed in the curious flower-work of Mr. *Gibbons* in the middst of the *Vestibule*, is very remarkable; and so are the Landskips of the Skreenes, representing the manner of living, & Country of the *Chinezes* &c: but above all his Ladys Cabinet, adorn'd on the fret, Ceiling & chimny-piece with Mr. Gib: best Carving; there is also some of Streeters best painting, & many rich Curiosities of Gold & sil: growing in the Mine: &c: Besides the *Gardens* are exactly kept, & the whole place very agreable & well watred: The *Owners* good and worthy neighbours, & he has also builded,ᶜ & endowed an Hospital

---

ᵃ Altered from *practice.*   ᵇ MS. *Jopan.*   ᶜ MS. *build*; the -*d* is a contracted form for -*ed*.

---

¹ Above, p. 245; but perhaps the son's wife (above, p. 219) is meant.

² Presumably Arthur Onslow (above, iii. 540); but Denzil (above, p. 255) is also possible.

³ On the status of the sermon in the service see below, 22 July 1705.

⁴ A slip for Titus iii. 2.

⁵ A slip for 1 Peter v. 5.

⁶ Christopher Boone: above, p. 180.

⁷ The varnish; the work was evidently Chinese.

for Eight poore people, with a pretty Chapell, & all accommodations:[1]

Aug: 1 To *Lond:* to see my Charges the late V: C: Mordaunts Children at Chelsey, & thence to *Fulham* to visite the
Bish: of *London*, & review againe the additions[a] which *Mr.
Marshall*[2] had made of his curious booke of flowers in miniature, and Collection of Insecta:[b] 2: I din'd with Sir *Ja: Shaen.*
3: At Mr. *Boscawens*: 4: With *Sir St:* Fox to survey the
foundation of the *Royal Hospital* begun at Chelsey,[3] and 5.
home: 6: Mr. *Saunders* preach'd on 1. Cor: 11. 28. The greate
necessitie & want of Laying Principles of Catechisme &c:
The bl: Communion follow'd: *Pomerid*: 13: Matt: 45. of what
inestimable value we ought account of the Gospel: &c:

9 To *Lond:* R: *Society*,[4] where Dr. *Tyson*[5] produced a *Lumbricus Latus*, which a Patient of his voided, of 24 foote in
length, it had severall joynts, at lesse than one inch asunder,
which on examination prov'd so many mouthes & stomachs
in number *400* by which it adhered to & sucked the nutrition
& juice of the Gutts, & by impairing health, fills it selfe with
a white Chyle, which it spewed-out, upon diping the worme in
spirit of Wine ; nor was it otherwise possible a Creature of that
prodigious length should be nourish'd, & so turgid, with but
one mouth at that distance: The part or joynt towards the
head was exceeding small: We ordered the Doctor to print
the discourse made upon it: The Person who voided it, indured such torment in his bowels, that he thought of killing

---

[a] Followed by *of* deleted.   [b] Or *Insectes*.

---

[1] In 1683 this institution consisted of a school for twelve children
and three almshouses for six poor
people, with an additional house for
the teacher. The charity was reorganized in 1868 and the almshouses were pulled down in 1877.
The chapel, which is said to have
been designed by Wren, still exists:
Drake's Hasted, pp. 225–6.

[2] Alexander Marshall, *fl.* 1660–
90. The British Museum possesses
some drawings of flowers by him.

[3] Cf. *Domestick Intelligence,* 7
Aug.; *True Protestant Mercury*,
12 Aug.

[4] Birch gives no notice of an
ordinary meeting this day and does
not mention Evelyn as attending
the council meeting: nor does he
mention the business relating to
Foubert.

[5] Above, p. 275. His account of
the tape-worm is published in
Philosophical Transactions, vol. xiii,
no. 146, 1683, pp. 113–41.

---

himselfe: There were likewise the Anatomies of other Wormes bred in humane bodys, which, *though* strangly small, were discoverd apparently to be *male* & *female*, had their *Penis, Uterus, Ovaries*[a] and seminal Vessels &c: so as no likely hood of æquivocal generations: There was also produced *Millipedes* newly voided by Urine, *per penem*, it having it seemes stuck in the neck of the blader & yard, giving a most intollerable itching to the patient; but the difficulty was, how it could possibly passe-through the bloud and the *Heart*, & other minute *ductus's* & strainers through the kidnies to the blader; which being looked on as impossible, was believed to be produced by an Egg in the bladder; The person who voided it, having ben prescribed *Millipedes* against suppression of Urine: &c: Then Dr. *King*[1] presented a sharp pointed *stone* that a day or two before had ben taken out of the *Ureters* of a Gent, who ⟨had⟩[b] no kidney at all: The *Council* this day had recomended to them the being *Trusteès* & Visiters or Supervisers of the *Academie*[c] which *Monsieur Faubert* did hope to procure to be builded by the subscription of worthy Gent: & noblemen, for the Education of Youth, & to lessen the vast expense the nation is yearely at, by sending their Children into *France*, to be taught these militarie Exercises: We thought therefore good, to give him all the Encouragement our recommendation could procure:[2] After this we *Adjourned* our meetings 'til *Michaelmas* according to *Costome* at this season: so I went home, where I found my Aunt *Hungerford* come to Visite us:

13 *Viccar* on 2: *Apoc:* 3. 4. 5. That the warning given to the Governors of the church, was also ment to the People; & that few, and (comparatively) small errors, without Gods infinite mercy, would be our ruine: shewing also the feare & care of the Primitive Saints, least after all their paines &

---

[a] Or *Ovaria*.   [b] MS. *hat.*   [c] Altered from *Acadamie*.

---

[1] Presumably Edmund King, 1629–1709: F.R.S. 1666; M.D. 1671?; knighted 1686: *D.N.B.*

[2] For the influence of the French and their academies see the notice in V. The Society does not appear to have assisted Foubert.

dilligence they should come-short and therefore how it imported, to be accurate in our Conversation: *Curate* on. 1. *Cor:* 2. 2. on the vanity of all worldly satisfactions, vilenesse in Comparison of *Christ*:

15 Came to visite me Dr. *Rogers*[1] an acquaintance of mine long-since at *Padoä*, he was there *Consul* of the English Nation students in that Universitie, where he proceeded Doctor in *Physic*; [a]presenting me now with the *Latine Oration* he lately made upon the famous Dr. *Harveys Anniversarie* in the Coll: of *Physitians* at *Lond:*

18 Came to Visite me the LL: Bishops of *London & Rochester*: My[b] A: *Hungerford* went away: 20 Our *Viccar* proceeded: shewing to how small purpose it was to professe[c] Religion, without living religiously: To have the *Creede* in our mouthes, and trample on Gods Commands in our lives:—*Curat* as above.

This night I saw another *Comet* neere *Cancer*, very bright, but the streame not so long:[2] 24 Came to Visite us, Dr. *Parr* of *Camerwell* that good man—

27 our *Viccar* on his former Text, The necessity of Repentance for averting Gods Judgements: That very greate sinns, are frequently punished in this life.—*Curate* of *Greenewich* on 5: *Matt ult.* A *Metaphysical* discourse of the Perfections of God, altogether unintelligible to most of our plaine Auditores. 29 Came to see me very much Company, as indeede there had, all this whole summer: &c:

September ⟨3⟩ Our *Viccar* on his former text; That Gods menaces by all that's terrible was to force, & work on our stubborn natures, not with designe to destroy, but reforme.

---

[a] Hand in margin here. [b] Preceded by *20* deleted. [c] Substituted for *have*.

---

[1] Above, ii. 464. The work now presented to Evelyn was his *Oratio Anniversaria*, 1682, the speech delivered by him on 18 Oct. 1681 (St. Luke's day) in commemoration of Harvey and other benefactors of the College of Physicians. He appended to it his speech at Padua, 30 April 1646, N.S., and commendatory poems by Englishmen there resident at the time, including a short Latin poem by Evelyn (p. 39).

[2] Halley's comet, observed at Greenwich from 15 August until 19 September: Carl, *Repertorium der Cometen-Astronomie*, pp. 366–7, 373.

(See your *Notes*) the holy *Sacrament* follow'd:—*Curate* on
10: *Pro:* 9. Against *hypocrisy.*

This weeke continual Companie to my house from *Lond:*

9 Being the Anniversarie of a deare friend, I was not a little
affected: & the Evening, I was at the funeral of my Neighbour Mr. *Sheeres*,[1] our *Vicear* preaching on a part of *Eccles:*
concerning the transitorienesse of all worldly things:

10 Dr.ª *White*ª[2] on 1. *Sam:* 3. 18. of submission to the Will
of God, from the reasonablenesse of it. *See your notes:*—
Curate on 11:ᵇ *Matt* 20, of Gods infinite mercy to penitents
&c.

15 To *Lond:* din'd at Sir R: *Claytons.* 17: Dr. *Tenison* at
St. *Mart:* 7 Eccles: 14, That the time of Adversitie, was a
proper time to Consider, namely, what sinn it is which brings
the Affliction to us &c: *Pomerid* at St. *Margarets* Dr. *Sprat*
on 119 *Psa:* 142 shewing how *Gods Law*, was the onely Truth;
That all Truthes flowed from him; Nothing in this world so
estimable, & worth persuit; that it did all things & prevailed
over all things. 22. I went home:

24 Our *Bishop* preached on 6 *Matt* 24. a very profitable
discourse of the impossibility of serving two Masters: Of the
Choice we have, of the Vile servitude of One, the freedome,
& easy Conditions of the other: Concluding with an exhortation to hold fast the choice we had made at our Baptisme;
& such especialy as now came to be Confirmed, addressing
his speech both to the Young who were not yet Confirm'd,
& to the rest who were: After this, he laied his hands on
about 600ᶜ young Children &c: There was also an Adult
Young man baptized: ᵈAlso my two Daughters, *Elizabeth*[3]
& *Susanna*[4] were now Confirmed. I dined with the *Bishop* at
our *Viccars*; *Pomerid*: Curat on his former: &c:

Octob: 1 *Viccar* on 5. *Jac:* 16: The duty, effect & power of

---

ª⁻ª Altered from *Viccar*.   ᵇ Reading doubtful.   ᶜ Followed by *per-*
deleted.   ᵈ Hand in margin here.

---

[1] Possibly John Sheere, clerk of
the survey in the Dockyard:
Drake's Hasted, pp. 39, 42.
[2] Apparently Dr. Thomas White,
later bishop of Peterborough: below, 28 March 1686.
[3] Born 13 Sept. 1667.
[4] Born 20 May 1669.

fervent Prayer both privat in the Closet, & pub: in the Church, also of Family devotion &c: The holy *Sacrament* follow'd. *Curate* of *Greenewich* on 17: *Gen:* 1. Describing the Omnipotency & Attributes of *God*, & that being himselfe the most perfect of beings, we were to imitate his perfections; That to live holily, was to Walke before him in the sense of the Text.—8: Mr. *Bohune* on 20: Act: 31. shewing very excellently, the nature of true faith & repentance, concluding with an Exhortation not to deferre it til death from the usual Topics &c: *Pomerid:* our *Viccar* as before: so also on the 15: See your *notes:* The *Curate* on 3. *Revel:* 16,[1] concerning the Christian Warfar, and the necessity of all Conditions to be striving for Victorie, the Encouragement comprehending all Sexes, Nations, Ages, by Fasting, Prayers, Almes, against Luxurie, Avarice, Satans tentations &c:

22 A stranger on 1. *Psal:* 1. Of the nature of true blessednesse, that all people sought it, but most in wrong objects; That it was not in bodily Pleasurs, Honor, Riches, nor any other sensual enjoyment, but in God alone, Virtue, Grace &c: Ending with a perswasion of pursuing them in time &c: &c:

25 To *Lond,* din'd with the R: *Society* (now againe ⟨meeting⟩[a] after reccssc).[2] After dinner a *French-man* produced some experiments for the raising of Water: Also we found, that Water put in *Vaccuo*[b] *Boyliano* & the glasse hermeticaly sealed, if jogged & shaken, made the same noise as if so many pibble stones had ben in the glasse, or some solid body beaten against the[c] bottom & sides of it: The reason; because the aire being exhausted both out of the water & the Vessel, the Contact of the water, was more immediate, & the body more solid; for it had ben easie to have broken the bottle with the water onely.

27 I suppd at the *Earle* of *Clarendons,* with my L: *Hide* his

---

a MS. *neeting.*   b Or *Vacuuo.*   c Followed by *glasse* deleted.

[1] Presumably a slip for Revelations ii. 16.
[2] Birch, iv. 161–2; Evelyn is not listed among those attending the meeting of the council this day. The Frenchman is Louis Hubin: Thieme, *Lexikon.*

bro, now the greate favorite,[1] who now invited himselfe to dine at my house the tuesday following:

29 I receiv'd the *B: Comm:* at St. *James's*, having some daies before ben in no small trouble & sorrow for the unkindnesse & ungratitude of one I deserved better from: Dr. *Tenison* preach'd at St. *Martin's*, on 11: *Rom:* 20 against *Atheisme* with the usual *Topics*, in which twas believ'd he met with a greate *Marques*[2] there present.

[a]30 Being my Birth-day,[3] and I now entering my greate *Climacterical* of 63, after serious Recollection of the yeares past, giving Almighty God thankes for all his mercifull preservations & forbearance; beging pardon for my sinns & unworthinesse, & his blessing & mercy on me the Yeare entering: I went with my Lady *Fox*, to survey her Bu⟨i⟩lding, and give some direction for the Garden at *Chiswick*:[4] The Architect is *Mr. May*, somewhat heavy & thick; & not so well understood: The Garden much too narrow, the place without water, neere an high way, & another greate house of my Lord *Burlingtons*;[5] little Land about it; so as I wonder at the expence; but Women will have their Will.

---

[a] Hand in margin here.

---

[1] Hyde's period of greatest power lasted from the defeat of the Exclusion Bill in November 1680 to the return of the duke of York in May of this year; he was still chief minister but James was the king's principal adviser.

[2] Halifax, created a marquis on 22 August of this year. On his religion, a sincere but rather sceptical Anglicanism, and his inability to suppress an epigram, 'however pungent or profane', see Foxcroft, i. 34–5, and the passages from Burnet and 'Saviliana' there quoted, i. 193; ii. 194, 196–8. As an inhabitant of St. James's Square he was a parishioner of St. Martin's until 1685, when the parish of St. James's was constituted. For his attendance at the service on 21 May

of this year see Foxcroft, i. 355–6.

[3] The date should be 31 October.

[4] Fox is said to have bought a copyhold estate in Chiswick in 1685; in 1691 he was lessee of the prebendal manor there: Lysons, *Environs*, ii. 209, 191. His house and garden are highly praised by Bowack (1705–6); the house was pulled down in 1812, the grounds being added to those of Chiswick House: W. P. W. Phillimore and W. H. Whitear, (*Chiswick*), 1897, pp. 12–13, 268. Part of it is shown on the extreme right of Knyff's view of Chiswick House: *Nouveau théâtre de la Grande Bretagne*, pl. 30.

[5] Burlington had this year bought a large old house here, called Chiswick House by 1708. It was rebuilt by the second earl, passed by

November 1 The Meeting of the *Foefees* for the poore of
Deptford, cald me home &c:

5 The *Anniversarie* of the *Pouder-plot* Mr. *Bohun* preaching
on 1. *Cor:* 10. 7. Comparing Popish Idolatrie, to that of the
Heathen: The peril of their doctrine; Their wicked & pernicious Conspiracys, The danger of our late *Dissenters* least
they bring us againe into that corrupt religion, by provoking
God to take away the light we have so long abused: The holy
Comm: follow'd: *Pomer: Curate* on 3 *Coloss:* 2. 12 our *Viccar*
on his former Text: (See your *notes*) expounding ἐνεργουμενη,
an expression taken from such as were possess'd, to signifie
that our prayers & devotions should be fervent &c: See your
notes. *Pomeridiano* the *Greenewich Curate* on 147: *Psal:* 5.
shewing Gods infinite Wisdome in all Created beings, & therefore knowledge of our Wants, & what was best for us: That
therefore we were to depend on him, & Observe the event;
& we should find it happen much better (all Circumstances
considered) than any thing we could have of our selves Contriv'd, had he permitted us to proceede after our owne
fancies.

13 To *Lond:*[a] about severall affaires: 19 At *Whitehall* Dr.
Coale[1] *coram Rege* on 41 *Jobe.* 5: Against *Atheisme*: how we
may every-day behold God in his Works, by the seeing of the
Eye, though we had never heard of him by the Eare: &c:
At St. *James's* in the Afternoone on 26 *Act:* 28, of the paucity
of intire *Christians* &c:

25 I was invited by Monsieur *Lionberg*[2] The *Swedish* Resident, who made a magnificent Entertainement it being the
Birth-day of his *King*: There dined the Duke of *Albemarle*,

---

a Followed by *19* deleted.

descent to the dukes of Devonshire in 1753, and is now public
property: Phillimore and Whitear,
pp. 263–7, &c.; view by Knyff.
  [1] A Dr. Cole appears as a chaplain in ordinary from *c.* 1679 to *c.*
1684. No doctor of divinity named
Cole is traceable at this time.

A man named Nathaniel Cole was
admitted as a chaplain to the king
on 1 Oct. 1672; several men of this
name appear in the Oxford and
Cambridge *alumni* lists.
  [2] Above, iii. 497. The king is
Charles XI, born 24 Nov. 1655,
king 1660–97.

D: *Hamilton*,[1] *Earle of Bathe*, E: of *Alesbery*,[2] Lord *Arran*,[3] Lord *Castlehaven*,[4] the sonn of him who was executed 50 yeares before for Enormous[a] Lusts &c: & sevveral greate persons: I was exceedingly afraide of *Drinking*, (it being a Dutch feast) but the *Duke* of *Albemarle* being that night to waite on his *Majestie*[5] Excesse was prohibited; & to prevent all, I stole away & left the Company as soone as we rose from Table: 26: At St. *Mart:* Dr. *Tenison* on 1. *Gal:* 10 Concerning innocent Complyances with our Neighbour, & all men, in innocent things, that were honest & of good report, against peevishnesse, & want of sweetenesse & easinesse of temper. 28: I went to Council of *R: Society*, for the Auditing the last yeares Accompts, where I was surpriz'd with a fainting fit, that for the present tooke away my sight; but God being mercifull to me, I recovered it after a short repose: 30: St. *Andrews* day, being our *Anniversar⟨i⟩e* for the Choice of new President; I was exceedingly indangr'd & importuned, to stand this Election, having so many Voices &c: But, by favour of my friends & reguard of my remote dwelling, & now frequent Infirmities, I desired their Suffrages for me, might be transferr'd on Sir *John Hoskins*, one of the Masters of the Chancery, a most learned virtuoso, as well as Lawyer, who accordingly was elected;[6] & then we all dined together according to Costome: & so on the

December 2 I returned home. 3: Mr. *Bohune* (formerly my

---

[a] Altered from *Enn-*.

---

[1] See above, iii. 254.

[2] Ailesbury, whom Evelyn had known in Venice in 1645 as Lord Bruce: above, ii. 449; iii. 166.

[3] James Douglas, 1658–1712; son of the duke of Hamilton (above); styled earl of Arran (Scotland) until 1698, when in succession to his mother he became fourth duke of Hamilton (Scotland); created duke of Brandon (Great Britain) 1711: *D.N.B.* Ormond's younger son, also earl of Arran (see above, iii. 2), was at this time in Ireland.

[4] James Touchet, *c.* 1617–84;

third earl of Castlehaven (Ireland) 1631; created Baron Audley of Hely (England) 1633 (an honour forfeited by his father); royalist: *D.N.B.* For his father see above, ii. 10.

[5] As a gentleman of the bedchamber (1670–85): above, iii. 366 n. His duties included sleeping in the king's bedchamber one week in every quarter.

[6] Birch, iv. 168. Hoskins (above, p. 212) was president for one year only. Evelyn's refusal to stand is not mentioned in Birch.

Sonns Tutor) preach'd on 11 *Matt: ult.* of the gentlenesse of *Christs* Yoake, compar'd with the *Jewish* dispensation: That yet it was a Yoake, as it had relation to the Law of *Christ*; but such as was sweete & infinitely rewarded &c: The holy *Sacrament* follow'd: *Pomer*: our *Viccar* as before, with no considerable addition.

7 To *Lond:* about affaires &c: 10: Dr. *Calamy*[1] *Cor: Rege*: on 4: *Eph:* 26 Against the passion of *Anger*: *Pomerid*: at St. *Jamess* a *Bishop* on 3[a] *Matt:* 14[b][2] Of the difficultie of the Way, & straitnesse of the gate & enterance &c:

I was this whole Weeke transacting buisinesse with Mr. *Brent*, about my *Arrere* due from his Majestie & made severall Visites: 17: A stranger at *W:hall* on *Judge not before the time*[3] &c & before his *Majestie* Dr. *Patrick* on *Greate is the Mysterie of Godlinesse*[4] &c: on which he made an incomparable discourse: I went to Visite, & Congratulate my Lord *Hyde* (the greate favorite) newly made *Earle of Rochester*,[5] & lately marrying his Eld: Daughter[6] to the Earle of *Ossorie*:

18 I sold my East India Adventure of 250 pounds, Principal for 750 pounds after it[c] had ben in that Companie 25 yeares, to my extraordinary Advantage: &[d] by the blessing of God:[7] 20: To our *Society*, where was an Experiment of the puritie of the *Æther* and a learn'd Discourse of Dr. *Tysons* red: proving that according to the newest & most accurate *Anatomists*, The *Embrio* was Nourish'd onely by the Mouth, of the liquor in the *Amnion* (not by the navil onely as the vulgar error) for that there was onely that liquor found in its Stomack & Intestines: & that the *Umbilical* Vessells carried blood onely, impregnated with *nitrous* aire for the supplie of life, but not at all for nourishment &c: 21 I supp'd with the new *Earle*

---

[a] Altered from *4*. [b] Altered from *34*. [c] Altered from or to *I*.
[d] Altered from *6*.

---

[1] Benjamin Calamy: above, p. 229.

[2] A slip for St. Matthew vii. 14.

[3] 1 Corinthians iv. 5.

[4] 1 Timothy iii. 16.

[5] On 29 November.

[6] Anne, b. 1668; married Ossory (above, p. 287) on 20 July of this year; died prematurely 1685: G.E.C.

[7] See above, iii. 201–2; below, p. 298.

of *Rochester* and much other Companie: & went home next day to my house:

24 Our *Viccar* on 5. *Jam:* 15. of the Antiquity & preference of Publique & set formes of Prayer in the Congregation; now much neglected by the Discenters &c: *Pomerid:* The *Curate* on 5: *John:* 14: That sinn was the cause of sicknesse, shewed by our *bl: Saviours* advising the impotent whom he restored, To sinn no more: &c:

25 *Christmas day*, our *Viccar* on 4: *Malachie* 2. How *Christ* was the Sunn of Righteousnesse &c: a discourse apposite to the festival, &c: The holy Communion followed:

29 I went to *Lond:* invited to dine with my good friend Mr. *Packer*, & returned the next day. 31. A stranger on 1. *Pet:* 2. 21, Concerning the sufferings of *Christ*, & in the *Afternoone* on 116 *Psal:* 4 a Preparatorie for Death &c: by Repentance: &c: This Evening recollecting the Passages of the former[a] yeare, I gave Almighty God thanks for his gracious preservation hitherto, being now advancing in yeares[b] apace: And on the

[*1683 January*][c] first, besought the continuance of his mercy & protection for the yeare now entering & which was my grand *Climacterical*. 3. I went to *Lond:* about my E: *India stock*, which I had sold to the *Royal Society* for 750 pounds: it being not to be paied 'til the 25 of *Mar:*[1] returned that evening: & Entertained severall of my Neighbours, according to costome:

7 our *Viccar* on 4: *Mal:* 2. how *Christ* was the Sunn of Righteousnesse, & how the light of the Gospel was spread by it, from its rising in the old Testament to its Meridian in the new, exhorting to walk as children of light. The holy Sacrament followed. *Pomerid: Curate* on 5: *John* 14. especialy on the word *behold*, inforcing the necessity & importance of Consideration. 14. *Viccar* on his former, The danger of Willfull blindnesse after such light is come into the World; & sinning against the light: *Christ* a sunn, as being like to the Sunne, *one̦* onely so Gods *onely* Sonne.—*Curate*, the peril of indulging

---

[1] Birch, iv. 174.

the least sinn, & greate difficulty of reforming habitual sinns.
16 To *Lond:* dind with some of the *R: Soc:*[1] 21. Sir *Jonathan
Trelany*[2] Baronet, preached *Cor: Rege* on   Rom: very
handsomely & well: he became Baronet, by the death of his
Bro: sonn, who I think was slaine at *Tangier*, when the
Moores besieged it. 23: Sir *Fran: North*,[3] sonn to the Lord
North & L:C. Justice, being upon the Death of the Earle of
Notingham late L. Chancelor,[a] now made Lord Keeper, and
my former Acquaintance, I went now to see, & Congratulate:
He is a most knowing, learned, ingenious gent,[b] & besides an
excellent person, of an ingenuous sweete disposition, very
skillful in[c] Musick, Painting, the new Philosophie[4] & politer
studies: He received me with all respect:

28 Dr. *Cave*[5] (Author of severall usefull bookes, as Primitive
Christianity, the life of the *Fathers* for the first 400 yeares &c)
preached on 16 *Luke* 25, upon the Parable of *Dives* & Lazarus,
very excellently: I dind at the Bish: of *Rochesters*, & then
heard a sermon in the *Abbey Church*. 29[d] Supped at Sir *Jos:
Williamsons*, where was a select companie[e] of our *Society* Sir

---

a Followed by *being n-* deleted.   b Substituted for *person*.
c Followed by *the* deleted.   d Hand in margin here.   e Altered
from *n-*.

---

1 Evelyn was in the chair at the meeting on 17 January: Birch, iv. 176–7.
2 Jonathan Trelawny, 1650–1721; succeeded his father as third baronet 1681; bishop of Bristol 1685; of Exeter 1689; of Winchester 1707: *D.N.B.* He had become heir to the baronetcy on the deaths of his brother, Captain John Trelawny, and of his nephew, both killed at Tangier in 1680: Routh, *Tangier*, pp. 170–7.
3 Above, iii. 613. He had been appointed lord keeper on 20 Dec. 1682; Nottingham having died on 18 December.
4 Modern natural science; not specifically Cartesianism. For North's interests see North, *Life of* *Guilford*, p. 284, &c. A paper by Guilford, with no name attached, is printed in *Philosophical Transactions*, vol. x, no. 114 (1675), pp. 310–11; for the authorship see North, p. 292.
5 Above, p. 192. The second work here mentioned is his *Apostolici: or, the history of . . . those who were contemporary with, or immediately succeeded the Apostles. As also the most eminent of the Primitive Fathers for the first three hundred years*, 1677; the half-title is 'The Lives of the Primitive Fathers' (2nd ed. 1682). A second volume, *Ecclesiastici*, covering the fourth century, was published this year; the half-title is 'The Lives of the Primitive Fathers. Volume II'.

Will: Petty, Dr. *Gale*[1] (that learned scholemaster of St. *Paule*)
Dr. *Whistler*,[2] Mr. *Hill*[3] &c: & the intire Conversation was
Philosophical & Cherefull, upon divers Considerable questions
propounded: as of the hereditarie succession of the *Roman
Empp*: The *Pica*[4] mention'd in the Præface to our *Comm:
Prayer*, which signifies onely the *Greeke Kalendarium*: of facetious things, The name of *Ninehamer*,[5] viz, *Anent-hammer*, he
that holds the hammer at the opposite point of a naile to
clinch it, being a thing of no art or skill, but such as any dull
fellow may do: This was upon an action at *Law*, against one
that calld a Greate Person, a *Ninehammer*, & interpreted by
a Smith in Dublin, upon which the Controversy fell, & no
damage recovered: Then we discoursed of *Rebus's* & *Ana-
gramms*;[a] That this sort of Trifling was seldom used by the
Romans or *Greekes*: The most natural being that which
usualy fell from Words, without literal Transpositions; such
as that which was made upon *John Bishop of Tuam* in *Ireland*: by one who asked him

Jo-an-es Tu amens is?[6] &c: in truth the discourse was perfect *Deipnosophisme*[7] & very harmelesse; nor without *Salt*, &
instruction.

30 The Anniversary of *Charles* the first his *Martyrdom*: The
B: of Rochester preached on 2: *Apoc:* 10. *cor: Rege*, appositely
to the Occasion:

Feb: 1 Returning with Sir *William Godolphin* from Visiting

---

[a] Or *Annagramms*.

---

[1] Thomas Gale, *c.* 1636–1702;
D.D. 1675; high master of St. Paul's
School 1672–97; dean of York
1697; F.R.S. 1677: *D.N.B.*
[2] Above, iii. 341; iv. 84.
[3] Above, p. 273.
[4] 'The Rules called the *Pie*':
preface, 'Concerning the Service of
the Church'; the form Pica (medieval
Latin) is not used in the *Book of
Common Prayer*. The rules governing the observation of saints' days,
&c., when they coincide with the
movable celebrations: *O.E.D.*
[5] The only form given in *O.E.D.*
is ninny-hammer; it is there suggested that the first element is
ninny, a simpleton.
[6] Since 1645 three archbishops of
Tuam had borne the name John.
[7] This refers to the *Deipnoso-
phistae* of Athenaeus, a late classical work giving an account of a
banquet in which the conversation
ranges from cooking to literary
matters of every kind.

Dr. *Burnet*[1] & P: Church-Yard among the Bookes,[2] being stop'd in *Fleetestreete*; a *Paver*, or inferior Labourer, working in a deepe Channell, by St. *Dunstans* in *Fleetestreete* flung in a greate stone to the Coach, and brake a greate glasse in pieces, which was drawn up, without doing either of us other harme, we being on the brink of the pit:

2 I made my Court at St. *Jamess* where I saw the Sea *Charts* of Cap: *Collins*,[3] which that industrious man now brought to shew the Duke, having taken all the Coastings from the mouth of the *Thames* as far as *Wales*, & exactly measuring every Creeke, Iland, Rock, Soundings, harbors, Sands, Tides & intending this next Spring, to proceede til he had finish⟨ed⟩ the ⟨whole⟩[a] Iland: & that measured by Chaine, & other Instruments: a most exact & usefull undertaking: He affirmed, that of all the Mapps, put out since, there are none extant, so true as those of *Jo: Norden*,[4] who gave us the first in Q: Eliz: time &c: all since him erroneous: hence I returned home:

4: Our *Viccar*, on his former 4: *Matt*:[5] That we were all sick to Death by sinn, that Christ onely could heale us: somewhat of the Soules Immortality &c: The holy Commun: follow'd— *Curate* on 1. *Pet:* 5. 6. on the Grace of Humility:

6 I went to *Lond:* 7 Dined with some of our *Society*, we had a very usefull Experiment how to describe any Spirals by a

---

[a] MS. *whale.*

[1] He had moved in 1682 to Brook Buildings in Greville Street, to the west of Hatton Garden: Clark and Foxcroft, p. 177.
[2] At this time about twenty-three booksellers, of whom five or six were important, had their premises in St. Paul's Churchyard, or facing the church: *Term catalogues*, 1682, 1683.
[3] Greenville Collins, *fl.* 1679–93; captain in the navy and hydrographer: *D.N.B.* He had commenced his survey in 1681 and published his charts as *Great Britain's Coasting Pilot*, 1693 (two parts;

some of the charts had already been published separately). He was helped by the Trinity House, as well as by Charles II, James II, William III, and private subscribers. For contemporary criticisms see Pepys, *Naval minutes* (Navy Records Soc., vol. lx, 1926).
[4] John Norden, 1548–1625 ?, the topographer: *D.N.B.* For his work and that of his more important contemporary Christopher Saxton see Sir H. G. Fordham, *Some notable surveyors*, &c., 1929, pp. 1–15.
[5] An error for Malachi: see above, p. 298.

Counter-poise upon *Mercurie*, which rising & falling the *Axis* after a new manner of motion of the poles describ'd the figure upon paper &c.[1] 11: Morning [at *Whitehall*][a] I came to the fragment of a sermon preached by Dr. *Cradock* Provost of Eaton on   perstringing the *Papists*, seeking to maintaine some erroneous conclusions by incompetent Arguments: *See your notes*: history of the Young rich man, *what shall I do to inherit Eternal life?*[2] &c.

Coram Rege preached Dr. *Cann*[3] on 138 *Psal:* 1. copiously & learnedly shewing, that by Gods were ment *Princes* & Kings, *Angels* &c: See your *notes*.

[b]12 This morning being at Mr. *Packers*, I received the newes of the death of my *Father* in Law, Sir *Rich: Browne* knight & Baronet, who dyed at my house at Says-Court this 12th of *Feb:* at 10 in the morning, after he had labour'd under the Gowt, and Dropsie for neere 6 monethes, in the 78th yeare of his Age,[4] upon which I returned home to comfort my disconsolate Wife; & take order about his Funerall.

18 I went not to *Church*, obeying the Custome of keeping at home 'til the Ceremonies of the Funerall were over: which were solemniz'd, on the 19th at *Deptford* with as much Decency, as the Dignity of the Person, & our Relation, required: There being invited the *Bishop* of *Rochester*, severall Noble Men, knights, & all the fraternity of the *Trinity Companie* (of which he had ben *Master*)[5] & others of the Country &c: The *Viccar* preaching on 39: *Psal:* 10, a short, but Proper discourse upon the frailty of our mortal Condition, Concluding with an ample, & well deserving Elogie upon the Defunct, relating to his honorable Birth, & Ancestors, Education, Learning in Gre: & Latin, Modern Languages, Travells, Publique Employments, Signal Loyaltie, Character abroad, &

---

[a] Interlined.   [b] Hand in margin here.

[1] Birch, iv. 180–2: 'a way of measuring the rise and fall of quicksilver in the barometer upon a spiral line.'

[2] St. Mark x. 17 or St. Luke xviii. 18.

[3] Thomas Ken, 1637–1711; D.D.

1679; chaplain in ordinary *c.* 1684; bishop of Bath and Wells 1684; deprived as a nonjuror 1691: *D.N.B.*

[4] Browne was baptized on 21 May 1606: Drake's Hasted, p. 38.

[5] In 1672–3: above, pp. 6, 11–12.

particularly the honour of supporting the *Church* of *England* in its publique Worship, during its pers⟨e⟩cution by the late[a] Rebells Usurpation, & Regicide, by the Suffrages of divers Bishops, Doctors of the church & others, who with it, found such an *Asylum* in his house & family at *Paris*, that in their disputes with the *Papists* &c (now triumphing over it, as utterly lost) they us'd to argue for its Visibility & Existence from Sir *R: Brownes* Chapell & Assembly there:[1] Then he spake of his greate & loyal sufferings during 19 yeares Exile with his present Majestie, his Returne with him, the signal yeare 1660; his honourable[b] Employment at home, his timely Recesse, to recollect, his greate Age, Infirmity, Death; He gave that land, to the *Trinity Corporation* in Deptford, to build upon it, those *Almes houses*, now standing for 24 Widdows of Emerited Sea-men &c:[2] He was borne the famous yeare of the Gun-powder Treason *1605*; & being the last of his Family, left my Wife his onely Daughter heire: His Grandfather Sir *Rich: Browne*[3] was the greate Instrument under the greate Earle of Licester (favorit to Quene *Eliz,*) in his government of the NetherLands: He was Master of the household to King James; & Coferer; (I think) was the first who regulated the Compositions through all England, for the Kings houshold provisions, Progresse &c, which was so high a service & gratefull to the whole Nation, as he had accknowledgements & publique thanks sent him from all the Counties; finaly he[c] died by the rupture of a Veine in a vehement speech he made about the Compositions, in a Parliament of K.

---

[a] MS. *lade* or *laste*. [b] MS. *hon^ll:* [c] Followed by *bro-* deleted.

---

[1] See above, iii. 248 n.
[2] See above, iii. 577.
[3] *c.* 1539–1604; a man or men named Richard Browne sat in all parliaments from 1572 to 1593; two men of the name in that for 1601; member for Harwich as Sir Richard Browne 1604. He was clerk of the green cloth at the time of his death: *Cal. S.P., Dom., 1603–10*, pp. 72, 76. He is not traceable (or at least identifiable) in Leicester's service, but it was from him that there descended to Evelyn the Elizabethan state papers which Evelyn later gave to Pepys, and which are now preserved at Magdalene College, Cambridge. Evelyn included him in the epitaph which he set up for the Browne family at St. Nicholas, Deptford: Drake's Hasted, pp. 7–8.

James's. By his Mothers side he was a *Gunson*,[1] Treasurer of the Navy in Hen: 8th: Q: *Marys*, Q: *Eliz:* reigne; & as by his large & noble Pedegree appeares, related to divers of the *English* peeres & nobility:[a][2] too tedious here to reherse: &c: Thus ended this honorable Person after infinite Changes & tossing too & froo, in the same house and place where he was borne: Lord teach us so to number our daies, that we may apply our hearts to Wisdome,[3] & sit so loose to the things & employments of this world, as to be ready & prepared for a better: *Amen:* By an especial Clause in his last Will, he ordered to be buried in the Church-Yard under the South-East Window of the Chancel, joyning to the burying places of his Ancestors, since they came out of *Essex* to Says-Court: being much offended at the novel Costome of burying every body within the body of the *Church* & chancel, as a favour hertofore granted onely to Martyrs, & greate *Princes*, this excesse of making *Churches Charnel-houses* being of ill & irreverent example, & prejudicial to the health of the living: besides the continual disturbance of the Pavement, & seates, the ground sinking as the Carcases consume, & severall other undecencies:[4] Dr. *Hall*, the pious *Bish:* of *Norwich* would also so be interr'd, as may be read in his Testament:[5]

23 I went to *Lond:* about severall buisinesses & return'd

---

[a] Followed by *from* deleted.

---

[1] Browne's mother, Thomazine Gonson, was granddaughter of William Gonson, who had been the principal navy official from 1524 until his death in 1545; her father Benjamin Gonson was surveyor of the navy in 1546 and treasurer from 1548(9) until his death in 1577; her brother Benjamin was clerk of the ships from 1588 to 1600: Oppenheim, *Hist. of the administration of the Royal Navy*, i. 84–5, 104, 144, 149; *Visitations of Essex*, i. (Harleian Soc.), 360–1; Drake's Hasted, introd., p. xix.

[2] Browne was apparently not himself related to any peer; he was connected with the Boyle family through his mother's first marriage: above, iii. 169. For his pedigree see Foljambe, p. 13.

[3] Psalms xc. 12.

[4] Evelyn had expressed his views on this subject already in 1666 in *London revived*, p. 40, and again in *Sylva*, 1670, p. 237. The latter passage is greatly expanded in ed. 1706, pp. 342–4 (sig. x x). See also below, 12 April 1689, 6 Nov. 1692.

[5] Joseph Hall: above, iii. 222. Evelyn apparently refers to the extract from his will published by Fuller: *Worthies*, Leics., p. 130.

next day: 25 The morning being bitter weather, I went not to Church til the Afternoone—Curate on 24 *Matt:* 42 of the Coming of *Christ*.

28 I went to *Lond*, about proving Sir R: *Brownes Will*.

Mar. 2. I heard Dr. *Tillotson* at St. *Michaels* in *Cornehill*,[1] but his Text I could not guesse what: his argument was the infinite goodnesse & mercy of God &c: It was not on a *Sunday*, but *lecture* & I steped in but casualy, as I was going by to the R: *Society*.[2]

3 I returned home: 4: our *Viccar* on 17: *Act*: 30: shewing how God, conniv'd, and oversaw as it were the invincible Ignorance of the heathen world for a time: they having even by the meere light of nature & Conscience light sufficient to forbeare some sinns, though not all others, as *Idolatry*, *Injustice*, *Intemperance*, &c: how far obliged to enquire the truth, & could not plead ignorance, if through sloth, supinesse,[a] or affected &c: (See your *notes*:) the holy Sacrament followd: *Pomer*: stranger on 1. *John* 1. 3. of the Easinesse of *Religion*, difficultys[b] of Vice &c:[3] 11. our *Viccar* on his former subject: That God conniv'd longer at the Heathen &c: because they had not the meanes his owne people had: See your notes:—Po: *Curat* 24. Matt: 42. Necessitie of preparation & Vigilance on Christ⟨s⟩ uncertaine time of Coming to Judgement: the vanity & sinn, of curiously enquiring or determining the time, which *God* will not permit us to know, but to prepare for; seing 'tis certaine he will come, uncertain when, &c. 14. To Lond: about buisinesse & probate of Sir R: Br: Will:

16 I went to see Sir *Josiah* Childs[4] prodigious Cost in plant-

----

[a] MS. *supine* | *esse*.   [b] Or *difficulty*.

----

[1] I cannot trace a lecturer here at this period, but this may have been a lenten sermon arranged by the bishop of London. In 1703 Morning Prayer was said here on Wednesdays and Fridays: *An account of the times . . . Morning and Evening Prayers . . . within the Bills of Mortality*, 1703 (reprinted in Strype's Stow, v. 19–21). The date should perhaps be Wednesday, 28 February: see next note.

[2] There was no meeting on this day; the date for the entry should probably be 28 February, when there was a meeting.

[3] The text may be wrong.

[4] Josiah Child, 1630–99; created

ing of Walnut trees, about his seate, & making fish-ponds, for many miles in Circuite, in Eping-forest, in a Cursed & barren spot; as commonly these over growne & suddainly monied men for the most part seate themselves: He from an ordinary Merchants Apprentice, & managements of the E. *India Comp:* Stock, being arived to an Estate of (tis said)[a] 200000 pounds: & lately married his daughter to the Eldest sonn of the Duke of *Beaufort*,[1] late Marques of Worcester, with 30000 pounds portion at present, & various expectations: This Merchant, most sordidly avaricious &c: I dined at one Mr. *Houblons*[2] a rich & gentile french Merchant, who was building an house in the Forest neere *Childs*, in the place where the Late Earle of *Norwich* dwelt some time, & which came from his Lady, the Widow of Mr. Baker: & where I had formerly ben with his Lordship: It will be a pretty Villa, about five miles from *White-Chapell*:

18. I received the *holy Comm:* at St. *James's* in the morning, then preached a stranger[3] at Court on 51 *Psal:* 3. a penetential discourse: In the afternoone I went to the *Savoy-Church* to heare Dr. *Horneck*[4] on 2: *Phil:* 5. most excellently shewing how we should perpetualy[b] carry the same mind, which was in *Christ Jesus*, & how farr most *Christians* were from it, the danger of neglecting: This Dr. *Horneck* (being a German

---

[a] Closing bracket supplied.   [b] Followed by *beare in mind* deleted.

---

a baronet 1678; director of the East India Company from 1677; deputy-governor or governor 1681–90: *D.N.B.* He bought the manor of Wanstead in 1673; the house had been rebuilt by Robert Dudley, earl of Leicester. It was entirely rebuilt *c.* 1715; the new house was pulled down *c.* 1822: Lysons, *Environs*, iv. 232–5; E. Walford, *Greater London*, 1894–5, i. 474–9.

[1] Child's daughter Rebecca, *c.* 1666–1712, had married in 1682 Charles Somerset, 1660–98, now styled marquis of Worcester, eldest surviving son of Henry Somerset, created duke of Beaufort 1682 (above, iii. 94); she married

secondly in 1703 John Granville, 1665–1707, created Baron Granville of Potheridge 1703: G.E.C. Luttrell gives the reputed dowry as £25,000: *Brief relation*, i. 192.

[2] Above, p. 162. For Norwich's house see above, iii. 538.

[3] The bishop of Llandaff (Dr. W. Beaw) was appointed to preach the lenten sermon this day: list of preachers in *London Gazette*, 14 Dec. 1682.

[4] Anthony Horneck, 1641–97; of German origin; D.D. 1681; curate of the Savoy 1671–97; F.R.S., 1669: *D.N.B.* The church is the Savoy Chapel.

borne) is a most pathetic preacher, a person of a sai⟨n⟩tlike
life; & hath written an excellent Treatise of *Consideration*:[1]
[20][a] I supped, at Sir Jos: *Williamsons*: Din'd at *Dr. Whistlers*[2]
at the Physitians Coll:[3] with[b] Sir *Tho: Mellington*,[4] both most
learned men, Dr, *Wistler* the most facetious man in nature;
& now *Censor* of the Colledge. I was here consulted, where
they should erect their Librarie: 'Tis pitty this Colledge is
bu⟨i⟩lt so neere new-gate Prison,[5] & in so obscure an hole, a
fault in placing most of our Publique buildings & Churches
in the Citty, through the avarice of some few men, & his
Majestie[c] not over-ruling it, when it was in his powre after
the dreadfull Co⟨n⟩flagration &c:[6]

21. Preached at W:hall: *Dr. Tenison* on 1. *Cor:* 6. 12,
shewing the lawfullnesse of the Use of every thing that God
has created, even our passions & appetites, Recreations,
Oathes, Actions, [Riches, Garments][a] &c: in a most incomparable discourse: in what Circumstances safe, & how perverted[d] by bringing our selves under their dominion, &
becoming Vassals, to our Servants &c: concluding in a most
heavenly exhortation, almost rapturous:[7] I esteeme this
Doctor to be absolutely one of the most profitable preachers
in the Church of England, being likewise of a most holy

---

a Interlined.   b Followed by *D^r*: deleted.   c Or *Majesties*.
d Followed by *them* deleted.

---

[1] *The Great Law of Consideration*,
1677 (*Term catalogues*, 22 Nov.
1676); further editions had appeared in 1678 and 1681. It reached
its eleventh edition in 1729.

[2] Whistler had been censor in
various years between 1657 and
1680; he was now treasurer; and
was elected president some time
this year.

[3] For the College see above,
iii. 337–8. The Warwick Lane buildings dated from 1670–c. 1678; the
theatre was designed by Hooke, and
probably the rest also: Walpole
Soc. xxv (1937), 89–90, and authorities there cited. The library was

built in 1684–8 to provide accommodation for an expected gift of
books: Munk, *Royal College of
Physicians*, iii. 331, 366–7.

[4] Thomas Millington, *c.* 1628–
1704; M.D. 1659; F.R.C.P. 1672;
knighted 1680; president, R.C.P.,
1696–1704: *D.N.B.*

[5] The College was on the west
side of Warwick Lane, at its
northern end, probably within
sound of the prison.

[6] Evelyn must have known that,
when the City was rebuilt, as many
improvements were adopted as the
authorities could afford.

[7] Lenten sermon at court.

Conversation,¹ very learned, & ingenious; but the insuperable paines he takes & care of his Parish, will I feare weare him out, which were an unexpressable losse.²

24,ᵃ I went to heare Dr. *Charletons*³ Lecture in the *Anatomie Theater* at the *Physitians Colledge*, upon the *heart*; & returned home:

25 Our *Viccar* as before: the infinite danger of deferring Repentance: See your notes: *Curate* as above, reproving the Curiositie of those who buisied them selves in calculating times when the world was to end, but neglecting to make up their owne accompts &c: 30. I went to *Lond:* in order to my passing the previous weeke for the Celebration of the *Easter* now approching; there being in the holy-Weeke, so many eminent Preachers, officiating at the *Court* &c:

30: Dr. *Tillotson* at *Whitehall* (*coram Rege*) on 1. *John*: 47.⁴ on the Testimonie *Christ* gave of *Nicodemas*, to recommend the grace of Truth & Sincerity in all our actions; perstringing the vaine & servile Complements crept in in this late ⟨depraved⟩ᵇ age, in this nation, from the Imitation of the *French* and other Nations; their submisse & servile expressions, when they intend nothing lesse, but shew their passions & revenges on every slight occasion: whereas we ought to be plaine, & intire in all our words & transactions, expressive of the simplicitie of our hearts &c:

Aprill 1. A stranger in the morning at Court, on 2. *Rom.* 4, of the infinite riches of the Grace, & long-suffering of *God*: danger of not accepting it; The blessed *Sacrament* followed: the B: of *Lond:* officiating: *Coram Rege* (it being *Dies Pal-*

ᵃ Altered from *23*?   ᵇ MS. *deproved*.

---

¹ In the obsolete sense, course of life: *O.E.D.*

² Tenison was born in 1636 and died in 1715. For his character see Burnet, *Own time*, 1833, i. 346; iv. 244; and Swift's and Dartmouth's notes. He was considered to be dull. Only three of his sermons survive.

³ Above, iii. 289. The date of the present notice is presumably wrong; Charleton delivered three lectures

on the heart, &c., at the college on 19, 20, and 21 March; they were published as *Three Anatomic Lectures*, 1683.

⁴ Lenten sermon at court. A sermon on this text delivered by Tillotson in 1694 is printed in his *Works*, ed. Birch, ii. 1–9; it was probably a repetition of the present sermon. Nicodemus is a mistake for Nathanael.

marum) the A: *Bish:* of *Canterbury* on 2: *Cor:* 6. 2. shewing
what was ment by the Accepted time; namely, that of the
Gospel, & of our present life: & peril of neglecting it, as what
will never be offred againe:[1] I dind at the B: of *Rochester*, and
after in the *Abby*, a Chaplaine of the *Earle* of *Bathe* made a
good sermon on 16 *Matt:* 24, concerning selfe-denyal, &
taking-up the Crosse: the greate benefit of it, & evident mark
of Discipleship:

4: *Wednesday* at Court, *Coram Rege*, the *Provost* of *Eaton*
(Dr. *Craddock*) on: 2: *Heb:* 14, explaining how we came to be
called Children; by what analogie partakers of *Christs flesh*
& *bloud* &c:[1] See *your notes*: ‡

5 ⟨*Thursday*⟩[a] before *Easter* at *St. Clements*,[2] Dr. *Burnet* on
6: *Rom:* 22, shewing how by *Christs* passion we were made
free from the slavery of sinn, & the honour of being prefered
to the service of *Christ*: see your notes: in a most excellent
discourse:

6 *Good Friday* morning at St. *Martines*, Dr. *Tenison* on
2: *Cor:* 8. 9 of the poverty of *Christ*, by all the instances of his
exinanition from his birth, to his burial, & what benefit we
reape by it: concluding in a most pathetical exhortation, &
that we should expresse our thankfullnesse, by our Charity
to the poore, who were his surviving Images. The blessed
Communion follow'd: The L: *Jesus* accept me! There was
(in the afternoone, according to Costome) a sermon *Coram
Rege* at *White-hall*: Dr.[b] Sprat[b] (for the Bish: of Rochester)
on   Peter   shewing the benefit of *Christs* Sacrifice; how
all the world, (even the very *Pagans*,) thought (as if by natural
instinct) that our Sinns could be expiated by nothing but
bloud, & death: &c:[3] See *your notes*: I return'd home to my
Family:

---

[a] MS. *Tuesday*.   [b-b] Substituted for *The.*

---

[1] Lenten sermon at court.
[2] St. Clement Danes, rebuilt
1680–2. Burnet held a Thursday
lectureship here for some time; he
was discharged about July of this
year: Clarke and Foxcroft, pp. 141,
197.

[3] Lenten sermon at court; the
preacher listed is the dean of Westminster, i.e. Dolben, who was also
bishop of Rochester; he is also
listed, as lord almoner, for the

8: *Easter-day* our *Viccar* on 8: *Rom:* 34.[1] shewing how *Elect* in H. *Scriptures*, signified what was approved, as the purest Gold, which one would choose for its refined-nesse & perfection with some thing of the benefit of *Christs Resurrection* &c apposite to the festivall: The holy Sacrament follow'd, of which I participated with my Wife & family: *Pomeridiano* our *Curate* on his former Text & Subject, concerning Watchfullnesse.

15. Our *Viccar* on his former *Text*, shewing the Confidence & assurance which the Chosen of God have[a] in the Intercession of *Christ*, since his Ressurection &c: See your notes: Pomer: Curate on 3. *Coloss:* 1. on the same subject: what was meant by the Rising of *Christ*; implying our necessity of being dead with him; that is mortified as to our former sinfull life, & rising as it were to a new & contrary state, manifested by the Effects of our Conversion &c:—17 I was at the Launching of the last ship of the 30, ordred to be new built, by Act of Parliament, & named the *Neptune*, a 2d rate, one of the goodliest vessels of the whole Navy, & of the world, & built by my kind neighbour [young][b] Mr. *Shish*, his *Majesties Master Ship-Wright* of this Dock:[2] 21. Came to Visite & Dine with me Sir *Joseph Williamson*, late *secretary* of state, & Plenepotentiary Ambassador at *Nimeghen*,[3] with my old fellow-Traveller Mr. *Henshaw* & Mr. *Hill*:[4]

22 our *Viccar* on his former text, describing the manner of *Christs* Intercession &c. See your notes:—*Pomeridiano*, one Mr. *Loton*[5] (Minister of Chattham, formerly Curate here) on

---

[a] Followed by *by* deleted.   [b] Interlined.

Easter Day sermon. Sprat succeeded Dolben as dean in September of this year.
[1] The text should be apparently vv. 33, 34.
[2] In 1677 parliament had voted nearly £600,000 for the building of thirty new ships; they were to be completed within two years: *Statutes of the Realm*, v. 802–36. Pepys, who was present at the launching, calls the *Neptune* the twenty-ninth of these ships: *Naval minutes*, pp.

192–3. She was 1,377 tons; 90 guns; rebuilt in 1710: Anderson, no. 628. The builder is John Shish, d. 1686: Drake's Hasted, p. 42; for his father see above, iii. 506; iv. 203.
[3] Williamson was a plenipotentiary at the abortive peace-conference at Cologne in 1673–4; he did not attend the proceedings at Nimeguen, which started in 1676.
[4] Presumably Abraham Hill: above, pp. 273, 300.
[5] Above, iii. 432, 468.

119 *Psal:* 73. How accountable we are to *God* for dignifying us with Reason, and making us Men, by which we are qualified to Glorifie our Creator, and enjoy those eternal & Intellectual Pleasures, & Preheminences no other Creature is capable of &c: See your notes: &c:

26 To *Lond:* To our *Society,*[1] return'd home. 29: The morning exceeding wett; Pomerid: *Curate* 23. *Pro:* 23. Of the Nature, & excellency of Truth; That the Truth here ment, is that which directs to Godlinesse: That like *Pilate*, many are ready to aske, what is truth? but stay not to learn it.

May: 1. Our *Viccar* on 7: Matt: 21: *not he that sayth Lord Lord* &c against hypocrisie, the vast difference 'twixt Saying, & Doing, & how considerable a way we may seeme to proceede in piety, and yet fall short: &c: The Foefees for the Poore met, with whom I was, & then went to *Black-heath*, to see the new *faire*, being the first, procured by the L: *Dartmoth*, this being the first day, pretended for the sale of Cattell;[2] but, I think in truth to inrich the new *Tavern* at the bowling-greene, erected by *Snape* his Majesties farrier,[3] a man full of projects: There appeared nothing but an innumerable assemblie of drinking people from *Lond*, Pedlers &c: & I suppose it too neere *Lond;* to be of any greate use for the Country: *March* was unaccostomably hott[a] & drie this spring &

---

[a] Spelling uncertain.

[1] There was a meeting on 25 April: Birch, iv. 201–3; Evelyn's date is presumably wrong.

[2] Dartmouth is George Legge, *c.* 1648–91; created Baron Dartmouth of Dartmouth 1682; admiral and friend of James II: *D.N.B.* He was lord of the manor of Lewisham and on 14 Dec. 1682 Charles II granted him the right to hold a fair twice a year on the part of Blackheath in Lewisham. In the eighteenth century (presumably from autumn 1752) it was held on 12–14 May and 11–13 October; but in 1772 was restricted to one day's cattle-fair in either month: Drake's Hasted, pp. 85, 243. It was suppressed in 1872:

W. Thornbury and E. Walford, *Old and new London*, n.d., vi. 228.

[3] Andrew Snape, *c.* 1644–*c.* 1709, 'a Son of that Family that hath had the honour to serve the Crown of this Kingdom in the Quality of *Farriers* for these two Hundred Years'; farrier to the king from at least 1685; author of *The Anatomy of an Horse*, 1683: *Notes and Queries*, 3rd ser., vi (1864), 309; &c. The Bowling Green was situated at the north end of what is now Dartmouth Row; the tavern later became the Green Man: Drake's Hasted, p. 64 n., and survey plan of 1695, pp. 42–3; L. L. Duncan, *Hist. of . . . Lewisham*, 1908, pp. 70–2.

all *April* hitherto, excessively Wet; I planted all the out limites of the Garden, & long Walks, with Holly:[1]

3 To *Lond:* about buisinesse, return'd the 5t: 6: Mr. *Bohune* on 20: *Act:* 21. Concerning Faith & Repentance: The bl: *Sacrament* followed: *Pomer*: a stranger, on: 3. *Colosse:* 1. shewing how *Christians* are already risen, that is, as certaine of rising, as if it were past:

7 To *Lond:* about affaires. 8. To our *Society.*[2] 9: Din'd at Sir *Gab: Sylvius*, & thence went to visite the *Duke* of *Norfolck*, & to know whither he would part with any of his *Cartoones* & other Drawings of *Raphael* & the greate masters: He answered me, he would part with & sell any thing for mony, but his *Wife* (the *Dutchesse* &c) who stood neere him; & I thought with my selfe, That if I were in his condition, it should be the first thing I would be glad to part with: In conclusion he told me, if he might sell them altogether, he would; but that the late Sir *Peter Lely* (our famous painter) had gotten some of his best:[3] The person who desir'd me to treate with the *Duke* for them was *Van der Douse*,[4] (Grand-son to that greate Scholar, Contemporarie, & friend of *Jos: Scaliger*,) a very ingenious *Virtuoso*: &c.

⟨10 ?⟩[a] I dined at my *Lord Keepers*[5] who treated me with

---

[a] MS. *3*.

---

[1] Evelyn's holly-hedge was already 'the boast of my *Villa*' in 1664; at that time it was 160 ft. long, 7 ft. high, and 5 ft. thick: *Sylva*, 1664, p. 66. The same measurements are given in the edition of 1670: p. 128. In 1679 it was 300 ft. long and 9 ft. high: ed. 1679, p. 133. Ultimately it was 400 ft. long: ed. 1706, p. 182.

[2] Birch gives a meeting on 9 May: iv. 203–4; Evelyn's date is presumably wrong.

[3] Lely (above, iii. 216) had died in 1680. 'Abundance of his capital things were of the Ld. Arundell and Vandyks collections': Vertue, *Note books*, i. 33. His collection of draw-

ings, &c., was sold in 1687.

[4] Presumably Johan van der Does, 1621–1704, politician, &c.; his grandfather is Johan van der Does, otherwise Janus Dousa, 1545–1609, politician and scholar, the first curator of the university of Leiden: for both see *Nieuw Nederlandsch biog. woordenboek*. It was he who induced Scaliger to come to Leiden in 1593: P. C. Molhuysen, *De komst van Scaliger in Leiden*, 1913.

[5] Francis North, created baron of Guilford on 27 September of this year. He was probably living in Chancery Lane: North, *Life of Guilford*, pp. 82–3.

extraordinary kindnesse, setting me the very next to him, & after dinner carrying me into his Withdrawing roome, we discoursed together of divers Philosophical subjects, as the Nature of Water, especialy, that of *Thames, That* onely, and the water of a River neere Bantam in the *East Indies* being of the same nature, to putrifie, & grow sweete againe, & is for all purposes the best we have in England:[1] That the most *dulcorus*[2] & milky tasted were not the best: There was here at dinner, my kindsman Sir *Humph: Forster*[3] a pretty Gent: newly come out of Spaine: I went home this Evening:

⟨13⟩[a] Our *Viccar* on 1. *Peter*: 2. 11. 12. Describing what were the Lust⟨s⟩ of the flesh, as not onely the incontinency of the lower man, but all other exorbitant desires &c: see your *notes*:

Curate on his former Text: Truth what it was, how to be found, namely, by quitting all prejudices, and taking heede of false appearances: I was so exceeding drowsy (as usualy I now am in the decline of my age) that I could hardly hold mine Eyes open: The Lord be gracious to me.

16 Came to dinner & Visite Sir *Rich: Anderson*[4] of *Pendley* & his Lady, with whom I went to Lond:

17 *Ascention* day I received the holy Comm: at St. *Martins*, The Reader preaching on 68 *Psal:* 18 How we ought to ascend in our Meditations, by taking off our Affections from Earthly things, clogs, & impediments &c: I return'd home this Evening: 20: our *Viccar* on his former, with little addition: *Pomerid*: the *Curate* on 4: *Eph:* 14. 15, shewing (very well) the peevishnesse of our present dissenters, & that private

---

a MS *11*.

---

[1] For the London water-supply at a slightly later date and the importance of the Thames see Strype's Stow, i. 22–8.

[2] Sweet. Evelyn also uses the word in *A Philosophical Discourse of Earth*, 1676, p. 112 (*Sylva*, 1679, p. 315).

[3] Humphrey Forster, *c.* 1649–1711; succeeded his grandfather

(Sir Humphrey: above, iii. 100) as second baronet 1663; his mother's mother was Elizabeth, d. 1630, sister of Sir John Evelyn of West Dean; he was also connected through the Tyrells and the Gonsons with the Browne family: G.E.C., *Baronetage*, i. 145; *Visitations of Essex* (Harleian Soc.), ii. 717.

[4] Above, p. 224.

opinions, though in themselves innocent & Indifferent, when they come to whart,[1] & set-up against the judgement of the *Church*, & Legal Authority, become occasions of greate Scandal, & instruments of evil Consequence, disagreable to Christian Charity, & Condescention. 23 To Lon: R: *Society*, when Mr. *Baker* (a most ingenious young man) that had ben at St. *Helenas*, shewed us some Experiments of the Variation of the[a] *Needles* plac'd betweene t⟨w⟩o equal *Magnets*, and Dr. *Tyson* brought in the *Anatomie* of a greene *Lizard*:[2] I return'd that Evening.

27 our *Viccar* (it being *Whitsonday*) preached on his former: How the Moral Virtues in the *Heathen*, became Divine in *Christians* &c. See your notes: The holy Comm: follow'd: *Pom*: *Curate*, as above, proceeding to shew the severall prejudices against *Truth*, & how *Reason* is eternaly the same:

June 1 Came the Duke of *Grafton* to see me: 3. our *Viccar* as before; of the Ennemies that most warred against the Soule, viz, whatever was opposite to either Moral or Divine Virtue: See Notes. The holy Comm: follow'd, of which with my wife I participated.

Curate[b] on his former &c: ⟨4⟩:[c] *Trinity Moneday*, was elected Master of that fraternity, the Lord *Dartmouth*[3] (sonn to Geo: Legg [late][d] Master of the Ordinance & one of the Groomes of the bedChamber) a greate favorite of the Dukes, an active & understanding Gent in sea affaires &c: our *Viccar* (as of costome) preaching on 11: *Heb: 7*: shewing how *Noach* was saved by faith, a sermon apposite to the occasion, being before sea-men: See your notes: Why so many yeares about building the *Arke*, in a place where so little appearance of a floud: That faith is a Christians best reason: That it was likely the

---

[a] Followed by *Magnet p-* deleted. [b] Preceded by incorrect date *11*.
[c] MS. *11*.   [d] Interlined.

---

[1] Presumably a form of thwart: *O.E.D.*
[2] Birch, iv. 205–6. Mr. Baker is an error for Edmond Halley, 1656–1742, the astronomer, who had been in St. Helena in 1677–8: *D.N.B.*
[3] Above, p. 311. The father is

William Legge: above, iii. 494. He was never master of the ordnance; he was lieutenant of the ordnance from 1660 until his death, and a groom of the bedchamber from 1645 to *c.* 1647, and from 1660 until his death.

first Vessel or ship that ever was made; we hearing nothing of
a *Ship-write* among the Inventors before; but of Tents &
Tabernacles, &c before houses, as fittest to remove when they
traveld for fresh pasture for their Cattell &c: That Iron-
worke was rather for the use of Agriculture &c than for
weapons of War: *Musique* for dauncing & revelling came in
after the Sonns of God, (i) Members of the true Church had
by lust corrupted their way: As to the dimensions of the
Arke for its being capable to containe so many species &c:
he referred to what Dr. *Wilkins* (late *Bish⟨o⟩p* of *Chester*) had
published &c:[1] to answer those objections: That it seem'd
flat-bottom'd, & covered like our houses, not with decks, as
needing neither Mast, nor saile, the Waters being calme, &
therefore stirr'd little from the place where it was made:
That thus all Arts had imperfect originals for the exercise of
mans Industrie, unlesse on occasions extraordinary: See the
excellent application &c: in your notes:

[a]6 To *Lond:* our *Society*:[2] an Experiment on the *Magnes*,
which immersed in filings, they so sated it, that it would take
up nothing more, 'til it was perfectly clensed from them:
Mr. *Hake*[3] brought a small *Magnes*, that being formerly of
great activity, being laied a side for severall yeares, lost all its
Virtue, as if sterv'd for want of foode; which being by little
& little applied to steele, from 2 ounces weight that it would
hardly take up, now suspended an yron of six pound, still
augmenting in power, as it recovered strength, he applying
weight after weight, & by degrees, not at once, as they treate
famished people, to whom if at first,[b] they give their fill of
Victuals, it indangers their lives: This we recorded as a noble
experiment: 8 I returned home where I found [a]Mr. *Wilbraham*,[4] a young gent: of *Chesshire*, &c—

---

[1] A paper by Wilkins on this subject is printed in M. Poole (Polus), *Synopsis criticorum aliorumque S. Scripturæ interpretum,* 1669–76, i. 84–90.

[2] Birch, iv. 208–9.

[3] Theodore Haak, 1605–90; mem-ber of the Philosophical Society 4 Dec. 1661; F.R.S., Original Fellow: *D.N.B.* Evelyn's notice differs from that in Birch.

[4] Identified by James Hall for Dobson as Randle Wilbraham of Townsend House, Nantwich, 1663–

10 our *Viccar* on 9: *Luke* 62: of the forward zeale of some proselytes, not allways a signe of perseverance, see your *notes*: *Curate* on 33: *Ezek:* 11, Exhortation to serious Repentance: 13 *Lond:* our *Society*, where we received the ⟨Count⟩[a] de *Zinzendorp*[1] *Ambassador* from the *Duke* of *Saxonie*, a very fine young Gent: we shew'd him divers Experiments on the *Magnet* on which subject the *Society* were upon:

16 I went to *Windsore*, dining by the way at *Chesewick*[2] at Sir St: *Foxes*, where I found Sir *Robert Howard*,[3] (that universal pretender) and Signor *Virrio* who brought his draught & designe for the painting of the Staire Case of Sir *Stephens* new house: &c: That which now at *Winsore* was new & surprizing to me since I was last there, was that incomparable fresca painting in St. *Georges Hall*, representing the Legend of *St. George*, & Triumph of the *black-Prince*, and his reception by *Edw:* the 3d, The *Volto* or roofe not totaly finished: Then the *Chapell* of the *Resurrection*, where the figure of the *Ascention*, is in my opinion comparable to any paintings of the most famous *Roman* Masters:[4] The Last-Supper also over the *Altar* (I liked exceedingly the Contrivance of the unseene Organs behind the Altar[5]) nor lesse the stupendious, &

---

[a] MS. *Cound.*

1732; sheriff of Cheshire 1714; he married in 1687: James Hall, *Hist. of ... Nantwich*, 1883, pp. 435, 438; note to *Diary*, ed. Dobson. Further notices below, pp. 324, 426.

[1] Apparently Georg Ludwig, Graf und Herr von Zinzendorf und Pottendorf, 1662–1700: Zedler, *Universal-Lexicon*. He was here again on a diplomatic mission in 1694.

[2] Chiswick; for Fox's house here see above, p. 294.

[3] Above, iii. 466. He 'pretends to understand every thing in the World': Wood, *Athenæ*, 1721, ii. 1018; see also below, p. 416.

[4] The King's Chapel lay to the west of St. George's Hall; the two rooms were united to form the present St. George's Hall. The chapel had been reconstructed and decorated between 1680 and 1682; the decoration of the hall was not completed until William III's reign or later. Verrio's paintings were greatly admired; they were destroyed when the hall was reconstructed for George IV: Hope, *Windsor Castle*, i. 320–3, 325, 337–9, 355–7; ii. 580–1. Further notice below, [6] Sept. 1685.

[5] 'The Room, which our Lord and the Apostles are suppos'd to be in [in Verrio's Last Supper], has a Dome, thro' which is seen the Real Organ belonging to the Chappel': G. Bickham, *Deliciæ Britannicæ*, 1742, quoted in Hope, i. 337.

beyond all description, the incomparable Carving of our *Gibbons*,[1] who is (without Contraversie) the greatest *Master*, both for Invention, & rareness of Worke, that the world ever had in any age, nor doubt I at all but he will[a] prove as greate a Master in the statuary Art:[2] *Virio* the Painters Invention is likewise admirable, his Ord'nance[3] full, & flowing, antique & heroical, his figures move; and if the Walls hold (which is the onely doubt, by[b] reason of the Salts, which in time, & in this moist ⟨climate⟩[c] prejudices) the Work will preserve his name to ages: There was now the *Terraces*[d] almost brought round the old *Castle*:[4] The Grafts made cleane, even, & curiously turf't, also the *Avenues* to the New-Park, & other Walkes planted with *Elmes* & limes, and a pretty Canale, & receptacle for fowle: nor less observable, & famous is the exalting of so huge a quantity of Excellent Water, to the enormous height of the *Castle*, for the Use of the whole house, by an extraordinary invention & force of Sir *Samuell More-land*:[5]

17 A Chaplaine preached in this glorious Chapell on 19: *Pro:* 11. [against Anger & passion, &][e] Concerning the danger of prosecuting worldly pleasures by Dr. *Woodroff*[6] on 16 Matt 26 *Coram Rege*:[7] I was invited, and dined at the *Earle* of

---

[a] Followed by *be* deleted.   [b] Followed by *the* deleted.   [c] MS. *clamate*.   [d] Altered from or to *Tarraces*.   [e] Interlined.

---

[1] For Gibbons's carvings in these two rooms see Hope, i. 321; Tipping, pp. 64–6. Some of them are now in the Waterloo Chamber.

[2] There exist three statues by Gibbons or from his studio: Charles II in marble at the Royal Exchange; Charles and James II in bronze in Chelsea Hospital and outside the National Gallery: Tipping, p. 94. The font in St. James's, Piccadilly, is also attributed to him.

[3] The arrangement of the parts of a composition in accordance with some plan: *O.E.D.*

[4] The North Terrace had been constructed by Henry VIII and reconstructed by Queen Elizabeth; it was again reconstructed and the east and south terraces were constructed between 1675 and 1682; there have been some nineteenth-century alterations: Hope, i. 327; ii. 578–80.

[5] Morland's engine brought up the water from the Thames; he was paid £1,500 for it: Hope, i. 322; see also *London Gazette*, 15 Dec. 1681; 14 Sept. 1682.

[6] Benjamin Woodroffe: above, p. 12.

[7] The court was at Windsor from 14 April until about 24 June: *London Gazette*, 16 April, 28 June, 2 July.

Sunderlands[1] where was the *Earles* of *Bath*, Castlehaven,[2] L. V: Falkonberg:[3] *Faulkland*,[4] *Bish:* of *London*: The *Grand Maistre* of *Malta*[5] brother to the Duke of *Vendosme* (a young wild spark) Mr. *Dryden* the Poet &c: After Evening Prayer I walked in the Park with my L. *Clarendon*, where we fell into discourse of the Bish: of *Salisbury* Dr. *Seth Ward*, his subtiltie &c[6]—Dr. *Durell* being now dead, late Deane of *Winsore*, Dr. *Turner* (one of the Dukes *Chaplaines*) was made *Deane*:[7] I visited my Lady[a] *Arlington* Groome of the *Stoole* to her *Majestie*,[8] who being hardly set downe to supper, word was brought her, that the *Queene* was going into the Park, to walke, it being now neere *Eleaven* at night; The *alarme* caused this *Countesse* to rise in all hast, leave her supper to us; by which one may take an estimate of the extreame slavery & subjection that Courtiers live in, who have not time to eate & drinke at their pleasure; & put me in mind of *Horac⟨e⟩'s* Mouse,[9] & to blesse God for my owne private Condition. Here was Monsieur *Del Angle*[10] the famous *Minister* of *Charen-*

---

a Altered from *Lord*.

---

1 He had been reappointed secretary of state on 28 January of this year.

2 Above, p. 296.

3 Above, p. 125.

4 Anthony Carey (Cary), 1656–94; fifth viscount of Falkland (Scotland) 1663; grandson of the Lord Falkland killed in the Civil War; English M.P., &c.; treasurer of the navy 1681–9: G.E.C.

5 Philippe de Vendôme, 1655–1727, brother of Louis-Joseph, duke of Vendôme, 1654–1712; on their father's side they were great-grandsons of Henri IV; their mother was Laura Mancini. Philippe became a knight of Malta in 1666; grand prieur de France (head of the French *langue*) 1678–1719: *Nouvelle biog. gén.* His character was excessively bad; for his adventures arising from the present visit here see Forneron, *Louise de Kéroualle*, pp. 208–15.

6 For Ward's character see Wood, *Athenæ*, iv. 247–9; Walter Pope's reply does not meet the real charges: *Life* of Ward, pp. 171–6. See also an anecdote in Aubrey, *Brief lives*, ii. 286–7; and Burnet, *Own time*, ed. Airy, i. 342–3.

7 Durel had died on 6 June of this year; Dr. Francis Turner was installed dean on 20 July.

8 Lady Arlington held this office from 1682 until the queen's departure for Portugal in 1692: Luttrell, i. 159; ii. 403.

9 *Satires*, II. vi. 79–117.

10 Samuel Baux, sieur de l'Angle, 1622–93; son of Jean-Maximilien de l'Angle, of Rouen, 1590–1674, author of sermons (*Nouvelle biog. gén.*); minister at Charenton 1671–82; D.D., Oxford, 12 Feb. 1683; prebendary of Westminster 1683–93: Douen, *La révocation de l'Édit de Nantes*, i. 367, 494–5, &c.; Agnew, *Protestant exiles*, ii. 341–2.

ton (lately fled from[a] the persecution in *France*) concerning the deplorable Condition of the Protestants there:

[b]18 I was present, & saw & heard the humble Submission & Petition of the *Lord-Major Sherifs & Aldermen* in behalfe of the Citty of *London*, upon the *Quo Warranto* against their *Charter*, which they delivered to his *Majestie* in the presence Chamber: It was delivered kneeling; & then the *King & Counsel*, went into the *Council-Chamber*, the *Major* & his Brethren attending still in the Presence: After a short space, they were called in, & my *Lord Keeper* made a speech, to them, exaggerating the dissorderly & royotous[c] behaviour in the late Election & polling for *Papillon & Du Bois*, after the Common hall had been formaly disolv'd, with other mis-demeanors, Libells on the Government, &c for which they had incurr'd upon themselves his Majesties high displeasure; and that but for this submission, and under such *Articles* which the *King* should require their obedience to: he would certainely, *Enter Judgement* against them; which hitherto he had suspended: which were as follows: That they should neither Elect *Major, Sheriff, Alderman, Recorder, Common Serjeant, Towne-Cleark,*[d] *Coroner* or *Steward of Southwark*, without his Majesties approbation; and that if they presented any, his Majestie did not like, they should proceede in wonted manner to a second choice, if that were disapprov'd, his Majestie to nominate them; & if within five daies they thought good to assent to this, all former miscarriages should be for-gotten &c: & so they tamely parted, with their so antient priveleges, after they had dined & ben treated by the *King* &c:[1] This was a signal & most remarkable period; what the

---

[a] Altered from *for*.   [b] Hand in margin here.   [c] Altered from *roiotous*.   [d] Followed by *Treas-* deleted.

---

[1] In November 1681 *Quo Warranto* proceedings had been started against the City of London, to inquire into its tenure of its liberties. After various pleadings the court of king's bench unanimously gave judgement for the king on 12 June of this year; the formal entry of the judgement was postponed in order to give the City an opportunity to make a voluntary submission. The result was this day's petition and the Lord Keeper North's declaration of the king's terms; the City accepted them on 20 June, but when they were found to include the surrender of the City's charter it rejected them. This was on 2

Consequence will prove time will shew, whilst there were divers of the old & most learned Lawyers & Judges, were of opinion that they could not forfaite their *Charter*, but might be personaly punish'd for their misdemeanors; but the pluralitie of the younger Judges, & rising Men, judg'd it otherwise:[1]

The *Popish Plot* also (which had hitherto made such a noise) began now sensibly to dwindle, through the folly, knavery, impudence & giddynesse of *Oates*; so as the *Papists* began now to hold up their heads higher than ever, & those who were fled flock'd to *Lond:* from abroad: Such suddaine Changes & eager doings there had ben, without any thing of steady, or prudent[a] for these last seaven yeares:[2] 19: I returned in Coach

---

ª Altered from *prudence*.

October. On 3 October the judgement was entered, and the City deprived of its charter.

North in his speech made only general charges against the City; he referred to the riots which had occurred when the court was gaining control over the City in the election of the sheriffs in June/July 1682. The defeated Whig candidates were Thomas Papillon (above, iii. 172) and John Dubois (d. 1683: Papillon, *Mem.*, p. 234; Agnew, *Protestant exiles*, i. 198; probably M.P. for Liverpool 1678/9–81). The riot mentioned in the text occurred on 24 June.

The City's petition and North's speech are printed in *London Gazette*, 21 June; accounts of the day's proceedings in *Hist. MSS. Comm.*, *Ormonde MSS.*, new ser., vii. 49–50; *Cal. S.P., Dom., 1683* (i), p. 322; general account in R. R. Sharpe, *London and the kingdom*, 1894, ii. 476–505; see also below, pp. 341–2. The lord mayor is Sir William Pri(t)chard: *D.N.B.*

[1] Evelyn probably refers to the removal from the court of king's bench of Sir Francis Pemberton (below, p. 342) on 22 January of this year and the dismissal of Sir

William Dolben (*D.N.B.*) on 20 April. The case was argued by Heneage Finch (below, 12 Jan. 1686) and Sir Robert Sawyer (*D.N.B.*) for the crown and by Sir George Treby (above, p. 227) and Henry Pollexfen (*D.N.B.*) for the City; the arguments are printed in *The Pleadings and Arguments . . . in the Court of Kings-Bench upon the Quo Warranto*, 1690. The view taken by Finch and Sawyer, that a corporation is liable to forfeiture, has prevailed: Sir W. S. Holdsworth, *Hist. of English Law*, vol. ix, 1926, pp. 65–7.

[2] The Popish Plot agitation died down after the dissolution of the Oxford Parliament on 28 March 1681; on 31 August of that year Oates was expelled from his lodgings in Whitehall; his pension, reduced in April to £2 per week, stopped on 2 September of the same year: L.C.C., *Survey of London*, xiii. 35–6; *Moneys . . . for secret services* of *Charles II*, &c. (Camden Soc., 1851). The cessation of the panic was due to time and to a growing suspicion of Oates's perjury.

The plot had begun in 1678; this passage was perhaps transcribed in 1684.

with the *Earle* of *Clarendon*, when passing by the glorious
Palace his father built, but few years before, which they were
now demolishing, being sold to certaine undertakers &c:[1]
I turn'd my head the Contrary way til the Coach was gon
past it, least I might minister occasion of speaking of it,
which must needes have grieved his Lordship that in so
short a time, their pomp was fallen &c: I went [20][a] next day
to my house:

24 Our *Viccar* on his former *Text*, shewed the danger of
Apostacie: See your notes: [b]He tooke occasion to speake of
the wonderfull tie of *Friendship*, & its effect upon the best,
& holiest of Men; namely St. *Paule*, whose heart was so knit
to *Titus*, ⟨that⟩[c] the *Apostle* who lived as it were the life of
an *Angel*, professes he had no rest in his Spirit, when he found
his friend absent; leaving even his purpose of Preaching the
Gospel at *Troäs*, & travelling to *Macedonia* to meete him
&c:[2] deploring, that there were now a daies, so few holy friend-
ships in the world &c—*Curat*, on his former:

26 I went to *Lond:* with my Bro: *Evelyn*, who came to visite
me, & next day to the *Society*,[3] where the *Curator* shew'd an
Experiment how to Calculate the *Saliences* & altitude of
Water, by the pressure of a small portable Pump which
crowding a small quantitie of Water, caused it to rise in a
slender *Tube* of Glasse, seal'd at the extreame, & marking by
the gradations on the Tube, what weight of Water was requisite to any height given, an exceeding usefull Instrument:
My affaires kept me in Towne 'til the end of the moneth.

[b]28 After the *Popish*-plot &c there was now a new (& as
they call'd it,)[d] *Protestant-Plot* discover'd, that certaine
Lords, & others should design the Assacination of his *Majestie*
& Duke, as they were to come from New-Market, with a

---

[a] Marginal date; there is also the date *19* in margin.   [b] Hand in
margin here.   [c] MS. *The.*   [d] Followed by *a* deleted.

[1] For the house see above, iii.
379–80; for its demolition, below,
pp. 338–9. The work of demolition
had begun in May.
[2] 2 Corinthians ii. 12, 13.

[3] Birch, iv. 211–12. For Hooke's
experiment see his *Philosophical
experiments*, ed. W. Derham, 1726,
pp. 90–1.

general rising of several of the Nation, and especialy the
Citty of *Lond:* disafected to the present Government &c:[1]
Upon which were committed to the *Tower* the Lord *Russel*,[2]
Eldest sonn of the *Earle* of *Bedford*: Earle of Essex,[a][3] Mr.
Algernon Sydnie,[4] sonn to the old Earle of *Licester*; Mr.
Trenchard,[5] *Hambden*:[6] Lord[b] Howard of *Eskrick*[7] & others;

---

[a] Followed by *Lord Grey* deleted.

[b] Followed by *Grey* deleted.

[1] This is the Rye-House Plot. Shaftesbury, before flying the country in November 1682, had formed projects for a general rising; and there had been treasonable consultations at a later date at which Lord Russell and others had been present; further, Russell and others had discussed the possibility of a rising with some disaffected Scots. In addition to these vague projects there was a plot formed by some old Cromwellian soldiers and other persons for the assassination of the king and the duke of York.

Evelyn's account is not strictly contemporary. The first information, that of Josiah Keeling, was taken on 12 June; Luttrell's date for the discovery, 'about' 19 June, indicates when it became public: i. 262. A proclamation for the arrest of the minor conspirators was published on 23 June; a second, for the arrest of Monmouth, Grey, Armstrong, and Ferguson, on 28 June: *London Gazette*, 25 June, 2 July. A full account, by Bishop Sprat, with an appendix of copies of the informations, &c., was published as *A true account and declaration of the horrid conspiracy*, &c., 1685.

[2] William Russell, 1639–83; styled Lord Russell from 1678: *D.N.B.* For his father see above, iii. 512. He was sent to the Tower on 26 June: *Cal. S.P., Dom., 1683* (i), pp. 347, 385.

[3] Essex was not sent to the Tower until 10 July: *Cal. S.P., Dom., 1683* (i), p. 385; (ii), pp. 85, 90.

[4] Algernon Sidney, 1622–83, the republican: *D.N.B.* For his father, the second earl, see above, iii. 72. He was sent to the Tower on 25 June: *Cal. S.P., Dom., 1683* (i), p. 385.

[5] John Trenchard, 1640–95; serjeant-at-law 1689; knighted 1689; secretary of state 1693–5: *D.N.B.* He was apparently arrested on 28 June and was sent to the Tower on 29 June: *Cal. S.P., Dom., 1683* (i), pp. 363, 385. He was not brought to trial owing to lack of evidence.

[6] John Hampden the younger, 1653–96, grandson of the opponent of ship-money: *D.N.B.* He was not sent to the Tower until 9 July: *Cal. S.P., Dom., 1683* (i), p. 385. He was tried on 6 Feb. 1684 for attempting to disturb the peace and was sentenced to a fine of £40,000; he was to remain in prison until it was paid. After Monmouth's rebellion in 1685, a new witness having appeared, he was tried for high treason, pleaded guilty, and was sentenced to death; he was pardoned in April 1686, on payment, it is said, of £6,000.

[7] William Howard, d. 1694 (matriculated at Cambridge 1646); third Baron Howard of Escrick 1678: *D.N.B.* He was taken apparently on 8 July and appeared before the Council on 9 July, where he turned informer: *Cal. S.P., Dom., 1683* (ii), pp. 72, 80–1; Luttrell, i. 265. He was the principal witness against Russell, Sidney, and Hampden.

with Proclamation¹ out against my Lord *Grey*,² the Duke of *Munmouth*,³ Sir *Tho: Arme-Strong*,⁴ and one *Ferguson*⁵ who had escaped beyond sea &c: of which some were said to be for the Killing of his Majestie, others for onely seasing on him, & perswading him to new Counsils, on pretence of the danger of Poperie, should the *Duke* live to succeede &c: who was now admitted to the Councils, & Cabinet seacrets againe &c:⁶ Much deplor'd were my Lords *Essex* & *Russell*,ᵃ few believing they had any evil Intention against his Majestie orᵇ the *Church*, & some that they were cunningly drawn in by their Enemies, for not approving some late Councils, & manegement of affaire⟨s⟩, in relation to France, to Popery, to the prosecutionᶜ of the Dissenters &c.⁷ They were discovered by the *Lord Howard*, & some false breathren of the Clubb,⁸ & the designe happily broken; since had all taken effect; it wouldᵈ inᵈ all appearance have indangered the

---

ᵃ Altered from *Roussell*.   ᵇ Substituted for *of*.   ᶜ Altered from or to *persecution*.   ᵈ⁻ᵈ MS. *would have in*.

---

¹ Dated 28 June: Steele, no. 3748; printed in *London Gazette*, 2 July.

² Forde Grey, 1655–1701; third Baron Grey of Warke 1675; created earl of Tankerville 1695: *D.N.B.* He appears to have been taken on 26 June; he escaped on the morning of 27 June when on his way to the Tower: *Cal. S.P., Dom., 1683* (i), pp. 347, 356–7.

³ Monmouth remained in hiding until October, when he negotiated with the king for his pardon.

⁴ Thomas Armstrong, 1624?–84; knighted 1660: *D.N.B.* He fled to Holland and was taken there in 1684: see below, p. 382.

⁵ Robert Ferguson, d. 1714, the 'Plotter': *D.N.B.* He escaped abroad.

⁶ All the men named except perhaps Ferguson were in the general plot, not the assassination plot. James had become Charles's chief minister on his return from Scotland in May 1682; about March of

this year the king promised to readmit him to the committee of foreign affairs; on the discovery of the plot he rejoined the privy council: James II, *Life*, ed. Clarke, i. 738; Luttrell, i. 264.

⁷ The general plot, in which Essex and Russell were concerned, at one time included a project for seizing the king. For Charles's present relations with France see below, p. 331; for the Roman Catholics, above, p. 320. Persecution of the nonconformists had recommenced about November 1681: Luttrell, i. 148, 151–3; it is reflected in some of the sermons noticed by Evelyn in 1682; and was now to be intensified.

⁸ For the 'Discoverers' see *A List of all the Conspirators . . . Seiz'd . . . since the Discovery of the . . . Plot*, n.d. [1683]. Besides Lord Howard and Keeling (above, p. 322 n.) the principal were Col. John Rumsey and Robert West.

Government to unknowne & dangerous Events: *which God avert*:

ª28 Was borne about 3 in the Afternoone, my *Grand-Daughter* at *Says* Court, & Christned by the name of *Martha Maria*,¹ by her two Grand-mothers, the *Lady Stonehouse* & my *Wife* &c:ᵇ our *Viccar* Officiating:

July: Our *Viccar* on his former with small addition, of the danger of *Recidivation*, and rejecting Gods *holy Spirit*:ᶜ That God seldome gives repentance to Double Apostacys, with the peril of repeted sinns: The bl: Sacrament followd. The *Curate* of Lee, of 28 *Pro:* 28. how the true feare of God, was the hight of Wisdome:

4 Was my *Grand-daughter* christned: The two Godmothers & Sir *Gabriel Roberts*² Susceptors, by the Name of *Martha Maria*, I pray God blesse it, & may she choose the better part: ª7: Came Sir *Tho: Bellot*³ to treate about Mr. *Wilbraham*⁴ proposed to my Daughter Mary:

8 Our *Viccar* pursues his Text; the difficulty of Lapsed sinners, recovery & peace with former joy, made out by the lamentable Complaints of *David* &c: *Curat* as above &c: 11: To *Lond:* din'd with a Club of our *Society*: Divers Experiments:⁵ ªone by *Dr. Slaer* attempting to demonstrate the several fermentations in our bodies, vizᵈ thatᵈ of our bloud in *Paroxysmes* of Agues & Feavors: He put an *extract* of humane *blood* & spirit of *Vinegar* drawn thro *Veredigreece* into fountain Water in a *Vescica*⁶ of Glasse, which all remained

---

ª Hand in margin here.   ᵇ Followed by *by* deleted.   ᶜ Followed by *The bl: Sacrament follow'd* deleted. The word *bis* occurs in the margin opposite this notice; it probably refers to the two notices of the christening. ᵈ–ᵈ Substituted for *&*.

---

¹ She died on 28 August: below, p. 335.
² *c.* 1629–1715; son of Lewis Roberts (*D.N.B.*); knighted 1678; deputy-governor of the Levant Company 1690–1715: *D.N.B.*, art. Roberts, Lewis; Beaven, *Aldermen*, ii. 111.
³ Thomas Bellot, 1651–*c.* 1709; second baronet 1674: G.E.C.,

Baronetage, iii. 278. He was related to Wilbraham.
⁴ Above, p. 315. Mary Evelyn was seventeen years old.
⁵ At the Society's meeting: Birch, iv. 213–14.
⁶ i.e. vesica, a vessel used in distilling, as a rule made of copper: *O.E.D.*

very cold: Then a pretty quantity of *sal armoniac*,¹ which set
it all a boiling like a pot, whilst in the meane time it grew more
cold than before; which sayd the Doctor is the cold fit of the
Ague, the *Pulse* being then higher by much: Then with a few
drops of Spirit of *Sulphure*, the *fermentation* & cold quite
ceasing, it became hot immediately: This says he is the hot
fit, succeeding the rigor of the Cold:² A most *luciferous*³ &
ingenious *Experiment*: It was then by Mr. *Waller*⁴ a young
modest, & most ingenious Gent: Suggested that the experiment should be repeated the next meeting, with a preparation of the *Cortex* (orᵃ *Jesuits Powder* as cald so famous for
Talbors curing Agues with it⁵) to trie whither it would hinder
both Ebulition & Fermentation: Then Mr. *Hooke* brought in
his new *Pump* that moved by Vanes or Wings, so contriv'd
as best to receive the full power of the wind, shewing the
defects of the ordinary way of ordering them: This did allways turne of it selfe the whole Mill, & tooke the Wind backward: & how it was applicable to all sorts of Mill-worke, for
grinding, sawing, drawing Water &c:ᵇ⁶ He also shewed, how
by the help of a small, but strong rope, to stop the fall of any
ponderous weight, in case of breaking theᶜ line which holds it;
by help of a small & simple piece of yron, fastned to the
Weight & running at the other end with an Eye *parallel* to

ᵃ Followed by *famous* deleted.   ᵇ There is a rough drawing of the
mill in the margin here.   ᶜ Followed by *roope on* deleted.

---

¹ Sal ammoniac. Evelyn uses
this form again in *Numismata*, p.
212.
² Slare's account of this experiment is printed in *Philosophical
Transactions*, xiii (1683), 297–300;
for his further experiment with
quinine see ibid., pp. 301–2.
³ This usage derives from Bacon:
O.E.D.
⁴ Richard Waller; perhaps b. *c.*
1646, and B.A., Cambridge, 1667;
F.R.S. 1681; secretary of the Royal
Society 1687–1709, 1710–14; editor
of *Philosophical Transactions*, vols.
xvii–xviii (1691–4); edited Hooke's
Posthumous works, 1705; last entered in Royal Society lists in 1714.
According to the minutes the proposal to experiment with quinine
was made by Herbert (above, p.
273): Birch, iv. 214.
⁵ Robert Tabor or Talbor, *c.*
1642–81; knighted 1678: *D.N.B.*
The Jesuits' powder is a common
name for quinine at this time
(Jesuits' bark, cortex, and quin-
quina, are also used): *O.E.D.* For
its introduction into Europe see
The Month, clvii (1931), 97–106.
Talbor was the first Englishman to
work out a proper method of using it.
⁶ See Hooke, *Philosophical experiments*, pp. 107–8.

the descending weight, upon the lines breaking, by altering the Center of gravitation, which would stop at the other line or stronger chord:[1] by this slight device he securd the vast weight of 2000 pounds which setts the *Chimes* of the R: *Exchange* a going, which before sometimes falling, had almost beaten-down the *Tower*.[2] 12. I dind at my L: Chamberlains with the *Duke* of *Grafton* &c:

13 ⟨*Friday*⟩[a], as I was visiting Sir Tho: *Yarbrow*[3] & Lady in Covent Garden, that astonishing newes of the *Earle* of *Essex* having Cut his owne Throat was brought to us,[b] having now ben but three dayes prisoner in the Tower, & this happning on the very day & instant that the Lord *Russel* was on his Trial, & had sentence of death: This accident exceedingly amaz'd me, my Lord of *Essex* being so well know⟨n⟩ by me to be a person of so sober & religious a deportment, so well at his ease, so much obliged to the *King*. It is certaine the *King* & *Duke* were at the *Tower* & pass'd by his Window about the same time this morning, when My Lord asking for a rasor he shut himselfe into a closet, & perpetrated the horrid fact: It was wondred yet by some how it was possible he should do it, in the[c] manner he was found; for the wound was so deepe & wide, as being cut through the Gullet, Wind-pipe, & both the jugulars, it reached to the very *Vertebræ* of the neck, so as the head held to it by a very little skin as it were, which tack'd it from being quite ⟨off⟩; The gapping too of the rasor, & cutting his owne fingers, was a little strange, but more, that having passed the Jugulars he should have strength to proceede so farr, as an Executioner could hardly have don more with an axe, and there were odd reflections upon it:[4]

---

[a] MS. *Thursday*.   [b] Followed by *th-* deleted.   [c] Or *that* (catchword at foot of page).

---

[1] *Philosophical experiments*, pp. 109–10.
[2] The clock and chimes were completed in 1671: C. Welch, *Illustrated Account of the Royal Exchange*, 1913, pp. 44–5.
[3] Thomas Yarborough, *c.* 1639–1716; knighted 1663: Miss Sampson, in *Life of Mrs. Godolphin*, pp. 269–71. For Lady Yarborough, a sister of Mrs. Godolphin, see above, p. 64.
[4] Essex had been examined and sent to the Tower on 10 July:

This fatal newes coming to *Hicks-hall*[1] upon the article of
my L: *Russels Trial*, was said to have no little influenc'd the
Jury, & all the bench, to his prejudice:[2] Others said, he had
himselfe upon some occasions hinted, that in case he should
⟨be⟩ in danger of having his life taken from him, by any publique misfortune, those who thirsted for his Estate, should
misse of their aime, & that he should long since speake
favourably of that D: of *Northumberland* & some others who
made away themselves:[3] But these are discourses so very
unlike his sober & prudent Conversation, that I have no
inclination to credit them: what might instigate him to this
develish fact I am not able to conjecture; since (as my Lord
Clarendon his bro: in Law, who was with him but the day

above, p. 322. His death led to
some discussion. The proceedings
of the coroner's inquest were published as *An Account how the Earl
of Essex Killed Himself*, 1683 (it is
from this that Evelyn takes his
account of the wound). As a result
of the general political situation,
the nature of Essex's wounds and
the circumstances of his death, the
evidence of two children, &c., one
Lawrence Braddon tried to prove
that he had been murdered; on
7 Feb. 1684 he and another man
were convicted of conspiring to
spread false reports (below, p. 367).
Further attempts to prove murder
were made in pamphlets published
in 1684, 1689, &c. (see notes below).
Burnet, who, at the request of Lady
Essex, had investigated the evidence for murder, was fully satisfied
that it was a case of suicide: *Own
time*, ed. Airy, ii. 398–9; *Supplement*, pp. 119–23; see also Clarendon, *Corr.*, ii. 277.

[1] The Sessions House of the
county of Middlesex from 1612 to
1779; situated in St. John Street,
Clerkenwell: Wheatley. But Russell
was tried at the Old Bailey.

[2] The suicide was mentioned by
the attorney-general (Sir Robert
Sawyer) in his opening speech after
the swearing in of the jury: *The
Tryals of Thomas Walcot*, &c., 1683,
p. 38. It caused Lord Howard to
falter when giving his evidence;
and was later referred to by Sir
George Jeffreys (below, p. 342) in
the final speech for the prosecution:
ibid., pp. 42, 59. For the alleged
influence of the news on the trial see
*An Enquiry into, and Detection of
the Barbarous Murther of the Late
Earl of Essex*, 1684, pp. 10–11; but,
as Ormond points out, one man
(Walcot) had been convicted for the
plot on the preceding day: *Hist.
MSS. Comm., Ormonde MSS.*, new
ser., vii. 73.

[3] With this compare Ormond's
letter, 14 July, as cited above.
Northumberland is Henry Percy,
1532 ?–85, eighth earl of Northumberland 1572: *D.N.B.*; he was
Lady Essex's great-grandfather;
his death was generally held to be
due to suicide, but murder was also
suggested. The supposed influence
of his death on Essex is also mentioned by Burnet and in *An Enquiry*
(as above), pp. 6–7. For Essex's
property see Ormond; the goods of
a suicide were as much liable to forfeiture as those of a traitor or of
any other felon.

before[1] assur'd me) he was then so very cherefull, & declared it to be the Effect of his innocence & loyalty: & most believe his *Majestie* had no severe intentions against him;[2] however he was altogether inexorable as to my *Lord Russell*[3] & some of the rest: For my owne part I believe the crafty & ambitious[a] Earle of *Shaftsbery* had brought them into some dislike of the present carriage of matters at Court, not with any designe of destroying the *Monarchy* (which *Shaftsbery* has in Confidence & for unanswerable reasons, told me,[4] he would support, to his last breath, as having seene & felt the miserie of being under [a][b] Mechanic Tyrannie &c) but perhaps of seting up some other, whom he might govern, & frame to his owne *Platonic*[5] fancie, without much reguard to the *Religion* establish'd under the *Hierarchie*, for which he had no esteeme:[6] But when he perceiv'd those whom he had engag'd to rise, faile of[c] his expectations, & the day past,[d] reproching his Complices, that a second day for an Exploit of this nature, was never successfull, he gave them the slip, & got into

---

^a Altered from *malicious.*   ^b Interlined.   ^c Followed by *th-* deleted.   ^d Followed by *tellin-* deleted.

---

[1] For this visit see Burnet, *Own time*, ed. Airy, ii. 371. Clarendon's first wife was Theodosia Capel, *b.* 1640, Essex's sister; she had died in 1662.

[2] The king '(as is said) declared, *He wondred the Earl should destroy himself, seeing he owed him a Life*': P.V., *Innocency and Truth Vindicated*, 1689, p. 84; the allusion is to Lord Capel's execution. Ormond thought that Essex might hope for pardon or at least that his honours would be restored to his son.

[3] Ormond on 14 July thought that Russell would not be spared: letter as above, p. 74. According to Rochester (in Burnet) and Dartmouth (note on the passage) it was the king who was inexorable: Burnet, *Own time*, ed. Airy, ii. 377 and n. But Monmouth stated that the king told him that he had yielded to the duke's insistence:

pocket-book, quoted in J. Welwood, *Memoirs*, 1700, pp. 375–6.

[4] Evelyn does not mention meeting Shaftesbury after the latter had been deprived of the Great Seal on 9 Nov. 1673; but Shaftesbury had continued to attend meetings of the Council of Trade and Plantations until the following March: Brown, *Shaftesbury*, p. 148. On his views on monarchy see ibid., pp. 221–2, 234–5.

[5] The allusion is to Plato's *Republic*, which Evelyn regarded as fantastic: so meaning 'that *Platonique Chimæra* of a *State*': *Of Liberty and Servitude*, To him that reades (*Misc. Writings*, p. 5): 'a *Platonic* Notion': *Numismata*, p. 235.

[6] He was 'a deist at best': Burnet, *Own time*, ed. Airy, i. 172. He was faithful to the cause of toleration for Protestant Dissenters.

Holland, where the fox died, three moneths before these unhappy Lords & others were discovered or suspected:[1] Every creature deplored *Essex*, & *Russell*, especialy the last, as being thought to be drawn in on pretence onely of endeavoring to rescue the King from his present Counselors, & secure Religion, from Popery, & the Nation from Arbitrary government, now so much apprehended; whilst the rest of those who were fled, especialy *Ferguson* & his gang, had doubtlesse some bloudy designe,[a] set up a Commonwealth, & turne all things topsie turvy; of the same tragical principles is Sidney &c:[2]

I had this day much discourse with *Monsieur Pontaque*[3] son to the famous & wise Prime President of *Bourdeaux*: This gent, was owner of that excellent *Vignoble* of *Pontaque* & *Obrien*, whence the choicest of our *Burdeaux*-Wines come and I think I may truely say of him (that was not so truely said of st. Paule) that much learning had made him madd: he had studied well in Philosophie, but chiefly the *Rabbines*, & was exceedingly addicted to Cabalistical fancies, an eternal *hablador*,[4] & halfe distracted with reading aboundance of the

---

[a] Followed by *&* deleted.

---

[1] According to the evidence at Walcot's and Russell's trials Shaftesbury projected a rising for some date in October 1682; the other conspirators refusing, the rising was to take place on 17 November; when it was again postponed Shaftesbury said that 'there was no dependance upon those Gentlemen that met, and he would leave *England*': *Tryals of Thomas Walcot*, &c., 1683, pp. 45–6, 5. He left Harwich on 28 November and died at Amsterdam on 31/21 Jan. 1683.

[2] See below, pp. 352–3. Sidney was a republican, whereas Ferguson was mainly a firebrand.

[3] Identifiable as François-Auguste de Pontac, d. 1694, *président aux requêtes du Palais de Parlement* at Bordeaux, only known son

of Arnaud de Pontac, 1599–1681, *premier président* of the *Parlement* of Bordeaux 1653–*c.* 1672. The two Pontacs were *seigneurs* of Haut-Brion, where they owned an important vineyard; its name was anglicized as 'O'Brien', &c. There was no vineyard of any importance properly called Pontac; the name was applied either to Haut-Brion, or to wines from other vineyards belonging to the family, or to clarets resembling it: *Notes and Queries*, clxxv (1938), 74. I have found no other notice of the son's studies. For Pontack's, the tavern, see below, 30 Nov. 1693.

[4] J. Minsheu gives *verbosus* as the equivalent: *Ductor in linguas*, 1617. Evelyn gives 'their great *hablador*' as his rendering of 'ce grand Diseur

extravagant Eastern Jewes: For the rest he spake all Languages, was very rich, an handsome person, & well-bred; aged about 45.

14 I visited this morning Mr. *Frazier*,[1] a learned Scots Gent: whom I had formerly recommended to my Lord Berkeley, for the Institution & government of his sonn, since dead at sea:[2] he had now ben in Holland, at the sale of the learned *Hiensius's* Library,[3] & shewed me divers very rare & curious bookes, & some *Manuscripts* he had purchas'd to good value: There were Three or foure Herbals in *Miniature* accurately don, divers *Roman* Antiquities, & of Verona[4] &c: very many books of *Aldus's* Impression &c:[5] hence I went home:

15 A stranger preached on 6. *Jer:* 8: The not harkning to Instruction, portentous of desolation to a people: The old man preached much after Bish: *Andrews's* method,[6] full of *Logical* divisions, in short, & broken periods, & latine sentences, now quite out of fashion in the pulpet;[a] grown into a far more profitable way, of plaine & practical, of which sort this[b] *Nation* nor any other ever had greater plenty, & more profitable (I am confident) since the *Apostles* time: so much has it to answer for thriving no better on it:

Pomerid: our *Curate* on 11: *Matt:* 28. The sweete Invitation of *Christ* to over laden sinners:

The whole Nation was now in greate Consternation, upon

---

[a] Followed by *&* deleted.   [b] Altered from *the*.

---

de rien' in R. Fréart de Chambray, *Idée de la perfection de la peinture*, 1662, p. 100; trans., p. 103.

[1] Probably the 'Mr. Frazier' mentioned by Hooke in *Philosophical experiments*, p. 111.

[2] Charles Berkeley, 1662–82, eldest son of John, Lord Berkeley of Stratton (above, iii. 445); second Baron Berkeley of Stratton 1678; he was captain of the *Tiger* man-of-war and died of small-pox while at sea: G.E.C.

[3] Nicolaas Heinsius the elder,

1620–81, classical scholar, poet, and diplomatist: *Nieuw Nederlandsch biog. woordenboek*. The auction-sale catalogue of his books was published as *Bibliotheca Heinsiana* (one issue dated 1682).

[4] 'Torellus de origine & amplitudine civitatis Veronæ 1540. *quo in libro passim extat manus Scaligeri*': *Bibl. Heinsiana*, ii. 137, no. 122. Torellus Sarayna: above, ii. 485 n.

[5] Aldo Manuzio, 1449–1515: *Encic. italiana*.

[6] See above, p. 166.

the late Plot & Conspiracy; his *Majestie* very Melancholic,
& not stirring without redoubled Guards, all the Avenues &
private dores about White-hall & the Park shut up; few
admitted to walke in it:[1] The *Papists* in the meane while
very jocond, & indeede they had reason, seeing their owne
plot brought to nothing, & turn'd to ridicule & now a Conspiracy of *Protestants*, as they cald them:[2] The Turk likewise
in hostility against the German Emperor, almost Master of
the upper *Hungarie* & drawing towards *Vienna*;[3] on the other
side the *French* (who tis believed brought in the Infidel)
disturbing their Spanish, & Dutch Neighbours, & almost
swallowed, all *Flanders*, pursuing his ambition of a fift [&
Universal][a] Monarchy;[4] & all this blood, & dissorder in
Christendome had evidently its rise from our defections at
home, in a Wanton peace, minding nothing but Luxurie,
Ambition, & to procure Mony for our Vices: To[b] this add
our *irreligion* & *Atheisme*, greate ingratitude & selfe Interest:
the Apostacie of some, & the Suffering the *French* to grow
so Greate, and the Hollanders so Weake.[5] In a word we
were Wanton, madd, and surfeiting with prosperity, every
moment unsettling the old foundations, & never constant to
any thing. The *Lord* in mercy avert the sad *Omen*; & that
we do not provoke him farther, 'til he beare it no longer:

This summer did we suffer 20 *French*-men of *Warr* to passe

---

[a] Interlined.   [b] Altered from *Thi-*.

[1] Luttrell notes late in June that the king 'hardly goes out but with a strong guard': i. 264.

[2] 'Spero che questo sarà di gran giovamento ai cattolici, mentre vengono adesso pienamente giustifi-cati della congiura di cui essi vennero accusati e che era falsissima': the duchess of York, 18 July, in Campana de Cavelli, i. 402.

[3] Apparently summarized from notices in *London Gazette* for June and July, especially 16 July.

[4] For the contemporary view of Louis's relations with the emperor and the Turks see Burnet, *Own time*, ed. Airy, ii. 387–8. He had helped to make the invasion possible and was prepared to profit from it. In March French troops were threatening Luxemburg; on 31 August, N.S., Louis opened an attack on the Spanish Netherlands. For the fifth monarchy see Daniel, ii. 44.

[5] Our foreign policy at this time was governed by Charles II's financial dependence on Louis XIV; the two treaties of 1681 were known only to Rochester and per-haps to the duke of York.

our Chanell towards the Sound, to help the Dane against the Swede, who had ⟨abandoned⟩[a] the ⟨French⟩[b] Interest; we having not ready sufficient to guard our Coasts, or take Cognizance of what they did; so as though the Nation never had more, or better Navy, the *Sea* never had so slender a Fleete:[1]

18 To *Lond:* Society:[2] some former Experiments repeated.

[c]19 *George Prince* of *Denmark*,[3] who landed this day, came to Mary the Lady *Anne* daughter to the *Duke*: so I return'd home; having seene the Young Gallant at dinner at *Whitehall*.

20 Severall of the Conspirators, of the lower forme, were Executed at *Tyburn*—[4]

21 And the next day was the *Lord Russell* decapitated in *Lincolns in fields*, the Executioner giving him 3 butcherly strokes: The Speech he made & Paper he gave the Sherif, declaring his Innocence, the noblenesse of the family, the piety & worthynesse of the unhappy[d] Gent: wrought effects of much pitty, & various discourses on the plot &c:[5]

22: A stranger on 11: *Pro:* 18. 19: how wicked designes, however covertly carried, end in the destruction of the Authors; with reflections on the late *plot*:

25 I went to Lond: saw againe *Prince George*, he had the Danish Countenance, blound; a young gent of few words, spake French but ill, seemed somewhat heavy; but reported Valiant, & indeede had bravely rescued & brought off his

---

[a] MS. *abondoned.*   [b] MS. *Fresh.*   [c] Hand in margin here.
[d] Altered from *h-.*

---

[1] The arrival of twenty-five French ships in the Sound (the channel leading into the Baltic) is reported in *London Gazette*, 12 July.
[2] Birch, iv. 215–17 (not dated).
[3] 1653–1708. Notice of his reception at Whitehall this day in *London Gazette*, 23 July. Princess Anne (above, p. 50) was now eighteen years old.
[4] Walcot (above, p. 327 n.) and two others: ibid.
[5] For the execution see ibid.; Luttrell, i. 270–1; *Hist. MSS. Comm.*, 7th rep., App., pp. 373–4. Evelyn

alludes not to Russell's speech, which was unimportant, but to a paper left by him; the two were published together as *The Speech of the late Lord Russel, to the Sheriffs: Together with the Paper deliver'd by him to them*, 'Printed for *John Darby*, by Direction of the Lady *Russel*', 1683. This is said to have been on sale in the streets within an hour of Russell's death; 20,000 copies were printed: Burnet, *Own time*, ed. Airy, ii. 384; *Cal. S.P., Dom., 1683* (ii), p. 432.

brother the K. of *Denmarke* in a battaile against the Swede, when both those Kings, were engaged very smartly:[1]

At the R: *Society* was repeated Dr. *Slaers* Experiment, which shewed the Cause of the Fitts in Agues & intermittent feavers; & the Effects of the *Cortex* mingled with a little *Chalk*, which qualified the Ebulition:[2] After this we adjourn'd 'til October, according to Costome, & I returned home.

28 Prince Geo: was *married* to the *Lady Ann* at Whitehall:[3] Her[a] Court & household to be moduled just as the Dukes her fathers &c: & to continue in England:

29 Preached Mr. *Meriton*[4] on 6: *Matt* 20, Answering divers *Atheistical* Objections, against the Providence of God &c: See your notes: *Pomerid: Curate* on 33 *Ezek.* 11 of the Danger of deferring Repentance &c:

August: 1 Came to see me Mr. *Flamested* the famous Astrologer from his Observatorie at Greenewich, to draw the Meridian[b] for my *Pendules* &c:[5]

2 Came to Visite me the Countesse of *Bristol*, & *Sunderland*, Aunt & Co: Germ: to the late Lord *Russell*;[6] & to Condole his sad fate:

5 Mr. *Saunders* preached on 1. *Hagg:* 7 of Consideration, a most excellent discourse. See your *notes: Pomeridiano* on 2 *Psal:* 6. Paralleling the preservation of his Majestie to that of K. *David* &c: a Politique discourse relating to the Plot &c: See your notes.

8 A Woman, who came from *Lond:* to speake with my Wife, was Arested for debt in my Hall, by one who pretended

---

[a] Altered from *His.*   [b] Or *Miridian.*

---

[1] Prince George and his brother King Christian V had distinguished themselves at the battle of Landskrona, 1677, both taking part in the fighting. Charles XI was in command of the Swedish forces.

[2] Above, pp. 324–5.

[3] *London Gazette*, 30 July. For the prince and princess's households see Chamberlayne, *Angliæ notitia*, 1684, i. 235–40. They resemble those of the duke and duchess of York, but are rather smaller.

[4] Presumably the preacher mentioned again below, p. 383. He appears to be distinguishable from Dr. John Meriton: above, p. 180; &c.

[5] He was presumably laying down some form of meridian line.

[6] Lady Bristol was a sister of Russell's father.

to be a Porter, & to deliver her a letter; but I rescued her from the Insolence &c:

12 A stranger preached on 2 *Cor:* 5. 11. describing the terrors of the last day, with the meanes of Escape: Afternoone the *Curate* of *Greenewich* on 22: *Matt:* 35 ad 41. exhorting to Love & Charity.

17 Came all the daughters of the late *Vicountesse* Mordaunt[1] to visite & dine with us &c:

19 Mr. *Bohune* preached on 33. *Isay* 14. a most profitable discourse on the dreadfull Judgments of God against *Atheists* & *Hypocrites*, paralleled with the sinns of *Israel* & *Judah* before the Captivity: *Pomerid*: our *Curate* on 33 Ezek. his former subject: [a]23d I went to *Bromely* to visite our *Bishop* our excellent neighbour, & to Congratulate his now being made *Arch-bishop* of York,[2] returnd that evening: 24 Dr. *Par*, Dr. *Bradford*[3] and some other friends dined with me;[b] Came to visite me Colonel Jo: *Russell*[4] unkle to the ⟨Late⟩[c] *Lord Russell*, & bro: to the Earle of *Bedford*, & with him Mrs. *Midleton*[5] that famous, & indeede incomparable beautifull Lady; Daughter to my Relation Sir Robert Needham.

26 Our *Viccar* preach'd on 5: *Psal:* 8, shewing that the most righteous man, has neede of Gods guidance & conduct, perstringing the *Pellagians*[6] & other sects, who ascribed too much to our owne will (se your *notes*)—*Curate* as before— not to deferr our turning to *God* &c:

---

[a] Hand in margin here.   [b] Followed by *26*? deleted.   [c] MS. *Lade*.

[1] There were four daughters apparently now living: Collins, *Peerage*, ed. Brydges, iii. 327–8.

[2] Dolben was elected archbishop on 26 July and confirmed on 16 August.

[3] The former schoolmaster of Camberwell: above, iii. 562. He was now rector of St. Edmund the King, London, and perhaps vicar of Bexhill, Sussex, also.

[4] John Russell, 1612–87; raised in 1660 the King's Own Regiment of Foot (Royal Regiment of Guards, now the Grenadier Guards), of which he was colonel until 1681: Sir F. W. Hamilton, *Origin and hist. of the . . . Grenadier Guards*, 1874, i. 43–4, 251, &c.

[5] Jane, 1646–92; married 1660 Charles Myddelton of Ruabon, d. 1691: *D.N.B.*; for her father see above, iii. 198. Evelyn had formerly praised her skill in painting: Pepys, 27 Sept. 1665.

[6] For Evelyn's description of the Pelagians see *Hist. of Religion*, ii. 237–8.

ᵃ28 Died my sweete little Grand-child *Martha Maria* of Convulsion fitts, an extraordinary pretty & foreward child: *Gods will be don*:

Came also this morning to take his leave of us his Grace the Archbishop of Yorke now preparing for his Journey:¹ & reside inᵇ his Province. 29 Was buried our Grand-child, amongst the rest of our sweete Infants in the *Parish-Church*:

September 2 This morning was read in the Church after the Office was don, the *Declaration* setting forth the late Conspiracy against his *Majesties Person* &c:² after which Dr. *Jackson*³ preach'd on 2: *Phil:* 1. 2. of the Nature of Love, friendship & Charity, very eloquently ending with an exhortation to Unitie, from the sad effects of devision, Examples of the *Saints*; greate decay & want of it in the World. The holy Comm: followed: *Pomerid*: the *Curate* 3: *Coloss:* 2. perswading to fix our hearts on permanent, & heavenly things.

3 I went (together with my Wife &c) to Chelsey, to see my Charge, the Daughters, and Children of my deare friends, the late V. Countesse *Mordaunt*: After dinner I walked to survey what had ben don as to repaires &c, by the *Duke* of *Beaufort* upon his late purchased house at ⟨*Chelsey*⟩,ᶜ of which I had once the selling for the Countesse of *Bristol*: I found he had made greate alterations, but might have built a better house with the Materials & that cost:⁴ at my returne to our Company, I found the Countesse of *Monte Feltre*,⁵ whose husband

---

ᵃ Hand in margin here.   ᵇ Followed by *that* deleted.   ᶜ MS. *chelsey*.

---

¹ Dolben arrived at Bishopthorpe (above, iii. 128) on 25 September: *London Gazette*, 1 Oct.

² *His Majesties Declaration*, &c., 28 July 1683 (ordered to be printed 27 July); reprinted in *London Gazette*, 6 Aug. It was ordered to be read in all churches this day.

³ Presumably John Jackson, the rector of Lee: above, p. 206.

⁴ For the house see above, pp. 161–2; for Beaufort, iii. 94. His

alterations do not appear to have affected the southern front, which is shown in Kip's view.

⁵ Elizabeth, daughter of Henry Savile of Bowlings, a half-brother of Halifax's grandfather; licensed to marry, 2 Sept. 1668, Charles Ubaldino, count of Monte Feltre (the spelling varies; 'Montesaltro' in the marriage licence is wrong): *Genealogist*, new ser., x (1894), 162. Monte Feltre was elected F.R.S. in

I had formerly known, & was a subject of the *Popes*, but Changing from his Religion, & become Protestant, resided here in England, & married into the familie of the *Savells* of York-shire: The Count (her late husband) was a very learned Gent: a greate Polititian; a goodly man: she was accompanied with her Sister,[1] exceedingly skild in painting; nor indeede did they seeme to spare for Colour on their owne faces: They had a greate deale of Wit, one of them especialy, who talked of a sparrow she had at home not inferior to *Lesbias*.[2]

9 It being the day of publique Thanksgiving for his Majesties late preservation, the former Declaration read the 2d time, there was a publique Office used compos'd expressly for the occasion;[3] & then our *Viccar* preached on 144 *Psal:* 10. Thou has⟨t⟩ preserved *David from the perill of the sword* &c, very learnedly seting forth the providence of God over Kings &c: & proving they were never set up, nor ought be pull'd downe by the *people*: he shew'd how the father of the Family was Monarch of his Tribe ab origine, that therefore the Eldest sonn, had a double portion, to sustaine the government, & as being Priest, the expense of Sacrifices: That from *Tribes* they grew to Nations, & that this patriarchal dominion continued 'til God himselfe chose the *Kings* &c so by divine right, The blessing of Monarchical Government above any other: That not one of all the murderers of J. *Cæsar* but came to untimly periods, or made themselves away: remarke[a] on the late Regicides: The strange discovery of plots against Q: Eliz: K: James, his present Majestie &c: & exhorting to obedience & loyalty, from the example & doctrine of the primitive Christians, & Church of England &c:[4] with much

---

[a] Or *remarks*.

1667; he appears in the annual *List* for 1668, but not thereafter; for him see also *Cal. S.P., Dom., 1667*, p. 142.

[1] The countess had two sisters: *Genealogist*, new ser., x (*c.* 1894), 162. Neither is traceable elsewhere as an artist.

[2] In Catullus, ii, iii.

[3] For the Declaration see above, p. 335 n.; a special *Form of Prayer, with Thanksgiving* was published for the occasion.

[4] The text is from the Prayer Book. The sermon was apparently strongly influenced by Sir Robert

more, See your *notes*:—*Curate* 21. *Psal:* 1. chiefly consisting
of the severall deliverances of his Majestie & that we should
continue to pray for his preservation: My little Grand-Child[1]
was very ill all yesterday, so as we feared his life, 'til this
day, that God was pleas'd to give us hopes: 15 Came to
visite & dine'd with us Sir W: *Godolphin* and my sweete charge,
little *Francis*:[2] also his Unkle *Henry* & Aunt Boscawen; came
also ⟨to⟩ visite me the learned Anatomist *Dr. Tyson* with
some other fellows of our Society:

16 Our *Viccar* on 5. *Psal:* 8: a former Text, what was meant
by the Wayes of God &c: See your notes: In the Afternoone
at *Lee*, the *Lecturer* on 34: *Psal:* 9,[3] shewing how signaly *God*
delivers the righteous out of all their troubles, & why many
times afflicts them in this life, viz. for their profit, fore-seeing
their neede of Chastizement or for trial, of their faith, or to
refine, & fit them for himselfe &c: See your *notes*: I passed
the Evening in a Visie of[a] my excellent neighbour Mr. *Bohun*[4]
at his elegant Villa, and *Gardens*; where upon sight of the
Zinnar Tree or *Platanus*, he told me that since their falling
to plant this[b] Tree about the Citty[b] of *Ispahan* in *Persia*, the
Plague (which formerly much infested that place) has exceedingly abated of its mortal effects, & rendered it very
healthy; & that they impute it to the salutarie shade of this
Tree.

18 I went to Lond: to visite & waite on the *Dutchesse* of
Grafton now greate with Child, a most vertuous & beautifull
Lady, & dining with her at my Lord Chamberlains met my
Lo: of *St. Albans*, now growne so blind, that he could not see

---

a Altered from *t-*.   b-b MS. *this Tree about the Tree about the Citty.*

Filmer's *Patriarcha*, which had been
published in 1680 (see below, p.
353); but the details are not derived
from the book.
   1 John: above, p. 272.
   2 Now five years old.
   3 A slip for verse 19.
   4 Christopher Boone: above, pp.
180, 288. His plane-tree was still
standing in 1886: Drake's Hasted,

p. 223. Evelyn repeats the present
statement, but as told him by 'a
worthy *Knight*', in *Sylva*, 1706, p.
133; it apparently originated with
Chardin: *Voyages*, iii. 294. For the
introduction of the plane-tree into
England see above, iii. 386. The
name zinnar is a variant of chenar:
O.E.D.

to the taking his meate:[1] It is incredible how easy a life this Gent: has lived, & in what plenty even abroad, whilst his Majestie was a sufferer; nor lesse, the immense summs he has lost at play, which yet at about 80 yeares old he continues, having one that sets by him to name the spot in the Chards:[2] He eate & dranke with extraordinary appetite.[a] He is with all this a prudent old Courtier, & much inrich'd since his Majesties returne.

After dinner I walked to survey the sad demolitions of *Clarendon* house that costly & onely sumptuous Palace of the late *L. Chancelor* Hydes, where I have often ben so cherefull with him, & so sad;[3] hapning to make him a visite but the day before he fled from the angry Parliament, accusing him of maladministration,[b] & envious at his grandure, who from a private lawyer, came to be fatherinlaw to the *Duke* of *York*; &, as some would suggest, designing his Majesties marriage with the Infanta of Portugal, not apt to breede:[4] To this they imputed much of our unhapinesse, & that being sole Minister & favorite at his Majesties Restauration he neglected to gratifie his Majesties suffering party, for the rewards he received of his richer, & disloyal subjects, who were the cause of our troubles:[5] But perhapps as many of these were injuriously laied to his charge; so he kept the Government far steadier than since it has proved: I could name some others who I thinke contributed greately to his ruine, The bouffones,

---

[a] Altered from *appetited*.   [b] Altered from *mall-*.

[1] St. Albans appears to have had a minor part in Charles's negotiations with France as late as 1681. He had 'at last renounced to the court' in March of this year: *Savile Corr.*, pp. 271–2. His affluence when in exile is also mentioned by Clarendon and by Anthony Hamilton.

[2] No other occurrence of this form is recorded.

[3] Clarendon occupied the house only from April to November 1667: above, iii. 481; Evelyn's final visit, iii. 502.

[4] In 1664 an attempt was made to prove that, before the king had married her, Clarendon was aware that Catherine would be sterile: Pepys, 22 Feb. 1664. The view that he had deliberately selected her for Charles's wife so that his own daughter should become queen, is without foundation; the marriage negotiations (which he had originally opposed) had begun before the duke of York's relations with Anne Hyde were known.

[5] See above, iii. 493.

and the *Misses* to whom he was an Eye sore: 'Tis true he was of a jolly temper, after the old English fashion; but *France* had now the ascendent, & we become quite another nation. The C⟨h⟩ancellor gon, & dying in *Exile*, the Earle his successor sold that which cost 50000 pounds building to the Young Duke of *Albemarle* for 25000, to pay his debts,[1] which how contracted remaines yet a Mysterie, his sonn being no way a prodigal;[2] some imagine the *Dutchesse* his daughter had ben chargeable to him; however it were, this stately *Palace* is decreede to ruine, to support the prodigious Wast the D: of *Albemarle* had made of his Estate, since the old man died;[3] so as selling it to the highest bidders, it fell to certaine inferior people,[a] rich bankers & Mechanics, who gave for it & the ground about it 35000 pounds; who designing a new Towne as it were, & the most magnificent *Piazza* in Europ, 'tis said have already materials toward it, with what they sould of the house alone, more worth than what they paied for it: See the Viccissitude of earthly things: I was plainely astonish'd as at this demolition, so noe lesse, at the little armie of Labourers, & Artificers in levelling ground, laying foundations, & contriving greate buildings at an expense of 200000 pounds, if they perfect their designe:[4]

19 I din'd at *Mrs. Boscawens*, visited Sir St: *Fox*: 20 did some buisinesse among the *Lawyers*, having a troublesome suite of an Accompt, with Mr. *Pretiman* my Wifes *Unkle*, pretending bills of Exchange not paied, during her Fathers Residence in *France*: This Controversie having now lasted for

---

[a] Followed by *though* deleted.

---

[1] Burnet also gives the cost as £50,000: i. 445; Clarendon had reckoned £20,000: Lister, iii. 452; this was the reason for the sale, which took place in August 1675, for the sum here stated: *Hist. MSS. Comm., 7th rep.*, App., p. 465.

[2] Henry Hyde, the second earl, mismanaged his own affairs in later life and was forced to sell Cornbury to his brother: *D.N.B.*

[3] The first duke of Albemarle.

[4] In February 1682 Albemarle is said to have sold the house for demolition: Luttrell, i. 167; the work began in May of this year: *Hist. MSS. Comm., 7th rep.*, App., pp. 481, 498. The principal purchaser was Sir Thomas Bond (above, pp. 93, 258). For the new streets on the site see above, iii. 380 n.; below, 29 Oct. 1690.

many Yeares, coming now to be defended by me, upon My Fa: in Laws decease, as executor in right of my Wife (whose land was engag'd, & Writings ⟨kept⟩[a] from us, on an imaginary debt) to put it to a final Issue, I was now to commence all a new; & for that end, did this day (among other Council) retaine Mr. *North*,[1] brother to my L: *Keeper*, & so referr the issue to the good providence of God, & return'd home to my house: Note, that by the way, I stepped in to a *Gold-beaters* work-house, who shewed me the wonderfull ductilitie of that spreading & oylie *Metall*: he said it must be finer than the standard; such[b] as was old *Angel* gold:[2] & that of such he had once to the value of 100 pounds, stamp'd with the Agnus Dei, & coyn'd at the time of the *holy-War*, which had ben found in a ruin'd Wall some where in the north, neere to *Scotland*: some of which he beate into leaves, & the rest sold to the *Curiosi* of Antiquities & *Medails*.

23 Our *Viccar* pursu'd his former subject, see your *notes*: & so the *Curate* 33: *Ezek:* 11. We had now the wellcome tidings of the *K: of Polands* &c raising the siege before *Vienna*,[3] which gave terror to all Europe, & uttmost reproch to the *French*, who 'tis believed brought him in, for diversion, that he might the more easilie swallow Flanders, & pursue his unjust conquests on the Empire &c, whilst we sate unconcerned, & under a deadly charme from somebody:[4] There was this day a Collection for the rebuilding of *New-Market* Consum'd by an accidental fire, which removing his *Majestie* thence sooner than was intended, put by the Assassinates,

---

a MS. *keept*. b Altered from *ye*.

---

[1] Roger North, 1653–1734, author of the *Lives* of the Norths, &c.: *D.N.B.*

[2] Angel-gold, the gold used for angels, which were coined between 1465 and 1634, as well as for some other coins, was of the standard 23 cts. 3½ grs. fine gold to ½ gr. alloy; the standard of crown-gold, in use since 1660, is 22 cts. fine gold to 2 grs. alloy. No gold was coined in England from before 900 until 1343, except for a tentative issue *c.* 1257. No English gold coin bears the Agnus Dei: R. L. Kenyon, *Gold coins of England*, 1884.

[3] John III (Sobieski), king of Poland, relieved Vienna on 2/12 September after a siege of two months: *London Gazette*, 20, 23 Sept., probably Evelyn's source.

[4] Cf. above, p. 331.

who were dissapointed of their *Rendezvous* & expectation, by a wonderfull providence:[1] This made the *King* more earnest to render *Wi⟨n⟩chester* the seate of his *Autum⟨n⟩al* field diversions for the future, designing a Palace there, where the antient Castle stood, infinitely indeede preferrable to *New-Market*, for Prospect, aire, pleasure, & provisions; The Surveior having already begun the foundations for a palace of 35000 pounds & his *Majestie* purchasing ground about it, to make a Parke &c:[2]

My right arme of late yeares bccoming very cold & weakened, it passed now into my left, with paine, & such weakenesse, that I had little force left in it, yet without the least appearance of any thing outwardly:

30 Our *Viccar* prosecutes his former subject, concerning the Ways of God; see your *notes*: our *Curate* on 13: *John* 34. That *Love*, the new Commandment of our B: *Saviour* and *Legislator*, was the oldest of all the rest; not only of those of *Moses*, written on *Tables* of stone, but the Table of our hearts before the *Decalogue* was in being, and therefore how indispensable a duty:

Octob: 4: I went to *Lond:* on buisinesse, having receiv'd a note from the Countesse of *Arlington*, of some Considerable Charge, or advantage I might obtaine, by applying my selfe to his Majestie on this signal Conjuncture, of his Majesties

---

[1] The fire took place on 22 March. Although the king's house was not damaged the town became too uncomfortable to stay in and he returned to Whitehall on 26 March: Hore, *Hist. of Newmarket*, iii. 64–71; for the collection for the sufferers, ibid., pp. 73–4. A brief was issued for the collection: Bewes, *Church briefs*, p. 289.

[2] Shortly before Christmas 1682 Charles ordered a preliminary examination to be made of the site of Winchester Castle, existing tenancies, &c.; the foundation-stone of his palace, which was designed by Wren, was laid on 23 March of this year. The estimate for the building 'to cover it in' was £30,144; by January 1685 the 'whole charge' amounted to £37,664. The park was to be to the south of the city. The structure was nearly complete when Charles died; it was thenceforward neglected and was burnt down in 1894. For it see Wren Soc., vii. 11–69. The plan closely resembled that of the central part of Versailles as existing at the time.

For the establishment of a race-meeting at Winchester, to be held annually on 31 August, 'the day sevennight after *Datchet-ferry*-Plate', see *London Gazette*, 31 July 1682.

entering Judgement against the *Citty Charter*:[1] The ⟨proposal⟩[a] made me, I wholy declin'd, not so well satisfied with these[b] violent transactions, & not a little sorry, his *Majestie* was so often put upon things of this nature, against so greate a *Citty*, the Consequences wheroff might be so much to his prejudice: so I return'd home againe: It was at this time the L: C. Justice *Pemberton*[2] was displac'd, held the very learnedst of the Judges, & an honest man: Sir *Geo: Geoffries*[3] advanc'd, reputed the most ignorant, though the most daring: Sir *Geo: Treby*,[4] Recorder of Lond: also put by, & one *Genner*,[5] an obscure lawyer set in his place: Eight of the richest & prime Aldermen remov'd, & all the rest made onely *Justices* of the Peace, & wearing[c] no more Gownes or Chaines of Gold: The *Lord Mayor* holding now his place & two Sherifes by new Grants, as *Custodes*, at the Kings pleasure;[6] the pompe &

---

[a] MS. *propasal*. [b] Followed by *hi-* deleted. [c] Altered from *mee-*.

---

[1] Judgement was entered against the City on 3 October: *Hist. MSS. Comm., 7th rep.*, App., p. 366; the king was informed of it on 4 October: *London Gazette*, 8 Oct.

[2] Francis Pemberton, 1624–97; knighted 1675; judge: *D.N.B.* He had been transferred to the chief justiceship of the common pleas on 22 January of this year and was superseded *c.* 29 September. Notice of his being superseded in *London Gazette*, 1 Oct.

[3] George Jeffreys, 1645–89; knighted 1677; recorder of London 1678–80; chief justice of Chester 1680–4; created a baronet 1681; appointed chief justice of the king's bench 29 September of this year (continuing until 1685); privy councillor 4 October of this year; created Baron Jeffreys of Wem 1685; lord chancellor 1685–8: *D.N.B.*; H. M. Hyde, *Judge Jeffreys*, 1940. His present promotions are mentioned in *London Gazette*, 1 Oct., 8 Oct.

Daring is about equivalent to audacious in the worst sense. So

Charles Hatton writes (in 1679) that Jeffreys 'hath, in great perfection, ye three cheif qualifications of a lawyer: Boldness, Boldness, Boldness': *Hatton corr.*, i. 199. Evelyn's testimony is valuable as dating (it cannot be later than 1685) from so long before Jeffreys's fall. See also below, p. 484.

[4] Above, p. 227. He was deprived of the recordership on 3 or 4 October (he is the recorder speaking on 2 October: Luttrell, i. 282); he was restored in 1688 and held the office until 1692.

[5] Thomas Jenner, *c.* 1638–1707; knighted and appointed recorder 4 October of this year; baron of the exchequer 1686; judge of the common pleas 1688; removed at the Revolution: *D.N.B.*, where his own acknowledgement of his insignificance is printed.

[6] The charter having been forfeited, the king on 13 October issued a commission reappointing the former lord mayor (Sir W. Prichard) and seventeen of the former aldermen; the eight who were not reappointed

grandure of the^a most august Cittie in the World chang'd face in a moment, & gave much occasion of discourse, & thoughts of heart, what all this would end in, & prudent men were for the old foundations.

Following his Majestie this morning through the Gallerie, ⟨I⟩^b went^c (with the few who attended him) into the Dutchesse of Portsmouths dressing roome, within her bed-chamber, where she was in her morning loose garment, her maides Combing her, newly out of her bed: his Majestie & the Gallants standing about her: but that which ingag'd my^d curiositie, was the rich & splendid furniture of this woman's Appartment, now twice or thrice, puld downe, & rebuilt, to satisfie her prodigal & expensive pleasures, whilst her Majestie dos not exceede, some gentlemens Ladies furniture & accommodation:¹ Here I saw the new fabrique of *French Tapissry*, for designe, tendernesse of worke, & incomparable imitation of the best paintings; beyond any thing, I had ever beheld: some pieces had *Versailles*, St. *Germans* & other Palaces of the French King with Huntings, figures, & Landscips, Exotique fowle & all to the life rarely don:² Then for *Japon Cabinets*, *Skreenes*, *Pendule Clocks*, huge *Vasas* of wrought plate, *Tables*, *Stands*, *Chimny furniture*, *Sconces*, *branches*, *Braseras*³ &c they were all of massive silver, & without number, besides of his Majesties best paintings:

---

^a Followed by *gr*- deleted.   ^b MS. &.   ^c Followed by *in* deleted.   ^d Altered from *me*.

---

included five former lord mayors, among them Sir Robert Clayton; eight new aldermen were appointed in their place: Beaven, *Aldermen*, ii. 109–10.

¹ For the position of these apartments see above, p. 74. There were reports that the duchess was about to rebuild them in 1678 and in 1680: L.C.C., *Survey of London*, xiii. 85; Burnet in *Camden Miscellany*, vol. xi, 1907, p. 15. For the splendour of her silver plate at this time see G. Leti, *Il teatro brittanico*, 1684, i. 132.

² The Gobelins had been refounded as a royal manufacture in 1662. The tapestries with views here mentioned belong to the series the *Maisons Royales* or *Months*, twelve pieces besides *entre-fenêtres*. A set of six principal and two subsidiary pieces was sent to England in December 1682 by Louis XIV's order: M. Fénaille, *État général des tapisseries de la manufacture des Gobelins, 1660–1900*, 1903–12, [i.] 128–65.

³ Properly braseros, the Spanish word.

Surfeiting of this, I din'd yet at *Sir Steph: Foxes*, & [5][a] went
contentedly home to my poore, but quiet *Villa.* Lord what
contentment can there be in the riches & splendor of this
world, purchas'd with vice & dishonor:

7 Our *Viccar* still pursues his former Text; passing from
Gods comands, as his Way, (& of which he had treated before)
to that of his Example: &c: See your *notes*: The holy *Sacrament* followed, of[b] which I participated, the Lord make me
worthy: *Pomeridiano* our *Curate* on his former also 33: *Ezek:*
11.—*Why will ye die?* &c on which he tooke occasion to
answer most of the objections of those who ⟨assert⟩ *Gods* secret,
& peremptorie Decrees; contrary to the tenor of all Scriptures, & infinite divine goodnesse, who invites all sinners to
Repentance & grace; See your notes:

10 I went to *Lond:* with my Wife, to put in our[c] Answer
to the Suite in *Chancery*:[1] Visited, the[d] *Dutchesse* of *Grafton*,
not yet brought to bed, & Dining with my *Lord Chamberlain*
(her Father) went with them to see *Montague-house*,[2] a Palace
lately built, by that *Gent:* who had married the most beautifull Countesse of *Northumberland*:[3] It is within a stately &
ample Palace, *Signor Virios* fresca Paintings, especialy the
funeral Pile of Dido, on[e] the Stayre Case & Labours of
Hercules, fight with the *Centaures*, *Effeminacy* with *Dejanira*,
& *Apotheosis* or reception amongst the Gods, on the walls &
roofe of the Greate roome above, I think exceedes any thing
he has yet don, both for designe, Colouring, & exuberance of
Invention, comparable certainely to the greatest of the old
Masters, or what they so celebrate at Rome: There are in
the rest of the Chambers some excellent paintings of Holbein
& other Masters: The Garden is large, & in good aire, but
the fronts of the house not answerable to the inside: The

---

[a] Marginal date.   [b] Altered from *at*.   [c] Altered from *mi-*.
[d] Altered from *&*.   [e] Altered from *of*?

---

[1] See above, pp. 339–40.
[2] Above, p. 90.
[3] Elizabeth Wriothesley, *c.* 1646–
90, daughter of the earl of Southampton (above, iii. 175) by his
second wife and half-sister of Rachel
Lady Russell; married, 1662, the
eleventh earl of Northumberland
(above, iii. 481), by whom she was
mother of Lady Elizabeth Percy
(above, p. 260); married Montagu
(above, p. 90) 1673.

Court at Entrie, & Wings for Offices seeme to neere the streete, & that so very narrow, & meanely built, that the[a] *Corridore* [is][b] unproportionable to the rest, to hide the Court from being overlook'd by neighbours, all which might have ben prevented, had they plac'd the house farther into the ground, of which there was enough to spare:[1] But in summ, 'tis a fine Palace, built after the *French* pavilion way; by Mr. *Hook*, the *Curator* of our Society: There were with us my *Lady Scroope*,[2] the greate Witt: & *Monsieur Jardine*[3] the greate Traveller; & so we came late to Says Court:

13 Came to Visite me, my old & worthy friend Mr. Packer, bringing with him his Nephew *Berkeley*,[4] Grandsonn to the honnest Judge; a most ingenious virtuous & religious Gent: seated neere *Worster*, & very Curious in Gardning &c:

14 Our *Viccar* preached on 1. *Cor: 15*: ult: That the paines *St. Paule* takes to cleare the certainty of both Christs, &[c] of Man-kinds Resurrection, was to establish a foundation, without which the superstructure of all Religion would fall to nothing, since it was the onely bridle which kept the wicked in awe, & gave assurance to the Righteous, of a glorious Reward: See your *notes*:

I accompanied my friends after dinner to *Greenewich*, where we heard the fragment of a sermon preached by a stranger, encouraging[d] an holy life:

15 Mr. *Packer* & his *Nephew*, return'd to *London*:

---

[a] Altered from *there*; followed by *is a* deleted.   [b] Interlined.
[c] Followed by *his s-* deleted.   [d] Altered from *encourading*.

---

[1] The outer wall of the court was on the line of the street; and the court was shallow as compared with that of Southampton House.

[2] Above, iii. 275.

[3] Chardin: above, p. 212.

[4] Robert Berkeley, 1650–95, of Spetchley, near Worcester; grandson of Sir Robert Berkeley, 1584–1656, judge of the king's bench 1632–41, a supporter of the royal prerogative (*D.N.B.*); nephew of Mrs. Packer (above, ii. 548); married *c.* 1679 Elizabeth, 1661–1709, daughter of Sir Richard Blake (she afterwards became third wife of Bishop Burnet; for her see *D.N.B.*): Nash, *Worcestershire*, ii. 358–62; T. Goodwyn, Life of Mrs. Burnet, prefixed to her *Method of Devotion*, 2nd ed., 1709. Eight letters from Berkeley to Evelyn, 1684–93, are printed in Bohn.

17 I was at the Court Leete of this *Mannor*: my L: Arlington his Majesties high steward:[1]

21 Our *Viccar* on his former, concerning perseverance: Tooke occasion to perstring⟨e⟩ our late sectaries and dissenters for going from one party to another, pretending to more purity, & finding fault that the Ch: of England admitted scandalous, & wicked men to her communion: That this was the same that was objected by the *Donatists*, which St. *Aug:* has long since fully answered [refuted]:[a][2] and that our Church dos not admit any such, whom she certainely knows to be such, but judges such as presume to come to the holy Table, to have repented: And that it is after severall admonitions, accurate examination and proofe, that the Church proceedes to excommunication, it being so weighty & solemn a Censure, as representing no lesse than the final Judgement of the last day: He prov'd that we are not to breake the Communion of the Christian Church[b] by separating, for every fault, no, not for many greate faults, by the example of the *Corinthians*, in which St. Paule reckons up severall: as going to Law before Infidels: excesse, nay, drunknesse even at the Lords Supper; baptizing for the dead; nay & for denying the Resurrection, even an Article of Faith, & yet for none of these dos the Apostle *Excommunicate*, or pronounce the dreadfull sentence, but[c] pitches on the Incestious person onely, to make him an example, & that with extraordinary reluctancey, and ready reconciliation, & all to shew the unreasonablenesse of our modern *Donatistical* separation &c: *Pomeridiano*, the *Curate* as before on 33: Ezek: 11. Gods mercifull offer of life to returning sinners: Sleepe exceedingly surpriz'd me.

---

[a] Interlined.   [b] Followed by *for e-* deleted.   [c] Followed by *for* deleted.

---

[1] The crown still owns the manor of Sayes Court: above, ii. 538 n.; iii. 59 n.

[2] This apparently refers to the *De Baptismo contra Donatistas*, bk. iv, c. xiii. There is a short account of this accusation and its refutation in T. Long, *The history of the Donatists*, 1677, pp. 97–9. Long regards the English dissenters as the 'proper Successors' of the Donatists: dedication. Evelyn regards '*Anabaptists* (and modern *Donatists*)' as forming a single, but varied, group of heretics: *Hist. of Religion*, ii. 264.

26 Came to visite, & dined with me Mr. *Brisbane* Secretary to the Admiralty, a learned, & knowing person:

28 Our Viccar on his former subject, with little addition, concerning the unreasonablenesse of Dissenting from the church communion: &c: *Pomeridiano* the Curate of *Greenewich* 1 *Sam:* 12: 24: Sleepe surprizing me, I was not so attentive as I ought to have ben, The Lord *Jesus* pitty me:

30 I went to *Cew*[1] to visite Sir *Henry Capell* bro: to the late Earle of Essex, but he being gon to *Cassioberry*, after I had seene his Garden, & the Alterations therein, I returned home. He had repaired his house, roofed his Hall with a kind of Cupola, & in a niche an artificiall fountaine; but the roome seemes to me over-melancholy; yet might be much improved by having the walls well painted a *fresca* &c: The two Greenehouses for Oranges & Myrtils[a] communicating with the roomes below are very well contriv'd: There is a Cupola made with pole work betweene two Elmes at the end of a Walk, which being covered by plashing the trees to them, is very pretty: for the rest, there ⟨are⟩[b] too many fir-trees in the Garden.

31 Being determin'd to passe this winter in London with my family, by reason of many important affaires; I invited divers of our Neighbours to dinner: ⟨it⟩[c] was likewise my Birth-day & the 63d or *greate Climacterical*, to w⟨h⟩ich through Gods infinite goodnesse I was now arived, & for which his holy name be praised.

November 1 Was a meeting of the fœfees for the poore, & according to Costome a sermon by our *Viccar*: on 2. I invited divers Neighbours, being purposed to spend the rest of the winter in London:

4: Our *Viccar* on his former Text, with little addition: The holy Sacrament followed, of[d] which I was participant, the Lord make me thankfull: *Pomeridiano*, our Curate as before: Sleepe also surprizing.

---

a Followed by *at th-* deleted.   b MS. *as.*   c MS. *I.*   d Altered from *at.*

---

[1] Kew. For it and Capel's garden see above, p. 144.

5 Our *Viccar* on 48 *Psal:* ult: (being the powder conspiracy) shewing how God alone gives all[a] deliverances; & particularly how signaly he is our God, as to the many deliverances of this Church: He suppos'd the *Psalme* to have ben indited by *Hezekiah*, after the slaughter of *Senacharibs* host:[1] Praysing God that though the danger was so iminent & greate, there was not the least detriment to the Citty, not an house, nor a tower beaten downe: This applied to the hellish powder plot, which intended to have laied all the Citty in ruinous heapes &c ending with an exhortation to prayse God, & to keepe the day in better remembrance, than of late we had don, as if we were not concerned with[b] a thing so long since, & before we were borne, which was greate Ingratitude: That the Israelites were from one age to another put in mind of their fathers deliverances out of Egypt, & other Calamities, as if not onely their fathers, but they themselves so many hundred yeares after had themselves ben the persons: This was the summ:

11 our *Viccar* proceedes, shewing the necessitie of perseverance, that Religion did not consist in furious Zeale, such as was *Jehus*, who served his Interest whilst he semed to serve God, but grew cold againe, when that was finish'd: but such as is signified by the beasts in the Revelations, whose wings were full of Eyes; signifying a readinesse of doing their duty, with speede & alacrity, but with judgement, & knowledge too, which the number of Eyes denoted: no ignorant or blind zeale: Sometimes indeede a suddaine & impetuous transport has succeeded, as in the Thiefe on the Crosse, in St. Paule, & some others, but they are to be looked on as Miracles rather than Examples: That[c] is true and pious zeale, which consists not so much in rapts & ec⟨s⟩tasies, & extraordinary transports, as in a Constant, sedate & permanent practise of all holy duties, a readinesse to obey God, to be Charitable, frequent

---

[a] Reading doubtful.   [b] Followed by *the* deleted.   [c] Altered from *The*.

---

[1] The association of the Psalm with the destruction of Senna-cherib's host is still occasionally suggested.

in good works, ready to suffer for righteousnesse: to[a] these
their labour shall not be in[b] vaine, that is their labour shall
be mightly rewarded in the other life, where[c] there shall be
no more labour at all, but ease, & peace, & joy, & pleasures
everlasting in the presence of God, in the joy of their Lord,
in the blessed society of the Saints & Angels, in Contemplation of his Workes, the mysteries not revealed, then to be
made manifest, in a full & consummat happinesse beyond all
that the heart or mind of the most inlightned man on Earth
can expresse or conceive: This was the summ: Afternoone
at *Greenewich* the *Curate* on 51 *Psal: 7*. Upon *Davids* sinn,
describing the progresse which it makes from small beginnings, as first from his evening Sloth, to the casting of his
Eyes, then lusting, lastly to Adulterie, & then to cover that,
the making poore Uriah drunke, & then murdering him:
See at how small an enterance this traine of sinn followes:
Men say of these beginnings, as *Lot* of *Zoare*, Is it not a little
one! What harme the looking on a Woman? but from this
little spark, we find how greate a flame was kindled: Therefore exhorted, to watchfullnesse, & greate care of not admitting the least sinn, or appearance of Evil, how small soever
the Instance appeare; since none knows where it may end:
obsta principijs: The result was, that no sin is little if it
seeme little, & that nothing but the bloud of *Jesus* Christ can
clense it, ment here by the Hyssope, relating to the use of
that plant, in the legal purifications:—I visited Sir William
Hooker:[1] whose Lady related to us of a Child laied to sleepe,
& [that][d] whilst the Nurse was a little absent, a Monkey had
bitten out its Eyes, torne the face, & eaten the head into the
brain: Those mischievous animals should not be kept by
Ladies that have young children, this being the second

---

^a Substituted for *for*.   ^b Followed by *these* deleted.   ^c Or *when*.
^d Interlined.

---

¹ William Hooker, *c.* 1612–97;
alderman of London 1664–89;
sheriff 1665–6; knighted 1666; lord
mayor 1673–4. His lady is presumably his second wife, Susanna,
daughter of Sir Thomas Bendish,
bart. His house was on Croom's
Hill, Greenwich: Drake's Hasted,
pp. 81, 100; Beaven, *Aldermen*, ii.
96; see also Pepys, 3 Sept., 13 Dec.
1665, &c.

accident of that nature I have ben told of, one of which happned in this Parish, a vile Monkey had killd a Nurse child in the cradle almost after the same manner, whilst the nurse went but out to draw a bucket of water: & what was most deplorable, it was the onely child remaining of one who had lost severall.

17 I came with my whole Family (except my little Grandson, & his Nurse & some servants to looke after the house) to be in London the rest of this Winter, having many important concernes to dispatch which I could not so well attend at home [& for the education of my daughters]:ᵃ I tooke therefore the house of one Mr. Dive's,ᵇ in Villars streete inᶜ Yorke-buildings in the Strand.¹

18 Dr. *Tenison* Viccar of St. Martines (being the Parish-church:) preached on 23: Pro: 2.² shewing the fatal Consequences of following others, be they never so greate & numerous, in Evil: *See your notes. Pomeridiano*: a stranger on 9: Rom: 14 shewing the injurie we do the justice & goodnesse of God by that doctrine of absolute reprobation &c: see your notes:

23 I went home to Says Court, to see my little family, and return'd next day: The Duke of Monmoth 'til nowᵈ proclaim'd Traytor upon the pretended plot, for which my L: Russell lately was be headed: Came this evening to white-hall & rendered himselfe, [24]ᵉ upon which were various discourses:³

Mr. *Forbus* shew'd me the plot of the Garden making at Burleigh at my L: of *Exesters*,⁴ which I looked on as one of

---

ᵃ Interlined. ᵇ Reading doubtful. ᶜ Followed by *Bui-* deleted.
ᵈ Followed by *proscrib'd &* deleted. ᵉ Marginal date.

¹ Villiers Street had been built mainly in 1674–5 on part of the site of York House (above, iii. 162): L.C.C., *Survey of London*, xviii. 61. I have not been able to identify Mr. Dive or his house.
² The text appears to be wrong.
³ Monmouth surrendered on the night of 24 November: *London Gazette*, 26 Nov.; Luttrell adds that

'his comeing in has surprized most people; some think he has not been out of Whitehall all this while': i. 292. For the proclamation against him see above, p. 323; and for his conduct at this time, Foxcroft, *Halifax*, i. 401–12.
⁴ John Cecil, *c.* 1648–1700; fifth earl of Exeter 1678: G.E.C.

the most noble that ever I had seene: The whole Court &
Towne[a] in solemn mourning for the death of the K. of
Portugal, her Majesties Brother.[1]

25 Dr. *Tenison* at St. *Martins* on 77: *Psal:* 8. 9.[2] shewing
what were sinns of Infirmity, what not, the danger & cure of
both in a most excellent discourse: See your notes:

Pomerid: Dr. Meriton[3] Coloss: shewing every Christians
dutie to admonish & teach his brother, Ministers, Magistrates,
People; as also their obligation to rejoice in giving praise to
God, expressly in Psalmes & Spiritual Melody, in the heart,[b]
when he spake also of the lawfullnesse of church Musique for
assistance of devotion &c: See your notes:

26 I went to complement the *Dutchesse* of *Grafton* now laying in of her first[c] child, which was a sonn,[4] which she cald
for me to see with greate satisfaction: She was become more
beautifull (if it were possible) than before, & full of vertue &
sweetenesse, discoursed with me of many particulars with
greate prudence, & gravity beyond her yeares:

30 Being St. Andrews, & our Anniversary at the R:
Society: Sir *Cyrill Wich*[5] was elected President. We din'd
together according to Costome &c: The King sent us two
does.

December ⟨2⟩[d] Dr. Tenison, on 13 Hosea 8.[6] perditio tua ex

---

[a] Substituted for *nation.*   [b] Followed by *to* deleted.   [c] Followed
by *son* deleted.   [d] MS. *r.*

---

[1] Dom Affonso VI, born 1643,
succeeded 1656, deposed 1667
(above, p. 130 n.). Notices of his
death in *London Gazette*, 8, 11 Oct.
The court went into deep mourning
on 21 October; this was to last for
three months and to be followed by
a similar period in 'second mourning': *Hist. MSS. Comm., 7th rep.,*
App., p. 367.
[2] Presumably a slip for Psalms
lxxix. 8, 9.
[3] Dr. John Meriton: above, p. 180.
He had been lecturer at St. Martin's
since about 1660. His text is Colossians iii. 16.
[4] Charles   Fitzroy,   1683–1757;

styled earl of Euston until 1690
when he succeeded his father as
second duke: G.E.C. Notice of his
birth (25 October), &c., in *London
Gazette*, 1 Nov. The duchess was
about sixteen years old.
[5] Cyril Wyche, *c.* 1632–1707;
knighted 1660; member of the
Philosophical Society 28 Aug. 1661;
F.R.S. (Original Fellow); statesman,
&c.: *D.N.B.* He was president for
one year only. He was named after
his godfather, Cyril Lucar (above, ii.
18). In 1692 he married Evelyn's
niece Mary. Further notices below.
[6] A slip for verse 9.

te: That God predestin'd none to destruction, that he willed the salvation of all, & gave them meanes to attaine it. (See notes) The holy Sacrament followed, at which I participated: I went to Court this Evening, visited my L: Chamb: &c:

[4 I was invited to dinner by my Lady Sunderland, wher was a most elegant entertainement:][a]

5 I was this day invited to a Weding of one Mrs. Castle, to whom I had some obligation, & it was to her fift Husband, a Lieutennant Coll: of the Citty: The woman was the daughter of one Burton[1] a Broome-man & of a Mother who sold Kitchin stuff[2] in Kent Streete, Whom God so blessed, that the Father became a very rich & an honest man, was Sherif of Surrey, where I have sat on the bench with him: Another of his daughters was Married to one Sir Jo: Bowles;[3] & this Daughter a jolly friendly woman: There was at the Wedding the Lord Major,[4] the Sherif, severall Aldermen and persons of quality, & above all Sir Geo: Jeoffries[b] newly[b] made Lord Chiefe Justice of England,[5] with Mr. Justice Withings,[6] daunced with the Bride, and were exceeding Merrie: These[c] greate men spent the rest of the afternoone til 11 at night in drinking healths, taking Tobacco, and talking much beneath the gravity of Judges, that had but a day or two before Condemn'd Mr. Algernoon Sidny,[7] who was

---

a Interlined.   b-b Or *Jeoffrie, newly*.   c Altered from *The*.

---

[1] James Burton, sheriff of Surrey in 1673. A man of this name was trading in Rotherhithe in 1666–8 (or perhaps two men): Boyne, *Trade tokens*, ed. Williamson, p. 1148.

[2] Materials used in cooking, especially vegetables; or waste materials from the kitchen, as dripping, &c.: *O.E.D.* For Kent Street see above, iii. 417.

[3] The only traceable person of this name is John Bolles, 1641–86; succeeded as third baronet 1663; of Scampton, Lincs., and St. Swithin's, London: G.E.C., *Baronetage*, ii. 47–8. His second wife had died in 1676; no marriage with any-

one named Burton is traceable.

[4] Sir Henry Tulse: Beaven, *Aldermen*, ii. 107.

[5] Above, p. 342; he was appointed lord chief justice on 29 September.

[6] Francis Wythens, d. 1704; knighted 1680; judge of the king's bench 1683–7: *D.N.B.*

[7] Above, p. 322. He had been tried on 21 November before Jeffreys, when Wythens, Holloway (below, 15 June 1688), and Sir Thomas Walcot (*D.N.B.*), were also on the bench; his sentence had been delivered by Jeffreys on 26 November. His trial was published as *The Arraignment, Tryal & Condemna-*

executed on the 7th on Tower hill upon the single Wittnesse
of that monster of a man the L: *Howard* of Eskrick,[1] and
some sheetes of paper taken in Mr. Sidnys study, pretended
to be writen by him, but not fully proov'd, nor the time when,
but appearing to have ben written before his Majesties
restauration, & then pardon'd by the Act of Oblivion:[2] So
as though Mr. Sidny was known to be a person obstinately
averse to government by a Monarch (the subject of the paper,
in answer to one of Sir E: Filmer)[3] yet it was thought he had
very hard measure: There is this yet observable, that he had
ben an inveterate enemy to the last King, & in actual
rebellion against him: a man of greate Courage, greate sense,
greate parts, which he shew'd both at his trial & death; for
when he came on the scaffold, in stead of a speech, he told
them onely, that he had made his peace with God; that he
came not thither to talk but to die, put a paper into the
Sherifs hand, & another into a friends, sayed one prayer as
short as a grace, laied downe his neck, & bid the Executioner
do his office:[4] The Duke of Monmouth now having his pardon, refuses to accknowledge there was any Treasonable plot,
for which he is banish'd White-hall:[5] This was a great diss-

---

tion, &c., 1684; for comments on it
see *D.N.B.*

[1] See above, p. 322. Burnet
describes him as behaving like 'a
monster of ingratitude' towards
Sidney: *Own time*, ed. Airy, ii. 294.
For his value as a witness in this
trial see Sidney's remarks, *Arraignment*, pp. 30–1.

[2] It was satisfactorily proved at
the trial, although Sidney contested
the point, that the papers found in
his study were in his handwriting;
he claimed that from the appearance of the ink the writing might
be twenty years old; but acknowledged that the papers were an
answer to Filmer (see below),
obviously referring to his *Patriarcha*,
which was first published in 1680:
Arraignment, pp. 32–3. A reply by
Sidney to *Patriarcha* was published
in 1698 as *Discourses concerning*

Government; the passage from his
papers quoted in the trial (*Arraignment*, pp. 23–6) does not occur in
the work as printed, but is obviously
closely related to it; see also *The
Very Copy of a Paper Delivered to
the Sheriffs*, by Sidney, 1683.

[3] A mistake for Robert Filmer,
d. 1653; knighted 1619: *D.N.B.* His
principal work is *Patriarcha: or the
Natural Power of Kings*, 1680.

[4] For accounts of the execution
see *Cal. S.P., Dom., 1683–4*, p. 137;
Hist. MSS. Comm., 7th rep., App.,
p. 375; Luttrell, i. 293; short notice
in *London Gazette*, 10 Dec.

[5] Monmouth submitted to the
king on 25 November, and further
proceedings against him were
stopped. The notice in the *London
Gazette* (26 Nov.) suggested that he
had turned king's evidence. Monmouth's remarks about this notice

appointment to some, who had prosecuted the rest,[a] namely
Trenchard,[1] Hampden[2] &c: that for want of a second wittnesse were come out of the Tower upon their *Habeas Corpus*.
The King had now augmented his guards with a new sort of
dragoons,[3] who carried also granados & were habited after
the polish manner with long picked Caps very fierce &
fantastical; & was very exotic:

I went to The Tower[b] & ([b]after 4 years Imprisonment,)
gave a visite to the Earle of Danby, late Lord H. Tresurer,[4]
who received me with greate kindnesse, I dined with him, &
staied with him til night: we had discourse of many things,
his Lady[5] railing sufficiently at the keeping her husband so
long in prison: Here I saluted the L: ⟨Dunblaines⟩[c] Wife, who
before had ben married to *Emerton*, & about whom was that
Scandalous buisinesse before the Delegates:[6]

---

[a] Followed by *th-* deleted.   [b-b] MS. *Tower* (&, followed by *gave*
deleted.   [c] MS. *Dunblaings* or *Dunblainys*.

---

led the king to demand a written
acknowledgement of his confession.
This he gave about 4 December, but
on learning Hampden's views about
it recanted and at length recovered
the acknowledgement; on the same
day, 7 December, he was forbidden
to appear at court. It was also the
day of Sidney's execution: Foxcroft, *Halifax*, i. 405–12.

[1] Above, p. 322. He was released
on bail on 28 November: *London
Gazette*, 29 Nov.; *The Proceedings
upon the Bayling the L. Brondon
Gerrard*, &c., 1683. He was never
brought to trial.

[2] Above, p. 322. He was released
on bail with Trenchard on 28
November but had previously been
compelled to plead to an indictment
of misdemeanour. He was tried on
6 Feb. 1684.

[3] The King's Own Royal Regiment
of Dragoons, now the First Royal
Dragoons, was being formed at this
time, partly from troops returned
from Tangier. Commissions are

dated 19, 21–4 November; the first
colonel was John Churchill, the
future duke of Marlborough (below,
12 Oct. 1690). For them see Walton, *British standing army*, p. 12,
&c.; for their arms, pp. 422–4; their
caps, p. 367. List of officers in
Dalton, *English army lists*, i. 301,
314.

[4] He had been in the Tower since
16 April 1679.

[5] Bridget, 1629–1704; daughter
of Montagu Bertie, second earl of
Lindsey; married Danby (Osborne)
1653.

[6] This refers to Bridget, *c.* 1662–
1734, daughter of Sir Thomas Hyde
of Aldbury, Herts., and stepdaughter of Sir Robert Viner
(above, p. 170). In 1674 she was
apparently abducted and married
to her cousin John Emerton; she
was rescued by her friends, Danby
also intervening. Emerton took
legal proceedings to regain possession of her, and possibly attempted
a new abduction. The case was

9 Preached a stranger at St. Martines on 1 Joh: 2. 15. shewing what was ment by our love of this world: & the things thereoff, not that all which God made, & pronounced good, were not objects of love by way of praise & admiration of the Creator; but that we should not love them with affection for any intrinsique virtue, & so as to take off our ⟨love⟩[a] from God, and shewing the meanesse & transitorinesse of all its enjoyments &c: Pomerid: a Young man, on 11: Luke 28. The unprofitablenesse & even danger of hearing sermons, & enjoying the meanes, without keeping, that is practising what we heare.

12 At our Society Dr. *Slaer* (an excellent chymist) having read a learned discourse concerning the production of the stone in the Kidnies, produced two very cleare liquors which being mingled together & shaken, turn'd into a curdled stone, so as none of the liquor (now all turnd to a white stone) would come out of the glasse, to shew the nature of some liquids, & that possibly there might be some such mixtures in the body, that produced the stone, the Experiment was universaly approv'd, & he was desired to ⟨improve⟩[b] the experiment: These two liquors were a sort of Spir: of Urine, & Spirit of Wine.[1] Here was the famous Naturalist Dr. Lister,[2] & some discourses concerning subterraneous shells &c:

---

a MS. *louue* (i.e. *lovve*).   b MS. *improves.*

---

brought before the Court of Delegates (above, p. 267) in 1680 and again in 1682. On 12 July 1682, while the case was still *sub judice*, she came before the court with Danby's second son, Viscount Osborne of Dunblane, and declared that they were married. Emerton withdrew his claims, perhaps being bought off, in April of this year. Osborne is Peregrine Osborne, 1659–1729; styled earl of Danby 1689–94; marquis of Carmarthen 1694–1712; summoned to the house of lords as Baron Osborne of Kiveton 1690;

succeeded as second duke of Leeds 1712; admiral: *D.N.B.*; *G.E.C.*; Marvell, *Poems*, &c., ed. Margoliouth, ii. 146–7, 316–17; *Hist. MSS. Comm., Finch MSS.*, ii. 91–3; Luttrell, i. 205, 233–4, 255.

[1] An abstract of Slare's paper is printed in *Philosophical Transactions*, xiv (1684), 523–31 (no. 157).

[2] Martin Lister, *c.* 1639–1712; not created M.D. until 5 March 1684, but practising medicine at York from 1670; F.R.S. 1671: *D.N.B.*

16 A Chaplaine, of my L: *Manchester*,[1] St. *Martine* on 1. Luke. 76—shewing that St. Jo: Bap: was both a *Prophet* & an *Apostle* in some sense: How Gods method was, and still is, to make gradual & natural changes, by intermediat & gentle meanes, and not all in an instant, & at once [not][a] passing from[b] one extreame to another, but as they speake of other Natures in the World, how by a certaine chaine of Causes, one species borders upon another, & unites to it, the Superior to the Inferior by parts participating of both Natures: Thus Jo: Baptist was a prophet of the old Testament, & an Apostle of the New, sent to prepare the way of the Lord, & be the precursor of his first Advent, to prepare for mens conversion, the reception of that greate prince the L. *Jesus*: Here he insisted long upon the necessity of Preparation before all our holy Addresses to God, by faith, repentance, humility & other virtues to make us acceptable: This he meant, where he speaks, of leveling the mountaines[c] & filling-up the vallies, such was the Tumor & pride of the *Pharesee* &c all which must be subdued & made even, and for this Message John sent to the obstinate Jewes: He tooke notice of our B: Saviours giving those two so different testimonies of the same man: That St. *John Bap:* was the greatest prophet of[d] the[d] whole[e] race of mankind, & yet He[f] that[f] was [the][g] least in the Kingdome[h] of heaven, was greater than hee: the meaning is, that as God Constituted him a Prophet, & dignified him with that signal office of being his Harbinger &c: he was greate indeede in the Jewish church; but that the Christian Faith did so exceede all the legal rites, that the least sincere christian, was of infinite higher account, than the most illustrious of the Prophets, so far did the Gospell exceede the law. Pomerid: Dr. Meriton on 55 *Isa:* 2 on the

---

a Interlined.　　　　b Substituted for *by*.　　　　c Or *mountaine*.
d-d Substituted for *the*, which is preceded by *in* left standing.　　e Followed by *kingdom of heaven* deleted.　　f-f Originally *he that*; altered to *that he*; again altered to *He that*.　　g Interlined.　　h MS. *Kdome*.

---

1 Charles Montague, *c.* 1662–1722; fourth earl of Manchester 14 March of this year; created duke of Manchester 1719: *D.N.B.* The chaplain is not identifiable.

exuberant & overflowing mercy of God, offer'd so freely to those that did come to him for refreshment &c:

20 I went to Deptford, return'd the 22d in very cold & severe weather: My poore Servant *Humphry Prideaux*[1] being falln sick of the small-pox some days before:

23 At White-hall *Coram Rege,* a Chaplaine of my L: *Manchesters* preached a most excellent sermon on 21 *Luke* 27. of Christs 2d Advent to Judgement; shewing the reason & certainty of it, for as much as innumerable transgressions Escaped justice among Men, which the righteous God, would not suffer to passe unpunish'd, as well as rewards to the godly, which not distributed here, should be herafter &c: See your Notes: *Pomerid* Dr. *Meriton,* as before, shewing the labour & slavery of sinn: &c: This night died my poore excellent servant of the small pox, that by no remedies could be brought out, to the wonder of the Physitians:[2] It was exceedingly mortal at this time; & the season was unsufferably cold. The Thames frozen, &c:[3]

25 *Christmas day* I received the Bl: Sacrament at St. James's chapel, with the Princesse[a] of *Denmark,*[4] The Dutchesses of Monmouth, & Grafton & severall others of quality: the Bishop of *Rochester* (Dr. Turner)[5] preaching on 9 *Isa:* 6. 7. Historicaly shewing how Christ was typified in

---

[a] Altered from *Du-*.

---

[1] He is described in the parish register as butler at Sayes Court: Drake's Hasted, p. 42.

[2] He was buried on 26 December. For the prevalence of small-pox at this time see also Wood, *Life and times,* iii. 83.

[3] This was an extremely severe winter in England, Holland, and Switzerland; the Thames above London Bridge was frozen over for about six weeks. Luttrell describes the frost as beginning about 15 December. For it see also Lady Newdigate-Newdegate, *Cavalier and Puritan,* 1901, pp. 233–40; W. Andrews, *Famous frosts and frost*

fairs, 1887, pp. 17–40; &c. Further notices below.

[4] Princess Anne.

[5] Francis Turner. He had been consecrated on 11 November of this year and was translated to Ely on 23 Aug. 1684. The allusion is to Virgil's fourth Eclogue; it is professedly based on a Sibylline oracle not now available; the interpretation that it refers to the birth of the Messiah goes back to St. Augustine or earlier: see J. Conington, commentary on Virgil. Princess Anne was generally known to be with child.

the old Testament, prophisied of even by heathens, as the *Sibylla Cumana,* by Virgil out of her, & that it could not be meant a complement to *Pollio* : that was but a simple Roman Gentleman onely: How our Saviour came just when the scepter was departed from Judah, as to lineal descent, & then explain'd the severall attributes given to him in the Text, & how he became truely the Prince of Peace &c:[a] I went[b] to visite the L: Chamberlaine this evening, where I met with a *Milaneze* Count, of a very pleasant humor.

26 I dined at my Lord *Clarendons* where I was to meete that most ingenious and learned Gent: Sir Geo: Wheeler,[1] who has publish'd that excellent description of Attica & Greece, and who being a knight of a very faire estate & young had now newly entred into holy Orders: I also now kissed the Princesse[c] of Denmarks hand, who was now with Child.[2]

27 I went to visite Sir *J. Chardin*[d] that *French* gent, who had 3 times travelled into *Persia* by Land, and had made many curious researches in his Travells, of which he was now setting forth a relation.[3] It being in England this yeare one of the most severe frosts that had happn'd of many yeares, he told me, the Cold in *Persia* was much greater, the yce of an incredible thicknesse: That they had little use of *Iron* in all that Country, it being so moist (though the aire admirably cleare & healthy) that oyle would not preserve it from rusting immediately,[4] so as they had neither clocks nor Watches, some padlocks they had for doors & boxes &c:

---

[a] Followed by *I received the holy Sacrament* interlined and expunged (i.e. the ink rendered faint by immediate blotting). [b] Followed by *then* deleted. [c] Altered from *Princesses.* [d] Altered from *J-.*

---

[1] George Wheler, 1651 ?–1723; knighted 1682; canon of Durham 1684; vicar of Basingstoke 1685–1702; D.D. 1702; &c.: *D.N.B.* In 1675 and 1676 he travelled in the Levant with Jacob Spon and published an account of his travels as *A Journey into Greece,* 1682. Further notices below; see also *Numismata,* pp. 241, 244.

[2] The child was born dead on 12 May: F. Sandford, *A genealogical history of the kings . . . of England,* ed. S. Stebbing, 1707, p. 859.

[3] See below, p. 369 n.

[4] This remark applies only to the province of Gilan, on the Caspian littoral: *Voyages,* ed. Langlès, iii. 279.

30 Dr. *Sprat*, now made Deane of *Westminster*[1] preached
to the King at White-hall on 6: *Matt:* 24 shewing the in-
competency of the service of God & Mammon &c:[a] vide
Notes: Afternoone a Chaplaine of the Bish: of *Elys*,[2] on
36 *Job*: 24: That good men are the most prosperous, & live
in the truest pleasure, which he made out very eloquently,
arguing from the End of their sufferings as either to trie their
graces, or reforme their lives, in order to a greate reward.

31 Recollecting the passages of the past yeare, I gave God
thanks for his Mercys, beging his blessing for the future &c:

1683/4 January 1 Beseeching the Continuance of Gods mercy
& protection the yeare now entred, after publique Prayer at
St. Martines, preached a young divine on 2. *Luke* 21. shewing
the Antiquity, use, & benefit of Circumcision, particularly
our Saviours, after which the Communion, at which I also
participated; The Lord make me thankfull:

My Daughter *Susan*[3] had some few small pox come forth
on her, so as I sent her out of the Family; The Weather continuing intollerably severe, so as streetes of Boothes were set
up upon the Thames &c: and the aire so very cold & thick,
as of many yeares there had not ben the like:[4] The small pox
being very mortal, many feared a worse Contagion to
follow &c:

2 I dined at Sir *St: Foxes*, after dinner came a fellow that
eate live charcoale glowingly ignited, quenching them in his
mouth, & then champing & swallowing them downe:[5] There
was a dog also that seemd to do many rational actions.

⟨6⟩[b] A stranger at St. Martines on 2 *Philip:* 7. 8. Upon the
wonderfull exinan⟨i⟩tion of our *B. Saviour*: The holy
Commun: follow'd at which I received. *Pomerid*: Dr. *Meriton* on 3 Colossians 18.[c] The duty of[d] Wives to their *husbands*:

---

[a] Followed by *Pom* deleted.   [b] MS. *5*.   [c] Substituted for *2*.
Phil: 7. 8.   [d] Followed by *greate* deleted.

[1] Sprat had been appointed dean
of Westminster on 14 September of
this year: *Cal. S.P., Dom., 1683* (ii).
396.
[2] Gunning. The chaplain is not
identifiable.

[3] She was now fourteen years old.
[4] Luttrell mentions the booths
on 7 January. For the fair see the
notice below, p. 362.
[5] Cf. Richardson, above, iii. 626.

6 I went home to Says-Court to see my Grandson, it being extreame hard weather, and return'd the next-day by Coach the river being quite frozen up:

8 Came Sir *Geo: Wheler* and Mr. *Ottwood* to visite me. 9 I went crosse the *Thames* upon the Ice (which was now become so incredibly thick, as to beare not onely whole streetes of boothes in which the⟨y⟩ roasted meate, & had divers shops of wares,ᵃ quite crosse as in a Towne, but Coaches & carts & horses passed over):ᵇ So I went from *Westminster* st ayers¹ to *Lambeth* and dined with my L. *Archbishop*, where I met my *Lord Bruce*,² Sir *Geo: Wheeler*, Coll: *Coock*³ and severall Divines; after dinner, and discourse with his Grace 'til Evening prayer, *Sir Geo:* and I returnd, walking over the Ice from *Lambeth* stayres to the Horse Ferry,⁴ and thence walked on foote to our Lodgings: 10: I visited Sir *Rob: Reading*,⁵ where after supper we had musique, but none comparable to that which Mrs. Bridgeman made us upon the Gittar, which she master'd with such extraordinary skill, and dexterity, as I hardly ever heard any lute exceede for sweetenesse.

13 Dr. *Pellin*⁶ *coram Rege* at Whitehall:ᶜ on 1. *Pet:* 5. 7:

ᵃ Followed by *on l-* deleted.   ᵇ Closing bracket supplied.   ᶜ MS. *Whall:*

---

¹ Leading out of New Palace Yard to the river.

² Thomas Bruce, 1656–1741; styled Lord Bruce from 1664; second earl of Ailesbury 1685; the author of the *Memoirs*: *D.N.B.*; G.E.C.

³ Edward Cooke, *c.* 1620–84, of Highnam, Glos.; 'sometime Colonel of a Regiment under *Oliver Cromwell*'; although serving in the parliamentary army he had participated in a scheme for the escape of Charles I from Newport, I.O.W., on 29 Nov. 1648; a commissioner for executing the Irish Act of Settlement 1662; friend and correspondent of Ormond; he died in London on 29 January: Fenwick and Metcalfe, *Visitation of Gloucester, 1682–3,* p.

47 ; C. H. Firth, *The regimental history of Cromwell's army,* 1940, pp. 578–9; Firebrace, *Honest Harry,* pp. 157–72; E. Thorne, *Funeral sermon,* 1684 (not seen); &c.

⁴ The Horse Ferry crossed the river nearly on the site of the present Lambeth Bridge; the Lambeth landing appears to have been slightly upstream, a pier called Lambeth Bridge (I have not found the name Lambeth Stairs elsewhere) occupying the site of the Lambeth end of the present bridge: see especially J. Moxon, *Map of the River Thames. Merrily cal'd Blanket Fair,* 1684.

⁵ Above, p. 140.

⁶ Presumably Pelling: above, p. 192; but he was not yet a doctor.

Against solicitude & over anxiety or despondency of the Gods assistance in all dangers & extremities, with the special care he had of *Princes* and his Church; in which he much insisted on the late Conspiracys; There was much of the Court in this sermon, calculated for the present conjuncture: &c: *Pomeridiano* Dr. *Meriton* on 3. *Coloss:* 19 concerning the duty of Husbands, a plaine honest discourse & usefull.

After sermon, came to Visite us, the *Dutchesse* of *Grafton*, & a daughter[1] of my late Earle of Ossory, my antient & deare friend:

14 I dined with my Lord Chamberlaine. 15 We had Mr. Hooks new balances produc'd and much approved of.[2] 16 Was my first tryal befor my L: Keeper at the Chancery for a rehearing of my Cause: I went thence to the Bishops of Lond, with whom I dined: endeavouring to procure some of his Majesties Charity for the poore of our Parish,[3] the severe weather still continuing, & now the *Thames* was filled with people & Tents selling all sorts of Wares as in the Citty it selfe: 16 I tooke a little Physick: 20 At white-hall *coram Rege*, preached a Chaplaine of the L:Keepers on 10 *Matt:* 16: concerning the nature of true & religious Wisedome, & how far human learning might be & was assistant to the knowledge of God; That when the extraordinary gift of Tongues &c Ceased: God made use of the most learned among the Gentiles, to Convert the Gentiles, and do service in his Church, such as St. *Justine, Cyprian, Augustine,* &c: *Pomeridiano* at *St. Martines* Dr. *Meriton* on 3. *Coloss:* 20, concerning the duty of children to parents, Catechisticaly &c:

24 The frost still continuing more & more severe, the Thames before London was planted with bothes in formal

---

[1] Two of Ossory's daughters were unmarried at this time: Collins's *Peerage*, ed. Brydges, ix. 130.

[2] This apparently refers to the meeting of the Royal Society; but it took place on 16 January: Birch, iv. 246–50.

[3] The king authorized Compton, Sprat, and Sancroft to make collections for the relief of the poor, and himself gave £200 for the poor of London and Westminster: *Cal. S.P., Dom., 1683–4,* p. 199; *Moneys . . . for secret services of Charles II and James II* (Camden Soc., vol. lii, 1851), pp. 81, 82.

streetes, as in a Citty, or Continual faire,[1] all sorts of Trades & shops furnished, & full of Commodities, even to a Printing presse, where the People & Ladys tooke a fansy to have their names Printed & the day & yeare set downe, when printed on the *Thames*: This humour tooke so universaly, that 'twas estimated the Printer gained five pound a day, for printing a line onely, at six-pence a Name, besides what he gott by Ballads &c:[2] Coaches now plied from Westminster to the Temple, & from severall other staires too & froo, as in the streetes; also on sleds, sliding with skeetes;[3] There was likewise Bull-baiting, Horse & Coach races, Pupet-plays & interludes, Cookes & Tipling, & lewder places; so as it seem'd to be a bacchanalia,[a] Triumph or Carnoval on the Water, whilst it was a severe Judgement upon the Land: the Trees not onely splitting as if lightning-strock,[4] but Men & Cattell perishing in divers places, and the very seas so locked up with yce, that no vessells could stirr out, or come in:[5] The fowle [Fish][b] &

---

[a] Followed by *or* deleted.   [b] Interlined.

---

[1] The principal group of booths was a double line extending from Temple Stairs (at the foot of Middle Temple Lane) to the Old King's Barge - House (Old Barge - House Wharf). Descriptive poems, &c., are reprinted in *Old Ballads illustrating the Great Frost of 1683-4*, ed. E. F. Rimbault (Percy Soc., no. xlii, 1844); see further *Roxburghe Ballads*, vol. v, pt. ii, ed. J. W. Ebsworth (Ballad Soc., 1884), pp. 457-69. Rimbault lists a number of views; many of them are in the Crace Collection and J. C. Crowle's extra-illustrated copy of Pennant's *Some account of London* in the British Museum.

[2] The chief printer appears to have been G. Croom. Two tickets printed by him (the royal family, 31 January; Lord Clarendon, &c., 2 February) are reproduced by Lady Russell, *Swallowfield and its owners*, pp. 146-7. Croom also published

a poem, *Thamasis's Advice to the Painter*; and a view with a poem, *The True and Exact Representation of the Wonders upon the Water* (a purchaser, probably Luttrell, paid five pence for this on 11 February; in the Crace Collection). Evelyn's notice appears to follow literary sources rather than to be entirely original.

[3] Cf. above, iii. 346-7. Skating was still evidently a novelty in England; the earliest occurrence of the verb in *O.E.D.* is dated 1696.

[4] Notices of the effects of the frost on trees and vegetation by Evelyn and by Plot (based on information supplied by Bobart and others) are printed in *Philosophical Transactions*, xiv (1684), 559-63, 766-79; for Evelyn's see below, p. 376.

[5] See notices in *London Gazette*, 28 Jan., 4 and 7 Feb.

birds, & all our exotique Plants & Greenes universaly perishing; many Parks of deere destroied, & all sorts of fuell so
deare that there were greate Contributions to preserve the
poore alive; nor was this severe weather much lesse intense
in most parts of *Europe* even as far as *Spaine*, & the most
southern tracts:[1] London, by reason of the excessive coldnesse of the aire, hindring the ascent of the smoke, was so
filld with the fuliginous steame of the Sea-Coale, that hardly
could one see crosse the streete, & this filling the lungs with
its grosse particles exceedingly obstructed the breast, so as
one could scarce breath:[2] There was no water to be had from
the Pipes & Engines, nor could the Brewers, and divers other
Tradesmen work, & every moment was full of disastrous
accidents &c:

25 I visited Sir Rob: *Southwell*, and my Lady *Berkeley*:[3]

26 I visited Mr. *Berkeley*[4] at St. *Johns*, his wives sister
paints very finely in Oyle:[5] In the Evening I went to see
Sir Geo: Wheeler.

27 Dr. *Dove*[6] *Coram Rege* on 1 John: 3. v: 3. in a very plaine
& honest discourse setting forth the necessity[a] of purity, in
reference to a well-grounded hope, & how most men deceived
themselves with a notional faith & opinion, that the bare
profession of Religion would carry them to heaven, however
they lived, as to interior purity, & righteousnesse, which
being the unsound doctrine of the *Gnosticks*, was the occasion
of St. *Johns* writing against them.[7]

---

[a] Substituted for *nature*.

---

[1] This statement appears to be
false; the winter was not extraordinary in the south of Europe:
Easton, *Les hivers*.

[2] I have found no other notices of
the fogs.

[3] Presumably the widowed Lady
Berkeley of Stratton.

[4] Robert Berkeley: above, p. 345.
Mrs. Berkeley bequeathed to her
second husband, Bishop Burnet, a
life interest in her estate at St.
John's, Clerkenwell; Burnet afterwards lived in a house there: Clarke

and Foxcroft, *Burnet*, pp. 439–40;
Pinks, *Clerkenwell*, pp. 319–22.

[5] Mrs. Berkeley had a sister Mary,
wife of Robert Dormer, of Lee
Grange, Bucks.: Le Neve, *Pedigrees*,
p. 299. She is not traceable as an
artist.

[6] Above, p. 100.

[7] Evelyn himself describes Gnosti-
cism as a second-century heresy;
but assimilates the first-century
Nicolaitans to the Gnostics: *Hist. of
Religion*, ii. 223, 225–6.

Pomeridiano Dr. *Meriton* proceeded on (3. *Coll:* 21) the Duty of Parents to their children, as to their Education, discipline, provision &c:

30 Dr. *Megot Coram Rege* on 2 *Reg:* 9: 31: Had *Zimri* peace that slew his Master? shewing, that though this were objected by a wicked woman, yet it was a true reproch for a Tretcherous Subject: Not because *Jehu* slew her husband, who was commanded by God to do it; but for the heynousnesse of others, who have imbrued their hands in their Sovraignes blood, applie⟨d⟩ to the present occasion, being his late Majesties martyrdom: shewing very historicaly the tragical ends of such monstrous Conspirators; & that upon no pretence whatever, subjects might resist their lawfull Princes &c: *Pomeridiano* a stranger at St. *Martines* on 13 Rom: 1. 2. on the former subject.

The frost still raging as fircely as ever, the River of *Thames* was become a Camp, ten thousands of people, Coaches, Carts, & all manner of sports continuing & increasing: miserable were the wants of poore people, Deare universaly perished in most of the parks thro-out England, & very much Cattell:[1]

February 3. At St. *Martins* preached that incomparable Divine Dr. *Sharp*[2] on 10 *Acts*: 34. 35 That Cornelius being an Heathen Roman, & Captaine, did upon the strength & perswasion even of Natural reason, not onely accknowledge one God, but praied constantly to him, giving much Almes, & with extraordinary Devotion served God, as far as by the light of nature he could: for this it was God in mercy Revealed the Mysterie of Christ to him: see your notes &c:—*Pomerid*: Dr. *Meriton* on 3. *Coloss:* 22. Concerning the Duty of Servants &c: I this morning received the B: Sacrament:

4 I went to Says-Court to see how the frost & rigorous weather had dealt with my Garden, where I found many of

---

[1] For the winter on Mendip see Andrews, *Famous frosts and frost fairs*, pp. 37–8.

[2] John Sharp, 1645–1714; D.D. 1679; rector of St. Giles in the Fields 1676-91; dean of Norwich 1681; chaplain in ordinary 1686–91; dean of Canterbury 1689; archbishop of York 1691: *D.N.B.*

the Greenes & rare plants utterly destroied; The Oranges & Myrtils very sick, the Rosemary & Lawrell dead to all appearance, but the Cypresse like to indure it out:[1] I came to Lond: the next day when it fir⟨s⟩t of all began to Thaw, and pass'd-over without[a] alighting in my Coach from Lambeth to the Horse-ferry at Mill-bank at Westminster; the Weather growing lesse severe, it yet began to freeze againe; but the boothes were allmost-all taken downe; but there was first a Map or Landskip cut in copper representing all the manner of the Camp, & the several actions, sports and passe-times thereon in memory of this signal Frost:[2]

6 I presented a Petition to his Majestie in Council, in behalfe of our Parish for reliefe of the poore:[3] [7 Invited by the Swedish Resident,[4] I dined at his house with the publique Minister of the *Emperor*,[5] *Venetian*,[6] *Genoan*[7] and other strangers, all persons of quality.][b]

⟨8⟩[c] I dined with my *L: Keeper*, in order to some further informing him concerning the state of our Parish, & then walking alone with him some time in his Gallery, we had discourse of Musique, his Lordship told me he had ben brought up to it from a Child, so as to sing his part at first sight: Then speaking of painting, of which he was also a greate lover, & other ingenious matters, I tooke leave of him, desiring me to come oftner to him &c:[8]

I went this Evening to visite that greate & knowing

---

[1] For the damage at Sayes Court see Evelyn's letter in *Philosophical Transactions*: below, p. 376 n.

[2] Luttrell also mentions the beginning of the thaw on this day; it was possible to go upon the ice at low water until 9 February; he states that the river was open for boats on 12 February. See also Wood, *Life and times*, iii. 88. For the views see above, p. 362 n.

[3] See above, p. 361.

[4] Johan Baron Leijonbergh: above, iii. 497; iv. 295.

[5] Franz Sigmund, Graf von Thun, 1639–1702, 'ablegatus' here from 1680 to 1685: J. Siebmacher, *Wappenbuch*, vol. iv, pt. v, Ober-oesterreichischer Adel, 1904, p. 464.

[6] Girolamo Vignola, secretary, here from 1681 to 1686.

[7] Carlo Ottone, 'proconsole', here from 1670 to 1695.

[8] Guilford still perhaps occupied his house in Chancery Lane: above, p. 312. For his interest in music and painting see North, *Life of Guilford*, pp. 296–300.

Virtuoso Monsieur *Justell*:[1] The weather now was set to an absolute Thaw & raine, but the Thames still hard:[a]

10 The *Bishop* of *Cork*[2] *Coram Rege* made an excellent practical sermon at *White-Hall* on 119 *Psal:* ver: 6. shewing how possible it was for a *Christian* to keepe all Gods Commandments, by making use of his natural powers, & reason,[b] which Gods special Grace would not faile of assisting, so as *Christians* under the dispensations of the Gospel, had no manner of excuse, from the plea of frailty &c. He shewed also, the true notion & nature of shame, & how misbecoming it was to Man-kind to dishonor his species by continuing & acting any known sin &c: *See your notes*: *Pomeridiano*, at St. *Martines*, the Lecturer on 8 *Rom:* 13. The necessity of sanctification, and mortifying the deeds of the flesh &c:

After 8[c] weekes missing the foraine posts, there came aboundance of Intelligence from abroad:[3] ⟨13⟩[d] Ash-Wednesday, an excellent sermon in the afternoone at St. Martins by Dr. L. On 119 *Psal:* 60. Against deferring Repentance 'til age &c:

11 I visited Dr. *Tenison* viccar of St. *Martins* newly recovered of the smal pox.

12 The E: of *Danby* late L: *Tressurer* together with the Rom: Cath: Lords impeach'd of high Treason in the popish-plot, had now their *Habeas Corpus*, and came out upon Baile, after 5 years Imprisonment in the Toure:[4] Then were also Tried and deeply fin'd Mr. *Hambden*[5] & others, for being supposed of the late Plot, for which my L: ⟨*Russell*⟩[e] and Coll:

---

[a] Altered from *frozen*?   [b] Followed by *to* deleted.   [c] Reading doubtful.   [d] MS. *14*.   [e] MS. *Rissell*.

---

[1] See above, p. 287.

[2] Edward Wetenhall, 1636–1713; D.D., Dublin, 1674; bishop of Cork and Ross 1679; of Kilmore and Ardagh 1699; F.R.S. 1683: *D.N.B.*

[3] Foreign news is given regularly in the *London Gazette* except in the period from 28 January to 7 February.

[4] Notice in *London Gazette*, 14 Feb. For the Roman Catholic peers see above, pp. 158–9; Stafford had been executed in 1680 and Petre had died on 5 January of this year; the other three were now released; Richard Power, earl of Tyrone (*D.N.B.*), was released at the same time.

[5] Notice in *London Gazette*, 14 Feb. Hampden had been tried and convicted on 6 February; the sentence was delivered this day.

⟨*Sidney*⟩ᵃ suffered: As also the person, who went about to prove that the E: of ⟨Essex⟩ᵇ had his Throat Cut in the Tower by others:¹ likewise Mr. *Johnson*,² the Author of that famous piece cald *Julian*.

13ᶜ Newes of the P: of Oranges having accus'd the Deputies of *Amsterdam* of *Crimen Læsæ Majestatis*, & being Pensioner to France.³

Dr. *Tenison* communicating to me his intention of Erecting a Library in St. *Martines* parish, for the publique use, desird my assistance with Sir *Chr: Wren* about the placing & structure thereof: a worthy & laudable designe: He told me there were 30 or 40 Young Men in *Orders* in his Parish, either, Governors to young Gent: or Chaplains to Noble-men, who being reprov'd by him upon occasion, for frequenting Taverns or Coffè-houses, toldᵈ him, they would study & employ their time better, if they had books: This put the pious Doctor upon this designe, which I could not but approve of, & indeede a greate reproch it is, that so great a Citty as *Lond:*

ᵃ MS. *Sindny*.　　ᵇ MS. *Exssex*.　　ᶜ Altered from or to *15*.
ᵈ Followed by *the* deleted.

---

¹ Notice in *London Gazette*, 11 Feb. This refers to Lawrence Braddon and Hugh Speke, who were tried on 7 February for conspiring to spread a false report that Essex had been murdered and for subornation of witnesses (above, p. 327 n.). Braddon was convicted on both charges and Speke on the former; they were sentenced to fines of £2,000 and £1,000 on 21 April: *London Gazette*, 24 April. For both men see *D.N.B.*

² Notice in *London Gazette*, 14 Feb. Samuel Johnson, 1649–1703, political divine; sometime chaplain of Lord William Russell: *D.N.B.* The work here mentioned is *Julian the Apostate: being a Short Account of his Life; the Sense of the Primitive Christians about his Succession; and their Behaviour towards him*. To-

gether with a Comparison of Popery and Paganism, 1682. On 20 Nov. 1683 he had been convicted of publishing a seditious libel, this work: *London Gazette*, 22 Nov.; on 11 February he was sentenced to pay a fine of 500 marks, &c. There were at least two editions of *Julian* in 1682; a fourth edition appeared in 1689.

³ The report appears to be inaccurate. Amsterdam was at this time opposing the proposal of the States of Holland to levy additional troops: *London Gazette*, 11, 14 Feb. It was reported in London that secret negotiations between Louis XIV and Amsterdam had been discovered: Luttrell, i. 302 (and see *London Gazette*, 18, 25 Feb.). The prince of Orange was leading the demand for the new levies.

should have never a publique Library becoming it:[1] There ought to be one at S. *Paules,* the West end of that Church, (if ever finish'd), would be a convenient place: 15. Dr. *Stillingfleete* Dean of *Paules Coram Rege* on 23[a] *Job* 15 an incomparable discourse against *Atheisme*: see[b] sermon printed:[2]

17 At St. *Martins* in the morning preachd a stranger on 103 *Psal:* 11. Magnifying the infinite mercy of God, to them who feare him, describing feare to signifie, the living a holy & religious life: The H. *Comm:* follow'd at which I participated:

Pomeridiano at St. *Giles's* the Curate on   *Sam:* Those who honour God he will honour:[3] shewing the nature of True honour, which being all deriv'd from him, was to be ascribed to him, & return'd: described the false honour of the world, & vanity of Titles, without virtue & Religion. &c:

19 I went to visite the Countesses[c] of *Ossory:*[4] 21 I had a tryal at the *Chequer* before the L: Chiefe *Barron*[5] against my Lady *Michelthwaite*[6] about an Accompt of Rent & asserted my Cause: This & other buisinesse on Friday hindred my hearing two *Lenten sermons.* [20 I went to visite & congratulate my Lo: *Danby,* after his coming out of Tower:][d]

---

[a] Followed by *Psal:* deleted. standing, *Notes* deleted.   [b] Followed by *your Notes* ; *your* left   [c] Or *Countesse.*   [d] Interlined.

---

[1] Tenison applied to the vestry in March 1685 and built his Library in Castle Street, with a room beneath it in which a school was opened in 1688 (below, 24 May 1688 n.); he also gave books. The library was eventually neglected and the books were sold in 1861; the school was moved in 1868, when the National Gallery acquired the site: J. Mc-Master, *Short hist. of . . . St. Martin-in-the-Fields,* 1916, pp. 263–6; view, p. 276; L.C.C., *Survey of London,* xx. 113–14; see also Strype's Stow, vi. 68, 73; further notice below, p. 369. According to Chamberlayne the Westminster Abbey library was open to strangers in term time (ed.

1684, ii. 308).
[2] Lenten sermon at court: list of preachers in *London Gazette,* 13 Dec. 1683. The sermon was published by May of this year: *Term catalogues,* ed. Arber, ii. 68. It is reprinted in Stillingfleet's *Ten sermons* (*Sermons,* vol. ii), pp. 484–529.
[3] 1 Samuel ii. 30.
[4] If the reading is correct, the mother and wife of the present earl of Ossory: above, pp. 102, 297.
[5] William Montagu: above, iii. 551.
[6] Ann, d. 1690, widow of Sir John Micklethwaite (1612-82, kt., M.D.: *D.N.B.*): *Genealogist,* i. (1877), 150.

23 I went to Sir John *Chardins,* who desired my Assistance
for the ingraving of the plates, the translation & Printing
of his historie of that wonderfull *Persian* monument neere
Persepolis, & other rare Antiquities, which he had Caus'd to
be drawne from the originals, at his 2d journey into *Persia:*
which we now concluded upon:[1] And afterwards I went to
Dr. *Tenison* (with Sir *Chr: Wren*) where we made both the
draught & estimate of the *Library* to be begun this next
spring, neere the *Mewes:*

Greate expectations of the *Prince* of *Oranges* attempts in
Holland, to bring those of *Amsterdam* to consent to the *new
Levies* ;[2] to which we were no friends by a *Pseudo*politic ad-
herence to the French Interest:

24 *Coram Rege* preached Dr. *Lloyd: Bishop* of *Peterborow,*[3]
once Curate of our Parish of Deptford; on 1. *Thessal:* 2: 12.
shewing in a most elegant, & practical discourse, what itt
was to walke Worthy of the Glory to be revealed, namely to
live religiously & holily, & such a life as becomes the Ends
& designe of God, to exhalt us to his heavenly Kingdome:

[1] Chardin had insuperable difficulties in publishing his travels.
French and English versions of his
account of part of his second journey to Persia were published in
London by Moses Pitt in 1686, in
each case as the first part of his
description of Persia (not advertised
until 1688: *Term catalogues,* ii.
230). In his preface to the English
version Chardin describes his difficulty in obtaining an accurate
translation. The plates (after Grelot's drawings: above, p. 213) were
unsatisfactory: 'The *Copper Plates*
are done by different *Gravers,* which
will not happen in the others of my
Volumes, where all of them will be
Engraven by that Hand which has
done the Draught of *Tauris,* and
Nine or Ten other *Figures*': preface
(the plate of Tauris is unsigned, but
is perhaps by P. P. Bouche, who
signs pls. xiii, xvi). No further parts
were published in the same form as
this volume. The second and third
parts first appeared, with a revised
version of the first, in French at
Amsterdam in 1711 (two editions,
3 vols., 4to, and 10 vols., 8vo); the
plates for the first part are newly
engraved throughout; those for the
other two parts appear to have been
engraved about the same time.
Chardin's other projected works on
Persia have never been published
in their original form. The account
of Persepolis occurs in pt. iii.

[2] For the new levies see above,
p. 367 n. Later reports deal with
the opposition of other towns to
them and with the dispute between
Amsterdam and the States of Holland following the seizure of the
papers of the deputies of Amsterdam: *London Gazette,* 25 Feb., &c.

[3] Lenten sermon at court. Lloyd
the nonjuror, bishop of Peterborough since 1679.

Pomeridiano Dr. *Meriton* at St. *Martins* proceeding in his former lecture.

26 Came to visite me Dr. *Turner* our new *Bishop* of *Rochester*:

27 *Coram Rege* preached Dr. *Hooper*[1] Parson of *Lambeth*, on 19: *Psal:* 13 shewing the danger of Presumptuous sinns, & how many more there were of them, than[a] men usualy believed: it was a quaint[2] & excellent discourse:

I went this Afternoone to the R: *Society*, where there were read severall learned discourses upon Experiments of Cold &c: of Optics, & Acoustics &c: Mr. Boyle presented me his booke or Natural historie of humane blood:[3]

28 I din'd at my *Lady Tukes*, where I heard Dr. *Wallgrave*[4] (physitian to the Duke & Dutchesse) play most incomparably on the Lute; I know not that ever I heard any to exceede him.

29 *Coram Rege* &c: *Dr. Sharp*[5] on. 2. *Cor:* 6. 2. Convincingly shewing the danger of deferring our Repentance 'til our old age or death-bed: That the good Theife ought to be no encouragement: whose Circumstances were so extraordinary, to believe in a dying Saviour, that to all appearance could not save himselfe: The Labourer cal'd at the 11th houre, no encouraging instance neither, for that related to the calling of the Gentiles; & besides they were never called 'til then, wheras we have ben long called on: Besids they had one houre to worke in, 'ere the day was spent, & therefore had a reward; but he that deferrs to the 12 houre (are there not 12 houres in the day: & then the night cometh) has no time to work; or if he should, would not be accepted, proved from the parable of the foolish Virgins, who sleeping and neglecting their Lamps, though they went to buy, & got oyle &c at last,

---

[a] Altered from *that*.

[1] Above, p. 260. Presumably a lenten sermon at court, but the preacher listed is Ken.
[2] Carefully elaborated, &c., in a favourable sense: *O.E.D.*
[3] *Memoirs for the Natural History of Humane Blood*, 1684: Fulton, *Bibliog. of . . . Boyle*, no. xxv.
[4] William Waldegrave: above, p. 48.
[5] Above, p. 364. Lenten sermon at court.

were yet shut out, because not ready with the rest. The
exhortation was to begin the worke of an holy life betimes,
in youth, at the first call, or at farthest in man hood, nay at
the first offer of grace in reguard of the uncertainty of our
lives, & difficulties of performing that absolutely necessary[a]
worke, when we are fit for nothing, by reason of age, sicknesse, & the disorder of our understanding at that time,
obnoxious as it is to so many sad accidents, it being at all
times, by Gods free grace that the most holy of men are saved,
and with difficulty enough, being all but unprofitable Servants; how much more Casuall & uncertaine would a wicked
& carelesse wretchs condition be, who begins to repent so
late, & [when][b] tis unpossible for him himselfe to be sure, that
his conversion is sincere, & that if he recover, he[c] shall not
relapse: Nothing but a Miracle or revelation can secure such
a person, the Priest may pray for & direct him, but none on
earth can divine the event:

March 2 Dr. *Tillotson* at St. *Martins* on 24 *Josh:* 15 shewing the folly of sinfull mens choice, the easinesse & happinesse of a holy & temperate life, above that of the sensual;
as I had heard him twice on This Text before;[1] but it could
not be preached too often; The holy *Communion* follow'd at
which I participated, The Lord be praised:

Pomeridiano Dr. Meriton proceeded on 3 *Colloss:* ult:
shewing that there was no respect of Persons with *God*,
exhorting every one of whatever degree to live uprightly:

5 The Deane of St. *Asaph*[2] at White-hall on

I went to visite Mr. *Ro: Boyle*, who had presented me with
his History of Experiments upon humane Blood: &c:

6 I went home to Says Court, returned the next day.

7 Dr. *Megot Deane* of *Winchester* preached an incomparable

---

a Or *nicessary*.   b Interlined.   c Followed by *do* deleted.

---

[1] Above, pp. 198, 277. Tillotson
also preached two sermons on
another part of the verse; he
preached them at St. Laurence
Jewry on 3 June and 13 July of this
year: *Works*, 1752, i. 473-88.

[2] Nicholas Stratford, 1633–1707;
D.D. 1673; dean of St. Asaph 1674;
bishop of Chester 1689: *D.N.B.*
Presumably a lenten sermon at
court; but the preacher listed is
Hooper.

sermon (the King being now gon to New-Market) on 12:
Heb: 15, shewing & patheticaly pressing the Care we ought
to have, least we come short of the grace of God, *see your
notes.*[1]

8 I went to visite Dr. *Tenison* at *Kensington* whither he
was retired to refresh after he had ben sick of the small-pox:

9 At White Hall preached a stranger on: 1. *Thess:* 1. 10,
concerning the certainty of Christs second Coming, as our
Highpriest to blesse his people, praying in the outward[a]
Court of the Temple, in alusion to which, the people prayed
& expected the Priests blessing:[2]

Pomeridiano: Dr. Meriton at St. Martines 4: *Coloss:* 1. of
the duty of *Masters* in giving their Servants due work,
wages, discipline &c:

12 At White-hall preached *Mr. Hen: Godolphin*[3] a preb: of
S. Pauls Bro: to my deare friend Sydnie, on 55 *Isa:* 7. very
excellently shewing the readynesse of God to pardon true
penitents, and the importance of reforming our ways
betimes:

15 I dined at my L. *Keepers* and brought to him *Sir John
Chardin*: who shewed him his accurate draughts of his travels
in Persia &c:

16 A stranger at *Whitehall* preached on 1. *Cor:* 22:[4] how
contemptible all earthly things were to the love & benefit of
Christ & his Gospell.

Dr. *Meriton* at S. *Martines* Pomerid: 4. *Coloss:* 2, on the
duty & benefit of Prayer and praises &c: 19. Dr. *Turner*[5] at

---

[a] Followed by *Temple* deleted.

---

[1] Meggot had been dean of Winchester since 1679. Lenten sermon
at court. Charles left for New-
market on 1 March: *London Gazette*,
3 March.

[2] Apparently a lenten sermon at
court; the preacher listed is the
bishop of Worcester, Dr. William
Thomas: above, p. 5.

[3] Godolphin (above, p. 181) was
a prebendary of St. Paul's from
1683 until his death. Lenten ser-

mon at court; the preacher listed is
Tenison.

[4] A slip perhaps for 1 Corinthians
ii. 2. The preacher listed for this
day's lenten sermon at court is the
bishop of Oxford, Dr. Fell.

[5] This can scarcely be Dr.
Francis Turner, now bishop of
Rochester; it is perhaps his brother,
Dr. Thomas Turner (below, p. 493).
Presumably a lenten sermon at
court; but the preacher listed is

W.hall, on   Eccl: very ex⟨c⟩ellently shewing the
preference of suffering in this life, to a vitious prosperity, for
the profitable effects thereof in bringing us to repentance, &
to a disesteeme of the vanities of this transitory world, this
by many examples illustrated, & advise for the practical use
of afflictions looking to their blessed & joyfull end.

21 At *Whitehall Dr. Tillotson* 16 *Luke*: 8,[a] most excellently
shewing the vanity of worldly wisedome, and paines men take
to pursue honours, wealth &c, to the neglecting of their
soules, & perstringing the folly of their prefering things temporal to things eternal, both by Arguments & Instances, &
that this wisedome of theires, was not spoken of as approving
it, but to shew the folly of it by the event.[1] *See your notes.*

23 Preached *Coram Rege* at Court: the *Bishop* of *Cork*,[2] on
19 Luke. 40, of the ingratitude and infidelity of the Jewes;
to which he compared many that made profession of Religion
in England, & ominating Judgements without timely
reformation.

Pomeridiano Dr. *Meriton* on his former Text, concerning
the certaine returne of fervent Prayer, and perseverance &c.

26 *Coram Rege*: Dr. *Cradock* provost of *Eaton* on[3]

28 *Good-friday*, at St. *Martines*, a Chaplaine of my L.
Manchesters[4] excellently on 12: *Heb:* 3 shewing the Contra-
dictions of Sinners which Christ sufferd, in a very ample &
profitable discourse. The holy *Sacrament* follow'd at which
I participated, the Lord accept me: *Pomeridiano coram
Rege* at *Whitehall* (Dr. *Sprat, deane* of *Westminster*) on 4:
Rom: 25 shewing how our B: Lord was deliver'd for us:
magnifying his infinite perfections, power, & glory, opposed
to his most stupendious contrary exinanition, & debasement

---

a Altered from *18*.

Dr. Montague (i.e. John Montagu, c. 1655–1728; D.D. 1682: *D.N.B.*; Venn).

[1] Lenten sermon at court. Printed in Tillotson, *Works*, 1752, ii. 481*–90.

[2] Wetenhall: above, p. 366. Presumably a lenten sermon at court;

the preacher listed is the archbishop of Canterbury, Sancroft. Charles had returned from Newmarket on 22 March: Luttrell.

[3] Lenten sermon at court.

[4] Above, pp. 356, 357.

for us, delivering himselfe to so ignominious a Condition & death to save us.[1]

There was so greate & eager a concourse of people with their children, to be touch'd of the *Evil*, that 6 or 7: were crush'd to *death* by pressing at the *Chirurgions* doore for Tickets. &c.[2] The weather began now onely to be more mild & tollerable, but there was not the least appearance of any Spring.

30 Easter-day, I received the B: Sacrament at *white-hall* early, with the Lords & household: the B: of *Lond:* officiating: Then went to St. *Martines* wher Dr. *Tenison* (now first coming abroad after his recovery of the small-pox) preached on 16: *Psal:* 11, an *Historical Resurrection* sermon, proving the truth of the fact, & how it engag'd us to believe, & consequently all the rest of the Christian doctrine:—Hence I went againe to *White Hall*, where *coram Rege*, preach'd the *B: of Rochester*[3] on a Text out of *Hosea* 6. 2. touching the subject of the day: After which his *Majestie*, accompanied with 3 of his natural Sonns, (viz. the Dukes of *Northumb:*[4] *Richmond*[5] & *St. Albans*,[6] base sonns of *Portsmouth, Cleaveland, Nelly*, prostitute Creatures) went up to the Altar; The three Boyes entering before the King within the railes,[a] at the right hand, & 3 Bishops on the left: viz: Lond: (who officiated) *Durham*,[7] *Rochester*, with the sub-Deane Dr. Holder: The King kneeling before the Altar, making his offering, the Bishops first received, & then his *Majestie*, after

---

[a] Followed by *where* deleted.

---

[1] Lenten sermon at court.

[2] By an order in council of 9 January there was to be no touching from 1 March until Passion week: *London Gazette*, 28 Jan.

[3] Dr. Francis Turner; lenten sermon at court. He was preaching as lord almoner, having been appointed in March: *Cal. S.P., Dom., 1683–4*, p. 311. The sermon was printed this year.

[4] George Fitzroy, 1665–1716,

Charles II's third son by the duchess of Cleveland; created earl of Northumberland 1674; duke 1683: *D.N.B.*

[5] Above, p. 268; the duchess of Portsmouth's son.

[6] Charles Beauclerk, 1670–1726, Charles's elder son by Nell Gwyn; created earl of Burford 1676; duke of St. Albans on 10 January of this year: *D.N.B.*

[7] Nathaniel Crew: above, p. 4.

which, he retir'd to a Canopied seate on the right hand &c:[1]
note, there was perfume burnt before the office began:
Pomeridiano, preached at St. *Mart:* the Lecturer Dr. *Meriton*
on 6: *Rom:* 4: Exhortatorie that as Christ was rissen from the
dead, so should we from sinns, as answering the ends &
intention of it.

Aprill 4[a] After 5 monethes being in *Lond:* this severe
winter, I return'd home with my family this day:[2] My sonn
with his wife &c: continuing behind, upon pretence of his
applying himselfe more seriously to his studying the Law,[3]
but wholy without my approbation:—hardly the least
appearance of any Spring.

6 Our *Viccar* preach'd on 14. *Rom:* 9. shewing how Christ
was Lord, after his Resurrection, and in how many glorious
& ruling capacities, not onely as Creator, but as Redeemer,
& giving laws to all man kind, exercising his powers here in
his Church, & over the wicked, &c at the last day: The
Application was to perswade us to obedience, & preparation
against his comming either at our death, or Day of Judgement. *Pomerid*: The *Curate* on 6 *Mich:* 8: That the whole
duty of Man, consisted in Sincerity, Justice, humility &
universal Charity:

12 Being much indispos'd this weeke, I tooke Physick, &
a Vomite, which did greately restore me, blessed be God:

13 A young stranger preached on 4: *Phil:* 5, describing the
nature, duty, & excellency of Moderation, in a very solid
discourse, onely a little too full of his *Greeke* for our Auditorie

---

a Reading doubtful.

---

[1] Queen Mary writes: 'One of my
grievances was the pomp and stir
was observed at receiving the Sacrament. There was an old custom left
since the time of Popery, that the
kings should receive almost alone;
this had been alwais observed, this
I could not resolve to do, but told
the Bishop of London [Compton],
who I found unreasonable upon that,
and would keep up the foolery, but
at last I got the better, and the king
[William III] being of my mind, we
resolved to make it a matter of as
litle state as possible, yet there is
to much left.' This was in 1689:
Memoirs, ed. R. Doebner, 1886,
p. 13.

[2] See above, p. 350.

[3] He had been called to the Bar
in February 1683.

&c. *Pomerid*: The same person on 6. *Matt:* 12, concerning Charity, and forgivenesse of Injuries: Sleepe surpriz'd me:

18 I went to Lond: about buisinesse, return'd in the Evening: 20, our Viccar & Curate preached on their former Texts, with small addition: 21. To Lond: return'd also that Evening:

27 Our Viccar proceeded on his former *Text*: See your notes: Also the *Curate*:

30 I went to *Lond:* To the *R: Society*, a letter of mine to it concerning the tirrible effects of the past Winter being read, they desire it might be publish'd in the next transactions.[1]

May 1 Being the meeting of the *Foefeès* for the poore, our *Viccar* preached on 7 *Matt:* 21. [the same as on the last yeare],[a] [shewing the greate mistake, of such as imagine it is enough to be a professor: that Christ will require what we sinners have done.][b]

4 Our *Viccar* proceeded with his former *Text*, without much addition: *pomerid*: The Curate of *Greene-wich* on 8. *John*: 34. shewing that our B: *Saviour*, meant habitual sinners, for that many of the Saints had don sinn, but continued not in it. I received the *B: Sacrament* this morning, after a most serious preparation, the L. *Jesus* make me ever mindfull of it.[2]

May 10th. I went to visite my Brother in Surry, caled by the Way at Ashstead[3] where Sir Robert Howard Auditor of the Exchequer entertain'd me very civily at his newly built

---

a Interlined subsequently to principal interlineation.　　b Interlined.

[1] For this day's meeting see Birch, iv. 290–2. But Evelyn's letter, which is dated 14 April, appears to have been read at the meeting on 23 April: ibid., p. 289 (Birch does not give the date for the meeting, but it must be of this date). The letter was published in *Philosophical Transactions*, no. 158, dated 20 April (vol. xiv, 1684, pp. 559–63; reprinted in Evelyn, *Misc. writings*, pp. 692–6).

[2] Ascension Day fell on 8 May.
[3] Sir Robert Howard had bought the manor of Ashtead from the duke of Norfolk in 1680. The house was rebuilt *c.* 1790 and no other description of its interior is known; the estate belonged to the Howards or their connexions until 1880: *V.C.H., Surrey*, iii. 249; [F. E. Paget], *Some Records of the Ashtead Estate*, 1873, pp. 64–8, &c.

house, which stands in a very sweete-park upon the downe, the avenue south though downe hill to the house exceedingly pleased me: The house is not greate but with the out-houses very convenient: The staire Case is painted by *Verrio* with the storie of *Astrea*, amongst other figures is the picture of the Painter himselfe, and not unlike him; The rest well don; onely the Columns did not at all please me; There is also Sir Roberts owne picture in an Oval, the whole in fresca: there is with all this one greate defect, that they have no Water save what is drawne with horses from an exceeding deepe Well. Hence I went to Wotton that night:

11 One Mr. Crawly[1] preached in the Morning at *Abinger* on 13 *Heb:* 18. concerning the necessity of having a good Conscience: In the Afternoone I went to visite Mr. *Higham* now sick in his Climacterical, whereof he died [about][a] 3 days after: his Grandfather & Father (who Christn'd me) with himselfe had now ben 3 generations Parsons of the Parish an hundred and foure years this *May*: viz: from 1584.[2]

12 I returned to Lond: where I found the Commissioners of the Admiralty abolished, & the Office of Admiral restord to the *Duke*, as to the disposal & ordering all sea buisinesse: But his Majestie signing all the Petitions, Papers, Warrants & Commissions, that the Duke not acting as Admiral by Com-mission, or Office, might not incurr the penalty of the late Act against Papists & Dissenters holding Office or refusing the Oath & Test: &c: every body was glad of this Change: Those in the late Commission being utterly ignorant of their duty, to the greate damage of the Navy royal:[3]

---

a Interlined.

[1] Presumably Thomas Crawley, d. 1685; admitted Cambridge 1672; B.A. 1676; M.A. 1679; rector of Abinger 1683; married 1683 Eliza-beth, d. 1688, daughter of the late rector Dr. Gabriel Offley, George Evelyn's brother - in - law: Venn; Abinger *Parish registers*; &c.

[2] Higham's date of burial is given as 15 and as 25 May: Wotton *Parish registers*, pp. 147, 201. His grand-father, Robert Higham, was insti-tuted rector of Wotton on 3 May 1583: Manning and Bray, ii. 158; his father George succeeded in 1612 and he himself apparently in 1659.

[3] *London Gazette*, 15 May (notice dated Windsor, 12 May). When James surrendered the office of lord high admiral in 1673 a committee of the privy council was appointed in his place (new commissions 1674

Now was also the utter ruine of the *Low-Countries* threatn'd, by the Seige of *Luxenburge* (if not timely reliev'd) & the Obstinacy of the Hollanders not to assist the Prince of Orange: Corrupted (as appear'd) by the French &c:[1]

16 I received 600 pounds of Sir *Charles Bickerstaff* for the Fee farme of Pilton in *Devon*:[2] & payed my Bro: 500 pounds which I owed him:[3]

18 Being W⟨h⟩*itsonday*, I received the B: Sacrament at St. Margarites, a stranger preaching on 15 *John* 26. shewing that the *H: Ghost* was no Created being, but God, co-equal with the Father & the Sonn: by many irrefragable testimonies;[a] against *Socinus*[4] & other heretics: *Pomerid*: another stranger on: 16: *John*: 7: Concerning the expediency of our B: Saviours absence for the Comfort of his Church &c:

19 At St. *Martines* my L: *Manchest*⟨*er*⟩*s* chaplain excellently on 14 *John*: 26 on the former subject, shewing how the H. Spirit has ben teaching the[b] Church ever since our

---

[a] Altered from *ar-*.   [b] Altered from *his*.

---

and 1677); then in 1679 this committee was superseded by a board of commissioners, of whom none was a member of the council (new commissions 1681, 1682, 1683, and 17 April of this year). Although the board in its latest form included two admirals it had been inefficient and the navy had fallen into decay: Pepys, *Memoires relating to the State of the Royal Navy* (1679–88), 1690 (new ed. by J. R. Tanner, 1906). James could not hold office without complying with the Test Act of 1673: above, p. 7.

[1] The siege of Luxemburg had begun on 27 April; the trenches were opened on 8 May. The city of Amsterdam had opposed the prince (see above, pp. 367, 369) and was said to have declared that, should the States General have joined in the war, it would not contribute to the cost. Luxemburg capitulated on 4 June, the garrison marching

out on 7 June (all dates N.S.): *London Gazette*, 1, 12, 19 May, 5 June.

[2] Pilton is near Barnstaple. Charles Bickerstaffe, c. 1632–1704 (1705), of Seale, Kent; knighted c. 1672; clerk of the privy seal or of the signet: Hasted, *Kent*, i. 336–7; *Cal. S.P., Dom.*; Chamberlayne. Bickerstaffe's deceased son-in-law, Sir John Chichester, was a member of a family formerly owning Pilton: Vivian, *Visitations of Devon*, p. 174.

[3] Cf. below, p. 380.

[4] Fausto Socino, known as Socinus, 1539–1604, one of the founders of Unitarianism: *Nouvelle biog. gén.*; *Encic. italiana* (his uncle Lelio Socino, 1525–62, held similar views). For the expansion of Unitarianism at this period—one of the most remarkable religious developments of the later seventeenth century— see A. Gordon, *Heads of English Unitarian History*, 1895.

Saviours Ascention:[1]—I return'd home this Evening: Praysed ⟨be⟩[a] God.

An excessive hot & dry Spring after so severe a Winter:

21 I visited the Bish: of Lond; & din'd with him at Fullham, return'd that evening:

25 Our Viccar on 1. *Cor:* 10: 12 shewing the danger of over Confidence of our own states[b] by[b] our pronesse to fall, and the hypocrisie & deceitfullnesse of our hearts: That God has pass'd no inevitable decree for the damnation of any: that opinion never heard of til of late: That tis utterly contrary to the goodnesse & Justice of God, to command us to be saved, and make the meanes of it impossible &c:

Pomerid: Curate on his former 6: *Mich:* 8: Concerning the love of *mercy*, and how it imported every Christian to be mercifull, as the 2d branch of the duty of Man &c.

26 Being Trinity monday *Dr. Can,*[2] preached before the Trinity Company (my L: *Dartmouth* being first chosen and continued Master for the Ensuing Yeare, now newly return'd with the fleete from blowing up, & demolishing Tangier)[3] Text 107[c] *Psal:* 31. After a very learned discourse about the dimensions of the Ark, compar'd with other Vessells of antient & later times, to obviate severall objections of Atheistical persons; he shewed the prophanesse of others, in the usual sarcasme, of calling an ignorant sayler on⟨e⟩ of St. *Paules* seamen,[4] for that description in 27 St. Luke *Acts Apost:* where 'tis said they cast Ankers out of the fore-ship, to proceede from utter ignorance,[d] that because we do not so in our seas, in stresse of Weather, & as our Vessels are built;

---

a MS. *by*.   b-b Or *state, by*.   c Reading doubtful.   d Followed by *bec-* deleted.

---

[1] The day is Whit Monday.

[2] Ken: above, p. 302. He had accompanied Dartmouth to Tangier as his chaplain. He was elected bishop of Bath and Wells on 16 December of this year, and was consecrated on 25 Jan. 1685.

[3] On account of the unwillingness of parliament to grant supplies, and of pressure from the Moors, Charles had been obliged to abandon Tangier; Dartmouth had been sent in 1683 to evacuate the population and to demolish the fortifications; he had returned in April. This was the expedition in which Pepys sailed.

[4] Fuller gives '*Saint* Pauls Mariners': *Worthies*, Kent, p. 61.

so they did in other seas; whereas it is at this day, and allways has bin the practise so to do in the Mediterranean seas, as St. Luke describes it: he also most rhetoricaly inlarg'd on the severall perils of sea Adventurers,[a] and Mariners, by Tempests, leakes, casual fires, Wracks; fights, [slavery],[b] diseases &c: thereby exciting those sort of men, to be above all others most religious, who were found usualy the most prophane: & what cause they had also above all others, to praise God for their deliverances; [He preached with much action:][c] Then we went to *Lond:* where we were magnificently feasted at the Trinity house, My L: of Dartmouth, Earles of Cravon & Berkely &c to the number of at the least of 100 at one table as I conjectur'd &c:

28 I paied my Bro: G: Evelyn 500 pounds more of the Mortgage:[1] Dined with severall of our Society of Gressham Coll, where after some Experiment: viz: by putting yron with A: fortis in *pleno*, & another piece of yron in *Vaccuo*, That in pleno, was rusted & eaten through[d] twenty times sooner than that in *vaccuo*, by w⟨h⟩ich was shew'd what a corrosive spirit there is in the common aire &c:[2] especialy about the Citty, so infected with steams of the seacoale &c: Now was *Luxemburg* rendered to the Conquering French,[3] which makes him Master of all the Neitherland, gives him entrance into Germanie; & a faire game for an universal Monarchy: which that we should suffer (who onely, & easily might have hindred) all the world were astonish'd at: But thus is the poore P: of *Orange* ruin'd, & this Nations, & all the Protestant Interest in Europ following, unless God of his infinite mercy (as by a Miracle) interpose; & that our Greate ones alter their Counsels.

29[e] Being his Majesties Birth-day & restauration, I went

---

a Or *Adventures*.   b Interlined.   c Later insertion.   d Followed by *in* deleted.   e Altered from *28*.

---

1 Cf. above, p. 378.
2 Birch, iv. 300. The allusion to the London atmosphere is presumably a reflection of Evelyn's.

3 *London Gazette*, 5 June. Luxemburg surrendered to the French on 28 May/7 June; the capitulation took place some days earlier.

to the Temple Church where a stranger[1] preached before all
the Judges & that Society on 1. 4. *Pet:* 15, a Theologo-
political[2] sermon, in order to obedience & Union; greately
celebrating the moderation of our first reformers, & perstringing our present dissenters; after which I returned
home, & found my Daughter much mended of her feavor,
God be blessed:

The *French fleete* were now beseiging *Genöa*: [burnt much of
that beautiful Citty with their bombs most maliciously, &
went off with disgrace.][a][3]

1 *June* Our Viccar, & Curate, upon the same subject &
Text with no greate addition. The B: Communion I receiv'd
&c:

8 Little improvement of either Text: My daughter now
wholy freed of her feavor and myselfe of an Indisposition, for
which God be ever praised.

10 I went to Lond, about my Law buisinesse, 11: At the
R: Society where was an experiment of the adhesion of a
plaine flat ground glasse to a Cucurbit emptyed in *Vaccuo
Boyliano*; & that so close, as to beare the weight of
almost 50 pound[b] hanging on the plate, nor did it
separate 'til aire was againe let in: 12 I went to
advise & give directions about the building of two
streetes in *Berkeley Gardens*, reserving the house, &
as much of the Garden as the breadth of the house; in
the meane time I could not but deplore that sweete place
(by farr the most pleasant & noble Gardens Courts and
Accommodations, [statly][c] porticos &c any where about the

---

a Added later, the writing similar to that of entry for 10 June.
b Followed by *drawing* deleted.   c Interlined.

---

[1] Perhaps Dr. William Sherlock
(below, p. 488), who had been
appointed master of the Temple in
April: *Cal. S.P., Dom., 1683–4*, p.
382. The text is perhaps wrong.

[2] A reminiscence of the *Tractatus
theologico-politicus* (1670) of Spinoza.
The work had attracted Evelyn's
notice: *Hist. of religion*, ii. 271; and
was probably the subject of his
manuscript 'Animadversions upon
Spinoza'.

[3] *London Gazette*, 29 May, 2, 5
June. The French fleet was before
Genoa from 17 to 24 May N.S.; the
French suffered some very slight
losses and Evelyn perhaps refers to
this; but later he speaks of bom-
bardments with detestation: 15 July
1694, 25 Aug., 15 Sept. 1695.

Towne) should so much of it ⟨be⟩ streitned & turn'd into
Tennements;[1] but that magnificent pile & Gardens contiguous to it (built by the late L. Chancellor Hyde with so
vast cost) being all demolish'd, & design'd for *piazzas* &
buildings, was some excuse for my Lady Berkleys resolution
of leting out her ground also, for so excessive a price as was
offerd, advancing her revenue neere 1000 pounds per Ann:
in meere Ground rents; to such a mad intemperance the age
was come of building about a Citty, by far too disproportionat
already to the Nation, I having in my time seene it almost as
large more than it was within my memorie.[2] I return'd home
this evening.

15 Our *Viccar* his former subject, most of it repetition:
Pomerid: the Curate of *Greenewich* on 10 *Pro:* 9, shewing the
benefit of uprightnesse: My Co: *Verney*[3] (to whom a very
greate fortune was fallen) came to take his leave of us; going
into the Country: a very worthy, and virtuous young Gent:

22 Our Vicc: & Curat proceeded on their former Text &
subject, without material addition:

The last friday was Sir Tho: Armstrong executed at
Tyburn for Treason, as outlaw'd and apprehended in Holland, upon the Conspiracy of the D. of Monmoth, Lord
Russell &c: without any Tryal, which gave occasion to
people & Lawyers of discourse, in reguard it being on an
outlawry, Judgement was given & execution don thereon:[4]

---

[1] For Berkeley House see above,
iii. 436, 624–5. The garden apparently ran only as far north as the
original end of Stratton Street. The
latter (formerly Stretton Street)
and Berkeley Street were the two
streets now laid out; each 'hath but
one Row of Buildings, and those
front the Garden' of Berkeley
House: Strype's Stow, vi. 78.

[2] For the growth in area, &c., see
Brett-James, *Growth of Stuart London*. The bills of mortality give, as
averages to the nearest hundred,
for the three years 1642–4, christenings 9,400; burials 12,100; for the
three years 1662–4, christenings

10,700; burials 16,700; for the three
years 1682–4, christenings, 14,000;
burials 21,500: [T. Birch, ed.],
*Collection of the Yearly Bills of
Mortality*, 1759.

[3] Presumably one of the three
sons of Richard Verney, who was
recognized as Lord Willoughby de
Broke in 1696, by his first wife,
Mary, daughter of Mrs. Evelyn's
uncle Sir John Prettyman; not
further identifiable: Muskett, *Suffolk manorial families*, ii. 302;
G.E.C., art. Willoughby de Broke.

[4] Notice probably suggested by
London Gazette, 23 June (see also
16 June). Armstrong (above, p.

27 Hearing my good & deare friend *Mr. Godolphin* (now Secretary of state[1]) was very ill of a feavor, I went immediately to Lond: in order to visite him at Windsore, where the Court now was:[2] 29 I got to Windsor by nine in the morning, where after I had visited my sick & deare friend, I went to the morning service, one Dr. Fuller[3] Deane of Lincoln preaching an excellent sermon on 10 *Matt:* 28: shewing the unreasonablnes of Atheisme, the necessity & effect of religious feare, the immortality of the humane soule, & the assurance of a future state: I din'd with the Earle of Sunderland, where was my L: Keeper, earle of Sussex,[4] young E. of Essex,[5] L. Alington[6] Constable of the Tower &c: after dinner I stayed with Mr. *Godolphin* now somewhat better; Visited my Lady Bristol, & Arlington, & came back to Lond: before nine at night; [30][a] returned next day home to my house.

July: 2 I went to the Observatorie at Greenewich, where Mr. Flamstead tooke his observations of the Ecclipse of the sunn, now hapning to be almost 3 parts obscur'd:[7] So greate a drowth still continu'd, as never was since my memorie:[8]

6 Our Viccar being now absent, Mr. Meriton[9] supplied on

---

[a] Marginal date.

---

323) had been indicted in London for high treason; for not appearing to plead he stood outlawed and attainted of high treason; his claim that he was now surrendering himself within the time permitted by law was rejected. Two bills for annulling the attainder were brought in in 1689, but failed to pass: *C.J.*, x. 110–11, 289–344; the attainder was reversed on technical grounds in 1694.

[1] He had been appointed on 14 April.

[2] The court had gone to Windsor on 5 April: *London Gazette*, 7 April; it went to Winchester on 26 August; and returned to London on 25 September: ibid., 28 Aug., 29 Sept.

[3] Identifiable as Samuel Fuller (or Fulwar), 1635–1700; D.D. 1679; chaplain in ordinary *c.* 1679–1700; he did not become dean of Lincoln until 1695, but had been chancellor of the diocese since 1670: *D.N.B.*

[4] Above, iii. 592 n. He was a gentleman of the bedchamber from 1680 to 1685.

[5] Above, p. 201.

[6] Above, iii. 553, &c. He was constable of the Tower from 1679 to 1685.

[7] Flamsteed published his observations of this eclipse in *Philosophical Transactions*, xiv (1684), 691–3 (no. 162).

[8] Cf. Luttrell's note in August: i. 314.

[9] Above, p. 333.

1. Pet. 4. 8. shewing the duty of Charity to be our love to
God, & our neighbour, (i) to all men, as his Images; That it
dos not signifie *Almes* to the poore in this place (as many
mistake) which one may do, without any benefit to our selves,
but our love &c to God, &c: The holy Comm: follow'd of
which I participated: *Pomeridiano* the *Curat* as above: I was
exceedingly drowsy; the Lord pardon me:

13 A stranger on 1. Phil: 27. That the chiefe & principle
thing requir'd in a Christian was his conversation, & tenor of
his life; what was meant by becoming, namely the whole
Institution, every Christian Virtue, and improvement: The
Curate afternoone 1. Phil: 27.[1] Concerning our love of God,
the vehemency, & constancy & unsatisfiable desire of frui-
tion, and care to please him.

Some small sprinkling of raine, never so dry a season in my
remembrance, the leaves droping from the Trees as in
Autumn.

20 A stranger preach'd on 1 *Tim:* 3. 4:[2] shewing the infinite
mercy of God, who exclud's none from Salvation; That we
are not to prejudge the very heathen, ill Christians in worse
estate. *Pomeridiano* our Curate on 2. *Matt:* 37.[3] our obligations to love God, & our Neighbour, that is every man, as
the image of God, & of our owne nature &c:

23 I went to Lond. to congratulate the recovery of my
Friend Mr. Godolphin, now made[a] principal Secretary of
state:

25 St. Jam: day Dr. *Meriton* Lecturer at St. *Martines*
preach'd on the 3d of S. *James*: 13. shewing that holy
conversation was wisdome &c. I din'd at my Lord Falklands,[4] Tressurer of the Navy, where after dinner we had
rare Musique, there being amongst others Signor *Pietro
Reggio*[5] and Signor Jo: Battist[6] bothe famous, the one for

---

[a] Followed by *a* apparently deleted.

[1] The text is presumably wrong.
[2] The text is wrong.
[3] A slip for chapter xxii.
[4] Above, p. 318. He was treasurer of the navy from 1681 to 1689.
[5] Above, p. 220.

[6] Identifiable as Giovanni Battista Draghi, *fl.* 1667–1706; organist
to the queen; composer for the
harpsichord, &c.: Eitner, *Quellen-
Lexikon*.

his Voice, & the other his playing on the Harpsichord, few if any in Europe exceeding him, there was also a Frenchman who sung[a] an admirable base.

26 I return'd home, where I found my Lord Chiefe Justice,[1] the Countesse of Clancartie, & the Lady Catharine Fitz Gerald,[2] who dined with me & went back in the Evening to Lond: late:

27 A *stranger* on 2: *Tit:* 11. Concerning the Universality of the Grace of the Gospel, against the prædestinarians: That the heathen have no excuse who live not up to the light of Nature, and the Law written in their heart, much lesse Christians, that sin against the light of Grace &c:

Pomeridiano another stranger on 119 *Psal:* 9, shewing the infinite advantage and happynesse of a Virtuous Youth, through all the successive periods of age, a very excellent discourse.

Aug: 3 Our Viccar on 5 Mat: 5.[b3]—*ne jurare omnino*—shewing what was ment by an Oath, and what our B: Saviour did meane by this prohibition, namely vaine swearing. *See notes*; The Curat afternoone on the former Text, of our obligation to Love God for his love to us: &c: I received the holy Sacrament this Morning, the Lord make me mindfull of my purposes:

8 Came my Lord Falkland to Visite me:

10 Both Viccar & Curate proceeded on their former Texts:

We had now raine after such a drowth as no man living had known in England, to the greate refreshing of the ground.

---

[a] Or *sang*.   [b] Altered from *3*.

---

[1] The lord chief justice of England was Jeffreys, but the person here intended is presumably Sir William Davis, the chief justice of the king's bench of Ireland from 1681 to 1687 and second husband of Lady Clancarty: above, p. 244 n.; F. Elrington Ball, *The judges in Ireland, 1221–1921*, 1927, i. 357–8.

[2] d. 1714 unmarried; sister of Lady Clancarty: Lodge, *Peerage of Ireland*, ed. Archdall, i. 103.

[3] A slip for verse 34. The wording is also wrong: the Vulgate reads 'non jurare omnino'; Beza, 'ne jurate omnino'.

15[a] Dined with us My L. Faulkland, & his Lady:[1]

17 one Dr. Hutchins[2] preached on 2. *Coloss:* 6, concerning walking with God, & what a Christians Walking signified, namely his universal Conversation to be holy and becoming his Calling, ⟨or⟩[b] the rules & precepts of the Gospel &c:

Pomerid: *Mr. Bohune*, on 17: Act: 30: shewing the Certaintie of a Judgement to Come, & therefore the necessitie of Repentance, a very excellent discourse, shewing how, were there no Law given by God, as derived to us from the Scriptures; yet that there is an evil & a good, a natural turpitude, & justice & virtue, writen in every mans heart, so as none are excusable before the righteous God, & thence inferr'd, that none were exempted[c] from reforming their lives & repentance, especialy Christians.

Feavors being now very rife, my Daughter[d] & severall of my family fell sick:

18 I went to see Mr. *Bohune* at Lee my excellent neighbour:

19 I dined at my L: Falklands at the Tressurers house in Deptford:[3] the next day I went to Lond: about buisinesse, returned 22d:

24 St. Bartholomews day our Viccar & Curate preached on their former Text, much of it repetition onely: I was exceedingly drowsy this afternoone it being most excessively hot: we having not had above one or two considerable showres (& they stormes) these eight or nine moneths so as the trees lost their leafe like Winter, & many of them quite died for want of refreshment.

---

[a] Altered from *12*.   [b] MS *oͬ* (abbreviation for *our*).   [c] Altered from *exc-*.   [d] Or *Daughters*.

---

[1] Rebecca, 1662–1709; daughter of Sir Rowland Lytton of Knebworth, Herts.

[2] No doctor of divinity of this name is traceable at this time. For a Dr. Hutchinson at Lee, 1680, see Drake's Hasted, p. 227 n.; he is not traceable elsewhere. The present man is mentioned several times below, and is presumably identical with the Mr. Hutchins, below, p. 460, &c.

[3] The treasurer of the navy's house in the Dockyard: above, iii. 312.

31 Our Viccar proceeded, Pomerid. a stranger on 20 *Exod:* against prophaning the Sabboth: &c.

Now was my deare friend Mr. Secretary Godolphin made Baron of Godolphin:[1]

September[a] 7 Viccar as before: I received the B: Sacrament: Curat 1. Cor: 11. 28. Concerning preparation to the Lords holy Supper:

14 Our Viccar finished his Text this day against Common Swearing, a Vice greately prevailing: The Curat proceeded.

The sister of my deare friend Mrs. Godolphin died on the same day of the moneth of the same distemper six-years[b] after.[2]

21. The Viccar being absent, the Curate preached on 18 *Pro:* 8: against Tale bearers, in which[c] 'tis believed, he reflected upon one who had reproved the scandalous life of his Wife: pomerid: 1. Thess: 4: 11. much to the same effect: [22 I dined at Dr. Parrs, visited Mr. Bowyer.[3]][d] 23: Lord & Lady Falkland came & dined with us:

26 I went to Lond, to Congratulate my deare friend Mr. Sidny Godolphins being created a Baron of England, the King being now returned from Winchester,[4] there was a numerous Court at White-hall where I saluted divers of my acquaintance: There was at this time a remove of the Earle of Rochester from the Treasury[e] to the presidentship of the Council,[f] & my L: Godolphin made first Commissioner of the Treasury in his place, my Lord Midleton a Scot, made Secretary of state:[g][5] These Alterations (being very

---

a Substituted for *Aug.*   b Or *six-yeare.*   c Followed by *he* deleted.   d Interlined.   e MS. *Tres:ry.*   f Followed by *which was* deleted.   g Followed by *in place of Godolphin* deleted.

---

[1] *London Gazette*, 8 Sept.; notice dated 6 Sept. His title was Baron Godolphin of Rialton.

[2] She is not identifiable.

[3] Presumably Anthony Bowyer of Camberwell, *c.* 1633–1709, son of Sir Edmund Bowyer (above, iii. 196) by his first wife; M.P. for Southwark 1685, 1690–8: Foster, *Alumni Oxon.*; Manning and Bray, iii. 408–9.

[4] The court had returned on 25 September: above, p. 383 n.

[5] These changes were made on 24 August: *London Gazette*, 28 Aug. Middleton is Charles Middleton, *c.*

unexpected & mysterious) gave greate occasion of discourse among the Politicians:[1] I supped this night at my *La: Sylvius*, with *Dr. Tenison*, & the afternoone taking the aire in Hide Parke, saw two bucks encounter each other very fiercely for a long willes 'til one was quite vanquished:

There was now an Ambassador from the King of *Siam* from the *E. Indias* to his Majestie.[2]

27 I returned home:

28 Our *Viccar* preach'd on 2: *Mar:* 17. concerning the Calling of Mathew the Publican, and our B: S: conversing with them, shewing how far Religious persons might without sinn, kepe-company or be in conversation with wicked men:[3] See Notes: The *Curate* on 55. *Isay* 6. of seeking the Lord, without procrastination; I was much oppress'd with sleepe:

29 I was let bloud about 8 ounces for the dizzinesse of my head.

Octob: 5 A stranger preached on 1. *Cor:* 11: 28: Concerning preparation to the H: Sacrament, at which I was participant: The Afternoone was so extreamely wet, that we had the Office, & a sermon at home:

6 I tooke a little preventing physick:

⟨12⟩[a] Our Viccar on his former Text, with no greate addition: In the Afternoone the *Curate* of Greenewich on 6. *Luke* 36, on a part of Christs Sermon in the Mount: Exhorting to Mercy, & benignity, from the Example of our B: Savior, & Almight⟨y⟩ God: &c. I afterward visited some friends:

14 I went to Lond: din'd at my Lord Falklands, made visits, & return'd: Mr Boile had now produced his Invention

---

[a] MS. *13.*

1650–1719; second earl of Middleton (Scotland) 1674; created by the Old Pretender earl of Monmouth 1701: *D.N.B.* He continued in office as secretary until 1688; and had been sworn a privy councillor of England on 11 July of this year.

[1] For the general bearing of these changes see Foxcroft, *Halifax,* i.

420–2.

[2] For this ambassador, a member of the Siamese embassy to France, see John Anderson, *English intercourse with Siam in the seventeenth century,* 1890, p. 243; *Cal. S.P., Dom., 1684–5,* p. 149.

[3] St. Matthew's Day falls on 21 September.

of dulcifying Sea-Water, like to be of mighty consequence:[1]

18 I went againe to Lond: about my suite in Chancery, returned in the Evening:

19 Mr. Bohune preached on a former Text: 29: 30,[2] shewing very pressingly the necessity of repentance, from the assurance of an approching Judgement to come, a learned Philosophico Theological discourse:

Afternoone the Curate on 9th Heb: 27: 28. upon almost the former subject, the necessity of preparation, from the frequent burials hapning at this time, by reason of much sicknesse in these quarters:

21[a] I went to Lond: about buisinesse at this Terme:[b][3]

22 Sir William Godolphin and I went to see the Rhinocerous (or Unicorne) being the first that I suppose was ever brought into England: It more ressembled a huge enormous Swine, than any other Beast amongst us; That which was most particular & extraordinary, was the placing of her[c] small Eyes in the very center of her[c] cheekes & head, her[c] Eares in her[c] neck, and very much pointed:[d] her[c] Leggs neere as big about as an ordinarie mans wast, the feete divided into claws, not cloven, but somewhat resembling the Elephants, & very round & flatt, her[c] taile slender and hanging downe over her Sex, which had some long haires at the End of it like a Cowes, & was all the haire about the whole Creature, but what was the most wonderfull, was the extraordinary bulke and Circumference of her body, which though very Young, (they told us as I remember not above 4 yeares old) could not be lesse than 20 foote in compasse: she had a set of most dreadfull teeth, which were extra-

---

[a] Altered from *22*.   [b] Altered from *Tr-*.   [c] Altered from *his*.
[d] Followed by *but* deleted.

---

[1] A machine for the purification of sea-water had been patented by a cousin of Boyle's, Captain R. Fitzgerald; Boyle himself was not immediately concerned, but a letter from him to Beale, approving of the results, is printed in Fitzgerald's *Salt-Water Sweetned*, 1683. For the machine see further *London Gazette*, 16 Oct., 17 Nov. 1684.

[2] Acts xvii. 29, 30: above, p. 386.

[3] Michaelmas Term, beginning on 23 October.

ordinarily broad, & deepe in her Throate, she was led by a ring in her nose like a Buffalo, but the horne upon it was but newly Sprowting, & hardly shaped to any considerable point, but in my opinion nothing was[a] so extravagant as the Skin of the beast, which hung downe on her[b] hanches, both behind and before to her knees, loose like so much Coach leather, & not adhering at all to the body, which had another skin, so as one might take up this, as one would do a Cloake or horse-Cloth to a greate depth, it adhering onely at the upper parts: & these lappets of stiff skin, began to be studdied with impenetrable Scales, like a Target of coate of maile, loricated like Armor, much after the manner this Animal is usualy depicted: she was of a mouse Colour, the skin Elephantine; Tame enough, & suffering her mouth to be open'd by her keeper, who caus'd her to lie downe, when she appeared like a [greate][c] Coach overthrowne, for she was much of that bulke, yet would rise as nimbly as ever I saw an horse: T'was certainly a very wonderfull creature, of immense strength in the neck, & nose especialy, the snout resembling a boares but much longer; to what stature she may arive if she live long, I cannot tell; but if she grow proportionable to her present age, she will be a Mountaine: They fed her with Hay, & Oates, & gave her bread.

She belonged to Certaine E. *Indian Merchants*, & was sold for (as I remember) above two-thousand pounds:[1]

At the same time I went to see a living Crocodile, brought from some of the W: Indian Ilands, in every respect resembling

---

[a] Followed by *more* deleted. [b] Altered from *his*. [c] Interlined.

---

[1] For this animal see Lady Newdigate-Newdegate, *Cavalier and Puritan*, pp. 245–6; North, *Life of Guilford*, p. 280. She was put up to auction, and sold for £2,320; but the purchaser failing to pay, no one would bid at a second auction. She was then put on view 'at twelve pence apiece, and two shillings those that ride him. They get fifteen pound a day'. This was at the Belle Savage Inn on Ludgate Hill: *London Gazette*, 13, 20, 30 Oct. She apparently remained on exhibition until 14 April 1686: ibid., 22 March 1686. For the rhinoceros as commonly represented at this time see J. Bontius, *Hist. naturalis* . . . *Indiæ orientalis*, p. 51, printed with G. Piso, *De Indiæ utriusque re naturali*, &c., 1658.

the Egyptian Crocodile, it was not yet fully 2 yards from head
to taile, very curiously scaled & beset with impenetrable
studds of a hard horny substance, & most beautifully ranged
in works especialy on the ridge of the back & sides, of a dusky
greene Colour, save the belly, which being tender, & onely
vulnerable, was of a lively & lovely greene, as lizards are,
whose shape it exactly kept: The Eyes were sharp & piercing, over which it could at pleasure draw up a thin cobweb
skinn: The rictus was exceeding deepe set with a tirrible
rank of sharp & long teeth: We could not discerne any
tongue, but a small lump of flesh at the very bottome of its
throate, which I suppose helped his swallowing: the feete
were divided into long fingers as the Lizards, & he went forward wadling, having a chaine about the neck: seemed to be
very tame; I made its keeper take up his upper jaw which he
affirmed did onely move, & so Pliny & others confidently
report;[1] but it[a] did not appeare so plaine to me, whither his
keeper did not use some dexterity in opening his mouth &
placing his head so as to make it seeme that the upper chap,
was[b] loose; since in that most ample & perfect sceleton in our
Repositarie at the R: Society,[2] it is manifestly fixed to the
neck & Vertebræ: the neither jaw onely loose: They kept the
beast or Serpent in a longish Tub of warme Water, & fed
him with flesh &c: If he grow, it will be a dangerous Creature.

Octob: 23 I dined at Sir Stephen Foxes with the Duke of
Nor⟨t⟩humberland[3] another of his Majesties natural sonns, by
that strumpet Cleaveland: He seemed to be a Young gent,
of good capacity, well bred, civile, & modest, had ben newly[c]
come from Travell, & had made his Campagne at the siege
of Luxemburg: Of all his Majesties Children, (of which he had

---

[a] Followed by *ap-* deleted.   [b] Followed by *the* deleted.   [c] Followed
by *in the* deleted.

---

[1] Pliny, *Nat. hist.*, bk. viii, ch. 25
(37).
[2] For it see Grew, *Musæum
Regalis Societatis*, pp. 42–5, where
the various features are discussed;
according to some writers some

Panama alligators attained a length
of a hundred feet: ibid., p. 41.
I have found no further notice of
the present animal.
[3] Above, p. 374; he was now
nearly nineteen years old.

now 6 Dukes[1]) this seemed the most accomplished, and worth the owning; he is likewise extraordinary handsome & perfectly shaped: what the Dukes of Richmond, & *St. Albans*, base sonns of the Dutchesse of Portsmouth a French Lasse, and of *Nelly*, the Comedian & Apple-woma⟨n⟩s daughter,[2] will prove their youth dos not yet discover, farther than that they are both very pretty[a] boys, & seeme to have more Witt than [most of][b] the rest:

25 I visited Mr. Rob: Boyle with whom I staied most part of the afternoone, discoursing of various Philosophical subjects:

26 At White-hall, *Coram Rege*, preached Dr. *Goodman*,[3] on 2: *James* 12 concerning the Law of liberty, namely, that it was the Law of Christ in the Gospel, in opposition to the ritual & Mosaical Law: and was so much easier & profitable than the other, that the offenders against it, should be judged by it, with all reasonable abatements, upon[c] true Repentance, which made it the more heynous in the offenders: It was an excellent discourse, & in good Method: This Doctor is Author of the Prodigal son; a Treatise worthy reading, [and another of the old Religion.][d]

I dined at my sonns, now newly being come to his new house & house-keeping:[4] My Daughter in Law ready to lie-in of her 4th Child: Thence I went to *St. Clements*[5] (that prettyly

---

[a] Followed by *youth* deleted.   [b] Interlined.   [c] Followed by *repe*- deleted.   [d] Apparently added to the original text.

[1] Besides the three here named there were Monmouth, Southampton (Charles Fitzroy, 1662–1730: *D.N.B.*), and Grafton.

[2] Nothing certain is known of Nell Gwyn's mother beyond the fact that she fell into a fish-pond and was drowned in 1679; contemporaries said that she was drunk at the time: Cunningham, *Story of Nell Gwyn*.

[3] Dr. John Goodman: above, p. 198. The books here mentioned are *The Penitent Pardoned: or a Discourse of the Nature of Sin, and the Efficacy of Repentance, under the*

Parable of the Prodigal Son, 1679 (new ed. 1683), and *The Old Religion Demonstrated in its Principles, and described in the Life and Practice thereof,* published this year (advertised in *Term Catalogues* for November: ii. 91).

[4] See above, p. 375; below, p. 395; for the child, p. 396.

[5] St. Clement Danes. The rebuilding of the church, with the exception of the tower, had begun in 1680; the principal part of the work appears to have been completed by now: Wren Soc., x. 108–11.

built & contrived Church) where a Young Divine gave us an eloquent sermon on 1. *Cor:* 6. 20: inciting to Gratitude, & glorifying of God for the fabric of our bodys & the dignitie of our nature:

26 I attended the Chancery in Westminster Hall, where I had a Cause pleaded, giving reasons for the changing of the Master who had made an injurious Accompt, in the difference betwixt me & Mr. Pretyman:[a] my L: Chan: was pleas'd to grant our plea:[1]

27 I din'd & went to Visite my Lord Chamberlaine now returned from the Countrie, where dined the black Baron,[2] & Monsieur Flamerin,[3] who had so long ben banish'd France for a duel:

28[b] Being S. Sim: & Judes, I carried my Lord Clarendon through the Citty amidst all the Squibbs & barbarous bacchanalia of the Lord-Majors shew, to the *R: Society*, where he was proposed a Member, and then Treated him at dinner:[4]

30[c] I returned home to Says-Court:

[31 I was this day 64 yeares of Age: Lord teach me to number my daies &c—][d]

November 1 Was a meeting of The Trustees for the poore: who dined together &c:

2 Our *Viccar* proceeded on his former Text: the holy

---

[a] MS. *Pretym̄:*   [b] Altered from *29*?   [c] Altered from *29*.
[d] Interlined (probably when notice for 4 Nov. was written).

---

[1] See above, pp. 339–40, &c. Lord chancellor is a mistake for lord keeper.

[2] I have not found this sobriquet elsewhere. About 1691 Halifax is called 'the black Marquis': Foxcroft, *Halifax*, ii. 134, 147; but he is scarcely admissible here. Perhaps it applies to a foreign nobleman.

[3] François de Grossolles, marquis de Flamarens, d. 1706; the duel for which he was exiled took place in 1662: de la Chenaye-Desbois and Badier, ix. 929; Hartmann, *Charles II and Madame*, pp. 59, 63. He is traceable here in 1686 and 1689: Dangeau, *Journal*, ed. Soulié, &c., 1854–60, i. 278, ii. 374.

[4] The lord mayor's swearing-in and show took place not on SS. Simon and Jude, 28 October, but—as usual—on 29 October: *London Gazette*, 30 Oct. The Royal Society's meeting was also held on 29 October: Birch, iv. 324–5. Clarendon's nomination is not mentioned in Birch; he was elected a fellow on 1 December.

Comm: followed at[a] which I was participant: So suddaine an alteration from temperate warme weather to an excessive cold, raine, frost, snow & storme, as had seldome ben knowne, this Winter weather beginning as early & firce, as the past did late, & neere christmas, till which there had hardly ben any winter at all: *Buda* in *Hungary* yet besieg'd: by the DD: of Lorrain & Bavaria, to the losse of many brave commande⟨r⟩s & men:[1]

4. I went to *Lond:* 5t Dr. Turner now translated from Rochester to Ely upon[b] the death of Dr. Peter Gunning,[2] preached *coram Rege* at W.hall on 3. *Rom:* 8, a very excellent sermon, vindicating the Church of England against the Church of Roomes pernicious Doct⟨r⟩ines, of the lawfullnesse of doing evil upon a good intent, proving that to be no ways justifiable in the least instance: one thing very observable, in reguard of the common imputation of the Episcopal Cleargies being inclin'd to Popery; He challenged the producing but of 5[e] Cleargy-men, ⟨who⟩[d] forsooke our church, & went over to Roome, during all the troubles & Rebellion in England, which lasted neere 20 yeares, among 10000 of them: And this was to my certaine observation a greate truth:

6[e] I delivered my Petition to his Majestie for reliefe against my grand suite, who referr'd it to the Lords Commissioners of the Treasury:[3] Supped with L: Clarendon &c:

---

a Altered from *of.*   b Substituted for *by.*   c Followed by *men* deleted.   d MS. *whô.*   e Altered from or to 7.

---

[1] *London Gazette,* 3 Nov., &c. The siege of Buda by the Imperialists began about 15 July, N.S., and was raised on 29 October, N.S. The duke of Lorraine is Charles V (IV) Leopold, 1643–90; duke 1675; imperial general: *Allgemeine deutsche Biog.* The duke of Bavaria is Maximilian II Emanuel, 1662–1726; elector of Bavaria 1679: ibid.

[2] Gunning had died on 6 July; Dr. Francis Turner was confirmed bishop of Ely on 23 August. His sermon was printed in 1685.

[3] The petition was made by Evelyn and his wife. There was owing to Sir Richard Browne, for his expenses and allowances while resident in France, the sum of £11,846. William Prettyman, who was now heavily in debt to the king, was suing the Evelyns for £4,181. 17s. and thirty years' interest, being money remitted by him to Browne in France. The Evelyns ask for the grant of an instalment on Prettyman's debt to the king, which they are willing to accept as so much paid on account of the sum owing to them. The petition was referred to

8 I returned home &c:

9 Our Viccar pursu'd his former Text: The Curate 6: *Gal:* 7:

12 I went to Lond: about my processe:

15 Being the Queenes Birth-day, there was such fire works upon the Thames before White-hall, with pageants of Castles, Forts, & other devices of Gyrandolas, Serpents, The King & Queenes Armes & mottos, all represented in fire, as had not ben seene in any age remembred here: but that which was most remarkable was the several fires & skirmishes in the very water, which actualy moved a long way, burning under the water, & now and then appearing above it, giving reports like Muskets & Cannon, with Granados, & innumerable other devices: It is said this sole Triumph cost 1500 pounds: which was concluded with a Ball, where all the young Ladys & Gallants daunced in the greate Hall: The Court had not ben seene so brave & rich in apparell since his Majesties restauration:[1]

16 I received the B: Sacrament at St. James: & then at White hall Dr. Jeane[2] (Regius professor Oxon:) preach⟨ed⟩ incomparably on 17: *Act:* 30, *see Notes*: I din'd at Sir W: Godolphins: returned home the 18: having made a Visite in the morning to The Arch-bishop of Canterbury at Lambeth &c:

21 I went to *Lond:* 23 Dr. *Ironside*[3] preach'd on 1. *Pet:* 4. 15.— 26 I went to the R: *Society*, where I was in the chaire in absence of the President:[4]

26[a] Was my Sons Wife brought to bed of a Daughter at hir house in Arundel streete neere *Norfolck house,*[5] & Christned

---

ᵃ Reading doubtful.

---

the commissioners of the treasury on 6 November: *Cal. S.P., Dom., 1684–5*, pp. 198–9. Further notices below.

[1] Luttrell, i. 320; for the finery at the ball see *Hist. MSS. Comm., Portland MSS.*, iii. 383; for the Great Hall, above, iii. 569 n.

[2] Jane: above, p. 260.

[3] Above, p. 87. The sermon was printed in 1685.

[4] Birch, iv. 333–7, where, however, Evelyn's taking the chair is not mentioned.

[5] Arundel House: above, iii. 234, 595. In Ogilby and Morgan's map, 1682, the east side and the northern part of the west side of Arundel

by the Curate of St. Clements in the Chamber, the Godfather
my Nephew Glanvil, Godmother the Lady Anderson, & my
Niepce Mary Evelyn, who named it Elizabeth,[1] the name of
my Lady Anderson: [30][a] St *Andrews Day*. It was Christned
on *Sonday* 30: November:—In the morning cor: Rege at
⟨White-hall⟩[b] preached *Dr. Finnes*[2] sonn of the L: Say &
Seale, on 21 *Joshua* 11:

December. St. Andrews day being on the Sonday, our
Election & meeting of the R: Society was on [1][a] Moneday,
when I brought the Duke of Norfolck & Earle of Clarendon
to the Society, who being first ballotted & chosen, tooke their
places, & were after chosen also of the Council for this yeare,
as was also myselfe: Mr. *Pepys*, Secretary of the Admiralty
elected President.[3]

3 I carried Monsieur *Justell*, & *Slingsby* Master of the Mint
to see Mr. Sheldons collection of Medaills;[4] The series of
Popes was rare, & so was[c] among the Moderns several,
especialy that of *John Husses* Martyrdome at Constance;[5]

---

[a] Marginal date. [b] MS. *Whate-hall*. [c] Or *were*.

Street are shown as built; the area
between it and Surrey Street and to
the south of (approximately) Howard Street is marked as the site for
a new Arundel House, which was
never built.

[1] d. 1760; married, 1709, Simon
Harcourt, 1684–1720, son of Simon
Harcourt, first Viscount Harcourt
(below, 2 March 1701), and father
of Simon Harcourt, first Earl Harcourt: *D.N.B.*, art. Harcourt, Simon,
first Viscount.

[2] No D.D. of this name is known.
Possibly Pharamus Fiennes, born *c.*
1647; grandson of William Fiennes,
1582-1662, eighth (or second) Baron
and first Viscount Saye and Sele;
B.C.L. 1674; rector of Weston-sub-
Edge 1685: Foster.

[3] Birch, iv. 337–8. Norfolk is
Henry Howard, the seventh duke
(above, iii. 329), having succeeded

on 13 January of this year. He had
been elected F.R.S. in 1672, and
was not re-elected. Pepys had been
reappointed secretary of the Admiralty on 10 June of this year, and
remained in office until 20 Feb. 1689.

[4] Ralph Sheldon, b. 1623; died
on 24 June of this year; he had bequeathed his collection to his cousin
Frances Sheldon, a sister of the
present Lady Tuke and at this time
a maid of honour to the queen:
E. A. B. Barnard, *The Sheldons*,
1936, pp. 56–72; for the collection
see also Evelyn to Pepys, 12 Aug.
1689 (Bohn, iii. 300); *Numismata*,
p. 245.

[5] John Hus, *c.* 1373–1415, the re-
former: *Nouvelle biog. gén.* There
were a number of medals showing
him being burnt: Count F. H. H. V.
Lützow, (*John Hus*), 1909, p. 319.

of the Roman Emp: Consulars; some Greeke, &c both Coper, Gold, Sil: not many of truely antient; a Medalion of *Otho*,[1] *P: Æmil*:[2]   , &c, hardly antient. They were held a thousand pound price, but not worth I judge above 200 pound, [there being many not truely antique:][a]

7 To the House-hold at W.hall preached *Dr. Calamy* on I. *Cor:* II. 29.[3] The holy Communion follow'd at which I was partaker: Then to his Majestie preached Dr. Patrick, on 15 *Rom:* 5: *Pomeridiano* I went to see the new church St. *James'*,[4] elegantly indeede built, especialy adorn'd was the Altar, the white Marble Enclosure curiously & richly carved, & the flowres & Garlands about the Walls by Mr. *Gibbons* in Wood, a *Pelican* with her young at her breast just over the Altar in the Carved Compartment and bordure, in-vironing the purple-velvet, richly frenged, with H$\overset{+}{\text{I}}$S richly embrodred, & most noble Plate were given by Sir R: Geere[5]— to the value (as was said) of 200 pounds: such an Altar was no were in any Church in England, nor have I seene any abroad more handsomly adorn'd: Dr. *Etcher*[6] preached an Excellent Sermon on: 119 *Psal:* 165 ver: concerning the

---

[a] Added later.

---

[1] For coins of Otho see *Numismata*, pp. 205, 211. The large copper Otho was rare: L. Jobert, *The knowledge of medals*, trans. O. Walker, 1697, pp. 15, 186–7.

[2] Lucius Aemilius Paulus (Paullus), *c.* 229–160 B.C., the general: Pauly.

[3] Possibly the sermon on this text printed in Calamy's *Sermons preached upon several occasions*, 1687, pp. 37–65.

[4] St. James's, Piccadilly; it had been consecrated on 13 July of this year: Newcourt, *Repertorium*. Descriptions in Wren Soc., x. 27 (following apparently C. Wren, *Parentalia*, 1750); [E. Hatton], *A new view of London*, 1708, i. 298–9; Strype's Stow, vi. 81–2; see also Luttrell, i. 313–14. Gibbons's carving

survives but the velvet has gone and modern painted decoration has been introduced; for what was apparently the original arrangement see Clayton, in Wren Soc., ix. 31. The exterior of the church has been somewhat altered; and the turret is not by Wren. [The church was badly damaged by German bombs in 1940.]

[5] Robert Gayer or Gayre, *d.* 1702 (admitted at Cambridge 1651); K.B. 1661: Venn; Lipscomb, (*Buckinghamshire*), iv. 554. The church still possesses some plate dated 1683.

[6] Presumably John Eachard, 1637–97; D.D. 1676; reputed author of *The Grounds & Occasions of the Contempt of the Clergy and Religion enquired into*, 1670: D.N.B.

internal peace of Religious persons: I went to visite my Lady Berkeley, & Yarborow:

8 My greate buisinesse was heard at the Treasury:

9 I returned home to my house whence my buisinesse had 'til now kept me.

12 I went againe to Lond, about my processe, and buisinesse with the Treasury &c:

14 Dr. *Patrick* deane of Peterboro, preach'd before the house-hold on 24 *Act:* 16 shewing what was meant by a good Conscience towards God; viz, all the duties of an holy man and Christian as to Faith and practise:[a] *Coram Rege*: Dr. *Calamie*, on 10: *Act:* 38,[1] of the virtue of Charity, and obligation of Doing good, from the example of our B: Saviour: That there was yet little hope of profiting by Preaching the duty &c. so long as Greate persons, Magistrates & men in high place lived ill lives, & gave so ill example, which was very boldly, but seasonably & truely said.

17 Early in the morning I went into St. James's Park to see three Turkish or Asian Horses, brought newly over, and now first shewed his Majestie: There were 4 of them it seemes in all, but one of them died at sea, being 9 weekes coming from Hamborow: They were taken from a Bashaw at the seige of *Vienna* in Austria, the late famous raising that Leaguer:[2] & with mine Eyes never did I behold so delicate a Creature as was one of them, of somwhat a bright bay, two white feete, a blaze; such an head, [Eye,][b] eares, neck, breast, belly, buttock, Gaskins,[3] leggs, pasterns, & feete in all reguards beautifull & proportion'd to admiration, spiritous & prowd, nimble, making halt, turning with that sweiftnesse & in so small a compase as was incomparable, with all this so gentle & tractable, as called to mind what I remember

---

[a] Followed by *Pomeridiano* deleted. [b] Interlined.

---

[1] Probably the sermon on this text printed in Calamy's *Sermons*, 1687, pp. 1–35.

[2] Sobieski had relieved Vienna in September 1683: above, p. 340.

The three horses cannot be identified or traced; the prices were 'exorbitant': C. M. Prior, *The Royal Studs*, 1935, p. 83.

[3] The hinder thighs: *O.E.D.*

Busbequius[1] speakes of them; to the reproch of our Groomes in *Europ* who bring them up so churlishly,[a] as makes our horse most of them to retaine so many ill habits &c: They trotted like Does,[b] as if they did not feele the Ground; for this first Creature was demanded 500 Ginnies, for the 2d 300, which was of a brighter bay, for the 3d 200 pound, which was browne, all of them choicely shaped, but not altogether so perfect as the first. In a word, it was judg'd by the Spectators, (among whom was the King, Prince of Denmark, the Duke of Yorke, and severall of the Court Noble persons skilled in Horses, especialy Monsieur Faubert & his sonn & Prevost, Masters of the Accademie and esteemed of the best in Europe), that there were never seene any horses in these parts, to be compared with them: Add to all this, the Furniture which consisting of Embrodrie on the Saddle, Housse, Quiver, bow, Arrows, Symeter, Sword, Mace or Battel ax a la *Tur⟨c⟩isque*: the Bashaws Velvet Mantle furr'd with the most perfect Ermine I ever beheld, all the Yron worke in other furnitur being here of silver curiously wrought & double gilt, to an incredible value: Such, and so extraordinary was the Embrodery, as I never before saw any thing approching it, the reines & headstall crimson silk, covered with Chaines of silver gilt: There was also a Turkish royal standard of an horses taile, together with all sorts of other Caparison belonging to a Generals horse: by which one may estimate how gallantly & ⟨magnificently⟩[c] those Infidels appeare in the fild, for nothing could certainely be seene more glorious, The Gent: (a German) who rid the horse, being in all this garb: They were shood with yron made round & closed at the heele, with an hole in the middle about as wide as a shilling; the hoofes most intire:

---

[a] Followed by *and* deleted.   [b] Reading doubtful.   [c] MS. *mignificently*.

---

[1] Ogier-Ghislain de Busbecq, 1522–92, imperial ambassador in Constantinople 1555–62: *Biog. nat. de Belgique*. The work here referred to is his *Legationis Turcicæ Epistolæ quatuor*, first published in 1589, and frequently reprinted (first English trans. 1694). The gentleness of the Turkish grooms is described in the third letter.

I dined with severall Gent: of the R: Society, going to[a] Gr: Colledge after, where was the experiment of *Dr. Papins* Syphon: &c:

18 Mr. *Faubert* having newly railed in a Manage & fitted it for the Academy,[1] I went with my Lord *Cornwallis*[2] to see the Young Gallants do their Exercise: There were the Dukes of Norfolck & Northumberland, Lord Newburge,[3] and a Nephew of the Earle of Feversham:[4] The exercises were first running at the ring, next flinging a Javlin at a Mores head, 3d, discharging a Pistol at a Mark, lastly, the taking up a ⟨Gauntlet⟩[b] with the point of the Sword, all these ⟨Exercises⟩[c] performed in full speede: The D: of Northumberland, hardly miss'd succeeding in every one a douzen times as I think: Next the D: of Norfolck did exceeding bravely: *Newburge & Duras* seemed to be nothing so dextrous: here I saw the difference of what the French call *bell-homme a Cheval*, & *bonn homme a Chevall*,[5] the D: of Norfolck being the first, that is rather a fine person on an horse; The D: of Northumberland being both, in perfection, namely a most gracefull person, & excellent rider:[a] But the Duke of *Norfolck* told me he had not ben at this exercise this twelve yeare[d] before:[6] There were in the fild the Prince of *Denmark* & the L: Landsdown,[7] sonn of

---

[a] Followed by *the* deleted.   [b] MS. *Gauntled*.   [c] MS. *Execrsises*, altered from *Execrc-*.   [d] Or *years*.

---

[1] The position of the manage is unknown. The ground to the north of Brewer Street (above, p. 257 n.) was still open about 1682, but was being built over as far north as Beak Street by about 1685: Kingsford, *Piccadilly*, pp. 117–18.

[2] See above, p. 219.

[3] Charles Livingston, *c.* 1662/6–94; second earl of Newburgh (Scotland) 1670: G.E.C. His mother was Catherine, daughter of Theophilus Howard, second earl of Suffolk.

[4] For Feversham (Duras) see above, p. 77. His nephew is probably Armand de Bourbon, marquis de Miremont, 1656–1732: (*Westminster Abbey registers*), pp. 355–6.

[5] Pluvinel explains to Louis XIII that to be 'bel homme de cheval' it is necessary to consider only 'la bonne grace', the rider's appearance and position on horseback; the 'bon homme de cheval' is the accomplished horseman, who will necessarily be also 'bel homme de cheval': A. de Pluvinel, *Le Maneige royal*, 1623, pp. 4–5; same, ed. Charnizay, as part of his *L'Exercice de monter à cheval*, 1660, ii. 13–15.

[6] He was born in 1655.

[7] Charles Granville, 1661–1701; son of John Granville, earl of Bath; styled Lord Lansdown from birth; created a count of the Holy Roman Empire 27 January of this year

the Earle of Bath, who had ben made a Count of the Empire last summer for his service before Vienna.

20 I returned home to my house to keepe Christmas now approching:

A villanous Murder perpetrated by *Mr. St. Johns*,[a] (eldest sonn to Sir Walter,[b] a worthy Gent:) on a knight of quality in a Tavern: The Offender being Sentenced, & Repriv'd, so many horrid murders & Duels about this time being committed (as was never heard of in England) gave much cause of complaint & murmure universaly.[1]

21 St. *Thomas's* day & *Sonday*, my Rheume & cold was so greate, that it kept me from Church:

25 *Christmas-day*, o⟨u⟩r *Viccar* preach'd on 11: *Matt:* 3. 4. 5. shewing why Christ was sent to by John the Bap: to know whether he was the *Messias*; not, 'tis likely, but that *John* knew he was, but to confirme his disciples, who might be in doubt: The wonders he did before them shewing plainely what he was without neede of farther answer: I received the B: Communion:

28 Our Viccar onely repeated: In the afternoone it was such terrible weather that we heard prayers at home: 29. I entertained my Neighbours: as accostom'd:

31 I spent this day (as usualy) in recollecting the passages of the yeare now past, making up all my Accompts, & giving God thanks for his greate mercys the last yeare &c:

---

[a] Or *St. Johne.*   [b] MS. has here a second opening bracket.

(presumably N.S.) on account of his services at the siege of Vienna; summoned to parliament 1689 as Lord Granville; second earl of Bath 1701: G.E.C.

[1] St. John is Henry St. John, of Battersea, 1652–1742; son of Walter St. John, *c.* 1622–1708, third baronet 1657; fourth baronet 1708; created Viscount St. John 1716; father of the statesman: G.E.C. On 14 October he and a Colonel Edmund Webb murdered Sir William Estcourt, third baronet (G.E.C. *Baronetage*, ii. 11), in a drunken quarrel at the Globe Tavern in Fleet Street. They were tried at the Old Bailey between 10 and 13 of this month and were convicted; but were reprieved by 13 and pardoned by 27 of this month; the king granted St. John a restitution of his estates on 30 December: *Notes and Queries*, clxii (1932), 57–9, and documents there quoted; *Cal. Treasury books, 1681–5*, p. 1472; see also Burnet, *Own time*, ed. Airy, ii. 447.

168⅘ *Jan:* 1 I implord the continuance of Gods mercy & providence for the yeare now enter'd; & went to the Publique Prayers &⟨c⟩. It proved so sharp weather and so long & cruel frost that the Thames was frozen crosse, but the frost often dissolved, & froze againe:[1]

4 Our *Viccar* altogether repeated, shewing the danger of the now universal neglect of the Lords Supper, of which I this day communicated, the Lord improve it to me: *Amen.*

There happn'd nothing this weeke worthy of note:

11 Mr. Bohune preached on his former Text & subject 17: Act: 30, *nunc omnibus ubique hominibus ut resipiscant:*[2] shewing the necessity of Repentance, & how we in this time of so much light have more obligation to live religiously than the former; deploring the Atheisme & evil Doctrines, & Schismes, especialy Socinianisme & Quakerisme broken in upon the Church &c:

Pomeridiano, a Young man upon 13. *Luke* 5. Concerning also the necessity of Repentance; after the presbyterian tedious method, & repetition:[3]

14 To Lond: about my tedious Chancery suit: 18th Dr. *Cave* preach'd before the King on 4: *Psal:* 8. shewing how infinitely the joy & satisfaction of Religious persons exceeded that of the Ungodly &c:[4] 23. I dind at my L: *Sunderlands:* 24 at my L: Newports,[5] who has some excellent pictures, especialy that of Sir Tho: Hanmers of V: Dyke, one of the best he ever painted:[6] another of our English Dobsons

---

[1] Luttrell notes the frost in the early part of January; it was possible to cross the Thames on the ice about Chelsea. See also Wood, *Life and times*, iii. 123.

[2] See above, pp. 386, 389. The text is quoted from Beza's translation.

[3] Nonconformist preaching from the middle of the century onwards appears to have been non-literary and dull; but Evelyn perhaps refers to the pre-Restoration period; by 1685 nonconformist sermons had become plain: Mitchell, *English pulpit oratory, passim.*

[4] The sermon was printed this

year (Evelyn cites the text from the Prayer Book).

[5] Above, iii. 526 (Lady Newport, p. 170). He was at this time treasurer of the household.

[6] For Hanmer see above, iii. 191. The present portrait is perhaps that now belonging to Mr. J. L. Severance of Cleveland, Ohio: Glück, *Van Dyck*, p. 438; it can scarcely be the destroyed portrait formerly belonging to Sir H. C. J. Bunbury, into whose possession it appears to have descended from the Hanmers: Sir T. Hanmer, *Garden book*, ed. Rohde, introd., p. xxxii.

painting:^a 1 but above all, that *Christo*^b in gremio² of *Pussine,*
an admirable piece, with something of most other famous
hands: 25. Dr. Dove preached *coram Rege* on 16. *Act:* 4: 5.
shewing that the Church ever had a power to make, and
impose her decrees, for the better government thereof; &
how her members are oblig'd to receive & observe them:³
[I saw this evening such a sceane of profuse gaming, and
luxurious dallying & prophanesse, the King in the middst of
his 3 concubines, as I had never before:]^c⁴

27 I dind at my Lord *Sunderlands*⁵ invited to heare that
celebrated voice of Mr. *Pordage*⁶ newly come from *Rome,* his
singing was after the Venetian Recitative, as masterly as
could be, & with an excellent voice both Treble & base:
Dr. Wallgrave^d accompanied it with his *Theorba Lute* on
which he perform'd beyond imagination, and is doubtlesse
one of the greatest Masters in Europ on that charming
Instrument: *Pordage* is a *Priest* as Mr. *Bernard Howard*⁷ told
me in private:

There was in the roome where we din'd, & in his bed-
chamber Those incomparable pieces of Columbus, a flagella-
tion, The Grammer schoole,⁸ The *Venus & Adonis* of *Titian,*⁹
& of Van Dykes That picture of the late Earle of Digby

---

¹ William Dobson, 1610–46; fol-
lower of Van Dyck: *D.N.B.*; Thieme,
Lexikon.

² i.e. the Virgin mourning over
Christ. The picture is not identifiable.

³ The sermon was printed this
year.

⁴ This passage was presumably
inserted at the same time as the
fuller account on pp. 413–14. The
date to which it is attached was
probably fixed by calculation.

⁵ As secretary of state Sunder-
land had lodgings in Whitehall.

⁶ There was in 1687 and 1688 a
singer or musician of this name on

the establishment of James II's
Roman Catholic Chapel Royal: *Cal.
Treasury books, 1685–9,* pp. 1442,
1822; he was probably not a priest.
For a Roman Catholic family of this
name see Foley, (*Jesuit records*), v.
565–6.

⁷ Above, iii. 329.

⁸ Presumably the 'Schoolmistress'
formerly attributed to Lodovico
Carracci and now to Michael
Sweerts; now belonging to Earl
Spencer at Althorp: *Catalogue of the
Exhibition of 17th century art in
Europe,* Royal Academy, 1938, no.
215.

⁹ See above, p. 162.

(father of the Countesse of Sunderland) & E: of Bedford,[1]
Sir Kenhelme Digby,[2] & 2 other Ladys,[3] of ⟨incomparable⟩[a]
performance, besides the Moses & burning bush of *Bassano*,[4]
& several other pieces of the best Masters: a Marble head of
M: Brutus &c:

28 I was solemnly invited to my L: Arundel of Wardour,[5]
(now newly releas'd of his 6 yeares confinement in the Tower,
upon suspicion of the plot, called Oates's plot) where after
dinner the same Mr. *Pordage* entertained us with his voice,
that excellent & stupendious Artist Signor Jo: Baptist,[6]
playing to it on the Harpsichord: My Daughter Mary being
with us, she also sung to the greate satisfaction of[b] both
Masters, & a world of people of quality present: as she also
did at my Lord Rochesters the Evening following, when we
had the *French boy*[7] so fam'd for his singing: & indeede he had
a delicate voice, & had ben well taught:

I also heard Mrs. Packer[8] (daughter to my old friend) sing
before his Majestie & the Duke privately, That stupendious
Base *Gosling*,[9] accompanying her, but hers was so lowd, as
tooke away much of the sweetenesse: certainely never woman
had a stronger, or better ⟨voice⟩[c] could she possibly have
govern'd it: She would do rarely in a large Church among
the Nunns:

30 Being the day of K. *Charles* Is Martyrdom, The Bish:

---

a MS. *inconparable*.   b Followed by *a num-* deleted.   c Reading
doubtful; perhaps altered to *eare*.

---

[1] See above, p. 162.
[2] Perhaps an error for the portrait
of Sir Kenelm Digby by Cornelius
Jansen: T. F. Dibdin, *Aedes Althorpianae*, 1822, p. 265.
[3] Presumably Van Dyck's double
portrait of Catherine, Countess
Rivers, and Lady Elizabeth
Thimbleby, bought by Sunderland
from Lely's collection in 1682 and
now belonging to Earl Spencer at
Althorp: *Catalogue . . . 17th century
art*, as above, no. 79.
[4] This is not traceable among the
pictures by Bassano in Dibdin's

Aedes Althorpianae.
[5] He had been released in February 1684: above, p. 366.
[6] Draghi: above, p. 384.
[7] Presumably the boy mentioned
below, p. 413.
[8] Packer had four daughters.
[9] John Gostling, *c.* 1650–1733;
minor canon of Canterbury 1674–
1733; minor canon of St. Paul's
1683–90; prebendary of Lincoln
1689–1733; a gentleman of the
Chapel Royal 1679 apparently
until death: *D.N.B.*

of Ely[1] preached on 5 *Matt:* 28. being an historical Oration, perstringing now & then the severall dangerous Tenents[a][2] of those pretended Reformists, who in divers of their Writings have favour'd the Killing of Kings, whom they found not complying with their discipline; among these (after he had deduced that wicked doctrine of divers Popes & their Doctors &c) he reckoned *Calvine* ⟨who⟩[b] implicitly verges that way; & observed that not one of all the Regicides exe- cuted for the Murder so barbarously perpetrated this day, shewed any signes of remorse. After Sermon I returned home.

Feb: 1 Our Viccar proceeded on his former Text 11: *Matt:* shewing the reasonablenesse of believing the Christian Reli- gion, by the Miracles don by our B: Saviour, and the truth of those Miracles, with such other Arguments as are usualy produc'd: & that there was as full demonstration of it, as the nature of any Historical truth is capable of, & in some sort more, viz, the suffering condition, & no human or secular advantages of the preachers & promoters of it: Thereupon upbraiding the Atheisme & incredulity of the Age; & how it would turne to their greater condemnation: The bl: Sacra- ment follow'd of which I was partaker:

Pomerid: the *Curate* on 1: *Jam:* ult: shewing how little all other acts of devotion would stead, without purity & charity: I was exceedingly drowsy: The Lord pardon my infirmitie:

4 I went to Lond, hearing his Majestie had ben the moneday before surpriz'd in his bed chamber with an Apoplectical fit,[3]

---

a MS. *Tenēts*.   b MS. *whô*.

---

[1] Turner. The sermon was printed this year; the text is Acts v. 28.

[2] At this time more frequently used than tenets: *O.E.D.*

[3] Charles had fallen ill on the morning of Monday, 2 February; the fact that he was ill appears to have been known in London that afternoon; the first printed state- ment is that in *London Gazette*,

5 Feb.

Most of the materials for the his- tory of Charles's death are listed by (Sir) Raymond Crawford, *The Last Days of Charles II*, 1909, which gives the best modern account of the death; the account of it by Sir Charles Scarburgh, the physician, is also there printed; there are also important dispatches in Campana de Cavelli. Crawfurd states that

& so, as if by Gods providence, Dr. King[1] (that excellent[a] chirurgeon as well as Physitian) had not ben accidentaly present [to let him bloud][b] (with his lancet in his pocket) his Majestie had certainely died that moment, which might have ben of direfull consequence, there being no body else with the King save this doctor & one more, as I am assured:[c] It was a mark of the extraordinary dexterity, resolution, & present-nesse of Judgment[d] in the Doctor to let him bloud in the very paroxysme, without staying the coming of other physitians, which regularly should have ben don, & the not doing so, must have a formal pardon as they tell me: This rescued his Majestie for that instant, but it prov'd onely a reprieve for a little time; he still complain'd & was relapsing & often fainting & sometimes in Epileptical symptoms 'til Wednes-day, for which he was cupp'd, let[e] bloud againe in both jugularies, had both vomit & purges &c:[2] which so relieved him, that on the Thursday hops of recovery were signified in the publique Gazett;[3] but that day about noone the Physitians conjectur'd him somewhat feavorish; This they seem'd glad of, as being more easily alaied, & methodicaly to be dealt with, than his former fits, so as they prescrib'd the famous *Jesuits* powder;[4] but it made his Majestie worse; and some very able Doctors present, did not think it a feavor, but the effect of his frequent bleeding, & other sharp opera-tions used by them about his head: so as probably the powder

---

[a] MS. *ex^t*:   [b] Interlined.   [c] Followed by *His Majesty after* *this revived* (or *received*) deleted.   [d] Altered from *Justic-*.   [e] Followed by *more* deleted.

---

the death was due to chronic granular kidney with uraemic con-vulsions. He also notes the wide connotation of the term apoplexy in this period.

[1] Edmund King: above, p. 290. Physicians and surgeons were in attendance to dress Charles's heel; when the seizure was first noticed they had all retired with the excep-tion of King; King's having a lancet available appears to have been un-expected: Thomas Bruce, earl of Ailesbury, *Memoirs* (Roxburghe Club, 1890), i. 88. A formal pardon does not appear to have been neces-sary. King was knighted on 2 Feb. 1686 as a reward for his service this day.

[2] For details of the treatment see Scarburgh in Crawfurd.

[3] *London Gazette*, 5 Feb.; notice issued by the Privy Council at 5 p.m. on 4 February.

[4] Quinine: above, p. 325.

might stop the Circulation, & renew his former fitts, which
now made him very weake: Thus he pass'd Thursday night
with greate difficulty, when complaining of a paine in his
side, the⟨y⟩ drew 12 ounces more of blood from him, this was
by 6 in the morning on friday,[1] & it gave him reliefe, but it
did not continue; for being now in much paine and strugling
for breath, he lay doz'd, & after some conflicts, the Physitians
desparing of him, he gave up the Ghost at halfe an houre-
after Eleaven in the morning,[2] being the 6 of Feb: in the
36t[a] yeare of his reigne, & 54 of his age:[3] [*Feb: 6*][b] 'Tis not to
be express'd the teares & sorrows of Court, Citty & Country:
Prayers were solemnly made in all the Churches,[4] especialy
in both the Court Chapells, where the Chaplaines relieved
one another every halfe quarter of an houre, from the time he
began to be in danger, til he expir'd: according to the forme
prescribed in the Church office:[5] Those who assisted his
Majesties devotion were the A: Bish: of Cant: of London,
Durrham & Ely; but more especialy the B: of Bath & Wells.[6]
It is sayd they exceedingly urged the receiving the H:
Sacrament but that his Majestie told them he would Consider of it, which he did so long, 'til it was too late:[7] others
whispered, that the Bishops being bid withdraw some time

---

[a] The *3* altered; from *2* to *5* to *3*.   [b] Marginal date.

---

[1] Scarburgh does not mention
this bleeding; it is mentioned by
Barillon: dispatch printed in C. J.
Fox, *Hist. of . . . James II*, 1808,
app., p. xv.

[2] The notice in *London Gazette*,
9 Feb., says about noon; Scarburgh,
shortly after noon.

[3] The thirty-seventh year of his
reign had commenced on 30 January;
and Charles was in his fifty-fifth
year.

[4] 'On Friday morning all the
Churches were . . . throng'd with
people to pray for him, all in tears
and with dejected looks': anonymous letter, 7 Feb., in *Original
letters*, ed. Henry Ellis, [1st ser.],

vol. iii, 2nd ed., 1825, p. 337.

[5] A form of *Prayers for the King*
was published on 4 February.
T. Horne (below, p. 414), preaching
in the chapel at Whitehall on
8 February, said: 'You carried your
Tears and Prayers, hour after hour,
from the Closet to this place with
some impatience, waiting for the
next opportunity of imploring God
again for him, and rejoycing when it
was come': *Sermon*, 1685, p. 32.

[6] Sancroft; Compton, Crew, Turner; Ken.

[7] Beside the Roman Catholic
accounts see W. Hawkins, *Short
account of . . . Thomas Ken*, 1713,
p. 11.

the night before, (except the Earls^a of Bath, & Feversham), *Hurlston*[1] the Priest, had presum'd to administer the popish Offices; I hope it is not true; but these buisie emissaries are very forewarde upon such occasions: [See September 16:]^b He gave his breeches & Keys to the Duke,[2] who was almost continualy kneeling by his bed side, & in teares; he also recommended to him the care of his natural Children, all except the D: of Monmoth, now in Holland, & in his displeasure;[3] he intreated the Queene to pardon him, [(nor without cause)]^c who a little before had sent a Bishop to

---

^a MS. *E^s:* perhaps later.   ^b Marginal note written later.   ^c Interlined,

---

[1] John Huddlestone, 1608–98, priest and Benedictine monk: *D.N.B.* He had assisted Charles in his escape from Worcester; his present intervention took place on Thursday, 5 February. The Modenese agent (Rizzini), writing on 16/26 February, states that the fact of Charles's dying a Roman Catholic is so widely known ('*palese*') in London that he need not hesitate to confirm it: dispatch in Campana de Cavelli, ii. 6. On the same date Barillon writes that the king (James II) does not try to contradict the reports, and gives the comments of 'les Protestans zélés': in Fox, *James II*, app., pp. xxxiii–xxxiv. Tories and Trimmers were hesitant. About 22–5 February Luttrell states that 'Some persons maliciously disposed have raised a story that the late king died a papist': i. 332; and about the end of the month Wood attributes reports of this nature to 'the whiggs, who live and get their ends by lying': *Life and times*, iii. 134. One of three editions (all undated) of *A True Relation of the Late Kings Death*, a Roman Catholic account, was apparently in circulation a few days later: ibid., cited in *The Month*, clx (1932), 522–3; according to Wood 'few believed it'.

Evelyn was apparently uncertain about the reports until 2 October: below, pp. 475–9.

[2] The Modenese agent mentions Charles's giving with his own hand the keys of his desk to James: Campana de Cavelli, ii. 5. But, unless there were two incidents of this kind, what Charles did was to make James take the contents of his breeches-pockets; Evelyn's marginal note refers to James's account of what he found in them: below, pp. 470–1. The time of the incident (or incidents) cannot be fixed; Crawfurd is probably correct in dating it late on the Thursday evening: p. 45.

[3] 'He recommended all his children to his [the duke's] care by name, except the Duke of Monmouth, whom he was not heard so much as to make mention of. He bless'd all his children, one by one, pulling them to him on the bed': the anonymous writer in Ellis, *Original letters*, as above, p. 336. The Modenese agent states that Charles recommended to James the dukes of Grafton, Northumberland, St. Albans, and Richmond: Campana de Cavelli, ii. 5. Barillon says Richmond especially; the rest, except Monmouth. This took place on the Thursday night.

excuse her not more frequently visiting him, in reguard of her excessive griefe, & with all, that his Majestie would forgive it, if at any time she had offended him:[1] He spake to the Duke to be kind to his Concubines the DD: of *Cleveland*, & especialy *Portsmouth*, & that *Nelly* might not sterve;[2] I do not heare he said any thing of the Church or his people,[3] now falling under the government of a Prince suspected for[a] his Religion, after above 100 yeares the Church & Nation had ben departed from Rome: Thus died K. Charles the 2d, of a Vigorous & robust constitution, & in all appearance capable of a longer life. A prince of many Virtues, & many greate Imperfections, Debonaire, Easy of accesse, not bloudy or Cruel: his Countenance fierce,[4] his voice greate, proper of person, every motion became him, a lover of the sea, & skill-full in shipping, not affecting other studys,[b] yet he had a laboratory and knew of many Empyrical Medicines, & the easier Mechanical Mathematics: Loved Planting, building,[5] & brought in a politer way of living, which passed to Luxurie

---

[a] Substituted for *of*.   [b] Followed by *besides* deleted.

---

[1] According to the Dutch ambassador (van Citters) it was Halifax, the queen's chancellor, who carried her message and the reply: Foxcroft, *Halifax*, i. 434–5. This was apparently during the early hours of Friday: Crawfurd, p. 45.

[2] Barillon states that Charles twice recommended the duchess of Portsmouth to James; according to Burnet he recommended her 'over and over again' to him, and also said, 'Let not poor Nelly starve': *Own time*, ed. Airy, ii. 461; these two mistresses are also named in *The Secret History of the reigns of K. Charles II. and K. James II.*, 1690, p. 143. Evelyn apparently alone mentions the duchess of Cleveland; the statement is questionable. Burnet and Evelyn probably had some informant in common. The time is very early on the Friday.

[3] Burnet states that 'he said

nothing of the queen, nor any one word of his people, or of his servants: nor did he speak one word of religion, or concerning the payment of his debts': ii. 461. He is said, however, at the bishops' prompting to have blessed 'all that were there present, and in them the whole body of his subjects': Ellis, *Original letters*, as above, p. 336; and to have 'asked his subjects pardon for any thing that had been neglected, or acted conterary to the best rules of a good government': Chesterfield (Philip Stanhope, the second earl), *Letters*, 1832, p. 279.

[4] In *Numismata* Evelyn describes Charles's countenance as showing 'a serious Majesty . . . attemper'd with . . . strokes of *Debonaire*': p. 305.

[5] Both *Sylva* and the translation of Fréart's *Parallel of Architecture* are dedicated to Charles.

& intollerable expense: He had a particular Talent in telling stories & facetious passages of which he had innumerable, which made some bouffoones and vitious[a] wretches too presumptuous, & familiar, not worthy the favours they abused: He tooke delight to have a number of little spaniels follow him, & lie in his bed-Chamber, where often times he suffered the bitches to puppy & give suck, which rendred it very offensive, & indeede made the whole Court nasty & stinking:[1] An excellent prince doubtlesse had he ben lesse addicted to Women, which made him uneasy & allways in Want to supply their unmeasurable profusion,[2] & to the detriment of many indigent persons who had signaly serv'd both him & his father: Easily, & frequently he changed favorites[3] to his greate prejudice &c: As to other publique transactions and unhappy miscarriages, 'tis not here I intend to number them; but certainely never had King more glorious opportunities to have made himselfe, his people & all Europ happy, & prevented innumerable mischiefs, had not his too Easy nature resign'd him to be menag'd by crafty men, & some abandoned & prophane wretches, who corrupted his other-

---

[a] Altered from *vic-*.

---

[1] 'A dozen dogs' spent the night of Sunday, 1 February, in the king's bedchamber: Ailesbury, *Memoirs*, i. 87.

[2] As a rule no distinction was made between the king's income from hereditary sources and his revenue from public grants; and the existing polity rendered impossible any distinction between what would now be regarded as the king's household and personal expenditure, on the one hand, and expenditure on national services, on the other. Parliament in 1660 had intended to grant Charles what was believed would produce, with the hereditary revenue, an adequate total revenue for times of peace; but this total was too low and the actual yield was considerably smaller than had been expected. As a result of parlia-

ment's distrust of Charles and his unwillingness to submit his accounts to its inspection he never obtained an adequate grant. His expenditure on his mistresses was comparatively small (the duchess of Portsmouth appears to have received £12,000 per annum from the Secret Service money about the year 1678; later £17,000); the nature of this expenditure increased the difficulty of asking parliament for grants.

[3] 'He showed his judgement in this, that he cannot properly be said ever to have had a *favourite*, though some might look so at a distance': Halifax, *Character of King Charles II*, on his ministers. Evelyn perhaps refers rather to Charles's personal friends, whether politicians or not.

wise sufficient parts, disciplin'd as he had ben by many afflictions, during his banishment: which gave him much experience, & knowledge of men & things; but those wiccked creatures tooke him [off]ᵃ from all application becoming so greate a King: the History of his Reigne will certainely be the most wonderfull for the variety of matter & accidents above any extant of many former ages: The [sad tragical]ᵃ death of his father, his banishment, & hardships, his miraculous restauration, conjurations against him; Parliaments, Warrs, Plagues,ᵇ Fires, Comets; revolutions abroad happning in his time with a thousand other particulars: He was ever kind to me & very gracious upon all occasions, & therefore I cannot without ingratitude [but]ᵃ deplore his losse, which for many respects (as well as duty) I do with all my soule:¹ [Seeᶜ 2. *Octob:* 1685:]ᵈ

His Majestie dead, The Duke (now K. *James* the 2d) went immediately to Council, & before entering into any buisinesse, passionately declaring his sorrow,² Told their Lordships, That since the succession had falln to him, he would endeavor to follow the exampleᵉ of his predecessor in his Clemency & tendernesse to his people: That however he had ben misrepresented as affecting arbitrary power, they should find the contrary, for that the Laws of England had made the King as greate a Monarch as he could desire; That he would endeavour to maintaine the Government both in Church & state as by Law establish'd, its Principles being so firme for Monarchy, & the members of it shewing themselves so good & Loyal subjects; & that as he would never depart from the just rights & prerogative of the Crown, so would he never Invade any mans propriety: but as he had often adventured his life in defence of the Nation, so he would still proceede, & preserve it in all its lawfull rites & libertyes:

ᵃ Interlined.   ᵇ Or *Plague*.   ᶜ Followed by *3* deleted.
ᵈ Apparently inserted later.   ᵉ Altered from *exane-*.

---

¹ This character was written within a few days of Charles's death. For Evelyn's later views on him see below, 2 Oct. 1685, and a passage in V.
² So Barillon, 9/19 Feb., in Fox, app., p. xvi.

This being the substance of what he said, the Lords desired it might be published as containing matter of greate satisfaction to a jealous people, upon this change: which his Majestie consented to:[1] Then were the Counsel sworn,[2] & a proclamation ordered to be publish'd, that all officers should continue in their station; that there might be no failure of publique Justice, 'til his farther pleasure should be known:[3] Then the King rose, the Lords accompanying him to his bed Chamber, where, whilst he reposed himselfe[4] (tired indeede as he was with griefe & watching) They immediately returned againe into the Council-Chamber to take order for the Proclayming of his Majestie which (after some debate) they consented should be in the very forme, his Grandfather K. *James* the first was, after the death of Q: *Elizabeth*, as likewise that the Lords &c: should proceede in their Coaches[a] through the Citty for the more solemnity of it;[5] upon this was I and severall other Gent: (waiting in the privy Gallerie), admitted into the Council Chamb: to be wittnesse of what was resolv'd on:[6] & Thence with the Lords (the Lord Martial[7] & the Herraulds & other Crowne Officers being ready) we first went to Whitehall gate, where the Lords stood on foote beareheaded, whilst the Herauld proclaimed His Majesties Titles to the Imperial Crowne, & succession according to the

---

[a] Followed by *as far* deleted.

---

[1] Paraphrased from *London Gazette*, 9 Feb.; the king's declaration and the council's request for its publication.

[2] So ibid. Barillon makes the oath precede the declaration.

[3] Ibid.

[4] This is questionable: see the Tuscan resident (Terriesi) in Campana de Cavelli, ii. 15; Barillon, in Fox, app., p. xvii.

[5] I have not found special accounts of the proclaiming of James I and Charles I, but the ceremonial for James I was perhaps fuller, and appears to have made a greater impression: cf. Sir Richard Baker, *Chronicle*, ed. 1670, pp. 424, 451. The proclaiming of Charles II was irregular, despite the full ceremonial.

[6] Barillon mentions the peers, apparently meaning those who were not members of the Council, as accompanying the latter when they went to proclaim James II: in Fox, app., p. xvi.

[7] The duke of Norfolk, Earl Marshal; being a Protestant he was able to discharge the duties of his office: see above, iii. 596 n.

forme: The Trumpets & Kettle drumms having first sounded
3 times, which after also ended with the peoples acclamations:
Then[a] an Herauld called the Lords Coaches according to
ranke, my selfe accompanying the solemnity in my Lord
Cornwallis Coach, first to Temple barr, where the Lord
Major[1] & his breathren &c met us on horseback in all their
formalities, & proclaymed the King; Thence to the Exchange
in Cornhill, & so we returned in the order we set forth: being
come to White-hall, we all went and kissed the King &
Queenes hands, he had ben on the bed, but was now risen,
& in his Undresse:[2] The Queene was in bed in her appartment, but put forth her hand; seeming to be much afflicted,
as I believe she was, having deported herselfe so decently
upon all occasions since she came first into England, which
made her universally beloved:[3] Thus concluded this sad, &
yet Joyfull day: [I am never to forget the unexpressable
luxury, & prophanesse, gaming, & all dissolution, and as it
were total[b] forgetfullnesse of God (it being Sunday Evening)
which this day sennight, I was witnesse of;[4] the King,
sitting & toying with his Concubines Portsmouth, Cleaveland, & Mazarine: &c: A french boy[5] singing love songs,
in that glorious Gallery, whilst about 20 of the greate
Courtiers & other dissolute persons were at Basset round a
large table, a bank of at least 2000 in Gold before them, upon
which two Gent: that were with me made reflexions with
astonishment, it being a sceane of uttmost vanity; and surely

---

---

[1] Sir James Smyth: Beaven,
Aldermen, ii. 107.

[2] Presumably the audience in the
'camera della Regina' described by
the Tuscan resident, who, however,
apparently places it immediately
after the king's retirement from the
council: in Campana de Cavelli, ii.
15. For the meaning of undress see
above, iii. 590 n.

[3] This presumably refers to the
new queen. For her grief see

Rizzini; and her letter to her
brother in Campana de Cavelli, ii.
18.

[4] This refers to 25 January:
above, p. 403.

[5] Macaulay describes this boy as
the Duchesse Mazarin's page and
identifies him with a boy named
Dery who was in her service probably about this time: pp. 423–4;
for him see Saint-Evremonde,
Oeuvres, 1739, iv. 211, 292–4.

as they thought would never have an End: six days after was all in the dust.]ᵃ

Feb. 8: Preached in the Chapell of W:hall *Mr. Horne*,¹ a fellow of Eaton Coll: on 1. Thess: 5. 19: *quench not the Spirit*, shewing that the publique Liturgie & formes of prayer were preferable to extemporarie; in which as to private devotions & emergencies, he was (in my opinion) a little too streite: he tooke occasion to speake of the prayers & office used, during his late Majesties sicknesse, & indeede they were most solemnly perform'd & with extraordinary & passionate devotion:

I dined at Sir W: *Godolphins*, & then heard *Dr. Patrick* in St. *James's* new Church:² on 1. *Thess*: 5. 3. describing the nature of Spiritual Sacrifices, and necessitie of puritie: withᵇ a pathetical exhortation to holinesse, constancy & perseverance in the true faith, & concluded in the Collect of the day, being the 5 *Sonday* after *Epiphanie*, That God would keepe the church continualy in his true Religion: &c:

9 I went home the next day to refresh, it being injoyned, that those who put on mourning, should weare it as for a father, in the most solemn & lugubrous manner:³

10 Being sent to by the Sherif⁴ of the County, to appeare, & assist the Proclayming the King; [11]ᶜ I went the next day to *Bromely*, where I met the Sherif, and the Commander of the Kentish Troope, with an appearance of (I suppose) above 500 horse, & innumerable people: Two of his Majesties Trumpets, & a searjeant, with other officers, who having drawn up the horse in a large field neere to towne, march'dᵈ thence [with swords drawn]ᵉ to the Market place, where

---

ᵃ Interlined as far as *forgetfullnesse*; the rest written in margin; the whole passage perhaps written later.   ᵇ Substituted for *ended in*.
ᶜ Marginal date.   ᵈ Followed by *these* deleted.   ᵉ Interlined.

---

¹ Thomas Horne, *c.* 1643–1720; fellow of Eton 1682(3?); vice-provost 1697–1708; sometime chaplain to Charles II: Venn. The sermon was printed this year: above, p. 407 n.
² Above, p. 397. Patrick was rector of St. Paul's, Covent Garden.

The text appears to be wrong.
³ The Earl Marshal's instructions for mourning are printed in *London Gazette*, 12 Feb.
⁴ The sheriff is William Rooke (later Sir William), father of Sir George Rooke the admiral: Hasted, *Kent*, iv. 670.

making a ring, after sound of Trumpets, & silence made, the high Sherif read the Proclaming Titles, to his Bailife, who repeated it alow'd, & then after many shouts of the people &c: his Majesties health being drunk in a flint glasse of a yard-long,[1] of the Sherif, Commanders, Officers & chiefe Gent: they all disperc'd and I returned:

13 I went to Lond: to passe a fine upon the selling of Honson-grange in Stafford-Shire, being about 20 pounds per ann: which lying at so greate distance I thought fit to part with, to one *Buxton*[a] a farmor there, it came to me as part of my Daughter in Laws portion, this being but a 4th part of what was divided betweene the Mother & 3 sisters:[2]

14 The King was [this night][b] very obscurely buried in a Vault under Hen: 7th Chapell in Westminster, without any manner of pomp, and soone forgotten after all this vainity, & the face of the whole Court exceedingly changed into a more solemne and moral behaviour: The new King affecting neither Prophanesse, nor bouffonry: All the Greate Officers broke their white-Staves on the Grave &c: according to forme:[3]

15 Dr. Tenison preach'd to the Household on 42. *Psal:* ult: shewing by the change and uncertainty of greatenesse,

---

[a] Or *Burton*.   [b] Interlined.

---

[1] For flint-glass see above, ii. 467. For beer-glasses a yard long see *Notes and Queries*, 6th ser., especially v. 368, 456.

[2] Presumably Hanson Grange in the parish of Thorpe, Derbyshire. The parish is in the valley of the Dove, on the Staffordshire boundary. It belonged earlier in the century to a family named Flacket: *Miscellanea gen. et her.*, new ser., i (1874), 134–6. I cannot trace any connexion with Evelyn's daughter-in-law.

[3] Charles was 'privately' buried on the evening of 14 February in a vault at the east end of the south aisle of Henry VII's chapel. Prince George was the chief mourner; the great officers of the crown, the members of the household, knights of the Garter, bishops, peers, &c., were in attendance; the Anglican service was used, the dean of Westminster apparently officiating; the breaking of the staves followed the service: notice in *London Gazette*, 16 Feb.; for the service see also Queen Mary, Chaillot MS., in Campana de Cavelli, ii. 11. The body had lain in state in the Painted Chamber and was carried thence under a canopy to the Abbey.

For James's reforms at court see Campana de Cavelli, ii. 19, 25; *Hatton corr.*, ii. 55; Burnet, *History of my own time*, 1833, iii. 13–14 (fol. i. 624).

& humane felicity, how necessary it was to make an Interest in Heaven, & that we should not disquiet ourselves to solicitude; but in all events have recourse to God:

The 2d sermon (which should have ben before the King, who to the great griefe of his subjects, did now the first time go to Masse publicly in the little Oratorie at the Dukes lodgings, the doores set wide open¹) was by Mr. Fox,² a young quaint Preacher, who made a very profitable sermon on Pro: *Fooles make a mock at sin*, against prophanes & Atheisme; now reigning more than ever through the late dissolutenesse of the Court:

I dined at my Friend Mr. Packers, & went in the afternoone to St. Margarites, where a stranger preached on 1. *Isa: 26.*

16 I din'd at Sir Rob: *Howards Auditor* of the Exchequer, a Gent: pretending to all manner of Arts & Sciences for which he had ben the subject of Comedy, under the name of Sir Positive; not ill-natur'd, but unsufferably boosting: He was sonn to the late Earle of Berkshire:³

This morning his Majestie restored the staffs & Key, to my Lord Arlington L: Chamberlaine, to Mr. Savell Vice-Cham: to my L: Newport, & Mainard Tressurer & Comptroller of the Household:⁴ [18]ᵃ And made my Lord

---

ᵃ Marginal date, altered from or to *17*.

---

¹ Barillon states that the service was held 'dans une petite chapelle de la Reine sa femme': in Fox, app., pp. xxxii–xxxiii. The Duke's, formerly known as the Prince's, Lodgings were on the river front of the palace, immediately to the south of the King's Lodgings: L.C.C., *Survey of London*, xiii. 80–1. He had generally lived at St. James's Palace, but the duchess had an oratory here.
² Identifiable as Henry Fox, *c.* 1657–*c.* 1687; M.A. 1681; chaplain in ordinary probably in succession to Ken, 1684, until his death: Foster.
³ The allusion is to 'Sir *Positive At-all*, A foolish Knight, that pre-

tends to understand everything in the world, and will suffer no man to understand any thing in his Company; so foolishly Positive, that he will never be convinced of an Error, though never so grosse'; in Shadwell's *The Sullen Lovers*, 1668. His father had died in 1669: above, iii. 529.
⁴ This notice is derived from *London Gazette*, 16 Feb., where, however, the reappointments (and the notice of them) are dated 15 February. Henry Savile (above, iii. 546) was vice-chamberlain from 1680 until 7 March 1687. Newport was treasurer of the household

Godolphin Chamb: to the Queene,[1] L. Peterborow Groome of the Stoole in place of the Earle of Bath:[2] Gave the Treasurers Staff to the E: of Rochester, & made his bro: the E: of Clarendon, Lord Privie-Seale, in place of the Marques of Hallifex, who was made President of the Council:[3] The Secretarys of State remaining as before:[4]

18 I was carried by my Lord Privy-Seale to congratulate my Lord Tressurer who [19][a] the next day, together with the other new Officers, were all sworne at the Chancery barr, & at the Chequer:[5] I return'd home in the Evening.

The late King having the revenue of Excise, Costomes, & other late duties granted for his life onely; were now farmed & let to severall persons upon an opinion that the late K: might let them for 3 yeares after his decease (some of the old Commissioners refusing to act) The major part of Judges, (but as some think, not the best lawyers) pronounced it legal; but 4 dissenting: The lease was made but the day before his Majesties death;[b] which seemes by the words of the statute to be invalid:[6]

---

^a Marginal date.   ^b Followed by *but* deleted.

from 1672 until 9 Feb. 1687 and again from the Revolution until his death. William Maynard, *c.* 1623–99, second Baron Maynard of Estaines and Turrim 1640, was comptroller of the household from 1672 until 9 Feb. 1687: G.E.C.; *London Gazette*, 10 Feb., 10 March 1687.

[1] Ibid., 19 Feb. He retained the office until the Revolution.

[2] On 17 February 'the place of Groom of the Stole is in suspense between my Lord of Bath, who has a patent for life . . . and my Lord of Peterborough': *Hist. MSS. Comm., Ormonde MSS.*, new ser., vii. 323. Luttrell mentions the change late in March; the appointment was made on 19 April: *London Gazette*, 23 April. Peterborough was a personal friend of the king.

[3] From ibid., 19 Feb. Rochester's appointment 16 February; the others 18 February. Halifax was dismissed on 18 October of this year; Rochester on 4 Jan. 1687; and the Privy Seal was put into commission when Clarendon was appointed lord lieutenant of Ireland in September of this year.

[4] Sunderland and Middleton.

[5] Notice of Rochester's taking the oaths in the two courts ibid., 23 Feb.; it does not appear that anyone else was sworn at the same time. The lord privy seal is Clarendon.

[6] Charles had been granted for life the customs (tonnage and poundage) and the excise by acts of parliament passed in 1660 and confirmed in 1661; the act for the excise provided that it could at any time be let to farm for a term of

Note that the Clearke of the Closset, had shut-up the late Kings private Oratory next the Privy-Chamb: above;[1] but the King caus'd it to be open'd againe, & that Prayers should be said as formerly: The Papists now swarmed at Court. &c:

22 Severall most usefull tractates against Dissenters, Papists & Fanatics, & resolutions of Cases, were now publish'd by the London divines:[2]

Our Viccar preach'd on 13 *Luke* 24, concerning the difficulty & necessity of governing our passions, in order to obtaining heaven &c: I was hindred from Church this evening. I stayed at home all this weeke:

March 1 Our ⟨Viccar⟩[a] proceeded with small addition, the holy Comm: followed. I participated together with my daugh⟨t⟩er Mary:

The Curate on[b] Jac: 27: shewing the duty of Charity to those who want.[3]

3 My daughter complain'd of her indisposition.

4[c] After Evening prayer Ash-wednesday I went to Lond: about my buisinesse:

---

[a] MS. *piccar.*   [b] Followed by 5 deleted.   [c] Substituted for 5.

---

three years. James issued a proclamation on 9 February for the payment of the customs, &c., to be continued until parliament, which was shortly to be summoned, should grant him supplies: *London Gazette*, 12 Feb. On 5 February, the day before Charles's death, the commissioners of the treasury had made an agreement for the farming the whole of the excise for three years. Eight of the twelve judges decided that this agreement was valid (the dissentients were Atkins, Jones, Levinz, and Montague) and a proclamation was issued on 17 February: ibid. 19 Feb.; for the judges' decision see *Ormonde MSS.*, new ser., vii. 324. Two of the commissioners for the customs had also raised doubts: ibid., p. 322.

[1] See above, p. 129. The clerk of the closet is Nathaniel Crew, bishop of Durham (above, p. 4, &c.); he held the office from 1669 until 29 December of this year.

[2] This presumably refers to an item advertised in the *Term catalogue* for Hilary (February): *A Collection of Cases and other Discourses Lately Written to Recover Dissenters to the Communion of the Church of England.* 'By some Divines of the City of London'; 2 vols., quarto, 1685. It consists of tracts against the Protestant dissenters of various dates, 1683–5, and issued by several publishers; bound up together with a general title-page and list of contents for each volume. There were new editions in 1694 and 1718.

[3] The text is James i. 27.

5 To my griefe I saw the new pulpet set up in the popish oratory at W—hall,[1] for the Lent preaching, Masse being publiqly saied, & the Romanists swarming at Court with greater confidence than had ever ben seene in England since the Reformation, so as every body grew Jealous to what this would tend; A Parliament was now also summond, and greate industry used to obtaine Elections which might promote the Court Interest: Most of the Corporations being now by their new Charters in power to make what returnes of members they pleased:[2] Most of the Judges likewise having given their opinions that his Majestie might still take the Costomes, which to foure Judges (⟨esteem'd⟩[a] the best Lawyers) seemed against the Act of Parliament which determines it with[b] the Kings life:

Now came over divers Envoyès & greate Persons to condole the Death of the late King: The Q: Dowager received them on a bed of mourning, the whole Chamber seiling & floore hung with black,[c] tapers lighted; so as nothing could be more Lugubrous & solemn: The Q: Consort sat out under a state on a black foot-cloth, to entertaine the Circle as the Q: used to do, & that very decently:[3]

6 Lent Preachers continuing as formerly in the Royal Chapell, The Deane of S. Paule[4] preached on 1. *Pet:* 3. 14: shewing that what ever Changes happn'd in the state or Government, an holy, & innocent life, was the greatest

---

a MS. *esteen'd.*   b Altered from *at.*   c Followed by *Wax* (?)
deleted.

---

[1] Presumably the oratory in the former Duke's Lodgings: above, p. 416.

[2] James had announced his intention of calling a parliament in his proclamation of 9 February: above, p. 418 n.; writs were issued on 14 February; returns are first published in *London Gazette* for 12 March. The effect of the new charters and the exercise of court influence on the elections have not been studied in detail; for a general statement see K. Feiling, *History of the Tory party, 1640–1714*, 1924, p. 205.

[3] Visits of condolence were paid by representatives of the Spanish Netherlands, of France, and of Denmark, on 2, 8, and 11 March, respectively: *London Gazette*, 5, 9, 12 March. The United Provinces also sent representatives: ibid., 2 March.

[4] Stillingfleet. List of Lenten preachers ibid., 24 Dec. 1684.

security; but in the meane time, Christians should endeavor to informe themselves in the faith they profess'd, and (behaving themselves thus inoffensively, & obediently to their Governers) when it came to suffering go through it with courage & meekenesse &c: I supp'd this night at my Lady Sylviu's with Dr. Tenison & other friends:

7 Newes coming to me that my Daughter Mary was falln ill of the Small Pox, I hastned home full of apprehensions, & indeede found her very ill, still coming-forth in aboundance, a wonderfull affliction to me, not onely for her beauty, which was very lovely, but for the danger of loosing one of extra-ordinary parts & virtue. &c: Gods holy will be don.

8 A stranger preach'd at our Parish on 4. *Gal:* 18, very solidly, concerning the notion of a well informe'd zeale, & how much good or evil depended upon the due & just regulation of it, &[a] what was according to knowledge: &c.

My Deare Child continuing ill, by reason of the Disseases fixing in the Lungs, it was not in the power of physick without more plentifull expectoration to recover her, insomuch as [9][b] Dr. Short[1] (the most approved & famous Physition of all his Majesties Doctors) gave us his opinion, that she could not escape, upon the Tuesday; so as on Wednesday she desired[c] to have the B: Sacrament given her (of which yet she had participated the Weeke before) after which disposing her selfe to suffer what God should determine to inflict, she bore the remainder of her sicknesse with extraordinary patience, and piety & with more than ordinary resignation, and marks of a sanctified & blessed frame of mind, rendred [up][d] her soule to the Lord Jesus on Saturday the 14 of March,[2] exactly at halfe-an houre after Eleaven in the fore noone, to our unspeakable sorrow & Affliction, and this not to ours

---

a Substituted for *or.* b Marginal date. c Here is an incorrect marginal date *10.* d Interlined.

---

[1] Thomas Short, 1635–85 (28 September); M.D. 1668: *D.N.B.*
[2] According to her epitaph she died on 17 March; but the Deptford parish register states that she was buried on that day: Foljambe,

pp. 37–8.
Mrs. Evelyn gives an account of Mary Evelyn's death and character, &c., in a letter to Lady Tuke, April 1685 (Bohn, iv. 40–1).

(her parents) onely, but all who knew her, who were many of the best quality,[a] greatest & most vertuous persons: How unexpressable losse I and my Wife sustain'd, the Virtues & perfections she was endow'd with best would shew; of which the justnesse[b] of her stature,[c] person,[c] comelinesse of her Countenance and gracefullnesse of motion, naturall, & unaffected (though more than ordinaryly[d] beautifull), was one of the least, compar'd with the Ornaments of her mind, which was truely extraordinary, especialy the better part: Of early piety, & singularly Religious, so as spending a considerable part of every day in private devotion, Reading and other vertuous exercises, she had collected, & written out aboundance of the most usefull & judicious periods of the Books she read, in a kind of Common place; as out of Dr. Hammonds *N. Test:*[1] and most of the best practical Treatises extant in our tonge: She had read & digested a considerable deale of History, & of Places, the french Tongue being as familiar to her as English, she understood Italian, and was able to render a laudable Account of what she read & observed, to which assisted a most faithfull memory, & discernement, & she did make very prudent & discreete reflections upon what she had observe'd of the Conversations among which she had at any time ben (which being continualy of persons of the best quality), she improved: She had to all this an incomparable sweete Voice, to which she play'd a through-base[2] on the Harpsichord, in both which she ariv'd to that perfection, that of all the Schollars of those Two famous Masters, Signor *Pietro* and *Bartolomeo:*[3] she was esteem'd the best; [for][e] the sweetenesse of her voice, and

---

[a] Followed by & deleted or blotted out.   [b] Substituted for *beauty* & *comelinesse.*   [c] Followed by & deleted.   [d] Altered from *ordinary.* [e] Interlined.

---

[1] Dr. Henry Hammond (above, iii. 105), *A Paraphrase and Annotations upon all the Books of the New Testament,* first published 1653; new editions had appeared in 1659, 1671, and 1675; later editions 1702 and 1845.

[2] Thoroughbass, here probably merely an accompaniment: see *O.E.D.*

[3] Pietro is presumably Pietro Reggio: above, p. 220; for Bartolomeo see above, pp. 186, 271.

manegement of it, adding such an agreablenesse to her
Countenance, without any constraint and concerne, that[a]
when she sung, it was as charming to the Eye, as to the
Eare; this I rather note, because it was a universal remarke,
& for which so many noble & judicious persons in Musique,
desir'd to heare her; the last, being at my Lord Arundels of
Wardours, where was a solemn Meeting of about[b] twenty
persons of quality, some of them greate judges & Masters of
Musique; where she sung with the famous Mr. *Pordage*,
Signor *Joh: Battist* touching the Harpsichord &c: with
exceeding applause:[1] What shall I say, or rather not say, of
the cherefullnesse & agreablenesse of her humor, that she
condescending to the meanest servant in the family, or
others, she kept still her respect without the least pride:
These she would reade to, examine, instruct and often pray
with, if they were sick; so as she was extreamely beloved of
every body: Piety was so prevalent an ingredient in her
constitution (as I may say) that even amongst superiors, as
equals, she no sooner became intimately acquainted; but she
would endeavour to improve them by insinuating something
of Religious, & that tended to bring them to a love of
Devotion; and she had one or two Confidents, with whom she
used to passe whole dayes, in fasting, reading and prayers,
especialy before the monethly Communions, & other solemn
occasions: She could not indure that which they call court-
ship, among the Gallants, abhorred flattery, & tho she had
aboundance of witt, the raillery was so innocent and ingenuous, as was most agreable; She sometimes would see a
play, but since the stage grew licentious, tooke greate scandal
at them, & express'd her being weary of them, & that the
time spent at the Theater was an unaccountable vanity, nor
did she at any time play at Cards, without extreame importunity & for the Company; but this was so very seldome,
that I cannot number it among any thing she[c] could name

---

a Followed by *was the* (or *she*) *most charming* deleted.   b Altered
from *above*.   c Substituted for *to her*.

---

[1] See above, pp. 384, 404.

a fault: No body living read prose, or Verse better & with
more judgement, & as she read, so she writ not onely most
correct orthography, but with that maturitie of judgement,
and exactnesse of the periods, choice expressions, & familia-
rity of style, as that some letters of hers have astonish'd me,
and others to whom she has occasionaly written: Among
other agreablenesses she had a talent of rehersing any
Comical part or poeme, as was to them[a] she might decently
be free with, more pleasing than the Theater: She daunc'd
with the most grace that in my whole life I had ever seene,
& so would her Master say, who was Monsieur *Isaac*;[1] but
she very seldome shew'd that perfection, save in the gracefullnesse of her Carriage, which was with an aire of spritefull
modestie, not easily to be described: Nothing of haughty,
nothing affected, but natural and easy, as well in her deportment, as her discourse, which was allways material, not
trifling, and to which the extraordinary[b] sweetenesse of her
tone, even in familiar speaking, was very charming: Nothing
was so pretty, as her descending to play with little Children,
whom she would caresse, & humor with greate delight: But
she most of all affected to be [with][c] grave, and sober men, of
whom she might learne something and improve herselfe:
I have my selfe ben assisted by her, both reading & praying
by me; and was comprehensive of uncommon notions,
curious of knowing every thing to some excesse, had I not
indeavor'd to represse it sometimes: Nothing was therefore
so delightfull to her, as the permission I ever gave her to go
into my Study, where she would willingly have spent whole
dayes; for as I sayd, she had read aboundance of History,
& all the best poets, even to Terence,[d] Plautus, Homer,
Vergil, Horace, Ovide, all the best Romances,[e] & modern
Poemes, and could compose very happily, & put in her pretty
Symbol,[2] as in that of the *Mundus Muliebris*,[3] wherein is an

---

ᵃ Substituted for *all*.   ᵇ Followed by *tone &* deleted.   ᶜ Interlined.   ᵈ Altered from *Terrenc*.   ᵉ MS. *Romanc,es*.

¹ Above, p. 271.   uses the word in *London revived*,
² Contribution (properly to a   p. 30.
feast): *O.E.D.*, Symbol, sb². Evelyn   ³ The piece published by Evelyn

enumeration of the immense variety of the Modes & ornaments belonging to the Sex: But all these are vaine trifles to those interior vertues which adorn'd her Soule, For she was sincerely Religious, most dutifull to her parents, whom she lov'd with an affection temper'd with greate esteeme, so as we were easy & free, & never were so well pleased, as when she was with us, nor needed we other Conversation: She was kind to her Sisters, and was still improving them, by her constant Course of Piety: Ô deare, sweete and desireable Child, how shall I part with all this goodnesse, all this Vertue, without the bitternesse of sorrow, and reluctancy of a tender Parent! Thy Affection, duty & love to me was that of a friend, as well as of a Child, passing even the love of Women, the Affection of a Child: nor lesse dearer to thy Mother, whose example & tender care of Thee was unparalleled; nor was Thy returnes to her lesse conspicuous: Ô how she mourns thy losse! ô how desolate hast Thou left us, Sweete, obliging, happy Creature! To the grave shall we both carry thy memory—God alone (in whose boosome thou art at rest & happy) give us to resigne Thee, & all our Contentments (for thou indeede wert all in this world) to his blessed pleasure: ô let him[a] be glorified by our submission, & give us Grace to blesse him for the Graces he implanted in thee, thy vertuous life, pious & holy death, which is indeede the onely remaining Comfort of our soules, hastning through the infinite love and mercy of the Lord Jesus, to be shortly with Thee deare Child, & with Thee (and those blessed Saints like thee,) glorifie the Redemer of the World to all Eternity. Amen:

It was in the nineteenth yeare of her Age, that this sick-

---

[a] Followed by *give* deleted.

---

as *Mundus Muliebris: or, the Ladies Dressing-Room unlock'd, And her Toilette spread. In Burlesque. Together with the Fop-Dictionary, Compiled for the Use of the Fair Sex,* 1690, with a preface apparently written by himself; the Fop-Dictionary is presumably by Mary.

There was a second issue of this edition and a second edition in this same year 1690; the latter was reissued, as *The Ladies Dressing-Room unlock'd,* in 1700. A reply, *Mundus Foppensis,* appeared in 1691: Keynes, pp. 214–19.

nesse happn'd to her, at which period *Dr. Harvy*[1] somewhere writes, all young people should be let blood; and to this we advised her; whilst to all who beheld her she looked so well, as her extraordinary beauty was taken notice of, the last time she appeared at Church: but she had so greate an aversion to breathing a veine, as we did not so much insist upon it as we should: being in this exceeding height of health, she was the more propence to change, & had ever ben subject to feavors; but there was yet another accident that contributed to the fixing it in this dissease; The apprehension she had of it in particular, & which struck her but two days before she came home, by an imprudent Gentlewomans telling my Lady Faulkland (with whom my daughter went to give a Visite) after she had entertained them a good while in the house,[a] that[b] she had a servant sick of the small pox above, who died the next day; This my poore Child accknowledged made an impression on her spirits, it being with all [of][c] a mortal & spreading kind at this time about the towne:

There were now no lesse than foure Gent: of Quality offering to treate with me about Marriage; & I freely gave her her owne Choice, knowing she was discreete: One (against which I had no exceptions) and who most passion-ately lov'd her, but was for a certaine natural blemish that rendered him very disagreable, she would in complyance to[d] me have married, if I did injoyne her; but telling me she should never be happy with him (observing[e] it seemes a neerenesse in his nature, and a little under-breeding) I would not impose it; for which she often expressed her satisfaction, & thanks to me in the most obliging & respectfull manner:[2] The other was one *Weston*[3] a Stafford shire Gent: of the

---

[a] MS. has closing bracket here.   [b] Followed by *a ser* deleted.
[c] Interlined.   [d] Followed by *my de* deleted.   [e] Altered from *no*.

[1] Dr. William Harvey. The passage occurs in the *Exercitationes de generatione animalium*, exercise lii; small-pox is there mentioned as one of the illnesses to which young people are liable if they are not relieved of their load of blood, either by haemorrhage or by being let blood.

[2] This presumably refers to John Hussey: below, p. 454.

[3] Presumably Charles Weston, born *c.* 1659, a great-grandson of Sir Richard Weston of Rugeley,

family, & I thinke heire (within one) to the Earles of Portland: This was but now just beginning: But the person who first made love to her, was Mr. *Wilbraham*[1] a Chesshire Gent: of a noble Family,[a] whose extreamely rich & sordid Fathers demands of Portion, I could by no meanes reach, without injury to the rest of my daughters, which[b] this pious, & good natured Creature, would never have suffered,[b] and so that match stood in suspense; I say in suspense, for the young Gent: still pursu'd, & would have married her in private, if either my Daughter, or We had don so disingenuously: She & we had principles that would by no meanes suffer us to harken to it: At last he's sent for home, continues his Affection, hop⟨e⟩s to bring his father to reasonable termes: My Child is taken with his Constancy, his Virtuous breeding, and good nature, & discretion, having beene a fortnight together in my house: This, made us not forward to embrace any other offers, together with the extraordinary indifferency she ever shewed of Marrying at all; for truely says shee to her Mother, (the other day),[c] were I assur'd of your lives & my deare Fathers, never would I part from you, I love you, & this home, where we serve God, above all things in the world, nor ever shall I be so happy: I know, & consider the vicissitudes and changes of the world, I have some experience of its vanities, & but for decency, more than inclination, & that You judge it expedient for me, I would not change my Condition, but rather add the fortune you designe me to my Sisters, & keepe up the reputation of our family: This was so discreetely & sincerely utter'd as, could not proceede but from an extraordinary Child, & one who loved her parents without example:[d]

---

[a] Followed by *to* deleted.   [b–b] These words were originally in brackets, afterwards deleted.   [c] Followed by *that* deleted.   [d] Followed by *In* deleted.

Staffs., and perhaps a very distant relation of the family of the earls of Portland (the latter were Roman Catholics): *Staffordshire pedigrees* (Harleian Soc., vol. lxiii, 1912), p. 238; S. Erdeswick, *Survey of Staffordshire*, ed. Harwood, 1844, pedigrees, pp. 164–5; *D.N.B.*, art. Weston, Richard, earl of Portland.

[1] Above, pp. 315, 324; Randle Wilbraham's father was Roger Wilbraham, 1623–1707; for him see Hall, *Hist. of ... Nantwich*, pp. 321, 428–35, &c.

At[a] London then it was she doubtlesse tooke this fatal dissease; and the Occasion of her being there at all was this:

My Lord Viscount Falklands Lady having ben our Neighbours (as he was Treasurer of the Navy)[1] she tooke so greate an Affection to my Daughter, that when they went back in the Autumn to the Citty, nothing could pacifie their uncessant importunity, but the letting of my ⟨daughter⟩[b] accompany my Lady, & the staying some time with her; so with the greatest reluctancy (as all can wittnesse) I ever refused any thing, I was almost forc'd to let her be with this Young Lady: Whilst she was there, my Lord being musical, and [that]ᶜ I[d] saw I could not prevaile with my Lady to part with her til ⟨Christmas⟩[e], I was not unwilling she should improve the opportunity of learning of Signor Pietro, an Italian who had an admirable way both of Composure & teaching; & when Christmas came, it was the end of February ere I could obtaine my Lady to part with her; But hearing she was to make a Step into Oxfordshire (when my Lord stood for knight of that[f] County)[2] my Daughter (who now longed to come home)[g] expressed her wearisom⟨n⟩esse of being in a Family, not so regular as to the due service of God, & religious duties, though otherwise exceedingly well govern'd, & where they were all of them infinitely fond, & pleased with her generous & obliging Way,[h] sent to her mother, that she had obtained of my Lady, she should come home; upon condition of returning to her againe, when she came out of the Country, hoping to prevaile with us, to continue with them 'til the Spring, when their family usualy lived at their house in Deptford: To this my Wife & I resolved not to Consent, finding likewise so greate a desire in my daughter to remove no more from her deare Parents, & which she expressed with a more than ordinary earnestnesse:

---

a Preceded by *Another Accident It the* deleted.   b MS. *daughters.*
c Interlined.   d Altered from *w-*.   e MS. *Christman.*
f Followed by *shire* deleted.   g Followed by *of a long time)* and deleted.   h MS. has closing bracket here.

---

[1] See above, p. 386.   [2] He was returned for the county on 18 March.

quite tired, as she confessed, with the vaine & empty
Conversation of the Towne, the Theaters, the Court, &
trifling visites which consum'd so many precious moments,
and made her sometimes (unavoidably) misse of that regular
Course of piety, which gave her the greatest satisfaction:
But this was the truth, that where ever she came, every body
was taken with her way, something appeared so charming
in her Conversation, & that modest freedome, which she
knew how to govern, & was indeede natural to her: This
made her contin⟨u⟩aly sought to [by]ᵃ severall persons of the
first rank, especialy my Lord Treasurers Lady,¹ my Lady
Rochester, Sunderland, Burlington,² Clarendon, Arlington,
Dutchesse of Grafton; besides other Ladys & persons lovers
of Musick, her two Italian Masters having (for their own-
sakes) spread the Talent she had: but the Child was starke
weary of this life, and went seldome, & I thinke not thrice
to Court all this time, except when her Mother, or my selfe
carryed her thither, when we came sometimes to Towne,
whither my occasions often brought me; for with all this she,
did not affect the shewing & producing of her-selfe, she knew
the Court well, passed one whole Summer at Windsore in it,
with my Lady Tuke (one of the Queenes Women of the Bed-
chamber) a most vertuous Relation of hers: so as she was
not fond of that glittering scene, now become abominablyᵇ
licentious: though there was a designe of my Lady Rochester
& Clarendon to make her Mayd of ⟨honour⟩ᶜ to the Queene,
so soone as there was a place empty: but this she did not in
the least set her heart upon, nor indeede upon any thing so
much as the service of God, a quiet regular life, & how she
might improve her selfe in the most necessary accomplishments, & to which she was arived in so great a measure, as
I acknowledge (all partiality of relation layed aside) I never

---

ᵃ Interlined.   ᵇ Altered from *abominable*.   ᶜ MS. *hononor*.

---

¹ i.e. Lady Rochester, formerly
Lady Henrietta Hyde.
² Elizabeth, 1613–91, daughter of
Henry Clifford, fifth earl of Cumberland; married in 1634 Richard
Boyle, at that time styled Viscount
Dungarvan, and later earl of Cork
and earl of Burlington; succeeded
as Baroness Clifford in her own
right 1643: G.E.C.

saw, or knew her equal, considering how universal they were;
save in *one onely Creature* of her Sex, Mrs. *Godolphin*, (late
the wife of my *Lord Godolphin*, whose life[a] for the singular
piety, Vertue & discretion, (& that she was to me a Friend,
in all the peculiar transcendencys of that relation) I have
written at large, and consign'd to my Lady *Sylvius* (whom she
loved above all her Sex) & who requested it of me: And this
I mention here, because the Example of that most religious
Lady: made I am assured deepe impressions in my deare
Child; and that I was told, she caused it to be read to her, at
the very beginning of her sicknesse, when She had taken that
bed, out of which she never risse, to my insupportable griefe
& sorrow; though never two made more blessed ends:[1] But
all this sorrow is selfe-love, whilst to wish them here againe,
were to render them miserable who are now in happinesse, and
above: This is the little History, & Imperfect Character
of my deare Child, whose Piety, Virtue, & incomparable
Endowments, deserve a Monument more durable than brasse
& Marble: *Precious is the Memorial of the Just*[2]— Much I could
enlarge on every period of this hasty Account, but thus I ease
& discharge my overcoming passion for the present, so many
things worthy an excellent Christian & dutifull Child, crowding upon me: Never can I say enough, ô deare, my deare
Child whose memory is so precious to me.

    This deare child was born at Wotton in Surry, in the same
house and roome where I likewise first drew breath, (my wife
being retir'd to my bro: there, the greate sicknesse yeare)

---

a Followed by opening bracket deleted.

[1] Allusions in the two texts of
the *Life of Mrs. Godolphin* place
the period of composition between
29 Nov. 1682 and 6 July 1684.
A rough date, 1686 or later, for its
sending to Lady Sylvius is provided
by the covering letter of the version
sent to Godolphin; but Evelyn's
language in this letter is too vague
and obscure for any reliance to be
placed upon it. In the present passage 'consign'd' may mean delivered, but possibly little more than
dedicated or assigned to the care
of. In any case Evelyn presumably
retained a copy of the work for his
own use. The manuscripts and the
dates of composition, &c., are discussed by Miss Sampson, *Life*, pp.
116–22.

[2] Perhaps a misquotation of Proverbs x. 7: 'The memory of the just
is blessed.'

upon the first of that moneth, & neere the very houre, that
I was borne, upon the last: viz: October:

16 Was my deare Daughter interr'd in the south east end
of the church at Deptford neere her Grand mother & severall
of my Younger Children and Relations: my desires were she
should have ben carried & layed among my owne Parents &
Relations at Wotton, where our Family have a Vault, where
she was born, & where I have desire to be interred my selfe,
when God shall call me out of this uncertaine transitory life;
but some Circumstances did not permit it; & so she was
buried here.[1] Our Viccar Dr. Holden preaching her Funerall
Sermon on: 1. Phil: 21. *For to me to live is Christ, & to die is
gaine,* upon which he made an apposit discourse (as those who
heard it assure me, for griefe suffer'd me not to be present)
concluding with a modest recital[a] of her many vertues, and
especialy her signal piety, so as drew both teares, & admiration from the hearers, so universaly was she beloved, & known
to deserve all the good that could be sayd of her: & I was not
altogether unwilling something of this should be spoken of
her, for the edification & encouragement of other young
people: There were divers noble persons who honor'd her
Obsequies, & funerall, some in person, others in sending their
Coaches, of which there were 6 or 7. of six horses viz. Countesse
of Sunderland, Earle of Clarendon, Lord Godolphin, Sir St.
Fox; Sir William Godolphin, Vis⟨c⟩ount Falkland &c [follow-
ing the hearse of 6 horses &c][b] there were (besides other
decenc⟨i⟩es) distributed among her friends about 60 rings:
Thus lived, died, & was buried the joy of my life & ornament
both of her sex & my poore family: God Almighty of his
infin⟨i⟩te mercy grant me the grace thankfully to resigne my
selfe & all I have, or had, to his divine pleasure, & in his good
time, restoring health & Comfort to my Family, teach me so
to number my days, as I may apply my heart to Wisdome, &
be prepared for my dissolution, & that into the hands of my
blessed Saviour I may recomend my Spirit. Amen:

---

[a] Altered from *remembrance*. [b] Interlined.

[1] Her monument was replaced in
a similar position when the church
was rebuilt *c.* 1697. For the date of
the burial see above, p. 420 n.

Having some days after opened her Trunks,[a] & looked into her Closset, amazed & even astonished we were to find that incredible number of papers and Collections she had made of severall material Authors, both Historians, Poets, Travells &c: but above all the Devotions, Contemplations, & resolutions upon those Contemplations, which we found under her hand in a booke most methodicaly disposed, & much exceeding the talent & usage of [so][b] young & beautifull women, who consume so much of their time in vaine things: with severall prayers, Meditations, & devotions on divers occasions; with a world of pretty letters to her confidents & others savoring of a greate witt, & breathing of piety & honor: There is one letter to some divine (who is not named) to whom she writes that he would be her Ghostly Father & guide, & that he would not despise her for the many errors & imperfections of her Youth, but beg of God, to give her courage, to acquaint him with all her faults, imploring his assistance, & spiritual direction: & well I remember, that she often desired me to recomend her to such a person, but (though I intended it) I did not think fit to do it as yet, seeing her apt to be scrupulous, & knowing the greate innocency & integrity of her life; but this (it seemes) she did of her selfe: There are many other books, offices & papers thus written by her selfe, so many indeede, as it is plainly astonishing how one that had acquired such substantiall & practical knowledge in other the ornamental parts of (Especialy) Music vocal & Instrumental, Dauncing; paying, & receiving visites, necessary Conversation,[c] & other unavoidable impertinences of life could find, much more employ, her time to accomplish a quarter of what she has left: but as she never affected Play, Cards &c: (which consumes a world of precious time) so she was in continual exercise, which yet abated nothing of the most free & agreable Conversation in the world: But as she was a little miracle whilst she lived, so she died with out Example:

---

[a] Or *Trunke*.   [b] Interlined.   [c] Followed by *often feavors* deleted.

26 I was invited to Cap: Gunmans[1] Funerall, that excellent
Pilot, & sea-man, who had behav'd himselfe so valiantly
in the Dut⟨c⟩h-Warr: taken away by the gangreene which
happn'd in his cure, upon his unhappy fall from the peere of
Calais: This was the Cap: of the yacht, whom they accused
for not giving timely warning, on the Dukes (now the King)
going into Scotland,[a] when his ship split upon the[b] Sands,
when so many perished: But of which I am most confident,
the Cap: was no ways guilty, either through negligence, or
designe; as he made appeare not onely at the Examination
of the matter of fact; but in the[c] Vindication he[d] shewed me
some time since, which must needes give any-man of reason
satisfaction: Our Doctor Preach'd the funerall sermon on

He was a sober, frugal, cherefull & temperat man; we
have few such sea-men left:

[e]There ⟨came⟩[f] to Condole the death of my deare Daughter
this Weeke moneday, & friday: The Countesses of Bristoll,
Sunderland, La: Sylvius, Mrs. Penelope Godolphin:[2] Sir
Stephen Fox & his Lady &c:

29 Our Viccar preach'd on his former Text 13: Luke. 24:
pursuing the greate difficulties of entring the straite gate, &
how we must resolve to subdue & conquer all impediments:
&⟨c⟩: The Curate on 1. *Cor*: 2. 6. shewing the infinite wisdome
of God in the Mysteries of Our faith, & how agreable to sound
reason:

A servant mayd of my Wifes fell sick of the very same

---

a Followed by *what ti-* deleted.   b Altered from *a rock*.
c Altered from *wh-*.   d Altered from *the* or *she*.   e Here is a
marginal date 27 deleted   f MS. *ccame* altered from *cacme*.

---

[1] Above, p. 80. He was master
of the *Prince*, the duke of York's
flagship, in the battle of Solebay
(above, iii. 616). When James sailed
to Scotland in the *Gloucester* in May
1682 (above, p. 282 n.) Gunman was
in command of the *Mary* yacht,
which accompanied her. He was
tried by a court martial on 6 and
13 June, and was sentenced to be
dismissed from his command, to be
imprisoned during pleasure, and to
forfeit a year's pay. The king
ordered him to send him his own
account of the proceedings against
him, and he was pardoned and
reinstated (apart from the loss of
pay) on 19 June: *Cal. S.P., Dom.,
1682*, pp. 247, 253; *Hist. MSS.
Comm., Dartmouth MSS.*, i. 74–5,
where a copy of Gunman's vindication is also mentioned.

[2] She died unmarried in 1697:
Marsh, *The Godolphins*, p. 11.

disease, of the same sort of S:pox, & in all appearance in as greate danger, though she never came neere my daughter: we removed her into the Towne with care:

Aprill: 5 Our Viccar proceeded: & the Curate on 2: Phil: 8: of the Exinanition of Christ: Drowsinesse much surpriz'd me: The Lord be gratious to me:

The mayd, by Gods greate mercy, but with extraordinary difficulty, recovered: Blessed be God:

7 Being now somewhat compos'd after my greate affliction, I went to Lond: to heare Dr. Tenison (it being [8]ᵃ a Wednesday in Lent) at Whitehall: who preached on 3. *Gen:* 3. Concerning the obedience exacted of our first parents, & that the sinn was not so frivolous as Atheistical men used to pretend:¹ Se your notes: I returned in the Evening: I observ'd that though the King was not in his seate above in the Chapell, the Doctor made notwithstanding his three congèes, which they were not us'd to do, when the [late]ᵇ King was absent, making then one bowing onely: I asked the reason; it was sayd, he had a special order so to do:² The Princesse of Denmarke yet was in the Kingsᶜ Closset, but sat on the left hand of the Chaire, the clearke of the Closset³ standing by his Majesties Chaire as if he had ben present: [I met Q: Dowager going now first from W.hall to dwell at Somerset house.]ᵈ⁴ This day was my Bro: of Wotton [& Mr. Onslow]ᵇ (candidates against Sir Adam Bro: & my Co: Sir Edward Evelyn) circumvented of their Elections standing for knights of *Surry* for the ensuing Parliament by a trick of the Sheriffs, taking advantage of my brother &c: partys going out of theᵉ small village of Letherhead to seeke shelter & lodging, the afternoone being very tempestious; to proceede to the Election when they were gon, expecting the next

---

ᵃ Marginal date.   ᵇ Interlined.   ᶜ Followed by *sea-* deleted.
ᵈ Inserted after text was written.   ᵉ Followed by *To-* deleted.

---

¹ Lenten sermon at court.
² Wood notes the order as being carried out already on 22 February: *Life and times*, iii. 132.
³ Nathaniel Crew, bishop of

Durham: above, p. 418.
⁴ This apparently took place on the evening of 7 April: the Tuscan resident, in Campana de Cavelli, ii. 36.

morning: where[a] as[a] before, & then they exceeded the other
party by (I am assured) many hundreds: The Duke of
Norfolck lead Sir Ed: E: & Sir Adam Browns party: but this
Election was very unfaire:[1] Indeede I writ to my Bro:
earnestly not to stand, finding the Court was unwilling he
should, & that I had observ'd by the account we had weekly,
what very meane & slight persons (some of them Gent:
Servants, Clearks, persons neither of reputation nor Interest)
were set up;[2] but the Country would choose him whether he
would or no: but thus he miss'd it, by an indirect trick, as
appeared; the other Candidate Sir Adam Browne, was so
deafe, that he could not heare one word: But Sir Ed:
Evelyn, an honest Gent: & much in favour with his Majestie,
& it had ben but decent in my Bro: to have transferred his
Votes to him, as I advised:[3]

10 Friday I went early to W:hall to heare Dr. Tillotson[4]
deane of Cant: preaching on 9: *Eccl:* 18: upon those words:

---

a-a Or *where-as* or *when as.*

---

[1] The election took place on
8 April. Adam Browne, d. 1690;
second baronet 1661; of Betch-
worth (above, iii. 143, &c.); previously M.P. for Surrey 1661:
G.E.C., *Baronetage*, ii. 29. Edward
Evelyn, 1626–92 ; son of Sir
Thomas Evelyn of Long Ditton, a
first cousin of George and John
Evelyn; knighted 1676; created a
baronet 1683: Foljambe, pp. 46–7,
55; this was the only occasion on
which he was elected M.P. The
sheriff was Samuel Lewen. The
duke of Norfolk was lord lieutenant
of Surrey from 1682 to 1701. For
the sheriff's trick on this occasion
see *English hist. review*, xxviii (1913),
62; the then sheriff had tried to trick
George Evelyn and Onslow in a
somewhat similar way in August
1679: ibid, p. 60.

[2] Returns of members are published in every number of the
London Gazette from 12 March to

4 May. The social status of the
members of this parliament has not
been investigated. According to
Burnet, 'they were neither men of
parts nor estates': *Own time*, 1833,
iii. 17; according to Ailesbury,
'there never was such an appearance
in any age, consisting of the prime
lords that were Commons, and the
top gentry of each county', this at
least for a very large informal
gathering, if not the whole house:
Memoirs, i. 100–1.

[3] Evelyn's letters to his brother
are not extant, but two letters from
George in reply, 20 February, 30
March, are printed by H. Evelyn,
pp. 48–51. For court influence in
the elections see above, p. 419 n.;
for alleged trickery Luttrell, i. 341.

[4] Lenten sermon at court. The
verse number should be 10; the
sermon is printed in Tillotson,
Works, 1752, iii. 363–70.

What soever thine hand findeth out to do, do it &c: *for there is nothing to be don in the Grave:* Applying most of it to the worke[a] of Charity, & exemplarinesse of a good life, & to the greate buisinesse of timely Repentance; especial pressing it to Noble & greate men, who had most opportunities; & how severe the account would be, if they neglected it: in as much as there could be no after act of retrivance[1] after this life: a very usefull discourse: I return'd in the Evening: I visited my Lady Tuke, and found with her Sir Geo: Wakeman[2] the Physitian, whom I had seene tried & acquitted amongst the plotters, about empoys'ning his late Majestie upon the accusation of the famous *Oates*: & surely, I believ'd him guiltlesse: Se 18 July:—79:

12 A stranger preach'd very well for-noone on 5. *Gall.* 24: concerning the necessitie of crucifying all sinfull desires of what sort soever, without the least indulgence to any: *pomeridiano*[3] The Comm: followed: at which I was participant: The Lord be praised:

The same person in the Afternoone on 24: *Act:* 25, S. Paules sermon to *Felix.* Drowsinesse so exceedingly surpriz'd me, that I could hardly hold up my head, at the sermon: The Lord pardon me:

14 According to my costome, I went to *Lond:* to passe the *Holy Weeke:*

15 Dr. *Craddock*[4] Provost[b] of *Eaton* preach'd at W:hall: on 1: *Heb:* 8, most excellently shewing That *Christ* is *God* against the *Arrians* of old & *Socinians* of late;[5] & proving by innumerable Scriptures (Especialy of this Chapter) the Deity of our *B: Saviour:* As by his joyning with the Father in the Creation; his eternity, by many places in the *Psal:* his power [& grace][c] in the work of our Redemption, in the *Prophets:* his Miracles; Adorations paied him even by the

---

[1] This word is not given in *O.E.D.*
[2] Above, p. 173. He gave evidence in Oates's first trial on 8 May.
[3] A mistake.

[4] Lenten sermon at court.
[5] Evelyn describes Socinus as a 'modern Arian, as well as Pelagian': *Hist. of Religion,* ii. 248.

Angels, & severall other ⟨manifest⟩[a] proofes through the new
Test: asserting it: He also forewarn'd of the Blasphemy,
Ingratitude, of those who denyed it, & made him but a
Phantosme, at best a mere[b] extraordinary man, but which
could never merit the pardon of sinns, & restauration to Gods
favour nor possibly performe the greate work of our
Redemption:

17 *Good Friday,* preach'd at the new Church (St. *Jame's*)
Dr. Tenison[1] on 1: *Cor:* 16: 22: Upon the infinite Love of
God to us, which he illustrated by many instances, especialy
that of his sending the Lord Jesus, & his coming, & being
Incarnate, to save us, dying that accursed death of the Crosse
for us: Obligations so transcendently greate and stupendious;
that those who made no returnes of Love to him againe were
worthy of the greatest malediction: *Anathema,* the one a
Greeke word; signifying devoted, or designed: *Maranatha* (a
Syriac expression) importing, *God shall come*; or reserved to
the final and greatest Curse at the day of Judgement:[2] Not
as an imprecation of the Apostle; but as a warning, what
those deserved, who loved not God, & that there was no
medium between it and absolute hatred of God, which he
also shewed by severall arguments: The holy Sacrament
follow'd at[c] which I participated: The Lord make me
thankfull:

In the Afternoone preached in *W:Hall:* Chap: (the Auditory very full of Lords; The two Arch-Bish: & many others,
now drawn to Towne upon the occasion of the *Coronation*
& ensuing *Parliament*) Dr. *Sprat* Deane of *Westminster* &
Bish: of Rochester:[3] on: 2. *Titus* 14: shewing That *Christs*
giving him-selfe for us was the most invaluable Gift not onely
that ever was given; but that God could Give: The purpose

---

a MS. *maniflest.*   b Or *more.*   c Altered from or to *of.*

---

[1] Listed among the divines to
preach here every Friday in Lent
this year: *Lent Preachers appointed
by the Lord-Bishop of London to
preach on Wednesdays and Fridays,
for the year 1684/5.*

[2] For Anathema Maranatha see
above, iii. 337; iv. 164.
[3] Sprat had been consecrated
bishop of Rochester on 2 Nov. 1684.
Lenten sermon at court.

of this Gift, being [not onely]ª to Redeeme wretched sinners, but to prepare them with such eminent & necessary graces & perfections, as might intitle them to Everlasting happinesse: He tooke occasion (speaking of the necessity of *Good-Works*, not as *meritorious*, but signes of our Faith & other Graces) to shew, that there had ben more Works of Munificent Charity of all degrees & kinds (bating [the]ª superstitious pomps,ᵇ & ostentation among the Papists) withinᶜ 100 yeares since the Reformation; than in all the ages which went before: & this was very well justified & applyed:

I supped with the Countesse of Sunderland & Lord Godolphin, & so returned home:

19 *Easter-day* our *Viccar* on 4: *Rom:* 25: Insisting chiefly on the nature & notion of Justification, & how through the sufferings of Christ for us, repentant sinners, are Justified, an undenyable proofe whereof was the Resurrection of our Lord: The H: Comm: followed, of which my *Wife*, (& my Daughter *Susan* the first time)[1] with my selfe received: Blessed be God:

Pomeridiano, the *Curate*: on 2: *Phil:* 8: upon our B: Lords exinanition &c: Drowsinesse exceedingly surpriz'd me:

23 Was the day of his Majesties Coronation, the Queene was also crown'd, the solemnity very magnificent, as the particulars are set forth in print:[2] The Bish: of Ely[3] preached, but (to the greate sorrow of the people) no Sacrament, as ought to have ben:[4] However the King beginns his reigne with greate expectations and hopes of much reformation as to the former vices, & prophanesse both of Court & Country:

ª Interlined.   ᵇ Or *pompe*.   ᶜ Substituted for *since*.

---

[1] She was now nearly sixteen years old.

[2] There is a notice of the coronation in *London Gazette*, 27 April; and *An Account of the Ceremonial at the Coronation* was 'published by Order of the Duke of *Norfolk* Earl Marshal' in 1685. The most elaborate account is F. Sandford, *The History of the Coronation of . . . James II . . .*

And . . . *Queen Mary*, 1687.

[3] Turner's sermon was printed this year.

[4] The king and queen are said to have been anointed and crowned in private by the king's confessor before the public ceremony began: Martin Haile, *Queen Mary of Modena*, p. 128.

Having ben present at our late Kings Coronation, I was not ambitious of seing this Ceremonie; nor did I think fit to leave my poore Wife alone, who was yet in greate sorrow:

⟨26⟩[a] A *stranger* preached on 13: *Heb:* 16. concerning the duty of Charity, the extent of it, how it became a Sacrifice, & how acceptable; how comfortable & advantagious to the Giver: That the realy wanting had title to all we could spare; how much more gratefull & gainefull which were don during our lives; The infinite blessing attending it here, & especially at the last day:

Hearing that my good neighbour, [the][b] painefull & charitable Dr. Par, minister of *Peccham*[1] was dangerously ill, We went first to church ther where the *Curate* preached on Phil: a Resurrection sermon:

29 I went to Lond: about my yet troublesome suite &c: returned 2d of May:

May: 3 Our Viccar preached on 4 Rom: 25 shewing how the Resurrection of Christ did Justifie us, what Justification also was, and saving faith &c: The bl: Communion follow'd of which I received: *Pomeridiano*, a young man (now going [chaplain][b] with Sir Jo: Wiburn[2] governor of *Bombain* in the East *Indias*) on 13. *Rom:* 8: in a very neate discourse exhorting to the vertue of love and charity:

5 To Lond: 7th: I was in Westminster Hall when *Oates* (who had made such a stirr in the whole Kingdome, (upon his revealing a plot of the Papists) as alarm'd several Parliaments, & had occasion'd the execution of divers persons, priests, noble men &c:)[c] was tried for Perjurie at the Kingsbench; but it being exceedingly tedious, I did not much endeavor to see the issue of it, considering that it would certainely be publish'd: Aboundance of R: Cath: were now

---

[a] MS. 27.   [b] Interlined.   [c] Closing bracket supplied.

[1] Peckham was only a hamlet in the parish of Camberwell; it was of the latter that Parr was vicar.

[2] John Wyborne, naval officer; apparently knighted in 1682; appointed deputy-governor of Bombay 1685 under Sir John Child (*D.N.B.*);

dismissed for insubordination 1687: *Cal. S.P., Dom.*; J. Bruce, *Annals of the Honorable East-India Company*, 1810, ii. 552-86; *Selections from the letters . . . in the Bombay Secretariat*, ed. G. W. Forrest, Home ser., 1887, i. 142-58.

in the Hall, in expectation of the most gratefull conviction
& ruine of a person who had ben so obnoxious to them; &
as I verily believe had don much mischiefe & greate injurie
to several by his violent & ill grounded proceedings, whilst
he was at first so unreasonably blowne-up, & encourag'd, that
his insolence was no longer sufferable:[1]

[6 I went to the R: Society, Dr. Wallis[2] presenting his
booke of *Algebra* &c:][a]

7 ⟨I⟩[b] went this Evening to visite my L. Arch: Bishop of
Yorke:

Roger Le Strange (a gent: whom I had long known, & a
person of excellent[c] parts, abating some affectations) appearing first against the Dissenters, in severall Tractates; had
now for some yeares turn'd his style against those whom (by
way of hatefull distinction) they called Whiggs & Trimmers;
under the title of *Observator*, which came out 3 or 4 days every
weeke: In which sheets,[d] under pretence to serve the Church
of England, he gave suspicion of gratif⟨y⟩ing another party,
by severall passages, which rather kept up animosities, than
appeased, especialy now that nobody gave the least occasion:[3]
[8][e] I return'd home:

---

a Inserted after next notice was written.   b MS. *A*.   c MS. *ext*:
d Or *sheete*.   e Marginal date.

---

[1] Oates was tried in the court of
King's Bench on 8 and 9 May on
two separate indictments for per-
jury and was found guilty in each
case: notice in *London Gazette*, 11
May; the trials were published as
*The Tryals, Convictions & Sentence of
Titus Otes*, 1685.

[2] Above, iii. 287, &c.; his book is
*A Treatise of Algebra both Historical
and Practical . . . With some Additional Treatises*, 1685 (some of the
treatises Oxford, 1684).

[3] For L'Estrange see above, iii.
167; iv. 35. For his attack on the
dissenters in 1661–3 see Kitchin,
pp. 75–87. He began *The Observator* on 13 April 1681 and continued
it until 9 March 1687; according to

his enumeration there were 931
numbers, an average of slightly
over three a week. It was in dia-
logue form; from 2 July 1681 to
6 Sept. 1682 between Whig and
Tory; from 13 Nov. 1682 to the
end between Trimmer and Observator. It was strongly loyalist—
Tory and Anglican—and marked
by its animosity against the dissenters. The numbers for 21 and
28 February of this year gave considerable offence; and L'Estrange,
while opposed to liberty of conscience or toleration, was obliged to
find some argument giving the
sovereign freedom for himself while
denying it to his subjects. He was
knighted on 30 April of this year;

10 Our *Viccar* preached on his former Text, shewing the necessity of ⟨an⟩[a] Apostolical Ministrie & order in the Church, in order to Conversion &c:

Pomerid: a Young stranger on 2 *Samuell* 2. 7. being a kind of funeral sermon on our late King, & elogies of his successor, without much to the purpose:

The *Scots*, valuing themselvs exceedingly to have ben the first Parliament called by his Majestie gave[b] the Excise Costomes &c: forever to the K. & successors; the Duke of *Queenesborow* &c making eloquent speeches, & especialy minding them of a speedy suppression of those late desperate fild Conventiclers, who had don so unheard of assasinations &c:[1] In the meane time Elections for the ensuing Parliament in England, were thought to be very indirectly carried on in most places, and persons chosen who had no interest in the Country & places for which they served:[2] God grant a better issue of it, than some expect:

12[c] To Lond: about my petition: 13. R: *Society*. Earle of Pembroque was admitted:[3]

16 Was sentenc'd *Oates* to be whip'd & pilloried with uttmost severity: &c:[4]

---

a MS. *on*.   b Followed by *him* deleted.   c Altered from *13* ?

in the number for 2 May he defends the Roman Catholics: besides *The Observator* see Kitchin, p. 358. L'Estrange remained an Anglican. He had been returned M.P. for Winchester on 16 March.

[1] From *London Gazette*, 7, 11 May. The Scottish parliament had met on 23 April; the duke was William Douglas, 1637–95; third earl of Queensberry (Scotland) 1671; created marquis of Queensberry (Scotland) 1682; duke 1684: *D.N.B.* He was acting as lord high commissioner. For the recusant Presbyterians since Bothwell Bridge (above, p. 171 n.) and the rise of the Cameronians see P. Hume Brown, *Hist. of Scotland*, 1911, ii. 326–34.

[2] Compare Luttrell's remarks made about this time: i. 341.

[3] Thomas Herbert, c. 1656–1733; eighth earl of Pembroke 1683; president of the Royal Society 1689–90: *D.N.B.*

[4] 'That he shall be divested of his Canonical Habit for ever, That on Monday next he be carried round *Westminster-Hall* with a Paper on his Head declaring his Offence . . . And that afterwards he stand in the Pillory before *Westminster*-Hall Gate, and on Tuesday before the *Royal Exchange*, That on Wednesday he be Whipt from *Aldgate* to *Newgate* by the Common Hangman, and on Friday following from *Newgate* to *Tyburn*, That he stand in the Pillory on every 24th of *April* during his

17 *Viccar* absent, The Curate pr: on: 2: Philip: 8 seting forth the bitter passion of our B: Lord &⟨c⟩: *pomeridiano*, I went to visite Dr. *Par* of *Camberwell*, now recovering of his long sicknes: after sermon there, a *Scotch*-young man preaching on 12 *Luke*. 32: Magnifying the infinite bounty of our Lord; exceeding all gifts, the bestowing no lesse than a Kingdome to every one of his flock:

20 To *Lond:* R: Soc: 21. Din'd at my Lord Privy-Seales,[1] with Sir *Will: Dugdale*[2] the ⟨Garter⟩[a] K: at Armes, Author of the *Monasticon*, & greate Antiquarie; with whom I had much discourse: he told me he was 82 yeares of age, had his sight & memory perfect &c: There was shew'd a draght of the exact shape & dimensions of the Crowne the Queene had ben crown'd withall, together with the Jewells & Pearles, their weight & value, which amounted to 100650 pounds sterling, an immense summ: attested at the foote of the paper by the Jeweller and Gooldsmith who set the Jewells &c:[3]

---

[a] MS. *Carter*.

Life before *Tyburn*, on every 9th of *August* in the *Palace-Yard* at *Westminster*, on every 10th of *August* at *Charing-Cross*, on every 11th of *August* at *Temple-Bar*, and on every second of *September* before the *Royal-Exchange* . . . That he pay a Fine of 1000 Marks for each Perjury, and that he suffer Imprisonment during his Life': *London Gazette*, 18 May. Oates was released at the Revolution and the judges declared that his sentence had been erroneous, cruel, and illegal; owing to his own bad management it was never formally reversed: see especially *Hist. MSS. Comm., House of Lords MSS., 1689–90*, pp. 78–80. On 19 Sept. 1689 King William, in response to an address of the commons, granted him an allowance of £10 per week; by 1695 this had sunk to £200 per annum; in 1698 it was fixed at £300 per annum: *Cal. Treasury Books, 1689–92*, p. 53;

1693–6, p. 1393; *1697–8*, p. 392.

[1] Clarendon.

[2] Above, iii. 171; he was Garter king-of-arms from 1677 until his death. The three volumes of the *Monasticon Anglicanum* were published in 1655, 1661, and 1673; for later editions see *D.N.B.* He was born on 12 Sept. 1605. For his presence in London at this time see his *Life, diary,* &c., pp. 146–7.

[3] This apparently refers not to the crown with which the queen was crowned, but to the 'Rich Crown' which she wore on her return to Westminster Hall; it was set with jewels valued at £111,900: Sandford, *Hist. of the Coronation*, p. 42, where nothing is said of the value of the other crown; Sandford figures both of them; he gives the jeweller's name, Richard Beauvoir. Most of the jewels were borrowed for the occasion: *Cal. Treasury Books, 1685–9*, pp. 157, 243.

22 In the morning, I went (together with a French gent, a person of quality) with my Lord Pr: Seale[1] to the house of Lords, where we were both plac'd by his Lordship next the barr just below the Bishops very commodiously both for hearing and seeing:[2] After a short space came in the Queene & Princesse of Denmark, & stood next above the Arch-Bishops, at the side of the house on the right hand of his Majesties *Throne*: In the interim divers of the Lords (who had not finish'd before) tooke the Test, & usual Oathes, so as her Majestie (Spanish Ambassador[3] & other forraine Ministers who stood behind the state) heard the Pope, & worship of the Virg: Mary &c: renounc'd very decently,[4] as likewise the following Prayers, standing all the while:[5] Then came in the King, the Crowne on his head &c and being sate, The Commons were let in, so the house being fill'd, he drew forth a Paper, containing his speech, which he ⟨read⟩[a] distinctly enough to this effect: That he resolved to call a Parliament from the moment of his brothers decease, as the best meanes to settle all the concernes of the Nation so as might be most easy & happy to himselfe & his subjects: That he would confirme what ever he had said in his declaration at the first Council, concerning his[b] opinion of the principles of the Church of England, for their Loyaltie, & would defend & support it, and preserve its government, as by Law

---

[a] MS. *reod*.   [b] Followed by *good* deleted.

---

[1] Clarendon. There is a notice of this day's proceedings in *London Gazette*, 25 May.

[2] For pictures of the sovereign in parliament see above, iii. 402 n. That nearest in date to 1685 is one belonging to the reign of Queen Anne: reproduction in Trevelyan, *Ramillies*. The sovereign occupied the throne near the upper end of the room, with the bishops sitting on his right and the temporal peers on his left; the bar was near the lower end of the room, and outside it stood the commons, the Speaker in the centre, facing the sovereign.

[3] Ronquillo: above, p. 242. The state is the chair of state or throne: cf. above, ii. 391.

[4] Members of both houses were required to take the oaths of supremacy and allegiance and to 'make subscribe and audibly repeate' a declaration under the parliamentary Test Act (1678; above, p. 159) in which they denied certain Roman Catholic tenets, some of them being described as 'superstitious and idolatrous'.

[5] Prayers apparently preceded the taking of the oaths, &c.

now establish'd: That as he would Invade no mans property, so he would never depart from his owne prerogative: & as he had ⟨ventur'd⟩ᵃ his life in defence of the nation so he would proceede to do still: That having given this assurance of his Care of our Religion (his word was *your* Religion) & propertie, (which he had not said by chance, but solemnly) so he doubted not of suitable returnes of his subjects duty & kindnesse, especialy as to the settling his Revenue for life for the many weighty necessities of the government which he would not suffer to be precarious: That some might possibly suggest that it were better to feede & supply him from time to time onely, out of their inclination to frequent Parliaments; but that that, would be but a very improper Method to take with him; since the best way to engage him to meete oftener, would be allways to use him well; & therefore expected their compliance speedily, that this session being but short, they might meete again to satisfaction: *At every period of this, the house gave lowd shouts* &c: Then he acquainted them with that mornings news of *Argiles* being landed in the West-highlands of *Scotland* from Holland, and the Treasonous declaration he had published, which he would communicate to them, & that he should take the best care he could it should meete with the reward it deserv'd, not questioning of the parliaments Zeale & readinesse to assist him, as he desired: *At which There followed another Vive le roy*, & so his Majestie retired: &c:[1] & I went into the Court of Requests &c:[2]

So soone as the Commons were return'd, & put themselves, into a grand Committè, they immediately put the Question,

---

ᵃ MS. *ventar'd*.

---

[1] The report of the speech from *London Gazette*, 25 May; the last words of the first part are that the revenue should be granted 'speedily, That this may be a short Session, and That We may Meet again to all Our Satisfactions'. The notice of the acclamations is original.

Argyll (above, iii. 318) had sent one of his sons ashore at Dunstaffnage in Lorne on 13 May and had there published two declarations: *London Gazette*, 25 May. For his rebellion see J. Willcock, *A Scots Earl . . . Archibald 9th earl of Argyll*, 1907, pp. 329–96.

[2] Above, iii. 435.

& unanimously voted the Revenue to his Majestie during life: Mr. *Seamour*[1] made a bold speech against many Elections, and would have had those Members who (he pretended) were obnoxious, to withdraw, 'til they had cleared their being legaly return'd, but no body seconded him: The truth is there were very many of the new Members, whose Elections & returnes were universaly censur'd; being divers of them persons of no manner of condition or Interest in the nation, and places for which they served, especialy in the Counties of Devon, Cornwell, Norfolck,[2] &c, said to have ben recommended from the Court, and effect of the new charters, changing the Electors: It was reported my L: of Bath, carried-down with him no fewer than 15 Charters, so as some cald him the Prince Elector:[3] whence *Seaymor* told the house in his speech, that if this were digested, they might introduce what Religion & Lawes they pleased, & that though he never gave heede to the feares & jealosies of the people before, he now was realy apprehensive of Popery &c: The truth is, by the printed List of Members of 505, there did not appear to be above 135 who had ben in former Parliaments, especialy that lately held at Oxon:[a][4]

In the Lords house, my Lord Newport made but an

---

[a] MS. *Oxoñ.*

---

[1] Edward Seymour: above, iii. 501. The best report of his speech is that given by Barillon: in Fox, app., pp. xciii–iv; see also Burnet, *Own time*, 1833, iii. 41. There was some other business before the house went into committee.

[2] Devon returned 26 members, of whom 22 had not sat for the same constituencies in 1681; Cornwall 44, of whom 31 were new; Norfolk 12, of whom 11 were new: cf. note below.

[3] On 25 Nov. 1684 Bath had returned from the west to Whitehall 'well loaden with western charters': Surtees Soc., *Misc.* (vol. xxxvii, 1861: Dr. D. Granville, pt. i), p. 190; *London Gazette*, 15 Dec. Burnet's

statement about his influence on the Cornish elections has never been questioned: *Own time*, 1833, iii. 16.

[4] Evelyn is probably following *A True and Compleat List of the Lords . . . Knights, Citizens, and Burgesses, of the Present Parliament*, 1685, the version printed by T. Newcomb. This prints 513 as the total number of the commons and marks 136 as having been members of the parliament at Oxford in 1681, but the latter figure is based on a crude comparison by constituencies. The turnover was probably in any case unusually large: a similar comparison for the Oxford parliament gives only 110 new members.

impertinent exception against two or three [young]ᵃ Peeres, who wanted some moneths, & some onely 4 or 5 daies of being of age:¹

The Popish Lords (who had some time before ben released from their Confinement about the Plot) were now discharg'd of their Impeachment: of which I gave my L. Arundel of Wardoer joy:²

Oates, who had but two days before ben pilloried at severall places, & whip't at the Carts taile from New-gate to Algate;³ was this day placed in a sledge (being not able to goᵇ by reason of his so late scourging) & dragd from prison to Tyburn, & whip'd againe all the way, which some thought to be very severe & extraordinary; but in case he were gilty of the perjuries, & so of the death of many innocents, as I feare he was; his punishment was but what he well deserv'd: I chanc'd to passe in my Coach, just as Execution was doing on him: *A strange revolution.*

Note, that there was no speech made by my *Lord Keeper*, after his Majesties as usualy:⁴ It was whispered, he would not long be in that station; & many believing the bold Chiefe Justice *Jeofries* (now made Baron of Wem in Yorkshire, & who went through-stitch in that Tribunal) stoodᶜ faire for that Office:⁵ I gave him joy theᵈ morning before of his new honor, he having always ben very civil to me &c:

ᵃ Interlined.   ᵇ Followed by *for* deleted.   ᶜ Or *stand*.
ᵈ Altered from *that*.

---

¹ I have found no other notices of Newport's speech and no specific cases of peers who were under age being present in this parliament. A standing order forbidding their attendance was made this day: *L.J.*, xiv. 10.

² On 19 March 1679 the lords had resolved 'that the Dissolution of the last Parliament doth not alter the state of the Impeachments brought up by the Commons in that Parliament'; on this day (22 May) it was resolved that this order should 'be reversed and annulled, as to Impeachments': *L.J.*, xiii. 466; xiv. 11.

³ It was from Aldgate to Newgate.

⁴ Guilford had prepared a speech; it is printed in North, *Life of Guilford*, pp. 256–8.

⁵ Jeffreys was created Baron Jeffreys 'of *Wem* in the County of *Salop*' on 15 May: *London Gazette*, 18 May. Already about 20 May Luttrell gives it as 'a very hot report' that Jeffreys would supersede Guilford: i. 343.

23 I supped this Evening with much Company at my L. Privy-Seales,[1] & return'd home next morning:

24 Our *Viccar* having lost his onely sonn, & one of his daughters, (who died I think[a] both in the same week of feavors, but at some greate distance each from the other),[2] a stranger supplied the pulpet, on 2. *Cor:* 4. 17. shewing the little proportion betweene all our sorrows, losses & suffering in this life, compar'd to the exceeding weight of glory & reward in the life to come; by many instances & proofes:[b] &c: The *Curate pomerid*: &c on 12: *Matt:* 20.

I fell into an exceeding drowsinesse after prayers:

We had hithertoo [not][c] any raine for many monethes, insomuch as the Caterpillar had already devoured all the Winter fruite through the whole land, & even killed severall greate & old trees; such two Winters, & Summers I had never known:

27 I went to Lond: There was newes of *Argiles* being landed in Scotland, having published a treasonous Declaration:[3] 29. A Loyal Sermon at St. *Martines* on 124: *Psal:* 8. rememorating the signal deliverances of the late & present King, & exhorting to thankfullnesse & obedience: The Office for the day being now newly fitted for the occasion since his late Majesties Restoration & death:[4] After Sermon I returned home.

My Lord Clarendon L. Privy-Seale was so obliging, as to give me the use of his intire Lodgings in White-hall, he having accommodation in another part of the house:[5]

30 I went againe to Lond: to resigne a Trust which concerned Mrs. *Thayre* & her husband;[6] return'd that evening:

---

[a] Followed by closing bracket.　　[b] Altered from *ex-*.　　[c] Interlined.

---

[1] Clarendon.

[2] The daughter, Rebecca, was buried at Deptford on 23 May: Drake's Hasted, p. 41.

[3] Besides the notice in *London Gazette*, 25 May, where Argyll's two declarations are printed, there are further notices of his movements in the issues for 28 May and 1 June.

[4] The new *Form of Prayer* was ordered to be published on 29 April. The king's order, which is printed with it, explains why a new form is necessary.

[5] The positions of Clarendon's sets of lodgings are unknown.

[6] A Mrs. Thyer is mentioned in Mrs. Evelyn's will, 1709.

31 Our Viccar preached on 13ᵃ Luke: 24: on which he had enter'd above a moneth before,[1] upon the word ἀγωνίζεσθε ἐισελθεῖν shewing the necessity of importunat prayer from the example of Jacobs wrestling, [Moses],ᵇ David, [Eliah,]ᵇ Hezekiah, Daniel, S. Paule & especialy our B: Saviour, for the obtaining the greatest Victories over our enemies spiritual or temporal; above all in conjunction with the Church & in the publique service of God; *Pomerid*: the *Viccar* on. 1. Cor: 2. 2. The importance of the knowledge of Christ above all other things:

June 4. Came to visite, and take leave of me Sir *Gab: Sylvius* now going Envoyè Extraordinary into Denmark:[2] with his secretary, & chaplaine, a french-man who related the miserable persecution of the Protestants in Fr:[3] not

---

ᵃ Altered from *12*.   ᵇ Interlined.

---

[1] See above, pp. 418, 432.

[2] He was appointed envoy extraordinary apparently in March and took leave of the king on 29 May: *Cal. Treasury Books, 1685–9*, pp. 42, 466. He remained in Denmark until 1689.

[3] The attack on French protestantism was inaugurated by the French Roman Catholic clergy about 1661 and was supported by Louis XIV when he assumed control of the government in that year. It increased in violence from about 1679, the dragonnades beginning in 1680; it was rapidly intensified in 1685, and culminated on 18 October, N.S., in the Revocation of the Edict of Nantes, an act by which the assembling of the Protestants for worship was declared illegal.

This edict of Revocation further ordered the immediate expulsion of the Protestant clergy from France. All other Protestants were forbidden to leave the kingdom; a clause granting freedom from interference to Protestants remaining there was rendered practically nugatory by the local officials; chil-

dren were henceforward to be baptized Roman Catholics. As a result of the persecution there was a large number of conversions; but many Protestants sought refuge in flight, while others, assembling as best they could, formed by degrees the churches of the Desert. The government's policy changed after a time; while relapsed converts were liable to be sent, the men to the galleys, the women to convents, from 1687 escape abroad was more or less tacitly permitted and in 1688 some of those who had refused to be converted were deported. The great majority of the conversions were at best superficial, and were very frequently fraudulent. Surveillance of the new converts and more or less active persecution of the remaining Protestants continued until the end of the reign.

The population of France in 1700 is estimated as 19 millions. By the end of 1685 Claude estimated that there were 150,000 refugees; modern French writers suggest 200,000 for the years immediately preceding and following the Revocation; and

above ten Churches left them, and they threatned to be also demolish'd: That they were commanded to christen their children within 24 houres after birth, or else a Popish-priest was to be call'd, & then the Infant brought-up in popery: and that in some places they were 30 leagues from any Minister or opportunity: That this persecution had dispeopled the most industrious part of the nation and dispers'd them into Swisse, Burgundy, Hollond, Ger: Denmark, England, Plantations & where not.[1] There were with Sir Gab: his Lady, Sir William Godolphin, and sisters, & my Lord Godolphins little son, (my Charge): I brought them to the water side, where Sir *Gab:* embarked for his Voyage, & the rest return'd to Lond:

7 Our *Viccar* proceedes—shewing the necessity of reading the Scriptures, and answering all objections of the papists forbiding it the laity &c: The holy Comm: follow'd of which

---

about a million for the period from 1680 to 1720. The Protestants were largely engaged in productive work and their flight resulted in a catastrophic decline of some manufactures.

The principal older work is [E. Benoist], *Histoire de l'Edit de Nantes*, 1693–5. There is a good modern account in Lavisse, *Histoire de France*, VII. ii. 39–80; VIII. i. 340–88; see further E. Guitard, *Colbert et Seignelay contre la Religion Réformée*, 1912. For the population of France see L. Schöne, *Histoire de la population française*, 1893; and for the fugitives, R. Lane Poole, *A History of the Huguenots of the Dispersion*, 1880.

Although no notice of the persecution appeared in the *London Gazette* in James II's reign and although very little printed matter relating to it can have circulated, knowledge of it must have been widespread; especially as there were general collections made for the refugees by the Briefs of 1686 and 1688. Probably six churches were established

in London and the neighbouring places between 1685 and 1688; and fifteen throughout the kingdom between 1686 and March 1688; 15,000 persons were said to have been relieved between May 1686 and December 1687: Huguenot Soc., *Proc.* vii (1901–4), 125, 139. Evelyn was in a good position to hear about the persecution, especially after the settlement of Ruvigny at Greenwich in 1686 and the establishment of a church there.

[1] The first statement, about the number of churches, is wrong; about sixty were suppressed between 1 June and October, when the Edict of Revocation was issued: list in J. Le Févre, *Nouveau Recüeil ... les Protestans*, 1686; others were destroyed in accordance with the first article of the Edict. The order for the baptism of children within twenty-four hours of birth was first issued in October 1684: Benoist, iii (v), 704. For the places of refuge at about the end of this year, see ibid., pp. 958–60.

my selfe, Wife & Child &c: participated, it being Whitsonday. *Pomerid*: Curate on: 2 *Heb:* 3. shewing with what care & dilligence we should work out Salvation: Drowsines sur-priz'd me: The Lord be gracious:

14 Our Viccar & Curate proceeded on their former Texts: There was now certaine Intelligence of the Duke of Mon-moths landing at Lyn in Dorset shire, & of his having set up his standart, as K. of England:[1] I pray God deliver us from the confusions which these beginings threaten:

Such a drowth for want of raine, was never in my memory:[2]

17 To *Lond:* at which time the D: of Monmoth invaded this nation landing with but 150 men at *Lyme* in Dorsetshire, which wonderfully alarm'd the whole Kingdome, fearing the joyning of dissafected people; many of the train'd bands flocking to him: he had at his landing publish'd a Declaration, charging his Majestie with Usurpation, & severall horrid crimes, upon pretence of his owne title, and the calling of a free-Parliament: This Decl: was condemn'd to be burnt by the hang-man, the Duke proclaim'd Traytor, a reward of 5000 pounds to him that should kill him &c:[3] Now were also those words in the Inscription about the *Pillar* (intimating the Papists firing the Citty) erased and cut out &c:[4]

---

[1] Monmouth disembarked at Lyme Regis on 11 June; the news reached Whitehall on 13 June, whereupon a proclamation declaring him a traitor was issued: *London Gazette*, 15 June. Monmouth in the declaration which he issued on landing claimed only 'a legitimate and legal right' to the crown; he was proclaimed king at Taunton on 20 June: G. Roberts, *Life . . . of Monmouth*, 1844, i. 235–50, 319–20. For the rebellion see further A. Fea, *King Monmouth*, 1902; *V.C.H., Somerset*, ii. 219–30.

[2] There was little rain at Oxford from 16 May to 21 June: Wood, *Life and times*, iii. 143, 144.

[3] See note above. The number of men landing with Monmouth is from *London Gazette*, as above. He

brought with him only eighty-two followers; there were in the ships sixty-seven sailors, most of whom did not land; he was almost immediately joined by about sixty townsmen of Lyme: Roberts, i. 202, 225, 253. By 18 June he was reported to have about 5,000 men: Luttrell, i. 347. On 15 June the lords ordered his Declaration to be burnt: *L.J.*, xiv. 41. An act for his attainder for high treason was passed on 16 June; the proclamation offering the reward for his capture was issued on the same day: *London Gazette*, 18 June.

[4] The Monument: above, p. 243. The additional inscription of 1681 was now obliterated; it was restored in 1689 and finally removed in 1830: Luttrell, i. 349; Welch, pp. 40–1.

The exceeding Drouth still continued: God grant a success-full conclusion to these ill-boding beginnings: I tooke the Chaire as Vice-President at the R: *Society*.[1]

18 I dined at my L: Sunderlands: 19: I heard the Appeale of my worthy friend Mr. Ch: Howard[2] (against the Duke of Norfolck his brother) pleaded in[a] the house of Lords, &c: and in the afternoone returned home, where I met a Warrant to send out an horse with 12 dayes provision &c:

21 Our Doctor proceeded on the later part of his former Text, shewing that therefore many sought to enter, but could not: because the⟨y⟩ sought not aright:

Pomeridiano, the Curate of Greenewich on 80 *Psal:* 4 shewing the many reasons, why men did not receive the returne of their prayers: Drowsinesse surpriz'd me:

28 We had now plentifull Raine after two yeares excessive drowth, & severe winters.[3] A stranger preached on 1: *Jam:* 25, That Christians were under a Law, against Libertines &c:—Argile taken in Scotland and[b] executed; his party desperssed:[b 4]

July 2 Came to Dine with me the Countesses of Bristoll, Sunderland, & little Clancartie[5] with Mrs. Boscauen, her sister, & the deare Child Godolphin: No considerable account of the forces sent against the D: of Mon: though[c] greate forces sent: there was a small ski⟨r⟩mish, but he would not be provok'd to come to an encounter, but still[d] kept in the

---

a Altered from *b-*.
c Followed by *th-* deleted.

b-b These words perhaps added later.
d Reading doubtful.

---

[1] Birch, iv. 407–8; Evelyn's taking the chair is not mentioned there.

[2] Of Greystoke. The present duke of Norfolk was his nephew. For the case see *Hist. MSS. Comm., House of Lords MSS., 1678–88*, pp. 299–300; *L.J.*, xiv. 26, 36, 48, 49–50.

[3] Wood notes slight showers on 20 and 21 June; an increase of rain on 22, 25, 28 June, &c.; the rivers were low in August and September: *Life and times*, iii. 144, 156, 163.

[4] The notice of Argyll's capture from *London Gazette*, 25 June; of his execution, &c., ibid., 6 July. He was taken on 18 and executed on 30 June.

[5] Elizabeth, *c.* 1673–1704, second daughter of Sunderland; married, 31 Dec. 1684, Donogh Maccarty, fourth earl of Clancarty (Ireland): below, 20 Aug. 1688. The Lady Clancarty whom Evelyn knew already (above, p. 244, &c.) was her mother-in-law.

fastnesses:[1] The Parliament prorogu'd til 4: Aug:[2] Danger-
fild whip'd & like *Oates* for perjurie:[3]

5 Our *Viccar* preached on 2. *Jacob:* 18. shewing the in-
utility of a speculative Faith onely: *Pomerid*: a stranger on
Judæ[a] 20. 21: Exhorting to Obedience, & reproving the error
of those who refused to joine in the Prayers of the Church as
not spiritual:

8 To Lond: Came now the newes of Monmouths Utter
defeate, and the next day of his being taken by Sir William
Portman & Lord Lumley, with the Militia of their Counties.[4]
It seemes the horse commanded by my Lord Grey, being
newly raised, & undisciplin'd, were not to be brought in so
short a time to indure the Fire, which exposed the foote to the
Kings: so as when Monmoth had led the foote in greate
silence and order thinking to surprise my Lord Feversham
Lieutenant Generall newly incamped, and given him a smart
charge, interchanging both greate & small shot; The horse
breaking [theire owne][b] ranks; monmoth gave it over, and
fled with *Grey*, leaving their party to be cut in pieces: to the
number of 2000: the whole number reported to be about

---

[a] Or *Jude*.   [b] Interlined; spelling doubtful.

---

[1] Apparently following *London Gazette*, 2 and 6 July. The skirmish was at Philips Norton on 27 June.

[2] *London Gazette*, 6 July. The two houses adjourned on 2 July until 4 August.

[3] Thomas Dangerfield, 1650?–1685: *D.N.B.* He was tried on 30 May, not for perjury, but for 'writing and publishing a most Villanous and Scandalous Libel, called his *Narrative*'; and on 29 June was sentenced to be whipped from Aldgate to Newgate and from Newgate to Tyburn, as well as to the pillory, a fine, &c.: *London Gazette*, 1 June, 2 July. He died as the accidental result of a blow given him when he was being brought back from his second whipping on 4 July.

[4] The second of these notices apparently derives from the report as originally circulated. Sedgemoor was fought early on 6 July; the report reached Whitehall early on 7 July: *London Gazette*, 9 July. Monmouth was captured in the morning of 8 July; the news reached Whitehall at midnight: ibid. For the capture see *An Account of the Manner of Taking the Late Duke of Monmouth, &c.*, 1685; *A True and Perfect Account of the Taking of James late Duke of Monmouth*, 1685. The part taken in it by Sir William Portman (above, p. 206) is not mentioned in *London Gazette*. Richard Lumley, 1650?–1721; second Viscount Lumley of Waterford (Ireland) 1663?; created, 1681, Baron, and, 1689, Viscount, Lumley of Lumley Castle; earl of Scarborough 1690: *D.N.B.*; I.H.R., *Bull.*, x (1933), 141.

8000: The Kings but 2700:[1] The slaine were most of them Mendip-miners, who did greate Execution with their tooles, and sold their lives very dearely:[2] whilst their leaders flying were pursu'd and taken the next morning, not far from one another: Mon: had walked 16 miles on foote changing his habite[a] with a poore coate, & was found by L.[b] Lumley[b] in ⟨a⟩ dry-ditch cover'd with fern-braken, but neither with sword, pistol, or so much as any Weapon,[c] and so might happly have passed for some country man, his beard being grown so long, & so gray, as hardly to be known, had not his George discovered him, which was found in his Pocket: Tis said he trembled exceedingly all over not able to speake:[3] Grey was taken not far from him:[4] Most of his party were Anabaptists, & poore Cloth-workers of the Country, no Gent: of account being come into him:[5] The Arch-*bouttefew*[6] Ferguson,[7] Mathews[8] &c: were not yet found: The 5000

---

[a] Or *habits*. deleted *Sir W:*   [b-b] Substituted for *Sir W: Portman*; Evelyn has not   [c] Followed by *yet* deleted.

---

[1] This notice is in part based on *London Gazette*, 9 July. Monmouth appears to have had only 3,620 men; the *Gazette* gives between 5,000 and 6,000 foot and 1,000 or 1,200 horse. Four hundred men are believed to have been killed on the field and 2,000 in the pursuit. For Grey see above, p. 323. Feversham was in command of the royal forces, with Lord Churchill (below, v. 35) as his subordinate. The best account of the battle is that given in *V.C.H., Somerset*, ii. 225–7.

[2] Lead was mined in the Mendips. Miners do not appear to have been prominent among the rebels; the men killed at Sedgemoor appear to have been mainly from Taunton: Roberts, ii. 77–8.

[3] Monmouth was captured early on 8 July near Ringwood, Hants, about sixty miles from the battle-field. Evelyn's notice appears to be related to that in *A True and Perfect Account*. Monmouth was apparently identified before the George was discovered; the notice of his beard is not found elsewhere.

[4] Grey was taken at Ringwood on 7 July: *London Gazette*, 9 July.

[5] In a list of sixty-six rebels with their trades about half are clothiers, weavers, or wool-combers: J. C. Hotten, ed., *Original lists of persons . . . who went . . . to the American Plantations, 1600–1700*, 1874, pp. 317 ff. For the strength of non-conformity in Somerset see *V.C.H., Somerset*, ii. 54, 219.

[6] Boutefeu, an incendiary; in frequent use in the seventeenth century: *O.E.D.*

[7] Above, p. 323. He escaped to Holland.

[8] Presumably Captain Edward Matthews, for whose arrest a warrant was issued about 8 June. He was a son-in-law of Sir Thomas

pounds to be given to whomsoever should bring Monmouth
in by Proclamation, was to be distributed among the Militia
by agreement twixt Sir William Portman & Lumley:[1] The
battail ended, some words first in jeast then in heate [passing][a]
twixt Sherrington Talbot a worthy Gent, (son to Sir Jo:
Talbot,[b] & who had behav'd himselfe very handsomly) and
one Capt: *Love*, both commanders of the Militia forces of
the Country, whose souldiers fought best: both drawing their
Swords, & passing at one another Sherrington was wounded
to death upon the spot; to the greate regrett[c] of those who
knew him, being also his fathers onely son:[2]

9 Just as I was coming into the Lodgings at Whitehall a
little before dinner my Lord of Devonshire standing very
neere his Majesties bed-Chamber-doore in the lobby: came
Coll: Culpeper & in a rude manner looking my Lord in the
face, Asked whether this were a time and place for Excluders
to appeare, my Lord tooke little notice of what he said at first,
knowing him to be a hot-headed fellow; but reiterating it
againe, Asked Culpeper whether he meant him? he said, yes,
he meant his Lordship: My Lord told him he was no Exclu-
der (as indeede he was not) the other affirms it againe: My
Lord told him he Lied; on which Culpeper struck him a box
o'th'Eare, my Lord him another and fell'd him downe: upon

---

a Interlined.   b MS. has closing bracket here.   c Spelling
doubtful.

Armstrong and was killed at
Philips Norton (above, p. 451 n.):
London Gazette, 8 June, 2 July;
Lauder, *Hist. observes*, p. 202. A
'Captain Matthews', an agent for
Monmouth in the United Provinces
and England, is probably the same
man: for him see Forde Grey, Lord
Grey, *The Secret History of the Rye-
House plot*, &c., 1754, pp. 74, 82,
91–2, 100–7, 110, 112, 121. There
was apparently a second man of this
name, the 'Sieur Mathieu, escuyer'
of Monmouth: Barillon, 10 Sept.
1685, N.S., in Fox, app., p. cxxii.
  [1] I have not found other reports
of this.

[2] The duel is also reported by
Luttrell, i. 354. Sharington Talbot,
b. *c.* 1656; M.P. for Chippenham
1685: *London marriage licences*. His
father is John Talbot, *c.* 1630–1714;
of Lacock Abbey; knighted 1660;
M.P. for Knaresborough 1661;
Chippenham 1679; Ludgershall
1681; Devizes 1685; F.R.S. 1663;
a participant in the duel between
Buckingham and Shrewsbury in
1668 (above, iii. 596 n.); intervened
in 1685 to save Thomas Rosewell,
the nonconformist divine: *A compleat history of Europe*, vol. for 1713
and 1714, pp. 406–7; &c. Love is
not identifiable.

which being soone parted: Culpeper was seiz'd and commanded by his Majestie (who was all^a the^a while in the B: chamber) to be carried downe to the Greenecloth Officer, who sent him to the Martialsea, as he deserv'd: My L: *Devon* had nothing said to him.[1]

I supped this night at Lambeth at my old friends Mr. Elias Ashmole with my Lady Clarendon,[2] the Bish: of St. Asaph, and Dr. Tenison rector of St. Martines, &c:[3] when we were treated at a greate feast:

10 The Count of *Castel Melior*,[4] that greate favorite and prime Minister of *Alphonso* late King of Portugal, after several Yeares banishment; now being againe received to grace & called home by *Dom Pedro* the present King (as having ben found a person of the greatest integrity after all his sufferings) desired me to spend part of this day with him, and assist him in a Collection of books, & other curiosities, which he would carry with him into Portugal: Mr. *Hussey*[5]

---

^{a-a} Spelling doubtful.

---

[1] William Cavendish, fourth earl, styled Lord Cavendish until 1684: above, iii. 65, &c. Thomas Colepeper, 1637–1708; royalist colonel prior to the Restoration: *D.N.B.* Colepeper had laid claim unsuccessfully to property purchased by Devonshire from his father-in-law. The present assault led to his imprisonment in the Marshalsea (in 1687 the quarrel broke out again and Devonshire was fined for assaulting Colepeper). As Lord Cavendish Devonshire had been a prominent member of parliament; he had belonged to the Country party and had become a Whig; but in the parliament of 1679 he had advocated limitation of the royal power as against exclusion; in that of 1680 he appears to have accepted exclusion as inevitable rather than as desirable; his attitude was probably that set out in *Reasons for His Majesties Passing the Bill of*

Exclusion 1681, which has been attributed to him.

The court of Green Cloth consisted of the principal officers of the lord steward's department of the royal household, and had general jurisdiction over the court and its verge: Chamberlayne.

[2] For her friendship with Ashmole see his *Diary*, ed. Gunther, p. 43 n.

[3] The other guests were Mr. Henshaw (presumably Thomas) and Mr. Frasier: Ashmole.

[4] Castelmelhor; for him and the kings see above, p. 130. Advertisement relating to his intended departure in *London Gazette*, 24 Aug.

[5] John Hussey, b. 30 Nov. 1658; eldest son of Peter Hussey (above, iii. 561; iv. 255); admitted at Trinity College, Cambridge 1677; at Lincoln's Inn 1677; inherited Sutton 1684; buried 9 July 1685: Manning and Bray, i. 497; Venn.

a young Gent: who made love to my deare Child, disseased of the small-pox in March-last; but whom she could not bring her selfe to answer his affection: died now of the same cruel dissease; for which I was extreamly sorry; because it is apparent, he never enjoy'd himselfe after my daughters death, nor was I averse to the Match, could she have overcome her inclinations:

11 I returned home:[a]

12 Our *Viccar* proceeded on his former Text and subject: The *Curate* on: 3. *Titus* 1: concerning subjection to Magistrates: I was surpriz'd with *sleepe*:

15 I went to Lond: to see Dr. *Tenisons* Library,[1] returned in the Evening:

This day was Monmoth brought to Lond:[2] examin'd before the King to whom he made great submission, accknowledg'd his seduction by Fergusson the Scot, whom he named the bloudy Villain:[3] thence sent to the Tower, had an enterview[b] with his late Dutchesse, whom he received coldly,[4] having lived dishonestly with the Lady Hen: Wentworth[5] for two yeares; from obstinatly asserting his conversation with that debauched woman to be no sin, seing he could not

---

[a] Followed by *I went* deleted.   [b] Or *interview*.

---

[1] See above, pp. 367–8.

[2] Evelyn has combined two events. Monmouth was brought to Whitehall during the afternoon of 13 July and was taken to the Tower that evening; he was beheaded on 15 July: *London Gazette*, 16 July. For his conduct from his arrival in London until his execution see the letter, 16 July, signed 'I. F.', in George Rose, *Observations on the Historical Work of . . . Fox*, 1809, app., pp. lxv–lxxv; and the letter of Lloyd, bishop of St. Asaph, in W. Hemingford, *Hist.*, ed. T. Hearne, 1731, vol. i, pp. clxxvii–clxxx.

[3] Compare I. F. and Reresby; and the notices in Campana de Cavelli,

ii. 70–2.

[4] There were two interviews, the first in the presence of Clarendon, the second apparently with the divines (see below) and other persons present: I. F.

[5] Henrietta Maria Wentworth, 1660–86; succeeded as Baroness Wentworth 1665 or 1667: *D.N.B.*; A. Fea, *The Loyal Wentworths*, 1928; for her father and grandfather (Lord Cleveland) see above, ii. 562; iii. 356. She had taken the part of Jupiter in *Calisto*. For Monmouth's remarks about her see I. F.; for those made by him when on the scaffold see further *An Account of what passed at the Execution of the Late Duke of Monmouth*, 1685.

be perswaded to his last breath, the Divines,[1] who were sent to assist him, thought not fit to administer the holy Communion to him: for the rest of his faults he professed greate sorrow, and so died without any apparent feare, would make use of no cap, or other circumstance, but lying downe bid the fellow[2] do his office better than to my late Lord Russell, & gave him gold: but the wretch made five Chopps before he had his head off, which so incens'd the people, that had he not ben guarded & got away they would have torne him in pieces: He made no Speech on the Scaffold (which was on Towerhill) but gave a paper (containing not above 5 or 6 lines) for the King, in which he disclaimes all Title to the Crowne, accknowledges that the late King (his Father) had indeede told him, he was but his base sonn, & so desire'd his Majestie to be kind to his Wife & Children:[3] This Relation I had from the Mouth of Dr. Tenison *Rector* of St. Martines, who with the Bishops of[a] *Ely* & *Bath* & *Wells*, was one of the divines his Majestie sent to him, & were at the execution: Thus ended this quondam Duke, darling of his Father, and the Ladys, being extraordi⟨na⟩rily[b] handsome, and adroit: an excellent souldier, & dauncer, a favorite of the people, of an Easy nature, debauched by lust, seduc'd by crafty knaves who would have set him up onely to make a property;[4] tooke this opportunity of his Majestie[c] being of another Religion, to gather a party of discontented; failed of it, and perished: He was a lovely person, had a vertuous & excellent Lady that brought him greate riches & a second Dukedome in Scotland;[5] Was Master of the Horse,[6] Gen. of the K. his fathers Army,[7]

---

[a] Followed by *Lond* deleted. [b] Spelling doubtful. [c] Or *Majesties.*

---

[1] Bishops Turner and Ken, sent by the King; Dr. George Hooper; and Tenison, sent at Monmouth's request. I. F. also states that it was on account of his views on his association with Lady Wentworth that he was refused the Sacrament.

[2] Jack Ketch, d. 1686: *D.N.B.* The fullest account of the execution is that given by I. F.

[3] This paper is printed in *An Account of what passed at the Execution.* [4] A cat's-paw: *O.E.D.*

[5] The dukedom of Buccleugh; strictly speaking, it was granted to him on his marriage with the countess of Buccleugh: above, p. 6.

[6] From 1674 to 1681.

[7] He was appointed captaingeneral of all land-forces in England and Wales in 1678 and of those in Scotland in 1679.

Gent: of the Bed chamber:[1] Knight of the Garter,[2] Chancellor of Camb:[3] in a Word had accumulations without end: Se what *Ambition* and want of principles brought him to. He was beheaded on Tuesday the 14th *July*:[4] His mother (whose name was Barlow,[5] daughter of some very meane Creatures) was a beautifull strumpet, whom I had often seene at *Paris*, & died miserably, without anything to bury her: Yet had this *Perkin* ben made believe, the King had married her: which was a monstrous forgerie, & ridiculous: & to[a] satisfie the world the iniquitie of the report, the King his father (if his Father he realy were, for he most resembld one *Sidny*[6] familiar with his mother) publiquely & most solemnly renounced it, and caused it to be so entred in the Council booke some yeares since, with all the Privy Counsel⟨o⟩rs attestation.[7]

17 Came my Lord Hatton[8] Governor of Gurnsey (a Worthy person) to Visite me:

19 Our Viccar absent, preached a stranger on 1: *Cor:* 16.

---

a Followed by *prevent* deleted.

[1] Apparently an error: Monmouth is not included in the lists printed in Chamberlayne.

[2] 1663.

[3] From 1674 to 1682.

[4] A mistake for Wednesday, 15 July.

[5] Lucy Walter: above, ii. 561.

[6] Colonel Robert Sidney, 1626–68: *D.N.B.*, art. Sidney, Robert, second earl of Leicester. The story that he was Monmouth's father apparently comes from James II: *Life*, ed. Clarke, i. 492; a rather better version in *Original papers*, ed. James Macpherson, 1775, i. 76; another allusion to it in James's instructions for his son, 1690, ibid., p. 77 n. It has never been widely accepted.

[7] On 6 Jan. 1679 Charles wrote a statement that he had never been contracted to or married to Monmouth's mother, or to any woman except Queen Catherine; he obtained the signatures of the archbishop of Canterbury, the chancellor, and the two secretaries of state a few days later. Then on 3 March 1679 he made a statement before the council, that he had never been contracted to or married to any woman except Queen Catherine; this was attested by all the members of the council then present. On 2 June 1680 he drew up *His Majesties Declaration to all his Loving Subjects*, which was published at once; it includes the two statements, which he caused to be enrolled in the records of the court of Chancery on 15 June: document in Rose, *Observations on Fox*, pp. lix–lxiv.

[8] Christopher Hatton, 1632–1706; second Baron Hatton of Kirby 1670; created Viscount Hatton of Gretton 1683: *D.N.B.* For his father see above, ii. 562. He was governor of Guernsey from 1670 to 1706.

13 shewing the necessity of Armour & Christian vigilancy, with a long narrative of the Disloyaltie of our late Rebellions[a] & the mischiefe of their principles:—

In the *Afternoone*, another stranger on 20: *Exod:* 8: of Sanctifying the Lords day:

I went the Saturday before to see the Muster of the 6 Scotch & Eng: Regiments, whom the Pr: of Orange had lately sent his Majestie out of Holland, upon this rebellion, but were now returning, having had no occasion to make use of them: They were all excellently clad, and perfectly disciplined, and were incamped on Black-heath most formaly with their Tents: The King & Queene &c: being come to see them exercise & the manner of Encamping, which was very neate & magnificent.[1]

By a grosse mistake of the Secretary of his Majesties forces,[2] they had ben ordred to quarter in private Houses (which was contrary to an Act of Parliament) but upon my informing his Majestie timely of it, it was prevented:

The two horse-men which[b] My Son & myselfe sent into the

---

[a] Altered from *Rebett-*. [b] Or *whom*; MS. *wʰ*.

---

[1] English and Scottish troops had been in the Dutch service almost continuously since the first rising against Spain in 1572. They were formed into three English and three Scottish regiments in 1674–5, and by an agreement made in 1678 could be recalled by the king. The Scottish regiments landed at Gravesend on 29 June; were reviewed by the king on Blackheath on 3 July; and then went westwards to join the army. The English regiments arrived later, but before 14 July. It was apparently only the English regiments that were reviewed here this day; the Scottish regiments were reviewed with the other forces on Hounslow Heath on 23 July. The English regiments were to embark for Holland on 25 July; the Scottish were to follow. All the regiments came to England in 1688, two of the three English becoming the Fifth and Sixth Foot; the Scottish returned to Holland in 1698 and continued in the Dutch service until 1782: James Ferguson, ed., *Papers illustrating the history of the Scots Brigade in . . . the United Netherlands* (Scottish Hist. Soc., 1899–1901), i. 470–8, 488, 536–41, &c.

[2] William Blathwayt: below, p. 554. Quartering soldiers on any persons without their consent was forbidden by the Petition of Right (1628) and again by act of parliament in 1679 (31 Car. II, c. 1, § xxxii). A complaint about it was made in the house of commons on 12 November of this year: *Faithfull Register* (see below, p. 488 n.).

County Troopes, were now come home, after neere a moneths being out, to our extraordinary charge:[1]

20 The Trinity Company met this day, as it should have indeede don on the moneday after Trinity Sonday, which was put off til now, by reason of the royal Charter, which being exceeding large could not be ready before:[2] some other immunities[3] superadded: Mr. *Pepys* (Secretary of the Admiralty) was a second time chosen Master:[4] present the Duke of Grafton, & Lord of Dartmouth[5] Master of the Ordnance, the Commissioners of the Navy & breathren of that Corporation: Then we went to Church according to costome when[a] preached Dr. Hicks,[6] on 72 Psal. v: 8. a most learned, excellent & instructive sermon, of the antiquity, usefullnesse & other benefits of shipping and Navigation, not onely in relation to commerce in general, & defence of this Iland, but as it had ben, & yet might be[b] an exceeding blessing in the propagation of the Christian religion, ending with an exhortation to sea-men (especialy the Vulgar) how they ought to govern themselves as to holinesse, who are in such continual hazards,[c] & much reproving the universal prophanesse among the vulgar, nor sparing their Commanders: The parallel between the Catholic Church & a ship was very handsome: but the sermon (I suppose) will be printed, as it deserves:

Then we tooke barge to the Trinity house in Lond: where

---

a Or *where*.   b Followed by *of* deleted.   c Or *hazarde*.

---

[1] See above, p. 450.
[2] Trinity Sunday had fallen on 14 June. The old charter of the corporation had been surrendered on 23 March; the present one, granted 8 July and published this year as *The Royal Charter of Confirmation granted . . . to the Trinity-House of Deptford-Strond*, is said to have been largely composed by Pepys, who is nominated first master in it; it is still in force, with a slight alteration: Barrett, *Trinity House*, pp. 104, 106–7.

[3] Presumably privileges or exemptions: *O.E.D.*
[4] He had been master in 1676–7.
[5] He was master-general of the ordnance from 1682 to 1688.
[6] George Hickes, 1642–1715; D.D. 1678 or 1679; supernumerary chaplain in ordinary 1681–9?; dean of Worcester 1683–90; the nonjuror and titular bishop of Thetford: *D.N.B.* The sermon is printed in Hickes's collected sermons: *A Collection of Sermons*, vol. ii, 1713, pp. 349–76.

we had a most plentifull & magnificent feast, There being above 80 at one Table; & so I return'd:

26 Being the day of Thanksgiving for his Majesties late victory over the Rebelles, Argyle in Scotland, & Monmouth in the West, according to a forme of Prayers composed for the Occasion;[1] one Mr. *Hutchins*[2] preached in the morning on 72 *Psal:* 10: shewing from what signal dangers, God had in all ages delivered his church: In the Afternoone the Curate on 64 *Psal:* 9. 10. relating much of the particulars of the late rising, and both concluding in Eucharistical exhortations: And most certain it is, that had not it pleased God to dissipate their beginnings, they had in all appearance gathered by an irresistable head, and desperately proceeded to the ruine of Church, & Government; so ⟨general⟩[a] was the discontent, and expectation of the opportunity:[3] For my owne part, I looked upon this deliverance as absolutely[b] most signal; such an innundation of Phanatics and men of impious principles, must needes have caused universal dissorder, cruelty, injustice, rapine, sacrilege & confusion, an unavoydable Civil-war, and misery without end: but blessed be God, the knot was happily broken, and a faire prospect of Tranquilitie for the future likely to succeede if we reforme, be thankfull, & make a right use of this Mercy:

27 This night when we were all asleepe went my Daughter Eliz: away, to meete a young fellow, nephew to Sir Jo: Tippet[4] (Surveyor of the Navy: & one of the Commissioners)

---

[a] MS. *generaly*.   [b] Followed by *the* deleted.

---

[1] Proclamation 11 July; published in *London Gazette*, 13 July. The *Form of Prayer* was published.

[2] Presumably the preacher called 'Dr. Hutchins' above, p. 386.

[3] Evelyn probably refers to the unpopularity of the reactionary measures of the government during the last four years. For the economic discontent in the west of England see G. N. Clark, *The Later Stuarts*, 1934, pp. 114-15.

[4] John Tippets; master-ship-wright at Portsmouth 1660; commissioner of the navy at Portsmouth 1668-72; surveyor of the navy 1672-92; knighted 1675; he had been granted arms in 1670: Sir G. Jackson, *Naval Commissioners, 1660-1760*, ed. Duckett, 1889; *Cal. S.P., Dom., 1675-6*, pp. 197, 198; J. Foster, *Grantees of Arms (to 1700)* (Harleian Soc., vol. lxvi, 1915). I have not traced the nephew. Elizabeth Evelyn was nearly eighteen years old.

whom she married the next day being Tuesday; without in the least acquainting either her parents, or any soule in the house: I was the more afflicted & ⟨astonish'd⟩ᵃ at it, in reguard, we had never given this Child the least cause to be thus diss-obedient, and being now my Eldest, might reasonably have expected a double Blessing: But it afterward appeared, that this Intrigue had ben transacted by letters long before, & when⟩ᵇ she was with my Lady Burton[1] in Licester shire, and by private meetings neere my house: She of all our Children had hitherto given us least cause of suspicion; not onely for that she was yet young, but seemed the most flattering, soupleᶜ and observant; of a silent & particular humor; in no sort ⟨betraying⟩ᵈ the levity & Inclination which is commonly apparent in Children who fall into these snares; having ben bred-up with the uttmost Circumspection, as to principles of severest honour & Piety: But so far it seemes, had her passion for this Young fellow made her forget her duty, and all thatᵉ most Indulgent Parents expected from her, as not to consider the Consequence of her folly & diss-obedience, 'til it was too late: This Affliction went very neere me & my Wife, neither of us yet well compos'd for the untimely losse of that incomparable & excellent Child, whichᶠ it pleased God to take from us by the small pox a few moneths before: But this farther Chastizement was to be humbly sub-mitted to, as a part of the burden God was pleased to lay farther upon us; in this yet the lesse afflictive, That we had not ben wanting in giving her an Education every way becoming us: We were most of all astonish'd at the suddaine-esse of this action, & the privatenesse of its manegement; the Circumstances also Consider'd & quality, how it was

---

ᵃ MS. *a stonish'd.*   ᵇ MS. *whan* or *wheen*?   ᶜ Or *soupple.*
ᵈ MS. *be traying.*   ᵉ Followed by *the* deleted.   ᶠ Or *whom*; MS. *wʰ.*

---

[1] Presumably Elizabeth, 1638–98, daughter of Mrs. Evelyn's uncle Sir John Prettyman, widow of Sir Thomas Burton of Stockerston, bart., and secondly of Sir William Halford of Welham, kt.; or her daughter-in-law, Anne, *c.* 1659–1720, daughter of Sir Thomas Clutterbuck (above, p. 156) and wife of Sir Thomas Burton, the third baronet: G.E.C., *Baronetage,* i. 204; Muskett, *Suffolk manorial families,* ii. 312.

possible she should be flattered so to her dissadvantage: He being in no condition sortable to hers, & the Blessing we intended her: The thing has given us much disquiet, I pray God direct us,[a] how to govern our Resentments of her dissobedience; and if it be his will, bring good out of all this Ill:

Aug: 2 So had this Affliction descompos'd us, that I could not be well at Church the next Lords day; though I had prepared for the B: Sacrament: I hope God will be more gracious to my onely remaining Child,[1] whom I take to be of a more discreete, sober and religious temper: that we may have that comfort from her, which is deny'd us in the other:

This Accident caus'd me to alter my Will; as was reasonable; for though there may be a reconciliation upon her repentance, and that she has suffer'd for her folly; yet I must let her see what her undutifullnesse in this action, deprives her of; as to the provision she else might have expected; solicitous as she knew I now was of bestowing her very worthily:

6 I went to Lond: next day to see Mr. Wats,[b][2] keeper of the Apothecaries[c] Garden of simples at Chelsey:[3] where there is a collection of innumerable rarities of that sort: Particularly, besids many rare annuals the Tree bearing the Jesuits bark,[4] which had don such cures in quartans: & what was very ingenious the subterranean heate, conveyed by a stove under the Conserveatory, which was all Vaulted with brick; so as he leaves the doores & windowes open in the hard⟨e⟩st frosts, secluding onely the snow &c:[5] I returned home by Clapham:

---

[a] Altered from or to *me*.   [b] Altered from *Watson*?   [c] Or *Apothecarie*.

---

[1] Susanna.

[2] John Watts, traceable as a member of the Society of Apothecaries from 1674 to 1693; in charge of the garden 1680–*c.* 1691: Field, *Mem. of the Botanic Garden*, ed. Semple, pp. 12–17; *Catalogue of the . . . Soc. of Apothecaries*, 1693.

[3] For the earlier history of the garden see above, iii. 217. It was transferred to Chelsea in 1673–6, where it still exists. For its history at this time, besides Field, see C. R. B. Barrett, *Hist. of the Soc. of Apothecaries*, 1905, pp. 98–104, 111.

[4] The cinchona. For the Jesuits' bark see above, p. 325.

[5] Presumably the building was of the kind described in 'A *New Conservatory*, or Greene-house', appended to *Kalendarium Hortense*, 8th ed., 1691, pp. 150–62 (reprinted in later editions).

9 one Mr. Meriton preach'd on 24 Act: 16. upon the necessity of having a good Conscience, instructing what it was;
with many practical Inferences.

14 [15]ᵃ came to visite us Mrs. Boscawen, with my Lord
Godolphi⟨n⟩s little son, with whose Education hitherto his
father had intrusted me:

16 Came newes to us that my undutifull daughter was
visited with the small-pox, now universaly very contagious:
I was yet willing my Wife should go visite & take care of her:

⟨16⟩ᵇ A stranger preached on 10. Rom: 6. 7. 8. 9. 10. 11.
shewing how we are justified by Faith and Repentance:
Pomerid: Curate on: 1.ᶜ *Cor:* 2. 2.

22 I went to Lond, to see my unhappy Child, now in greate
danger, and carried our Viccar with me, that according to
her earnest desire, (being very sensible & penitent for her
fault) he might administer to her the H: Sacrament, which
he did; & after some time, and her greate submissions &
agonies, leaving herᵈ toᵈ the mercys of God, & her mother
with her I returned in the Evening: We had now the newes
of Newhausels being taken by the Christians:¹ There was
also this day an universall appearance of the Kings forces at
Brainford:²

23 Our *Viccar*ᵉ preached on 2. Jam: 18 shewing the vanity
of relyances on any speculative faith, without workes: [V:
Notes]ᶠ *Pomerid*: Curat: on 10: *Pro:* 9. shewing the necessity of Integrity, & that all our observances of the first Table
is not sufficient, without obedience & practise of the second:
in which charity, justice, temperance &c are equaly en-
joyned us:

28 My poore unhappy Daughters sickness increasing, a
violent feavor succeeding when her other distemper appeared
to be past danger; I went up againe to see, & comfort her,

ᵃ Marginal date below *14*; apparently both dates belong to this notice.
ᵇ MS. *17*.   ᶜ Substituted for *2*.   ᵈ⁻ᵈ MS. *her in to*.
ᵉ Followed by *being* deleted.   ᶠ Interlined.

---

¹ From *London Gazette*, 24 Aug.   ² The review was probably held
Neuhäusel in Hungary, taken by the   at Hounslow: *Hist. MSS. Comm.*,
Imperial forces on 19 August, N.S.   *Portland MSS.*, iii. 387.

together with our Minister: My disconsolate Wife I left with her, who had ben almost all her sicknesse with her; so I return'd home in greate doubt how God would deale with her, whom the next morning he was pleased to take out of this vale of misery, I humbly trust, to his infinite mercy, though to our unspeakeable affliction, loosing another Child in the flower of her age, who had never 'til now given us cause of any displeasure, but many hopes of Comfort: & thus in lesse than 6 moneths were we depriv'd of two Children for our unworthinesse, & causes best known to God, whom I beseech from the bottome of my heart that he will give us grace to make that right use of all these[a] chastisements that we may become better, and intirely submitt [in][b] all things to his infinite wise disposal. She departed this life on ⟨Saturday⟩[c] 29: Aug: at 8 in the Morning: fell sick [& died][b] on the same day of the weeke, that my other most deare & dutifull daughter did, and as also one of my servants (a very pious youth) had don the yeare before: I beseech God of his mercy Sanctifie this and all other Afflictions & dispensations to me. His holy will be don *Amen*.

30 This sad accident kept me from the publique service this day being Sonday.

My Child was buried by her sister on 2d September in the Church of Deptford:

The 3 of Sep: I went to Lond, being sent to by a Letter from my Lord Clarendon (Lord privy-seale) to let me know that his majestie being pleased to[d] send him *Lord Lieutennant* into *Ireland*, was also pleased to Nominate me one of the Commissioners to execute the office of *Privy-Seale* during his *Lieutenancy* there:[1] It behoving me [4][e] to waite upon his Majestie & to give him thanks for his greate honor (returning home that Evening) I accompanied his Lordship [5][f] the next

---

a Altered from *this*.   b Interlined.   c MS. *friday*.   d Followed by *Nominate* deleted.   e Marginal date.   f Marginal date; apparently altered from *4*.

---

[1] Clarendon was appointed lord lieutenant about 20 August: *Hist. MSS. Comm., Ormonde MSS.*, new ser., vii. 355. For Evelyn's fellow commissioners see below, p. 493.

morning to *Windsore* (dining by the Way at Sir *Hen: Capels*
at *Cue*)[1] where his Majestie receiving me with extraordinary
kindnesse, I kissed his hands:[a] I told him how sensible
I was of his Majesties gracious favour to me: that I would
endeavour to serve him with all sincerity, dilligence &
loyalty, not more out of my duty, than Inclinations: He
said, he doubted not of it, & was glad he had this opportunity
to shew the kindnesse he had for me: After this came
aboundance of the greate Men to give me Joy, particularly[b]
L: *Tressurer*, L: *Sunderland*, L. *Peterborrow*, L: *Godolphin*,
L: *Falkland* & every body at Court who knew me: [6][c] The
next day being *Sonday*, I went to Church in the[d] Cathed:[2]
where preached Dr. Standish[3] on   after which follow'd the
H: Communion of which I participated, beseeching God to
be gracious to me &c: The 2d sermon was preached by Dr.
Creighton[4] on 1: *Thess:* 4: 11. perswading to unity & peace,
and to be mindfull of our owne buisinesse, according to the
advise of the Apostle:[e] Then I went to heare a *French* man,
who preached before the *King* & *Queene* in that splended
Chapell[5] next St. *Georges Hall*, his discourse was on the
Gospel of the day, describing the leaprosies of sin &c:[6] Their
Majesties going to *Masse*, I withdrew, to consider the stupendious painting of the *Hall*, which both for the Art & Invention deserves the Inscription, in honor of the Painter *Signior
Verrio*: The History is Edw:[f] the ⟨3rd's⟩[g] receiving the black-
prince, coming towards him in a Roman Triumph &c. The
whole roofe, the Hist: of St. George, The Throne, the Carvings
&c are incomparable, & I think equal to any & in many
Circumstances exceeding any I have seene Abroad:[7]

ᵃ Followed by *the* deleted.   ᵇ Followed by *D: of Norfolck* deleted.
ᶜ Marginal date.   ᵈ Followed by *Castle* deleted.   ᵉ Followed by *Bein-* deleted.   ᶠ Altered from *Hen-*.   ᵍ MS. *3ᵗʰˢ:*; the *3* altered from *4* in pencil only.

¹ Kew. Capel was a brother of
Clarendon's first wife.
² i.e. St. George's Chapel.
³ Above, p. 75.
⁴ Above, iii. 623.
⁵ Above, pp. 316–17.
⁶ Twelfth Sunday after Trinity.

⁷ Above, p. 316. The decoration
(apart from an additional portrait of
William III by Kneller) had been
completed in 1684: Hope, *Windsor
Castle*, i. 322–3. The Triumph of the
Black Prince occupied the north
wall; St. George the part of the east

I was invited to Dinner by the *Duke* of *Norfolck*, but had ben engaged before to dine at my L: *Sunderlands*, where also dined my L: Clarendon, L: Arran,[1] L: *Middleton*,[2] & Sir W: *Soames*,[3] design'd Ambassador to Constantinople ; After[a] dinner,[a] I visited the Countesse of *Bristol*, & then went to Evening prayers. About 6 a Clock came Sir *Dudley* & his Bro: *Roger North* & brought the *Greate*[b] Seale[b] from my *L: Keeper*, who it seemes died the day before at his house in *Oxfordshire*:[4] The King went immediately to *Council*, and everybody guessing who was most like to succeede this greate officer; most believing it could be no other than my L: Ch: Justice *Jeoffries*, who had so vigorously prosecuted the late Rebelles, and was now gon the Western-Circuit, to punish the rest that were secured in the severall Counties; and was now neere upon his returne:[5] I tooke my leave of

---

a-a Substituted for *After Evening prayer*.   b-b *Greate* ends one line ; *Seale* begins the next.

---

wall above the throne; the ceiling was painted with Charles II and allegorical figures and with panels relating to the Garter. The inscription, on the west wall, ran: Antonius Verrio Neapolitanus | non ignobile stirpe natus | Augustissimi Regis Caroli Secundi | et | Sancti Georgii | Molem hanc fælicissima manu | Decoravit: Pote, *Windsor Castle*, pp. 423–5; W. H. Pyne, *Hist. of the Royal Residences*, 1819, vol. i, with plate.

[1] Presumably the duke of Hamilton's son; but the duke of Ormond's younger son was also in England at this time. For them see above, iii. 2; iv. 296.

[2] Above, p. 387, &c.

[3] William Soame, *c.* 1645–86; of Thurlow, Suffolk; knighted 1674; created a baronet 5 February of this year; envoy extraordinary at Turin 1678–80, 1681; appointed ambassador at Constantinople late 1684?; died at Malta on his way there, June 1686: G.E.C., *Baronetage*, iv. 136;

English hist. review, xl (1925), 544.

[4] Guilford had died at Wroxton on 5 September: *London Gazette*, 10 Sept.; for an account of the bringing of the seal see also North, *Life of Guilford*, p. 268. Dudley North, 1641–91; sheriff of London 1682–3; knighted 1683; financier, &c.: *D.N.B.* For Roger North see above, p. 340.

[5] Jeffreys was appointed lord chancellor on 28 September: *London Gazette*, 1 Oct. But he appears to have been chosen as Guilford's successor before the latter's death and was apparently notified about the impending appointment as soon as the death was known: see his letter to Sunderland, 8 [Sept.]; cf. North, *Life of Guilford*, p. 268. The 'late rebels' are presumably the Rye House plotters (Jeffreys tried only Sidney and Armstrong). The dates of the Bloody Assize are Winchester 25 August; Salisbury 28 August; Dorchester 3 September; Exeter 12 September; Taunton 17 Septem-

his Majestic who spake very graciously to me; & supping that night at Sir Stephen Foxes; promising to dine at his house [7]ᵃ the next day: [which I did]ᵇ on Moneday,ᶜ returningᵈ with my Lord Clarendon,ᵉ thro Cheesewick, and [9]ᵃ the next day home to my house:

13 Our Viccar preached on 12: Heb: 1: shewing that no man was naturaly as man, inclined to one Vice more than to another; though constitution might sometimes sway, [& that]ᵇ seing God had provided satisfactions suitable to all needes,ᶠ it was onely our disorderly Appetites, & evil costomes, which perverted us: reckoning up the sin, or heavy weight,ᵍ which beset us of lust, pride, Avarice &c. against which we were to combate, & strive:ʰ The *Curate* proceeded on his former: I was exceedingly sleepie: The Lord pardon me:

15 I went to Lond: accomp⟨a⟩nied Mr. *Pepys* (Secretary of the *Admiralty*) to *Portsmouth*, Whither his Majestie was going the first time since his coming to the Crowne, to see in what state the Fortifications were:¹ Wee tooke Coach & 6 horses, late after din⟨n⟩er, yet got to *Bagshot*² that night: whilst supper was making ready I went & made a Visite to Mrs. Grahames, some time Maideⁱ of honorⁱ to the queen Dowager, now wife to Ja: Gr: Esquire of the Privie-purse to the King:³ her house being a Walke in the Forest, within a little quarter of a mile from Bagshot Towne: very impor-

---

ᵃ Marginal date.   ᵇ Interlined.   ᶜ Followed by *we I* both deleted.   ᵈ Altered from *returned.*   ᵉ Followed by *&* deleted. ᶠ Substituted for *Appetites.*   ᵍ Altered from *weights.*   ʰ Followed by *against* deleted.   ⁱ⁻ⁱ MS. *Maide-honor*; *of* interlined.

---

ber; Wells 22 September (Jeffreys was also at Bristol on 21 September): F. A. Inderwick, *Side-lights on the Stuarts*, 1888, pp. 398–424.

¹ The king left Windsor for Winchester on 14 and returned on 18 September: *London Gazette*, 17, 21 Sept.

² By Brentford and Staines Bagshot was twenty-nine miles distant from the Standard in Cornhill.

³ Bagshot Park is part of Windsor Forest; Graham was appointed keeper and ranger of it in 1682 and in 1687 was given a lease of the lodge for thirty-one years; he probably ceased to occupy it soon after 1688: G. M. Hughes, *Hist. of Windsor Forest*, 1890, pp. 334–6, &c. Graham was master of the privy pack of Royal Buckhounds from 1685 to 1688: *V.C.H., Berks.*, ii. 285.

tunate she was that I would sup, & abide there that night;
but being oblig'd by my companion, I return'd to our Inn,[a]
after she had shew'd me her house which was very commodious, & well furnish'd, as she was an excellent housewife,
a prudent & vertuous Lady: There is a parke full of red deare
about it: Her eldest son,[1] was now sick there of the small
pox, but in a likely way of recovery; & other of her Children
ran about, & among the infected, which she said she let them
do on purpose that they might whilst young, passe that fatal
dissease, which she fancied they were to undergo one time or
other, & that this would be the best: The severity of this
cruel dissease so lately in my poore family confirming much
of what she affirm'd:

16 The next morning early seting out, we ariv'd early
enough[b] at *Winchester* to waite on the King, who was lodg'd
at the Deanes, (Dr. Megot) I found very few with him besides
my Lord *Feversham*, *Arran*,[2] *Newport*, & the *Bishop* of *Bath*
and *Wells* to whom his Majestie was discoursing concerning
Miracles, & what strange things the *Saludadors*[3] would do in
Spaine, as by creeping into [heated][c] ovens with[out][c] hurt
&c: & that they had a black Crosse in the roofe of their
mouthes: but yet were commonly, notorious & prophane
wretches: upon which his Majestie farther said, that he was
so extreamely difficult of Miracles, for feare of being impos'd
on, that if he should chance to see one himselfe, without
some other wittnesse, he should apprehend it some delusion

---

a Altered from *lo-*.   b Followed by *to* deleted.   c Interlined.

1 For Graham's children see
D.N.B.
2 See above, p. 466 n.
3 The Saludadores were Spaniards
of low class who claimed that they
were able to cure diseases, especially
hydrophobia, by means of their
saliva; they were distinguished by
markings like a St. Catherine's
wheel on the roof of the mouth and
a crucifix beneath the tongue, and
were able to enter hot ovens, walk
on hot iron, &c. They were probably simply charlatans. They are
fully discussed by B. G. Feyjoó
(Feijoo) y Montenegro, *Teatro critico
universal*, vol. iii, 1773, pp. 1–18.
See further Franciscus a Victoria,
Relectiones theologicae, vol. ii, 1557,
De arte magica, ch. xi, xvi; M. A. Del
Rio, *Disquisitionum magicarum libri
sex*, 1612, pp. 14–15. They are mentioned by M. Casaubon, *Of credulity
and incredulity, in things natural*,
1668, p. 147.

of his senses: Then they spake of the boy who was pretended
to have had a wanting leg restor'd him, so confidently asserted
by *Fr: de Santa Clara*,[1] & others: To all which the Bishop
added a greate Miracle happning in that Citty of Winchester
to his certaine knowledge, of a poore miserably sick & de-
crepit Child, (as I remember long kept un-baptized) who immediately on his Baptisme, recover'd;[2] as also of the sanatory
effect of *K. Charles* his Majesties fathers blood, in healing one
that was blind:[3] As to that of the *Saludador* (of which likewise I remember[a] Sir *Arthir Hopton*,[4] formerly Ambassador
at Madrid had told me many like wonders) *Mr. Pepys* passing
through *Spaine*,[5] & being extreamely Inquisitive of the truth
of these pretended[b] miracles of the *Saludadors*; found a very
famous one of them at last, whom he offered a considerable
reward to, if he would make a trial of the *Oven*, or any other
thing of that kind, before him: The fellow ingenuously told
him, that, finding he was a more than ordinary curious person, he would not deceive him, & so accknowledg'd that he
could do none of those feates, realy; but that what they pretended, was all a cheate, which he would easily discover,
though the poore superstitious people were imposed upon:
yet have these Impostors, an[c] allowance[c] of the Bishops, to
practise th⟨e⟩ir Juggleings:[6] This Mr. *Pepys* affirm'd to me;

---

a Followed by *my* deleted.   b Followed by *Salu-* deleted.
c-c Altered from *a pr-*.

---

[1] Christopher Davenport, 1598–
1680, Franciscan, better known as
Franciscus a S. Clara: *D.N.B.* The
reference is to a miracle discussed
in his *Religio Philosophi Peripati
discutienda*, 1662; an account of it
is given with the reprint in his *Opera
omnia*, vol. ii, 1667; it took place at
Saragossa in 1640.

[2] This is Matthew Cante, baptized
by Ken himself; see his mother's
account of his recovery in *Life of
Thomas Ken*, by a Layman (J. L.
Anderdon), 2nd ed., 1854, i. 97–8.

[3] Presumably Mary Bayly of
Deptford, a sufferer from the king's

evil: *A Miracle of Miracles Wrought
by the Blood of King Charles I*, 1649;
G. J., *Letter Sent into France to the
Lord Duke of Buckingham*, 1649; the
same writer, in *A second Letter*,
1649, gives further cures, all apparently for the king's evil.

[4] Above, ii. 555.

[5] Pepys spent a few weeks in
Cadiz and Seville early in 1684,
when on his way home from Tangier: Pepys, *Life, journals, &c.*, ed.
Smith, ii. 9–30.

[6] The bishops certified that they
were not guilty of superstitious
practices: Feyjoó, iii. 12.

but said he, I did not conceive it fit, to interrupt his Majestie, who told what they pretended to do, so solemnly: Then there was something said of the second[a]-sight, happning to some[b] persons, especialy *Scotch*: Upon which both his Majestie & (I think) my Ld: *Arran,*[c][1] told us, that Monsieur a French Nobleman lately here in England, seeing the late Duke of Monmoth, come into the Play-house at Lond: suddainly cryed out to some sitting in the same box: *Voila Messieurs comme il entre sans tete*: After this his Majestie speaking of some Reliques, that had effected strange cures, particularly a *Thorne* of our B: S: Crosse; that healed a Gentlewomans[d] rotten nose by onely touching; & speaking of the Golden Crosse & Chaine taken out of the Coffin of St. *Edward the Confessor* at *Westminster,* by one of the singing-men, who[e] as the scaffolds were taking-down, after his Majesties Coronation, espying an hole in the Tomb, & something glisten; put his hand in, & brought it to the Deane, & he to the King:[2] his Majestie began to put the Bishop in mind, how earnestly the [late][f] King (his brother) call'd upon him, during his Agonie, to take out what he had in his pocckett: [See Feb: 6:][g] I had thought (says the King) it had ben for some keys, which might lead to some Cabinets, which his Majestie would have me secure; but (says he) you well remember that I found nothing in any of his pockets but onely a Crosse of Gold, & a few insignificant papers;[3] & there-

---

a Substituted for *first,* apparently some time after the passage was written.   b Followed by *people* deleted.   c MS. has closing bracket.   d Or *Gentlemans*; reading doubtful.   e Followed by *after* deleted.   f Interlined.   g Marginal note; apparently added later.

---

[1] From this it would appear that the present is the Scottish Lord Arran. I have not found the story reported elsewhere.

[2] The finding of this relic is described in C. Taylour, *A True and Perfect Narrative of the Strange and Unexpected Finding the Crucifix & Gold-Chain of . . . St. Edward the King and Confessor,* 1688; for an attempted reading of the inscription as there given see Soc. of Antiquaries, *Proc.,* 2nd ser., ix (1883), 227–30. It was still in the possession of the exiled Stuarts in 1715: Martin Haile, *Queen Mary,* p. 520.

[3] See above, p. 408; Ken had been present at the time. This cross was believed to be one which Sir William Waller the younger (*D.N.B.*) had seized in a Roman Catholic house at the time of the

upon shewed us the Crosse, & was pleased to put it into my hand; it was of Gold about 3 Inches long, having on one side a Crucifix enameled & embossed, the rest was graved & garnished with gold-smith worke & two pretty broad table Amethists (as I conceived) & at the bottome a pendant pearle; within was[a] inchas'd[a] a little fragment (as was thought) of the true Crosse: & a latine Inscription, in Gotic & roman letters:[1] How his Majestie came by it I do not remember;[2] for more company coming in this discourse ended: Onely I may not forget, a Resolution which his Majestie there[b] made, & had a little before entered upon it, at the Counsel board at Windsor or White-hal: That the Negros in the Plantations should all be Baptized, exceedingly declaiming against that impiety, of their Masters prohibiting it, out of a mistaken opinion, that they were then *ipso facto* free: But his Majestie persists in his resolution to have them Christn'd, which piety the *Bishop*, deservedly blessed him for;[3] and so I went out, to see the New Palace his late Majestie had began, and brought almost to the Covering: It was placed on the side of the Hill, where formerly stood the old Castle; a stately fabrique of 3 sides, & a Corridor, all built of brique, & Cornished, windoes, Columns at the break & Entrance, of freestone: intended for a Hunting House,

---

a–a MS. *was in inchas'd.*   b Or *then.*

Popish Plot: Terriesi, 2/12 March 1685, in Campana de Cavelli, ii. 25. A gold cross said to contain a piece of the True Cross was plundered from James when he was stopped off Sheppey in 1688 and was destroyed for the gold: James's relation, ibid., ii. 390; *Notes and Queries*, 3rd ser., v (1864), 392.

[1] This appears to be a rather loose description of St. Edward's cross; it contained no relic, however, when it was found, although there was a space for one.

[2] If the preceding note is correct Evelyn appears not to have grasped that the cross shown to him was St. Edward's.

[3] I cannot trace James's order. In March Louis XIV had issued such an order as art. ii of his edict for the French West Indies: *Le Code noir*, 1767, p. 30. The '*supposed Right*' to liberation on their being baptized is given as one of the planters' arguments against the proselytizing of the slaves in M. Godwyn, *The Negro's & Indians Advocate*, 1680, p. 138; he holds that Christianity and slavery are not incompatible. Baxter insists on proselytizing, but allows only a restricted penal or contractual slavery, whether the slaves are Christian or heathen: *Christian Directory*, 2nd ed., 1678, ii. 71–4.

when his Majestie came to those parts, & having an incomparable prospect: I believe there had already ben 20000 pounds and more expended; but his now Majestie did not seeme to encourage the finishing of it; at least for a while; & it is like to stand:[1] Hence I went to see the Cathedrall, a reverend pile, & in good repaire: There is still the Coffines of the 6 Saxon kings, whose bones had ben scattered by the sacrilegious Rebells of 1641, in expectation (I suppose) of finding some valuable Reliques; & afterward gather'd-up againe & put into new chests, which stand above the stalls of the Quire:[2] Here lies the body of their Founder,[3] of Card: [4] & severall other Bishops &c: & so I went to my Lodging, very wett, it having rained the whole day:

17 Early next morning we went to *Portsmouth*, some thing before his Majestie arived: we found all the way full of people, the Women in their best dresse, multitudes of all sorts, in expectance of seeing his Majestie passe by, which he did, riding on horse-back, a good part of the way:[5] We found the Major, his Aldermen with[a] their Mace, & in their formalities standing at the Entrance of the Fort,[6] a Mile on this side the Towne, where he made a speech to the King, & then went off the Guns of the fort, as did all those of the Garison, so soone

---

[a] Altered from *in*.

[1] Above, p. 341. Work had been stopped on James's accession.

[2] Winchester Cathedral was defaced by Sir William Waller's troops in December 1642. According to a writer of 1635 there were ten chests containing the bones of the kings and bishops: *Camden Miscellany*, xvi. 46–7. There are now six of them, four dating from the time of Bishop Foxe (1501–28) and two said to be copies made in 1661; one of them bears an inscription of that date, commemorating the regathering of the bones dispersed in 1642: *V.C.H., Hants.*, v. 56; H. Hyde, earl of Clarendon, *Antiq. of the Cathedral Church of Winchester*, 1714, p. 29, &c. Clarendon quotes Bruno Ryves's

account of the damage done by the parliamentarians.

[3] Evelyn presumably refers to the supposed tomb of King Lucius behind the choir; he was believed to have founded a church here consecrated in 189: Clarendon, pp. 3, 34.

[4] Henry Beaufort, d. 1447; bishop of Winchester 1404; cardinal 1426.

[5] The distance by Fareham and Cosham is about twenty-eight miles.

[6] Presumably the fort at Portsea Bridge, four miles from Portsmouth, guarding the bridge leading to Portsea Island: J. Ogilby, *Britannia*, 1675, p. 60.

as he was come into *Portsmouth*, all the souldiers (which were neere 3000)[1] drawn up, and lining the streetes, & platforme[a][2] to *Gods-house* (which is the name of the Governors house)[3] where (after his Majestie had viewed the new Fortifications, & Ship-yard) he was Entertained at a Magnificent dinner, by Sir   Slingsby,[4] the Lieutenant Governor; all the Gent: of any quality, in his traine setting downe at Table with him, & which I also had don, had I not ben before engag'd to *Sir Robert Holmes* (Governor of the *Isle of Wight*) to dine with him at a private house, where likewise we had a very sumptuous & plentifull repast of excellent[b] Venison, Fowle, Fish, fruit, & what not: After dinner I went to waite on his Majestie againe, who was pulling[c] on his boots in the Towne hall joyning to the house where he dined, & then having saluted some Ladys &c: that came to kisse his hand; he tooke horse for Winchester, whither he returned that night: This hall is artificialy hung round, with Armes of all sorts, like the Hall & keepe of Windsor, which looks very finely:[5]

I went hence to see the Ship-yard, & Dock, the Fortifications, and other things; What I learned was, the facility of an armies taking the Ile of Wight, should an attempt be made by any Enemy, for want of due care in fortifying some places of it, & the plenty of the Iland, able to nourish 20000

---

[a] Or *platforms*.   [b] MS. *ext:*   [c] Or *putting*.

---

[1] I have been unable to check this statement.

[2] The esplanade at the harbour end of the High Street.

[3] It had been a hospital in the middle ages; it was used as the governor's house from 1540 and was demolished in 1826 except for the chapel, now the Garrison Church: *V.C.H., Hants.*, iii. 191.

[4] Henry Slingsby; identified as a younger son of the Sir Henry Slingsby executed in 1658 (*D.N.B.*); cornet in the Royal Regiment of Horse (Oxford's) 1661; captain 1674; lieutenant-governor of Portsmouth from 1682; colonel of a regiment of horse 4 Oct. 1688; perhaps a groom of the bedchamber to James as duke and king, from *c*. 1682 onwards; probably M.P. for Portsmouth 1685, 1689: Dalton, *English army lists*, i. 5, 178; &c. He was never a knight or baronet.

[5] For the town-hall at this time see W. G. Gates, *Illustrated hist. of Portsmouth*, 1900, pp. 147–8; but possibly a special armoury is intended; for one at a later date see L. Allen, *Hist. of Portsmouth*, 1817, p. 145.

men, besides its inhabitants:[1] *Portsmouth* when finished will be very strong, & a Noble Key: There were now 32 Men of war in the Harbour: I was invited by Sir R: Beach,[2] the ⟨Commissioner⟩[a] where after a greate supper, Mr. Secretary and my selfe lay-all that night: & the next morning set out for Gildford [18][b] where we arived in good houre, & so the day after to Lond: whence [19][b] taking leave of Mr. Pepys, I came home to my house, after a journey of 140 miles:[3]

I had twice before ben at *Portsmouth*, Ile of Wight &c: many yeares since:[4] I found this part of *Hampshire* bravely wooded; especialy about the house and estate of *Coll: Norton*,[5] who (though now in being, having formerly made his peace by meanes of Coll Legg) was formerly a very fierce Commander in the first Rebellion: His house is large, & standing low, as one goes from Winchester to ⟨Portsmouth⟩:[c]

By what I observed in this Journey; I find that infinite industry, sedulity, gravity, and greate understanding & experience of affaires in his Majestie, that I cannot but predict much happinesse to the Nation, as to its political Government, & if he so persist (as I am confident he will) there could nothing be more desired, to accomplish our prosperity,

---

a MS. *Commissioners.*   b Marginal date.   c MS. *Ports mouth.*

[1] Camden notes the various castles, the natural defences provided by the cliffs, and the numbers of the militia available for the defence of the island: *Britannia*, p. 198.

[2] Richard Beach, d. 1692?; rear-admiral 1672; commissioner of the navy 1672–92; at Portsmouth 1679–90; knighted *c.* 1677: J. Charnock, *Biographia navalis*, 1794–6, i. 51; &c.

[3] Ogilby gives the distance from London to Portsmouth as 73½ miles: *Britannia*, pp. 59–60. The whole distance travelled was about 165–70 miles.

[4] In 1638 and 1642: above, ii. 21, 79.

[5] Richard Norton, *c.* 1615–91; matriculated at Oxford 1631; ad-mitted at Gray's Inn 1634; colonel under Manchester in the first Civil War; M.P. for Hampshire 1645–8 and for Hampshire or Portsmouth in all parliaments, except that of 1685, from 1653 until his death. He was a friend of Cromwell's and helped to arrange Richard Cromwell's marriage. A sister was married to Robert Legge, younger brother of Col. William Legge (above, iii. 494). His house was at Southwick near Portsdown Hill: *Hampshire Notes and Queries*, v (1890), 54, 64–5; G. N. Godwin, *Civil War in Hampshire*, 1904; Cromwell, *Letters and Speeches*; Collins, *Peerage*, ed. Brydges, iv. 109; *V.C.H., Hants*, iii. 161–3; &c.

but that he were of the national Religion: for certainely such a Prince never had this Nation since it was one:

20: Our *Viccar* had a stranger preached for him: on: 9 Jo: 4: shewing the greate necessitie of holinesse in this life, before it be too late: Afternoone the same on 4: Heb: 1: almost to the same effect: that the day of Grace dos not allways last: inciting to make sure of our estate &c:

My Wifes & Daughter Susans pictures were drawn: This Weeke:

27 A *stranger* preached on 3. *John* 31: & pomerid: on: 3. *Eph:* 19: concerning the knowledge, & Love of Christ, how it is term'd past Understanding &c: *See notes*:

30 I went to *Lond*, dind at Mrs. Boscawens; went to visite Dr. Tenison: sup't at my Lord Clarendon, whose Commission for Lieutenant of Ireland, was this day sealed: I also went to waite on my Lord *Tressurer*, who receiv'd me very kindly:

Octob: 1: This day I din'd at Mr. Slingsbys: Visited the *Dutchesse* of *Grafton*: Came in my absence to see me The *Duke* of *Norfolck*, neither my wife nor my selfe being at home; There were with him and much company:

2 I spent this morning in Devotion, preparing for the Communion, when having a letter sent me by Mr. *P[epys]*,[a] with this expression at the foote of it: *I have something to shew you, that I may not have againe another time*: &c & that I would not faile to dine with him:[b]1 I went accordingly: After dinner he had me, and one Mr. *Houblon*[2] (a very rich & considerable Merchant, whose Fathers had fled out of *Flanders* upon the persecution of the *Duke* of *Alva*) into a private roome: & being sate downe, told us that being lately alone with his Majestie and upon some occasion of speaking

---

[a] Interlined, apparently later.

[b] Hand in margin here.

[1] The letter is dated 'Thursday night, 2nd Oct. 1685': Bohn, iii. 279.

[2] Identifiable as James Houblon: above, p. 162; he was an intimate friend of Pepys. His great-grandfather had come to England from Lille, then part of Spain's Netherlandish possessions, in 1567, during the governorship of the duke of Alba (1506–82: *Nouvelle biog. gén.*): Lady Houblon, *Houblon family*, i. 41, 53, &c. Evelyn perhaps derived his statement from G. Burnet, *A Sermon Preached at the Funeral of Mr. James Houblon*, 1682, p. 24.

concerning my late Lord *Arlingtons* dying a *R: Cath*, who had all along seemed to professe himselfe a Protestant, taken all the Tests &c: 'til the day (I think) of his death:[1] His Majestie say'd, that as[a] to[a] his inclinations he had known him long wavering, but ⟨for⟩ feare of loosing his places [he][b] did not think convenient to declare himselfe: There are (says the King[c]) who believe the Ch: of R: gives Dispensations, for going to church, & many like things; but that it was not so; for if that might have ben had, he himselfe had most reason to make use of it:[2] Indeede he said, As to some Matrimonial Cases, there are now & then Dispensations, but hardly in any Cases else: This familiar discourse encourag'd Mr. P: to beg of his Majestie (if he might aske it, without offence, and[d] for that his Majestie could not but observe how it was whispered among many), [whither][e] his Late *Majestie* had ben reconcil'd to the *C. of Rome*:[3] He againe humbly besought his Majestie to pardon his presumption, if he had touch'd upon a thing, did not befit him to looke into &c: The *King* ingenuously told him, That he both was, & died a *R: Cath:* & that he had not long since declared it was upon some politic & state reasons, best known to himself [(meaning the King his Brother)][b] but that he was of that persuasion, he bid him follow him into[f] his Closett, where opening a Cabinet, he shew'd him two papers, containing about a quarter of a sheete on both sides, written in the late Kings owne hand,[g] severall Arguments opposite to the Doctrine of the *Church of Eng:* Charging her with heresy, novelty, & [the][b] phan⟨tas⟩ticisme of other Protestants: The chiefe whereoff (as I remember) were, our refusing to accknowledge the Primacy & Infallibility &c

---

a-a Substituted for *in*. b Interlined. c Followed by *further* deleted. d Preceded by opening bracket. e Interlined; in text *The As if* all deleted. f Followed by *ano a* all deleted. g Followed by *containing* deleted.

---

[1] Arlington had died on 28 July of this year. He had taken the oaths enabling him to sit in parliament on 23 May of this year; the report that he had died a Roman Catholic seems to have been generally accepted by his contemporaries.

[2] James's biographer gives a report of a conversation on this subject between James and a Jesuit in 1669: *Life*, ed. Clarke, i. 440-1.

[3] See above, p. 408 n.

of the Church of Rome, how impossible it was so many Ages should never dispute it, til of late; how unlikely our B: Saviour would leave his Church without a Visible Head & guide to resort to during his absence, with the like usual *Topics*; so well penn'd as to the discourse, as did by no means seeme to me, to have ben put together by the Late King: Yet written all with his owne hand, blotted, & interlin'd, so as if indeede, it were not given him by some Priest; they happly might be such Arguments and reasons as had ben inculcated from time to time, & here recollected, & in the conclusion shewing his looking on the Protestant Religion, (& by name the Church of Eng:) to be without foundation, & consequently false & unsafe: When his Majestie had shew'd him these *Originals*, he was pleas'd to lend him the Copies of those two Papers, attested at the bottome in 4 or 5 lines, under his owne hand: These were the papers I saw & read:¹ This nice & curious passage I thought fit to set downe; Though all the Arguments, and objections were altogether weake, & have a thousand times ben Answerd irreplicably by our Divines; though such as their Priests insinuate among their Proselytes, as if nothing were Catholique but the C. of Rome, no salvation out of that, no Reformation sufferable &c: botoming all their Errors on *St. Peters* Successors unerrable dictatorship; but proving nothing

---

¹ The contents of the two papers were published by the king's command as *Copies of Two Papers Written by the Late King Charles II*, 1686; a paper left by Anne, duchess of York, is appended; James certifies both papers (they are reprinted in the *Harleian Miscellany* and elsewhere). Although Evelyn appears to mean that what Pepys showed him were transcripts of Charles's papers certified by James it is possible that they were the originals with James's certification added; Burnet writes: 'Tenison told me that he saw the originals in Pepys's hand, to whom King James trusted them for some time. They were interlined in several places: and the interlinings seemed to be writ in a hand different from that in which the papers were writ. But he was not so well acquainted with the king's hand as to make any judgment in the matter, whether they were writ by him or not': *Own time*, ed. Airy, ii. 472 (added passage). On the whole Evelyn appears to be more likely to be correct than Tenison as reported by Burnet. On the originality of the compositions see Sancroft, as reported by James, *Life*, ii. 9; and on the other side Halifax, *Character of King Charles II*; &c.

with any sort of Reason, or the taking notice of any Objection which could be made against it: Here was all taken for granted, & upon it a Resolution & preference implied: I was heartily sorry to see all this; though it were no other, than what was long suspected, by his late Majesties too greate indifference, neglect & course of Life, that he had ben perverted, & for secular respects onely, profess'd to be of another beliefe; [See 6: *Feb* 168⅘]ᵃ & thereby giving infinite advantage to our Adversaries, both the Court, & generaly the Youth, & greateᵇ persons of the nation becoming dissolute & highly prophane;ᶜ God was incensed to make his Reigne very troublesome & improsperous, by Warrs, plagues,ᵈ fires, losse of reputation by a universal neglect ofᵉ the publique, for the love of a voluptuous & sensual life, which a vitious Court had brought into credit. I thinke of it with sorrow & pitty, when I consider of how good & debonaire a nature that unhappy prince was,ᶠ what opportunities he had to have made himselfe the most renouned King, that ever sway'd the British Scepter; had he ben firme to that Church, for which his Martyred & Bl: Father suffer'd; & gratefull to Almighty God, who so miraculously Restor'd him, with so excellent a *Religion* had he endeavored to owne & propagate it, as he should, not onely for the good of his Kingdomes, but all the Reformed Churches in Christendome, now weaken'd, & neere utterly ruind, through our remissnesse, & suffering them to be supplanted, persecuted & destroyed; as in *France*, which we tooke no notice of: The Consequence of this time will shew, & I wish it may proceede no farther: The Emissaries & Instruments of the C. of R: will never rest, 'til they have crush'd the Church of Eng: as knowing that alone able to cope with them: and that they canᵍ never answer her fairely, but lie aboundantly open to ⟨irresistible⟩ʰ force of her Arguments, Antiquity, & purity of her doctrine: so that albeit it may move God (for the punishment of a Nation so unworthy) to eclipse againe the profession of her here; &

ᵃ Marginal note.   ᵇ Followed by *men* deleted.   ᶜ Followed by *but* deleted.   ᵈ Or *plague*.   ᵉ Followed by *all* deleted.   ᶠ Followed by *&* deleted.   ᵍ Altered from *cannot*.   ʰ MS. *irresistoble*.

darknesse & superstition[a] prevaile; I am most confident the Doctrine of the *Church of Eng:* will never be extinguish'd, but remaine Visible, though not Eminent, to the consummation of the World: I have innumerable reasons that confirme me in this opinion, which I forbeare to mention here: In the meane time, as to This discourse of his Majestie with Mr. Pepys, & those Papers; as I do exceedingly preferr his Majesties free & ingenuous profession, of what his owne Religion is, beyond all Concealements upon any politique accounts what so ever; so I thinke him of [a][b] most sincere, and honest nature, one upon whose word, one may relie, & that he makes a Conscience of what he promises, to performe it: In this Confidence I hope, the Church of England may yet subsist; & when it shall please God, to open his Eyes, & turne his heart (for that is peculiarly in the Lords hands) to flourish also: In all events, whatever do become of the C. of Eng: It is certainely of all the Christian Professions on the Earth, the most Primitive, Apostolical, & Excellent:

I[c] returned home this Evening.

4: Our *Viccar* proceeded on his former Text: 12: Heb: 1: shewing what that ὄγγος[1] and *Encompassing weight* was; namely whatsoever darling, or unsubdued Sin remaind, that might hinder a Christian Course; & how to provide against it, recommending especialy [to][b] the care of parents &c: the Education & Institution of their Children: & how difficult it would be to hinder Vice,[d] & prevent evil habites:

The holy Sacrament foll: at which my Wife, & Daughter received with me:

Afternoone the *Curate* on 3: *Pro:* 17: of the peace & security of Godly wisdome &c: I was exceedingly drowsy: The Lord be gracious to me:

8 To Lond: return'd that Evening: I had my picture drawn this Weeke: [by the famous Kneller:][e][2]

---

a Followed by *agai-* deleted.   b Interlined.   c Perhaps preceded by a date *3*.   d Altered from *evi-*.   e Added later.

1 An error for ὄγκος.
2 Godfrey Kneller, 1646–1723; knighted 1692; created a baronet

1715: *D.N.B.* He had settled in England *c.* 1675 and since Lely's death had been the best portrait-

11 Our Viccar on his former subject:[a] Stranger Afternoone on 5: Matt: 4: the blessednesse of those who mourne for their sinns &c:

Octo: 14 I went to Lond: about my Suite, & finishing my Lodgings at *White-hall.*[1]

15 Being the Kings birth-day, was a solemn Ball at Court; And Musique of Instruments & Voices before the Ball: At the Musique I happen⟨ed⟩ (by accident) to stand the very next to the Queene, & the King, who ta⟨l⟩ked with me about the Musick:

18: Dr. *Good-man* [at *Whitehall*:][b] preached on 2: *Cor:* 4: 18, shewing in an excellent[c] discourse, the vanity of all earthly visible things, & proving, that there were real, though invisible now to us, which were solid & permanent:

The King was now building all that range from East to west by the Court & Garden to the streete, & making a new Chapel for the Queene, whose Lodgings this new building was: as also a new Council Chamber & offices next the South end of the Banqueting-house:[2]

20. I returned home: [21][d] Next morning againe to *Lond:*

22 I accompanied my Lady Clarendon to her house at Swallow-field in *Berkeshire,* dining by the way at Mr. *Grahams's* Lodge at *Bagshot*:[3] Where his Lady (my excellent & long acquaintance when maide of honour) entertain'd us at

---

[a] Followed by *Cur-* deleted.   [b] Interlined.   [c] MS. *ext.*
[d] Marginal date.

---

painter working in England. The portrait mentioned above is presumably that now at Wotton. The portrait owned by the Royal Society is a copy of part of it; it was given by Mrs. Evelyn in 1707. For another portrait of Evelyn by Kneller see below, 9 July 1689.

[1] Presumably the lodgings lent to him by Clarendon: above, p. 446.

[2] James had begun the work of rebuilding in May, but demolition of the old buildings and digging the foundations had occupied the inter-

vening months, and it was in October that the masons began. The principal building was completed by March 1687, but an additional annexe to the chapel only in November of that year. The whole was burnt down in the Whitehall fire of 1698. For the buildings and their progress see L.C.C., *Survey of London,* xii. 102–5; Wren Soc., vii. 73–7, 86–134. Queen Catherine had occupied lodgings near the waterside.

[3] Above, pp. 467–8.

a plentifull dinner: The house, new repaired, and capacious of a good family, stands in a Park: Hence we went to Swallow-fild[1] the house is after the antient building of honourable gent: houses where they kept up the antient hospitality: but the Gardens & Waters as elegant as 'tis possible to make a flat, with art & Industrie and no meane Expenses, my Lady being so extraordinarily skilld in the flowry part: & the dilligence of my Lord in the planting: so that I have hardly seene a seate which shews more toakens of it, then what is here to be found, not onely in the delicious & rarest fruits of a Garden, but in those innumerable & plentifull furniture of the grounds about the seate of timber trees to the[a] incredible ornament & benefit of the place: There is one Ortchard of a 1000 Golden & other cider Pepins: Walks & groves of Elms,[b] Limes, Oake: & other trees: & the Garden so beset with all manner of sweete shrubbs, as perfumes the aire marvelously: The distribution also of the Quarters,[2] Walks, Parterre &c is excellent: The Nurseries, Kitchin-garden, full of the most desireable plants; two[c] very noble Orangeries well furnish'd; but above all, The Canale, & fishponds, the one fed with a white, the other with a black-running water, fed by a swift & quick river:[3] so well & plentifully stor'd with fish, that for Pike, Carp, Breame, & Tench; I had never seene any thing approching it: We had Carps & Pike &c of size fit for the table of a Prince, every meale, & what added to the delight, the seeing hundreds taken in the drag, out of which the Cooke standing by,[d] we pointed what we had most mind to, & had Carps every meale, that

---

[a] Reading doubtful.   [b] Or *Elme*.   [c] Altered from *a*.
[d] Followed by *po-* deleted.

---

[1] Swallowfield, six miles south of Reading, had come to Clarendon through his present wife (above, p. 2). In 1719, ten years after his death, it was sold to Thomas Pitt, the father of Chatham; it now belongs to the Russell family. The house was largely rebuilt by Clarendon after 1689 and was greatly altered in the early nineteenth century: Lady Russell, *Swallowfield*.

[2] The beds or plots: *O.E.D.*

[3] The Loddon. The canal was filled in in the nineteenth century. By a white running water Evelyn perhaps means a light-coloured stream, not a clear one: *O.E.D.*, White, adj., 2.

had ben worth at London twenty shill a piece: The Waters are all flag'd about with Calamus arromaticus;[1] of which my Lady has hung a Closset, that retaines the smell very perfectly: Also a certaine sweete willow & other exotics: There is to this a very fine bowling-greene; Meadow, pasture,[a] Wood, in a word all that can render a Country seate delightfull:

25 The minister preached on 1. *Cor:* 6. ult a very honest & excellent[b] sermon against irreverence in Gods presence, after which the holy Sacrament, at which I was particip⟨a⟩nt: There is also a well furnished library in the house.

26 We return'd to Lond, having ben treated with all sorts of Cheare, & noble freedom, by that most religious & vertuous Lady, whom I beseech God to blesse & prosper: She was now preparing to go for Ireland with her husband; now made Lord Deputy,[2] & went to this Country house, and antient seate of her Fathers & family, to set things in order during absence, but never were good peopl⟨e⟩ & neighbour⟨s⟩ more concern'd, than all the Country (the poore especialy) for the departure of this Charitable woman; every body were in teares, & she as unwilling to part from them: There was amongst them a Maiden of primitive life: The daughter of a poore labouring man who sustain'd her parents (sometimes since dead) by her labour; & has for many yeares continued[c] a Virgin (though sought by severall[d] to marriage) & refusing to receive any assistance of the Parish (besides the little hermitage my Lady gives her rent-free) lives on foure pence a day which she getts in spinning: She says she abounds, & can give almes to others, living in strange humility and contentednesse, without any apparent affectation or singularity; she is continualy working, or praying, or reading; gives a good account of her knowledge in Religion; Visites the sick; is not in the least given to talke; is wonderfull modest, & of a simple, not[e] unseemly[e] behaviour; is of a Comely counte-

---

[a] Reading doubtful.   [b] MS. *exc*:   [c] Perhaps altered to *continues*.
[d] Above this word *substant-* interlined and deleted.   [e-e] MS. *not, unseemly.*

---

[1] Presumably Sweet Flag or *O.E.D.* Sweet Rush (*Acorus Calamus*):   [2] Properly lord-lieutenant.

nance, clad very plaine, but cleane & tight; in summ,
appeares a *Saint* of an extraordinary sort, in so religious a
life as is seldom met with in Villages now a daies:

27 I was invited to Sir St: Foxes, with my L. Lieutennant,
where was such a dinner for variety of all things, ⟨as⟩[a] I had
seldome seene, & it was so, for the triall of a Master-Cooke,
which Sir Stephen had recommended to go with his Lordship
into Ireland: There was all the Dainties not onely of the
season, but of what[b] art could add: Venison, & plaine solid
Meate, Foule, Baked & boiled meates; banquet &c in exceeding plenty, & exquisitely dressed: There also din'd my
Lord Ossory & Lady the Duke of Beauforts daught⟨e⟩r,[1] my
Lady Treasurer, Lord Cornbery[2] &c:

28 I went to the R: Society,[3] being the first meeting after
our Summer recesse, & was very full: An Urn full of bones,
was presented, for the repository, dug up in an high way, by
the repairers of it: in a field in *Camberwell* in *Surry*: This
Urn & cover was found intire among many others; believed
to be truely Roman & antient: Sir Ri: Bulkeley,[4] described
to us a model of a Charriot he had invented, which it was not
possible to overthrow, in whatsoever uneven way it was
drawn: giving us a stupendious relation, of what it had perform'd in that kind; for Ease, expedition, & Safty: There
was onely these inconveniences yet to be remedied; that it
would not containe above one person; That it was ready to
fire every 10 miles, & being plac'd & playing on no fewer than
10 rollers, made so prodigious noise, as was almost intollerable: These particulars the Virtuosi were desir'd to

---

[a] MS. *&*.   [b] Followed by *was* deleted.

---

[1] Mary, *c.* 1665–1733; married
Ossory as his second wife 3 August
of this year; for her father see
above, iii. 94. The first Lady
Ossory (above, p. 297) was a daughter of Rochester.

[2] Edward Hyde, 1661–1723;
styled Lord Cornbury 1674–1709;
third earl of Clarendon 1709:
D.N.B., art. Hyde, Henry, second

earl of Clarendon.

[3] Birch, iv. 424–6.

[4] Richard Bulkeley, 1660–1710;
second baronet 17 March of this
year; F.R.S. 25 November of this
year: *D.N.B.* He was not the in-
ventor of the calesh; he gives an
account of its powers in *Philosophical Transactions*, xv (1685),
1028–9 (no. 172).

excogitate the remedies, to render the Engine of extraordinary Use: &c:

31 I dind at our greate Lord Chancellors,ᵃ who us'd me with greate respect: This was the late L: C. Justice Jeofries, who had ben newlyᵇ the Western Circuite, to trie the Monmoth Conspirators; & had formerly don such severe Justice amongst the obnoxious in Westminster Hall &c for which his Majestie dignified him with creating him first a Baron, & now L. Chancellor:¹ He had some yeares past, ben conversant at Deptford:² is of an assur'd & undaunted spirit, & has serv'd the Court Interest upon all the hardiest occasions: [of nature cruell & a slave of this Court.]ᶜ

I had now accomplish'd the 65t yeare of my Age: Lord teach me to Number my daies so, as to employ their remainder to thy glory onely. Amen:

November 1 Being Sonday Dr. *Jeane*³ R: *Profess:* in *Oxford*, preached in W:hall Chapell on 13. *Heb:* 18: shewing what Conscience was, how to be directed by it: with what extraordinary nicenesse to be dealt with, & secur'd in all our actings: A discourse of greate & solid matter, perspicuous, full, & Instructive: I received the holy Communion:

3 I returned home: The *French* persecution of the Protestants, raging with uttmost barbarity, exceeding what the very heathens used: Innumerable persons of the greatest birth, & riches, leaving all their earthly substance & hardly escaping with their lives, dispers'd thro' all the Countries of Europe: The Fr: Tyrant, abrogating the Edicts of Nants⁴ &c in favour of them, & without any Cause on the suddaine, demolishing all their Churches, banishing, Imprisoning,

---

ᵃ Here *Jeoffries* interlined and deleted.   ᵇ Substituted for *just*.
ᶜ Added later.

---

¹ He was created Baron Jeffreys of Wem on 16 May of this year; and was appointed lord chancellor on 28 September.

² Jeffreys had no known connexion with Deptford, unless through James Burton: above, p. 352.

³ Jane.

⁴ The Edict of Nantes (1598) was revoked by an edict signed on 18 October, N.S. (registered 22 October). Luttrell mentions the outbreak of persecution about 19 October: i. 360.

sending to the Gallies all the Ministers: plundring the common people, & exposing them to all sorts of barbarous usage,
by souldiers sent to ruine & prey upon them; taking away
their children; forcing people to the Masse, & then executing
them as Relapsers: They burnt the libraries, pillag'd their
goods, eate up their filds & sustenance, banish'd or sent to
the Gallies the people, & seiz'd on their Estates: There had
now ben numbred to passe through *Geneva* onely, from time
to time by stealth onely (for all the usual passages were
strictly guarded by sea & land) fourty thousand, towards
Swisserland:[1] In Holland, Denmark, & all about Germany,
were dispersed some hundred thousands[a][2] besids here in
England, where though multitude of all degrees sought for
shelter, & wellcome, as distressed Christians & Confessors,
they found least encouragement; by a fatality of the times
we were fall'n into, & the incharity & indifference of such,
as should have embrac'd them: and I pray, it be not laied
to our Charge:[3] The famous Claude[4] fled to Holland: Alex[b][5]

---

[a] Followed by *not* deleted.
doubtful.

[b] Altered from *Alexan*; reading

---

[1] This figure is apparently grossly
exaggerated. About 24 November
it was reported in London that
20,000 fugitives had escaped into
Switzerland; 6,000 had passed
through 'Geneva and Genoa': *Hist.
MSS. Comm., Portland MSS.*, iii.
390. Geneva and the neighbouring
towns sheltered 60,000 fugitives
between 1682 and 1720: J. Gaberel,
Hist. de l'Église de Genève, 1853–62,
iii. 369. Most of these moved on,
but the population of Geneva was
permanently increased by over
3,000: Lane Poole, p. 115.

[2] Lane Poole reckons that Germany received altogether about
75,000, but this covers the whole
migration: p. 169. D'Avaux in
1686 reported that there was the
same number in the United Provinces: Lavisse, VIII. i. 343.

[3] A writer on 24 November says
that 'very few' refugees come to

London: *Hist. MSS. Comm., Portland MSS.*, iii. 390. Burnet states
that so many came that James II
openly condemned the persecution:
Own time, 1833, iii. 87. On 6
November he ordered a Brief to
be prepared for a general collection:
Huguenot Soc., *Proc.*, vii (1901–4),
177. For the delay in issuing it see
below, p. 508.

[4] Jean Claude, 1619–87; pastor
of Charenton 1666–85; theologian
and author: *Nouvelle biog. gén.*;
E. and E. Haag, *La France Protestante*. On 21 October, N.S., he had
been exiled, being ordered to leave
Paris within two days.

[5] Pierre (Peter) Allix, 1641–1717;
minister at Charenton 1671–85;
ordered to leave Paris by 24 October,
N.S.; conformed to the Church of
England; D.D., Cambridge, 1690;
treasurer of Salisbury 1690; author:
D.N.B.

& severall more came to Lond: & persons of mighty estates came over who had forsaken all: But France was almost dispeopled, the bankers so broaken that the Tyrants revenue exceedingly diminished:[1] Manufacture ceased, & every body there save the *Jesuites* &c. abhorring what was don: nor the Papists themselves approving it ;[2] what the intention farther is time will shew, but doubtlesse portending some extraordinary revolution: I was now shew'd the Harangue that the *Bishop* of *Valentia* on Rhone, made in the name of the Cleargie, celebrating the Fr: King (as if he were a God) for his persecuting the poore protestants; with this Expression in it: That as his Victories over Heresy was greater than all the Conquests of[a] Alexander & Cæsars &c: it was but what was wished in England: & that God seem'd to raise the French King to this power & magnanimous action, that he might be in capacity to assist the doing of the same here:[3]

---

[a] Followed by *a* interlined.

---

[1] The direct influence of the persecution of the Huguenots on Louis XIV's revenue cannot be estimated. The persecution was a contributory, but not the principal, cause of the economic decline of France in the later part of Louis's reign: Lavisse, VIII. i. 201–13.

[2] This is not true; approval of the Revocation was almost unanimous in France. The Pope, Innocent XI, appears to have been aware of the use of force in many of the conversions; his attitude at best was equivocal: *Revue des questions historiques*, xxiv (1878), 417–18, 423–4.

[3] The bishop is Daniel de Cosnac, *c.* 1630–1708; bishop of Valence and Die 1655; archbishop of Aix 1687: *Nouvelle biog. gén.*; *Mém.*, ed. Cosnac, 1852. The reference is to his speech to the king, 14 July, N.S., on behalf of the Assembly of the French clergy; published as *Harangue*, &c., 1685. Evelyn misrepresents the passage relating to England:

'Mais comme si ce n'étoit pas assez pour vous d'avoir ramené dans le sein de l'Église tant de milliers d'âmes égarées qui vivoient sous votre empire, vous avez encore voulu conquérir de nouvelles provinces pour y rétablir les prélats, le culte et les autels. La Hollande et l'Allemagne n'ont servi de théâtre à vos victoires que pour y faire triompher Jésus-Christ. Que ne doit-on pas attendre encore? L'Angleterre est sur le point d'offrir à Votre Majesté une des plus glorieuses occasions qu'elle puisse désirer. Le plus triomphant, le plus hardi, le plus grand de tous les monarques de l'univers, avant que le ciel eût donné Votre Majesté à la terre, souhaitoit pour comble de bonheur de rencontrer une fois dans sa vie un péril digne de lui; le roi d'Angleterre, par le besoin qu'il aura du secours et de l'appui de vos armes pour se maintenir dans la religion catholique, vous fera

This paragraph is very bold & remarkable; severall reflecting on *Æ: Ushers Prophecy*[1] as now begun in France, & approching the orthodox in all other reformed Churches: &c: One thing was much taken notice of, That the *Gazetts* which were still constantly printed twice a weeke, & informing[a] us what was don all Europ over &c: never all this time, spake one syllable of this wonderfull proceeding in France, nor[b] was any Relation of it published by any, save what private letters & the persecuted fugitives brought: Whence this silence, I list not to conjecture, but it appeared very extraordinary in a Protestant Countrie, that we should know nothing of what Protestants suffered &c: whilst greate Collections were made for them in forraine places more hospitable & Christian to appearance.[2]

5 It being an extraordinary wett morning, & I indisposed by a very greate rheume, I could not go to Church this day, to my greate sorrow, it being the first Gunpouder conspiracy Anniversary, that had ben kept now this 80 yeares, under a Prince of the Roman Religion: Bonfires forbidden &c:[3] What[c] dos this portend?[c]

7 I went to Lond:

---

[a] Followed by *the world* deleted. words possibly added later.

[b] Substituted for *&*.   [c–c] These

bien trouver le moyen de donner une protection digne de vous': *Mém.*, ii. 319–20.

The speech attracted the attention of the members of parliament: d'Adda (below, p. 494), 9/19 Nov., quoted by Macaulay, p. 678.

[1] Ussher's earliest biographer, N. Bernard, is inclined to believe that he was divinely inspired with the gift of prophecy: *Life . . . of . . . Usher*, 1656, pp. 90–1. The prophecy relating to the coming persecution of the Protestant churches is an alleged report of a conversation with him, possibly based on genuine remarks of his; it was apparently first published in 1678 (licence 16 November) in *Strange and Remarkable Prophesies and Predictions of . . . James Usher*,

pp. 5–7 (there are three editions all belonging to 1678); slightly varying versions were published in other tracts, with Ussher's name, in 1681, 1682, &c.; see also Elrington's remarks in Ussher, *Whole Works*, 1847–64, i. 295–8.

[2] The statement as regards the *London Gazette* is correct. Luttrell gives only two notices, both rather slight. Noteworthy collections were made for the fugitives in the various places of refuge abroad: notices in Lane Poole; Benoist, iii (v), 958–60.

[3] The old form of service remained in use. In London orders were circulated by the parish officials on 4 November, forbidding bonfires, squibs, &c., for the following day: Luttrell, i. 362. On 6 November an order was made in

8 Dr. *Birch*[1] preached at Whitehall on: 12: *Heb:* 1: shewing the necessitie of throwing off the greate weight & impediment of our Christian race, in an excellent[a] discourse:

The second: Dr. *Smith,*[2] on: 2: *Heb:* 3: The danger of Ingratitude, especialy of this Nation, having such wonderfull meanes above others:

9 Began the Parliament; The King in his Speech requiring continuance of a standing force in stead of a *Militia*, & indemnity & dispensation to Popish Officers from the Test; Demands very unexpected & unpleasing to the Commons; He also requird a Supply of Revenue, which they granted; but returned no thanks to the King for his Speech 'til farther consideration:[3]

10 I dined at my L. *Arch-Bishops* of *York*, w⟨h⟩ere were The *Bishops* of *London*, & St. *Asaph* &c:

11 I went to Gressham Colledge.[4]

12 The Commons postpon'd the finishing the bill for the Supply, to consider of the Test, & popish Officers: this was carried but by one voice:[5]

14[b] They voted an Addresse to the King about it:

I dined at Lambeth my Lord *Arch Bish:* carrying me with him in his barge: there were my L: Deputy of Ireland:[6] The *Bishops* of Ely,[7] & St. Asaph, Dr. Sherlock[8] & other divines,

---

a MS. *ex^t:*   b Altered from *13*.

---

the Privy Council forbidding bonfires, &c., on all festivals henceforward; it was published in *London Gazette*, 9 Nov., and also separately. Similar orders had been issued in 1680, 1682, and 1683.
[1] Presumably Peter Birch, c. 1652–1710 ; B.D. 1684; D.D. 1688; chaplain in ordinary c. 1692–c. 1694: *D.N.B.*
[2] Presumably Dr. Smith of Christ Church: above, p. 240.
[3] For this day's proceedings see *C.J.*, ix. 755–6, where the king's speech is printed. The supply was not voted until 12 November; owing to the prorogation on 20

November no act for it was passed. Reports of debates in the commons during this session are printed in *The Faithfull Register*, [1689], and are reprinted in the various parliamentary histories.
[4] For the Royal Society's meeting.
[5] By 183 to 182; but this took place on Friday, 13 November: *C.J.*, ix. 757.
[6] Clarendon, the lord-lieutenant.
[7] Turner.
[8] Presumably William Sherlock, c. 1640–1707; D.D. 1680; master of the Temple 1684–1705; chaplain in ordinary c. 1687–9, c. 1694–1707; dean of St. Paul's 1691: *D.N.B.*

Sir William *Hayward*,[1] Sir Paule Rycot[2] &c: The Dinner was for cheere extraordinary.

I returned home this Evening:

15 Our *Viccar* on 8: Mar: 38: something impertinent to the Text, he much insisted on our B: Saviours Miracles, shewing that Miracles[a] being wrought to convince our Understandings, They were such as were obvious to our senses: an unanswerable objection to the doctrine of Transubstantiation.

Pomeridiano: the Curate of Greenewich: 1: *John*: 5: 3: shewing the easinesse of the Commands & injunctions of the Gospell:

This day 65 years, was I Baptized: &c: Blessed be God:

17 I went to Lond: 18 I din'd at the Bishops of Londons:

20 Was the Parliament adjourn'd to ffeb: Severall both of Lords & Commons, excepting against some passage of his Majesties Speech, relating to the Test, & continuance of Popish Officers in Command:[3] This was a greate surprize to a Parliament, which people believed would have complied in all things:

Popish pamphlets & Pictures sold publiqly: no books or answers against them appearing &c:[4] [till long after:][b]

21 I returned home, having ben at a Triall of my La: Tukes Cause in Chancery the morning, with doubtfull successe; and also resigned my Trust for the Composing of a difference betweene Mr. Thayre & his Wife:[5]

22 Our Viccar proceeded on his former text: & in the After-

---

a Followed by *were* deleted.   b Added later.

---

[1] Sir William Hawarde: above, iii. 598.

[2] Paul Rycaut (Ricaut), 1628–1700; F.R.S. 1666; appointed secretary to Clarendon (as lord-lieutenant) early in October of this year; knighted 8 October; diplomatist and author of works on Turkey: *D.N.B.* He had been consul at Smyrna from 1667 to 1677. He was the author of the account of Sabatai Sevi which Evelyn published in *The*

History of the three late famous impostors (above, iii. 522).

[3] Parliament was prorogued, not adjourned: *L.J.*, xiv. 88; *C.J.*, ix. 761. For the lords' debates see Macaulay, pp. 690–4; Foxcroft, *Halifax*, i. 458–9.

[4] Cf. Wood, *Life and times*, iii. 131, 176. The chief publisher was apparently Henry Hills senior: below, p. 504 n.

[5] Above, p. 446.

noone the Curate on 2: *Heb:* 3. shewing the danger of neglecting the grace of the Gospel:

Hitherto was a very wett, warme season:[1]

29 Our Viccar proceeded: Curate on: 2. *Tim:* 2. 19, shewing the necessity of an holy life.

30 To *Lond:* it being St. *Andrews* the Patron of the R: Societies day: to choose Officers for the ensewing yeare: which we did, continuing our former President *Mr. Pepys*, who had ben a bountifull benefactor to us:[2] There was a very full meeting:

December 3d: I din'd at Lord *Sunderlands*, where din'd L: *Chancellor*, L: *Midleton*, *Abergavenie*[3] &c: 4th Lord *Sunderland* was declar'd President of the Counsel, & yet to hold his *Secretaries* place &c:[4] The forces disposed into severall quarters through the Kingdome, are very insolent, upon which greate Complaints:[5] Lord *Brandon* (tried-for the late conspiracy) condemn'd & pardoned;[6] so was L: Grey his accuser: & wittnesse:[7] Persecution in France raging: The French insolently visite our Vessels, & take away the fugitive protestants: Some escape hidden in barills &c:[8]

5 I return'd home:

6 Our Viccar & Curate prosecuted their former subjects: The H: Sacrament follow'd, of which I participated: The Lord make me Thankfull & carefull:

10 I went to *Greenewich* being[a] put into the new Com-

---

[a] Followed by *of the Comm-* deleted.

---

[1] There was a green Yule this year: Wood, *Life and times*, iii. 180.

[2] For Pepys as benefactor of the Society see Weld, i. 299.

[3] George Nevill, 1665-95; twelfth Lord Bergavenny (Abergavenny) 1666: G.E.C.

[4] Notice in *London Gazette*, 7 Dec.

[5] There were complaints in the commons on 16 November: *Faithfull Register*.

[6] Charles Gerard, *c.* 1659-1701; styled Viscount Brandon 1679-94; second earl of Macclesfield 1694: *D.N.B.* He had been tried for high treason (conspiring against the late king) on 26 November and had been sentenced to death on 28 November: *London Gazette*, 30 Nov.; report of the trial in Luttrell. He was now reprieved and was pardoned in 1687.

[7] Above, p. 323. He appears to have been pardoned in time to give evidence at Brandon's trial: Luttrell, i. 363, 365.

[8] Apparently James II in October permitted the French to visit all his ships calling in the Normandy ports: Guitard, *Colbert*, &c., pp. 129-30. For the escapes by sea besides Guitard see Benoist, iii (v), 948.

mission of Sewers, where I tooke the Oathes of Alegeance
&c:[a] din'd with the Commissioners:

12 I went to Lond, to take leave of my L: Deputy of Ireland:

13 Dr. Patric Deane of *Peterborow* preached at W:hall
before the Princesse of Denmark, who since his Majestie came
to the Crown, allways sate in the Kings Closset, (and had the
same bowings &[b] Ceremonies applied to the place where she
was, as if his Majestie had ben there in person)[1] on 1. Tim:
3. 9. shewing that by the Mysterie of faith, was meant, the
Christian religion; a Mysterie, in reguard it was then but
newly publish'd &c: the application, exhorting to a sincere
profession &c:

15 Dining at Mr. *Pepyss* Secretary of the Admiral⟨ty⟩, &
still president of our Society: Dr. *Slayer*[2] shew'd us an
Experiment of a wonderfull nature; pouring first a very cold
liquor into a Matras,[3] & superfusing on it another (to appearance) cold & cleare liquor also, it first producd a white
clowd, then boiling, divers Corruscations & actual flames of
fire mingled with the liquor, which being a little shaken
together fixed divers sunns & starrs of real fire perfectly
globular upon the walls of the Glasse to our greate astonishment, & which there stuck like so many Constellations burning most vehemently, & exceedingly resembling starrs &
heavenly bodys, & that for a long space: It seem'd to exhi-
bite a Theorie of the eduction of light out of the *Chäos*, & the
fixing or gathering of the universal light, into luminous
bodys: This matter of *Phosphorus*, was made out of human
blood & Urine, elucidating the Vital flame or heate in
Animal bodys: a very noble Experiment:

16 I accompanied my L: Lieutennant as far as St. Albans,
there going out of Towne with him neere 200 Coaches, of all
the Greate Officers & Nobilitie:[4]

---

[a] Followed by *&* deleted.   [b] Followed by *applications* deleted.

---

[1] Cf. above, p. 433.
[2] i.e. Slare: above, p. 251, &c.
[3] A glass vessel with a round or oval body and a long neck, used for

distilling, &c.: *O.E.D.*
[4] There is a notice of Clarendon's departure this day in *London Gazette*, 17 Dec.

17 Next morning taking leave, I return'd to Lond.

18 I dind at the greate entertainement his Majestie gave the Venetian Ambassadors Signors *Zenno* & *Justiniani*,[1] accompanied with 10 more Noble *Venetians* of their most illustrious families *Cornaro*, *Maccenigo* &c, who came to Congratulate their Majesties coming to the Crowne &c: The dinner was one of the most magnificent & plentifull that I have ever seene, at 4 severall Tables with Music, Trumpets, Ketle-drums &c which sounded upon a whistle at every health: The banquet was 12 vast Chargers pild up so high, as those who sat one against another could hardly see one another, of these Sweetemeates which doub⟨t⟩lesse were some dayes piling up in that exquisite manner, the Ambassadors touched not, but leaving them to the Spectators who came in Curiosity to see the dinner, &c were exceedingly pleas'd to see in what a moment of time, all that curious work was demolish'd, & the Comfitures &c voided & table clear'd: Thus his Majestie entertain'd them 3 dayes, which (for the table onely) cost him 600 pounds as the Cleark of the Greene-Cloth Sir W: Boreman,[2] assur'd me: Dinner ended, I saw their procession or Cavalcade to W:hall, inumerable Coaches attending: The 2 Ambassadors had 4. Coaches of their owne & 50 footemen, as I remember, besides other[a] Equipage as splended as the occasion would permitt, the Court being still in mourning,[3] Thence I went to the Audience[4] which they had in the Queenes presence Chamber:[5] The banqueting-house being full of goods & furniture til the Galleries on the Garden side, Council Chamber & new Chapell,

---

[a] Followed by comma in MS.

---

[1] Girolamo Zen and Ascanio Giustinian, here from 15 December to *c.* 16 January. They came to offer condolences and congratulations and to request help for the war against the Turks. Their train included Sebastian Mocenigo: N. Barozzi and G. Berchet, *Relazioni . . . ambasciatori Veneziani*, ser. iv, Inghilterra, 1863, pp. 471–[85].

There are notices of their entry, leave-taking, &c., in *London Gazette*, 17 Dec.–18 Jan. For Giustinian, *c.* 1640–1715, see Barozzi and Berchet, ser. ii, Francia, iii. 283.

[2] Above, iii. 270.
[3] Presumably for Charles II.
[4] Notice in *London Gazette*, 21 Dec.
[5] See above, iii. 494.

were finish'd, now in building:[1] They went to their Audience in those plaine black Gownes, [& Caps][a] which they constantly weare in the Citty of Venice:[2] I was invited to have accompanied the two Ambassadors in their Coach to supper that night, returning now to their owne Lodgings, as no longer at the Kings expense, but being weary, I excus'd my selfe:

19 My Lord Tressurer made me to dine with him, where I came acquainted with Monsieur *Barillon*,[3] the French Ambassador, a learned & crafty Advocate:

20 Dr. *Turner*[4] bro: to Bishop of Ely, & sometime Tutor to my Son, preached at W.hall on 8: *Mar:* 38: concerning the submission of Christians to their persecutors, in which were some passages indiscreete enough, considering the time, & the rage of the inhumane French Tyrant against the poore protestants:

22 Our pattent for executing the Office of the Lord Privy-Seale, during the absence of the L: Lieutennant of Ireland, being this day sealed by the L: Chancellor:[5] We went afterwards to St. *Jame's*, where the Court then was, upon occasion of the building at White-hall;[6] where his Majestie deliverd *The Seale* to My L: *Tiveat*[7] & my-selfe (the other Commissioner being not come) and then, gave us his hande to kisse: There[b] was the 2 *Venetian Ambassadors* & a world of Company, amongst the rest, The first *Popes Nuntio*

---

[a] Interlined.   [b] Altered from *This*.

---

[1] See above, p. 480.

[2] For Venetian costume see above, ii. 448–9.

[3] Above, p. 128.

[4] Thomas Turner, 1645–1714; D.D. 1683; vicar of Milton, near Sittingbourne, 1672–95; chaplain in ordinary, *c.* 1687(1685)–*c.* 1692; president of Corpus Christi College, Oxford, 1688–1714: *D.N.B.* Evelyn does not mention him elsewhere as his son's tutor.

[5] See above, p. 464. A notice,

dated 18 December, of the appointment is printed in *London Gazette*, 21 Dec.

[6] The court had moved to St. James's Palace on Saturday, 19 December: *Hist. MSS. Comm., Rutland MSS.*, ii. 98.

[7] Robert Spencer, created Viscount of Teviot (Scotland) on 20 October of this year: above, iii. 37, &c. The third commissioner was Col. Robert Phelips: below, p. 513.

Signor ¹ that had ever ben³ in England since the Reformation; so wonderfully were things chang'd, to the universal jealosie &c:

24 We were all three Commissioners sworn on our knews by the Cleark of the Crowne² before my Lord Chancellor, 3, severall Oathes, Allegeance, Supremacy, & the oath belonging to the L: Privy-Seale,³ which we onely tooke standing: After which the L. Chancellor invited us all to dinner; but it being Christmas Eve, we desir'd to be excus'd; at 3 in the afternoone intending to Seale divers things which lay ready at the Office: So attended by three of the Clearks of the Signet,⁴ we met, & sealed; amongst other things, one was a Pardon to *West*⁵, who being privy to the late Conspiricy, had reveald the Complices, to save his owne neck: There was also another pardon, & two Indenizations: & so agreeing to a fortnights vaccation, I return'd home to my house:

25 Christmas-day, our Viccar preach'd on 1: *Heb:* 1: subje⟨c⟩t apposite to the occasion, The holy Communion following, at which I participated, the *Lord* grant me acceptance:

27 Our Viccar proceeded on his former subje⟨c⟩t: & in the

ª Followed by *own'd* deleted.

---

¹ Ferdinando, conte d'Adda, 1650–1719, a Milanese; apostolic minister here from November of this year until 14/24 May 1687, when he was appointed nunzio (public audience 3 July); left England at the Revolution; created a cardinal 1690: M. Guarnacci, *Vitæ . . . Pontificum . . . et . . . Cardinalium*, 1751, i. 335–8; &c. Some of his despatches are printed in Sir James Mackintosh, *History of the Revolution in England in 1688*, [1834], pp. 631–77; additional despatches and omitted passages in Campana de Cavelli, vol. ii; some excerpts in Macaulay.

² Henry Barker. For the office see Chamberlayne (ed. 1687, ii. 126–7).

³ The substance of the oath is given in Sir E. Coke, *The fourth part of the Institutes of the Laws of England*, 1644, p. 55.

⁴ There were four clerks of the privy seal and four clerks of the signet (under its keeper, the principal secretary of state): lists in Chamberlayne, 1684, i. 191: 1687, i. 169. It is not clear why the latter should be employed on this occasion; perhaps an error on Evelyn's part.

⁵ Robert West of the Middle Temple, barrister, one of the Rye House conspirators who turned king's evidence. Informations given by him are printed in Sprat, *True account of the horrid conspiracy*, [ii]. 27–48, 55–62 (23 June, &c.).

afternoone, the Curate of Greenewich on: 7: *Isa:* 14, apposite
to the season, & Incarnation &c:

29 I invited our Viccar, & other friends to dinner:

31 Recollecting the passages of the yeare past [I][a] made
up Accompts, humbly besought Almighty God, to pardon
those my sinns, which had provok'd him to discomposse my
sorrowfull family, that he would accept of our humiliation,
& in his good time restore comforte to it: I also blesse God
for all his undeserved mercys & preservations, beging the
continuance of his grace & preservation: The winter had
hitherto ben extraordinarily wett, & mild:[1]

1 *Jan: 1685/6.* Imploring the continuance of Gods Mercy,
& providential care for the yeare now entred, I went to the
publique Devotions: some neighbours din'd with us. The
Deane of the Chapell, & Cleark of the Closset put out, viz.
Bishop of Lond: and   & Rochester & Durham put in their
places; They had opposed the Tolleration intended,[b] &c &
shew'd a worthy zeale for the reformed religion established:[2]

3 Our *Viccar* proceeded, shewing by many Scripture⟨s⟩ the
Godhead of Christ against the *Socinians* and Jewes: That
his coming and vocation of the Gentils was foretold by
severall of the Prophets from Abraham forewards, signified
by Job, Naaman, Jethro, of other heathen proselytes, how-
cver thcy could not indurc to hcarc that any should be the
people of God, but themselves, & therefore oppos'd their
Conversion all they were able, & even with spite; Though
even at this day their owne Doctors have acknowledg'd that
a little before the destruction of their rites & temple, three
things were ominous: 1 That the scarlet wooll used to be tied
to the head of the scape goate, & which was wont to be
changed white in token of their sinns being pardoned, still

---

[a] Interlined later.   [b] Followed by *as* deleted.

---

[1] See above, p. 490 n.
[2] Compton was discharged from
his place as dean of the chapel on
16 December; he was succeeded by
the clerk of the closet, Crew, who
was succeeded by Sprat; Crew and
Sprat were sworn on 29 December:
London Gazette, 31 Dec. Compton
had spoken against the court in the
house of lords on 19 November:
Macaulay, pp. 692–3.

kept its Colour: 2: That the perpetual light or lamp extinguish'd of[a] it[a] selfe, & the dores of the Temple opened of their
owne accord,[1] all of them intimating, that grace & pardon
was no longer to them alone, but light, & admission even into
the holiest admitted to all the world: The use was our thankfullnesse for admitting us into his Church, & giving us the
light of the Gospel: The holy Communion follow'd, at which
I participated, in order to the *Test*, as a Commissioner of the
Sewers, by a late Commission now renew'd &c:[2] The *Curat*
preach'd on 1. *Joh:* 4. 9, drowsinesse surprizing me:

6 I went to Lond: to our Office,[3] din'd with the L. Arch-
Bish: of Yorke, where was Peter-Walsh[4] that[b] Romish Priest,
who was so well known for his moderation; professing the
Ch: of England to be a true member of the Chatholique
Church; he is used to go to our publique prayers without
scrupule, did not acknowledge the Popes Infallibility, &
onely primacy of Order &c. I returned this Evening:

10 Our Viccar & Curate proceeded on their former Texts:

13 I went to *Lond:* to a Seale, return'd that Evening:

16 I went to Lond: invited by the Trinity Comp: a greate
dinner, return'd:

Jan: 17 Our *Viccar* proceeded on his Text; se your notes:

Pomerid: Curate of Greenewich 1 Jam: 22: of the duty of
practising what we heare:

19 I went to Lond: pass'd the Privie Seale amongst others,
the Creation of Mrs. *Sidly*[5] (concubine to . . .) Countesse of

---

a-a Or *of-it*.   b Altered from *a J-*.

[1] The preacher refers to a passage
in the treatise Yoma in the Talmud;
for it see *Le Talmud de Jérusalem*,
trans. M. Schwab, vol. v, 1882,
p. 234.
[2] See above, pp. 490-1; for the
Test Act, p. 7.
[3] The Privy Seal.
[4] Peter Walsh, 1618?-88, Irish
Franciscan: *D.N.B.* His views are
set out in the preliminary matter
to his *History & Vindication of the
Loyal Formulary, or Irish Remon-*

strance, 1674; and in the preface to
his *Four Letters*, 1686. He himself
does not mention attending Anglican services.
[5] Catharine Sedley: above, p.
13; the patent for her peerage is
dated 20 January. For the supposed
reasons for the grant and for the
queen's distress, &c., see the diplomatic documents; especially the
French dispatches in Pinto, *Sedley*,
pp. 352-62.

Dorchester, which 'tis certaine the Queene tooke very
grievously: so as for two dinners, standing neere her, she[a]
hardly eate one morsel, nor spake one word to the King, or
to any about her, who at all other times was us'd to be
extreamely pleasant, full of discourse & good humor: The
Roman Cath: were also very angrie, because the⟨y⟩ had so
long valu'd the Sanctite of their Religion & Proselytes &c:

Dryden the famous play-poet & his two sonns, & Mrs.
Nelle (Misse to the late . . .) were said to go to Masse; & such
purchases were no greate losse to the Church.[1] This night
was burnt to the Ground my Lord Montagues Palace in
Bloom⟨s⟩bery; than which for Painting & furniture, there
was nothing more glorious in England:[2] This happen'd by
the negligence of a servant, airing (as they call it) some of
the goods by the fire, in a moist season; for indeede so wett
& mild a Winter had scarce ben ever seene in mans memory:[3]

At this *Seale* there also passed, the creation of Sir *H:
Walgrave*[4] to be a Lord: He had married one of the Kings

---

[a] Altered from *I.*

---

[1] This report was wrong as regards Nell Gwyn and was perhaps
premature as regards Dryden;
Wood dates his conversion as May
or June 1686: *Life and times*, iii.
191; see also a story in *Hist. MSS.
Comm., Le Fleming MSS.*, p. 202,
which also requires a later date;
Luttrell, however, notes, 14–19
January, 'Severall persons have
appear'd publickly to be papists,
which have been only suspected
before'. For Dryden's religious
development see L. I. Bredvold,
*The Intellectual Milieu of John
Dryden*, 1934; see also Sir L.
Stephen in *D.N.B.* Dryden had
three sons, all living at this time;
the dates of their reception into the
Roman Catholic Church are unknown; for them see *D.N.B.*, art.
Dryden, John.

[2] For Montague House see above,
p. 90. Fuller notices of the fire in

Rachel, Lady Russell, *Letters*, 1853,
i. 179–80, and Sir John Bramston,
Autobiography (Camden Soc., vol.
xxxii, 1845), pp. 220–1; see also
Luttrell. Lord Devonshire had
taken a lease of the house. An
advertisement relating to property
lost at the time of the fire in *London
Gazette*, 28 Jan.
[3] For the weather see *An Account
of the Dreadful Storm* (18 Jan.),
1686; and above, p. 490 n.
[4] Henry Waldegrave, *c.* 1662–90;
married 1683 Henrietta FitzJames,
c. 1667–1730, daughter of the king
by Arabella Churchill; fourth baronet *c.* 1684; created 20 January of
this year Baron Waldegrave of
Chewton; comptroller of the household 1687–8; ambassador extraordinary to France 1688 (credentials
7 November); Jacobite; died in
Paris: G.E.C.; C. E. Lart, (*Jacobite
extracts*), 1910–12, i. 133. Arabella

3811.4   K k

natural Daughters, begotten on Mrs. *Churchil*: These two Seales, my Bro: Commissioners pass'd in the morning before I came to Towne, at which I was not at all displeas'd; We likewise pass'd privy seales for 276000 pounds upon severall accounts, Pensions, Guards, Wardrobes, Privie purse &c, besids divers Pardons: & one more which I must not forget (& which by providence, I was not present at) one Mr. *Lytcott*, to be Secretarie to the Ambassador to *Rome*:[1] we being three Commissioners [any][a] two were a *Quorum*.

23 I din'd at my Lady *Arlington*, Groome of the Stole to the Queene Dowager, at Somerset house, where dined the Countesses of Devonshire,[2] Dover[3] &c in all 11 Ladys of qualitie, no man but my-selfe: & return'd home after dinner:

24 Our *Viccar* proceeded to the Application: se your notes, & the Curate to his former text: Unheard of Cruelties to the persecuted protestants of France, such as hardly any age has don the like even amongst the pagans.[4]

It began to freeze sharply:

25 I went to *Lond*: 27: After the Seale, I went to the R:

---

[a] Interlined.

Churchill, 1649–1730, sister of John Churchill, the future duke of Marlborough; mistress of James *c.* 1665–73; married, probably before 1685, Col. Charles Godfrey: *D.N.B.*

[1] John Litcott, b. 1646, at Leigh, Kent; fellow of King's College, Cambridge, 1669; M.A. 1673; appointed secretary to the proposed embassy to Rome (Lord Castlemaine's: below, p. 558) *c.* 13 January of this year; knighted 13 May; appointed agent at Rome 24 Feb. 1687; agent there June 1687–October 1688; later at St. Germain: Venn; *Cal. Treasury Books, 1685–9*, pp. 523–4, 1223, 1233; Lart, *Jacobite Extracts*; &c.

[2] Presumably Mary, 1646–1710, daughter of the duke of Ormond; married in 1662 the present (fourth) earl of Devonshire (the future first duke); she was now occupying lodgings in Somerset House: Lady Russell, *Letters*, i. 180. Otherwise her mother-in-law Elizabeth, *c.* 1619–89, daughter of William Cecil, earl of Salisbury; married the third earl 1639.

[3] Presumably Judith, 1654–1726, daughter of Sir Edmund Poley; married in 1675 Henry Jermyn, created Baron Dover of Dover 1685 (above, iii. 482); she was related to the late Lord Arlington. Otherwise Abigail, 1610–88, daughter of Sir William Cokayne; married in 1630 John Carey, *c.* 1608–77, second earl of Dover 1666: G.E.C.

[4] For the severer persecution beginning late in 1685 see Lavisse, VIII. i. 356–7; Guitard, pp. 78–91.

Society[1] where was entertain'd the *Count Caponi*[2] Envoyè Extraordinary[a] from the Duke of Florence: Some experiments were shew'd him &c:

30 Being the Anniversarie of the Martyrdom of K. Char: ⟨I⟩[b] the Bish: of Ely preach'd in White-hall Chap: before the Princesse on: 3: *Apoc:* 31 shewing the blessed estate & glory of suffering for the Truth:[3] *Pomerid:* St. Martins the Lecturer[4] on: 4: *Gen:* 8: of Abels murder &c: all applied to the occasion:

31 At St. Martines, a stranger, on 1. *Phil:* 27: shewing how much it behov'd Christians to live holily in all conversations: I din'd at my Lady Mordants[5] &c: pomerid: St. Mart: Dr. Merideth[6] on: *Jude:* 15. Threates against the Ungodly for their actions & words: &c.

Feb: 3 A Seale: 6:[c] Being his Majesties day, on which he began his Reigne; By Order of Council, it was to be solemniz'd with a particular Office, & sermon,[7] which the Bis: of *Ely* preached at W:hall: on 11: *Numbers:* 12: a Court-*Oration*, upon the Regal Office &c: It was much wonder'd at; that this day which was that of his late Majesties death, should be kept as festival, & not the day of the present Kings Coronation: It is said, that it had formerly ben the costome, though not 'til now, since the Reigne of K. James. 1.[8]

---

[a] MS. *Ex^t:*   [b] MS. *2d.*   [c] Followed by *At St. Martine* deleted.

---

[1] Birch, iv. 454; Capponi's presence is not mentioned there and is presumably wrong; he was present and was shown an experiment at the next meeting, on 3 February, when Evelyn attended the preliminary meeting of the council: ibid., pp. 454–6.

[2] Pietro Capponi. He had his first audience on 3 January and his audience of leave on 2 February: *London Gazette*, 7 Jan., 4 Feb.

[3] The text should presumably be Revelations iii. 21.

[4] Presumably Dr. Meriton: above, p. 180, &c.

[5] Carey, c. 1658–1709, daughter of Sir Alexander Fraiser (*D.N.B.*; I.H.R., *Bull.*, v (1928), 183–5); married Mordaunt c. 1678.

[6] Presumably a mistake for Meriton, the lecturer.

[7] On 23 Dec. 1685 James ordered that the day of his accession should be celebrated annually and published a Form of Prayer (printed with *A Form of Prayer* for 30 Jan. 1685, i.e. 1685/6).

[8] The day of accession was commemorated by Elizabeth and by Charles I; there appears to be no evidence for James I; an act of

7 Being the first Sonday of the Moneth, Dr. *Tenison* preach'd at St. *Mart:*[1] on 11: *Rom:* 8 Caution against insensiblenesse & sloth in the Christian Progresse, from divers examples and danger of spiritual negligence &c: The holy Communion follow'd, at which I participated in order also to the *Test*, as Commissioner of the Privy-Seale, with my L: Tiveat[2] &c:

The Dutchesse of *Munmoth* being in the same seate with me, appeared with a very sad & afflicted countenance:

8 I tooke the Test, in *Westminster Hall* before the *L: C. Justice* &c:[3] [I now came to Lodge in White hall, in the Lord privy-seals Lodging][a]

12 My greate Cause was heard by my Lord Chancellor, who granted me a Rehearing:[4] I had 6 Eminent Lawyers, my Antagonists 3. whereof one the smoth-tong'd Soliciter,[5] whom my Lord Chancellor reprov'd in greate passion for a very small occasion: Blessed be God for his greate goodnesse to me this day:

13 I return'd home: [having ben the longer absent, about fitting my Lodging in White-hall &c:][b]

Feb: 14 Mr. *Hutchin*,[6] on 3. *Apoc:* 20: Upon the Condescention, and infinite patience of *Christ*, waiting so long without, knocking & importuning for enterance into our hearts, with such proposals & offers of intimate grace &

---

[a] Interlined.   [b] These words form part of a notice immediately following that of 8 February, and beginning *13 I return'd home*; these first words are deleted and the latter part of the notice left standing; I have attached it to the later entry for 13 February.

Convocation of 1640 (declared void in 1661) also ordered it to be kept; it was also kept from the accession of Queen Anne: T. Lathbury, *The Authority of the Services*, &c., 1843.

[1] Tenison was both vicar of St. Martin's and rector of St. James's; the former, as the parent parish of the latter, presumably took precedence.

[2] Teviot; for the Test Act see above, p. 7.

[3] The lord chief justice is Sir Edward Herbert: below, p. 517.

[4] Presumably Evelyn's action against William Prettyman: above, pp. 339–40, 394.

[5] Heneage Finch, *c.* 1649–1719; second son of Heneage Finch, first earl of Nottingham; created Baron of Gernsey 1703; earl of Aylesford 1714: *D.N.B.* He had been appointed solicitor-general in 1679 and was dismissed on 21 April of this year.

[6] See above, pp. 386, 460.

favours; notwithstanding our long, & unkind denyals: with exhortation to admitt him, and not[a] so to weary[a] him, as to make him depart, upon our ungratefull neglect of the day of his Grace, Exaggerated by the consideration of so unspeakable mercy &c: The same Text pursued in the Afternoone:

19 I went to *Lond:* The deane of S. *Paules* Dr. Stillingfleete preach'd on 15. *Luke*: 18. of the infinite mercy of God to repenting sinners from the parable of the prodigal, & the effect of a firme resolution, would sinners seriously set themselves to returne from their evil courses:[1] I return'd home the next morning:

Many bloody & notorious duels were fought about this time, The D: of Grafton kill'd Mr. *Stanley*, bro: to the E: of Shrewsbery, indeede upon an almost unsufferable provocation:[2] It is hop'd his Majestie will now at last, severely remedy this unchristian Custome:

21 Our *Viccar* preach'd on 11: *Matt:* 30: on the Easinesse of a Christian & vertuous life:

The *Curate* (afternoone) on 1. *Joh:* 4: 9. of the purity, & holy lives of the first *Christians* & how very unlike to the prophane & wiccked[b] age we now lived in.[3]

23[c] Came the Countesse of Sunderland (whose Lord was now Secretary of State, Lord pres: of the Council, & premier Minister)[4] to diner at my house:

---

a–a MS. *not to so to weary*; the word *so* is altered from *go.*　　b MS. perhaps *wicceked.*　　c Followed by *I went to Lond* deleted.

---

[1] Lenten sermon at court: list of preachers in *London Gazette*, 31 Dec. 1685. The sermon was printed this year and is reprinted in Stillingfleet's *Thirteen sermons*, 1698, pp. 1–39.

[2] Mr. Stanley is a mistake for John Talbot, b. *c.* 1665, brother of Lord Shrewsbury (above, p. 181). The duel, in which a pair of seconds was also engaged, took place on 2 February; another duel took place on the same day: notices in *Hist. MSS. Comm., Rutland MSS.*, ii. 103;

Luttrell, i. 370–1. Stanley is the surname of the earls of Derby.

[3] The text appears to be wrong.

[4] Marvell used this phrase in 1672 in 'Nostradamus's Prophecy', and a variant slightly earlier in 'The Kings Vowes': *Poems*, &c., ed. Margoliouth, i. 167, 170, and notes. Sunderland had been secretary of state continuously from 1683; and had been appointed lord president on 4 Dec. 1685. He held both offices until 1688.

24 I went to Lond: Mr. *Chetwin*[1] preached before the Princesse of Denmark in his Majesties Chapel at White-hall, on 4: *Job*: 6, a penetential discourse, shewing the vanity of all earthly things &c: even of human sciences & learning &c:

I went to the R: Society:

26:[a] Friday: Dr. *Sharp*[2] preached excellently on 12. *Rom:* 2: shewing the danger of conforming to the fashions, and formes of this world.

28: Sonday: Dr. *Chetwood*[3] 24: *Act:* 25. on the necessity of repentance without deferring:

After[b] sermon[b] Bishop of *Chichester*[4] on: 17: *Acts*: 30. on the same subject:

March 1 Came Sir Gilb: Gerrard[5] to treate with me about his sonns marying my Daughter *Susanna*; The father being obnoxious, & in some suspicion & displeasure of the King, I would receive no proposal, 'til his Majestie had given me leave, which he was pleas'd to do: but after severall meetings, we brake off, upon his not being willing to secure any thing competant[c] for my daughter⟨s⟩ Children: besides that I found his estate to be most of it in the Coale-pits as far as N. Castle,[6] & leases from the *Bishop* of Durrham, who had

---

a Altered from *27*. substituted for *noon*. b–b MS. originally *Afternoon*; the word *sermon* c Or *competent*.

---

[1] The only traceable clergyman of this name is John Chetwynd (*D.N.B.*); but perhaps an error for Knightly Chetwood (see below). Evelyn mentions 'Mr. Chetwin' again below, p. 539, where he should certainly be Chetwood. The preacher listed is Dr. Creighton.

[2] Above, p. 364, &c. Lenten sermon at court. It is perhaps that printed in Sharp's *Theological works*, 1829, iv. 205–31.

[3] Knightly Chetwood, 1650–1720; D.D. 1691; chaplain in ordinary *c.* 1687 (as 'Dr. *Chetwood*'); dean of Gloucester 1707: *D.N.B.*

[4] Lake; bishop of Chichester October 1685. Lenten sermon at court.

[5] Gilbert Gerard, d. 1687; created

a baronet by 1660? (recorded grant 1666); married as his second wife Mary, d. 1680, daughter of Bishop Cosin. His son is presumably Gilbert Cosin-Gerard, *c.* 1662–*c.* 1730, who succeeded as second baronet: G.E.C., *Baronetage*, iv. 38–9; Cosin, *Corr.*, vol. ii. The father had been accused of 'being at a consult to make an insurrection'; he pleaded not guilty on 28 Nov. 1685, and proceedings against him were stopped in February of this year. Earlier he had been said to possess a black box containing a certificate of Charles II's marriage to Lucy Walter; he had also been an active whig: Luttrell, i. 31, 42, 366, 371.

[6] Newcastle.

power to make concurrent Leases¹ with other difficulties,
so as we did not proceede to any conclusion:

3 Dr. *Montague*² preached on 4: *Jam:* 3: shewing what our
asking amisse was, & how our devotions prov'd ineffectual;
we praying more for things of this life, than for heavenly
graces &c:

7 Dr. *Fitzwilliams*,³ [to the Household]ᵃ on: 7: *Luke* 7: a
penetential sermon:

Dr.ᵇ Frampton⁴ [2d sermon]ᵃ Bish: of Glocester on 44:
Psal: 17: 18. 19: shewing the severall afflictions of the Church
of Christ, from the primitives to this day, and her Constancy & deliverance, applyed exceedingly to the present
conjuncture, when many were wavering in their minds,
& greate temptations appearing, through the favour the
Papists now found; so as the people were full of jealosies,
& discouragement; The Bish: magnified the Ch: of England
exhorting to constancy & perseverance,ᶜ &c:

I din'd at the Lord *Treasurers*.

10: At Council of the R: Society, about disposing of Dr.
Rays book of fishes, which was printed at the charge of the
Society &c:⁵ I was at morning Pr: but heard not the sermon:

11 I din'd at Mr. Pepys Secretary of the Admiralty:

12ᵈ There was a doquett⁶ to be sealed importing a Lease of

ᵃ Interlined.   ᵇ Preceded by date *10* deleted.   ᶜ Followed
by *in* deleted.   ᵈ Altered from *13*.

---

¹ Leases made before others have
expired and so existing for a time
side by side with them: *O.E.D.*

² Presumably John Montagu, *c.*
1655–1728; younger son of the first
earl of Sandwich; D.D. 1682?;
master of Trinity College, Cambridge, 1683–1700; dean of Durham 1700: *D.N.B.*; Venn. Lenten
sermon at court; but the preacher
listed is Dr. Jane.

³ John Fitzwilliam, d. 1699;
matriculated at Oxford 1652; D.D.
1677; chaplain in ordinary *c.* 1687;
canon of Windsor 1688–90; the

nonjuror; tutor and friend of
Rachel, Lady Russell: *D.N.B.*

⁴ Above, iii. 604, &c.; he was
bishop of Gloucester from 1681.
Lenten sermon at court.

⁵ Birch, iv. 463–4. The work is
Francis Willoughby, *De Historia
Piscium libri quatuor*, completed
and edited by Dr. John Ray, and
published this year at Oxford.

⁶ Here an abstract of the contents of the proposed letter-patent,
written upon the king's bill which
authorized the preparation of such
letter for the Great Seal: *O.E.D.*

21 yeares to one Hall,[1] who styled himselfe his Majesties Printer (& lately turn'd Papist) for the printing Missals, Offices, Lives of Saints, Portals,[2] Primers &c: books expressly forbidden to be printed or sold, &c by divers Acts of Parliament: which I refused to put the seale to, & made my exceptions against, so it was laied by:

14 The Bish: of Bath & Wells preach'd on 6: Joh: 17: (being the Gospel of the day) in a most excellent & pathetical discourse, ⟨after⟩[a] he had recommended the duty of fasting, & other penetential dutys; he exhorted to Constancy to the protestant religion, detestation of the French unheard of Cruelty, & stirring up to a liberal contribution:[3] This sermon was the more acceptable, as it was unexpected, from a Bish: who had gon through the censure of being inclin'd to popery; the contrary whereoff no man could more shew, as ⟨indeede⟩[b] did all our Bishops, to the disabusing & reproch of all their delators, none more zealous against popery than they:

15 Came my Lady Sunderland to house-warming to my new Lodgings in White-hall:

16 I was at the [review of the][c] Army about Lond: which was in Hide-parke, the whole consisting of about 6000: horse & foote in excellent order &c: his Majestie & an infinity of people present:[4]

17 I went to my house in the Country, refusing to be present at what was to passe the next day at the Privy-Seale:

This morning preached at W:hall, Dr. *Tenison* on 2: *Tim:*

---

[a] MS. *aster*.   [b] MS. *endeede*.   [c] Interlined.

---

[1] A mistake for Henry Hills, the elder, *d*. 1688 or 1689; active from *c*. 1640; printer to the council of state, the parliament, &c., 1649–60; to the king from 1670: H. R. Plomer, *Dictionary of . . . Booksellers and Printers, 1641–1667*, 1907; ibid., *1668–1725*, 1922 (Bibliographical Soc.); *D.N.B.*

[2] The word portal is an erroneous form of portas, a portable breviary in the medieval church: *O.E.D.*

[3] Lenten sermon at court. The text is wrong, as the Gospel for the fourth Sunday in Lent is St. John vi. 1–14. Ken presumably refers to the collection for the French Protestants about to be made in accordance with the Brief of 5 March: below, pp. 506, 508.

[4] The review is also noticed by Luttrell: i. 373.

3. 4. in an incomparable discourse perswading to the Love of God, before the vaine pleasure of this World:¹

Mar: 21 Our Viccar preached on 1. *Cor:* 5: 7: shewing the meaning of the Jewish Passover, in what particulars applicable to Christ: why a Lamb, to denote our Saviours innocency, why to be rosted with fire, intimating Gods fierce wrath against sinners &c:

Pomerid: Curate on 12: Heb: 14. The duty of universal charity:

23 I went to *Lond:* 24: Dr. *Cradoc* (Provost of Eaton) at W-hall on 49 *Psal:* 13. in an excellent discourse shewing the vanity of Earthly enjoyments &c.¹

26 Dr. *Tillotson,* 33 *Job:* 27: folly of all Vices, danger of late Repentance, &c:¹ See your notes:

28 [Dr. Littleton first Sermon on 6. *Gal:* 14. Glory in the Crosse—see notes]ᵃ Dr. White,² Bishop of Peterborow on 26: *Matt:* 29. Submission to the will of God on all Accidents, and at all times, a very eloquent style &c:

I supped this night at my L: Tressurers: discoursed with my Lady *Tennet,*³ who pretended to some more than ordinary talent of knowledgeᵇ &c:

29 I return'd home:

The Duke of Northumberland (a Natural sonn of the late King, by the Dutchesse of *Cleaveland,* an impudent woman) marrying very meanely, with the helpe of his bro: *Grafton,* attempted to spirit away his Wife &c:⁴

ᵃ Interlined.   ᵇ Followed by *in* deleted.

---

¹ Lenten sermon at court.

² Thomas White, 1628–98; D.D. 1683; bishop of Peterborough 1685–90; nonjuror: *D.N.B.* The text should be St. Matthew xxvi. 39. Lenten sermon at court; but the preacher listed is the archbishop of Canterbury.

³ Either Catherine, 1665–1712, fourth daughter of Henry Cavendish, second duke of Newcastle, married, 1684, Thomas Tufton, 1644–1729, sixth earl of Thanet

1684; G.E.C.; or her sister-in-law Elizabeth, widow of the third earl: above, p. 222.

⁴ Northumberland married (as his first wife) Catherine, d. 1714, daughter of Robert Wheatley of Bracknell, Berks., and widow of Thomas Lucy of Charlecote, who died in 1684. Wheatley is said to have been a poulterer near Fleet Bridge. The marriage is first mentioned on 13 March; it displeased the king, who had been trying to

A Briefe was read in all the Churches for Relieving the French Prostestants who came here for protection, from the unheard-off, cruelties of their King:[1]

31 To Lond: Dr. *James*[2] preached at *W:hal:* on 23. Luke. 42. 43. of the good Theife: &c:

Aprill 2: Dr. Tenison at St. *Martins* (being *Good-friday*) on 6: *Eph:* 24:[a] our manifold obligation to love The L. Jesus, above all things, for his infinite love to us: excellently: The holy Sacrament follow'd at which I participated: The L. Jesus be prais'd.

Pomerid: at W.hall, the Bish: of Rochester Dr. Sprat: Elegantly on 1. Peter: 2. 21. 22. To follow, & Imitate our B: Lord, in his exemplary purity, truth & holinesse &c:[3] I return'd home this Evening:

A papist made Governor òf Dover Castle: *Sir Ed: Hales*:[4]

4 our *Viccar* on 1. *Cor:* 5. 7. shewing how Christ was our Passover &c: The Bl: Sacrament follow'd of which I was (with my family) participant: The Lord make me thankfull:

Pomeridi⟨a⟩no a stranger on 14: *Joh:* 19, of the assurance of a future life, by the Resurrection to life of Christ:

11 Viccar on his former: the necessity of sincerity in all

---

a Or *21*.

---

arrange a marriage between Northumberland and one of the second duke of Newcastle's daughters. The reason for Northumberland's taking the duchess abroad is not clear. In April the king ordered her to be sent for, and she was at court on 16 June: G.E.C. and sources there cited, especially *Hist. MSS. Comm., Rutland MSS.*, ii. 107, 110; *Downshire MSS.*, i. 135–69; Luttrell, i. 374.

[1] The present notice is apparently premature. The letters patent ordering the collection are dated 5 March. A copy of the printed brief in the British Museum is dated —apparently in Luttrell's hand— 15 April; he mentions the collection as beginning between 8 and 12 April: i. 374. Evelyn mentions the reading of the brief in church on 25 April: below, p. 508. For it see further Huguenot Soc., *Proc.*, vii (1901–4), 122–3, 172–7.

[2] Above, p. 86. Lenten sermon at court.

[3] Lenten sermon at court.

[4] Above, p. 171. The date of his appointment is unknown, but his predecessor, Col. John Strode (above, iii. 395), was buried on 30 March of this year: (*Westminster Abbey registers*), p. 215. Hales had been reconciled to the Roman Catholic Church on 11 Nov. 1685: C. Dodd (Hugh Tootell), *Church history of England*, 1737–42, iii. 451.

our words as well as actions; against officious lies & sinns of
that sort, or for sport & raillery &c:

The Curate of Lee on 22: Matt: 36 &c: concerning the love
of God, & our Neighbour &c:

15 I went to Mr. Cooks funerall, a Merchant my kind
Neighbour at Greenewich where our Viccar preach'd the
sermon: 2. Tim: 4:—6. 7. 8: proper on the Occasion: Little
Fr: Godolphin was now sick of the small pox, I pray God be
gracious to that precious Child:

The Arch-Bish: of Yorke now died of the small-pox, aged
62 yeares, a Corpulent man; My special loving Friend, &
whilst our Bish: of *Rochester* (from whence he was translated)
my excellent Neighbour, an unexpressible[a] losse to the whole
Church, & that Province especialy, he being a learned, Wise,
stoute, and most worthy Prelate; so as I looke on this as a
greate stroke to the poore Church of England now in this
defecting period:[1]

18 Our *Viccar* on his former Text & most of it repetition:

Afternoone I went to Camberwell to visite *Dr. Par*: but
sate so inconveniently at Church, that I could very hardly
heare his Text, which was 5. *Heb:* 9: After sermon I went to
the Doctors house, where he shew'd me The life and Letters
of the late learned Primate of *Armagh, Usher,* and among
them that letter of *Bish: Bramhals* to the Primate, giving
notice of the popish practises to pervert this nation, by sending an hundred priests &c into England, who were to con-
forme themselves to all Sectaries, and Conditions for the more
easily dispersing their doctrine amongst us: This Letter was
the cause of the whole Impressions being seiz'd on, upon pretence, that it was a political or historical account, of things,
not relating to Theologie, though it had ben licenc'd by the
Bish: &c: which plainely shewe'd what an Interest the Popish
now had, that a Protestant Booke, containing the life, &
letters of so eminent a man was not to be publish'd. There

---

[a] Altered from or to *unexpressable.*

---

[1] Dolben died on 11 April at   until November 1688.
Bishopthorpe. The see was vacant

were also many letters to & from most of the learned persons
his correspondents in Europ: but The Booke will, (I doubt
not) struggle through this unjust impediment.[1]

20 To Lond: a seale—& to see little Godolphin now,
I blesse God, in an hope full way of Escape: Severall[a]
Judges put out, & new complying ones put in.[a][2]

24 I returned home, found my Coach-man dangerously ill
of vomiting greate quantities of blood:

25 St. *Mark*: this day was the Briefe for a collection of
reliefe to the Persecuted French Protestants (so cruely,
barbarously & inhumanly oppressed, without any thing laied
to their charge) read in our Church; but which had ben so
long expected, & difficultly at last procur'd to be publish'd,[b]
the interest of the French Ambassador & cruel papists
obstructing it:[3]

Our *Viccar* preached on 13. Heb. 16. exhorting to a liberal

[a-a] This sentence perhaps added later. [b] Followed by *by* deleted.

---

[1] *The Life of . . . James Usher,
Late Lord Arch-Bishop of Armagh,
Primate and Metropolitan of all Ireland. With a Collection of Three
Hundred Letters.* The book appears
to have been ready for printing by
24 April 1684, the date of the
original dedication. A large part of
it had been printed off when the
Licensing Act was revived in 1685;
the licence was delayed by Sunderland, and Parr suggested making
some alterations: letters of 22, 24
Feb. 1686. The original sheet N 2,
pp. 91–4 of the Life, has been replaced by a freshly set sheet; the
letter from Bramhall (above, iii. 253)
and another of a similar nature
from Sir W. Boswell to Laud, both
presumably forgeries, are retained:
Ussher, *Whole works*, i. 315–19.
Bramhall's letter, dated 20 July
1654, describes the supposed
methods used by the Roman
Catholic missionaries to destroy the
Church of England. See further

below, 9 March 1690.

[2] Four judges were superseded by
new ones on 21 April, and two more
judges were appointed on 26 April:
London Gazette, 22, 29 April, where
the names are given (the entries are
repeated by Luttrell).

[3] See above, p. 506. The king
had ordered the brief to be prepared
on 6 Nov. 1685; the draft was submitted to Sancroft on 1 March:
Huguenot Soc., *Proc.*, vii (1901–4),
177. At court Barillon was believed
to have had some share in causing
the delay: *Hist. MSS. Comm.,
Downshire MSS.*, i. 130. He himself
remarks that the king would have
liked to cancel the collection if it
had been possible: despatches, 25
Feb., 4 March N.S., in Macaulay, p.
733. The brief was to run for a
year. A supplementary order for
the collection was issued on 15
April 1687, and the total amount
realized was £42,889: Huguenot
Soc., *Proc.*, vii. 123, 109.

Charity, to these persecuted Christians:[1] Afternoone, the Curate, on 12. *Heb:* 14. Exhorting, to holinesse of life &c:

27[a] I received the B: Sacrament with my sick servant:

29[b] To Lond, a Seale [I din'd at my Lord presidents,[2] &c:][c] &c: returnd the 30th.

May. 1. Being the day the foefees for the poore of Deptford met, our Viccar (according to custom) preached, the Text, as on the last Sunday, with little alteration:

Hitherto a very wett Spring.

2 our *Viccar* preached on 4: Matt: 3. 4. shewing how we should behave our selves in time of Satans temptations, by the Example of our Saviour: The holy Sacrament follow'd, I received:

Pomerid: the Curate on 12: *Heb:* 14, Exhortation to charity, and other Christian duties:

5 To Lond: There being a Seale, it was feared we should be required to passe a Doquett,[3] Dispensing with Dr. Obadia Walker[4] & 4 more, wheroff one an Apostate Curate at Putney,[5] the other Master of University Coll: Ox: to hold their Masterships, fellowships & Cures, & keepe pub: schooles & enjoy all former emoluments &c, notwithstanding they no more frequented, or used the pub: formes of Prayers, or Communion with the Church of England, or tooke the Test, & oathes of Allegeance & Supremacy, contrary to 20 Acts of Parliaments &c: which Dispensation being likewise repugnant to his Majesties owne gracious declaration at the begining

---

a Altered from 22.   b Altered from 28.   c Interlined.

---

[1] By an order issued by the archbishop of Canterbury the clergy were forbidden to preach on the contents of the brief: F. A. J. Mazure, *Histoire de la révolution de 1688, en Angleterre*, 1825, ii. 124, following Barillon.

[2] Sunderland.

[3] See above, p. 503.

[4] Walker had been master of University College since 1676. He appears to have attended the usual Anglican services until the end of

1685, to have determined to declare himself a Roman Catholic in January of this year, and to have done so in March: Wood, *Life and times*, iii. 176–7, 182–3.

[5] Edward Sclater, 1623–99?: *D.N.B.* He had been perpetual curate of St. Mary's, Putney, since 1663; Luttrell reports his conversion to Roman Catholicism at the end of February of this year. He reverted to Anglicanism in 1689.

of his Reigne, gave umbrage (as well it might) to every
good Protestant: nor could we safely have passed it under
the Privy-Seale: wherefore it was don by Immediate warrant, sign'd by Mr. Soliciter &c at which I was not a little
glad:[1] This *Walker* was a learned person, of a munkish life,[a]
to whose Tuition I had more than 30 years since, recommended the sonns of my worthy friend *Mr. Hyldiard* of
Horsley in Surry: believing him to be far from what he
proved, an hypocritical concealed papist, by which he perverted the Eldest son of Mr. *Hyldyard*,[b] [2] Sir *Ed. Hales's* eld:
son[3] & severall more [&][c] to the greate disturbance of the
whole nation, as well as the University, as by his now publique defection appeared: All engines being now at worke
to bring in popery amaine, which God in mercy prevent:

This day was burnt, in the old Exchange, by the publique
Hang-man, a booke,[d] (supposed to be written by the famous
Monsieur Claude) relating the horrid massacres & barbarous
proceedings of the Fr: King against his Protestant subjects,
without any refutation, that might convince it of any thing
false: so mighty a power & ascendent here, had the French
Ambassador: doubtlesse in greate Indignation at the pious

---

a Followed by *under* deleted.   b Followed by *& son* deleted.
c Interlined.   d Followed by *goin-* deleted.

---

[1] Walker, two fellows of University College, and one of Brasenose,
were licensed to hold their mastership and fellowships without attending Anglican services, taking oaths,
&c.; Sclater was licensed to retain
the curacy of Putney (and the rectory of Esher) and to keep a school
or schools; he was, however, to provide curates to discharge the duties
of his two preferments: documents
in J. Gutch, *Collectanea curiosa*,
1781, i. 287-8, 290-3. The licences
are by letters patent under the
Great Seal. Normally they would
have had to pass the Privy Seal
before the Great Seal could be
affixed to them. It was Evelyn's
unwillingness to pass dispensations
of this kind that made the use
of immediate warrants necessary:
Reresby to Halifax, 22 May 1686,
in *Diary*, pp. 426-7. Mr. Solicitor
is Thomas Powys, c. 1649-1719;
appointed solicitor-general and
knighted 25 April of this year;
attorney-general 1687-8; judge of
the queen's bench 1713-14: *D.N.B.*

[2] Henry Hildyard; he was appointed a captain in a regiment of
horse in 1688 and went into exile at
the Revolution.

[3] Edward Hales, c. 1670-90;
matriculated from University College, Oxford, 1684.

& truly generous Charity of all the Nation, for the reliefe of those miserable sufferers, who came over for shelter:[1]

About this time also, The Duke of Savoy, instigated by the Fr: King to exterpate the Protestants of *Piemont*, slew many thousands of those innocent people,[2] so as there seemed to be a universal designe to destroy all that would not Masse[3] it, thro⟨ugh⟩ out Europ, as they had power, *quod avertat D.O.M.*

I procur'd of my L. president of the Council, the nomination of a son of Mrs. Cock, a Widdow (formerly living plentifully, now falln to want) to be chosen into the Charter-house Schoole, which would be a competent subsistence for him:

7 I return'd home:

8 Died my sick Coachman of his feavor, to my greate griefe, being a very honest, faithfull servant: I beseech the Lord, to take-off his afflicting hand, in his good time.

9 Our *Viccar* proceeded on his former subject, & in the Afternoone the Curate of Greenewich on 13: *Rom:* 13, exhorting to a religious walking & conversation:

The Duke of Savoy, instigated by the French ⟨king⟩,[a] put to the sword many of his protestant subjects: No faith in Princes.

---

a MS. *kind.*

---

[1] *London Gazette*, 10 May, where the ambassador's (Barillon's) complaint is mentioned. For Claude see above, p. 485. His book is *Les Plaintes des Protestans, cruellement opprimez dans le royaume de France*, published this year at Cologne; the translation, much abridged, is *An Account of the persecutions and oppressions of the Protestants in France*, published without the publisher's or printer's names. Copies of both original and translation were burnt. For bibliography, &c., see the reprint, ed. Puaux, 1885; for Barillon's part see Mazure, ii. 122-3.

[2] The duke of Savoy at the instigation of Louis XIV had issued an edict against the Waldenses on 31 January, N.S., prohibiting the exercise of their religion, ordering all new-born children to be baptized Roman Catholics, &c.; a second edict of 9 April, N.S., provided for the exile of the resolute. As a result of resistance French and Piedmontese troops were sent on 22 April, N.S., to exterminate the Waldenses. Those who were imprisoned were sent into exile in December. The Waldenses returned to their homes in August 1689 and were re-established legally in 1694: *Hist. of the Persecution of the Valleys of Piedmont*, 1688; &c.; C. Rousset, *Hist. de Louvois*, 1862-3, iv. 5-28. Luttrell notes reports of the massacres early in May.

[3] This use of the verb is rare: see *O.E.D.*

12 To Lond: Memorand, I refus'd to put the P: Seale to Dr. Walker⟨s⟩ licence[a] for the printing & publishing divers Popish Books &c:[1] of which I complain'd both to my L: of Canterbury (whom I went to[b] advise with, which was in the Council-chamber) and to my Lord Treasurer that evening at his lodging: My Lord of Cantorburies advise was that I should follow my owne Conscience therein; my L: Tressurer, that if in Conscience I could dispence with it; for any other hazard, he believed there was none: Notwithstanding which I persisted not to do it:

13 I received the B: Sacrament at St. *Martines*, it being Ascention-day, after an excellent[c] sermon, by a young man on   *Luke*   on Christs Ascention, & the benefits thereoff &c:

15 I return'd home:

16 A stranger on: 2: *Zeph:* 1. 2. 3. Afternoone, on: 2. *Tit:* 11. 12 &c: both practical sermons exhorting to Repentance upon prospect of the ruines threatning the Church, & drawing on for our prodigious Ingratitude, & doubtlesse Never was England so perverted, through an almost universal face of prophanesse, perjury, luxurie, unjustice,[d] violence, hypocrisie, Atheisme, & dissolution: A kingdome & people so obliged to God, for its long prosperity, both in Church & state: so signaly delivered, and preserved: & now threatn'd to be destroyed, by[e] our owne folly & wickednesse: How strangely is this nation fallen from its antient zeale & Integritie! ô unhappy, unthankfull people!

18 To Lond: returned the next day: [19][f] I was not at the seale, but returned home.

23 Our Viccar preached on 8. Rom: 9: concerning the divers manners of having the Spirit: It being Whi⟨t⟩sonday, & a Communion, at which I & family received: Pomerid: Curate on 16: Mark: 19: about Christs Ascention: Sleepe so

---

a Altered from *license*.   b Followed by *con-* deleted.   c MS. *ex^t*:
d Altered from *vi-*.   e Followed by *its* deleted.   f Marginal date.

---

1 Gutch prints a note of the licence granted to Walker and a list of the books to which it applied: *Collectanea curiosa*, i. 288–9.

surprizing me that I could scarse hold up my head; which I pray God pardon.

26 Came *Coll: Phelips*[1] my Bro: Commissioner to ⟨me⟩ with the Seale, to dispatch some buisinesse and din'd with me &c.

29 There was no sermon at this *Anniversary*—as usualy was, even since the reigne of our present *King*:[2]

30 Both *Viccar* & *Curate* repeated their former Argument &c: the one on 4: *Matt:* [*See 2d. May*:][a] the other *Mark*: who toke occasion to say something against Transubstantiation, & how since Christs Ascension, his body was localy [to be][b] in heaven, 'til the last day:

31 Our *Viccar* at the *Anniversary* of the Trinity Society,[3] on 107 psal: 22. 23: A very learned & proper discourse on the occasion:

June 2 To Lond: passing divers Pardons & other doquetts:[c]

Such stormes, ⟨raine⟩[d] & foule weather hardly ever know⟨n⟩ at this season:[4] The Camp now on Hounslo-Heath forc'd for sicknesse and other inconveniences of Weather to retire to quarters:[5]

6 Both *Viccar* & *curate* proceeded on their former Text: the Viccar most insisting of the necessity of searching & reading the holy Scriptures: The Sacrament follow'd, of which I was participant: I pray God make me thankfull:

9 To Lond: a Seale, most pardons, & discharges, of

---

a Marginal note. b Interlined. c Altered from *s-*.
d MS. *raile.*

---

[1] Robert Phelips, 1619–1707; royalist colonel; assisted Charles II in his escape after Worcester; M.P. for Stockbridge 1661; for Andover 1685; chancellor of the duchy of Lancaster 1687–9: *D.N.B.*, art. Phelips, Sir Robert; Le Neve, *Monumenta, 1650–1718*, p. 219.

[2] This was probably only an accidental and local omission. Wood records a sermon this day at St. Mary the Virgin's at Oxford: *Life and times*, iii. 187.

[3] Trinity House.

[4] Wood notes the very cold weather from 27 May to 3 June; the last three days were also wet and stormy: *Life and times*, iii. 187–8.

[5] The date on which the camp was formed is not stated, but a market for it was to begin on 27 May and the king visited it on 28 May: *London Gazette*, 20, 31 May. The rumours of illness in the camp led to a special notice, dated 17 June, contradicting them: ibid., 21 June. Reresby visited the camp on 5 June.

Knight[a] Baronets[a] fees; which having ben pass'd over for so many yeares, did greately dissoblige several families who had serv'd his Majestie.[1]—The Camp now at *Brainford* [Hounslow][b] after exceeding ⟨wet⟩[c] & stormy weather, now as excessively hott;[2] many grew sick: greate feasting there, especialy in my L: Dunbarton⟨s⟩ quarters:[3] many jealosies & discourse what the meaning of this incampment of an army should be:—L: Terconell[4] gon to Ireland with greate powers & commissions—giving as much cause of talke as the other: especialy 19 new Pr: Councelors being now made & Judges, among which but three protestants:[5] & Terconell made [L.][b] Generall: New-Judges also here, among which *Milton* a papist, & bro: to the Milton who wrot for the Regicides, who presum'd to take his place, without passing the Test:[6]—Scotland, refuse to grant Liberty of Masse to the Papists in Scotland:[7]—The French persecution more in-

---

[1] When the order of baronets was founded by James I each recipient was required to pay a sum of £1,095, commonly called his fee; from the Restoration the fees were generally remitted, a special warrant being issued for the remission: F. W. Pixley, *Hist. of the Baronetage*, 1900. At this period process was being issued against those baronets who had not paid their fee or obtained remission for it: *Cal. Treasury Books, 1685-9*, pp. 540, 850-1. It does not appear that many of them paid fees as a result of the proceedings.

[2] Cf. Wood, 6-9 June: *Life and times*, iii. 188.

[3] Lord George Douglas, *c.* 1635-92; created earl of Dumbarton (Scotland) 1675; appointed commander-in-chief of the army in Scotland 1685; went into exile at the Revolution: *D.N.B.*

[4] The former Richard Talbot: above, p. 23; created earl of Tyrconnel (Ireland) 1685; he had now been appointed lieutenant-

general of the army in Ireland and had arrived in Dublin about 5 June. He was a Roman Catholic and was independent of Clarendon the lord lieutenant: R. Bagwell, *Ireland under the Stuarts*, 1909-16, iii. 158-9.

[5] Twenty men, including Tyrconnel and three judges, were ordered to be added to the Irish privy council in May: list in Clarendon, *Corr.*, i. 400.

[6] No new judges had been appointed since April (see above, p. 508); but those then appointed were sworn in on 8 June, with the exception of Milton: Luttrell. He is Christopher Milton, 1615-93, younger brother of the poet; apparently a Roman Catholic; appointed a serjeant-at-law 21 April; knighted 25 April; appointed a baron of the exchequer 26 April—all of this year; appointed a judge of the common pleas 1687; discharged 6 July 1688: *D.N.B.*

[7] A letter from the king asking, among other matters, for the repeal of the penal laws against the Roman

humane than ever &c: The Protestants in Savoy, success-
fully resist the French Dragoons, perfidiously murdering
them.[1]—The booke written by[a] *Monsieur*[b] *Claude* to informe
the world of the cruel persecution in France: Translated
here burnt by the hangman, so greate was the Interest of
the Fr: Ambassador, as was said: It seem'd to relate onely
matter of fact, very modestly: & was thought a severe treate-
ment; his Majestie having both given[c] protection, & reliefe
to the Refugies:[2] It was thought hard, the people should
not know for what & to whom they gave so bountifully.—
The Kings chiefe physitian in Scotland, Apostatizing from
the protestant Religion, dos of his owne accord publique[d]
Recantation at Edenbrugh.—[3]

11 I went to see Midletons—receptacle of Waters at the
New River:[4] & the new Spà wells neere it.[5]

---

[a] Altered from *to*.   [b] MS. *M*[r]:   [c] Followed by *the* deleted.
[d] Or *publish*.

Catholics was read when the Scottish parliament met on 29 April.
The parliament made a non-
committal reply on 6 May: *Acts of
the Parliaments of Scotland*, 1814–75,
viii. 579–82.

[1] Similar notice in Luttrell, 8/12
June. For the Waldenses see above,
p. 511. It refers presumably to
the resistance near St. Germain in
the valley of Peirouse on 22 April,
N.S., or that at Boby in the valley
of Lucerne about 12 May, N.S.:
Hist. of the Persecution, pp. 19, 29.

[2] James is reported to have himself given £500 towards the relief
of the refugees: Lauder, *Hist.
observes*, p. 249. I can find nothing
to confirm this.

[3] This refers to Robert Sibbald,
1641–1722; M.D. 1662; knighted
(Scotland) 1682; physician (Scotland) to Charles II and to James
VII and II. He was converted to
Roman Catholicism about September 1685; fled to London in February of this year; returned about
April or May to Edinburgh, where
he declared to friends his reversion

to the Scottish (Episcopalian)
Church; received into it formally in
September. He was also an author
of some note: *D.N.B.*; *Memoirs*, ed.
F. P. Hyett, 1932. According to
Burnet he made a public recantation on account of his conversion;
he certainly offered to do so: Sir
J. Lauder of Fountainhall, *Hist.
notices* (Bannatyne Club, 1848), p.
725.

[4] The New River Head at Islington, a reservoir still existing in an
enlarged form. It was fed by
springs at Chadwell and Amwell,
Herts., and was constructed in
1609–13 by Sir Hugh Myddelton
(1560?–1631: *D.N.B.*). It was owned
by a company; the water was laid
on to private houses; by 1682 the
growth of London had rendered the
supply inadequate: Aubrey, *Brief
lives*, ii. 60. James issued a
proclamation, dated 5 March of
this year, protecting the company
against stealing their water, pollu-
tion, &c.: Steele, no. 3827 (published 8 April: Luttrell).

[5] Either Islington Spa, otherwise

12ᵃ I returned from Lond—

13 Our *Viccar* proceeds, still insisting on the duty of reading Scriptures, & that it belonged to all. The Curate on 3. *Apoc:* 21. concerning Constancy & perseverance &c:

16 To Lond, a seale, return'd 18.

20 Our Viccar, excellently on 4 Gal: 18. shewing the whole scope of the Galatians dissagreeing with St. Paule, looking on him as an intruder, because he pretended not his calling from any Apostle, but immediately from God; for which he blames their mistaken zeale:

An extraordinary season of violent & suddaine raines: The Camp still in Tents.

23 To Lond, To a seale.

24 My L: Tressurer settled my greate buisinesse with Mr. Pretyman, toᵇ which I hope God will at last give a prosperous issue:ᶜ

Now his Majestie beginning with Dr. Sharp¹ & Tully,² proceeded to silence & suspend divers excellent Divines for preaching against Popery:

ᵃ Date altered.   ᵇ Substituted for *of*.   ᶜ MS. *issue to:*

---

called Islington Wells and New Tunbridge Wells, or Sadler's Wells, both close to the New River Head and both in operation in 1684 and the following years. The waters at the former retained their importance for a considerable period and it is now commemorated by Spa Green; those at the latter went out of use about 1700, a pleasure-resort and later the theatre occupying the site: Wroth, *London Pleasure Gardens*, pp. 15–24, 43–53.

¹ He had preached two sermons against Roman Catholicism on 2 and 9 May at his church, St. Giles in the Fields; on 14 June Compton, the bishop of London, was ordered by the king to suspend him, but refused to do so; in July Sharp retired to his deanery, Norwich.

No further action was taken against him and in January 1687 he was reinstated in 'that liberty of his function which the rest of your [i.e. the king's] Clergy enjoy': T. Sharp, *Life of John Sharp*, 1825, i. 88. That is, he could again officiate at St. Giles without fear of molestation.

² George Tully (Tullie), *c.* 1653–95; sub-dean of York and prebendary 1680; suspended (apparently by 18 June: Luttrell) on account of a sermon preached at Oxford on 24 May; appointed to a lectureship in Newcastle 2 Dec. 1687; reinstated at York (at the Revolution?): *D.N.B.*, art. Tully, Thomas; I.H.R., *Bull.*, ix (1932), 140. There were no other suspensions at this time.

The New [very]ᵃ young L. C. Justice Herbert,¹ declared
these positions on the bench for Laws viz:

at which every body were astonished; by which the Test was
abolished.ᵇ Times of greate Jealosies, where these proceedings would end.

26 I return'd home:ᶜ

27 Our Viccar proceeded on his former Text: The afternoone wet, Dr. Bohune read the Office & a sermon (to the
family) out of Dr. Barrow,² concerning our obligation to submitt to the will of God, by the Example of our B: Savior:

I had this day ben married 39 yeares: Blessed be God for
all his mercys.

July:ᵈ 3 To Lond: 4: Dr. Megot preach'd on   & I received the holy Sacrament inᵉ St. Georges Chapell:³ returning
next day to Lond: my buisinesse being with my L: Godolphin
&c: By the way saw the Camp, was in the Generalsᶠ Tent &c.⁴

6 I supp'd with the Countesse of Rochester where was also
the Dutchesse of Bouckingham⁵ & *Madame de Governè*⁶ whose

ᵃ Interlined.   ᵇ Followed by *and* deleted.   ᶜ Altered to *to Lond:*
the alteration cancelled.   ᵈ Followed by *1 July I went to visite my L.
of Cant: at Lambeth where I din'd, there was Mr. Alexen the French famous
& great divine* deleted; the notice perhaps inserted after the notices for
3 July, &c., were written.   ᵉ Followed by *the Colledge* deleted.
ᶠ MS. *Gensˢ*?

---

¹ Edward Herbert, *c.* 1648–98;
son of Charles II's lord keeper
(above, iii. 1); chief justice of
Chester 1683; knighted 1684; lord
chief justice of the king's bench
23 Oct. 1685; transferred to the
common pleas 1687; went into exile
at the Revolution; created earl of
Portland by James, 1689?: *D.N.B.*
Evelyn refers to his judgement,
21 June, in the case *Godden* v. *Hales*
(Sir Edward: above, p. 506), in
which he declared the king's right
of dispensing with the laws.

² Above, p. 62. Apart from
occasional publications and smaller
collections, there were now available the earlier volumes of his col-

lected theological writings (*Works*,
ed. Tillotson, 4 vols., 1683–7).

³ Evidently at Windsor, where
the court was at present; Meggot's
tour of duty fell in July.

⁴ The general is probably Feversham.

⁵ Mary, 1638–1704, daughter of
Thomas Fairfax, third Lord Fairfax
of Cameron (Scotland), the parliamentary general; married the
second duke of Buckingham 1657.

⁶ Esther, *c.* 1636–1722, daughter
of Bartholomew Hervart, a banker
at Paris, and widow of Charles de
la Tour, marquis de Gouvernet; she
had come here as a refugee early
this year: *Hist. MSS. Comm., Down-*

daughter was married to the Marq⟨u⟩esse of Halifax's son. She made me a Character of the French King, & Dauphine,[1] & of the Persecution: That they kept much of the cruelties from the Kings knowledge: That the Dauphine was so afraid of his Father, that he durst let nothing appeare of his sentiments; that he hated letters and Priests, spent his time in hunting, & seem'd to take notice of nothing that passed &c:

This Lady of a greate family & fortune, was now fled for refuge hither:

8 I went to waite on my L: A: Bish: at Lambeth, where I dined, and met the famous Preacher & Writer Dr. *Alexer*:[a][2] doubtlesse a most excellent & learned person: The A Bish. & he spake Latine altogether, & that very readily:

9 I dined at Clothyers Hall,[3] with Mr. Bridgeman the Master, at a most sumptuous Entertainement.

10 I went againe to Windsore to speake with my L: Tressurer:

11 Dr. Megot Deane of Winchester preach'd before the Household in St. Geo: Chapell; the late Kings glorious Chapell,[4] now seiz'd on by the Masse-priests &c: his Text: was 24: Matt: 35, shewing the stability & certainty of the Scriptures, prophesies &c;

To the Greate men of the Court, in the same place preached Dr. Cartwrite[5] Deane of Rippon, on *Let every one that names the name of Christ depart from evil:*

---

[a] Spelling uncertain.

---

shire MSS., i. 119, 136. Her daughter is Esther, 1666–94, married 1684 to Henry Savile, 1661–87, styled Lord Eland from 1679, eldest son of Lord Halifax: (*Westminster Abbey registers*), p. 306, &c.; Foxcroft, *Halifax.*

[1] The Dauphin is Louis de France, 1661–1711. He was uninterested in business, and at the same time was excluded from it by Louis XIV. His principal amusement was hunting.

[2] Allix: above, p. 485.

[3] The Clothworkers' Company.

Bridgeman (above, p. 197), a freeman of the company, had been appointed a member of its governing body (an 'Assistant') by the charter given to it by Charles II on 5 Feb. 1685: *The Charters . . . [of] the Clothworkers' Company,* 1881, p. 51.

[4] Charles II's chapel, already used by James II in 1685: above, p. 465.

[5] Thomas Cartwright, 1634–89; D.D. 1661; dean of Ripon 1676; chaplain in ordinary *c.* 1663–86; named bishop of Chester privately

We had now the sad newes of the Bish: of Oxfords death,[1] an extraordinary losse at this time to this poore Church: Many candidate⟨s⟩ for his Bishoprick & Deanery, Dr. Parker,[2] South,[3] Aldrich[4] &c: Dr. Walker, (now apostatizing) came to Court, & was doubtlesse very buisy:

12 I went to visite Dr. Godolphin vice-Provost of Eton, & dined with him in the Colledge: among the Fellows: It is an admirable foundation:

13 I return'd to Lond: Note, that standing by the Queene at Basset (Cards) I observ'd that she was exceedingly concern'd for the losse of 80 pounds: her outward affability much changed to statelinesse &c since she has ben exalted:

The season was very rainy, & inconvenient for the Camps: his Majestie cherefull:

14 Was sealed at our Office the Constitution of certaine Commissioners to take upon them the full power of all Ecclesiastical Affaires, in as unlimited a manner, or rather greater, than the late High-Commission Court, abbrogated by Parliament: for it had not onely faculty to Inspect & Visite all Bishops diocesses, but to change what lawes & statutes they shold think fit to alter, among the Colledges, though founded by private men; to punish [suspend][a] fine &c give Oathes, call witnesses, but the maine drift was to ⟨suppresse⟩[b] zealous Preachers &c—In summ, it was the whole power of Viccar General, note the Consequence—The Commissioners were of the Cleargy, the *A Bish of Cant: Bishops of Duresme, Rochester*:—of the Temporal: L: Tressurer,

---

[a] Interlined.   [b] MS. *suspresse.*

---

11 and publicly 22 August and consecrated 17 October of this year: *D.N.B.*; *London Gazette*, 26 Aug. His text is 2 Timothy ii. 19.

[1] Fell; he had died on 10 July. He was dean of Christ Church as well as bishop of Oxford.

[2] Samuel Parker, 1640–88; F.R.S. 1666; D.D. 1671; named bishop of Oxford 22 August and consecrated

17 October of this year; author: *D.N.B.*; *London Gazette*, 26 Aug.

[3] Above, iii. 365, &c.

[4] Henry Aldrich, 1648–1710; canon of Christ Church 1682; D.D. 1682; dean of Christ Church 1689: *D.N.B.* The successful candidate for the deanery at this time was John Massey, a recent convert to Roman Catholicism (*D.N.B.*).

Chancellor (who alone was ever to be of the quorum) Chiefe Justice, L: President:[1]

17 I returned home to my house:

18 Dr. *Bohune* preach'd on 14 *Rom:* 17 excellently, against the Idolatrie & other errors of the Roman Church: Afternoone the Curate of Greenewich on 16 *Deut:* 13, Duty of gratitude for temporal blessing⟨s⟩. I went to see Sir Jo: Chardin at Greenew⟨ic⟩he:[2]

19 To Lond: to a Seale.[a] Came this morning to visie me Sir W: Godolphin, L. Sylvius: Mrs. Boscawen; Dr. Tenison, with divers Ladys & Gent: After dinner, I went to Lond, to a *Seale*. &c. Return'd 21: Evening, having ben at the R: Society, where was a Wind Gun brought & tried, which first shot a bullet with a powder Charge, & then discharged 4 severall times with bullets, by the wind onely, every shoote at competent distance piercing a thick board: The Wind-Chamber was fastned to the barrill through the stock, with Valves to every ⟨charge⟩[b] so as they went off 4 successive times: I⟨t⟩ was a very curious piece, made at Amsterdam, not bigger than a pretty Birding piece: Note, that the drawing up of the Cock alone ⟨admitted⟩[c] so much aire into a small receptacle at the britch of the piece out of the Cham-

---

[a] Followed by *return'd the 21th:* deleted. *shot* altered to *charge*. [b] MS. *shorge*, presumably [c] MS. *admittened*.

[1] This was the Commission for Ecclesiastical Affairs (Commissionarii ad Causas Ecclesiasticas), which first met on 3 August; it was established by letters patent issued on 15 July of this year, and made public on 17 July. The Court of High Commission, established at the Reformation, had been abolished in 1641 by an act of parliament which also prohibited the establishment of any similar court thereafter; an explanatory act of 1661 was now held by James's adherents to have restored to the crown the right to establish such a court. The new commission was, however, almost certainly illegal. For it see *Hist. of*

King James's Ecclesiastical Commission, 1711, where the king's commission is printed; J. S. Burn, *The High Commission*, 1865, pp. 71–8. The members were Sancroft (who refused to take part in proceedings), Crew, Sprat, Rochester, Jeffreys, Sir Edward Herbert, and Sunderland. New commissions were appointed in January and October 1687.

[2] Chardin was presumably living here during the summer. In 1687 he had lodgings in the Queen's House: below, p. 561. He was here again in the summer of 1689: Dumont de Bostaquet, *Mémoires*, p. 246.

ber or magazine of aire underneath as suffic'd for a charge, which was exploded by pulling downe the Cock by the Triccker: (a) the wind Chamber [of brasse]ᵃ, to scrue into the barrell thro the stock, at (b): note, that it was fill'd with an [aire]ᵃ pumpe.

25 Our *Viccar* in 4: *Gal:* 18ᵇ, concerning the duty of zeale, and the mischiefes of it, if not well guided: Instancing in that of *Irene*[1] against her husband, son &c: about Images, & so of some persecuting Popes and others, Enthusiasts &c:

The *Curate* in the afternoone on 1. *Philip:* 27, the necessity of a real holinesse, preferrable to all outward formes &c: Came to visite me Sir J. *Chardin*, & Monsieur *Ruvigny*[2] the son:

27 This day was bound Apprentice to me, & serve as a Gardner, *Jonathan Mosse*, to serve from 24 June 1686: to 24 June –92, being six yeares:[3]

28 I went to Lond, to a Seale, return'd by the R: Society: having seen the ⟨e⟩xperiment of a bullet droven out of a gun, by the external aire, the barill of the piece having a perforation by which the aire within it was sucked out by the Boylean pump, the two extreames shut close with corks:ᶜ Then one of the ends, viz, the breech part suddainly opned, the aire in the roome rushed in with that extreame ⟨swiftnesse⟩ᵈ as forced out the bullet to a greate distance:

ᵃ Interlined.   ᵇ Altered from *19*.   ᶜ Or *corke*.   ᵈ MS. *swistnesse*.

---

[1] Irene, *c.* 752–803, empress of the Eastern Empire 775–802. She headed the Image-worshippers in opposition to her husband and brought about the deposition and blinding of her son.

[2] Henri de Massue, seigneur de Ruvigny, 1648–1720; second marquis de Ruvigny 1689; created Viscount Galway (Ireland) 1692; earl of Galway (Ireland) 1697: *D.N.B.*

[3] This appointment led Evelyn to compile his 'Directions for the Gardiner at Says-Court, but which may be of use for other gardens', which was published by Mr. Geoffrey Keynes in 1932.

Aug: ⟨1⟩ Our Viccar proceeded on his Text, against in-discreete zeale, & our duty in complying with *res mediæ* & things indifferent, but not so, when injoyn'd by the Magistrate, because of order, & to avoid Confusion, the discretion of the Primitives in such case: The[a] holy *Comm:* follow'd at[b] which I participated:

Afternoone the Curate on 6. *Gal:* 7: recommending sincerity: Sleepe surpriz'd me: Came my Lady Tuke to be some time with us, being in an ill state of health.

4 I went to *Lond*, to a seale, din'd at Signor *Verrios* the famous Italian Painter, & now settled in his Majesties Garden of St. ⟨James's⟩,[c] which he had made now a very delicious Paradise:[1] I return'd in the Evening:

8 Our Viccar being gon to dispose of his country living in Rutlandshire, & now having an addition of St. Dunst: East, given him by the Arch Bishop of Cant:[2] Dr. *Bohune* supplied his place here, preaching on 14: Rom: 17: perstringing both Papists, & Dissenters, the one for their needlesse superstition, and the other their Scrupules at Indifferent things, to the ⟨disturbance⟩[d] of the Church: In the Afternoone a young Stranger on: 4: *John:* 22, exceedingly well proving that the Papists in the Eucharist, knew not what they worship'd, there going so many contradictious difficulties to Justifie their doctrine of Transubstantiation; in summ proving the adoration of it grosse Idólatrie: I went to visite the *Marquis de Ruvignie* now my Neighbour at Greenewich, he had ⟨been⟩ 'til this cruel persecution in France (whence he was now retir'd) the Deputy of all the Protestants of that Kingdome in the Parliament of Paris, & severall times

---

a Followed by *Curate* deleted. b Perhaps altered to *of.*
c MS. *Janes's.* d MS. *distrubance.*

---

[1] For the garden see above, iii. 573. Verrio already occupied it in 1685: Newcourt, *Repertorium*, i. 659.

[2] Holden's successor at Great Casterton (above, pp. 4 n., 179 n.) was instituted on 18 December of this year. Holden himself was insti-tuted rector of St. Dunstan in the East on 28 October of this year. He had been a student under Sancroft at Emmanuel College about 1642–5: St. John's College, Cambridge, *Admissions*, 1882– , i. 74.

Ambassador in this & other Courts; a Person of greate Learning & experience:[1]

12 To a Seale at Lond, dind at my Sons, return'd that
evening:

15 Mr. Meriton preached in the morning on: 12: Pro: 26.
of the Excellency of a Righteous man above another:
pomeridiano, on 3: Heb: 7: 8. exhorting to Repentance in
time:

18 To Lond: to a Seale, return'd in the afternoone:

19 Came to Visie us, The Marq: de Ruvignè, & his Lady:[2]

22[a] A stranger preach'd on 18: *Gen:* 14, concerning the
infinite power of God, how sure a Refuge, & how able to deliver his Church & people on all occasions, & difficulties, for
the encouragement of our Faith & Reliance &c:

25 To Lond: a Seale: I went after to Hamer-Smith to see
some gardens: & the next day to Fullham:

28 Spake with my L. Tressurer about my buisines, &
returned home on Saturday:

29 Our *Curate* preach'd on 119 *Psal:* 60: pressing the
importance of repentance: The wet weather hindred my
going to Church in the afternoone:

Sept: 1 to Lond: There was nothing at our Office ready to
passe the Seale, so I immediately returned home.

5: our Viccar yet absent a stranger preach'd on 5: *Matt:*
44 concerning charity, in forgiving injuries, and forbearing
revenge: The same young man In the Afternoone on 14:

---

[1] Henri de Massue (or Massué),
c. 1610–89; succeeded as baron
and created marquis de Ruvigny
(France); deputy-general of the
Protestant Churches of France
1653–79, and thenceforward in conjunction with his eldest son; on
special missions in England 1660,
1662, 1664–5; envoy extraordinary
1667–8; ambassador in ordinary
1674–6: D. C. Agnew, *Henri de
Ruvigny, earl of Galway*, 1864, pp.

1–27, 203–8; &c. He came to England about March. James granted
him the use of the 'Reale palazzo'
of Greenwich: *Hist. MSS. Comm.*,
Downshire MSS., i. 138; Campana
de Cavelli, ii. 292, 293. Evidently
the Queen's House is intended:
below p. 565.

[2] Marie Tallemant, d. *c.* 1698;
married Ruvigny 1647; accompanied him into exile: Agnew, pp. 4,
84, &c.

Jo: 15. Of shewing our Love to Christ: I received the B:
Sacrament in the morning, Dr. Bohune officiating:

8. I went to Lond: to a Seale: The Bish: of Lond was on
Monday suspended on pretence of not silencing Dr. Sharp of
St. Giles's, for something of a sermon, in which he zealously
reproov'd the Doctrine of the R.C. The Bish: having consulted
the Civilians, who told him, he could not by any Law proceede against Dr. Sharp, without producing wittnesses, &
impleading according to forme &c: But it was over-ruled by
my L: Chancelor & the Bishop sentenc'd, without so much as
being heard to any purpose: which was thought a very extraordinary way of proceeding, & universaly resented; & so
much the rather, for that 2 Bish: Durham, & Rochester,
sitting in the Commission, & giving their suffrages: The
AB: of Cant: refusing to sit amongst them: What the issue
of this will be, Time will shew:[1]

12 Both our *Viccar* & *Curate*, preached on their former
subject:

Budâ now taken from the Turks; A forme of Thanksgiving was ordered to be used in the (as yet remaining)
protestant Chapells, & Church of White-hall & Winsor:[2]

The K. of Denmark, was now besieging Hambrow:[3] no

---

[1] On 9 May Sharp had preached
in his parish church (St. Giles in the
Fields) on the claim of the Roman
Catholic Church to be the only visible
church. On 14 June James wrote to
Compton ordering him to suspend
Sharp. Compton refused on the
ground that he was obliged to pro-
ceed according to law. The Commissioners for Ecclesiastical Affairs
(above, pp. 519–20) summoned him
to appear before them on 9 August;
after further proceedings on 16 and
31 August Compton was sentenced
on 6 September to suspension from
his episcopal functions. He was
represented by counsel, but the
proceedings were summary: reports
of proceedings in *An exact account
of the whole proceedings against . . .
Henry Lord Bishop of London*, 1688

(this gives the dates correctly) and
in *A true narrative of all the proceedings against the Lord Bishop of London*, 1689 (a Dutch translation of this
text, *Verhael vande Proceduren*, was
published in 1686); see also Sharp,
Life of John Sharp, i. 71–86; *Hist.
MSS. Comm.*, 7th rep., App., p. 503;
Downshire MSS., i. 207, 210–11, 216.

[2] Buda was taken on 2 September, N.S.: *London Gazette*, 9 Sept.;
see also 20, 27 Sept. *A Form of
prayer and thanksgiving* was issued
for the services to be held on 12
September in St. George's, Windsor,
Westminster Abbey, and St. Mary
le Bow.

[3] The siege had begun on 31
August, N.S.: *London Gazette*, 6 Sept.
The king is Christian V: above,
iii. 342.

doubt but by the French contrivance, to embroile the protestant princes in a new warr, that Holland &c being ingag'd, matter for new quarrell might[a] arise: The unheard persecution against the poore Prot: still raging more than ever:

15 To Lond, to a Seale, return'd immediately:

19 Both Viccar & Curate proceded as last Sonday.

22 To Lond, to a Seale, return'd that Evening: My deare Bro: came from Wotton to visite me. The Dane Troops retire from Hambrow, The Protestant Princes appearing for their succor, & the Emperor sending his Minatories to the K: of *Denmark*, & also requiring the Restauration of the D: of Sax-Gottorp:[1] thus it pleas'd God to defeate the French designes, which was evidently to kindle a new warr:

25 Receiving a Letter from the Secretary of my Lord President; that the two Bishops Elect Oxford[2] & Chester[3] could not have the Royal assent for the *Conge d'elire* without a privy Seale: I made a step to Lond: & return'd immediately:

26 Our *Viccar* preached on 8: *Matt: ult:* shewing by the example of the *Gadareenes* how dangerous it was, to make light of Grace when offer'd: our *B: Saviour* coming to preach amongst them, and they desiring him to depart: which immediately he did, & we reade not of his ever coming among them againe: A dangerous thing to reject the meanes of Salvation:

The Curate proceeded on his former subject, shewing the preference of vertue, to the most specious vices, & exhorting to embrace the first, & that as early as might be: I went to

---

[a] Followed by *be to* deleted.

---

[1] The emperor's 'Monitoria' for the king of Denmark, warning him to withdraw his troops, reached Hamburg on 18 September, N.S.; the siege was broken up by 27 September, N.S.: ibid., 23, 27 Sept. Sax-Gottorp is an error; Evelyn refers to Christian Albrecht, 1641–94, duke of Gottorp from 1659 (family of Holstein-Gottorp); driven into exile by Christian V from 1675 to 1679 and again from 1684 to 1689: *Allgemeine deutsche Biog.* He is not mentioned in the *London Gazette* in this connexion at this time.

[2] Parker: above, p. 519.

[3] Cartwright: above, p. 518.

take my Leave of *Monsieur Ruvignie* now going to Winter in Lond: who had ben to complement me a little before:

28[a] My Brother went home: My La: Tuke (who had ben most of this summer with us [for her health][b]) went away.[c][1]

30[d] To Lond, a Seale; little buisinesse: The King returned from Windsor to White-hall.[2] I went home in the Evening:

October 3 Our *Viccar* proceeded as before: Communion follow'd, I received: Blessed be God: Curate of *Grenewich* Afternoone: 5. *Eccl:* 1: of the Reverence due to Gods house & service.

6 To Lond, a Seale, where buisines kept me 'til 8th, when I returned home:

10 Our Viccar proceeded on his Text: with small addition:[e] A stranger Afternoone on 19 Gen: 23,[3] Lots-wife, her disobedience, love of sensual enjoyments, &c:

13: To Lond: a Seale:

14: His Majesties Birth day, I was at his Majesties rising in his Bed-Chamber: Afterwards in the [Hide][f] Parke where his Majesties 4: Comp: of Guards were drawn up: Such horse & men as could not be braver: The Officers &c: wonderfully rich & gallant: They did not head their troops, but their next officers; the Colonels &c: being on Horse ⟨back⟩[g] by the King, whilst they marched: The Ladys not lesse splendid at Court, where was a Ball that night;[4] but small appearance of qualitie: This day all the shops both in Citty & suburbs shut up, and kept as solemnly as any holy-day: Bone-fires at night in Westminster &c: but forbidden in the Citty:[5]

17 Dr. *Patric* Deane of *Peterborow* preach'd at Co: Garden

---

a Altered from 27.   b Interlined; closing bracket supplied.
c Followed by an entry 27 *My Lady* deleted.   d Altered from 28 ?
e Altered from *edition*? Spelling doubtful.   f Interlined; MS. *hide*.
g MS. *by*.

---

[1] She had come on 1 August: above, p. 522.

[2] The king returned to Whitehall on 1 October, having been at Windsor since 14 May, apart from a short progress, 23–31 August: *London Gazette*, 17 May, 4 Oct., &c.

[3] A slip for verse 26.

[4] Notice from ibid., 18 Oct. The guards are the four troops of Horse Guards; for them see Chamberlayne, 1687, i. 176–86.

[5] The shutting of the shops is also mentioned in *London Gazette*.

Ch:[1] on 5: *Eph:* 18. 19 shewing the costome of the Primitive
Saints of serving God with Hymns, & their frequent use of
them upon all occasions: perstringing the prophane way of
mirth & Intemperance of this ungodly age:

In the Evening I went to prayers at W:Hall:

I visited my L: Chiefe Justice of Ireland,[2] with whom I
had long & private discourse concerning the Miserable condition that Kingdome was like to be ⟨in⟩ if Tyrconnells Counsels should prevaile at Court: I also waited on the Countesse
of Clancartie, & return'd home on [18]ᵃ Moneday, St.
Lukes Day.

22 To Lond: the next day with my Lady the Countesse of
Sunderland, I went [23]ᵃ to Cranburne, a Lodge & walke of
my Lord Godolphins, in Windsor parke:[3] there was one
roome in the house, spared in the pulling-downe the old one,
because the late Dutchesse of York, was borne in it,[4] the rest
was build & added to it by Sir Geo: Carteret, Tressurer of the
Navy:[5] & since the whole purchased by my Lord Godolphin,
who spake to me to go see it, and advise what trees were fit
to be cut downe, to improve the dwelling, it being invironed
with old rotten pollards, which corrupt the aire:[6] It stands
on a knowle, which though insensibly rising, gives it a prospect over the keepe of Windsore, which is about three miles
north-east of it: The ground is clayy & moist, the water
stark nought: The Park is pretty; The house tollerable &

ᵃ Marginal date.

[1] Patrick was still vicar of St.
Paul's, Covent Garden.

[2] Sir William Davis, husband of
Lady Clancarty: above, pp. 244 n.,
385. Tyrconnel, after having remodelled the Irish army, was now
in England intriguing to supersede
Clarendon.

[3] Cranbourn. A tower, which still
exists, was built here in the fifteenth
century; the lodge attached to it
was rebuilt *c.* 1665 by Sir George
Carteret. Godolphin was granted
the keepership of it for thirty-one

years in 1688 but ceased to occupy
it before his death. It was pulled
down *c.* 1830: Hughes, *Windsor
Forest*, pp. 298–311.

[4] Anne Hyde, born here 12 March
1637, when it was occupied by her
maternal grandfather, Sir Thomas
Aylesbury: *D.N.B.*

[5] Carteret was granted the keepership in 1664: *Cal. S.P., Dom., 1664–
5*, p. 50.

[6] It was decided to cut down
twenty trees: *Cal. Treasury Books,
1685–9*, p. 1107.

gardens convenient: after dinner we came back to Lond, having 2[a] Coaches both going and coming, of 6 horses a-piece, which we changed at Hounslow:

24 Dr. Warren[1] preached before the *Princesse*, at Whitehall, on 5 *Matt:* of the blessednesse of the pure in heart, most elegantly describing the blisse of the beatifical vision:

Afternoone preached *Sir Geo: Wheeler*[2] knight & Baronet at St. *Margarets*, on 4: *Matt:* upon the necessity of Repentance, to prevent the future Judgement: an honest & devout discourse, & pretty tollerably perform'd: This Gent: married a Niepce of the Earle of Bath, Sir Tho: Higgins's daught⟨e⟩r:[3] who being his Majesties Resident at *Venic*, & this Gent: coming from his travells out of Greece, of which he has published a very learn'd & ingenious book; fell in love with Sir Tho: daughter, & when they return'd into England, being honor'd with knighthood, would needes turne preacher, & tooke Order accordingly:[4] He is a very worthy, learned, ingenious, person, a little formal, and particular, but exceedingly devout:

25 I returned home:

27 To Lond:

29 Was a Triumphant shew of the Lord Major, both by land & water with much solemnity, when yet his power was so deminish'd, by[b] the losse of their former charter:[5]

31 Was my Birth-day, which I kept fast: in order to my

---

[a] Followed by *setts of* deleted. [b] Altered from *as.*

---

[1] Richard Warren, 1649–*c.* 1692; D.C.L. 1676; chaplain in ordinary *c.* 1682–*c.* 1687: Foster; Clutterbuck, (*Hertfordshire*), ii. 224.

[2] Wheler: above, p. 358. He was not a baronet. His text is verse 17.

[3] Thomas Higgons, 1624–91; knighted 1663; envoy extraordinary at Venice from 1674 to 1679; married 1661 Bridget, d. 1692, sister of John Grenville, earl of Bath, and widow of Symon Leach of Cadeleigh: *D.N.B.* His daughter was Grace, *c.* 1663–1703; married

Wheler 1677: *London marriage licences*; *Memoir of Sir George Wheler*, [*c.* 1820].

[4] Wheler appears to have been in deacon's orders by about 21 July 1683: *Memoir.*

[5] Notice in *London Gazette*, 1 Nov. The show was devised by Matthew Taubman, who published an account of it as *London's Yearly Jubilee*, 1686. The mayor is Sir John Peake: Beaven, *Aldermen*, ii. 107.

receiving the holy Sacrament on [November 1]ᵃ the next day,
which I did at St. James's Chapel: It being the 66t yeare of
my age;¹ dining at Sir William Godolphins; after I had
heard Mr. Branstonᵇ² (grand-son of the late Judge) preach
excellently on 15. Rom: 1. before the Princesse of Denmark
at White-hall: Thence I went [2]ᵃ to visite the Countesse of
Clancartie & the 3d home, [4]ᵃ The next day dined with us the
Countesse of Sunderland & other company: whom I left to
waite on my Lord Tressurer at the Treasury Chamber³ about
my long processe, where appear'd against me the Attorney
Generall;⁴ but my Cause was comitted to Referrees:

5 I went to St. *Martines* in the Morning, where preached
Dr. Birch⁵ on 16 *Joh:* 2 very boldly, Laying open the wiccked
stratagemms, & bloudy proceedings of the Papists in that
devlish conspiracy: a more pertinent discourse could not be:
In the afternoone I heard Dr. *Tillotson* in Lincolns-In Chapell
on the same Text, but more cautiously:⁶ I din'd at the Countesse of Clancarties:

6 I returned home:

7 A *stranger* preached on 55 Esay: 6ᶜ Exhorting to embrace
the present opportunity to repent, and reforme &c: The
Communion follow'd of which I was participant: The Lord
make me thankfull: *Pomeridiano*, the Curate on: 4: *Phil:* 11.
upon Contentment: &c:

14 The Viccar on his former Text 8. *Mat:* ult., with little

ᵃ Marginal date.   ᵇ Altered from *Brapston*?   ᶜ Altered from
or to 7.

---

¹ There is an error in the dates:
the Sunday fell on 31 October,
Evelyn's birthday. Presumably he
kept the preceding day as a fast.
² William Bramston, *d.* 1735;
nephew of Francis Bramston
(above, ii. 470); admitted at Cambridge 1673; M.A. 1680; chaplain
in ordinary *c.* 1704–*c.* 1710; D.D.
1705; at this time rector of Willin-
gale Spain: Venn. His grandfather
was John Bramston, 1577–1654;
knighted 1634; lord chief justice of

the king's bench 1635–42: *D.N.B.*
³ The Treasury Chamber (Office)
was in Whitehall palace, on the
ground floor of the Privy Gallery
wing, of which the rebuilding was
now nearly finished.
⁴ Robert Sawyer, 1633–92;
knighted 1677; attorney-general
from 1681 to 1687: *D.N.B.*
⁵ Presumably Peter Birch: above,
p. 488.
⁶ The sermon is printed in Tillotson, *Works*, 1752, ii. 181–7.

variation: & likewise the Curate: urging that nothing ought more reconcile us to our present condition, than the consideration of the sufferings & misery of most people in the world, & the natural vicissitute of worldly things:

16 I went with part of my family to passe the melancholy winter in Lond: at my sonns house in Arundel Buildings:[1]

17 I was at the Seale: In the afternoone I went to Gressham Coll: where was shew'd the *pineal glandule* taken out of a mans head, petrified, on which the *Cartesians* fell to reasoning about it:[2]

21 Dr. *Tenison* [at S. Martins][a] preached according to his costome excellently, on 10: *Heb:* 23. shewing how faithfull God was in his promises, & therefore we should rely on him in well doing:

24 Was a Seale: *Pomerid:* at St. *Clements* a stranger: on: 4: *Jam:* 13. 14: Touching the uncertainties of this life:[3]

25[b] Was the Triall of my *Lady Tukes* buisinesse; which was now for the present dismiss'd:

26[c] I din'ed at my L. Chancelors, where being 3 other Serjants at Law, after dinner being cherefull & free, they told their severall stories, how long they had detained their clients in tedious processes, by their tricks, as [if][a] so many highway thieves should have met & discovered the[d] severall purses they had taken: This they made but a jeast of: but God is not mocked:

28 Dr. *Tenison* at St. *Mart:* on: 1: *Pet:* 5. 6. Concerning the grace of humility: the holy Communion followed, of which I was partaker:

December 2[4] At white-hall *Dr. Patric:* on: 2. *Heb:* 3. 4. as

---

---

[1] See above, pp. 392, 395.

[2] In *Les passions de l'âme* (first published in 1649) Descartes states that the pineal gland is the seat of the soul: arts. xxxi–xxxiii.

[3] This sermon presumably belongs to Sunday, 21 November.

The church is St. Clement Danes.

[4] The dates of this and some of the following entries are wrong. Patrick's and Tenison's sermons presumably belong to Sunday, 5 December; the visit to the Savoy to that or the following Sunday.

I remember: The holy Sacrament[a] to the household, among whom I received:[b] Dr. *Tenison* at St. *Martins* on: 6. *Gal:* 14. How we should glory in the Crosse of Christ:[c]

5 I dind at my Lady *Arlingtons* Groome of the Stole to the Q. Dowager at Somerset-house, where dined Divers French Noble men driven out of their Country by the Persecution: In the Afternoone I went to the French-Church in the Savoy,[1] where a young man preached on: 26. *Act:* 29 Concerning *Paules* bonds, & Apologie before Agrippa, much relating to the Persecution &c: & encouraging the Sufferers: &c:

⟨12⟩[d] I went to St. James's[e] New Church, where Dr. *Tenison* preach'd on: 1. Pet: 5:[f] 7 Encouraging us to cast all our Care upon Gods Providence these dangerous times &c: The holy Sacrament being administred, I did also participate: God make me Thankfull: I dined at Sir William Godolphins &c:

15 I dined at Sir Will: Pettys: Visited my Lord C. Justice of Ireland,[2] and the Countesse of ⟨Clancartie⟩,[g] who had both ben to visite me:

16 I carried the Countesse of Sunderland to see the rarities of one Mr. Charleton[3] at the Middle Temple, who shewed us such a Collection of Miniatures, Drawings, Shells, Insects, Medailes, & natural things, Animals whereoff divers were kept in glasses of Sp: of wine, I think an hundred, besids, Minerals, precious stones, vessels & curiosities in Amber, Achat, chrystal &c: as I had never in all my Travells abroad seene any either of private Gent: or Princes exceede it; all being very perfect & rare in their kind, espec⟨i⟩aly his booke of Birds, Fish: flowers, shells &c drawn & miniatured to the

---

[a] Followed by *of* deleted.　　　　[b] Followed by *Pomerid:* deleted.
[c] Followed by *I dined* deleted.　　[d] MS. *13*.　　[e] Spelling doubtful.
[f] Altered from *1*.　　[g] MS. *Clincartie*.

---

[1] Above, iii. 545.
[2] Sir William Davis.
[3] William Courten, 1642–1702, who called himself Charleton at this time: *D.N.B.*, s.v. Courten. Evelyn mentions him in letters to Pepys, 12 Aug. and 4 Oct. 1689 (Bohn, iii. 299, 315), and in *Numismata*, p.

246. There is an interesting notice in R. Thoresby, *Diary*, ed. Hunter, 1830, i. 299. To Courten Obadiah Walker dedicated *The Greek and Roman History illustrated by Coins & Medals*, 1692. Further notices below.

life, he told us that one book stood him in 300 pounds: it was painted by that excellent[a] workeman whom the late Gastion duke of Orleans emploied:[1] This Gent:'s whole Collection (gathered by himselfe travelling most parte[b] of Europe) is[c] estimated at 8000 pounds: He seem'd a Modest and obliging person:

This Evening I made a step to my house in the Country, where I stayed[d] some dayes:

19 I went to *Greenewich*, where Dr. *Plume* preached on 2: *Eph:* 20, shewing how our holy Religion owned no Institutor but Christ, & that no other foundation could be lasti⟨ng⟩.[e]

21 I return'd to Lond: a seale:

25 Dr. Tenison at St. Martins preach'd on 8: *Joh:* 56. upon the joy of *Abraham* in prospect of Christs Incarnation, an heavenly discourse &c. The Communion follow'd at which I received:

26 At Whitehall in the Morning Dr. *Turner*[2] on 7: Acts: ult. forgivenesse of Enemys. Coram principiss: Dr. Leake: 4: *Gal:* 4: Gods punctual performances: concerning the coming of our B: L: in the fullnesse of Time: &c. [29][f] See next moneth at *

1686/7. Jan: 1 At St. Martines Mr. *Wake*[3] (who wrot so excellently in answer to the Bish: of *Mea⟨u⟩x*) on 1. *Tim:* 3.

---

a MS. *ex*[t]:   b Or *parts.*   c Preceded by *was* deleted.
d Followed by *till the* deleted.   e Reading doubtful.   f Marginal date.

---

[1] The principal artist employed by Gaston (above, ii. 128) for drawings of flowers, &c., was Nicolas Robert, 1614–85: Thieme, *Lexikon.*
[2] Presumably Dr. Thomas Turner: above, p. 493.
[3] William Wake, 1657–1737; D.D. 1689; bishop of Lincoln 1705; archbishop of Canterbury 1716: *D.N.B.* He had been chaplain to the English ambassador in Paris from 1682 to 1685. The work here referred to is *An Exposition of the Doctrine of the Church of England, in the Several Articles proposed by Monsieur de Meaux . . . in his*

Exposition of the Doctrine of the Catholick Church, 1686 (fourth ed. 1688). The bishop is J. B. Bossuet (*Nouvelle biog. gén.*) whose *Exposition de la Doctrine de l'Eglise catholique* had been written *c.* 1668 and first published in 1671; it had been translated into English in 1672 and anew in 1685: V. Verlaque, *Bibliog. raisonée . . . de Bossuet,* 1908, pp. 4–7, 14–15, 23. Wake notices the alterations made in Bossuet's work after the first edition. For the ensuing controversy see T. Jones, *Catalogue* (below, p. 541 n.), pp. 112–17.

16, concerning the Mysterie of Godlinesse, an admirable discourse: I receiv'd this Communion:

2 *White-hall* a stranger: on 1. *Tim:* 4. 8: The little profit of bodily exercise, perstringing the Papists superstitions, & particular⟨ly⟩ *Bellarmins* who expo⟨u⟩nds this Text as meaning the Roman & heathnish Spectaccles, & Theatrical Contentions:[1] The same morning I also received:

Dr. Tenison on

3 A Seale to confirme a gift of 4000 pounds per ann for 99 years to L. Tressurer out of the post office, and 1700 per Ann for ever out of L. Greys Estate—

Now was there another change of that greate Officer The *L. Treasurer*:[2] It being now againe put into Commission, two professed Papist⟨s⟩ among the rest, viz, the Lord *Bellasis*[3] & Dover,[4] joyned with the old ones, L: *Godolphin*, Sir *S. Fox*: and Sir J. Earnley:[5]

5 The French K. now sayd to be healed or rather patch'd up of the fistula in *Ano*, for[a] which he had ben severall times cutt: &c:[6] The persecution still raging:

---

[a] Altered from *of*.

---

[1] Bellarmine, *Opera omnia*, 1620, &c., iv. 1245.

[2] The grants to Rochester were made under the great seal by royal warrant to the attorney-general or solicitor-general; that for the £4,000 per annum was for ninety-nine years terminable on the lives of himself and his eldest son; the other was for lands in Northumberland, &c., conveyed to the king by Lord Grey: *Cal. Treasury Books, 1685–9*, p. 1103. The annual value of this second grant was variously estimated.

Rochester's dismissal is not mentioned in the *London Gazette*, only the appointment of his successors on 5 January.

[3] Belasyse: above, iii. 351, &c.

[4] Formerly Henry Jermyn: above, iii. 482; iv. 498 n.

[5] John Ernle, d. 1696/8; of Whetham, in Calne, Wilts.; perhaps M.P. for Wiltshire 1654, 1660; M.P. for Cricklade 1661; Great Bedwin 1681; Marlborough 1685, 1689 (Convention), and 1690; knighted 1665; a commissioner for the treasury 1679–85, 1687–9; chancellor of the exchequer 1679–89: (*Westminster Abbey registers*), p. 8; Le Neve, *Pedigrees*, p. 200.

[6] Te Deums for Louis's complete recovery were sung at Versailles on 20/30 December and in Barillon's chapel in London on 2 January: *London Gazette*, 3 Jan., 6 Jan. There is a full account of his illness, which lasted from 15 Jan. 1686 to 15 January of this year (both dates N.S.), in A. Vallot, &c., *Journal de la santé du roi Louis XIV*, ed. J. A. Le Roi, 1862, pp. 166–77. See also notices in Luttrell.

*a I was to heare the Musique of the Italians in the new Chapel, now first of all opned at White-hall publiquely for the Popish Service: Nothing can be finer than the magnificent Marble work & Architecture[b] at the End, where are 4 statues representing st. Joh: st. Petre, st. Paule, & the Church, statues in white marble, the worke of Mr. Gibbons, with all the carving & Pillars of exquisite art & greate cost: The history or Altar piece is the Salutation, The Volto, in *fresca*, the Asumption of the blessed Virgin according to their Traditions with our[c] B: Saviour, & a world of figures, painted by *Verio*. The Thrones[d] where the K. & Q: sits is very glorious in a Closset above just opposite to the Altar:[1] Here we saw the Bishop[2] in his Miter, & rich Copes, with 6 or 7: Jesuits & others in Rich Copes[e] richly habited, often taking off, & putting on the Bishops Miter, who sate in a Chaire with

---

[a] In MS. the asterisk is opposite the line beginning *5 The French K.*
[b] Followed by *before* deleted.   [c] Altered from *a*.   [d] Or *Throna*.
[e] End of page in MS.

---

[1] The chapel formed part of the new buildings begun in 1685 (above, p. 480) and was situated at the north-west corner of the Privy Garden. It was consecrated probably on 24 December and opened for worship on Christmas Day. An annexe was built on its south side in 1687. It was destroyed in the Whitehall fire of 1698. No plans or views of its interior are known. The marble altar-piece (or, rather, reredos), the work of Grinling Gibbons and Arnold Quellin, was later re-erected, with necessary alterations, in Westminster Abbey. Some parts of it are now preserved in St. Andrew's, Burnham, Somerset; the four principal figures are probably the statues now in the College Garden, Westminster School; if so, they represent Faith, St. Peter, St. Paul, and Hope. Benedetto Gennari (1633–1715) was paid £150 for a picture of the Nativity for the altar-piece in 1688; this may have replaced an older picture by him; or Evelyn may have mistaken the subject of the picture. His pictures for the chapel are now lost. Some other furnishings were removed elsewhere, but are now lost: L.C.C., *Survey of London*, xiii. 105–10; *Ellis correspondence*, ed. G. A. Ellis, 1829, i. 213; Wren Soc., vii. 73–6, &c.; xi. 118–19; *Moneys . . . for secret services of Charles II and James II, 1679–1688*, ed. J. Y. Akerman (Camden Soc., vol. lii, 1851), pp. 175, 209; Martin Haile, *Queen Mary*, p. 156. The chapel had its proper establishment of clergy, musicians and singers, sacristans, &c.: list in *Cal. Treasury Books, 1685–9*, pp. 1822–3.

[2] Perhaps John Leyburn, 1620–1702; D.D.; bishop of Adrumetum *in partibus* 1685; vicar-apostolic of all England 1685–8; of the London district (England having been divided into four districts) 1688–1702: *D.N.B.* For the Jesuits being given charge of this chapel see Campana de Cavelli, ii. 125.

Armes pontificaly, was adored, & censed by 3 Jesuits in their
Copes, then he went to the Altar & made divers Cringes there,
censing the Images, & glorious Tabernacle placed upon the
Altar, & now & then changing place; The Crosier (which was
of silver) put into his hand, with a world of mysterious Ceremony the Musique pla⟨y⟩ing & singing: & so I came away:
not believing I should ever have lived to see such things in
the K. of Englands palace, after it had pleas'd God to in-
lighten this nation; but our greate sinn, has (for the present)
Eclips'd the Blessing, which I hope he will in mercy & his
good time restore to its purity.   This was on the 29 of
December:

Little appearance of any Winter as yet:

9 A Chaplain[1] of the Dutchesse of Monmoth at St. Martins
on 12: Heb: 14, shewing the necessity of holinesse, preparatory to our admission into the holy heaven &c:

15 Trial at the L. Chancelor[a] for L. Tuke, going for her:

16 At White-hall, a *stranger* on 16 *Luke 8*, shewing by the
parable of the Unjust stuard, the method which the faithfull
should observe, for the securing his eternal Condition: not,
from his defrauding his Masters Debtors; but the Industry
worl⟨dl⟩ings use to attaine their secular ends, & secure themselves:[b]

Then Dr. *Tenison* on 2. *Apoc:* 10, encouraging us to perseverance &c:

17 We had a Private Seale: & I open'd my buisinesse[2]
againe to my L. Godolphin, now againe made one of the Lords
Commissioners of the Treasury; My Lord of Rochester being
layd aside:

Greate expectations of severall greate-mens declaring
themselves Papists:[3] and L: Tyrconell gon to succeede my
Lord Lieutennant in Ireland, to the astonishment of all sober
men, & to the evident ruine of the Protestants in that King-

---

a Spelling uncertain.   b Altered from *their*.

---

[1] Perhaps John Mandevile: be-   ture in France.
low, p. 539.   [3] Luttrell records only one con-
[2] Presumably his claims relating version this month: i. 391.
to Sir Richard Browne's expendi-

dome, as well as of its greate Improvement:[1] Much discourse that all the White-staff-Officers and others should be dismissed for adhering to their Religion:[2] Popish Justices of Peace established in all Counties of the meanest of the people:[3] Judges ignorant of the Law, and perverting it: so furiously does the Jesuite[4] drive, & even compell[a] Princes to violent courses, & distruction of an excellent Government both in Church & State: God of his infinite mercy open our Eyes, & turne our hearts, Establish his Truth, with peace: The *L: Jesus* Defend his little flock, & preserve this threatned church & Nation.

23[b] Dr. Tenison at St. Martin: on 18 *Pro:* 14: the misery of a gilty and wounded spirit, against which ⟨no⟩[c] natural power can contest, to be onely healed by Gods infinite mercy, upon unfain'd Repentance:

Afternoone the Lecturer of St. *Clements* 12 *Eccles:* 13— That the feare of God is the whole duty, & consummation of a Christian man &c:

---

[a] Followed by *our* deleted.   [b] Reading doubtful; altered from *21*?
[c] MS. *now.*

---

[1] On 1 January a notification was sent to Clarendon that Tyrconnel was to succeed him, but as lord deputy. Tyrconnel left London on 11 January: Clarendon, *Corr.*, ii. 134, 146; *Ellis corr.*, i. 225, 229–30.

[2] White staffs were carried as part of their insignia by the lord high treasurer and possibly by some others of the great officers of the crown, by the lord steward, the treasurer, and the comptroller, of the household. Evelyn is probably thinking of the last two; the present officers, Newport and Maynard (above, iii. 526; iv. 402, 416), were superseded on 9 February of this year: *London Gazette*, 10 Feb. The lord steward was Ormond.

[3] A committee of the Privy Council was appointed about 13 Nov. 1686 to inspect the justices of the peace throughout England; it finished its work apparently about

30 November: *Ellis corr.*, i. 181–3, 197. Luttrell names three Roman Catholics appointed for Middlesex in January; they are Tyrconnel and two men of good social standing: i. 391–2. They were granted a dispensation from taking the usual oaths; the Protestant justices asked for a similar dispensation: *London Gazette*, 3 March; presumably some of them were nonconformists. Reresby on 6 January notes the appointment of ten Roman Catholic justices for the North Riding. The statement about social rank is probably greatly exaggerated.

[4] The reference is presumably general, not to an individual. For the influence attributed to the Jesuits see articles by B. Duhr on Father Edward Petre in *Zeitschrift für katholische Theologie*, vols. x, xi (1886–7).

24 I din'd at the Duke of Norfolcks: where was my L. Yarmoth[1] &c: I saw the Queenes new appartment at W-hall with her new bed, the embrodery cost 3000 pounds: the carving about the Chimny piece is incomparable of Gibbons:[2]

27 I had an hearing of my buisinesse before the Lords of the Treasury.

30 At W-hall: Dr. Hooper to the Household on 2: Cor: 4. 3. If the Gospel be hid[a] it is hid to them that perish &c: excellently shewing how freely it has ben promulged,[b 3] how easy to understand, and that it is from our owne negligence if we miscarry:

At St. Martins, Dr. Tenison: on 2. Cor: 2: ult, shewing the Truth of the Scriptures, & most learnedly defending our Translation, clearing divers Controversies about ⟨it⟩, & proving that there is no neede of an Infallible Interpreter:[4] *vide Notes*:

I heard the famous *Cifeccio*[5] (Eunuch) sing, in the new popish chapell this afternoone, which was indeede very rare, & with greate skill: He came over from Rome, esteemed one of the best voices in *Italy*, much crowding, little devotion:

31[c] At S: Clements: Dr. Harscot,[6] (Deane of Windsore) on: 116. Psal: 15, the Anniversary of K. Char: I. Martyrdom, shewing the preciousnesse of the death of the Saints &c:

I made a step home this Evening: return'd next day.

---

[a] Substituted for *lost*.   [b] Or *provided*.   [c] Altered from *21*.

---

[1] William Paston, c. 1652–1732; second earl of Yarmouth 1683: G.E.C.; Ketton-Cremer, *Norfolk portraits*, pp. 37–56.

[2] This carving cost £48: Wren Soc., vii. 120. For the bed see ibid., p. 133.

[3] For this form see *O.E.D.*

[4] Tenison had already discussed this topic briefly in *A Discourse concerning a Guide in Matters of Faith*, 1683; and returned to it in his introduction to *Popery Not Founded on Scripture*, 1688.

[5] Giovanni Francesco Grossi, 1653–97, called Siface (i.e. Syphax) from his performance in some opera: *Grove's Dict. of Music*; A. Ademollo, *I Teatri di Roma nel secolo XVII*, 1888, pp. 141–4; *Nuova Antologia*, April 1889, pp. 782–93; C. Nardini, *Il musico Siface*, 1891.

[6] Gregory Hascard, d. 1708; matriculated at Cambridge 1657: D.D. 1671; rector of St. Clement Danes 1678–1708; chaplain in ordinary c. 1679–1708; dean of Windsor 1684: Venn.

Feb: 2: Candlemas-day, a stranger preached at St. Martins on   shewing the inconsistence of sin, with the service of God:

6 At St. Mart: Dr. Tenison: 107 *Psal:* 31. An Exhortation to Praise God for his infinite benefits &c: The holy Comm: follow'd at which I receiv'd: &c:

9 W-hall, Ashwednesday B: of Durham¹ 18. *Gen:* 17. proper for the Season.

11 I went home.ª

13 Dr. Hutchins preached on: 4. *Gal:* 4. 5, on the Incarnation &c:

15 I return'd to Lond: 16 Dr. Tenison [at W-hall]ᵇ preached on 10: *Jer:* 2. against superstitious feares &c:²

18 W.Hall Dr. *Jane* on 2. *Cor:* 7. 10: The necessity of repentance, & the severity of it among the primitive Christians, perstringing the Papists who give Absolution before pennance is performed:²

Feb: 20 At St. *James's* Dr. *Tenison*, on 2. *Reg:* 5. 1. shewing by the example of that valiant General *Naman*, and greate favorite of the King of *Syria* (who notwithstanding all this, was a Leper) That there neither is, nor ever was any perfect & compleate happinesse in this life, but that there is & of ⟨necessity⟩ᶜ both for the Glory of God, & the benefit of man, some affliction or Imperfection interwoven & mingled among all sublunary enjoyments: The bl: Sacrament follow'd of which I participated: The Lord make me thankfull:

27ᵈ Dr. Tenison at St. *Martines* 1. *Cor:* 11. 19: shewing what heresy & Schisme was; the necessitie of them, for the approbation of those who avoide them: The false notion of the words among the papists, & how wrongfully they reproch the true worshipers of God, by their hard censure: That we

---

ª Followed by *returned* deleted.   ᵇ Interlined.   ᶜ MS. *necesisity*.
ᵈ This notice is written over three short lines written in pencil: *22 I . . . 23 At W:hall preach . . . was Affliction. . . .*

---

¹ Crew, preaching as dean of the chapel. Lenten sermon at court. The list of preachers was not published in the *London Gazette* this year, but is given in H. L. Benthem, *Engeländischer Kirch- und Schulen-Staat,* 1694, pp. 231–2.

² Lenten sermon at court.

are not now to expect miracles to evince the Truth, but to
follow the Scriptures, for the rule of faith: how far ignorance
unaffected is to be pitied, & abated for: An incouragement
to search the Truth and persist therein &c: *Pomeridiano,* at
St. *Jamess* by Mr. *Mandivel*[1] (Chaplain to the Dutchesse of
Monmouth:) on 119 *Psal:* 71. The benefit of Afflictions.

Mar: 2: At W-hall *Mr. Chetwin*[2] on 1. *Rom:* 18. a very
quaint neate discourse of moral Righteousnesse &c:

Came out now a Proclamation for Universal[a] liberty of
Conscience in Scotland and dispensation from all Tests &
Lawes to the Contrary; as also capacitating Papists to be
chosen into all Offices of Trust: &c. *The Mysterie operats.*[3]

[3 I went out of Town to meete my Lord Clarendon returning from Ireland, &c:][b 4]

4: At *W.hall* Dr. *Megot* deane of *Winchester,* before the
Princesse of *Denmark*—on 14: *Matt:* 23: The benefit &
necessity of religious Recesse:[5] *See your notes:*

6 Dr. *Tenison* at St. *Martines* on. 22: *Luke:* 19. to prove
that the Sacramental Elements remain'd in their natural
substance & qualities, & that there could be no transubstantiation, which he proved both from Scriptures, Antient
Fathers, and even from the antient Offices celebrating &
consecrating the Elements, even in the Church of Rome it
selfe: That which I tooke to be an excellent[c] observation
was, that if (as now the C. of Rome holds) after the consecration, it be no bread, & that before it the body of Christ was
not there, they consecrate nothing: There is no Text in

---

[a] Altered from *L-.*   [b] Interlined after next notice was written.
[c] MS. *ex*[t]*:*

---

[1] Presumably John Mandevile,
c. 1655–1725; D.D. 1694; chaplain
in ordinary 1690–1725; dean of
Peterborough 1722: Venn. He is
later (30 March 1690, 29 Nov. 1691)
described as the duchess of Buckingham's chaplain.

[2] Benthem gives 'Mr. Chetwood':
above, p. 502. Lenten sermon at
court.

[3] The proclamation, dated 12

February and published at Edinburgh on 18 February, is printed in
London Gazette, 3 March. The field-
conventicles, at which the extreme
presbyterians met, remained illegal.
The Mystery is 'the Mystery of
Jesuitism', a subject to whose literature Evelyn had contributed:
above, iii. 393.

[4] He arrived this night.

[5] Lenten sermon at court.

Scripture where it is shewed that God ever turn'd one body into another, the body still remaining: nor was Moses rod any more a rod, but a Serpent, when it was turn'd: he spake also of the Indignity they put on our B.S. body: &c:[1] See your note⟨s⟩: The holy Sacrament followed ⟨of⟩[a] which I participated: God mak⟨e⟩ me thankfull:

10 His Majestie sent[b] to the Commissioners of the Privy-Seale this morning into his bed-chamber, & told us that [tho][c] he had thought fit to dispose of the Seale, into a single hand, yet he would [so][c] provide for us, as it should appeare how well he accepted of our faithfull & loyal service, with many gracious expressions to this effect: upon which we delivered[d] the Seales into his Majesties hands[e]—It was by all the world both hoped & expected his Majestie would have restor'd it to my Lord Clarendon againe; but they were astonish'd to see it given to my L. Arundel of Wardour, a zealous Rom: Catholique: & indeede it was very hard, and looked very unkindly, his Majestie (as my L: Clarendon protested to me, going to visite him & long discoursing with him about the affaires of Ireland) finding not the least failor of duty in him during all his government of that Kingdome: so as his recalling, plainely appeared to be from the stronger Influence of the Papists, who now got all the preferments:[2]

Most of the greate officers both in the Court, [& Country,][c] Lords & others, dismissed,[f] who would not promise his Majestie their consent to the repealing the Test, & penal statutes against the Romish recusants: There was to this end most of the Parliament men, spoken to in his Majesties Closset, & such as refused, if in any place or office of Trust,

---

a MS. *af*, altered from *at*. b Followed by *for* deleted. c Interlined.
d Followed by *his M-* deleted. e Followed by *&* deleted.
f Followed by *& wh-* deleted.

---

[1] Tenison sets out his views on Transubstantiation incidentally in his controversy with Father Andrew Pulton (1687) and at large in *Six Conferences concerning the Eucharist*, 1687 (but this is said to be a translation from Jean la Placette).

[2] A notice that Arundell of Wardour, having been appointed keeper of the privy seal, was sworn in on 11 March, occurs in *London Gazette*, 14 March. For James's conduct towards Clarendon see the comment in *Ellis corr.*, i. 247.

Civil, or military, put out of their Employments: This was
a time of greate trial: Hardly one of them assenting, which
put the Popish Interest[a] much backward:[1] The English
Cleargy, every where very boldly preaching against their
Superstition & errors, and wonderfully follow'd by the people,
not one considerable proselyte being made in all this time.[2]
The party so exceedingly put to the worst by the preaching
& writing of the Protestants, in many excellent Treatises,
evincing the doctrine & discipline of the Reformed Religion,
to the manifest disadvantage of their Adversarys:[3] & to which
did not a little contribute [13][b] the Sermon preached now at
W-hall before the Princesse of Denmark, & an innumerable
crowde of people, & at least 30 of the greatest nobility, by
Dr. Ken: Bish: of Bath & Wells, upon 8: *John*: 46 (the
Gospel of the day)[4] all along that whole discourse describing
the blasphemies, perfidie, wresting of Scriptures, preference
of Traditions before it, spirit of persecution, superstition,
Legends & fables, of the Scribes & pharisees; so as all the[c]
Auditory understood his meaning of paralleling them with
the Romish Priests, & their new Trent Religion: Exhorting
the people to adhere to the Written-Word, & to persevere in

---

a Followed by *to* deleted.   b Marginal date.   c Followed by
world deleted.

---

[1] James was apparently 'closeting' members of parliament by
1 February; the term is used in a
letter of 5 March: *Ellis corr.*, i. 235–
6, 256; see also pp. 259, 265.
Reresby describes the process:
9–18 March.

[2] The only English peers known
to have been converted about this
time are Peterborough and James
Cecil, 1666–93, fourth earl of Salisbury 1683 (*D.N.B.*; converted at
Rome: Luttrell, i. 400), who was
generally considered contemptible.
The other converts about this time,
including Dryden, Wycherley, and
Obadiah Walker, were not very important socially.

[3] On the controversial writings
see Macaulay, pp. 762–6. The best
list is *A catalogue of the collection of
tracts for and against Popery*, by
Thomas Jones (Chetham Soc., vols.
xlviii, lxiv, 1859, 1865; it in-
corporates F. Peck, *A complete catalogue*, 1735; it lists about 794
separate works, but a few were
published before 1685 or after
1688). There seems to be little
ground for questioning the claim
to superior literary ability made on
behalf of the Anglicans. Cardinal
Howard acknowledged the Roman
Catholics' defective command of
English: Burnet, *Own time*, 1833, iii.
84–5. Lingard mentions their principal writers.

[4] Fifth Sunday in lent. Lenten
sermon at court.

the Faith tought in the Church of England, whose doctrine for Catholique & soundnesse, he preferr'd to all the Communit⟨i⟩es & Churches of Christians in the whole-world; & concluding with a kind of prophesy, that whatsoever it suffer'd, it should after a short trial Emerge to the confusion of her Adversaries, & the glory of God:

I went this Evening to see the order of the Boys & children at Christs hospital,¹ there was neere 800 of them, Boys & Girles: so decently clad, cleanely lodged, so wholesomly fed, so admirably taught, some the Mathematics, Especialy the 40 of the late Kings foundation;² that I was plainly astonished to see the progresse some little youths of 13 & 14 years of age, had made: I saw them at supper, visited their dormitories, admired the order, Oeconomie, & excellent government of this most charitable seminary: The rest,ᵃ some are tought for the Universitie, others designed for seamen, all for Trades & Callings: The *Girles* instructed in all such worke as became their Sex, &ᵇ as might fit them to make good Wives, Mistresses, & a blessing to their generation: They sung a Psalme before they sat downe to supper, in the greate hall, to an Organ which played all the time, & sung with that cherefull harmony, as seem'd to me a vision of heavenlyᶜ Angels:³ & I came from the place with infinite Satisfaction, having never in my life seene a more noble, pious, & admirable Charity: All these consisting of Orphans⁴

ᵃ Comma supplied.   ᵇ Followed by *such* deleted.   ᶜ Partially deleted.

---

¹ See above, iii. 192. The school buildings had been greatly damaged by the Fire and had been largely rebuilt; the hall had been rebuilt *c.* 1680: Pearce, *Annals of Christ's Hospital*, pp. 56, 208–10. At Easter this year there were 789 children in the hospital and at nurse: *Notes and Queries*, clxxvii (1939), 362.

² This was the Mathematical School founded in 1673 by Charles II at the instigation of Sir Robert Clayton, and training forty boys from the hospital in navigation, &c., to prepare them for the navy and the mercantile marine; these boys wore special badges. The position of the premises occupied by it at this time is unknown; it is now scarcely distinguished from the rest of the school: Pearce, pp. 59, 99–134, &c.

³ Cf. the account of the Sunday supper in Strype's Stow, i. 182.

⁴ Apparently the requirement at

onely: The foundation (which has also had & still has many
Benefactors) was of that pious Prince, K. Edward the 6:
whose picture, (held to be an Original of Holbeins) is in the
Court,¹ where the Governors meete to consult of the affairs
of the Hospital, & his stat⟨u⟩e in White-marble stands in a
Nich of the Wall below,² as you go to the Church which is a
modernª noble & ample fabric.³

16 I made a step home,ᵇ 10th Saw the trial of those devlish
murdering mischiefe-doing engines *Bombs,* shot out of the
Morter piece on black-heath: The distance that they are
cast, the destruction they make where ever they fall is most
prodigious:⁴

19 I return'd: 20 The Bish: of Bath & Wells *Dr. Ken,*
preached at St. *Martines*; the Crowd of people is not to be
expressed; nor the wonderfull Eloquence of this admirable
preacher: The Text: 26: Matt: from ver: 36 ad 40: Describing the bitternesse of our B: S. Agonie, the ardour of his love,
the infinite obligations we have toᶜ imitate his patience, and
resignation: the meanes by watching against temptations,
& over our selves, with fervent prayer to attaine it; & the
exceeding reward in the end: upon all which he madeᵈ most
pathetical discourses:⁵ The Communion follow'd, at which
I was participant: And afterwards din'd with the Bishop,
& that young, most learned, pious & excellentᵉ Preacher
*Mr. Wake,*⁶ at Dr. Tenisons,ᶠ who invited me: In the Afternoone, I went to heare Mr. *Wake,* at the New-built Church

---

ª Followed by *&* deleted.   ᵇ Followed by *returned Saturday the*
19 deleted.   ᶜ Followed by *him & the* deleted.   ᵈ Followed by
the deleted.   ᵉ MS. *exᵗ:*   ᶠ Followed by *to* deleted.

---

this time was that one of the child's
parents should be dead: Pearce,
p. 43.

¹ The portrait of Edward VI, not
the picture of Edward granting the
hospital its charter: Hatton, *New
view,* pp. 740, 741. Neither picture
is by Holbein.

² It occupied a niche over the
main entrance to the hospital.

³ The rebuilding of the church

had begun in 1677; it was not completed until 1691.

⁴ The date of this notice is presumably wrong. There were later
trials of grenades, &c., on Black-
heath on 15 and 28 April: *Hist.
MSS. Comm., Downshire MSS.,* i.
238, 241–2.

⁵ The day is Palm Sunday.

⁶ Above, p. 532.

St. Anns:¹ on 8: *Mar:* 34: upon the subject of taking up the Crosse, & strenuously behaving our selves in times of persecution: such as this now threatned to be: His majestie having againe prorogu'd the Parliament,² forseeing it would not remitt of the Laws against Papists, by the extraordinary, zeale & bravery of its members, & [free]ᵃ renuntiation of greate officers both in Court & State, who would not be prevailed with for any temporal concerne:³

23 Dr. *James coram Pr: Daniæ* W:hall: on: 5: Rom: 8: shewing the infinite & stupendious love of God, to exceede all Examples & Instances of Charity in the love of Christ, whilst we were yet Enemies, & wretched sinners.⁴ I went to visite my L: Clarendon &c:

24: At St. *James's* a Chaplaine of the Dutchesse of *Monmoths*,⁵ on. 1. Lament: 1. describing the sufferings of our B Saviour &c.

25 At St. Martines Dr. *Tenison* (Goodfriday) on: 1: Pet: 2. 24. A most pathetical discourse, describingᵇ how our B: Saviour had our sinns transferred on him, as a Sacrifice for our sinn, & in our behalfe, as the sacrifices not onely in the old Law, but amongst the very Gentiles, were suppos'd to be substituted in the place of the sinner, by a kind of natural Law; generaly agreeing that there could be no attonement without sheding of blood, & forfaiture of life: In his describing the infinite Charity of God in sending his son for this end & our ingratitude in being no more affected with it, he drew teares from many Eyes: The H: Sacrament follow'd, ⟨of⟩ᶜ

ᵃ Interlined.   ᵇ Followed by *the* deleted.   ᶜ MS. *af*, altered from *at*.

---

¹ The parish of St. Anne, Soho, was created by an act of parliament, 1678 (further act 1685); the church was consecrated on 21 March 1686: Newcourt, *Repertorium*, i. 572–4. The building has undergone various alterations.

² By proclamation dated 18 March: *London Gazette*, 21 March. Parliament was prorogued until 22 November but was dissolved on

2 July.

³ For the closeting see above, pp. 540–1; for displacements, Luttrell, &c.

⁴ Lenten sermon at court.

⁵ Presumably Mandevile: above, p. 539. At St. James, Piccadilly; in 1703 there was a sermon here every Thursday in Lent: *An account of the times*, &c. (cited above, p. 305 n.).

which I participated after a very solemn preparation & to my extraordinary Comfort: The Lord make me mindfull & thankfull:

There came in a man (whilst we were at divine service) with his sword drawn to neere the middle of the Church, with severall others in that posture; which in this jealous time, put the Congregation into a wonderfull Confusion; but it appear'd to be one who fled into it, for Sanctuary, being pursued by Baylifs &c:

Pomeridiano, Dr. *Sharp*,[1] at White-hall, (*Coram Pr: Daniæ* &c) on 1. *Cor:* 1. 2. shewing the stupendious efficacy of the Gospel, that the Scandal of the Crosse & the preaching there-off so plainely, & inartificialy; should prevaile so infinitely beyond all the Rhetoric & Eloquence of other Sects, Philosophers & Orators; & with all seting forth the sufferings of Christ with the practical inferences flowing from the Text: I went & visited my Lady Ossorie:[2]

27 At St. Martines Easter-day: Mr. Hall[3] (chapl: to Sir W: Trumbul[4] Ambassador of Constantinople) on: 1. Cor: 15. ult: shewing very eloquently, & by way of Character, what a Christian should be as to Constancy, & other active & passive Vertues in expectation of the resurrection & future reward: The H: Sacrament follow'd of which I participated: *Pomeridiano*, the[a] Lecturer at St. Clements on: 28 *Matt* 5. 6. apposite to the Day:

Aprill: 3. Dr. *Tenison* at St. *Martin*: on: *1. Rom:* 8. shewing the novelty of Error, & the Truth of Antiquity, & that

---

[a] Followed by *Curate* deleted.

[1] Sharp had been restored to favour in January: see above, p. 516; this probably refers to his chaplaincy in ordinary. Luttrell also notes his preaching here this day.

[2] Either the widow of Thomas, the late Lord Ossory, or the second wife of James, the present lord.

[3] William Hayley, *c.* 1658–1715; fellow of All Souls College; D.D. 1695; rector of St. Giles in the Fields 1695–1715; dean of Chichester 1699; chaplain in ordinary *c.* 1700–15?: Foster. He was chaplain to Trumbull at Paris and Constantinople; letters, &c., in *Hist. MSS. Comm., Downshire MSS.*, vol. i.

[4] Above, p. 110. He embarked for Constantinople on 16 April of this year and remained there as ambassador until 1691.

onely the Scripture must be our Rule, what ever doctrine be pretended:[1] *See your notes*: The H: Communion followed, I received: I dind at Sir William Godolphins:

8 Had a tryal of re-hearing my greate Cause at the C⟨h⟩ancery in Westminster hall, I had 7. of the most learned Council, my Adversary five, among which the Attourney Gen:[2] & late Soliciter Finch[3] son to the L: Chancellor Earle of Notingham: The Accompt was at last brought to one Article of the Surcharge, & referr'd to a Master, the Cause lasting two houres & more:

9 After 5 monethes Absence, of my Family, wintering at my Sons in Lond: we all returned home, (I thank God) in health: for which the Lord be blessed:

10 Our *Viccar* in the morning preached on 2. *Pet:* 2. 21, shewing, the greate danger of willfull sinns:

Pomerid: Mr. *Hutchins*, on 1. *Pet:* 2: 31,[4] Exhorting to an imitation of our B: Savior.

There having the last weeke ben issu'd forth a dispensation from all Obligations and Tests, by which dissenters & Papists especialy, had publique liberty of exercising their severall ways of Worship, without incurring the penalty of the many Laws, & Acts of Parliament to the Contrary ever since the Reformation;[5] & this purely obtained by the Papists, thinking thereby to ruine the C. of England, which now was the onely Church, which so admirably & strenuously oppos'd their Superstition; There was a wonderfull concourse at the Dissenters meeting house in this parish, and the Parish-Church left exceeding thinn:[6] What this will end in, God

---

[1] Tenison had dealt with the last subject in *A Discourse concerning a Guide in Matters of Faith*, 1683.

[2] Sir Robert Sawyer: above, p. 529.

[3] Heneage Finch: above, p. 500. He had been dismissed from the solicitorship on 21 April 1686.

[4] Presumably a slip for verse 21.

[5] James's first Declaration of Indulgence, dated 4 April; published in *London Gazette*, 7 April (also separately, without date of publication). Besides granting freedom of worship it abrogated the Test Acts.

[6] In 1672 Henry Godman (Goodman) was licensed as a Congregationalist to hold services in Upper Deptford. In 1683 he was fined £20 for preaching before forty persons and more. In 1690 his congregation numbered 500 and his salary was £40 per annum. This church still flourishes: Matthews, *Calamy revised*, p. 225; Dews,

Almighty onely knows, but ⟨it⟩[a] lookes like confusion, which
I pray God avert:

11 To Lond: about my Suite, some termes of Accommodation being proposed:

17 Dr. *Tenison* at St. Martines on 9: *Mar:* 50: shewing
how the truely religious were the salt spoken of by our B:S.
according to all the preserving, & uniting qualities of Salt,
and of the insipidnesse of ungodly, & unregenerate men:
The holy Communion follow'd at which I staied: *Pomerid:* at
St. *Anns* Mr. *Wake:* on 24 *Acts* 14 of *Heresy* &c:

19 I heard the famous Singer the Eunuch *Cifacca*,[1]
esteemed the best in *Europe* & indeede his holding out &
delicatenesse in extending & loosing a note with that incomparable softnesse, & sweetenesse was admirable: For the
rest, I found him a meere wanton, effeminate child; very Coy,
& prowdly conceited to my apprehension: He touch'd the
Harpsichord to his Voice rarely well, & this was before a
select number of some particular persons whom Mr. Pepys
(Secretary of the Admiralty & a greate lover of Musick)
invited to his house, where the meeting was, & this[b] obtained
by peculiar favour & much difficulty of the Singer, who much
disdained to shew his talent to any but Princes:

20 I dined with my L. Godolphin &c.

21 My Petition was heard by the Lords of The Treasury:
I din'd at my L. Sunderlands:

22 I made a step home for a few-daies:

24 Our *Viccar* on his former Text 2. *Pet:* 2. 21 22 shewing
the danger of presumptuous sinns, and the mercys of God to
common frailties, which do not remaine in that number if
habitual: &c:

---

[a] MS. *is.*   [b] Followed by *favour* deleted.

Deptford, pp. 131–8. A General
Baptist church is said to have
existed here from the time of
Charles II, but the earlier ministers
listed by Dews (p. 127) belong to
the Shad Thames congregation in
Bermondsey: for it see W. Wilson,
Hist. . . . of Dissenting Churches . . .
in London, 1808–14, iv. 256–7,
342–3.

[1] Siface: above, p. 537. Early
in March Lady Tuke had been
arranging for him to play for Pepys:
Pepys, *Life, journals*, &c., ed. Smith,
ii. 65–6.

Pomerid: at *Greenewich* the Curate on 5. *Mat:* 5. perswading to the grace of meekenesse & humility &c: After this, I staied to heare the *French* sermon, which succeded (in the same place, & after use of the English[a] Liturgie translated into French) the congregation consisting of about 100 French Protestants refugiès from the Persecution, of which Monsieur de *Rouvigny* (present) was the chiefe, & had obtain'd the use of the Church after the Parish had ended[b] their owne[c] Service &c: The Preachers text was 16: *Psal:* 11, patheticaly perswading to patience, constancy & relyance on God, for the comfort of his Grace, amidst all their Sufferings, & the infinite reward to come:[1]

25 To *Lond:* about my Affairs at Law:

1 *May* Dr. *Tenison* at St. Martines: on[d] 73. Psal: 1. 2. 3. shewing Gods indifferent dealing as to things of this world, both with the Godly, and Wicked; 'til the end of their race, & then the infinite reward of those who love & serve him through all circumstances; besides the inward comforts which religious men enjoy, amidst all their outward sufferings: The holy Sacrament follow'd & I received:

2 I dined at Myn heere *Dickvelts*[2] the Holland Ambassadors: a prudent and worthy person: There din'd, my Lord Middleton Prin⟨ci⟩pal Secretary of state; Lord Pembrock,[3] L: Lumly,[4] L. Preston,[5] Coll Fitz-Patrick,[6] Sir J: Chardin:

---

[a] Substituted for *French*. [b] Substituted for *heard*. [c] Followed by *Li-* deleted. [d] Followed by *5: Matt:* deleted.

---

[1] Very little appears to be known about the French church in Greenwich beyond what is to be derived from Evelyn and Dumont de Bostaquet; the latter names several ministers. A list of ministers from 1686 to 1720 is given in Huguenot Soc., *Proc.*, viii (1909), 54–5.

[2] Everard van Weede, heer van Dijkveld, &c., 1626–1702: van der Aa, *Biog. woordenboek*. He was here as ambassador from 21 February to 19 May.

[3] The eighth earl: above, p. 440.

[4] Above, p. 451.

[5] Richard Graham, 1648–95; third baronet 1658; created Viscount Preston (Scotland) 1681: *D.N.B.* He was the elder brother of Col. James Graham.

[6] Presumably Edward Fitzpatrick, d. 1696; elder brother of Richard Fitzpatrick, first Baron Gowran (*D.N.B.*); captain, Holland regiment, 1678; distinguished himself at Steenkirk; colonel, Royal Fusiliers, 1 Aug. 1692; drowned at sea: Collins, *Peerage*, ed. Brydges, viii. 307; Dalton, *English army lists.*

After dinner the Ambassador discoursed [of]ᵃ & deplored the stupid folly of our Politics, in suffering the French to take Luxembourg: it being a place of the most concerne to have ben defended for the Interest of not onely the Netherlands, but of England also:¹

5 Being Ascension day, a stranger preached at St. Martinesᵇ on: 2. *Cor:* 5. 11, terribly describing the state of the Wiccked in Hell, and the happinesse of the Saints in Heaven: The H: Communion follow'd, at which I participated:

6 I returned home.

8 A stranger 10 Heb: 36. shewing the necessitie of Christian Patience, and the difference of that Virtue from that of the heathen Moralists, & fortitude:

11 Lond: 12 I came downe with the Countesses of Bristol & Sunderland, whose husband being Lord President [& Secretary of state]ᵃ was made knight of the Gartir, & prime favorite:² The two Countesses &c: dined at my house: Memorandum: this day was such a storme of wind as had seldome happened in an age for the extreame violence of it, being as was judged a kind of Hurocan: It also kept the floud out of the Thames that people went on foote over several places above bridge, the tide was so low.³ I return'd this evening with the Ladys:

14 and went home againe against Whitson Sonday, the 15:

15 Preached at Deptford a young man, Lecturer at our Viccars London Parish,⁴ excellently well on 2. *Ephes:* 14. shewing what the gifts of the Spirit were in the primitive times,ᶜ extraordinary then, for the planting of the Gospel,

---

ᵃ Interlined.　　ᵇ Altered from *Marg-*.　　ᶜ Followed by *necess-* deleted.

---

¹ See above, p. 380. On 12 April, N.S., Louis XIV announced his intention of visiting Luxemburg in May; he was there from 21 to 26 May, N.S.: *London Gazette*, 7 April, &c.

² He had been elected K.G. on 26 April and was installed on 23 May: ibid., 28 April, 26 May.

³ So Luttrell, i. 403; see also Wood, *Life and times*, iii. 219.

⁴ St. Dunstan in the East. The lecturer is probably the gifted William Strengfellow: below, p. 641. There is perhaps a slip in the verse number in the text.

not necessary now, & therefore ceased & more rare: & what gifts are now requisite, & continu'd, namely those *Dona gratum facientia* as Humility, patience, Charity, faith, Hope &c. The H: Sacrament follow'd, at which I received: Afternoone on 2. *Cor:* 5. 10. Describing the certainty of a future Judgement: I being much wearied, was extreamely sleepy: The Lord[a] pardon all my Infirmities:

17: Lond: about my P: Seale &c:[1] stayed all this weeke: An Earthquake in severall places of England about the time of the great storme 11th past:[2]

22 Trinity Sonday: at St. Martins, Dr. Tenison preached on 28 *Matt:* 19. Explaining the Mysterie of the holy Trinity, & shewing how its beliefe was necessary in order to practise:[b] [3] I went immediately home to Deptford; & in the afternoone a Stranger preached on 4: Ephes: 30: shewing how many ways the H. Spirit might be said to be grieved, though as God impossible,[4] and the danger of it:[c] I received the B: Sacrament in the Morning at St. Martins: The Lord make me mindfull & thankfull. [24 Returned home:][d]

26: To Lond: about my Agreement with[e] Mr. Pretyman after my tedious suit:

28 I returned home: 29 our *Viccar*   shewing the unhappinesse of Anarkie, & duty of Obedience to Governors: It was the Anniversary of the Late Kings returne, & still continu'd to be observed: 1 *Tim:* 2—1. 2. 3. *Pomerid*: A stranger: on 1. Thess: 5. 19: shewing, what is meant by quenching the Spirit; not as if (with the Anabaptists & other Inthusiasts) the Spirit of God were essentialy as he is the third person in the S. Trinity, in them; but the fruites & graces of the spirit, which we should endeavour to cherish

---

a Spelling doubtful.   b Followed by (*See note:*) deleted.
c Opposite this line a deleted date *23* in margin.   d Interlined later.
e Followed by *the* deleted.

---

[1] See below, p. 551.
[2] I have not found any other notices of this earthquake.
[3] Tenison had recently published *The difference betwixt the Protestant and Socinian methods: in answer to*

a book written by a Romanist, and intituled, The Protestants plea for a Socinian (1687; licensed 14 Dec. 1686).
[4] Perhaps a mistake for impassible.

& improve, so as to be able to instruct & edifie others &c. as
the following verses shew, by the warning us not to despise
Prophecy:

June: 2: I went to Lond: it having pleas'd his Majestie to
grant me a Privy-Seale for 6000 pounds, for the discharging
the Debt, I had ben so many yeares persecuted for.[a][1] It being
indeede for Mony drawne over by my F. in Law Sir R:
Browne during his Residence in the Court of France, & so
(with a much greater summ, due to[b] Sir Richard from his
Majestie & now this part of the Arrere payed) there remaining
yet due to me (as Excecutor to Sir Richard) about 6500 more:
But this determining a tedious & expensive Chancery suite,
has ben so greate a mercy & providence to me (through the
kindnesse & friendship of my L. Godolphin one of the Lords
Commissioners of the Treasury), that I do accknowledge it,
with all imaginable thanks to my gracious God:

5 I receiv'd the B: Sacrament at St. *Martines,* Dr. *Tenison*
preaching on 3: Heb. 4: Exhorting to contemplate the
Workes of the Creation in the aspectable world, for the stirring up of our Thankfullnesse, & confirmation of our Faith
in the Deity, against Atheists:

Pomerid: Lecturer at St. Clements o⟨n⟩ 1. *Jam:* 17.
Shewing how God was the onely Author of all Good things
&c:

6 I visited my Co: Pierpoint, Daughter to Sir Jo: Evelyn
of Deane, now widdow of Mr. Pierpoint, & mother of the
Earle of Kingston: she was now marrying my Cousen Evelyn
Pierpoint her 2d son.[2]

---

a Followed by *up-* deleted.   b Followed by *his* deleted.

---

[1] The royal warrant for the privy
seal was issued on 14 June. The
sum was apparently to be paid out
of the debt owing to the crown by
William Prettyman on account of
the revenue from the First Fruits
and Tenths, of which he was remembrancer (above, ii. 538 n.; iv.
394 n.); Evelyn and Mrs. Evelyn
were to be empowered to sue Prettyman for the sum: *Cal. Treasury
books, 1685–9,* pp. 1404–5.

[2] The present earl was William
Pierrepont, *c.* 1662–90; fourth earl
1682: G.E.C. Evelyn Pierrepont,
c. 1665–1726, Mrs. Pierrepont's
third, but now second surviving son,
succeeded as fifth earl of Kingston in
1690, and was created marquis of
Dorchester in 1706 and duke of

I also visited my Co: Hales[1] & her Daughter, & severall other of my Relations, now happning to be in Towne:

7 My Lord Clarendon (late Lord Lieutennant of Ireland) inviting himselfe & Lady &c to dinner to my house, I returned home this evening:

8 I went back to Lond: about my Privy-Seale, return'd home the 11th.

12 Our Viccar preach'd on 2. *Pet:* 2. 21, upon the danger of relapsing into sin: *Pomerid:*[a] a stranger on: 8. *Rom:* 19: of the unsatisfactorienesse & vanitie of all earthly things:

After this I went & heard *Monsieur La Mot,*[2] an Eloquent French Preacher at Greenewich, on: 30: *Pro:* 8. 9: A consolatory discourse to the poore & religious *Refugieès* who escaped out of France in the cruel persecution, & shewing how we ought to be content with daily bread, & chiefly seeke the bread of Life: The fullnesse of this World being dangerous, & its enjoyments so uncertaine:

After sermon, I went to see old *Monsieur de Ruvignèe,* who had ben to visite me the weeke before:

There was about this time brought into the Downes, a Vast treasure which after 45 yeares being sunk in a Spanish Galioon, which perish'd somewhere neere Hispaniola [or B⟨a⟩hama *Ilands*][b] coming home; was now weighed up, by certaine Gentlemen & others, who were [at][b] the Charge of Divers[c] &c: to the suddaine enriching of them, beyond all expectation: The Duke of Albemarles share came (tis believed) to 50000, & some private Gent: who adventured but 100 pounds & little more, to ten, 18000 pounds, & proportionably;[d] [his Majesties tenth to 10000 pounds:][e] [3]

---

[a] Followed by *the* deleted. [b] Interlined. [c] Substituted for *Engines.* [d] Or *proportionatly.* [e] Inserted after next line was written.

Kingston in 1715: *D.N.B.* He married, as his first wife, by licence dated 27 June of this year, Mary, *c.* 1668–97, daughter of William Feilding, earl of Denbigh.

[1] Above, iii. 174. She had three daughters now living: Hasted, *Kent,* ii. 434.

[2] Probably Claude-Grôteste de la Mothe, 1647–1713; refugee 1685; minister at St. Martin's Orgars 1686–9; &c.; at the Savoy 1694–1713: *D.N.B.*; Huguenot Soc., *Proc.,* xi (1915–17), 285.

[3] Hispaniola is the modern Haiti. The ship bringing the treasure home

The Camp was now againe pitch'd at Hounslow, The Commanders profusely vying in the expense & magnificence of Tents:[1]

16 I went to Lond: thence to Hampton-Court to give his Majestie thanks for his late gracious favour, though it was the granting but what was a due debt to me, [18][a] & so return'd home: Whilst I was in the Council-chamber came in a formal person, with a large roll of Parchment in his hand, being an Addresse (as he said, for he introduc'd it with a Speech) of the people of Coventry, giving his Majestie their greate Acknowledgements for his granting a liberty of Conscience: He added, that this was not onely the Application of one party, but the unanimous Addresse of C. of England men, Presbyterians, Independents, & Anabaptists, to shew how extensive his Majesties Grace was, as taking in all parties to his Indulgence & protection, had also taken a way all dissentions & animosit⟨i⟩es, which would not onely unite them in bonds of Christian Charity, but exceedingly incourage their future Industry to the Improvement of Trade in his Majesties dominions, & spreading of his Glory through out the world, & that now he had given to God his Empire, God would establish his, with Expressions of greate loyaltie & submission: and so gave the King the roll: which being return'd him againe, his Majestie caused him to reade: The Addresse was short, but much to the substance of the speech of their foreman: To whom the K. (pulling off his hatt,) sayed; That what he had don in giving liberty of Conscience, was, what was ever his judgement ought to be don, & that as he would preserve them in their injoyment of it during his reigne; so he would indeavor so to settle it by Law, that it

---

a Marginal date.

---

arrived at Deal on 7 June: *Hist. MSS. Comm., Downshire MSS.*, i. 245. For contemporary notices see Luttrell, i. 407; Bramston, pp. 282–3; modern account by C. H. Karraker, *The Hispaniola treasure*, 1934, especially pp. 54–6, where the amounts are very different from those given by Evelyn. There is an incidental notice in *London Gazette*, 4 July.

[1] The camp was to begin for the foot on 7 June, for the horse on 22 June: ibid., 2 June.

should never be alter'd by his successors: After this he gave
them his hand to kisse: It was reported the subscribers were
above 1000:¹ But this is not so remarkeable as an Addresse
of the Weeke before (as I was assured by one present) of some
of the Family of Love; His Majestie asked them what their
Worship consisted in, & how-many their party might consist
of: They told him, their costome was to reade the Scriptures,
and then to preach, but did[a] not give any farther account,
onely sayed, that for the rest, they were a sort of refined
Quakers, but their number very small, not consisting (as
they sayed) of above threescore in all, and those chiefly
belonging to the Ile of Ely:²

I din'd this day at Mr. Blathwaites³ (two miles from
Hampton); the Gent: is Secretary of Warr, Cl: of the Counsel
&c having raised himselfe by his Industry, from[b] very moderate
Circumstances: He is a very proper handsome person, and
very dextrous in buisinesse, and has besids all this married
a very greate fortune, his incomes [alone][c] by the Army, & his

---

a Substituted for *would*.　　　　　b Followed by *low ci-* deleted.
c Interlined.

---

¹ The address is printed in *London Gazette*, 20 June (notice dated 18 June; not necessarily the date on which the address was delivered).
² The Family of Love was a sect founded by Henrick Niclaes (Henry Nicholas), who is described as teaching 'an anabaptist mysticism, entirely without dogma, yet of exalted ideals'. It was introduced into England about 1555, and spread chiefly in East Anglia; there was a second flowering-time during the Commonwealth: *D.N.B.*, art. Nicholas. Evelyn describes the sect in *Hist. of Religion*, ii. 229. The address was not published in the *London Gazette*, and the king's receiving it shocked Dr. Ironside: 'When . . . I waited on your Majesty as Chaplain [in June] I was amazed to see what countenance your Majesty gave that monstrous

and scarce Christian sect, called the Family of Love, and with what respect you received an Address from them': Ironside's narrative, September 1687, in *Magdalen College and James II*, ed. J. R. Bloxam (Oxford Hist. Soc., 1886), p. 91.
³ William Blathwayt, *c.* 1649–1717; secretary at war from 1683 to 1704 (a short break in 1689); clerk of the council from 1686 to 1717 (clerk in extraordinary from 1678); clerk to the lords of trade and plantations 1675; secretary from *c.* 1679 to 1696; member of the Board of Trade, &c. He was a nephew of Thomas Povey; he married in December 1686 Mary Wynter, *c.* 1650–1691, of Dyrham Park, Somerset: *D.N.B.*; G. A. Jacobsen, *William Blathwayt*, 1932 (with portrait). The position of his house is unknown.

being Cl: of the Counsel, & Secretary to the Committeè of
Foraine Plantations brings him in above 2000 pounds per
Annum:

19 A stranger preached at Deptford excellently well both
morning & afternoon on: 7: *Matt:* 17:[1] By their fruites, you
shall know them, chiefly applied to the superstitions &
novelties of the present C: of Rome, and warning people to
take heede of their Doctrine, which (for all their pretences
⟨to⟩[a] more sanctitie and Infallibilitie) did manifestly tend to
the promoting of secular Interests, viz Indulgences, pilgrimages, Image & Relique worship; & all the Additional
Articles of the Trent Counsell, & that when ever they were
tempted by the emissaries of that party, though they should[b]
shew Miracles, they were not to be believed: because contrary to the expresse word of God, & to the rule given by the
H. Scriptures, which commands us to trie whether they will
beare the test of the Law & Prophets, & this of our B:
Saviour in the Gospel: for if what they taught, did end in
the promoting of Pride, Avarice, secular pomp, tyrannie,
[merits,][c] superstition, Idolatrie, power, deceit, [prayer to
Saints & . . . in unknown tongues][d] &c: (as the Popish Religion did) though a[e] miracle accompanied them, they were to
be detested: because any of those doctrines brought to the
touch-stone of Gods word, would be found false coyne; by
their fruits ye shall know them: Concluding with an Elogie
of the C: of England for the puritie & soundnesse of her doctrine &c:

23[f] I went to Lond: which day was his Majesties grant of
6000 pounds part of the debt due to me, passed to me by
Privy-Seale, so as that tedious affaire being dispatched & the
Privy-Seale Inrolled, I returned home the 25: Giving thankes
to God for his gracious mercy in delivering me at last from
my ruinous suite:

---

a MS. &.   b Followed by *endeavour to* deleted.   c Interlined.
d Interlined; the word omitted is illegible.   e Followed by *true*
deleted.   f Altered from *22.*

---

1 The text quoted is verse 20.

26 A stranger preached on 12: *Heb:* 5. 6. concerning the greate benefit of afflictions.

This had hitherto ben a very windy tempestuous summer: *July.* 3. Our *Viccar:* 13[a] *Luke.* 6. 7. shewing the danger of persisting in sin, by the Example of the whole Jewish nation, of whom that parable of the Tree which the Master of the Vine⟨y⟩ard spared from cutting-downe so long, seemes to have ben spoken: & is now fullfill'd to the uttmost, in their utter Excision, & in so signal a manner, as never was since the beginning of the world:

The holy Sacrament follow'd, at which I communicated: *Pomeridiano* a stranger (the Curate being dead) on 3. *Coloss:*[b] 1. shewing the vanite & ⟨unsatisfactorinesse⟩[c] of all ⟨sublunary⟩[d] things, & that there is no true repose here below:

8: To Lond, to seale an Agreement with *Sir Ch: Porter*[1] and Mr. Pretyman, returning the same day:

10 Our *Viccar* on his former Text, applying to the present danger of having the purity of the Gospel preached, taken from us, by reason of the universal profanesse, and neglect of walking religiously, having so long enjoyed the meanes. One note he had: That it being asked why God drave out the wicked Canaanites with wasps,[2] and plagued Egypt with lice & froggs & such despicable creatures; whereas he might at once [have][e] used[f] his thunder & lightning and so made a quick end of them: T'was Answered, that indeede Gr⟨e⟩ate Princes

---

 a Substituted for *15*.   b Altered from *Philip.*   c MS. *unsatisfactoriensse.*   d MS. *sublinary.*   e Interlined.
f Altered from *use.*

---

[1] Charles Porter, 1631–96; barrister, Middle Temple, 1663; knighted 1686; appointed lord chancellor of Ireland 1686; dismissed January of this year, when he returned to England; lord chancellor of Ireland 1690–6: *D.N.B.*; Le Neve, *Pedigrees*, p. 401. He had been appointed to execute the office of Remembrancer of the First Fruits and Tenths while Prettyman was suspended, and appears to have made himself responsible for the debt (or some part of it) owing by Prettyman to the crown (above, p. 551 n.); eventually Evelyn had to take action to obtain payments due from him: *Cal. Treasury books, 1681–5*, p. 471; *1689–92*, p. 434, &c.

[2] In the Bible hornets: Exodus xxiii. 28; &c.

& earthly Warriers, make use of men, & weapons of destruction, and put themselves to extraordinary charges & troubles to ruine their Enemys; but when God[a] is provoked to chastize the strongest nation & proudest Tyrannies, to shew his infinite & Almighty power, & how weake & piteous creatures men are, he[b] has no more than to bid silly flies, or an army of locusts, or any the most despicable Insect to make the warr, against the mightiest power in the Earth: so dangerous it is to provoke the greate God:

Pomerid: Our *Curate* being lately dead, a Young man[c] preached on 17: *Job*: 9. shewing what was meant by the Righteous holding on his way, perswading to perseverance: I was exceedingly drowsie, The Lord forgive:

17 our Viccar on his former Text, with no greate addition:

Pomerid: A young man who was to be Curate on 2 James 14 of the severall kinds of Faith, even to worke Miracles, yet none saving, but what worke by obedience: which he pressed reasonably well:

I went afterwards to heare the french sermon at Greenewich, coming after the sermon was newly begun, but by the discourse found the Text to be 1. Jam: 8: of the danger & sin of Inconstancy, applied to such as apostatiz'd to Popery, & the glory of suffering for the gospell:—Then I went to take leave of Monsieur Rovigny & some other French, before my Journy to my Bro:

19 I went to Wotton [with wife, daughter, son, daughter in law &c:][d] to visite my deare Bro: in the way dined at Ashsted with my Lady Mordant:[1]

24: At *Wotton* church preached one Mr. *Lucas*[2] on 5. *Eph*: 16: a very trim preacher & though very young, likely to make a good preacher:

---

a Followed by *has* deleted.
c Followed by *succeeded* deleted.

b Followed by *can* deleted.
d Interlined.

[1] No Lady Mordaunt can be traced at Ashted at this date. See above, iii. 425 n.

[2] Identifiable as Anthony Lucas, b. *c*. 1661; B.A. 1681; rector of Ribbesford, Worcs., 1689–95; a son of his was baptized at Wotton in 1687 and buried there in 1688: Foster; Wotton *Parish registers*, pp. 146, 201; &c.

31. By the same 1. *Thess:* 5. 21. & in the Afternoone at Abinger: 1 *Eccles:* 1.

3. Aug: I went to see *Albury* now purchased by Mr. Finch, son to the late L. Chancelor & Kings Soliciter: I found the Garden (which I first designed for the L. Duke of Norfolck) nothing improved:[1]

4: I went to Clandon[2] to visite Mr. Onslow, where we dined:

7 Mr. *Duncomb,*[3] Parson of Wotton, preached on 18 *Ezek:* 30, very indifferently & buisily, a very ill choise of my Bro: for that excellent living: In Afternoone at *Abinger* I heard Mr. Lucas on: 13. *Rom:* 13.

8[a] I went from Wotton to Bagshot,[4] a house [in a desolate forest:][b] & parke belonging to Mr. *Ghrame,* Master of the Buck-hounds & Privy-purse to the King; where I went to visite his Lady & her sister, formerly both Mayds of Honor, & my deare friends: [9][c] the next day to *Windsor* about buisinesse with my L. Godolphin & L: Sunderland with whom I dind[5] [(as also Lord Castle maine,[6] late Ambassador to Rome)][b] & returned by *Cranburn* an house of my L. Godolphin, & thence again to Bagshot:

14 Went again to Cranburn, & dined there, return'd to Bagshot:

15 I went to visite my L. Clarendon &c at Swallowfild,[7]

---

[a] Substituted for *3*. [b] Interlined. [c] Marginal date; substituted for *4*.

---

[1] For Evelyn's work at Albury see above, iii. 496, 561–2. Heneage Finch, no longer solicitor-general, presumably bought the estate about 1680, when Norfolk conveyed it to trustees for sale: *V.C.H., Surrey,* iii. 73.

[2] West Clandon: above, iii. 561 n. Its owner, Arthur Onslow, came into possession of his baronetcy on 12 October of this year.

[3] William Duncombe, *c.* 1648–99; M.A., Oxford, 1671; rector of Ashted 1683–99; of Wotton 1684–99: Wotton *Parish registers*; &c. He was a first cousin of George

Evelyn's first wife.

[4] Above, p. 467. The distance is about twenty miles. Mrs. Graham's sister is Lady Sylvius.

[5] The court was at Windsor from 19 May to 16 August: *London Gazette,* 23 May, 8, 18 Aug.

[6] Roger Palmer, 1634–1705; husband of Barbara Villiers (afterwards duchess of Cleveland); created earl of Castlemaine (Ireland) 1661; a Roman Catholic; ambassador at Rome 1686; left Rome 20/10 June of this year: *D.N.B.*

[7] Swallowfield: above, pp. 481–2. Lord Cornbury (above, p. 483) was

where was my L: Cornbery just then arived[a] from Denmark, whether he had accompanied the Prince of Denmark two months before & now came back: The miserable Tyrannie under which that nation lives, he related to us: the King keeping them under by an Army of above 40000 men all Germans, not daring to trust his owne subjects: notwithstanding which, that the *Danes* are exceedingly proude: The whole Country very poore & miserable: &c:[1] here was my L: *Montrah*[2] & Lady, after dinner I returned to[b] Bagshot: 17th I went back to Wotton:

21 Mr. *Lucas* on: 11. Heb: 22: & so on 22 returned home to Says-Court, having ben 5 weekes absent, with my Bro: & friends, who entertained us very nobly: God be praised for his goodnesse, & this refreshment: after my many troubles, & let his mercy & providence ever preserve me.

27 I went to Lond, to resigne a Mortgage of 1000 pounds to my Lord Sunderland, being mony lent him in my name, but belonging to my Lord Godolphin, as part of his late Wifes (my ever dearest friend) portion: & now by his Lordships desire lent to the ⟨Exchequer⟩,[c] in my name againe, the product both of this and 2000 pounds more, for the maintenance of his sonn & heire Francis Godolphin &c:[3] I returned this Evening:

---

[a] Followed by *at* deleted.   [b] Followed by *Cran-* deleted.
[c] MS. *ExChequer*, altered from *Chequer*.

---

at this time master of the horse to Prince George of Denmark: G.E.C. The latter embarked for Denmark on 17 June and returned on 15 August: *London Gazette*, 20 June, 18 Aug.

[1] For the condition of Denmark about this time see the very unfavourable *An account of Denmark, as it was in the year 1692*, by R. Molesworth (later Viscount Molesworth), 1694. This account was attacked at the time, but the general condition of the peasantry was very bad: C.-F. Allen, *Histoire de Danemark*, 1878, ii. 126–8. Molesworth gives the total for the army in Denmark and Norway as 39,500 men; they were largely of foreign origin.

[2] Charles Coote, c. 1655–1709; third earl of Mountrath (Ireland) 1672; married, 1679, Isabella, 1663–91, daughter of Charles Dormer, second earl of Carnarvon, and a granddaughter of Arthur, Lord Capel: G.E.C.

[3] A loan of £1,100 is entered on 31 August: *Cal. Treasury books, 1685–9*, p. 2183.

28 Our Viccar preached on 4: *Heb:* 1 & the Curate 2: Eph: 1. 2: floridly, like a young preacher:

The King went his greate progresse, Addresses of Dissenters every where:[1] Queene at the Bath:[2]

Sept. 3 The Lo: Mayor &c sent me an Officer with a staff to be one of the Governors of St. Tho: Hospital:

4 Our Viccar proceeded on his former Text: The B: Comm: succeeded at which I participated:

Pomerid: The Curate ⟨on⟩[a] 1. *Cor:* 5. 7. concerning the due preparation for the Sacrament.

The *Turkes* beaten this summer by Emp: & Venetians exceedingly:[3] persecution raging in France. Divers churches in France fired by lightning, Priests strucken, Consecrated hosts &c. burnt and destroyed, both at St. Malo, & *Paris* at the grand procession on *C. Christi* day.[4]

11 The *Viccar* proceeded on his former Text, concerning the danger of neglecting timely reformation:

The Curat on: 6: Rom: *ult.*

13 I went to *Lambeth* & dined with my Lord Arch-bishop, after dinner I went into the Library[5] which I found was exceedingly improved; there are also divers rare *Manuscripts* in a roome a part:

18 The *Curat* of *Deptford* morning on 9: *Heb:* 27. a florid discourse of death: *pomerid*: A stranger: on: 1. *Peter*: 4. 16. describing, & reproving the profanesse of the age: I was exceedingly Drowsy:

---

[a] MS. *of.*

---

[1] The king was on progress or at Bath from 16 August to 17 September. The *London Gazette* prints for the period from 18 August to 19 September thirty-three addresses, of which fifteen are explicitly from bodies of dissenters, the rest from boroughs or non-sectarian groups; eighteen of the addresses are due to the progress; the rest come from other parts of England, &c.

[2] Queen Mary was at Bath from 18 August until a day or two before 6 October: *London Gazette*, 8, 22

Aug., 10 Oct.

[3] This refers to the victory of the Venetians in the gulf of Lepanto about 21–4 July, N.S., and to the great Imperial victory at Harkány near Mohács on 12 August, N.S.: *London Gazette*, 22, 25 Aug., 1 Sept. The Venetians captured Athens on 28 September, N.S.

[4] This year Corpus Christi fell on 26 May, N.S. I have found no other notices of any mishaps.

[5] Above, iii. 527.

20 I went to Lond, return'd that evening:

25 Our Viccar proceeded on his former Text: The Curate on 119 Psal: 54 how becoming prayses is, whilst we are in this pilgrimage: drowsinesse surpriz'd me:

2 *Octob:* Our *Viccar* on 119 *Psal:* 68, shewing the greate attribute of God, to be his Goodnesse, & that *that*, consisted in his holinesse; & the goodnesse of man in imitating it, as being that[a] which made him the Image of his Maker: He shewed how man was[b] like to God, not as God the Sonn is like him, who is of his substance, & as our sonns &[c] children are like their fathers [(being of the same natures)];[d] but as *Cæsars* Image was like to *Cæsar*, ressembling him &c: that not onely the most inlightned of the Heathen, but[e] *Aristotle* himselfe, acknowledges that there was aliquid θεῖον, something of divine, & more than animal nature in man &c: This applied to encourage holinesse: The blessed Sacrament follow'd, of which I participated, the Lord make me thankfull:

6 I was Godfather to sir Jo: Chartins sonn[1] (the greate French Traveller), with the Earle of Bath, and the Countesse of Carlile:[2] The Child was Christn'd in Greenewich Church with much solemnitie, and it was named *John*, which was also my L: of Bathes name &c: we all dined at sir Johns in the Queenes house, where was the Marquisse of Ruvignie,[f] Young Lord Carteret,[3] Sir Jo: Fenwick,[4] & other persons of quality:

---

a Followed by *Image* deleted.   b Followed by *Gods* deleted.
c Substituted for *is*.   d Interlined.   e Substituted for *&*.
f Altered from *Ro-*.

---

[1] John Chardin, d. 1755; created a baronet 1720: G.E.C., *Baronetage*, v. 48.

[2] Either Anne, d. 1703; daughter of Edward Howard, first Baron Howard of Escrick; widow of the first earl (above, iii. 239); or Elizabeth, 1646–96; daughter of Sir William Uvedale; married first Sir William Berkeley; secondly, in 1668, Edward Howard, c. 1646–

92, second earl of Carlisle 1685: G.E.C.

[3] George Carteret, 1667–95; created Baron Carteret of Hawnes 1681; grandson of Sir George Carteret: G.E.C.

[4] John Fenwick, c. 1645–97; third baronet c. 1677; soldier and conspirator: *D.N.B.*; I.H.R., *Bull.*, v (1928), 118–20. His wife was a daughter of the first earl of Carlisle.

9 Our *Viccar* proceeded very well on his former Text:

Afternoone the Curate of Greenewich, on 4: *Matt:* 10, concerning the outward, as well as inward reverence to God. &c:

I went to Visie Coll: Roussell[1] &c:

16 Our Viccar proceeded on his former Text, perstringing the Papists for their errors in their doctrine of Repentance, Attrition[2] & Confession without amendment, as also their prayers in a language they understand not; so as they have no publique prayers in their church: *Zuares*[3] affirming it enough that the people are present, though they understand not what is sayd, contrary to all tenor of Scripture, sense of the fathers, & reason itselfe:

I was hindred by an impertinent Visit from Lond: from going to Church this afternoone, The Lord be gratious to me:

23 Our Viccar proceeded, shewing the wonderfull longsuffering & unwillingnisse of God to punish, in expectation of amendment by many example⟨s⟩:

The Curate, on 8 *Rom:* 11. that Sanctification was the surest signe of our Resurrection to Eternal life: I was very drowsy:

I tooke a Vomite & other preventing Physic, the weeke before:

26 I went to Lond: return'd the next-day:

29 Was an Anabaptist very odd[a] ignorant Mechanic, I thing a   made Lord Mayor;[4] The K: Q: Invited to feast

---

[a] Reading doubtful.

---

[1] Presumably Col. John Russell: above, p. 334. He was buried at Chenies on 25 November of this year.

[2] Horror of sin through fear of punishment, as contrasted with contrition, when it is due to the love of God: *O.E.D.*

[3] Francisco Suarez, 1548–1617, Spanish Jesuit: *Nouvelle biog. gén.* I have not traced the reference; but see *Popery not founded on Scripture*, 1688, p. 681.

[4] John Shorter, *c.* 1625–88; goldsmith; knighted 1675; sheriff of

London 1675–6; alderman 1676; superseded 1683; restored 6 August of this year; died as a result of an accident 4 Sept. 1688: Sir J. J. Baddeley, *Aldermen of Cripplegate Ward*, 1900, pp. 79–81. He had been one of the Whig candidates for the mayoralty in 1681. Luttrell describes him as 'a great presbyterian' and notes that he was permitted in the patent appointing him lord mayor 'to have whom he pleases to preach before him': i. 128–9, 411, 414; John Bunyan is described as his 'teacher, or chap-at Guild-hall, together with *Dadi*, the *Popes Nuncio*—ô strange turne of affaires, That these who scandaliz'd the Church of England, as favourers of Popery (the Dissenters[a]) should publiqly invite an Emissary from Rome, one who represented the very person of their Antichrist!

30 Our Doctor proceeded on his text, shewing the exceeding readinesse of God to pardon penetent sinners: The *Curate* on 14. *John*: 15, a Discourse of the H: Spirit:

31 I was this day sixty-seaven yeares old: ô Lord, I beseech thee, teach me so to number my daies, that I may apply them to Wisedome, & prepare for my last day, & that of thy blessed Coming:

Nov: 5 Our[b] Curate on 64 Psal 9 shewing the wonderfull deliverance[b] that God gave his Church in this Nation from that most execrable designe: the History whereof he related at large; Inviting us to depend upon God, and celebrate this mercy &c.

6 Our Viccar proceeded on his Text 119 *Psal:* 68 shewing the transitorynesse of all worldly things; the little value of them in reguard of the Soule & the making them meanes of promoting our endeavor for the world to come, with divers Arguments proving the Immortality of the Soule & a future state: with Application of the Whole: being now going to his Living at London[1] during the Winter: The Holy Communion follow'd of[c] which I participated. Blessed ⟨be⟩[d] God:

The Curate, on 13 *Heb:* 5 exhorting to Contentation in moderate things, without murmuring, distrust, or Carking & solicitude &c: I was exceeding drowsy:

I went in the Evening to pay a Visite to the Marquis de *Ru⟨v⟩ignie* &c:

13 Our *Viccar* being gon to his other living in Lond: The *Lecturer* made an excellent discourse upon Gods providence,

---

a Or *Discenters*.   b–b Altered, partly by substitution, &c., from *Our Viccar proceeded on his former Text, shewing the transitorinesse of all worldly things*; the number *64* doubtful.   c Altered from *a-*.   d MS. *by*.

---

lain': *Ellis corr.*, ii. 161. For his feast see *London Gazette*, 31 Oct.; for d'Adda, above, p. 494. The queen was not present on account of an indisposition.
[1] St. Dunstan's in the East.

from Jobe 34–27: & in the Afternoone the *Curate* on 19 *Psal:* 8 of the righteousnesse of Gods *Law* &c:

20 Our Lecturer on 27: *Job*: 56[1] made an excellent sermon against revolting from the Faith, particularly applied to the temptations of the times, & dangers of Popish Error, perswading to constancy & perseverance in the profession of the Doctrine of the Church of England, as most consonant to the Rule of Fa⟨i⟩th ⟨and⟩ the H. Scriptures, which he exhorted to examine the doctrines of our Adversaries by, with the aid, of our Spiritual Guides &c:

Pomerid: the Curate on 10. Act: 38 exhorting to the Imitation of Christ, who went about doing good: Sleep surprized me, having sate very late up, upon my daughter Susans, Indisposition &c:

24: To Lond: to finish some buisinesse: & visite severall friends:

27: Dr. Tenison at St. Martines on 25 *Eccles:* 10,[2] concerning the vanity of riches & ease and peace of moderation & discreete frugality, for Charity & good works, that never any man yet was fully satisfied, but rather more desirous & thirsty after aboundance: I dind at Sir W: Godolphins:

30 Was our Annual feast of the R: Society: we continued my L: Carbery president another Yeare:[3]

December 1 I went to visite severall of my friends, & returned home [2][a] The next day, leaving both my poore Wife & daughter very much Indisposed:

This season was Extraordinarily Wett & Tempestious.[4]

4 The Lecturer on 119 *psal:* 59. shewing the necessity of indeavoring to take the right way, which could not be don without greate Consideration, & examining & pondering our

---

[a] Marginal date.

---

[1] i.e. Job xxvii. 5, 6.
[2] An error, probably for Ecclesiastes v. 10.
[3] Birch, iv. 555. Carbery is John Vaughan, 1639–1713; presumably the John Vaughan elected a member of the Philosophical Society 20 March 1661; styled Lord Vaughan

1667–86; F.R.S. 1685; third earl of Carbery (Ireland) 1686; president of the Royal Society 1686–9: *D.N.B.*, art. Vaughan, Richard, earl of Carbery; &c.
[4] The whole of November was wet and stormy: Wood, *Life and times*, iii. 242, 244.

steps, there being so many deviations, & turnings, in our Journey, & the infinite importance of keeping the right part, for which he gave severall excellent directions: The holy Sacrament follow'd, of which I was participant, the Lord make me thankfull:

Pomerid: the Curat, on 22. Luke 19. magnifying the infinite condescention and goodnesse[a] of God our Saviour in giving us this pledge of his love, & admission to so neere relation to him, as every one had, who worthily prepares himselfe for that holy feast, & the solemnities following it, being now Advent:

10 I went to Lond to see my Wife who was Indisposed with a rhume, & staying some while to take the physitians Advice: My Son was now returned out of Devon Shire, where he had ben upon a Commission, from the Lords of the Tressury, about a Concealement of Land: I dined with the Secretary of the Admiralty[1] [upon a petition for Mr. Fowler:][b] & returned home late:

11 Our Lecturer on 12: *Rom:* ult: about forgiving Injuries: In the Afternoone, I went to visite the Marq: de Ruvigny, & heard our Comm⟨on⟩[c]-prayers[c] in French in his Chapell, that is in a Rome of the Queenes house:

19 I went to Lond: 20: that learned young-man Mr. Wake, preached at St. Martins on 11. *Matt:* 5. 6. An Advent sermon asserting Christ to be the true Messias:

I din'd at my Lady Arlingtons at Somer-set house &c:

20 I went with my Lord Chiefe-Justice Herbert,[2] to see his

---

a Spelling doubtful.   b Interlined.   c-c MS. *Com̄-prayers*.

---

[1] Pepys.

[2] Above, p. 517, &c. His estate was that attached to the palace of Oatlands; the palace itself was in the parish of Weybridge, but the greater part of the land was in Walton. The palace had been largely destroyed during the Commonwealth. In 1660 the estate reverted to Queen Henrietta Maria, who granted a lease to Henry Jermyn, Lord St. Albans; ultimately St. Albans obtained a lease extending to 1712. Herbert acquired this lease from him, and in 1688 was granted a reversionary lease for seventy-six years from 1712. It is not clear whether he occupied the remains of the palace or an older house. After the Revolution his estates were forfeited; Oatlands was granted in 1696 to his brother Arthur Herbert, earl of Torrington (below, p. 609):

house at Walton on the Thames: It is a barren place, he had
built, to a very ordinary house a very handsome Library,
designing more building to it, than the place deserves in my
opinion: He desired my advice about the laying out of his
Gardens &c: next day, we went to Waybridge, to see som
pictures of the Dutchesse of Norfolcks,¹ especialy the statue,
or Christo in Gremio,² said to be of M: Angelos; but, there
are reasons to think it rather a copy, from some proportion
in both the figures ill taken: I⟨t⟩ was now exposed to sale:
I came to Lond: the thursday after, having be⟨en⟩ exceedingly
well treated by my L. C. Justice: and so

22 Return'd to Deptford.

25 Our *Lecturer* on 72. *Psal:* 6: explaining the Incarnation
of our B: Lord: The holy Sacrament follow'd of which I
participated; the Lord make me thankfull: *Pomerid*: our
Curate *on Psal 119*: 58, shewing the necessity of serving God
with the heart:

31 I went to Lond:

[Post annum 1588, 1660, 1688. Annus mirabilis Tertius viz]ᵃ

1688. *Jan:* 1. Dr. Tenison at St. Martines; on: 1 Cor: 14.
40: shewing the good and necessity of Order & government,
& applying to the observation of the Christian festivals: The
H: Sacrament followed, at which I communicated:

4 I having visited my Wife, (who had ben still Indispos'd)
returned home:

[7 Came Sir Gilb: Talbot,³ & Sir Fr: Lawly⁴ to visite me:]ᵇ

8 The *Lecturer* on 27. *Job:* 6 vigilance against Temptations:

ᵃ This line is a later insertion at the head of the next page of the MS.;
it occurs immediately above the notice *I stirr'd not out this week* (preceding
notice for 29 Jan.).　　ᵇ Inserted after next line was written.

Manning and Bray, ii. 786–7;
V.C.H., Surrey, iii. 478; *Ellis corr.*,
ii. 60–1.
¹ Evidently the former Jane
Bickerton, widow of the sixth duke.
For her house here see above, pp.
140–1.
² i.e. Christ in the Virgin's lap,
the Pietà. Besides the group in St.
Peter's there are two unfinished
groups by Michelangelo of this subject. A sale by auction of Arundel's
collection of paintings, limnings,
and drawings, is advertised in
London Gazette, 17 Jan. 1689.
³ Above, iii. 332, 626.
⁴ Francis Lawley, d. 1696; second
baronet 1646: G.E.C., *Baronetage*,
ii. 141.

Pomerid: *Curate* on 5. *Matt:* 11. Patience & humble fortitude in persecution:

12 I went to Lond. to visite my Wife still under her course of Physick, but (I tha⟨n⟩k God) growing better:

Mr. Slingsby, Master of the mint, being now under very deplorable circumstances, upon the Account of his Creditors, & especialy the King; I did my endeavor with the Lord⟨s⟩ of the Treasury, to be favorable to him:[1]

My Lord Arran (eldest son to the Duke of Hamilton) being now married to my Lady Ann Spencer, eldest daughter of the Earle of Sunderland, Lord President of the Council: I & my family had most glorious favours, sent us: This wedding being celebrated with extraordinary splendor[2]

14[a] I went to salut & felicitate the new Lady Bride, & was most civily received by my Lord her husband, & the duke of Hamilton:[3] which ceremony perform'd I returned home:

15[b] Was a solemn & particular office used at our, & all the Churche⟨s⟩ of London, & 10 miles about it, for thankgiving to God for her Majesties being with child:[4]

Our Lecturer preached on 5 John: 22. shewing by many reasons why our Saviour, God the Son, onely, was to sit Judge at the last Assises, with a profitable Application:

The Afternoone being very tempestious, I went not to church:

22 I stayed at home all this weeke.

The Lecturer 4. Psal. 5. shewing how the Psalmes had a double respect, one, as it concerned David, & his exigencies (as this, giving God praise for his many deliverances) and

---

a The date should perhaps refer to *This wedding being celebrated.*
b Followed by *I* deleted.

[1] Slingsby had been suspended from his office of master and worker of the Mint in 1680 and had surrendered it in 1686; he was now required to account for £12,697: *Cal. Treasury Books, 1685–9*, pp. 736, 1760.

[2] For Arran see above, p. 296, &c. Lady Anne Spencer, 1666–90. The date given by G.E.C. for the marriage is probably wrong: cf. Luttrell, i. 427.

[3] Above, iii. 254; iv. 296.

[4] Proclamation for the service 23 December (reprinted in *London Gazette*, 5 Jan.). *A Form or Order of Thanksgiving, and Prayer*, 1687, was published for it. The child was the future Prince James Edward, the Old Pretender.

another respecting the future as well as present Church, & so typif⟨y⟩ing the Afflictions of our B. Saviour, in those of David, ending with a profitable exhortation:

This Afternoone I went not to Church, being to finish a Religious Treatise I had undertaken.[1]

I[a] stirr'd not out this week.

29. Our *Lecturer* pre⟨a⟩ched on 5 Gal: 24: shewing excellently well the benefit[b] of humane Passions & affections, and the care we ought to have to regulate and governe them. I went In the Afternoone to Greenewich to visite the Marquis de Ruvigny, where was publique prayers in the Chapell:

30: Being the Martyrdome day of K. Charles the First, our *Curate* made a florid Oration against the murder of that excellent Prince, with an Exhortation to Obedience: from the example of David 1. *Sam:* 24. 6.

I was not from home all this weeke:

Feb: 5 Our Lecturer proceeded on his ⟨former⟩[c] Text in Jobe, shewing the nature of Conscience, & the danger of violating it &c: The holy Sacrament followed, I received: Pomerid: a stranger: on: 14. Joh: 6. shewing how Christ is our way &c:

6: I went to Lond: about my *Quietus*.[2]

12 At St. Jame's new church forenoone Dr. Tenison on 12. Pro: 10: shewing the difference of the Mercy of the Righteous from that of the Wicked &c: The holy Sacrament (of which I participated) followed:

Din'd at the E: of Clarendons: Afternoone preached on⟨e⟩ Dr. Needham[3] Chap. to the A: Bish: of Cant: on: 2. *Rom:* 29: which I could hardly heare:

Wednesday[d] before[d] My Daughter Evelyn, going in the

---

a See note above, p. 566.   b Substituted for *necessitie*.   c MS. *forner*.   d–d Substituted for *17 After about*, which was altered before being deleted.

---

[1] This may perhaps be the work published by R. M. Evanson in 1850 as *The History of Religion*; but the wording of the notice suggests a short treatise, perhaps one to be given in manuscript to a friend.

[2] See below, p. 571.
[3] William Needham, d. 1727; matriculated at Cambridge 1671; B.D. 1685; chancellor of St. David's 1690–1727; &c.: Venn.

Coach to visite in the Citty, a Jolt (the doore being not fast-shut) flung her quite out of the Coach upon her back, in such manner, as the hind-wheles passed over both her Thighes a little above the knees: Yet it pleased God, besides the bruse of the Wheele upon her flesh, she had no other harme: We let her blood, anointed, & made her keepe bed 2 days, after which ⟨s⟩he was able to walke & soone after perfectly well: Through God Almightys greate mercy to an Excellent Wife & a most dutifull & discreete daughter in Law:

17 After above 12 Weekes Indisposition, we now returned home much recovered:

I now receiv'd[a] the sad tidings of my Niepce Montagues death, who died at Woodcot the 15th: There had ben unkindnesses & Injuries don our family by my Sister-in Law, her mother, which we did not deserve; & it did not thrive to the purposes of those who instigated her, to cause[b] her da⟨u⟩ghter to cut-off an Intaile clandestinely:[1] But Gods will be don, she has seene the ill effect of it, & so let it passe:

19 Our Lecturer preached on 1. *John*: 2. 15. upon the caution of our seting our love on any thing in this world, as a stipulation obliging all that are baptised, & the necessity, of continuing the same forme still in the Christian Church, by reason of the manyfold temptations to the love of outward things, & our proclivity to be inticed by them:

The Curate on 11: *Matt*: 22: shewing the danger of Ingratitude & neglect of Christs gracious offers &c: Sleepe exceedingly surpris'd me:

21[c] Came the Countesse of Sunderland, & other Ladys to dine with us:

26 Our Lecturer preached on 5: Ephes: v: 30: Concerning the union of Christ with the Faithfull, & thence inferring the necessity of preserving our selves pure and holy becoming so neere a tye: with encouragements to rely on Christ, as head and husband of his Church[d] as his spouse, which he would never desert &c:

---

[a] Spelling doubtful.   [b] Reading doubtful.   [c] Substituted for *26*.
[d] Followed by *&* deleted.

[1] See below, pp. 582–3; v. 86.

Mar. 4. The Lecturer preached on 1. Joh: 3. 1. shewing in paralelle[a] with paternal & filial relations on Earth; how the Saints become & in what relation they are the sonns & children of God: How Christ is Gods onely son, by Eternal Generation & nature; How we by Grace & adoption: & in the Afternoone[b] from 8. Rom: 17, what Inference we were to derive from this heavenly relation, namely our Obedience, Confidence, love & gratitude to our heavenly father: &c: The⟨re⟩ was a Communion in the morning (it being the first Sonday of Lent & of the moneth) at which I participated: The Lord blesse it to me Amen.

7[c] To Lond about my Accompt to the Lords Commissioners. I step'd in to the R: Society,[1] where a paper of Mr. Lewenhooks[2] concerning Insects &c was read:

8[c] I visited Lo: Clarendon & Mr. Boile:[3]

9 The nineth Dr. Harscat[4] preachd in W-hall Chap: before the Princesse of Denmark &c: on 16 Act. 30 about the converted jaylor, shewing in how small a compasse the primitive Christian Religion lay, as to the Credenda, perstringing the Romish & Trent addition &c: I returned home in the Evening:

11 The Lecturer on his former Text 27 Job. 6. exhorting to the searching scriptures and accordingly to make choice of our Religion, & not be impos'd upon for any secular interest &c. The Curate on 23 *Pro:* 6:[5] Concerning the care & Education of Children.

13 I went to Lond in the Evening: 14. preached Dr. Sherlock, on 24: Luke 47. shewing, that no repentance is valid, of

---

[a] Or *parabelle*; blotted.   [b] Followed by *a* deleted.   [c] Substituted for *2*.

[1] Birch's *History of the Royal Society* stops at the end of 1687; I have not attempted to check later notices of meetings in the Diary.

[2] Antony van Leeuwenhoek, 1632–1723, the naturalist; F.R.S. 1680: *Nieuw Nederlandsch biog. woordenboek.*

[3] Presumably Robert Boyle; his nephew, Henry Boyle of Castle-martyr (d. 1693; *D.N.B.*, art. Boyle, Henry earl of Shannon), is also possible, being at this time rather closely associated with Clarendon: Clarendon, *Corr.*, ii. 167, 169.

[4] Hascard; above, p. 537. Lenten sermon at court: list of preachers in *London Gazette*, 16 Jan.

[5] An error for chapter xxii.

itselfe, but through the Sacrifice of Christ: & that therefore the Sacrifices of the Jewes, did not conciliate Gods favor for presumptuos sinns; all the Mosaic rites being too narrow, & Imperfect, 'til the better Covenant tooke place: That there was no remission without blood, which those Sacrifices shed in relation to Christ, nor was this sacrifice valid til carried into Heaven, by our High Priest, & there presented befor God the Father: typified under the Law, by the Aronical[a] H. Priests entring into the S. Sanctorum: That otherwise, if upon Repentance onely, sinners should be forgiven, no Society of men could subsist: There must be blood shed & severe Justice to keepe the World in order: And Gods detestation of sinn was so greate, as he would never have pardon'd it, without the Sacrifice of his Sonn, Repentance & contrition[b] upon that account being onely available: & This an infinite[c] Comfort to penetents, that thro faith & Repentance the Sacrifice of Christ dos away & propitiats for the greatest sinns,[d] without any other Mediators, a priviledge which never was under the Law &c:[1]

14 I dined with the Countesse of Bristol:

15 I gave in my Account about the Sick & Wounded, in order to my quietus: & Visited some friends:

16 Dr. Jeane[2] Divinity Profess: at Oxon: preached at W-hall on 3: *Mal:*[e] 16 concerning the Integrity & patience of Christians in difficult times, with the certainty of Gods deliverance of them, & an happy Issue, when things seem'd to be most desperate: That by the Providence of God; The most wicked Tyrants & men, did frequently bring about, God Almightys purposes for the good of his children, defeating their Intentions. Instancing in the Malice of the Jewes against our B. Saviour to be the Instruments of the greatest blessing, that ever was bestowed on Mankind, & that by ways, contrary to all human reason, shewing the manyfold wisdome of God, & the folly of worldly pollicie,[f] concluding

---

[a] Or *Aronial.* [b] Followed by *for his sake* deleted. [c] Followed by *cause of* deleted. [d] Or *sinne.* [e] Or *Mat:* [f] Spelling doubtful.

---

[1] Lenten sermon at court. [2] Jane. Lenten sermon at court.

with an exhortation, to holy life & perseverance in our Religion, as[a] the most pure, primitive & True, of all Professions of Christians under heaven.

I return'd home in the Afternoone:

18 The Lecturer on 17: Matt: 21. of the vertue of Fasting & prayer when joyn'd together: That about the time of our B: Saviours coming, & preaching among them, There were extraordinary disseases among the people, as Leaprosies, Epilepsies, Lunatics & possessed, more than at other times, & such as were Incurable by Physic & the Skill of man; for the greater setting forth of the power of Christ, & to convince the world of his being[b] the true Messias: He shewed the wonderfull effect of Prayer joyn'd with faith, & Mortification for the performing of wonderfull difficulties, subduing Enemies, delivery from dangers, pardon of sinns, obtaining of graces &c from many Scripture Instances: Recommending frequent chastizements, selfe denyal, and vacation,[c][1] the exercises of abstinence & mortifications of our appetites, & sensual enjoyments, for spiritual advantages, & by the example of our Saviour himselfe & his Apostles &c, who used extra⟨or⟩dinary fastings and devotions before his entring into his greate office, after which followed that admirable Sermon in the mount; & so at this day dos the Church Indict a fast before Ordination, & for the obtaining of blessing to the more sollemn undertakings [as of][d] ⟨especial⟩[e] Efficacy when joyned also with Almes: upon [which][f] he tooke occasion to Exhort, to a liberal & charitable Contribution to the reliefe of the French Protestants flying from the continual raging persecution at this time; for which there was a second Briefe, read in all the Churches:[2]

---

a Altered from *&*.   b Followed by *sent* deleted.   c Comma supplied.   d Interlined.   e MS. *especialy*.   f Added later.

---

[1] Here apparently abstention from ordinary occupations: see *O.E.D.*

[2] The letters patent for the king's second brief for a general collection were sealed on 31 January. The amount collected was £19,634: Huguenot Soc., *Proc.*, vii (1901–4), 109.

I went in the Afternoone to prayers to the French Congregation at Greenewich, visiting the Marquis de Ruvigny: &c:

21 I went to Lond: heard that excellent[a] man Dr. Tenison at W:hall.[1]

23 At white-Hall Dr. Sharp on 18: ⟨*Ezek*⟩:[b] 27. 28, Excellently describing the infinite mercy of God to true penitents; with the danger of being decived by the many mistakes about it: That Teares, & even transports & satisfaction in holy performances, are not that Repentance God requires, without a perpetual progresse, an intire Reformation, an holy, usefull & Innocent life: And that for the rest of Mankind, passing under the name of Christians, there were very few, who could have any solid assurance of Salvation, whilst they indulged any the least known sin: That it was strange that any who pretended to be Christians should imagine[c] ever to come to heaven upon lesse termes than the Apostles & primitive Christians did; for no sooner did any embrace that profession, but they were immediatly changed from all their former Courses, meeke, serious, sober, & devout persons, where as now, what numbers do we see every where, who go under that name that live in abominable sinns,[d] luxury, & prophanesse: And that the reason & cause of all this, God has set downe in this text; the want of Consideration, a vertue & thing so absolutely necessary, that even in all the affaires & actions of human life,[e] all the expectation & hopes of it, we seldom or never[f] do any thing, or hope to obtaine any benefit; but men sit downe & consider, weigh and contrive by what meanes it may be accomplish'd, & shall we think that so greate & so momentous a Concerne as our Eternal Salvation should be secured to us, without thought & deepe, study of attaining;[g] Is it not worth some serious Consideration: Yes, the horrid perplexitie & confusion which

---

a MS. *ex^t*. deleted.   b MS. *Elek:* badly written.   c Followed by *to* deleted.   d Or *sinne*.   e Followed by *in* deleted.   f Followed by *obtaine* deleted.   g Or *altering*.

---

1 Lenten sermon at court. The space is left presumably for a note of it.

those who have neglected it (til they come to die) is a convincing demonstration, that it had ben worth their more timely seting about it, though to the neglect of all the rest of their Enjoyments in the world; besides the heavenly & unexpressible Contentment & satisfaction of living a truly Christian life: This was the sum:[1] I returned home.

The Bish: of Oxford, Parker who so lately published, his extravagant Treatise about Transubstantiation & for abbrogating the Test & penal Laws, died: esteem'd a Violent, passionate haughty man, but[a] being [yet][b] pressed to declare for the C. of Rome; he utterly refus'd it: A remarkable end:[2]

The Fr: Tyrant, now finding he could make no proselytes amongst those Protestants of quality & others whom he had caused to be shut up in Dungeo⟨ns⟩ & confin'd to Nunneries & Monastries; gave them after so long Tryal a general releasement, & leave to go out of the Kingdom, but Utterly taking away their Estates, & their Children; so as greate numbers came[c] daily into England & other places, where they were received & relieved with very Considerable[d] Christian Charity: This providence and goodnesse of God to those who thus constantly held out; did so work upon those miserable poore soules, who to avoy'd the persecution, sign'd their renuntiation, & to save their Estates, went to Masse; That reflecting on what they had don, grew so afflicted in their Consciences, as not being longer able to support it; They Unanimously in infinite number thro all the french provinces; Acquaint the Magistrats & Lieutenants that being sorry for their Apostacy; They were resolved to returne to their old Religion, that they would go no more to Masse, but peaceably assemble where they could, to beg pardon & worship

---

a Substituted for &.   b Interlined.   c Substituted for *coming*.
d Or *Considerate*.

---

[1] Lenten sermon at court.
[2] Parker (above, p. 519) died at Oxford on 20 March. A notice of the death, the day not stated, in *Publick Occurrences*, 27 March. Evelyn refers to his *Reasons for abrogating the Test, Imposed upon*

All Members of Parliament Anno 1678. Octob. 30, 1688 (published 16 Dec. 1687: Wood); in it Parker attempts to reconcile the Roman Catholic doctrine of Transubstantiation with the Anglican conception of the Real Presence.

God, but so without weapons, as not to give the least umbrage of Rebellion or sedition, imploring their pitty & com-
misseration: And accordingly meeting so from time to time,
The Dragoon Missioners, popish[a] Officers & Priests, fall upon
them, murder & put to death who ever they could lay hold
on, who without the least resistance embrace death, torture
& hanging, with singing ⟨psalmes⟩[b] & praying for their persecutors to the last breath; yet still continuing the former
Assembly of themselves in desert places, suffering with
incredible Constancy, that through Gods mercy they might
obtaine pardon for this Lapse: Such Examples of Christian
behaviour has not been seene, since the primitive Persecution, by the Heathen: & doub⟨t⟩lesse God will do some sig-
nall worke in the end, if we can with patience & christian
resolution hold out, & depend on his Providence:[1]

25 Our Lecturer pursued his former subject, with excellent[c]
advise concerning the necessity, order & effect of prayer:

28 I went to Lond: in the Evening, the next morning with
Sir Charles Littleton[2] to *Sheene* an house & estate given him
by my Lord Brounchar, one who was ever noted for an hard,
covetous, vicious man, had severall Bastards; but for his
worldly Craft, & skill in gaming &c: few exceeding him:
Coming to die,[d] he bequeathed all his Land, House, furnitur
&c intirely to Sir Charles, to whom he had no manner of
Relation, but an antient friendship,[e] contracted at the famous
siege of Colchester 40 yeares before:[3] It is a pretty place,[f]
fine gardens and well planted, & given to one worthy of them,
Sir Charles being an honest Gent, & souldier; & brother to

---

a Altered from *pr-*   b MS. *plalmes*.   c MS. *ex^t*.   d Altered
from *dy*.   e Followed by *ever* deleted.   f Comma supplied.

---

[1] For the failure to convert the
Protestants, the expulsion of the
unconvertable, and the formation of
the assemblies of the Desert, see
Benoist, iii (v). 989–1002; Lavisse,
VIII. i. 349–60.

[2] Charles Lyttelton, *c*. 1629–1716;
knighted *c*.1662; third baronet 1693;

soldier, &c.: *D.N.B.* For his house
at Sheen see above, pp. 142–3.
Brouncker is Henry, the third viscount, who died on 4 January of
this year: above, iii. 578, &c.

[3] In 1648. I have found no other
notice of the presence of either man
at the siege.

Sir Hen: Littleton[1] of Worster shire, whose greate Estate he is to Intaile, his Bro: being without Children: They are ⟨descendents⟩[a] of the greate Lawyer of that name[2] & give same Armes & motto: He is married to one ⟨Mrs⟩.[b] Temple[3] (formerly maide of Honor to the late Queene,) a beautifull Lady, & has many fine Children; so as none envy his good fortune.

After dinner (at his house) we went to see Sir William Temples, neere to it:[4] The most remarkeable thing, is his Orangerie & Gardens; where the wall Fruite-trees are most exquisitely nailed & applied, far better than in my life I had ever noted:

There are many good Pictures, especialy of V. dykes, in both these houses, & some few statues & small busts in the later:[5]

From hence we went to *Kew*, to Visite Sir Hen: Capels, whose Orangerie & Myrtetum,[6] are most beautifull, & perfectly well kept: He was contriving very high palisados[c] of reedes, to shade his Oranges in during the Summer, & painting those[d] reedes in oyle:

We return'd to Lond: in the Evening:

⟨30⟩[e] Dr. Megot, Deane of Winchester, preached at W: hall, on 10: Heb: 36 Recommending patience & perseverance, in time of trouble, & persecution of the Church: magnifying the Reforme'd, who though requiring Repentance, & holynesse, exacted no superstitious pennances, Pilgrimages, but for-

---

[1] Henry Lyttelton, *c.* 1624–93; second baronet 1650; royalist: *D.N.B.*, art. Lyttelton, Sir Thomas.

[2] Sir Thomas Littleton, 1422–81, the judge and author of the 'Tenures': *D.N.B.* The descent, arms, &c., are given in J. Wotton, *English Baronets*, 1727, i. 125–9.

[3] Anne, *c.* 1649–1718; daughter of Thomas Temple of Frankton, Warwickshire; married Lyttelton (as his second wife) 1666; she had previously been a maid of honour to the duchess of York: G.E.C., *Baronetage*, i. 117–18; see also Grammont.

[4] Above, p. 143. The house was occupied at this time by Sir William's son, John Temple, *c.* 1655–89 (*D.N.B.*, art. Temple, Sir William): Woodbridge, *Sir William Temple*, p. 53 n.

[5] Lyttelton's pictures included a copy of Vandyck's portraits of Charles I: *Hatton corr.*, ii. 169, 171–2.

[6] The Latin word; apparently not found elsewhere in English.

saking of sinn, Innocence, Integrity and persistence ⟨in⟩[a] the
Faith, as what would certainly leade to inherite the
promises:[1]

Aprill 1 In the morning the first sermon[2] was preach'd by
Dr. Stillingfleete: Deane of St. Paules on 10: Luke 41. 42.
Insisting on a Speedy Turning from sin, without delay, from
the approbation of our B. Saviour, concerning Mary, who had
taken the better part, that one thing Necessary; The prefer-
ring the hearing her[b] blessed Lord & Saviour, to all the enjoyments of Secular things whatsoever; about which so many
buisie themselves, leaving the maine thing undon, or put off
to the last; & exaggerating the infinite danger of it, by this,
That we never read, or have any encouragement, almost to
hope, of the Salvation of death-bed penitents, the Thiefe on
the Crosse excepted, upon the Circumstance of which he
much delated, shewing, that there could never be the like
after it, & thence the danger of presuming on it: He tooke
also occasion to shew, by the parable of Lazarus, & the words
of our Saviour to the faithfull Thiefe, That departed soules
of the Saints, were immediately received into Paradise,
places of infinite Joy & comfort, without any such thing as
passing Purgatory &c: The H. Communion follow'd, but was
so interrupted, by the rude breaking in of multituds[c] into the
Chapell, zealous to heare the second sermon, to be preached
by Dr. Ken: Bish: of Bathe & Wells; that the latter part of
that holy Office could hardly be heard, or the Sacred Elements
distributed, without greate trouble: The Princesse being
come, The Bishop preached on 7: Mich: 8. 9. 10: Describing
the Calamity of the Reformed Church of Judah, under the
Babylonish persecution, for her sinns; &[d] Gods certainely
delivering her, upon her Repentance & patience, and therefore advising that her Enemy should not Insult over her
calamity; for that though the Church should sit in the darke,
& under all imaginable Circumstances of being deserted for

---

[a] MS. *on.*   [b] Altered from *our.*   [c] Or *multitude.*   [d] Followed
by *th-* deleted.

---

[1] Lenten sermon at court.   [2] To the household.

her sinns; though the time should be long; she should certainly rise againe & be delivered, by him who would avenge her Enemys, as God did, upon the Edomites her apostate brother & neighbours, rejoicing in her Calamity, & the Babylonians designing her destruction: That yet by Gods providence from this Captive desolate state as[a] Juda emerged; So should[b] the now[c] Reformed Church, where ever persecuted & Insulted over: & therefore exhorting to patience, & Reformation, and waiting on Gods Providence, for that Salvation should come, even out of the dust: Victory without [other][d] Weapons[e] of his people [than prayer & ⟨reformation⟩] ;[f] That when they threw away their Swords, submitted to Tyrannous princes, God would take them up in his Churches defence, & revenge their wrongs: & therefore Exhorted all degrees of men, to a serious amendment of life; for the more speedy & Effectual deliverance: This he preached with his accustom'd action, zeale & Energie, so as people flock'd from all quarters[g] to heare him.[1]

I Return'd this Evening home:

6 I went to Lond: Dr. Patrick preached [Whitehall][d] on 9. *John*: 4 shewing the exceeding danger of procrastinating repentance & reformation of life, & deferring til death bed Repentance:[2]

8: A stranger preached on: 1. *Cor:* 9. 24: shewing, the greate difficulty & hazard of attaining Eternal life, & that amongst all the Contenders, in a race, but one gets the prise: &c: second sermon: By Dr.[h] Leven,[3] Bish: of Man: on 5 *Eph:* 14: Inciting to Vigilancy &c:

11. Dr. Cradock, Provost of Eaton: on: 2. *Heb:* 14. 15.

---

a Followed by *the* deleted.   b Followed by *now* deleted.   c Or *new*.   d Interlined.   e Followed by *from* deleted.   f Interlined; MS. has *reformate*.   g Or *quarter*.   h Altered from *B-*; preceded by *the*, not deleted.

---

[1] Lenten sermon at court. It is printed in Ken, *Prose works*, ed. J. T. Round, 1838, pp. 174–206. The text is verses 8 and 9 only.

[2] Presumably a lenten sermon at court; but the preacher listed is Tillotson.

[3] Baptist Levinz, *c.* 1644–93; D.D. 1683; bishop of Sodor and Man 1685: *D.N.B.* Lenten sermon at court; but the preacher listed is Archbishop Sancroft.

&c: Concerning Christs undertaking the Salvation of man-
kind by becoming man, & the Assurance, & comfortable
hopes the Faithfull have & even the greatest of sinners, by
being partakers of Christs humane nature, so they take hold
of this relation by a timely sincere conversion &c:[1]

13 Good friday at St. *Martins* Dr. Tenison, on 9 Heb: 25.
26 &c The infinite Comfort & Assurance Penetents have,
by Christs death, Resurrection & Ascention,[a] by all which he
has expiated the greatest sinns, sinns for which the Mosaic
dispensation had no sacrifice to propitiate for, as Murder &
Adultery &c: upon which David gos to God for Pardon: If
sacrifice & burnt offeringes (which were available for other
lesser faults) would have don it, he would have given them
in aboundance; but God would have none of them: & There-
for he flies to his Mercy to a broken & Contrite heart: That
the blood carried into the Sanctuary by the Priest once a
yeare, & was a type of what Christ should do,[b] was of those
Sacrifices which could not make those perfectly holy, who
offer'd & presented them in the name of all the people;
because this was yet imperfect ⌊& the offerer himself a mortal
man][c] & was to be yearely reiterated: Til Christ, who was the
most pure [immortal][c] & Eternal High-priest, offer'd himselfe, & when he asscended carried in the blood into heaven,
& truely holy place,[d] that is, the merits of that blood &
sacrifice which he shed & offered on the Crosse, which,[e] not
as of old in figure & with the blood of Bulls & beasts, offered
by a fraile mortal High Priest; but by Christ our Immortal
High-priest: mortal indeede for our sakes, but not of his
owne Nature, & therefore the grave could not hold him, nor
his blessed body corrupt: as ours dos: This offering of that
Efficacy therefore, not to be repeated; but being Once alone[f]
imolated, was sufficient; had it not ben so, it would neede to
be renew'd, as the Aaronical H. priests yearely was, but this

---

a Comma supplied.   b Followed by *who* deleted.   c Interlined.
d Followed by *whi-* deleted.   e Followed by opening bracket
f Followed by *offer-* deleted.

---

[1] Lenten sermon at court.

being perfect and aboundantly expiatory, How greatly dos the late Council of Trent, derogate from the validity of this sacrifice, whilst in their Masses, they repeate this offering of Christ, as if what he once offered,[a] ware not enough; except they helped it out by their pretended sacrifices: There is indeede frequent mention of sacrifices amongst the antients writings, but they are onely Commemorations of this of our Saviours, as was shewed, by divers Instances, & the Sacrifice of the H: Eucharist is no other, in relation to this one, once alsoficient oblation of Christ: in vertue of what he our Eternal H. Priest, has Carried in to Heaven, where he sits to make Intercession for us by that Sacrifice, & is so Interceding til he comes to Judgement; & therefore cannot come bodily downe into the Popish Masse to be every day sacrificed anew, as they most erroneously & dangerously opine: Concluding with an Exhortation of accesse to this onely propitiatory[b] Sacrifice: of Christ at the Right hand of God: The Holy Communion follow'd, at which I participated: & it was a blessed day to me, The L: Jesus be praised:[c]

Afternoone at White-hall, Dr. *Sprat* Bish: of *Rochester*:[1] on 3 *Phil:* 8. 9. 10 &c shewing the invaluablenesses of the merit of Christs sufferings, for the reward of those who love him & obey him, in comparison of this wretched world, by S. Paules undervalluing all those greate privileges he had by his birth,[d] acquired parts, & Interest he had in being a Jew: He shewed that this Conformity to the death of Christ, was our imitation of his blessed life, which was the application: I returned home after this Sermon was don:

15 *Easter day*, at *Deptford*, our *Viccar*, on 14. Rom: 9. The whole discourse being touching the power & dominion of *Christ*, whom God had made Lord & Judge of all things: The holy Communion follow'd, of which I participated:

---

[a] Followed by *had* deleted.   [b] Or *propitiating*.   [c] Followed by *I return'd home this Evening:* deleted.   [d] Followed by *&* deleted.

---

[1] Sprat, as dean of Westminster, is listed to preach this day's lenten sermon at court. Afternoon in Evelyn's text is perhaps wrong, but I have met with no evidence for the hours of services at this date.

Pomeridiano our Curate on: 1. *Cor:* 15. 20, a florid discourse on the Resurrection.

It was now a very dry, cold easterly windy, backward Spring:[1]

The Turkish Empire in greate intestine Confusion:[2] The French persecution still raging, multitud⟨e⟩s of Protestants & many very Considerable greate & noble persons flying[a] hither, produced a second general Contribution: The papists, (by Gods providence)[b] as yet making small progresse amongst us.

22 Dr. Huttchins on 14. *Joh:* 6. shewing how Christ was the true way to life Eternal, all other ways, deviations &c:

29 Dr. *Hutchins* on his former Text, with Application of keeping in the way which Christ has directed, in these deviating times, especialy by following his voice in the Gospel, where we can onely heare ⟨it⟩[c]; & to beware of Seducers, which would now forbid people to looke into it: The Curate on 16: *Mark:* 15. shewing in what sense the Disciples were to preach to all the Creatures, (i) to man kind; his chiefe scope being, to[d] insinuate that the Word read is as much Gods, as if it were preached: some of the parish (I suppose) taking exceptions that he allways read his sermons &c:[3]

The weather was until now so cold & sharp, by an almost perpetual East wind, which had continued many moneths, that there was little appearance of any Spring; & yet the winter was very favourable as to frosts or Snow:[4]

May 1: Met the foefees for the poore of Deptford:

2 To Lond: about my petition for allowances upon the

---

[a] Or *slipping*.   [b] Closing bracket supplied.   [c] MS. *of*.
[d] Followed by *tell* deleted.

---

[1] Cf. Wood, *Life and times*, iii. 263.

[2] There were disturbances at Constantinople in February: *London Gazette*, 23 April.

[3] Anglican preachers at this time generally preached by memory or from notes; Tillotson is said to have read his sermons, but this was very unusual in a preacher of his eminence: Mitchell, *English pulpit oratory*, pp. 22–6. The Deptford curate's florid style (above, p. 560) presumably made reading indispensable.

[4] Wood notes heavy snowfalls at Oxford on 3–5 April, followed by storms: *Life and times*, iii. 263.

Accompt of Commissioner for sick & wounded in the former war with Holland:

6 Dr. Tenison preached on 8: *Pro:* 11: concerning the True Wisedome, which was the feare of God, directing to all other prudence: The Holy Sacrament follow'd, I received: blessed be God:

8: I returned home: His Majestie alarm'd by the greate Fleete of the Dut⟨c⟩h (whilst we had a very inconsiderable one & to our greate reproch) went down to chatham:[1]

13 Mr. *Winnell*[2] on 13: *John:* 35, exhorting to mutual love & charity:

Pomeridiano, the Curate, on 2. Joell. 12: Exhorting to mortification & Repentance:

The Hollanders did now al'arme his Majestie with their fleete, so well prepar'd & out before we were in any readinesse, or had any considerable number to have encounter'd them had there ben occasion, to the greate reproch of the nation, whilst being in profound peace, there was a mighty Land Army, which there was no neede of, & no force by Sea, where onely was the apprehension;[3] [at present, but was doub⟨t⟩-lesse kept & increased in order to bring in & Countenance Popery, the K beginning to discover his intention by many Instances, perverted[a] by the Jesuites against his first seeming resolution to alter nothing in the Church Established,[b] so as it appeared that there can be no relyance ⟨o⟩n Popish promises.][c]

17 I went to Lond, to meete my Bro: G. Evelyn about our mutual concerne in the will of my Bro: Richard, by which,

---

[a] Reading doubtful. [b] MS. *Estab^l.* [c] Inserted later, mainly in margin.

---

[1] The king was at Chatham from 8 to 10 May: *London Gazette,* 10 May. The rumours about the Dutch preparations are dismissed in *Publick Occurrences,* 15 May, as being the usual setting out of convoys in the spring. This was certainly an understatement. For the English preparations about this time see *English hist. review,* viii (1893), 272 ff.

[2] The name is generally spelled Whinnell. The most likely identification is with Philip Wynell, b. *c.* 1647; B.A., Oxford, 1667: Foster.

[3] The army appears to have numbered nearly 35,000 officers and men about this time: Walton, *British standing army,* p. 496.

my Niepce Montague dying without issue, a considerable Estate ought to have returned to our Family, after the decease of her husband: but thro the fraude[a] & unworthy dealing of her mother, (my[b] sister in-Law), the intaile had ben cut off & a recovery pass'd & consequently the Estate given to her husband Montag⟨u⟩e, through the perswasion of my sister[c] contrary to the intent of her husband my brother, & that to a son-in law who had lived dissolutly & Scandalously with another woman, & his dishonesty made publiquely notorious: What should move my sister in Law, professing so greate love to the memory of her husband, to [cause my Niepce to][d] give away not onely this, but considerably more, to a son in law, who had no Issue, from all her husbands relations, was strangely spoken off, especialy to one who had so scandalously & so basely abused her da⟨u⟩ghter:[1]

18 The King injoyning [the ministers][d] the Reading his declaration for giving liberty of Conscience (as it was styled) in all the Churches of England: This Evening six *Bishops*, *Bath* & Wells, *Peterborow, Ely, Chichester, St. Asaph*, & *Bristol*, (in the name of all the rest) came to his Majestie to petition him that he would not impose the reading of it to the[e] severall Congregations under their diocesse: not that they were averse to the publishing of it, for want of due tendernes towards dissenters, in relation to whom they should be willing to come to such a temper, as should be thought fit, when that matter might come to be consider'd & settled in parliament & Convocation: But that the *declaration being founded upon such a dispencing power, as might at pleasure*[f] *set aside all Lawes Ecclesiastical & Civil*, it appeared to them *Illegal*, as doing so to the parliaments in

---

a Or *frauds*.   b Some words and parts of words in this and the following lines are lost in a blot.   c Followed by *whilst* deleted.
d Interlined.   e Altered from *their*.   f Followed by *be* deleted.

[1] For Anne Montagu's death see above, p. 569. From an abstract of Richard Evelyn's will (Foljambe, p. 46) it appears that Baynards (above, ii. 539), with some other property, was settled on him and his wife for their lives, with remainder in default of heirs male to George Evelyn; it was this entail that Anne Montagu broke: see below, 29 Jan. 1692.

-61 & 72; & that it was a point of such Consequence, as they could not so far make themselves parties to it, as the Reading of it in the Church in the time of divine service amounted to.

The King was so far incensed at this Addresse, that he with threatning expressions commanded them to obey him in reading of it at their perils; & so dismis'd them:[1]

20[a] I went to Church in White-hall Chapell, where after the morning lessons; The Declaration was read, by one of the *Coire* who used to reade the Chapters:[2] Then followed the sermon, preached by Dr. *Scott*[3] on 14 *John*: 17 making an eloquent [& pious][b] discourse upon the vicissitudes of worldly things. I heare it was also read in the Abby at Westminster; but almost universaly forborne throughout all London;[4] the Consequences of which, a little time will shew:

I returned home in the Evening:

23 I went to Lond, 24 Ascension-day to Lond:[c] the Scholemaster of St. Martines[5] preached an excellent sermon, shew-

---

a Followed by *After the Lessons, one of the m-* deleted.   b Interlined.
c Followed by *the Lecturer* deleted.

[1] James reissued his Declaration of Indulgence on 27 April; and on 4 May ordered in Council that it should be read at the time of divine service in all churches and chapels in and near London on 20 and 27 May; and in all other churches and chapels on 3 and 10 June: *London Gazette*, 30 April, 7 May. On this day a meeting of some of the bishops and other clergy was held at Lambeth; the petition was drawn up and was presented to the king by the six bishops, i.e. Ken, Thomas White, Francis Turner, Lake, William Lloyd the apocalyptic, Sir Jonathan Trelawney (above, p. 299); it was also signed by Sancroft. For it and the king's reception of it see Gutch, *Collectanea curiosa*, i. 336-40; it was printed and circulated this night. The passage quoted by Evelyn runs: 'That Declaration is founded upon such a dispensing power, as hath often been declared illegal in parliament . . . and is a matter of . . great moment and consequence to the whole Nation, both in Church and State.'

[2] 'At Whitehall the Declaration was read by one of the *singing men* —by special order from the Lord Chamberlain': Thomas Smith, bishop of Carlisle, in *Hist. MSS. Comm., Le Fleming MSS.*, p. 210.

[3] Probably John Scott, *c.* 1639-95; D.D. 1685; chaplain in ordinary *c.* 1692-5: *D.N.B.*

[4] Bishop Sprat was dean of Westminster; for the reading of the declaration in the Abbey see Dartmouth's note to Burnet, 1833, iii. 229. It is reported to have been read in only about half a dozen churches and chapels in London.

[5] Presumably John Postlethwayt, 1650-1713; master in charge of Tenison's school 1688-97?; high master of St. Paul's School 1697-

ing how Piety & religion contributed to thriving [& happi-
ness]ᵃ evenᵇ in this world amongst Christians, as well ⟨as⟩
among the Jewes, by divers Instances, on   It was not so
proper for the day, as profitable to the Auditorie, in this
vicious age: The holy Sacrament followed, of which I
participated:

25 I visited Dr. Tenison, Secretary Pepys, of the Admiralty,
Mr. Boile, Coll: Philips¹ and severall of my Friends, all the
discourse now being about the Bishops refusing to reade
[the injunction for the abbrogation of]ᶜ the Test &c:² It
seemes the Injunction came so crudely from the Secretarys
office, that it was neither sealed nor sign'd in forme,³ nor had
any Lawyer ben consulted; so as the Bishops who tooke all
imaginable advice, put the Court to greate difficulties how to
proceede against them: Greate were the Consults, and a
Proclamation expected all this day;⁴ but no thing don: The
action of the Bishop⟨s⟩ universaly applauded, & reconciling
many adverse parties, Papists onely excepted, who were now
exceedingly perplex'd, & violent courses every moment expected: Report was the Protestant Secular Lords & nobility
would abett the Cleargy: God knows onely the event.

The Queene Dowager obstinately bent hitherto on her
returne into Portugal, now on the suddaine, upon pretence o
a greate debt owing her by his majesties,ᵈ disabling, declares
her resolution to stay:⁵

Newes of the most prodigious Earthquake, that was almost

ᵃ Interlined.   ᵇ Followed by *in this world, as well as* deleted.
ᶜ Interlined, probably later.   ᵈ MS. *maᵗˢ.* apparently.

1713: *D.N.B.* Tenison's school was
opened on 23 April in reply to the
opening of the various Roman
Catholic free schools: Luttrell, i.
437; Patrick, Autobiography, in
Works, ix. 506; see also above, p.
368 n.; for the masters, Strype's
Stow, vi. 73.
   ¹ Above, p. 513.
   ² The Declaration suspended the
Test Acts as well as the penal laws.
   ³ The Injunction is presumably
the Order in Council of 4 May:

above, p. 584 n. This point was
not raised at the trial of the bishops.
   ⁴ On 27 May it was decided to
prosecute the bishops; for the period
before this decision was made and
a proposed declaration see Mackintosh, *Hist. of the Revolution*, pp.
253–6.
   ⁵ Queen Catherine announced
her intention of remaining in England on 24 May: *Publick Occurrences*, 29 May.

ever heard of, subverting the Citty of *Lima* & Country inᵃ
Perù, with the dreadfull Innundation following it:¹

26 I returned home.

27 Our *Curate* on 12 *Matt:* 36, against swearing & idle
words: my Wife being indispos'd weᵇ hadᵇ prayers & sermon
at home this afternoone: Came Sir J. Jardin² to visite us:

June ⟨3⟩ᶜ Whitsonday, our *Viccar* on 4: *Eph:* 30, shewing
the meaning of the Spirit in that Text, & how it was a seale
of Gods promises in Christ; through all the resemblances &
effects of a seale, to convey grace & establish us in the
heavenly Inheritance &c: The holy Communion followed at
which I participated: The Lord make me thankfull:

In the afternoone the Curate:

7 Dined at my house the Countesse of Sunderland, Bristol,
Clancartie³ & severall other Ladys:

8 This day were the Arch-Bishop of Canterbery together
with the Bishops of Ely, Chichester, St. Asaph, Bristol,
Peterborow & Bath & Wells, sent from the Privyᵈ Council,
Prisoners to the Tower, for refusing to give baile for their
appearance (upon their not reading the Declaration for
Liberty of Conscience) because in giving baile, they had pre-
judiced their Peerage: Wonderfull was the concerne of the
people for them, infinite crowds of people on their knees,
beging their blessing & praying for them as they passed out
of the Barge; along the Tower wharfe &c:⁴

10ᵉ A young Prince borne &c.⁵ [which will cost dispute.]ᶠ

10 Dr. *Bohune* preached this Trinity-Sonday on 2. *Rom:*
15. making an excellent discourse upon the operation of

ᵃ Followed by *Ame-* deleted.   ᵇ⁻ᵇ Altered from *I read.*   ᶜ MS. *2.*
ᵈ MS. *Pr.*   ᵉ Followed by *A little after dinner* deleted.   ᶠ Added
later.

---

¹ Notice from *London Gazette,*
24 May. Lima was ruined by earthquakes on 20 Oct. 1687, while
Callao, &c., were flooded by the sea.
² Chardin.
³ Presumably the younger Lady
Clancarty: above, p. 450.

⁴ For the proceedings at the
council see Gutch, *Collectanea
curiosa,* i. 347–53. For the bishops'
progress to the Tower see Mackintosh, p. 258.
⁵ James Francis Edward Stuart,
d. 1766, the Old Pretender.

Conscience approving or disapproving all our actions, for the convincing men of a Deity, & of a judgement to Come:

About two a clock, we heard the Toure Ordnance discharge, & the Bells ringing; for the Birth of a Prince of Wales; This was very surprizing, it being universaly given-out, that her Majestie did not looke til the next moneth:[1]

Dined with me the young *Marq: de Ruvigny* & Sir J. Jardine:

In the Afternoone, preach'd a very young man: on 2. Heb: 3:

13 I went to the Tower to see the Bishops now there in Prison, for not complying with his Majesties commands to Cause his declaration to be read in their Diocesse;[a] where I visited the *A: Bish:* B: of Ely, Asaph, & Bath & Wells:

[14 Dined with my L. Chancelor—][b]

15 The Bish: came from the Tower to Westminster upon their *Habeas Corpus* & after divers houres dispute before the Judges, by their Counsel, upon security to appeare friday fortnight, were dismiss'd: Their Counsel alledged false Imprisonment & abatement of their Committment for want of some words: Denyed the paper given privately to the K. to be a seditious libel or that it was ever published: but all was over-ruled: W⟨r⟩ight, *Alibon*, Hollowell & Powell were the Judges: Finch, Sawyer, Pollixfen & Pemberton, their Counsel, who pleaded incomparably, [so as the Jury quitted them.][c 2] There was a lane of people from the Kings Bench to

---

a Punctuation supplied.   b Interlined.   c Interlined later.

[1] The prince was born about 10 a.m.: *London Gazette*, 11 June. According to Anne the queen expected him to be born a month later: Queen Mary II, *Lettres et mém.*, ed. Bentinck, 1880, pp. 42–3.

[2] Evelyn apparently brings together the proceedings on 15 June, when the bishops were brought before the court of king's bench by writ of habeas corpus, and urged false imprisonment, &c.; and those on 29 June, when they were tried and the questions of publication

and of the nature of the petition were discussed; the verdict was delivered on 30 June: *The Proceedings and Tryal*, &c., 1689. The judges are Sir Robert Wright; Sir Richard Allibone, Sir Richard Holloway, and Sir John Powell; the bishops' counsel Heneage Finch, Sir Robert Sawyer, (Sir) Henry Pollexfen, and Sir Francis Pemberton, as well as Sir Creswell Levinz and John Somers, the future lord chancellor: for them all see *D.N.B.*

the water-side, upon their knees as the Bishops passed & repassed to beg their blessing:[1] Bon fires made that night, & bells ringing, which was taken very ill at Court[2] and an appearance of neere 60[a] Earles & Lords &c upon the bench in honor of the Bishops, & which did not a little comfort them; but indeede they were all along full of Courage & cherefull:[3]

Note that they denyed to pay the Lieutennant of the Tower: (Hales[4] who us'd them very surlily) any Fees, denying any to be due:

I[b] Introduc'd Sir Jo: Hoskins[5] Master of the Chancery to my Lord[c] President, who received him being in bed: &c:

Supped at the E: of Clarendons, where I found the Bishops of St. Asaph, and Norwich[6] &c:

16[d] I return'd home.

17 Was the day of Thanksgiving in Lond: & 10 miles about, for the young Princes Birth, a forme of prayer made for the purpose by the B: of Rochester:[7]

---

[a] Perhaps altered from *70*.
[c] Followed by *Sun-* deleted.
[b] Preceded by date *16* deleted.
[d] Altered from *17*.

---

[1] This was on 15 June: 'All the way, as they came from the bridge [the pier, probably Westminster Stairs], where they landed, to the very court, the people made a lane for them, and begged their blessings': Clarendon, *Corr.*, ii. 177. It is not clear whether Evelyn was present at any part of the trial; the similarity of his language to Clarendon's suggests that he derived his information from Clarendon. There was a similar scene in Westminster Hall after the acquittal: Luttrell.

[2] The great rejoicings took place on 30 June after the acquittal. For the king's displeasure at them see Reresby, 10 July. There were also bonfires on the night of 15 June, for the bishops' release on bail: Luttrell; and on 17 June for the prince's birth: see below.

[3] Eighteen peers are named as having been present on 15 June and twenty-nine on 29 June: *Proceedings and Tryal*. The latter number is probably nearly correct. The bishop of Carlisle expected the bishops to be found guilty: *Hist. MSS. Comm.*, *Le Fleming MSS.*, p. 211.

[4] Hales took up office as lieutenant of the Tower on 14 May 1687: *Ellis corr.*, i. 297.

[5] Hoskins (above, pp. 212, 296) was a master in chancery from 1677 to 1703.

[6] Lloyd the apocalyptic and Lloyd the non-juror. Clarendon mentions the former as supping with him; but not the latter or Evelyn.

[7] Proclamation for the celebration 10 June (reprinted in *London Gazette*, 14 June). The service was published as *A Form of Prayer with*

Our Viccar preached on 4: *Eph:* 30: of the danger of grieving the H: Spirit: [& how he was a Seale of Redemption.]ᵃ
Afternoone the Curate on

[The two Judges Holloway & Powel, who dissented from
Alibon about the Bishops Adresse not being a scandalous
libell, had their writs of Ease:]ᵃ ¹

The night was solemniz'd with Bonfires & other Fire
workes &c:²

23 Came Dr.   Master of Balliol Coll:³ Oxon to visite me.

24: Our Viccar being indisposed, Dr. Hutchins preached
on: 14: John: 6. &c:

28 I went to Lond: about my petitions & grants: &c:

July 1 Dr. Tenison preach'd at St. Martines 10: Heb: 23:ᵇ
exhorting to a stedfastnesse in the Faith. The holy Communion followed,ᶜ which I received: The Lord blesse it to
me:

2 I dind at my L. Godolphins where was the Duke of
Grafton, L: Dover, &c:

3 I went with Dr. Godolphin [(& his bro: Sir William)]ᵃ to
St. Albans to see a library which he [would have]ᵃ bought of
the Widow of Dr. Cartwrite,⁴ late Arch-deacon of St. Albans,
a very good collection of Books, especial Divinity: he wasᵈ
to giveᵈ for them 300 pounds: so having seene the greate
Church now newly repaired by a publique Contribution,⁵ we
return'd that Evening:

8 In the morning at W. hall, preached Dr.   one of the

ᵃ Interlined.   ᵇ Altered from *25*.   ᶜ Followed by *at* deleted.
ᵈ–ᵈ Substituted for *gave*.

Thanksgiving, &c., 1688; the attri-
bution to Sprat is presumably
correct.

¹ The two judges were dismissed
on 7 July: *London Gazette*, 9 July;
the reason for their dismissal is not
there stated but was their findings
in the trial: Barillon, in Mazure, ii.
473. For them and Allibone see
above, p. 587 n.

² The night of 17 June, for the
prince's birth; for the celebrations

see *London Gazette*, 18 June.

³ Roger Mander, *c.* 1649–1704;
master of Balliol 1687–1704; D.D.
7 July of this year: Foster.

⁴ Edward Carter, d. 1687; matriculated at Cambridge 1634; arch-
deacon of St. Albans 1683: Venn.

⁵ A general brief for a collection
for repairing the church was issued
on 26 Feb. 1681; for it and the
repairs see Clutterbuck, (*Hertfordshire*), i. 71–2.

Kings Chaplains before the princesse: on: 14 Exod: 13. Stand still & behold the salvation of the Lord: which he applied so boldly to the conjuncture of the Church of England, as more could scarse be said to encourage desponders:

In the meane time more viru⟨le⟩ntly did the popish priests, in their sermons against the C. of England, raging at the successe of the Bishops, as being otherwise no ways able to carry their Cause[a] against their learned Adversaries confounding them by both disputes & writings:

In the afternoone Preached (for Dr. Tenison, at St. ⟨James's⟩[b] new church) Dr. *Bohune* ⟨the⟩[c] same sermon he preached at Deptford, the 10th of the last moneth:

12 I return'd home; The Camp now began at Hounslow,[1] but the nation in high discontent:

The 2 Judges, who favour'd the Cause of the Bish: had their writ of Ease:[2] greate wroth meditating against the Bish: Cleargy & Church:[3]

Coll: *Titus*, Sir *H. Vane* (son of him who was executed for his Treason) & some others of the Presbyt: & Indep: party, Sworn of the Privy[d] Council, hoping thereby to divert that party, from going-over to the Bishops & C: of England, which now they began to do: as foreseeing the designes of the papists to descend & take in their most hatefull of heretiques (as they at other time believed them) to effect their owne ends, which[e] was now evidently, the utter extirpation of the C. of Eng: first, & then the rest would inevitably follow:[4]

---

a Followed by *by* deleted.　　　b MS. *Janes's*.　　　c MS. *se*.
d MS. *Pr:*　　　e Altered from *&*.

---

[1] The encampment appears to have begun on 27 June: *Ellis corr.*, ii. 1. It had been delayed by the bad weather: ibid., i. 355. It was broken up on 8 August: *Publick Occurrences*, 14 Aug.

[2] Holloway and Powell: above, p. 589.

[3] On 12 July the Ecclesiastical Commission ordered returns to be made as to the reading of the Declaration for Liberty of Conscience: *London Gazette*, 16 July.

[4] There is a notice of the swearing-in of three new privy councillors on 6 July in *London Gazette*, 9 July. They are Titus (above, iii. 526); Christopher Vane, 1653–1723; only surviving son of the younger Sir Henry Vane; created Baron Barnard of Barnard's Castle 1698: G.E.C.; and Sir John Trevor, 1637–

14[a] Came[a] to Visite me my Lord Chief-Justice Herbert.

15 One Mr. *Turner*[1] (Schole-Master of Lewsham) preached an excellent[b] sermon (our Viccar being sick) on 1. Cor: 15. ult: Exhorting to perseverance in the profession of our Religion: In the Afternoone the Curate on 11: *Matt.* 21, the Effects of Repentance:

16 Came to dine with us the Countesse of Sunderland, who staied 'til night:

17 I went to Lond: with my Wife &c: & This night were the fire-works plaied, which were prepar'd for the Queenes up-sitting: We[c] stood at Mr. Pepys's Secretary of the Admiralty to greate advantage for the sight, & indeede they were very fine, & had cost some thousands of pounds about the pyramids & statues &c: but were spent too soone, for so long a preparation:[2]

19 We returned home:

22 Preached Dr. Hutchins on his former Text, shewing how Christ was the life of believers: In the afternoone the Curate on: 10: Act: 38: recommending the doing ⟨good⟩,[d] by the example of our B: Lord:

26 I went to Lambeth to visite the ArchBish: of Canterbery, I found him very cherefull: There was likewise at Dinner my Lord Clarendon & few others: I returned after evening prayers:

---

a–a Substituted for *15 One M*[r]*:*   b MS. *ex*[t].   c Preceded by *I* altered
to *We* and deleted.   d MS. *goad.*

1717, at this time master of the rolls, a first cousin of Jeffreys: *D.N.B.* The Imperial envoy writes that these three have always been so hostile to the court and so great plotters among the Presbyterians, that 'man sich dann verwundert, wie diese Leuthe sich umbkehren, undt beym König versöhnen können, vielmehr aber wie der König ihnen wohl trauen darf': Compana de Cavelli, ii. 239. On 13 July another privy councillor was sworn, Sir Thomas Strickland: *London Gazette*, 16 July. He was a Roman Catholic.

[1] John Turner, 1660–1720; M.A., Cambridge, 1683; headmaster of Colfe's Grammar School at Lewisham from 1687 to 1704; vicar of Greenwich 1704–20; D.D. 1706: Venn; L. L. Duncan, *Hist. of Colfe's Grammar School*, 1910, pp. 106–12.

[2] There is a notice in *London Gazette*, 19 July; see also *Ellis corr.*, ii. 52; *Publick Occurrences*, 17 July. Pepys was now living in no. 14 Buckingham Street, by York Stairs: L.C.C., *Survey of London*, xviii. 71, &c.

29 Came to visite me Sir Fra: *Loylie*:[a][1]

⟨29⟩[b] Preached, our Ministers Lond: Lecturer[2] a very excellent sermon on 2 *Judges*, 1. 2. 3 shewing what calamaties befell the Israelites upon breach of the Covenant, God made with them: which he most pertinently applied to the danger the sinns of this nation expos'd the Church & Religion to[c] after so many signal mercies, especialy its[d] being brought out of the Egyptian darknesse of popery & superstition;

My Wife was ataqu'd with a suddaine fit of fainting, at dinner, but without any sensible convulsion; which yet to prevent, she was immediately let blood, & I blesse God soone restored:

The *Curate* preached, or rather declaim'd on 19 *Psal:* 1 in a very unedifying philosophical discourse, about *Atomes* &c that Chance could not create the World &c:

Aug: 5 Our *Vicar* on 5 *Matt:* 8 Concerning purity of heart: The holy Communion follow'd of[e] which I participated: The Curate on 9. Heb: 27. Concerning the C⟨e⟩rtainty of death and preparation for it:

10[f] To Lond. Din'd with Sir William Godolphin, return'd: [Dr. Tenison now told me there would suddainly be some greate thing discovered, which happened to be the P: of O: intended coming:][g][3]

12 Our Viccar on his former Text: Pomerid: Went to visite the Marquis of Rouvigny: heard a [french][h] sermon in his Chapell on the Lords prayer: very well preached by a young man, fled for his Religion:

14 I went to Lond: [15][i] the next day to *Althorp* in Northampton shire, it being 70 miles, which in 2 Coaches one [of 4 horses][h] that ⟨tooke⟩[j] me & my son up at white-hall &

---

a Or *Longlie*?   b MS. *30*.   c Altered from *too*.   d Substituted for *on*.
e Altered from or to *at*.   f Altered from *19*; reading doubtful.
g Interlined later.   h Interlined.   i Marginal date.   j MS. *toake*.

---

[1] Presumably Sir Francis Lawley: above, p. 566.
[2] See above, p. 549.
[3] On 7 August Tenison told Patrick, as 'an important secret', that the prince of Orange 'intended to come over with an army to our relief': Autobiography, in *Works*, ix. 513.

carried us to Dunstaple, where we arived & dined at noone, & another there of 6 horses, which carried us to Althorp 4 miles beyond N-hampton, by 7 a clocke that evening; both these Coaches laied for me alone, by that noble Countesse of Sunderland, who Invited me to her house at Althorp, where she entertaind me & my son with very extraordinary kind-nesse, and convey'd us back againe to London in the very same noble manner, both going & coming, appointing a Dinner for us, at Dunstaple, which we found ready for us, as soone as we came to the Inn:[1] I stayed with her Ladyship 'til the Thursday following.

18 Dr. Jessup[2] the Minister of Althorp, who was my Lords Chaplaine, when Ambassador in France, preached on the shortest discourse I ever heard: but what was defective in the amplitude of his sermon, we found supplied in the largenesse, & convenience of the[a] Parsonage house, which the Doctor (who had in spiritual advancements, at least 600 pounds per Annum) had new-built, fit for any[b] person of quality to live in, with Gardens & all accommodations according.

20 My Lady carried us to   my Lord of Northamptons Seate, a very strong large house built of stone, not altogether modern:[3] they were now inlarging the Gardens, in which was nothing extraordinary but the Yron gate, opening into the Parke, which is indeede very good worke, wrought in flowers,

---

[a] Altered from *his*.   [b] Substituted for *a*.

---

[1] For Althorp see above, pp. 69–70. Dunstable is 34 miles from London (Cornhill), and Northampton 32 miles farther; Althorp another 5 miles: Ogilby, *Britannia*, pp. 41, 79, 122.

[2] Constantine Jessop, *c.* 1640–96; D.D. 1685; rector of Brington (to which parish Althorp at this time belonged) 1676–96; prebendary of Durham 1686. His rebuilding of the rectory is commemorated in his epitaph: Longden, *Northamptonshire and Rutland clergy*;

Baker, (*Northamptonshire*), i. 91, 93–4. Sunderland was ambassador extraordinary in Paris in 1672–3 and again in 1678–9.

[3] Identifiable as Castle Ashby; its present owner was George Compton, 1664–1727, fourth earl of Northampton 1681: G.E.C. The house still belongs to his descendant, the present marquess of Northampton, and has been comparatively little altered; the garden has twice been re-planned: *V.C.H., Northants.*, iv. 230–3.

painted with blew & gilded; & there is a very noble Walke
of Elmes towards the front of the house by the Bowling
Greene: I was not in any roomes of the house besides a lobby
looking into the Garden, where my Lord, and his new
Countesse (Sir St: Foxes daughter,[1] whom I had known from
a very Child) entertained the Countesse of Sunderland & her
daughter the Countesse of Arran, (newly married to the son
of the Duke of Hammilton)[2] with so little good grace, & so
dully, that our Visite was very short, & so we return'd to
Althorp: which is 12 miles distant:

The Earle of Sunderlands House, or rather palace at
Althorp, is a noble uniforme pile, in forme of an 𝕳 built
of brick & freestone, balustred,[a] & a la moderne;[3] The Hale
is well, the Staircase incomparable, the[b] roomes of State,
Gallerys, Offices, & Furniture such as [may][c] become[d] a
greate Prince: It is situated in the midst of Gardens, exquisitely planted & kept, & all this in a parke wall'd with
hewn stone; planted with rows & walkes of Trees; Canales
& fish ponds, stored with Game: & what is above all this,
Govern'd by a Lady, that without any shew of solicitude;
keepes every thing in such admirable order both within &
without, from the Garret, to the Cellar; That I do not believe
there is any in all this nation or any other, exceeds her: all
is in such exact order, without ostentation, but substantialy
greate & noble; The meanest servant lodged so neate &
cleanely, The Services at the several Tables, the good order
& decenccy,[e] in a word the intire Oeconomie perfectly becoming, a wise & noble person, & one whom for her distinguishing
esteeme of me from a long & worthy friendship; I must ever
honour & Celebrate: & wish, I do from my Soule; The Lord
her Husband (whose parts & abilit⟨i⟩es are otherwise conspicuous) were as worthy of her, as by a[f] fatal Apostacy, &

---

a Or *balustraded*.   b Followed by *Offices* deleted.   c Interlined.
d Altered from *becomes*.   e Or *decencey*.   f Followed by *pro-* deleted.

---

[1] Jane: above, p. 245, &c. She
had married Northampton in 1686.
[2] See above, p. 567.
[3] See the views mentioned above,
p. 69 n., and the plan in Dibdin.
For the plantations see Dibdin, pp.
vii–xi.

Court ambition, he has made himselfe unworthy:[1] This is
what she deplores, & renders her as much affliction, as a Lady
of a greate Soule & much prudence is capable of: The
Countesse of Bristol her mother, a grave & honorable Lady
has the comfort of seing her daughter & Grand-children
under the same Oeconomie, especialy, Mr. Charles Spencer,[2]
a Youth of extraordinary hopes, very learned for his age &
ingenious, & under a Governor of Extraordinary worth:
Happy were it, could as much be said, ⟨of⟩[a] the Elder Bro: the
Lord Spencer,[3] who rambling about the world, dishonors both
his name & family, adding sorrow to sorrow, to a Mother, who
has taken all imaginable care of his Education: but vice
more & more predominating, gives slender hopes of his
reformation: He has another sister very Young, married to
the Earle of Clancartie[4] to a greate & fair Estate in Ireland,
which [yet][b] gives no greate presage of worth; so universaly
contaminated is the youth of this corrupt & abandoned
age: But this is againe recompens'd by my *Lord Arran*, a
sober & worthy Gent: & who has Espoused the Lady Ann
Spencer, a young lady of admirable accomplishments &
vertue:

23d I left this noble place, & Conversation on the 23d,

---

[1] Sunderland had declared himself a Roman Catholic on 26 June,
a fact immediately made common
knowledge: d'Adda, in Mackintosh,
p. 659. Barillon states that he had
abjured heresy a year earlier: in
Mazure, ii. 463–4. Princess Anne
considered that Lady Sunderland
and her husband were 'well
matched': letters to Princess Mary,
in Sir J. Dalrymple, *Memoirs of
Great Britain*, &c., Appendix (vol.
ii), 2nd ed., 1773, [ii]. 299–302.

[2] Charles Spencer, *c.* 1674–1722;
styled Lord Spencer after the death
of his brother this year; succeeded
as third earl of Sunderland 1702:
D.N.B. Evelyn gives him a second

place in the dedication of *Numismata*. Two letters from Evelyn to
him, 1688, 4 Sept. 1693 (Bohn,
iii. 293–4, 336), reflect his literary
interests. His governor is presumably Charles Trimnell (*D.N.B.*).

[3] Above, p. 245. He died at Paris
on 15 September, N.S., from drinking too much brandy: Dangeau,
Journal, ii. 168.

[4] Donogh Maccarty, *c.* 1668–
1734; fourth earl of Clancarty (Ireland) 1676; married, 1684, Elizabeth, Sunderland's second daughter
(above, p. 450); converted to
Roman Catholicism 1685; attainted
and honours forfeited 1691: *D.N.B.*;
G.E.C.

passing through Northampton, which having lately ben burnt & reedified, is now become a Towne, that for the beauty of the buildings especialy the Church, & Towne-house, may compare with the neatest in Italy itselfe:[1]

24 Hearing my poore wife, had ben ataqu'd with her late Indisposition I hasted home this morning, & God be pra⟨i⟩sed found her much amended.

Dr. Sprat: Bish of Rochester, writing a very honest & handsome letter to the Commissioners Ecclesiastical; excuses himselfe from sitting no longer among them, as by no meanes approving of their prosecution of the Cleargy who refus'd to reade his Majesties declaration for liberty of Conscience, in prejudice of the Church of England &c:[2]

The French Arme & threaten the Election of the Elect: of Colin:[3] The Dutch make extraordinary preparations both at sea & land,[4] which (with the very small progresse popery makes amongst us) puts us to many difficulties:

The popish Irish Souldiers commit many murders &

---

[1] It had been burnt in 1675: see above, pp. 69–70; for the rebuilding see *V.C.H., Northants.*, iii. 31–3. The church is All Saints, rebuilt by 1680, except for the tower and crypt, which had survived the fire; the portico and cupola were added *c.* 1701: R. M. Serjeantson, *Hist. of . . . All Saints, Northampton*, 1901, pp. 246–8. The town-hall was an unimportant building which had survived the fire; Evelyn presumably refers to the County Hall, built *c.* 1675–8: C. A. Markham, *Hist. of the County Buildings of Northants.*, 1885, pp. 39–41.

[2] Published as *The Lord Bishop of Rochester's Letter*, n.d.; it was dated Bromley, 15 August: *The Bishop of Rochester's Second Letter to . . . the Earl of Dorset*, 1689, p. 22.

[3] Cologne. The archbishop-elector had died on 3 June, N.S. There were two candidates for the succession, Joseph Clemens, 1671–1723, brother of Maximilian, elector of Bavaria; bishop of Freising 1684(5)–94; of Ratisbon 1685–1716; archbishop of Cologne 1688–1723; bishop of Liège 1694–1723; and of Hildesheim 1714–23: *Allgemeine deutsche Biog.*; and Wilhelm Egon von Fürstenberg, 1629–1704; bishop of Strassburg 1682; cardinal 1686: ibid. The emperor supported Joseph Clemens, Louis XIV Fürstenberg. The election on 19 July, N.S., was indecisive and the decision was referred to the pope. The succession was now the immediate point at issue in the European conflict. By 21 August, N.S., Louis had ordered a new levy of 16,000 horse and foot in order to release troops to support Fürstenberg. The pope gave his decision in favour of Joseph Clemens on 18 September, N.S. Louis declared war on the emperor on 24 September, N.S.

[4] Cf. *Ellis corr.*, ii. 141–3, &c.; Luttrell, i. 457.

Insolences;[1] The whole Nation dissaffected & in apprehensions: what the event will prove God onely knows:

After long trials of the Doctors, to bring up the little P: of Wales by hand (so-many of her Majesties Children having died Infants) not succeeding: A country Nurse (the wife of a Tile-maker) is taken to give it suck:[a][2]

26 our *Curate* on 4: *Eph:* 24. describing the new man &c: our Viccar being sick.[b] I went to evening prayer to Monsieur Ruvignies:

September 2 Our Viccar preached on his former Text: 5: *Matt:* 8: The holy Sacrament followed, at which I received, the L. Jesus make me thankfull:

9 He continued on the same Text:

16 On the same: I went to Greenewich to the French Evening service;

18 I went to Lond: where I found the Court in the uttmost consternation upon report of the Pr: of Oranges landing, which put White-hall into so panic a feare, that I could hardly believe it possible to find such a change:[3]

Writs issued now in order to the Parliament, & a declaration to back the good order of Elections, with greate professions of maintaining the Ch: of England: but without giving any sort of satisfaction to people, who now began to shew their high discontent at several things in the Government: how this will end, God onely can tell:[4]

---

a Spelling doubtful.   b End of line; punctuation supplied.

---

[1] Luttrell records only one murder by an Irish soldier since 1 July: i. 449. For the soldiers' alleged misconduct see *Ellis corr.*, ii. 139.

[2] For the prince's nourishment and health see Campana de Cavelli, ii. 221, 225, 227, 248–50. The nurse's name was Cooper: Luttrell, i. 453.

[3] It was the news that the Dutch fleet was almost ready to sail that caused this day's alarm at court: *Ellis corr.*, ii. 191–2; Campana de Cavelli, ii. 263–4.

[4] On 24 August the king ordered writs to be issued for a parliament to meet on 27 November: *London Gazette*, 27 Aug.; they were sealed on 18 and sent to the sheriffs on 19 September: *Ellis corr.*, ii. 201, 207. Evelyn refers to the king's declaration of 21 September (reprinted *London Gazette*, 24 Sept.) setting out his objects in summoning the parliament. The writs were recalled on 28 September: see below.

[21 I heard an excellent sermon on 1. Cor: 9: Chap: 8. ver: at St. *Martins* it being St. Matthew:]ᵃ

22 I returned home: 23:ᵇ Our Doctor concluded his former Text with a proper exhortation: I went to Common prayer to the French church in Afternoone.

News of the French Investing Philipsburge:¹ & of the Mar: Shombergs putting in 3000 men into Collin, upon the dispute of that Electors Interest against the Prince of Firstenberge:² Appearances of wonderfull stirrs in this part of Europe, whilst the Emp: was successfull in Hungarie, having taken Belgrade:³ Earthquakes had now utterly demolished the antient *Smyrna*, & severall other places, both in Greece, Italy, & even the Spanish Indies, forerunners of greater Calamities:⁴ God Almight⟨y⟩ preserve his Church, & all who put themselves under the shadow of his Wings, 'til these things be over-past.

30 Our *Viccar* on 3: *Apoc:* 20, Christs gracious Invitation of sinners &c:

I went to *Greenewich* where at Monsieur *Rovignies* a French sermon on 20. *Apoc:* 6 shewing the dignity of a true Christian, & where in his Ro⟨y⟩alty consisted &c:

The *Court* &c in [so]ᵃ extraordinary consternation upon assurance of the Pr: of Oranges intention of Landing, as the Writs which were sent forth to choose Parliament men, were recalled &c:⁵

Octob: 6: I went to Lond: [7]ᶜ The next day being Sonday

ᵃ Interlined. ᵇ Altered from *22*. ᶜ Marginal date.

---

¹ Philippsburg, in Baden. The French army invested it on 23 September, N.S.: notices in *London Gazette*, 24, 27 Sept.

² Frederick Herman Schomberg (Schönberg), 1615–90, count of Schönberg (Empire); created count of Coubert, &c., by Louis XIV; field-marshal, France, 1675; Huguenot refugee; created duke of Schomberg 1689: *D.N.B.* On 20 September, N.S., he brought 2,700 men into Cologne to increase the garrison: *London Gazette*, 20 Sept. For Fürstenberg see above, p. 596 n. The elector is presumably Joseph Clemens.

³ It was taken from the Turks on 6 September, N.S.: ibid., 17 Sept.

⁴ Smyrna was largely destroyed by an earthquake on 30 June, N.S.: ibid., 20 Sept.; see also ibid., 27 Aug. For other earthquakes at Naples and Lima, &c., see ibid., 25 June, 13 Aug., 13 Sept., &c.

⁵ The writs were recalled in a proclamation of 28 September (reprinted ibid., 1 Oct.). For the disorder at court see *Ellis corr.*, ii. 218–20, 229, 230.

Dr. Tenison viccar of St. Martins, preached on 2: *Tim:* 3. 16. shewing the Scripture to be our undoubted & onely Rule of Faith, & its perfection above all other Traditions & Writings, most excellently proved; after which the Communion was celebrated to neere 1000 devout people. This sermon chiefly occasioned by an impertinent Jesuite who in their Masse-house the Sunday before had disparaged the Scripture & railed at our Translation with extraordinary ignorance and impudence; which some present contradicting, they pulled him out of the Pulpit, & treated him very coursely, insomuch as it was like to create a very greate disturbance in the Citty:[1]

Hourely dreate on expectation of the Pr: of Oranges Invasion still heightned to that degree, as his Majestie thought fit to recall the Writes of Summons of Parliament;[2] to abbrogate the Commission for the dispencing power,[3] [but retaining his owne right still to dispense with all Laws &][a] restore the ejected Fellows of Magdalen College Oxon:[4] But in the meane time called over 5000 Irish, 4000 Scots;[5] continue⟨s⟩ to remove protestants & put papists in to Portsmouth & other places of Trust:[6] & retaines the Jesuites about

---

a Interlined; & followed by *removing none of the Jesuit or Popish officers now placed in all the places of trust:* interlined and deleted.

---

[1] The offending preacher was Charles Petre (*D.N.B.*, art. Petre, Edward), preaching at the Elector Palatine's chapel in Lime Street: Campana de Cavelli, ii. 282, 290; *Hist. MSS. Comm., Le Fleming MSS.*, p. 214; Luttrell, i. 465.

[2] This belongs to 28 September: see above. The word 'dreate' is perhaps a bad rendering of dread.

[3] The Commission for Ecclesiastical Affairs is intended; it was dissolved on 5 October: *London Gazette*, 8 Oct. In his statements at this period James never mentions the dispensing power.

[4] Notice dated 12 October, ibid., 15 Oct. For James's dealings with Magdalen see *Magdalen College and King James II*, ed. Bloxam.

[5] For reports and notices relating to these troops see Luttrell, i. 465, 468; *Ellis corr.*, ii. 245, 250, 255; *Hist. MSS. Comm., Le Fleming MSS.*, pp. 213–17.

[6] James had recently issued five commissions for raising regiments. One colonel was Henry Gage, who was almost certainly a Roman Catholic; his regiment and the duke of Newcastle's, also new, were largely composed of Roman Catholics: *London Gazette*, 4 Oct.; Dalton, *English army lists*, ii. 171, 175. In September James had provoked a strong protest by introducing Irish troops into a regiment at Portsmouth, and six officers were

him,[1] which gave no satisfaction to the nation, but increasing the universal discontent, brought people to so desperate a passe as with uttmost expressions[a] even passionately seeme to long for & desire the landing of that Prince, whom they looked on as their deliverer from popish Tyrannie, praying uncessantly for an Easterly Wind, which was said to be the onely remora of his expedition, with a numerous Army ready to make a descent;[2] To such a strange temper & unheard of in any former age, was this poore nation reduc'd,[b] & of which I was an Eye witnesse: The apprehension was (& with reason) that his Majesties Forces, would neither at land or sea oppose them with that viggour requisite to repell Invaders:[3]

The late Imprisoned Bishops, were now called to reconcile matters, & the Jesuites hard at worke to foment confusions amongst the Protestants, by their usual tricks &c: [Leter sent the AB. of Cant informing from a good hand what was contriving by the Jesuits: &c][c][4]

---

[a] Followed by *of* deleted.   [b] Followed by *to* deleted later.
[c] Interlined, perhaps on 21 or 28 October.

---

cashiered: Macaulay, pp. 1071–2. On his intention of making Portsmouth a place of retreat see Mazure, iii. 76, 134.

[1] About 11 October the queen advised James to dismiss Father Edward Petre, but he refused: Campana de Cavelli, ii. 290.

[2] For notices of the wind from the time of the Dutch fleet's being ready until 19/29 October, when it first set sail for England, see *Ellis corr.*, ii. 230–63. Wood notes, as early as 27 September, 'All publick houses are full *waiting for good news*': *Life and times*, iii. 278.

[3] For the disaffection in the navy in October see *Memoirs relating to the Lord Torrington* (G. Byng), ed. J. K. Laughton (Camden Soc., new ser., vol. xlvi, 1889), pp. 26–8; for that in the army, Campana de Cavelli, ii. 306–7.

[4] Interviews between the king and the bishops (various numbers of them) took place on 28 September, 3, 8, 10, and 11 October. The bishops apparently sought that on 3 October, when they recommended the king to cancel his innovations and to keep within the law. On 8 October the king ordered them to prepare a form of prayers for use in this time of public danger. Evelyn wrote to Sancroft on 10 October, warning the bishops not to act without the concurrence of the secular peers, calling Sancroft's attention to the report that the prince of Orange was to be named as the invader in the form of prayer, and advising that the Church of England should be described as Protestant or Reformed whenever mentioned in these extraordinary forms of prayer. The draft form was submitted to the king on the afternoon of 10 October and was accepted on

9 I return'd the 9th—A paper of what the Bishops advised his Majestie [was publish'd]ᵃ¹

A [forme of]ᵇ prayer, the Bishops were injoy⟨n⟩'d to prepare [an office]ᶜ against the feared Invasion.²

A pardon published:³ Souldiers & Mariners daily pressed &c.

14 The Kings Birth-day, no Gunns from the Tower, as usualy: The sunn Eclips'd at its rising:⁴ This day signal for the Victory of William the Conqueror against Herold neere Battel in Sussex: The wind (which had hitherto ben West)ᵈ all this day East, wonderfull expectation of the Dutch fleete.⁵

Our *Viccar* proceeds ⟨on⟩ᵉ his former Text: a stranger in the afternoone on 1. Cor: 15. ult: concerning the Resurrection, exhorting to an unmoveablenesse in our Re⟨l⟩igion, these difficult times, &c:

Continual apprehensions of the Dutch Invasion, there were pub: prayers ordered to be read in the Church [against it.]ᶠ⁶

21 Our Viccar proceedes on his former Text:

27 I went to Lond: the 28th Dr. Tenison at St. Martins preached on 9 *Jer:* 3. shewing what mistakes men made byᵍ their false conceptions of the Deity, that if they truly knew

---

ᵃ Interlined at same time as previous interlineation.　ᵇ Interlined.
ᶜ Interlined later.　　ᵈ Closing bracket supplied.　　ᵉ MS. *one*.
ᶠ Added later.　　ᵍ Altered from *in*.

---

11 October; neither specific invader nor Church is named. Jeffreys on 27 September thought that the king would not come to terms with the bishops; on 12 October Anne thought that this was still the case: notices in Clarendon's diary, in *Corr.*, ii. 191, 194; documents, including Evelyn's letter, in Gutch, i. 409–18; draft version of Evelyn's letter in Bray's editions of the *Diary*; for Sancroft's thanks for it see below, p. 614.

¹ Presumably *An Account of the Proposals of the Arch-bishop of Canterbury, with some other Bishops, to his Majesty*, n.d., signed N. N. It was intended as a vindication of the

bishops from the reports mentioned in Evelyn's letter. The material was obtained surreptitiously and the recommendations are paraphrased.

² See note above.

³ On 2 October (reprinted in *London Gazette*, 4 Oct.).

⁴ This was not a true eclipse.

⁵ See also *Ellis corr.*, ii. 253, 255.

⁶ No special order is traceable other than that appearing in the title of the form of prayers, *Prayers to be used . . . during this time of Publick Apprehensions from the danger of Invasion*; the order for printing is dated 11 October.

God, they could not go from Evil to evil which[a] the prophet assignes for the effect of their ignorance:

I din'd with Sir W: Godolphin: [A Tumult in Lond on the rabble demolishing a popish Chapell set up in the Citty.][b][1]

29 My Lady Sunderland acquainted me at large his Majesties taking away the Seales from her husband, & of her being with the Queene to interceede for him: It is conceiv'd he grew remisse of late in pursuing the Interest of the Jesuitical Counsels, some reported one thing, some another; but there was doubtlesse some seacret betraied, which time may discover:[2]

There was a Council now cald, to which were summon'd the A:Bish of Cant. &⟨c⟩: Judges, Lord Major &c: Q: Dowager, all the Ladies & Lords, who were present at the Q: Consorts labour, upon oath to give testimonie of the Pr: of Wales's birth, which was recorded, both at the Council board, & at the Chancery a day or two after:[3] This procedure was censur'd by some, as below his Majestie to condescend to, upon the talke of Idle people: Remarkable on this occasion, was the refusal of the A Bish: Marq: Halifax, Earles of Clarendon & Notinghams refusing to sit at the Council Table in their places, amongst Papists, & their bold telling his Majestie that what ever was don whilst such sate amongst

---

a Altered from *as*.   b Added after next entry was begun.

---

[1] The mob demolished, and burnt the altar furnishings of, the Carmelites' chapel in Bucklersbury on 29 October, after the lord mayor's show: Campana de Cavelli, ii. 317; Luttrell, i. 472; see also *Ellis corr.*, ii. 269.

[2] Sunderland was superseded as secretary on 28 October: *London Gazette*, 29 Oct.; he had been dismissed on 26 October, and at the same time from the presidentship of the council: Clarendon. The reasons for his dismissal remain unknown. The king is said to have exonerated him from the widespread charge of treachery: *Ellis corr.*, ii. 237-8, 268; *Hist. MSS.*

Comm., Rutland MSS., ii. 122; Mazure, iii. 164. For Lady Sunderland's interest in Evelyn about this time see her two letters to him, 10 ? and 11 ? October, in Sidney, *Diary*, ii. 279-80.

[3] This meeting took place on 22 October. Besides the privy council there were present Queen Catherine, such peers spiritual and temporal as were in town, the lord mayor and aldermen of London, the judges, &c. The depositions, &c., were ordered to be enrolled in Chancery, and this was done on 27 October. A formal report was published as *The several declarations*, &c.; see also *London Gazette*, 25 Oct.

them was unlawfull, & incurr'd præmunire: if at least, it be true, what I heard:[1]

I din'd with[a] my Lord Preston,[2] now made Seccretary of state in place of the E. of Sunderland:

Visited Mr. Boile, where came in[b] Duke Hamilton[3] & E. of Burlington:[4] The Duke told us many particulars of Mary Q: of Scots, and her amours with the Italian favorite[5] &c:

30. I dined with the Secretary of the Admiralty,[6] visited Dr. Tenison:

31. My Birthday, being the 68 yeare of my age: ô Blessed Lord, grant, that as I advance in yeare⟨s⟩, so I may improve in Grace: Be thou my protector this following yeare, & preserve me & mine from these dangers and greate confusions, which threaten a sad revolution to this sinfull Nation: Defend thy Church, our holy Religion, & just Lawes, disposing his Majestie to harken to sober & healing Counsels, that yet if it be thy blessed will we may still enjoy that happy Tranquility which hitherto thou hast continued to us. Amen: Amen:

I din'd at my sonns:[c]

November 1.[d] Dined with my L: Preston againe, with other company, at Sir St: Foxes:

Continual al'armes of the Pr: of Oranges landing, but no certainty: reports of his greate losses of horse in the storme; but without any assurance.[7] A Man was taken with divers

---

a Followed by *Mr. Pepys at the Admiralty* deleted.   b Followed by *th-* deleted.   c Followed by *Sup'd at Sir St: Foxes:* deleted.
d Altered from *2*.

[1] Clarendon and Nottingham (above, p. 171) refused to sit at council with Father Petre; Sancroft also sat with the peers: notice in Clarendon, who was presumably Evelyn's informant. Halifax was not a privy councillor at this time but was the most eminent of the peers not councillors. Father Petre was absent, but other Roman Catholics, members of the council, were present.

[2] Above, p. 548. He had been appointed secretary on 28 October: *London Gazette*, 29 Oct.

[3] He was now a member of the English privy council.

[4] He was Boyle's eldest brother.

[5] Rizzio.

[6] Pepys.

[7] The prince had set sail on 19/29 October, but had been driven back by a storm on the following day; 400 horses were lost. For the damage see *Hist. MSS. Comm., Dartmouth MSS.*, pp. 175–8; *London*

papers & printed Manifests, & carried to Newgate after examination at the Cabinet-Council:[1] There was likewise a declaration of the States, for satisfaction of all publique Ministers in their Dominions, the reason of their furnishing the Prince with their Vessels & Militia on this Expedition, which was delivered to all the Ambassadors & publique Ministers at the Hague except to the English & French:[2]

There was in that of the Princes, an expression as if the Lords both Spiritual & Temporal &c had invited him over, with a deduction of the Causes of his enterprise: This made his Majestie Convene my L: of *Cant:* & the other Bishops now in Towne, to [give][a] them an account of what was in the *Manifesto*: & to enjoyne them to cleare themselves by ⟨some⟩[b] publique writing of this disloyal charge.[3]

2 It was now certainly reported by some who saw the Pr: imbarke, and the fleete, That they sailed from Brill on Wednesday Morning, & that the Princesse of Orange was there, to take leave of her Husband,[4] [3][c] & so I returned home.

4[d] A stranger preached at Depford on: 8. *Luke*: 18: directing how we ought to heare &c: The H: Sacrament follow'd,

---

a Interlined.   b MS. *same.*   c Marginal date.   d Followed by *Our Vi-* deleted.

Gazette, 29 Oct.; a later and exaggerated report, ibid., 1 Nov. For reports as to where the prince intended to land see *Dartmouth MSS.* as above and pp. 180–1; I have not found any reports of a supposed landing at this date (1 November).

[1] Humphrey Lanham, a captain in one of the English regiments in Dutch service, was sent to Newgate about 29 October. He was brought before a grand jury on 17 November, but they refused to find a bill against him: Dalton, *English army lists*, ii. 228–9; Luttrell, i. 472; *Hist. MSS. Comm., Le Fleming MSS.*, p. 218.

[2] The document was published in Dutch, French, and English—in English as *Extract of the States General their Resolution. Thursday, 28th. October 1688.*

[3] This was on 2 November. Compton, who had been questioned by the king on 1 November, had then equivocated or lied as to his share in the invitation to the prince. The bishops now were silent when asked to publish a paper expressing their abhorrence of the prince's design; at a further meeting on 6 November they refused to publish anything: documents in Gutch, i. 422–45.

[4] The prince and princess parted at the Brill on Wednesday, 31 October/10 November; the prince sailed from Helvoetsluis on 1/11 November. The present report is also given in a letter (from London?) of 3 November: *Hist. MSS. Comm., Rutland MSS.*, ii. 123: see also *Ellis corr.*, ii. 274, 276–7.

at which I participated, the L. Jesus blesse it to me: My Wife (not yet out of her Chamber) received at home &c:

Fresh reports of the Pr: being landed somewher about Portsmouth or Ile of Wight: wheras it was thought, it would have ben north ward:[1] The Court in greate hurry—

5 Being the Anniversary of the powder plot, our *Viccar* preach'd on 76. Psal. 10. by divers Instances: shewing the disasters & punishments overtaking perfidious designes.

8[a] I went to Lond: heard the newes of the Prince of Oranges being landed at Tor-bay, with a fleete of neere 700 saile, so dreadfull a sight passing through the Channell with so favorable a Wind, as our Navy could by no meanes intercept or molest them:[2] This put the King & Court into greate Consternation, now employed in forming an Army to incounter their farther progresse: for they were gotten already into Excester, & the season, & wayes very improper for his Majesties forces to march so greate a distance:[3]

The A Bish of Cant, &[b] some few of the other Bishops, & Lords in Lond: were sent for to White-hall, & required to set forth their abhorrency of this Invasion; They assured his Majestie they had never invited any of the Princes party or were in the least privy to this Invasion, & would be ready to shew[c] all testimonies of their Loyalty &c: but as to a publique declaration, they being so few, desired that his majestie

---

[a] Reading doubtful; perhaps altered from *9*.   [b] Followed by *the* deleted.   [c] Followed by *him* deleted.

---

[1] See Pepys's letter of 3 November, 'Past midnight', in *Hist. MSS. Comm., Dartmouth MSS.*, pp. 183–4. William appears to have depended on the weather to decide where to land.

[2] William landed at Brixham in Tor Bay on 5 November; the news reached London by 4 p.m. on 6 November: *Hist. MSS. Comm., Le Fleming MSS.*, p. 218. His fleet consisted of 65 men-of-war, 500 fly-boats, and 70 other ships: *London Gazette*, 8 Nov. The winds prevented the English fleet from en-countering it: *Hist. MSS. Comm., Dartmouth MSS.*, pp. 184, 186; Campana de Cavelli, ii. 314–15; *Hatton corr.*, ii. 98–9. There are various accounts of the passage of the expedition along the Channel.

[3] William did not reach Exeter until 9 November: *Correspondentie van Willem III en van . . . Portland*, ed. Japikse, ii. 626 (Rijks Geschiedkundige Publicatiën, kleine serie, vol. xxiv, 1928). News of his marching towards the city in *London Gazette*, 12 Nov.

would call the rest of their brethren & peeres, that they might consult what was fit to do on this occasion, not thinking it convenient to publish any thing without them, & untill they had themselves seene the Princes[a] Manifest, in which it was pretended[b] he was invited in by the Lords Sp: & temporal: This did not please his Majestie: So they departed:[c][1] There came now out a Declaration, prohibiting all people to see or reade the Princes Manifest;[2] in which was at large setforth the cause of his Expedition, as there had ben on⟨c⟩e before one from the States: These are the beginnings of Sorrows,[d] unlesse God in his Mercy prevent it, by some happy reconciliation of all dissentions amongst us, which nothing in likelihood can Effect but a free Parliament, but which we cannot hope to see, whilst there are any forces on either side: I pray God protect, & direct the King for the best, & truest Interest of his People: [I saw his Majestie touch for the Evil, Piters the Jesuit & F. Warner officiating in the Banqueting house][e][3]

I dined at Dr. Godolphins, with Mrs. Boscawen &c at her house warming in his prebends house near S. Paules:[4] Lay at my sonns, & [9][f] returned home the next day.

11[g] Our *Viccar* proceeded on his former Text: 76: Psal: our Curate on 2. Joel, exhorting to mortification:

---

a Followed by *decl-* deleted.   b Followed by *th-* deleted.   c Followed by *It* deleted.   d Followed by *&* deleted.   e Inserted later, perhaps when the entry for 18 November was made.   f Marginal date.   g Altered from *10.*

[1] This was the meeting on 6 November: see above, p. 604 n.

[2] This was a proclamation dated 2 November (reprinted *London Gazette*, 5 Nov.). James also issued on 6 November a declaration, a counterblast to the prince's declaration (reprinted ibid., 8 Nov.).

[3] The date of this notice is questionable. Despite Crawfurd's statement to the contrary, Roman Catholic clergy using a Roman Catholic service officiated when James touched for the evil, at any rate in the later part of the reign; a conscientious Anglican could not have taken an active part in the service which he reprints: *King's evil*, pp. 132–7; see also Campana de Cavelli, ii. 108. The present officiants are Edward Petre, 1631–99, and John Warner, 1628–92, both Jesuits; for them see *D.N.B.*; for Petre see further the articles by B. Duhr cited above, p. 536 n.

[4] Godolphin had been a prebendary of St. Paul's since 1685; presumably he had now been appointed a residentiary.

My deare Wife fell very ill of the gravell &c in her kidnies this afternoone. God in mercy give her ease & comfort:

The Pr. of Orange increases every day in forces, several Lords go in to him;[1] The King gos towards Salisbery with his Army;[2] doubtfull of their standing by him, Lord Cornbery carrys some Regiments from him, marches to Honiton, the Princes head quarters;[3] The Citty of Lond: in dissorder by the rabble &c who pull-downe the Nunery at St. Johns, newly bought by the Papists of my Lord Berkeley:[4] The Queene [prepare⟨s⟩ to]ᵃ ⟨go⟩ᵇ to Portsmouth for safty: to attend the issue of this commotion, which has a dreadfull aspect:[5]

18 Our Viccar on his former Text, shewing the wonderfull deliverances of Gods church in its greatest necessities:

I went afternoone to Greenewich to visite the Marq: de Ruvigny, wher a young man preached very excellently on 11. *Heb:* 6. shewing the greate effects of Faith & relyance upon God:

It was now very hard frost:[6]

ᵃ Interlined when the entry for 25 November was made.   ᵇ MS. *gos.*

---

[1] At first it was stated that no 'Person of Quality' had joined the prince; later that none of 'the Gentry' but some of 'the Rabble' had joined him; at the same time Lord Lovelace was arrested at Cirencester on his way to join him: *London Gazette*, 12, 15 Nov.

[2] The king left London on 17 November and arrived at Salisbury on 19 November: ibid., 19, 22 Nov.

[3] Cornbury on 12. November tried to take three regiments of horse to join the prince; many of the officers and men turned back, but Cornbury with the remainder joined the prince's forces at Honiton: ibid., 17 Nov.; the news reached Clarendon on 15 November.

[4] The mob attacked the chapel at St. John's, Clerkenwell, on 11 November; as some of the contents were being removed to safe-keeping on 12 November they were seized and burnt in the street: *Hatton corr.*, ii. 99–100. The earl of Berkeley's house was situated at the east end of the present Berkeley Street: Pinks, *Hist. of Clerkenwell*, pp. 279–81. To what order its occupants belonged is unknown; they appear to have been men, not nuns.

[5] It was reported as early as 3 November that, when the king went to oppose William, the queen was to go to the neighbourhood of Portsmouth: *Hist. MSS. Comm., Rutland MSS.*, ii. 122, 123. The prince of Wales was sent there on 17 November; the queen remained in London until her flight on the night 9–10 December.

[6] '. . . bey diesem harten Frost und Schnee . . .': the Imperial agent, London, 29 November N.S., in Campana de Cavelli, ii. 336.

The King gos to Salisbery to rendevouze the Army, and returning back to Lond:[1] Lord De la Mare appears for the Pr: in Cheshire:[2] The nobility meete in Yorkshire:[3] The ABish & some Bishops, & such peeres as were in Lond: addresse to his Majestie to call a Parliament:[4] The King invites all forraine nations to come over:[5] The French take all the Palatinat, & alarme the Germans more than ever:[6]

25 Our Doctors Lond:[a] Lecturer preached an excellent sermon on 122 Psal 6: shewing the ruine that the dissentions[b] of Christians has brought upon their profession &c.

29 I went to the R: Society, we adjourn'd Election of Præsident til 23. Aprill by reason of the publique commotions, yet dined together as of custome on this day:[7]

December 2 Dr. Tenison at St. Martins on: 36 Psal: 5. 6. 7: concerning providence: I received the B: Sacrament.

Visited my L. Godolphin, then going with the Marquis of Halifax, & E: of Notingham as Commissioner to the Prince of Orange: He told me, they had little power:[8] Plymoth

---

[a] Followed by *Curate* deleted.   [b] Spelling doubtful.

---

[1] The king returned to London on 26 November: *London Gazette*, 29 Nov.

[2] Ibid., 22 Nov. De la Mare is Henry Booth, 1652–94; succeeded as second Baron Delamer 1684; created earl of Warrington 1690: *D.N.B.* He had been tried for high treason in connexion with Monmouth's rebellion.

[3] See especially *The Declaration of the nobility, gentry, and commonalty at the rendezvous at Nottingham, Nov. 22. 1688.*

[4] A petition signed by Sancroft and five other bishops, and by twelve temporal peers, was presented to the king on 17 November: printed petition, 1688.

[5] This is misleading. In his proclamation of pardon of 22 November (reprinted *London Gazette*, 24 Nov.), James offers his pardon and protection to all foreigners who shall 'come over' to him; those forming part of the prince's expedition being intended.

[6] The principal fortresses in the Palatinate had been taken by 17 November, N.S. Evelyn probably refers to a report made to the Diet of the Empire about 13 November, N.S.: ibid., 22, 24 Nov.

[7] This meeting probably took place on 30 November; about twenty-three fellows were present: Hooke, diary, 30 Nov. 1688, in Gunther, *Early science in Oxford*, x. 77.

[8] The appointment of this mission is noticed in *Universal Intelligence*, 11 Dec. For its history see Foxcroft, *Halifax*, ii. 17–33; its instructions have not been preserved.

declared for the Prince & L: Bath:[1] Yorke, Hull, Bristoll,[2] all the eminent nobility[a] & persons of quality throout England declare for the Protestant Rel⟨i⟩gion & Laws, & go to meete the Prince; who every day sets forth new declarations &c: against the Papists:[3] The Greate favorits at Court, priest⟨s⟩ & Jesuites, flie or abscond:[4] Every thing (til now conceiled) flies abroad in publique print, & is Cryed about the streetes:[5] Expectations of the Pr: coming to Oxon:[6] Pr: of Wales & greate Treasure sent daily[b] to Portsmouth, Earle of Dover Governor:[7] Addresse from the Fleete not gratefull to his Majestie:[8] The Popists in offices lay down their Commissions & flie: Universal Consternation amongst them:[c] it lookes like a Revolution: Herbert, beates a french fleete:[9]

7 My son went towards Oxon:[10] I returned[d] home:

---

[a] Word altered; spelling doubtful. doubtful.   [c] Punctuation supplied.   [b] Word blotted; reading   [d] Followed by *the 8.* deleted.

---

[1] Bath gained control over the garrison at Plymouth on 24 and declared for the prince on 26 November: *English Currant,* 12 Dec. The news had reached London by 30 November: Campana de Cavelli, ii. 356.

[2] For Bristol and Hull see *Universal Intelligence,* 11 Dec., paragraphs dated 3, 6 Dec.; *English Currant,* 12 Dec. The garrison at York was secured on 22 November, and the city joined in a declaration published on 25 November: Reresby.

[3] The prince issued only two declarations, those made at The Hague on 10 and 24 October, N.S. They are general vindications of the expedition. Evelyn refers to the spurious 'third declaration', dated from Sherborne Castle, 28 November; it was circulating in London by 3 December: Macaulay, pp. 1176–8; Campana de Cavelli, ii. 363.

[4] Cf. *Universal Intelligence,* 11 Dec.; *English Currant,* 12 Dec.

[5] Cf. the Imperial agent, 3/13 December, in Campana de Cavelli, ii. 364. Four newspapers started

between 11 and 15 December.

[6] When at Littlecote (8–10 December) William spoke of marching to Oxford on 11 December: *Universal Intelligence,* 15 Dec. He did not go there at this time.

[7] The prince of Wales was sent to Portsmouth on 17 November. He was brought back to London on 8 December: Campana de Cavelli, ii. 334, 371; *English Currant,* 12 Dec. Dover was appointed governor of Portsmouth on 27 November: *Ellis corr.,* ii. 340.

[8] There is a notice of the address in *Universal Intelligence,* 11 Dec., paragraph dated 3 December; it is printed with date 1 December, ibid., 18 Dec.

[9] This report, which was false, was circulating on 22 November: *Ellis corr.,* ii. 310. Herbert is Arthur Herbert, *c.* 1647–1716; elder brother of Sir Edward Herbert, James II's lord chief justice; vice-admiral 1678; admiral 1680; created earl of Torrington 1689: *D.N.B.*

[10] To join the prince of Orange.

9 Our Lecturer on 122. Psal: 6: Pray for the peace of Jerusalem: Lord Sunderland meditating flight, I writ to my Lady, advised an Apologie:[1]

13 I went to Lond: [The rabble people demolish all Papists Chapells & severall popish Lords & Gent: house⟨s⟩, especialy that of the Spanish Ambassador, which they pillaged & burnt his Library &c:][a][2] 16 Dr. Tenison at St. Martins on: 8: Isay: 11. shewing the reverence we ought to have of the greate God, in all our Addresses to him:[3]

I din'd at my L. Clarendons:[b][4] The King flies to[c] sea, [putts in at Feversham for ballast is rudely detained by the people: comes back to W⟨hite⟩hall.][d][5]

The Pr: of Orange now advanc'd to Windsor, is invited by the King to St. James,[e] the messenger sent was the E. of Feversham the general of the forces: who going without Trumpet or passeport is detained prisoner by the Prince: The Prince accepts the Invitation, but requires his Majestie to retire to some distant place, that his owne Guards may be quartered about the palace & Citty: This is taken heinously, so the King gos away privately to Rochester: Is perswaded to come back: comes on the Sunday;[f] Goes to masse & dines in publique, a Jesuite says grace: [I was present][g] That night

---

[a] Interlined, probably when entry of 24–6 December was made; the word *rabble* is a further interlineation.   [b] Followed by *This evening his* Ma[je]: deleted.   [c] Followed by *Fra-* deleted.   [d] Interlined; the reading *detained* is doubtful.   [e] Followed by *by* deleted.   [f] Substituted for *Saturday*.   [g] Interlined.

---

[1] This letter is not traceable. Sunderland's movements at this time are uncertain. He apparently occupied his Whitehall lodgings as late as 23 November: Campana de Cavelli, ii. 340; and reached Rotterdam by 19 December (o.s.?): letter in Winston S. Churchill, *Marlborough*, 1933–8, i. 344–5.

[2] The outburst took place on the night of 11 December: notices in the newspapers, especially *English Currant*, 14 Dec. The Spanish ambassador (Ronquillo) occupied Wild (or Weld) House, near Lincoln's Inn Fields: above, p. 242 n.

[3] The text is doubtful.

[4] This was on 18 December. Clarendon had left London on 16 December for Windsor; and returned to London after dark on 17 December. See also Evelyn's letter to his son, 18 December (Bohn, iii. 289).

[5] James left London at about 3 a.m. on 11 December; was taken at sea near Faversham on the following night; and arrived back in London on 16 December.

a Council, [17][a] his Majestie refuses to assent to all proposals; gos away againe to Rochester:[b][1]

18[c] The Pr: comes to St. James, fills W-hall (the King
taking barge to[d] Gravesend at 12 a Clock) with Dut⟨c⟩h
Guard:[2] A Council of Peres meete about an Expedient to
call a parliament: Adjourne to the House of Lords:[3] The
Chancelor, E. of Peterbor, & divers Priests & other taken:[4]
E: of Sunderland flies[5] & divers others, Sir E: Hales, Walker
& other taken &[e] secured:[6] All the world go to see the Prince
at St. Jamess where is a greate Court, there I saw him &

---

[a] Marginal date. [b] Followed by *I saw him take barge a sad sight*,
added later and deleted. [c] Altered from *17*. [d] Followed by
Roche- deleted. [e] Followed by *Imp-* deleted.

[1] This paragraph is confused.
The prince was at Windsor from 14
to 17 December; James on 15
December sent Feversham from
Rochester to invite the prince to
come to London on 17 December;
and himself reached London on
16 December. That day Feversham
had delivered his message and been
arrested; his arrest had been ordered
on 13 December on account of his
disbanding the king's army without
having proper authority or providing for them. The prince sent a
letter by W. van Zuylestein (*D.N.B.*),
asking the king to stay at Rochester
but refusing to answer his message.
On the night of 17–18 December the
prince sent a message to James requiring him to remove next day to
Ham; the king asked to be allowed
to go to Rochester and left Whitehall
for the second and last time on 18
December: besides other sources see
James II, *Life*, ed. Clarke, ii. 262.
Evelyn saw James at dinner on 17
December and his departure from
Whitehall next day: letter of 18
December, as above (the passage in it
relating to Feversham is incorrect).
James held his council on 16 Decem-
ber after his arrival at Whitehall:
London Gazette, 17 Dec. The king's
attending mass in public on 17

December is mentioned in *Universal
Intelligence*, 22 Dec.
[2] The prince came to St. James's
Palace between 2 and 4 p.m. on
18 December (he remained there
until February 1689). The Dutch
guards had taken charge at White-
hall late at night on 17 December:
*His Majesties reasons for withdraw-
ing himself from Rochester*, dated
22 Dec. 1688; *Reflections on . . . his
Majesty's reasons*, 1689.
[3] The peers met at St. James's
on 21 December when the prince
asked them to advise him about
summoning a parliament. They met
again at Westminster on 22 December and later: *London Mercury*,
24 Dec.; *English Currant*, 26 Dec.
[4] Jeffreys was taken at Wapping
on 12 December: *London Gazette*,
13 Dec. The newspapers give
various reports as to where Peterborough was taken; he was in cus-
tody at Ramsgate by 18 December:
London Courant of that date, which
gives a list of captives.
[5] Above, p. 610 n.
[6] Hales was taken with the king
off Faversham on 12 December:
ibid., 15 Dec. Obadiah Walker was
taken on the same day, apparently
at Sittingbourne: *London Mercury*,
15 Dec.

severall of my Acquaintance that come over with him:[1] He is very stately, serious, & reserved: The Eng: souldiers &c. sent out of Towne to distant quarters:[a] not well pleased:[2] Divers reports & opinions, what[b] all this will end in; Ambition & faction feared:

21[c] I visited L. Clarendon where was the Bishops of Ely & St. Asaph: we had much discourse of Afairs:[3] I returned home:

23 Our Lecturer at Deptford: on: 1. Mark: 3. an Advent Sermon:

24 The King passes into France, whither the queen & child wer gon a few days before.[4]

25 Christmas day, our Lecturer on his former Text; The holy Communion followed, at which I received:

26 The Peeres & such Commons as were members of the Parliament at Oxford, being the last of Charles the first: meeting, desire the Pr: of Orange to take on him the Government, & dispose of the publique Revenue 'til a[d] Convention of Lords & Commons should meete in full[e] body,[e] appointed by his Circulary Letters to the Shires & Borrowghs 22. Jan:[5]

---

[a] MS. *q^rs:*   [b] Followed by *it* deleted.   [c] Altered from *19*.
[d] Followed by *P*- deleted.   [e-e] MS. *fullbody*.

---

[1] For the concourse see the newspapers, Campana de Cavelli, ii. 443, and Clarendon, 18 December. Burnet apparently came to London with the prince and notes his reserve. Lord Mordaunt came to London by 13 December: *London Courant*, 15 Dec.

[2] The prince had assumed control of military affairs. A list of quarters for the English, Scottish, and Irish forces is published in *London Gazette*, 20 Dec. The replacement of the English by Dutch guards at Whitehall, &c., displeased the English regiments: Mazure, iii. 288; Burnet, iii. 359. Clarendon states on 19 December that some officers and men were expressing their dislike of the prince's treatment of the king.

[3] Clarendon mentions Turner's visit this morning; he does not mention Lloyd or Evelyn. As a high tory, trying to combine loyalty to the king with Anglicanism, he was seeking a suitable Roman Catholic agent to persuade the king not to leave the country.

[4] James left Rochester about 1 a.m. on 23 December: *Universal Intelligence*, 26 Dec. The news reached London by the afternoon of the same day: *London Courant*, 25 Dec. The queen had left Whitehall with the prince of Wales early on 10 December, and arrived in Calais next day.

[5] The peers presented their address on 25 December; a second assembly, consisting of surviving members of Charles II's houses of

I had now quartered upon me a Lieutenant Coll: & 8 horses:

30 Our Lecturer on 122. *Psal:* 6 concerning the returne of assiduous Prayers of good men: Pomerid: a Stranger on 6. Eccles: not to judge according to successes in this life: This day Prayers for the Prince of Wales were first left off in our Church pew & pulpet.[1]

Greate preparations of all the Princes of Europ, against the French &c: the Emp: making peace with the Turke:[2]

168⅘ Jan: 1 Dined with me severall friends.

3 I went to Lond: about buisinesse, & to visite divers friends:

6. Epiphany, Dr. Tenison at St. Martins on 2: Psal: 8: shewing the calling of the Gentiles & how we were concerned there⟨i⟩n &c: The holy Communion followed, at which I received &c: [Lord make me worthy:][a]

7 I returned home: on foote, it having ben a long frost & deepe snow, ⟨so⟩[b] as the Thames was almost quite frozen over.[3]

13 Our Lecturer on 6 Matt. 21. concerning the Soveraigne good, & the way of attaining it.

15 I went to visite my Lord Archbish of Cant: where I found the Bishops of St. Asaph, Ely, Bath & Wells, Peterborow & Chichester;[4] The Earle of Alesbery[5] & Clarendon,

---

[a] Added later.   [b] MS. *as.*

---

commons and the aldermen and some members of the common council of London, presented a similar address on 27 December: *London Gazette,* 31 Dec. The prince announced on 28 December that he would send out letters for elections for a new parliament; they were ready for issue on 29 December.

[1] Luttrell states that an order to this effect by the bishop of London was being observed by the clergy in January: i. 496.

[2] Notices of the negotiations in *London Gazette,* 10 Sept. onwards; they were broken off in 1689.

[3] The river was frozen over for a few days but there was a thaw on 8 January: *English Currant,* 9 Jan. See also Wood, *Life and times,* iii. 291.

[4] Sancroft; Lloyd the apocalyptic, Francis Turner, Ken, White, and Lake; all except Lloyd became nonjurors. There is a short notice of this meeting in Clarendon; for Sancroft's views see G. D'Oyly, *The Life of William Sancroft,* 1821, i. 414–22.

[5] Above, p. 360; for his activities at this period see his *Memoirs,* i. 229.

Sir Geo: Makenzy[1] Lord Advocate of Scotland, & then came in a Scotch Archbishop:[2] &c. After prayers & dinner, were discoursed divers serious matters concerning the present state of the publique: & sorry I was to find, there was as yet no accord in the judgements of those who both of the Lords & Commons were to convene: Some would have the princesse made Queene without any more dispute, others were for a Regency, There was a Torie part (as then called so) who were for ⟨inviting⟩[a] his Majestie againe upon Conditions, & there were Republicarians,[3] who would make the Prince of Orange like a State-holder: The Romanists were also buisy among all these severall parties to bring them into Confusion; most for Ambition, or other Interest, few for Conscience and moderate[b] resolutions:[c][4] I found nothing of all this in this Assembly of Bishops, who were pleas'd to admitt me into their Discourses: They were all for a Regency, thereby to salve their Oathes, & so all publique matters to proceede in his Majesties name, thereby to facilitate the calling of a Parliament according to the Laws in being; this was the result of this meeting: My Lord of Cant: gave me greate thanks for the advertisement I sent his Grace in October, & assur'd me they tooke my counsel in that particular,[d] & that it came very seasonable:[5]

I found by the Lord Advocate of Scotland that the Bishops of Scotland, who were indeede very unworthy that Character & had don much mischiefe in that Church, were

---

[a] MS. *inviitting* altered from *admitting.* deleted.   [c] Followed by *I speak?* deleted.   [b] Followed by *Coun-*   [d] Followed by *I foun-* deleted.

---

[1] Mackenzie: above, iii. 475. He was lord advocate (i.e. king's advocate) from 1677 until the Revolution.

[2] Presumably John Paterson, 1632–1708, archbishop of Glasgow from 1687: *D.N.B.* He was at this time a political associate of Mackenzie: see C. Lindsay, earl of Balcarres, *Memoirs touching the Revolution in Scotland* (Bannatyne Club, 1841). For his leaving London in March see *Cal. S.P., Dom., 1689–90*, p. 13.

[3] This word is also used in *London Gazette*, 1682: *O.E.D.* Evelyn uses below a variant, republicary, which is not recorded elsewhere.

[4] This refers to the general state of opinion in the country. For the bishops' views see the paper in D'Oyly, as above.

[5] See above, p. 600.

now coming about to the True Interest, more to save themselves in this conjuncture, which threatned the abolishing[a]
the whole Hierarchy in that Kingdome, than for Conscience:
& therefore the Scotish Archbish: & Lord Advocate requested
my L. of Cant: to use his best endeavors with the Prince, to
maintaine the Church there in the same state as by Law at
present settled:[1] It now growing late, I after some private
discourse, tooke my leave of his Grace, most of the Lords
being gon: I beseech God of his infinite mercy to settle truth
& peace amongst us againe:

It was now that the Triall of the Bishops was published in
print:[2]

20 Our Lecturer proceeded on his former text; shewing the
greate importance of finding the way to the sovraine good, &
the difficulty:

In the A⟨f⟩ternoone I went to the French Congregation at
Grccnewich, The Preachers Text was 17: *Matt:* 9. giving
reasons why our B: Lord prohibited the divulging of this &
other his miracles 'til he should be raised from the dead; that
is, 'til his ⟨omnipotent⟩[b] power should be so manifestly
asserted, that none but the most obstinate should refuse the[c]
Gospel[c]: That after that they were to preach the Christian
faith, with all boldnesse, reproving the coldnesse & want of
zeale of the present age &c:

I visited the Marquis de Ruvignie:

---

[a] Followed by *that* deleted.   [b] MS. *omnipotend.*   [c-c] Substituted
for *to be convicted.*

---

[1] On 3 November the Scottish
bishops sent James a letter in which
they styled him 'the Darling of
Heaven' and expressed the hope
that God would preserve and
deliver him by giving him 'the
Hearts of your Subjects and the
Necks of Your Enemies': *London
Gazette,* 12 Nov. The rabbling and
dispossession of the Scottish episcopalian clergy took place about
Christmas. Members of their party
now came to seek William's protection against 'their implacable enemies', who were now 'getting the
Government, both in Church and
State, into their hands': Balcarres,
Mem., as above, pp. 18–19.

[2] *The Proceedings and Tryal in
the case of . . . William Lord Archbishop of Canterbury,* &c., 1689;
advertised in *London Gazette,* 17
Jan. The shorthand report was
taken for the bishops by Mr.
Blaney: Gutch, *Collectanea curiosa,*
ii. 378.

23ᵃ I went to Lond, The greate Convention being assembled the day before, falling upon the greate Question about the Government, Resolved that K. *Jam:* 2d, having by the advise of Jesuites & other wicked persons, endeavored to subvert the Lawes of church & state, and Deserting the Kingdome [carrying away the Seales &c]ᵇ withoutᶜ taking any care for the manegement of the Government, had by demise, abdicated himselfe, and wholy vacatedᵈ his right: & They did therefore desire the Lords Concurrence toᵉ their Vote, to place the Crowne upon the next heires: The Prince of Orange for his life, then to the Princesse his wife, & if she died without Issue to the Princesse of Denmark, & she failing to the heires of the Pr: Excluding for ever all possibility of admitting any Ro: Cath:ᶠ 1

27 Dr. Tenison preached at St. Martines, on 6: *Gen:* 5, shewing the universal Corruption of mens hearts, & exhorting to a serious watchfullnesse over them: I din'd at the Admiralty,² where was brought, a young Child not 12 yeares old, the sonn of one Dr. Clench,³ of the most prodigious

---

ᵃ Or *21*. In the margin opposite the following passage are dates *24, 25, 26*; and *27* deleted. ᵇ Interlined. ᶜ Altered from *&*. ᵈ Followed by *the* deleted. ᵉ Altered from or to *in*. ᶠ Followed by *These were the debates, and* [*29*] *the Vote was accordingly carried up to the Lords, which* deleted.

¹ The Convention met on 22 January; on 28 January the commons resolved that James, having attempted to subvert the constitution, &c., and having withdrawn himself out of the kingdom, had abdicated the government, and that the throne was vacant (Evelyn's rendering is inexact); they desired the lords' concurrence and the resolution was carried up on 29 January (see below). On 29 January the commons resolved that it was 'inconsistent with the Safety and Welfare of this Protestant Kingdom, to be governed by a Popish Prince'; on the same day this resolution was carried up to the lords, who immediately concurred in it. The conferring of the crown and the determination of the succession were first voted by the commons in this form (for a correct rendering see p. 622 n.) on 8 February as part of the Declaration of Rights; the lords concurred in the vote on 9 February. James probably took away the great seal on his first flight on 11 December; it was dropped into the Thames; and was recovered and altered to serve William and Mary: *Antiquaries Journal*, xxiii (1943), 1–13; Luttrell, i. 529.

² Pepys continued as secretary of the Admiralty until 20 February.

³ Andrew Clench, d. 1692; matriculated at Cambridge 1663; M.D. 1671; F.R.S. 1680: *D.N.B.*; see

maturity of memorie, & knowledge, for I cannot call it
altogether memory, but [something more]ᵃ extraordinary;
Mr. Pepys & my selfe examining him not in any method, but
[by]ᵃ promiscuously questions, which required judgement
& wonderfull discernement, to answere things so readily &
pertinently: There was not any thing in Chronologie,
Historie, Geographie, The several systemesᵇ of Astronomers,ᶜ
Courses of the starrs, Longitudes, Latitudes, doctrine of
the Spheares, Sourses & courses of Rivers, Creekes, harbors,
Eminent Citties, staples, boundaries & bearings of Countries,
not onely in Europe but any other part of the Earth, which
he did not readily resolve & demonstrate his knowledge of,
readily drawing out, with his pen any thing that he would
describe: He was able not onely to repeate the most famous
things which are left us in any of the Greeke or Roman
histories, Monarchie, Repub, Warrs, Colonies, Exploitsᵈ by
sea & land; but readily, besides all the Sacred stories of the
Old & New Test: the succession of all the Monarches, Babylonish, Persian, Gr: Roman, with all the lower Emperors,ᵉ
Popes, Heresiarches, & Councils; What they were cald about,
what they determined, [&]ᵃ in the Controversie of Easter,
The Tenets of the Gnostics, Sabellius,ᶠ Arius, Nestorius;ᵍ
The difference twixt St. Cyprian & Stephen¹ about rebaptiza-
tion; The Schismes, we leaped from that to other things
totaly different: To Olympic yeares, & Synchronismes; we
asked him questions which could not be resolved without
considerable meditation & judgement: nay, of some particulars of the Civil Lawes, of the Digest & Code: He gave
aʰ stupendous account of bothⁱ Natural, & Moral Philosophie,
& even in Metaphysics: Having thus exhausted our selves,

ᵃ Interlined.   ᵇ Or *systemas*.   ᶜ Altered from or to *Astronomie*.
ᵈ Altered from *pe-*   ᵉ Altered from *Empi-*.   ᶠ Or *Sabellians*.
ᵍ Or *Nestorians*.   ʰ Followed by *prodi-* deleted.   ⁱ Followed by
the deleted.

---

also below, 6 Jan. 1692. Two sons, Edmund and John, had both been admitted at Cambridge and at Gray's Inn in 1688. Nothing more is known of the present boy.
¹ Stephen I, pope from 254 to 257. For the controversy see St. Cyprian's epistles.

rather than this wonderfull Child, or Angel rather, for he was
as beautifull & lovely in Countenance, as in knowledge; we
concluded, with asking him, if in all he had read, or heard of,
he had ever met with any thing which was like, this Expedition of the Pr: of Orange; with so small a force, to obtaine 3
greate ⟨Kingdoms⟩,ᵃ without any Contest: He after a little
thought, told us, that he knew of nothing did more resemble
it, Than the coming of Constantin the Greate out of Brittane,
thro: France & Italy, so tedious a March, to meete Maxen-
tius, whom he overthrew at ponteᵇ Milvij,ᵇ with very little
conflict, & at the very gates of Rome, which he entered &
was received with Triumph, & obtained the Empire, not of
3 Kingdomes onely, but of all the then known World: He
was perfect in the Latine Authors, spake french naturaly, &
gave us a description of France,ᶜ Italy, Savoy, Spaine,
Antient & modernly divided; as also of the antient Greece,
S⟨c⟩ythia, & Northern Countries & Tracts, in a word, we left
questioning farther with astonishment: This the child did
without any set or formal repetition; as one who had learned
things without booke, but, as if he minded other things going
about the roome, & toying with a parat there, & as he was at
dinner [(*tanquam aliud agens* as it were)]ᵈ seeming to be full
of play, of a lively & spiritfull temper, allways smiling, &
exceedingly pleasant without the least levity, rudenesse or
childishnesse: His father assur'd us, he never imposed any
thing to charge his memorie, by causing him to get things by
heart, no, not the rules of Grammer; but his ⟨Tutor⟩ᵉ (who
was a French-man) reading to him, in French first, & then
in Latine: That he usualy plaied, amongst other boys 4 or
5 hours every day & that he was as earnest at play, as at his
study: He was perfect in Arithmetic, & now newlyᶠ entered
into the Greek: In sum [(*Horesco referens*)]ᵈ I had, read of
divers, forward & præcoce, Youthes, & some I have known;
but in my life, did never either heare or read of any like to
this sweete Child, if it be lawfull to call him Child, who has

---

ᵃ MS. *Kingdunes.*　　ᵇ⁻ᵇ Spelling doubtful.　　ᶜ Spelling doubtful.
ᵈ Interlined.　　ᵉ MS. *Tutors.*　　ᶠ Or *neerely*; spelling uncertain.

more knowledge, than most men in the world: I counseled his father, not to set his heart too much upon this Jewell,[a] *Immodicis brevis est ætas, et rara senectus*,[1] as I my selfe learn'd by sad experience in my most deare child Richard many yeares since, who dying before he was six years old, was both in shape & Countenance, & pregnancy of learning, next to prodigie[b] even in that tender-age, as I have given ample account in my præface to that Golden book of St. Chrysostome, which I published on that sad occasion &c:[2]

28 The Votes of the House of Comm: being Carried up, by their chaire-man Mr. Hamden, to the[c] Lords,[3] [29][d] I got a station by the Princes lodgings at the doore of the Lobby to the House, to heare much of the debate which held very long; The Lord Danby being in the chaire (for the Peres were resolved into a grand Committee of the whole house) after all had spoken, it comming to the question: It was carried out by 3 voices, again⟨s⟩t a *Regency*, which 51 of 54 were for, aledging the danger of dethroning   Kings, & scrupuling many passages & expressions of the Commons Votes; too long to set downe particularly, some were for sending to his Majestie with Conditions, others, that the K. could do no wrong, & that the maladministration was chargeable on his Ministers.[e] There were not above 8 or 9 Bish: & but two, against the Regency;[4] The *Arch Bishop* was absent:[5]

---

a Followed by *with* deleted.   b Followed by *as these* deleted.
c Followed by *Hous-* deleted.   d Marginal date.   e Or *Minister*.

---

[1] Martial, *Epigrams*, bk. vi, no. xxix, l. 7.

[2] For Richard Evelyn see above, iii. 206–9; for the *Golden Book*, iii. 220.

[3] This is the resolution that James II had abdicated and that the throne was thereby become vacant: see above, p. 616. It was carried up to the lords on 29 January by the chairman of the committee of the whole house (which had voted it), Richard Hampden: above, p. 227.

[4] The lords were debating not the commons' resolution, but a motion for establishing a regency, while James should continue as king in name. The motion was defeated, but the numbers are uncertain; there were 103 peers present; Clarendon names 49 peers forming the minority, and states that the motion was defeated by 2 votes; the House of Lords MSS. give 51 and 48. Twelve bishops voted for and 2 against the motion.

[5] Sancroft refused to attend the council of peers held on 21 December or the house of lords in the Convention or afterwards.

& the Cleargie now began a new to change their note, both in pulpet & discourse, upon their old passive Obedience:[1] so as people began to talke of the Bishops being cast out of the House:[2] In short, things tended to dissatisfaction on both sides, add to this the morose temper of the Pr: of Orange, who shewed so little Countenance to the Noblemen & others, expecting a more gracious & cherefull reception, when they made their Court:[3] The English Army likewise, not so in order, & firme to his Interest, nor so weaken'd, but that it might, give interruption:[4] Ireland in a very ill posture, as well as Scotland; nothing yet towards any settlement: God of his infinite mercy, Compose these ⟨things⟩,[a] that we may at lastt be a Nation & a church under some fixt and sober establishment:

30 Was the Anniversary of K: Ch: the Is Martyrdome; but in all the publique Offices & pulpet prayers, The Collects [& Litanys][b] for the King & Queene, were curtailed & mutilated: Dr. Sharp preached before the Common⟨s⟩; but was disliked & not so much as thanked for his sermon:[c][5]

---

a MS. *thigns.*   b Interlined.   c Followed by *Dr. Lloyd Bishop*
deleted.

---

[1] Evelyn presumably means that, having surrendered the doctrine of passive resistance in the summer of 1688, the clergy were now reverting to it. Although there were to be only about 400 nonjurors in 1689–90, the clergy in general apparently disliked what was going forward: see Grey, *Debates*, ix. 98–101, 112.

[2] I have found no other notices of any proposal of this kind.

[3] On William's coldness of manner, and especially as it would affect the English, see Burnet, *A supplement to Burnet's History of my own time*, ed. H. C. Foxcroft, 1902, p. 193 (passage written in 1686 or 1687).

[4] In January and February Luttrell notes the disaffection and desertions in the army; the latter include the Roman Catholics; his figures for the wastage are, however, probably much exaggerated: i. 494–5, 505. Only one regiment mutinied.

[5] Sharp had prayed for James as 'his most excellent Majesty', despite the commons' vote of 28 January that he had abdicated. He was voted the thanks of the house on 1 February, but only after some debate: *C.J.*, 1 Feb.; Grey, *Debates*, ix. 37–40; Sharp's memorandum in Sharp, *Life of Sharp*, i. 99–100. From the debate it appears that any modification of the service for the day was irregular if not illegal; but by 5 February prayers for the king were being omitted at the chapel royal at Whitehall and elsewhere: *London Intelligence*, 5 Feb. See also Clarendon, 23, 25, 28 Jan.

I went to St. Martin, where a stranger preached on *2: Apoc: 10* much against popery, with a touch at our Obligation of Loyalty to the King &c:

I came home afternoone, & at our church (the[a] next[a] ⟨day⟩ being appointed a Thanksgiving for deliverance by the P: of Orange, prayers purposly composed)[1] our Lecturer, preached on 97: Psal: 1. a very honest Sermon, shewing our duty to God for the many signal deliverances of his Church, without entering into the politics.

Feb: ⟨3⟩[b] Our[c] Lecturer on his former Text, shewing how all power flowes from God, & how absolutely necessary it is, that he should ⟨constitute⟩[d] his Vicegerents here, & how responsible they are that they governe justly; The fatal ends of those who have in all ages abused their power, & the hapinesse of religious Princes &c: The holy Communion follow'd, at which I received: Blessed be God.

6 The Kings Coronation day was ordred not to be observed, as hitherto it yearely had.[2]

The Convention of L: & Comm: now declare the Pr: & princesse of Or: Q: & K of England,[e] Fr: & Ireland (Scotland being an Independent Kingdome) The Pr & Princesse to enjoy it jointly during their lives, but the executive[f] Authority to be vested in the Prince during life, though all proceedings to run in both names: & that it descend to the heires of both, & for want of such Issue to the Princesse Ann of Denmark, & in want of such to the heires of the body of the Pr: of Or: if he survive, & for defect, to devolve to the Parliament to choose as they think fit: These produc'd a Conference with the Lords, when also there was presented

---

[a]-[a] Substituted for *there being it.*   [b] MS. *2.*   [c] Followed by *Viccar* deleted.   [d] MS. *constitude.*   [e] Followed by *but* deleted.
[f] Altered from *execution.*

[1] On 22 January both houses ordered the thanksgiving to be celebrated this day (14 February in the country): *L.J.,* xiv. 102; *C.J.,* x. 11; notice in *London Gazette,* 24 Jan. A *Form of Prayer and Thanksgiving* was published.

[2] This was the day of James's accession, not his coronation. The non-observance was ordered by the house of lords on 2 February: *L.J.;* the order is printed in *London Gazette,* 4 Feb.; notice in *London Intelligence,* 5 Feb.

heads of such [new][a] laws as were to be enacted: & upon those
Conditions they tis thought will be proclaim'd:[1] There was
much contest about the Kings abdication, & whether he had
vacated the Government: E. of Notingham & about 20
Lords & many Bishops, entred their protests &c, but the
Concurrence was greater against them—[2] The Princesse
hourely Expected:[3] Forces sending to Ireland, that K⟨ing⟩-
dome being in greate danger, by the E. of Tyrconnells Armie,
& expectations from France:[4] which K. is buisy to invade
Flanders, & encounter the German Princes comming now to
their Assistance:[5] so as this is likely to be one of the most
remarkable summers for action, as has happed for many
Ages:

---

[a] Interlined.

---

[1] This is an inaccurate rendering
of the section of the Declaration of
Rights relating to the holding of the
crown. It was to be held by the
prince and princess of Orange during
their lives and the life of the sur-
vivor; after their decease it was to
devolve on the heirs of the body of
the princess; in default of such issue,
to the Princess Anne and the heirs
of her body; and in default of such
issue, to the heirs of the body of the
prince of Orange. There is no provision for the further succession.
The complete draft of the Declaration was presented to the commons
on 8 February, and after a conference on 11 February, in which
the course of the succession was not
discussed, was adopted by both
houses on 12 February. It was presented to the prince and princess on
13 February and on the same day
they were proclaimed king and
queen: *C.J.*; *L.J.*; *London Gazette*,
14 Feb. Abbreviated versions of
the section of the Declaration relating to the succession are printed in
Orange Gazette, 12 Feb.; *London Intelligence*, 12 Feb.

[2] This refers to the crucial debate
of 6 February, when twenty-six lay

and twelve spiritual peers entered
their dissents against the vote that
James had 'abdicated' and that
the throne was 'thereby vacant'.
Ninety-five lay and seventeen spiritual peers were present in the house
on that day: *L.J.*, xiv. 118–19;
Clarendon, 6 Feb. This year was
published *A List of the Lords that
Enter'd their Protest against the
Vacancy of the Throne*.

[3] She arrived on 12 February,
going immediately to Whitehall.
For her journey see *Orange Gazette*,
12 Feb.; *Universal Intelligence*,
13 Feb.

[4] A report from St. Germain-en-
Laye of 13 February, N.S., gives a
notice relating to Ireland and the
projected French expedition: *Universal Intelligence*, 15 Feb. On 20
February it was reported that some
forces were to be sent from England;
some regiments set out a few days
later: *Orange Gazette*, 22 Feb., 5
March.

[5] Notices in *London Gazette*, 11,
14 Feb., &c. The declaration of
war against France made by the
Imperial Diet at Ratisbon was published on 12 February, N.S.: ibid.,
28 Feb.

10 Our Lecturer preached on 26. Matt: 11ᵃ concerning our dutie to all the members of Christs Mystical body, whilst he is no more conversant with us in his natural:[1]

Pomerid: Curate ⟨on⟩ᵇ 119 Psal: 105. shewing the perfection & use of the H Scriptures:ᶜ

16 I went to Lond: 17th Dr. Tenison [at St. Martin]ᵈ on 19 Psal: 12. Concerning the danger, & necessity of begging pardon of God, to clense us from our seacret sinns, not such onely, as we have don in seacret, but such as are seacret & unobserv'd & unknown to us:

21 At St. James's church preached Dr. Burnet, on 5. *Deut:* 29 relating to the obligation lying upon the nation, to walke worthy of Gods particular & signal deliverances of this Nation & Church:[2]

22 Dr. Stillingfleete (Deane of S Paules) on 1. *Pet:* 4. 18: Resolving that Text, If the Righteous scarcely be saved, where shall the sinner &c appeare; to meane not as if there were any doubt of a good-mans Salvation; but the difficultie of a good mans continuance to be religious, amidst such temptations, snares, & almost inevitable dangers inticing to sin & the being perverted, which all men meete with in this life, & that are so hard to Escape; so as if a righteous man escape them with such difficulty, howᵉ shall the wiccked, who are lesse solicitousᶠ & go on in sin, be able to encounter them, & consequently hope for Salvation?[3]

I saw the new Queene & King, so proclaim'd, the very next day of her coming to White-hall, Wednesday 13. Feb. with wonderfull acclamation & general reception, Bonfires, bells, Gunns &c:[4] It was believed that they both, especialy the

---

ᵃ Reading doubtful.　ᵇ MS. *of.*　ᶜ Or *Scripture.*　ᵈ Interlined.
ᵉ Followed by *have we* deleted.　ᶠ Followed by *to* deleted.

---

[1] The text is doubtful.

[2] Ash Wednesday had fallen on 13 February. For the sermons here on Thursdays in Lent see above, p. 544.

[3] Lenten sermon at court; but the preacher listed is the dean of Norwich, Dr. Sharp; Stillingfleet was to have preached on 15 February: list in *London Gazette*, 17 Jan. The new queen was present. Printed as *A sermon preached before the Queen*, 1689.

[4] The princess had arrived on 12 February; the offer of the crown was made to William and her on

Princesse, would have shewed some (seeming) reluctancy at
least, of assuming her Fathers Crowne & made some Apologie,
testifying her regret, that he should by his misgoverment
necessitat the Nation to so extraordinary a proceeding,
which would have shewed very handsomly to the world,
(and according to the Character give⟨n⟩ of her piety &c) &
consonant to her husbands first Declaration, that there was
no intention of Deposing the King, but of Succoring the
Nation;[1] But, nothing of all this appeared; she came into
W-hall as to a Wedding, riant[2] & jolly, so as seeming to be
quite Transported:[3] rose early[a] on[a] the next morning of her

---

[a-a] Or *earlyer*.

---

13 February; and they were proclaimed king and queen the same
day. She occupied the queen's
apartments at Whitehall from her
arrival; William was still at St.
James's Palace on 6 February and
probably did not move to White-
hall until her arrival: *London
Gazette*, 11, 14 Feb.; *Universal
Intelligence*, 13, 15 Feb.

[1] I have found no other reference
to the expected apology. The prince
in his first *Declaration* (10 Oct. 1688,
N.S.) declared that his expedition
was 'intended for no other Designe,
but to have a free and lawfull Parliament assembled, as soon as is possible'; the king's 'Evill Councel-
lours' are attacked, but it was
assumed—as it was expected—that
James would continue to occupy the
throne. The prince changed his
views apparently about 16 December: Foxcroft, *Halifax*, ii. 37–8.
For his reluctance to accept the
crown see below, p. 625 n. If
Mary's piety is not mentioned in
contemporary pamphlets, Evelyn
may have heard about it from
Compton or Burnet or from one of
her chaplains: for the last see Sir
C. H. Firth, *A Commentary on
Macaulay's History of England*,
1938, pp. 309–10.

[2] Occurrences of this as an
English word in 1567 and from 1720
onwards are recorded in *O.E.D.*

[3] 'The next day after I came, we
were proclaimed, and the goverment put wholy in the princes hand.
This pleased me extreamly, but
many would not believe it, so that
I was fain to force my self to more
mirth then became me at that time,
and was by many interpreted as ill
nature, pride, and the great delight
I had to be queen. But alas, they
did litle know me, who thought me
guilty of that; I had been only for
a regency, and wisht for nothing
else . . . but the good of the public
was to be preferd and . . . I have had
more trouble to b[r]ing my self to
bear this so envyed estate then I
should have had to have been reduced to the lowest condition in the
world': Mary, *Memoirs*, ed. Doebner, p. 11. Burnet says that Mary
told him that William had written
to her asking her 'to put on a cheer-
fulness' on her arrival; this was in
order to counteract reports that
'she was not well pleased with the
late transaction, both with relation to her father, and to the present
settlement': iii. 406. Mary accepted
'the lawfulness of the design' of the
expedition to England: ibid., iii.

arival, and in her undresse (as reported) before her women were up; went about from roome to roome, to see the Convenience of White-hall:[1] Lay in the same bed & appartment where the late Queene lay: & within a night or two, sate downe to play at Basset, as the Q. her predecessor us'd to do: smiled upon & talked to every body; so as no manner of change seem'd in Court, since his Majesties last going away, save that the infinite crowds of people thronged to see her, & that she went to our prayers: This carriage was censured by many: she seemes to be of a good nature, & that takes nothing to heart whilst the Pr: her husband has a thoughtfull Countenance, is wonderfull serious & silent, seemes to treate all persons alike gravely:[2] & to be very intent on affaires, both Holland, & Ireland & France calling for his care: Divers Bishops, & Noble men are not at all satisfied with this so suddain Assumption of the Crown, without any previous, sending & offering some Conditions to the absent King: or, upon his not returning & assenting to those Conditions within such a day: to have proclaim'd him Regent &c:[3] But the major part of both houses, prevailed to make them King & Q: immediately, and a Crowne was tempting &c—[4] This was

---

311; she was distressed by her father's misfortunes and was aware of the invidiousness of her position; but was supported by her love of her husband, her sense of duty towards the public, and above all by her belief in God's guidance. Besides Mary's *Memoirs* see Firth, *Commentary on Macaulay*.

[1] For Mary's examining her apartment at Whitehall see also Sarah Churchill, duchess of Marlborough, *Account of the Conduct, &c.*, 1742, pp. 25–6.

[2] Apart from his natural bad manners William was in ill health at this time: Mary, *Mem.*, p. 10.

[3] Arguments for negotiating with James are put forward in [W. Sherlock], *A letter to a member of the Convention* (published before 24 Jan. 1689, the date of *An answer* to it);

they appear either naïve or disingenuous. Sancroft at least at one time held that king and subjects were indissolubly bound to one another, but that if the king should prove unable to carry on the government, a regent or regents might be appointed to take his place; he might be incapacitated by lunacy, &c., or 'by some invincible prejudices of mind': D'Oyly, *Sancroft*, i. 418–21.

[4] Mary's attitude is made clear in her *Memoirs*, William's in a private letter of 24 or 25 December, O.S.: 'Si j'avois voulu donne le moindre encouragement je suis persuade qu'ils m'auroient declare Roy ce que je n'embitione point n'estant pas venu pour cela icy. Ce qu'ils fairont a l'Assemble de la convocation [i.e. the Convention] je ne scai

opposed & spoke against with such vehemency by my L. Clarendon (her owne Unkle) as putt him by all preferments, which must doubtlesse, ⟨have⟩ been as greate, as[a] could have ben given him:[1] My L: of Rochester his bro: overshot himselfe by the same carriage & stiffnesse,[2] which, their friends thought, they might have well spared, when they saw how it was like to be over-ruled, & that it had ben sufficient to have declared their dissent with[b] lesse passion, acquiescing in due time: The Æ B of Cant, & some of the rest, upon scrupule of Conscience, & to salve the Oathes they had taken, entred their protests, & hung[c] off:[3] Especially the Arch-Bishop, who had not all this while so much as appeared out of Lambeth: all which incurred the[d] wonder of many, who observed with

---

a Followed by *he* deleted.   b Altered from *to*.   c Or *hang*.
d Followed by *ad-* deleted.

point, mais je crains qu'ils voudront m'oblige a accepter une chose que je ne demande nullement, quoyque je prevois fort bien que le monde en jugera autrement. Si j'accepte le Gouvernement [the interim government until the meeting of the Convention] je poures vous envoyer incessament le secour qu'en cas de geurre l'Angleterre est oblige de donner a la Hollande . . .': P. L. Müller, *Wilhelm III von Oranien und Georg Friedrich von Waldeck*, 1873–80, ii. 126; see also William's letter of 14 February, o.s.: he has accepted the crown: 'Je vous asseure que ce n'est pas un petit fardeau, et que je le considere très bien mais je n'ay peu m'en dispenser . . .': ibid., p. 137; so 15 February, o.s.: 'Je m'imagine que vous me cognoisses asses de croire que l'Eclat d'une couronne ne m'eblouit point. et si ce n'avoit esté une absolue necessite je ne l'aurois poi⟨n⟩t accepte': ibid., p. 139.
1 In the conference between the two houses on 6 February one of Clarendon's speeches was probably

unnecessarily outspoken: *The Debate at large, between the House of Lords*, &c., 1695, pp. 125–9. His utterances in the house of lords are not recorded; but, as a strong legitimist, he was deeply afflicted by the turn of events and deliberately absented himself from London from 12 to 16 February; as a result Mary refused to see him in private: Diary, 6, 8 Feb., &c. William, who in December described him and his brother as 'Knaves', had offended him by refusing to hear his representations concerning Ireland: Foxcroft, *Halifax*, ii. 202; Burnet, *Own time*, iii. 368–9.
2 In the conference on 6 February Rochester had spoken against the view that the throne was vacant; he kissed the new king's hand but Mary refused to see him in private: Clarendon, 16 Feb. William's distrust of him probably dated from the later years of Charles II.
3 Sancroft had refused all along to have any part in present events. On 6 February twelve bishops had joined in the protest against the abdication vote: above, p. 622 n.

what zeale they contributed to the Princes[a] Expedition, &
all this while also, rejecting any proposals of sending againe
⟨for⟩[b] the absented King: That they should now boggle &
raise scrupuls, & such as created much division among[c] people,
greatly rejoicing the old Courtiers, & Papist⟨s⟩ especialy:

Another objection was the invalidity of what was don, by
a Convention onely, & the as yet unabrogated Laws: which
made them on the 22, make themselves a parliament, the
new King passing the act with the Crowne on his head: This
lawyers disputed; but necessity prevailed, the Government
requiring a speedy settlement:[1] And now innumerable were
the Crowds who solicited for & expected Offices, most of the
old ones turn'd out: Two or 3. White Staves were disposed
of some days before, as L: Steward to the E. of Devonshire,
Tress: of the Household to L: Newport, L. Cham: to the K,
to my L: of Dorset &c: but there were yet none in offices of
the Civil government, save: Pr: Seale to the Marq: of Halifax: A Council of 30 was chosen, L. Danby Presedent:[2] but
neither Chancellor, Tressurer, Judges &c not yet declared,
A greate seale not yet finished:[3] Thus far went things when
I returned home (having visited divers of my old acquaintance &c) which was [23][d] on the Saturday:

24 St. *Matthias*, our Viccar preached on 12. *Luke*. 21 shewing the vanity and[e] uncertainty of riches, &c:

Mar. 2 To Lond: 3d Dr. *Tenison* at St. Martins on: 16:
Matt 26: of the foolish exchange of the soule, for temporal

---

[a] Followed by *commin-* deleted.   [b] MS. *from.*   [c] Followed
by *the* deleted.   [d] Marginal date.   [e] Followed by *unsafety &*;
the word *unsafety* deleted.

---

[1] The bill was presented to the
lords on 18 February and was
passed by them on 19 February; it
was passed by the commons on 22
and by the king on 23 February:
L.J.; *C.J.*; *London Gazette*, 25 Feb.;
commons' debates in Grey, *Debates*,
ix. 84–106. The act was further
confirmed by an act passed in 1690
by the first parliament summoned
by royal writ: 2 William and Mary,
c. 1.

[2] The list of the privy council is
printed in *London Gazette*, 18 Feb.;
the offices held by various members
of it are appended to their names;
these appointments were not published separately. For Dorset see
above, iii. 466.
[3] So *Harlem Currant*, 19 Feb.
For the technical importance of the
great seal see Grey, *Debates*, ix.
7, 10; *Antiquaries Journal*, xxiii
(1943), 5.

things: The holy Communion follow'd, of[a] which I participated.

6: Dr.   at White-hall before the new Queene: 2. Thess: 5. pray continualy &c.[1]

8. Dr. Tillotson deane of Cant: an excellent discourse on 5. Matt: 44: exhorting to charity and forgivenesse of Enemies;[2] I suppose purposly, The new Parliament now being furiously about Impeaching those who were obnoxious:[b] & as their custome has ever ben going on violently, without reserve or moderation:[3] whilst wise men were of opinion that the most notorious Offenders being named & excepted, an Act of Amnesty were more seasonable, to paciffie the minds of men, in so generall a discontent of the nation, especialy of those who did not expect to see the Government assum'd without any reguard to the absent King, or proving a spontaneous abdication, or that the Pr: of Wales was an Imposture, &c: 5 of the Bishops also still refusing to take the new Oath:[4] In the interim to gratifie & sweeten the people, The Hearth Tax was remitted for ever: but what intended to supply it, besids present greate Taxes on land: is not named:[5]

---

[a] Altered from or to *at*.   [b] Or *abnoxious*.

[1] The preacher listed is Dr. Grove, i.e. Robert Grove, c. 1634–96; D.D. 1681; chaplain in ordinary c. 1690–1; bishop of Chichester 1691: *D.N.B.*

[2] Lenten sermon at court. The sermon was printed this year (reprinted in Tillotson, *Works*, 1752, i. 303–13).

[3] On 5 March the commons appointed a committee to examine some grievances already reported and to determine what persons were responsible for them: *C.J.*; Grey, *Debates*, ix. 137–41. The committee reported on 29 May.

[4] On 26 February the lords ordered that they should take the new oath of allegiance to William and Mary, &c., on 2 March. On 2 and 4 March the archbishop of York and seven other bishops took

the oath: *L.J.*, xiv. 133, 137, 138. A notice, that the archbishop of York and four bishops (by name), took it on 4 March, appears in *Orange Gazette*, 5 March.

[5] The Hearth Money or Chimney Tax had been established by an act of 1662; it was abolished by an act passed on 24 April of this year. The abolition had been suggested on 1 March in a message from the king: *C.J.*, x. 38; the commons' reply is printed in *Orange Gazette*, 5 March; *London Gazette*, 7 March. The taxes on land probably refer to the aid which was granted by an act passed on 21 March. Mention of a land-tax is first reported by Grey on the same day; a bill to establish it was introduced in the commons on 13 May.

The King abroad furnished with[a] mony & officers by the French King going now for Ireland,[1] Their wonderfull neglect of more timely preventing that from hence, and disturbances in Scotland, gives men apprehension of greate difficulties before any settlement can be perfected here: [whilst][b] The Parliament men dispose of the greate Offices amongst themselves: The Gr: Seale, Treasury, Admiralty put into commission, of many unexperienc'd persons to gratifie the more:[2] So as, by the present prospect of things (unlesse God Almighty graciously interpose, & give successe in Ireland, & settle Scotland) more Trouble seemes to threaten this nation, than could be expected: In the Interim, the New K. referrs all to the Parliament in the most popular[3] manner imaginable: but is very slow in providing against all these menaces, besides finding difficulties in raising men to send abroad, The former army (who had never don any service hitherto, but received pay, and passed the summers in an idle scene of a Camp at Hounslow) unwilling to engage, & many of them dissaffected, & scarce to be trusted:[4]

9: I returned home: [10:][c] our[d] *Viccar*: on his former subject 21. Matt:

The *Curate* 90 Psal: 12: of the brevity of [this][b] life, & the wisdome of providing[e] for another more lasting.

24:[f] Palme[g]-Sonday: I went early to Lond: according to my custome, to passe the Holy-Weeke in Lond: At St. Martines preached Dr. Tenison on: 2. Cor: 4. 8. shewing the Troubles & afflictions happning to the faithfull, and difference of their troubles[h] from that of the wiccked whose troubles were ⟨intollerably⟩[i] greater, & [thus][b] fuller of anxiety:

---

[a] Followed by *men* deleted.   [b] Interlined.   [c] Marginal date.
[d] Altered from *D*r.   [e] Followed by *of* deleted.   [f] Altered from *25*.
[g] Substituted for *Lady day*.   [h] Or *trouble*.   [i] MS. *intollerable*.

[1] Reports in *Orange Gazette*, 5, 9 March.
[2] Commissioners for the great seal were appointed on 2 March; for the admiralty on 8 March; for the treasury not until 8 April: *London Gazette*.
[3] Here presumably seeking to gain the favour of the people: see *O.E.D.*; used in an unfavourable sense.
[4] Desertions were numerous at this time: Reresby, 10 March; Clarendon, 10 March.

which the godly were freed from, especialy from despaire &c.

25 Lady-day, preached a Young man: at St. Martin on: 1. Luke: 30. 31 concerning the Incarnation & Annuntiation, the ministry of Angels:

27: At White-Hall, Dr. Jeane,[1] Regius professor at Oxon: before the new Queene: &c: on: 1. *John*: 5. 4. shewing in what consisted that Victory, which over-came the world, namely our Faith, & obediencial relyance on Christ: insisting on those three, the world, the flesh, & the devil: in the[a] lust of the Eye, lust of the flesh & pride of life:

[28 I visited[b] Mr. Boile where an Italian Traveller described how farr he had ben in the desert of Africa and saw a Creature, bodied like an ox, head like a pike fish, taile like a peacock:][c]

29 Good friday Morning at St. Martin, Dr. Tenison: on: 53.[d] Isah: ver: 3.[d] shewing how our B: Saviour was by innumerable Instances a man of the greatest sorrow that ever appeared on the Earth, & that for our sake,[e] with proper application:

The Holy Sacrament follow'd at which I received:

Pomeridiano at W.hall, before the Princesse of Denmark: The Bish: of *St. Asaph* Almoner:[2] on: 12[f] Zech:[f] 10: Describing the cruelty & malice of the stubborn Jewes, through all the sad Circumstances of their Crucifying our B: Lord, & how they who had don this then, & crucifie him still by their sinns, shall see him whom they pierced so ungratefully; describing the horror of the last day & the appearing of Christ, with exceeding patheticalnesse:

I returned home after this:[g] sermon:

The new King, much blamed for neglecting Ireland, now like to be ruined by the L. Tyrconnel,[h] & his popish party;

---

a Followed by *pride* deleted.   b Or *visied*.   c Interlined.
d–d Substituted for *12 Zech. 10.*   e Or *sakes*.   f–f Substituted for *53 John:*   g Altered from *di-*.   h Altered from *Tyrconnels.*

[1] Jane. Lenten sermon at court.   [2] Lloyd the apocalyptic. He appears to have been appointed almoner before 25 March: Wood, *Athenæ*, iv. 716.

too strong for the Protestants; wonderfull uncertainty where King James was, whether in France or Ireland:[1] The Scotts seeme as yet to favor King William, rejecting K James letter to them:[2] yet declaring nothing positively: Souldiers in England, discontented: Parliament preparing the Coronation Oath:[a][3] Presbyterians & Dissenters displeased at the vote to preserve the protestant Religion as established by Law; without mentioning what they were to have as to Indulgence:[4] The Arch-Bishop of Cant, & the other 4: refusing to come to Parliament, it was deliberated whether they should incurr premunire: but this was thought fit to be let fall, & connived at, for feare of the people, to w⟨h⟩om these prelates were very deare, for their oppo⟨s⟩ing poper⟨y⟩:[5] Court Offices, distributed among the Parliament men:[6] no Considerable fleete as yet set forth: in summe: Things far from [the][b] settlement was expected by reason of the slothfull sickly temper of the new King:[7] and unmindfullnesse of

---

[a] Or *Oaths*.   [b] Interlined.

---

[1] News of his arrival at Kinsale on 12 March reached London by about 17 March: Luttrell, i. 512, 515. No positive statement appeared in *London Gazette* until 6 May.

[2] Notice ibid., 25 March; the proceedings in Edinburgh on 16 March; fuller notice, with James's letter, in *An Account of the proceedings of the meeting of the Estates in Scotland*, 1689 (this forms no. 1 of a periodical, *A Continuation of the proceedings of the Convention of the Estates in Scotland*, which continued, with slight changes of title, to 18 Oct. 1690; further citations below).

[3] The act for establishing the Coronation Oath (1 William and Mary, c. 6) received the royal assent on 9 April: *London Gazette*, 11 April.

[4] This presumably refers to the votes of the two houses on 27 February and 1 March, to 'stand by and assist the King . . . in Defence of the Protestant Religion, and the Laws

of the Kingdom': *C.J.*, x. 36, 39; *L.J.*, xiv. 136; but possibly to a clause in the new Coronation Oath.

[5] On 22 March Sancroft was ordered to attend the house of lords on the following day. He did not attend, pleading illness as the reason for his not doing so: *L.J.*, xiv. 158, 159; *Hist. MSS. Comm., House of Lords MSS., 1689–90*, p. 39. No further proceedings in the house against him or any other bishops are traceable, apart from some answers to the original summons to attend.

[6] Very few appointments are announced in *London Gazette* about this time; the most important were those of the commissioners for the treasury, three peers and two members of the house of commons, on 8 April: issue for 11 April. See also issue for 28 March.

[7] For William's health see above, p. 625 n. His slothfulness is contradicted by his letters to Waldeck.

the Parliament, as to Ireland,[1] which is like to prove a[a] sad omission. The Confederats, beate the French out of the Palatinate, which they had most barbarously ruined:[2]

31 Easter day: Our Viccar on 22 Matt: 29 Concerning the infinite power of God, in effecting the Resurrection: The holy Communion follow'd, at which I received. The Curate on 1. Cor: 15. ver: 56. 57. a Resurrection sermon.

Aprill 7: Having taken cold after some preventing physick: I was not at Church this day, to my greate sorrow:

10[b] I went to Lond: was at the R. Society, where the very ingenious Mr. Waler brought in his Tables of knowing plants by a peculiar method: There was an extraordinary greate[c] scorpion, sent the Society out of Africa, whose Eyes were in his back, like to spiders, but not so prominent:[3]

11 I saw the procession both to, & from the Abby church of Westminster, with the greate feast in Westminster Hall &c: at the Coronation of the new K William & Q. Mary:[4] That which was different from former Coronations, was, something altered in the Coronation Oath, concerning maintaining the Prot: Religion: &c:[5] Dr. Burnet (now made L.B. of *Sarum*)[6] preached on   with infinite applause: The parliament men

---

[a] Followed by *sore* deleted.   [b] Altered from *19*.   [c] Followed by *Afri-* deleted.

---

[1] The commons were concerned with the state of Ireland, and providing a supply for it, from 19 or 20 March onwards: *C.J.*, x. 53, &c.

[2] Perhaps from *London Gazette*, 21 March. Notices of the French evacuation and devastation of the Palatinate appear frequently in February and March.

[3] Hooke mentions this meeting. Richard Waller (above, p. 325) was apparently making limnings or coloured drawings of plants about this time: Hooke, diary, 14 March, 4, 13, 30 April, in Gunther, *Early science in Oxford*, x. 106, &c.

[4] There is a notice of the coronation, processions, &c., in *London Gazette*, 15 April.

[5] The new oath was prescribed by the act of parliament passed on 9 April. It differs considerably from that used in 1660: and the king promises to maintain 'the Protestant reformed religion established by law': for texts see C. Grant Robertson, *Select Statutes*, &c., pp. 118–20. Evelyn had urged the importance of this phraseology in his letter to Sancroft of 10 Oct. 1688: above, p. 600 n.

[6] Burnet had been nominated bishop of Salisbury about 5 March and had been consecrated on 31 March: Clarke and Foxcroft, *Burnet*, pp. 265, 267; *London Gazette*, 1 April. His sermon this day was printed this year.

had Scaffolds & places which tooke up one whole side of the Hall:[1] & when the K & Q. had din'd. The Ceremonie of the Champion, & other services upon Tenures: The Parliament men were also feasted in the Exchequer Chamber: and had each of them a Medaile of Gold given them worth five & fourty shill: the K. & Q: effigies inclining one to another, on one side, the Reverse Jupiter throwing a bolt at Phaeton, the Word   which was but dull seing they might have had[a] out of the poet something[b] as apposite   The sculpture also very meane:[2] Much of the splendor of the proceeding was abated, by the absence of divers who should have made it up: There being but as yet 5 Bish:[3] 4. Judges, (no more at present, it seemes [as yet][c] sworn)[4] & severall noblemen & greate Ladys wanting: But indeede the Feast was magnificent: The next day, went the H of Commons & kissed their new Majesties hands in the Banqueting house:[d][5]

12 I went the next day afternoone [with the B: of St. Asaph][c] to visite my L. of Canterbery at Lambeth, who had excused himselfe from officiating at the Coronation, (which the Bishop of Lond: performed assisted by the A.B: of Yorke)[6] we had much private & free discourse with his Grace, concerning severall things, relating to the Church, there being now a Bill of Comprehension to be brought[e] to the Commons

---

a Followed by *it* deleted.   b Followed by *more* deleted.   c Interlined.
d Followed by *And* deleted.   è Followed by *be-* deleted.

---

[1] This was the first coronation, at least since 1485, to take place while parliament was in session.

[2] Evelyn describes the medal incorrectly; the busts of William and Mary both face to their left, William's being partially superimposed on Mary's. The inscription is 'Ne totus absumatur'. The medal is by John Roettiers (above, p. 138): Hawkins, *Medallic illustrations*, i. 662–3. The busts face one another on two Dutch medals commemorating the coronation: ibid., pp. 668–9, 672.

[3] The archbishop of York and the bishops of London, St. Asaph, Rochester, Winchester, Bristol, and Salisbury (Lamplugh; Compton, Lloyd, Sprat, Mews, Trelawny, Burnet) are mentioned in the notice in *London Gazette*.

[4] The only appointments appear to have been those of the master of the rolls and of one judge in each of the three courts.

[5] Ibid., 15 April.

[6] Lamplugh, promoted from Exeter by James II on 16 November and enthroned on 19 December. Compton was the presiding cleric at the coronation.

from the Lords:[1] I urg'd, that when they went about to reforme some particulars in the Liturgie,[a] Church discipline, Canons &c: The Baptising in private Houses, without necessity, might be reformd: as likewise the Burying dead bodies so frequently in the Churches: The one proceeding meerely from the pride of [the][b] Women, bringing that into Custome, which was onely indulged in case of iminent danger: & out of necessity, during the Rebellion and persecution of the Cleargy,[c] in our late Civil Warres &c: The other from the Avarice of the Minister, who made[d] in some opulent parishes, almost as much of permissions[e] to bury in the chancels & churches, as of their livings, and were paid with considerable advantage & gifts, for baptising in Chambers: To this the two Bishops, heartily assented: and promised their indeavors to get it reformed: utterly disliking both practice⟨s⟩, as novel, & undecent:[2] We discoursed likewise concerning the greate disturbance & prejudice it might cause should the new oath (now[f] upon the anvile) be imposed upon any, save such as were in [new][b] office; without any retrospect to such as either had no office; or[g] had ben long in office, who likely had some scrupules about taking a new othe, having already sworn fidelity to the Government, as established by Law:[3] and this we all knew to be the case of my L. Arch Bishop & some other worthy persons, who were not so fully satisfied with the Conventions abdicating the late K James, To whom they had sworn alegiance &c: So I[h] went back to Whit hall, & thence home:

K. James now certainly in Ireland; with the Marshall

---

[a] Followed by *&* deleted.   [b] Interlined.   [c] Followed by *du-* deleted.   [d] Substituted for *had*.   [e] Or perhaps *permissing* (for 'permitting').   [f] In MS. the opening bracket precedes *should*.   [g] Followed by *were* deleted.   [h] Altered from *we*.

[1] The Protestant Comprehension bill, sent down to the commons on 8 April, and laid aside by them after a first reading on that day: *Hist. MSS. Comm., House of Lords MSS., 1689–90*, pp. 49–52.

[2] For private baptisms see above, ii. 5; *Hist. of Religion*, ii. 381; and works by E. Arwaker, 1687, and M. Strong, 1692. For burial in churches see above, p. 304.

[3] The oath of allegiance to William and Mary, appointed by 1 Will. and Mary, c. 8. It was at present in committee in the house of commons.

d'Aveaux, whom he made a Pr: Counselor,[a] who immediatly caused the King to remove the protestant Counselor⟨s⟩ (some wheroff it seemes had continued to sit) telling him that his Master the K of France would never assist him, if he did not immediatly do it:[1] by which tis apparent how this poore Prince is menag'd by the French:

Scotland declare for K. William & Q: Mary, with the Reasons of their laying K James aside [not as Abdicating but forfaiting his right by maladministrat⟨ion⟩, the particulars mentioned][b] which being published, I repeate not:[2] proceeding with much more caution & prudence than we did; who precipitated all things to the great reproch of the Nation, but all[c] that was plainly menaged by some crafty, ill principled men: The new Pr: Council having a Republican Spirit,[3] & manifestly undermining all future Succession of the Crown, and prosperity of the Church of England: which yet, I hope, they will not be able to accomplish so soone as they hope: though they get into all places of Trust and profit:

14: Our Viccar on 22. Matt: 29. 30: asserting the Resurrection:

The Curate in the Afternoone on 13. Romans 12: Exhorting to timely Reformation: This was a more Seasonable Spring, than any we have had since the Restauration of K. Char. IId:[4]

---

[a] Followed by *& upon the French* deleted.   [b] Interlined, probably contemporaneously.   [c] Followed by *men-* deleted.

---

[1] James landed at Kinsale on 12 March: *A full and true account of the Landing . . . of the Late King James,* 1689. His companion is Jean-Antoine de Mesmes, comte d'Avaux, 1640–1709: *La grande encyclopédie.* He went as ambassador extraordinary and, although one of James's principal advisers, was not officially a member of his council. His instructions were to conciliate the Protestants. They were printed with a selection from his dispatches, *c.* 1845; facsimile, Irish MSS. Comm., 1934.

[2] *London Gazette,* 11 April. These votes were included in the Instrument of Government (Claim of Right), passed on 11 April; published in London *c.* 20 April as no. 12 of *A Continuation of the Proceedings of the Convention.*

[3] Evelyn apparently refers to such extreme whigs as Thomas Wharton, Richard Hampden, and William Harbord.

[4] At the beginning of April Wood writes that the spring is 'very backward' and mentions heavy rain and floods: *Life and times,* iii. 301.

21 The Viccar proceeded on his former Text & sub: as also did the curate:

This was one of the most seasonable Springs, free from the usual sharp Eastern winds: that I have observ'd since the yeare 1660; at the Restauration of K. C. II: which was much such another:

24 I went to Lond: about buisinesse: [25]ᵃ Next day dined at the Countesse of Bristolls.

26 I heard the Lawyers plead before the Lords, theᵇ Writ of Error, in the Judgment of *Oates*, as to his charge of Perjurie, which they after debate referred to the Answer of Holloway &c: who were his Judges:¹

Then went with the B: of St. Asaph to Lambeth to visie the A Bishop: where they both entred into a discourse concerning the final destruction of Antichrist: both of them concluding, that the 3 Trumpet & Vial was now powering out; and my L. S. Asaph attributing the Killing of the two Witnesse⟨s⟩, to the utter destruction of the Cevenes Protestants, by the French & Duke of Savoy, & the other, the Waldenses & Pyrennean Christians (who by all appearances from good history had kept the Primitive faith from the very Apostles times till now):ᶜ The doubt his Grace suggested, was whether it could be made ev⟨i⟩dent, that the present persecution had made so greate an havock of those faithfull people as of the other, & whether as yet, there were not some among them in being who met together:ᵈ it being expedient from the Text: 11: Apoc: that they should be both slaine together: The⟨y⟩ both much approved of Mr. Meads way of Interpretation, and that he onely failed in resolving too hastily, upon the King of Swedens successes, (Gustavusᵉ Adolphus), in Germany: That It were good to employ some intelligent French

---

ᵃ Marginal date. bracket supplied. ᵇ Followed by *reversing the* deleted. ᶜ Closing bracket supplied. ᵈ Followed by *They* deleted. ᵉ Opening

---

¹ Oates was trying to obtain a reversal of the verdicts given against him in an action for *scandalum magnatum* brought against him by the Duke of York in 1684, and in the two trials for perjury in 1685. His counsel was heard by the lords this day; the order for the judges to attend was given on 27 April: *L.J.*, xiv. 193-4.

Minister, to travell even as far as the Pyrennes, to understand
the present state of the Churches there: It being a country,
where no body almost traverses.[1]

There now came certaine[a] newes of K: James's being not
onely landed in Ireland, but that by surprizing London
Derry, he was become absolute Master of all that Kingdome:[2]
to the greate shame of our new King & Assembly at Westminster, who had ben so often solicited to provide against it,
by timely succors, & which so easily they might have don:
This is a terrible beginning of more troubles, especialy should
an Armie come thence into Scotland; People being so generaly dissafected here & every where else; so as scarse would
sea, or Landmen serve without compulsion:

A new Oath was now fabricating, for all the Cleargy to
take, of obedience to the present Goverment, in abrogation
of the former Oathes of Alegeance: which it is forseene, many
Bishops, & others of the Cleargy will not take, the penalty
being the losse of their dignit⟨i⟩e & spiritual preferment:[3] so
as this is thought to have ben[b] ⟨driven⟩[c] on by the Presbyters
& Comm: welth party, who were now in much[d] credite with
our new Governors: God in mercy, send us help, & direct the
Counsel to his glory, & good of his Church:

---

a Followed by *Int-* deleted.   b Followed by *a dev-* deleted.
c MS. *drauen* (i.e. *draven*), perhaps for *drawn.*   d Followed by *pow-*
deleted.

---

[1] The reporting appears to be
faulty. The Protestants of the
Cevennes were Huguenots, belonging to the French Reformed Church;
those of Savoy were Waldensians.
It was the latter and the Albigensians
who were generally identified as the
Two Witnesses; the Albigensians
were said to live in the Pyrenees
(they had long been extinct). For
the prophecies see especially Luttrell, ii. 213; W. Whiston, *An Essay
on the Revelation of Saint John*,
1706, pp. 204–8, where Lloyd is
specially mentioned; E. Waple, *The
Book of the Revelation Paraphrased*,
1693, p. 238; works by P. Boyer,
&c.; for the alleged primitive origin
of the two churches see the works
on them by P. Allix, 1690, 1692.
Joseph Mead, 1586–1638, was
author of *Clavis Apocalyptica*, first
published 1627; for him see *D.N.B.*

[2] For James's landing see above,
p. 635. A rumour—untrue—that
Londonderry had fallen was circulating about 9 April: *Hist. MSS.
Comm., Le Fleming MSS.*, p. 236.

[3] For the oath see above, p. 634;
the bill for it received the royal
assent on 24 April.

I[a] returned this evening home, finding my sick servant recovered:

28 Our Viccar on 6: Matt: 14: concerning Charity, in[b] forgiving Injuries: The Curate on 9. Dan 9. The Confession of sinne[c] of that prophet & applying it to our duty & necessities:

May: 1 Being the Anniversary[d] of the Feffees, for the poores Rents proceeding from the Charity of divers persons, our[e] Viccar preached on: 11: Matt: 30: shewing the Ease of Christs Yoake: &c:

5 Our Viccar proceeded on his former Text 6: Matt: 14. perstringing the passions of Divers Christians of these times, for their quarells, censoriousnesse, and ill language: Shewing how St. Paule, whose spirit, though[f] stirr'd up, upon his seeing the monstrous superstitions of the Heathens, & greate pretenders to philosophy & knowledge, above others: did not raile at them, call them wicked Idolaters, &c: but (not so much as naming any Scripture, to men whom he knew, they were ignorant of) tooke that gentle, & discreete way of reproving, & convincing them, by a Text out of one of their owne Poets & philosophers,[1] by which he avoides all dissorder & hubbubs, which ill language & indiscreete passion might have caus'd, & made his preaching unsuccessfull: Other like Instances he produces out of Scripture; as that of Nathans reproving David, of those horrid crimes, by a familiar similitude of the poore mans Lamb; without lowd, & publique denouncing against him, by which meanes, he caused David, to accknowledge his sin, & be his owne accuser: Then as to Dissenters dividing from the legal, & establish'd Worship, in the Church, he aledges the Example of St. Paule, & his dealing with the Corinthians, in Which, he[g] dos by no meanes, dehort them from frequenting the publique Assemblies, upon that Churches many, & greate corruptions: guilty of Incest, Intemperance at the Lords Supper, quarelling, & litigating before the Heathen Tribunals; but still advises them, not to

---

[a] Preceded by a date 27 deleted.   [b] Reading doubtful.   [c] Or *sinns*.
[d] Followed by *for* deleted.   [e] Followed by *Curate pr-* deleted.
[f] Substituted for *was*.   [g] Substituted for *I*.

[1] Acts xvii. 28.

forbeare the communicating one with another in all Christian
Charity, & by no means to make those inormities, occasion
their separation: The H: Sacrament follow'd, at which I received, The Lord be praised:

Being indisposed in my health, I went not this afternoone
from home: [19]ᵃ nor was I in condition to go to church 'til
Whitsonday, when, though very weake, I got thither, the
Viccar preaching a sermon apposite for the Day: on 2: Act:
1. 2. 3. 4. 5. verses, shewing the history, designe, & effects of
the holy Spirits miraculous appearing in his power, this day,
& the consequence of it, to the Conversion of the world, with
Instructions how to entertaine his graces &c: The H: Sacrament follow'd of which I received: The Lord make me
thankfull:

Matters publique went very ill in Ireland, Confusion &
dissention amongst ourselves, stupidity, unconstancy, emula-
tion, in the Governours, employing unskillfull men in greatest
offices: No person of publique spirit, & ability appearingᵇ
&c: threaten us with a very sad prospect what may be the
conclusion: without Gods Infinite mercy: A fight by Admiral
Herbert with the French, imprudently setting on them in a
Creeke as they were landing men &c in Ireland: by which we
came off with greate slaughter, & little honor:¹ so strangely
negligent, & remisse in preparing a timely & sufficient fleete.
The S⟨c⟩ots Commissioners offer the Crowne &c to the new
King, & Queene, upon Condition.ᶜ² [Act of Pole mony came
forth sparing none:³]ᵈ

ᵃ Marginal date.   ᵇ Spelling uncertain.   ᶜ Or *Conditions.*
ᵈ Interlined.

---

¹ The indecisive skirmish in
Bantry Bay on 1 May: *London
Gazette,* 9 May. Evelyn's criticism is
rather unfair. Herbert (above, p.
609) was created earl of Torrington
on 29 May.

² The Scottish Convention proclaimed William and Mary king and
queen of Scotland on 11 April.
Commissioners were then sent, with
a letter dated 24 April, 'to attend

Your Majesties with the chearful
Offer of the Crown, and humbly to
present the Petition, or Claim of
Right of the Subjects of the Kingdom'. The letter was delivered on
11 May: *An Account of what passed
in the Banqueting-House* (no. 22 of
*A Continuation of the proceedings of
the Convention*); for William's reply,
&c., see *London Gazette,* 16 May.

³ The act was passed on 1 May:

Trinity[a] Sunday,[1] our Viccar on[b] 2. Acts, proper for the day: the holy Comm: followed, which I received:

June 2: Our Viccar on 6: Heb: Last 3 verses, shewing that the most godly men, though they had assured hope, yet they had not allways a presumptious Confidence of their Salvation: That assurance being not allways imparted to all alike, & that yet those who had that humble hope, were many times as certaine of Gods mercy, & perhaps upon better grounds, as the most confident: The greatest Saints having often ben in doubts & feares, considering their frailties and to what Temptations they were liable: An humble fiducial hope & resignation upon doing our uttmost duty, being our best relyance: I received the holy Sacrament: Went in the afternoone to Greenewich to visite some French Gent: refugies:

Now came forth the Act of Indulgence for the disscenters, but not exempting them from paying dues to the Ch: of Eng: Cleargy, or serving in offices &c: according to law, with severall other Clauses:[2]

A most splendid Ambassy from Holland to congratulate the Kings accession to the Crowne.[3]

4. I went to Lond: [in my way Visited L: Arran, L. Peterboro, L: Preston in the Toure[4] &c][c] the solemn Fast for Successe of the Fleete &c:[5] was on [5][d] the next day carried

---

[a] Substituted for *Whitsun*. [b] Followed by *his former text* deleted.
[c] Interlined. [d] Marginal date.

London Gazette, 2 May; a proclamation was issued on 13 May for appointing commissioners to execute it: ibid., 20 May.
[1] 26 May.
[2] The Toleration Act, passed on 24 May: ibid., 27 May.
[3] The ambassadors made their entry on 27 May and had their public audience in the Banqueting House on 30 May: ibid., 30 May, 3 June.
[4] Arran (the Scots lord) was sent to the Tower on 28 February and

escaped on 11 November; Preston was ordered to be arrested on 13 May and was released on bail on 25 October; both were arrested for treasonable practices: *Cal. S.P., Dom., 1689-90*. Peterborough had been taken prisoner in December 1688: above, p. 611; and remained in the Tower until 1690.
[5] The fast, to be held on 5 June in and about London, and on 19 June elsewhere, was ordered by a proclamation of 23 May: *London Gazette*, 30 May.

on by the Bishop of Salisbury[1] at Westminster[a] Abby, before the Lords, and at St. Margarites before the Convention or Parliament by Dr. Tenison in the morning on   In which he did incomparably shew the sinn of selfe love, and how it was prejudicial to all brave and heroick actions &c:[2]

In the Afternoone by Mr. Wake on   shewing with greate Eloquence & Zeale[3]

6 I din'd with the L. Bish: of St. Asaph. Monsieur Capellus,[4] the Learned son of the most learned Ludovicus, presented to him his Fathers workes, not til now published:

7 I visited my L. A Bish: of Canterbery, to recommend Mr. Stringfellow[5] to him, staied with him til about 7: a clock: he read to me, the Popes Excommunication of the French King &c:

8 I din'd with Mr. Pepys.

9 Went to Covent Gard: Church, an Irish deane preached on 28. Pro: 13.

---

[a] MS. *Wes*ʳ.

---

[1] An error. Burnet preached this day before the king and queen at Hampton Court; it was Lloyd of St. Asaph who preached before the lords.

[2] This sermon, on 2 Tim. iii, 1, 2, was printed immediately.

[3] This sermon, on Joel ii. 12, 13, was printed immediately.

[4] Presumably Jacques-Louis Cappel, 1639–1722, teacher of Hebrew, &c.; son of Louis Cappel, 1585–1658, Protestant theologian: *Nouvelle biog. gén.*; E. and E. Haag, *La France protestante*. Evelyn here refers to the father's *Commentarii et notæ criticæ in Vetus Testamentum*, &c., edited by the son, Amsterdam, 1689; it is dedicated to Sancroft. For the son's family see Pepys, *Private corr.*, ii. 306.

[5] William Strengfellow, *c.* 1658–1731; M.A., Oxford, 1684; curate and, later, lecturer at St. Dunstan in the East during Holden's incumbency (1686–98); minister at Trinity

Chapel, in the parish of St. Martin in the Fields, 1691–9; perhaps Tuesday lecturer at St. Antholin, Watling Street, *c.* 1692 (as Strongfellow); rector of St. Dunstan in the East 1698–1731; lecturer at St. Andrew Undershaft *c.* 1714; perhaps preacher to the Clothworkers' Company, *c.* 1714 (as Strongfellow): A. G. B. West, (*St. Dunstan in the East*), p. 88; *The Hours of Daily Prayer in and about the city of London*, 1692; James Paterson, *Pietas Londinensis*, 1714, pp. 23, 131; notices below. His only printed sermon was preached before the lord mayor at St. Lawrence Jewry on St. Michael's Day, 1693, the day of the election of the lord mayor for the ensuing year. Evelyn, who greatly admired his preaching, had written to Sancroft on 10 May, recommending him for the rectory of Coulsdon, Surrey: B.L., MS. Tanner 27, f. 37.

Dind at my L: Gorges:[1] 10: at Mr. Povys, 11: At my Sons, now at his new house:[2] Visited Dr. Burnet Now B. of Salisbery, got him to let Mr. Kneller draw his picture.[3]

⟨12?⟩[a] I went with my Lady Sunderland,[4] & Sir W: Godolphin to Cranburne in Windsor forest; to visite Mrs. Boscawen &c: returned to Lond, that Evening: and [13][b] the next day home.

16 Our Viccar proceeded on his former Text, shewing the Comfort of Hope & that doing our duty, we might have a full & solid Assurance, & that we should be carefull to Cast Ankor on a firme ground, which is Christ, & in him to Hope to the end:

Afternoone, the Curate of Greenewich on 1. John: 16. That it was our duty to add grace to Grace; not to sit downe with one Grace, but making continual progresse, towards perfection:

K: James's declaration was now dispersed, offring pardon to all if upon his landing or 20 days after, they should returne to their obedience:[5]

Our Fleete, not yet at sea, & thro some prodigious sloth, & mens minding only their present Interest: The French riding master at Sea, taking many greate prises, to our wonderfull Reproch: No certaine newes from Ireland, various reports of Scotland, discontents at home: The K. of Denmark at last joyning with the Confederates:[6] [& the two Northern Princes reconciled:][c]

---

[a] MS. *10*; the dates *11*, *12*, and *13* are placed below one another in the margin opposite this paragraph.   [b] Marginal date; see preceding note.   [c] Added later.

[1] Richard Gorges, 1620–1712; second Baron Gorges of Dundalk (Ireland) *c*. 1650: G.E.C.

[2] Presumably his house in Dover Street: below, v. 37.

[3] Burnet had been consecrated bishop of Salisbury on 31 March: above, p. 632. A portrait of him by Kneller is mentioned in his will: Clarke and Foxcroft, *Burnet*, p. 475.

[4] Sunderland was still in exile in the Netherlands.

[5] The declaration dated Dublin Castle, 8 May. There were at least two editions. The text is reprinted, with date 18 May, in James II, *Life*, ed. Clarke, ii. 362–5. Luttrell notes its dispersal about this time: i. 548, 549. A proclamation for apprehending two men who were distributing copies was issued on 24 June: *London Gazette*, 1 July.

[6] Ibid., 4 July. Treaty between the king of Denmark and the duke

The E. India Company like to be disolv'd by the Parliament for many arbitrarie actions:

Oates acquitted of perjurie to all honest mens admiration.[1]

20 Dined with me the Countesses of Bristoll & Sunderland, Sir W: Godolphin, Dr. Tenison & Mrs. Penelope Godolphin:[2] Brought newes of a plot discovered, upon which divers were sent to Tower & secured:[3]

Twas now also reported that Col: Kirke had gotten into Lond:Derry with supplies: [but this proved false.][a][4]

23: Mr. Stringfellow preach'd an excellent[b] ser: on 16 Luke 13.[5] upon the Comming of the H: Ghost at Pentecoste, and the severall powers he imparted to the Apostles [who guided them into all Truth][c] for the planting of the Gospel: that nothing was deficient in the Scriptures, but what was made knowne by their preaching, against the doctrine of the Papists & their superstructure, with an exhortation to cleave to it &c:

Pomeridiano a Young Ship Chaplaine (I suppose) on 24: *Pro:* 21. Against mens being given to change, to the disturbers of Government; a Text not so apposite, upon our so often changes:

An extraordinary Drowth, to the threatning of greate Wants, as to the fruits of the Earth:

---

a Added later.   b MS. *ex*[t]:   c Interlined.

---

of Holstein, signed 30 June, N.S. The king of Denmark at the same time offered to support the emperor with 8,000 troops.

[1] This refers to a resolution of the house of commons on 1 June, that Oates's two trials for perjury in 1685 were 'a Design to stifle the Popish Plot; And that the Verdicts . . . were corrupt', &c.: *C.J.*, x. 177. The lords on 31 May voted that the two verdicts in 1685 were to be maintained: *L.J.*, xiv. 228.

[2] Above, p. 432.

[3] Cf. Luttrell, i. 552. Two men sent to the Tower about 25 June.

Some other men had been arrested a few days earlier: ibid., p. 549.

[4] Percy Kirke, 1646?–91; colonel of the Queen's Regiment (now the Queen's West Surrey; 'Kirke's Lambs') 1682–91; brigadier-general 1685; major-general 1688 (William); lieutenant-general 1690: *D.N.B* He had sailed from Liverpool for the relief of Londonderry on 31 May: *London Gazette*, 6 June. He entered Lough Foyle on 14 June: *A particular journal of Major Gen. Kirks Voyage*, 1689. He did not succeed in relieving the city until 28 July.

[5] An error for St. John xvi. 13.

30: Our Viccar on ⟨his⟩ª former Text: we had now good showers God be praised:

⟨July⟩ 7 Viccar proceeded in his former Text; shewing, that none could have any assurance of Salvation, but from the holinesse of his life & performance of the Condition of the Gospell: I received the B: Sacrament:

8 To Lond: [9]ᵇ I sat for my Picture to Mr. *Kneller*, for Mr. Pepys late Secretary of the Admiralty, holding my *Sylva* in my right hand: It was upon his long and earnest request; & is plac'd in his Library: nor did Kneller ever paint better & more masterly work:¹

11 I dind at my L: Clarendons, it being his Ladys Weding day:² when about 3 in the afternoone, so greate & unusual a storme of Thunder,ᶜ raine and wind suddainly fell, as had not ben known in an age: many boates on the Thames were over wh⟨e⟩lmed, & such was the impetuosity of the wind, as carried up the waves in pillars & spouts, most dreadfull to behold, rooting up Trees, ruining some houses, & was indeede no other than an Hurocan:ᵈ³

The Co: of Sunderland told me, that it extended as far as *Althorp*, that very moment, which is about 70 miles from Lond: But I blesse Almighty God it did us no harme at Deptford, but at Greenewich it did much mischefe:

14 Dr. Tenison preached at St. James's on: 4: Eph: 25: exhorting to speaking Truth sincerely, & without any doubtfullnesse or Equivocation, one to another &c: The B: Sacrament followed, at which I was present:

I din'd at the Countesse of Sunderlands.

16 I went to Hampton Court, about buisinesse, the Coun-

ª MS. *this*.   ᵇ Marginal date; it occurs opposite the line beginning 'of the Admiralty' and its incidence is uncertain.   ᶜ Followed by & deleted.   ᵈ Or *Hurecan:*

---

¹ Evelyn refers to this portrait in his letter to Pepys of 12(?) August (Bohn, iii. 294–5). Pepys had been deprived of his secretaryship between 20 and 28 February.

² This is incorrect: Clarendon was married to his present wife on 19 Oct. 1670: Russell, *Swallowfield*, p. 137. He was at Tunbridge Wells from 17 June to 29 July continuously: diary, in *Corr.*, ii. 280–4.

³ This storm is not traceable elsewhere; the date is questionable: see preceding note.

cil[a] being there;[1] A greate appartment, & spacious Garden with fountaines, was beginning in the Parke, at the head of the Canale:[b2] I return'd to Lond that evening:

19 I returned home: The Marishall de Scomberge, went now Generall towards Ireland, to the reliefe of Lond: Derry:[3] Our Fleete lie before Brest:[4] The Confederates, now passing the Rhyne, beseege Bonn, and Maence to obtaine a passage into France:[5] A greate Victory gotten by the Muscovite, taking & burning *Procop*:[6] A new Rebell against the Turks, unkle to Yegen[c] Bassha threatens the destruction of that Tyrannie:[7] All Europe in armes against France; & hardly in memory of an⟨y⟩ Historie, so universal a face of Warr: The Convention (or Parliament as some called it) sitting, exempt the Duke of Hanover from the Succession to the Crowne,[8] which they seeme to confine to the present New King, his Wife, & Princesse Ann of Denmark, who is so monstroustly s⟨w⟩ollen, that its doubted, her being thought with child, may

---

[a] Altered from *Couns-*.   [b] Altered from *Chanale*.   [c] Reading doubtful; altered from *Segen*?

---

[1] The king was in residence at Hampton Court at this time.

[2] For the palace in Charles II's time see above, iii. 322–5. William and Mary began to rebuild it on 1 April of this year. Work stopped on Mary's death in 1694, when the interiors were largely unfinished; it was resumed in 1699–1702, and the interiors were completed in the eighteenth century. Work on the gardens began on 1 May of this year. It also stopped on Mary's death, but was resumed in 1699–1702: Wren Soc., vol. iv.

[3] *London Gazette*, 18 July. Schomberg (above, p. 598) set out on 17 July.

[4] So ibid.

[5] Notice from ibid. The Rhine was bridged at three or more places. The siege of Mainz began on 17 July, N.S.; that of Bonn on 22 July, N.S.:

ibid., 25, 29 July. The former is always called Mentz there.

[6] Ibid., 22 July; the correct name is Pericop (i.e. Perekop in the Crimea). It was taken from the Tartars by 2 June, N.S.: ibid., 15 July.

[7] Ibid., 22 July; the notice refers to Yedic Bassa, who was leading a rising in Asia; for his relationship to Yeghen Bassa, who had recently been executed, see ibid., 24 June.

[8] Evelyn apparently refers to a conference between the two houses of parliament on 16 July concerning a bill for the succession to the crown. The lords tried to add a clause naming Sophia, duchess of Hanover (the future Electress), as next heir; this was rejected by the commons: *Hist. MSS. Comm., House of Lords MSS., 1689–90*, pp. 345–7.

proove a Tympane onely:[1] so as the [unhappy][a] family of
Steuarts, seemes to be extinguishing: and then what government next, is likely to be set up, whether Regal & by Election, or otherwise, The Republicaries & Dissenters[b] from the
C. of England looking evidently that way: The Scots
having now againe newly, voted downe Episcopacy there:[2]
Greate discontent still through the[c] nation, at[d] the[d] slow
proceedings of the King, & the incompetent Instruments &
Officers he advances to the greatest & most necessary charges:

21 Our Viccar on former Text, shewing that Christians
may expect and hope for a Reward: Curate on: ⟨1⟩ Cor: 15:
55 &c benefit of the Resurrection:

24 I went to Lond; sate at Mr. Knellers for my picture,
dined at Mr. Pepys', return'd that evening:

25 Came Mr. Knellar, with two other painters to visite me:

27 My son, & both daughters[3] went to Tunbridge to drink
the waters:

28 Our Viccar, on 27: *Jobe*: 6, describing what Conscience
was, no word but Heart, in the Hebrew to signifie it: The
terrors of an evil, and comfort of a good Conscience &c:

The Curate on 22: *Luke*. 19. Preparatory to the H. Communion:

[29 Countesse of Sunderland, Sir W: Godolphin, Dr. Tenison came to dine &c:][a]

⟨August⟩ 2 I went to Lond, return'd that evening:

4 Mr. *Stringfellow* preached on: 16: *John*[e] 13. shewing why
the gifts of Tongues & other miraculous χαρίσματα ceased after
the Gospel was throly embraced; that men might themselves
study the Scriptures &c & not wholy rely upon extraordinary
meanes, when they had the ordinary: blaming Enthusiasts,
& perstringing the C: of Romes pretence to Infallibility, by

---

a Interlined.　　b Altered from *Dissenting*.　　c Altered from or
to *this*.　　d–d Reading doubtful; possibly *as to*.　　e Altered from *Luke*.

---

[1] She gave birth to a son on
24 July: *London Gazette*, 25 July.
He was William, duke of Gloucester,
who died in 1700.
[2] Ibid., 1 Aug. The act for abolishing episcopacy was passed on 22
July. See also *A Continuation of
the proceedings of the Parliament in
Scotland*, nos. 37, 42.
[3] i.e. Evelyn's daughter and
daughter-in-law.

assistance of the H. Ghost, the Scriptures being aboundantly sufficient for the determining all necessary doctrines &c: The H: Communion followed, at which I participate⟨d⟩, *Deo laus & gloria*:

Marishal Schomberg went with forces to⟨w⟩ards Ireland, London Derry in exceeding want of reliefe:[1]

6 I went to Lond: about buisnesse, returned the 8th: Lond: Derry relieved,[2] Dundee slaine in Scotland.[3]

11 Our Curate preached on 1. *Cor:* 3. 7, concerning the dignitie of the Ministerial office, and the respect due to them, a very handsome discourse; The extreame heate of the Weather hindred me from Church in the Afternoone:

18 Our Viccar[a] proceeded on his former text out of Jobe.

21: I went to Lond: to take leave of the Countesse of *Sunderland* going next day to Holland.[4] I returned that Evening:

23[b] Came to visite me Dr. Tenison, & an Irish Bishop, Mr. Firmine[5] & others.

25 Our Viccar proceeded on his former Text, to shew what Conscience was, and in what cases it might erre even in the best men: shewing also the infinite extent of Gods mercy, in forgivenesse of sinns, upon repentance, & that such as did so repent & amend, might truely & comfortably affirme, they had a good Conscience.

The Curate of Woo⟨l⟩wiche preached on: 2. Cor: 1. 22: very well, concerning Gods giving us his holy Spirit, in so especial a manner under the Gospel: and in what sense, some morral heathen might be said to receive some beame of it:

---

[a] Followed by *not well the* deleted.   [b] Altered from *25.*

---

[1] See above, p. 645. Schomberg was now at Chester preparing his forces; he did not sail until 12 August.

[2] *London Gazette,* 5 Aug. The town was relieved on 28 July.

[3] Ibid. John Graham of Claverhouse, born 1648; created Viscount of Dundee (Scotland) 1688; mortally wounded at the battle of Killiecrankie

on 27 July.

[4] A pass for her to go there was issued on 18 August: *Cal. S.P., Dom., 1689–90,* p. 223.

[5] Presumably Thomas Firmin, 1632–97, the philanthropist: *D.N.B.* His interest in the relief of the fugitive Irish bishops and clergy led him to distribute the briefs for it: *London Gazette,* 12 Sept.

Hithertoo it has ben a most seasonable Summer:

1: *Sept:* our Vicar[a] on his former Text on Jobe, Shewing that there was no word in old Test, to expresse Conscience save Spirit & heart: That God commandes many Good[b] things which every one is not to take on them to do: as to punish offenders not being Magistrates, or Imitating the Zeale of some who had special callings to justifie[c] them: God determined the death of his sonn, but the Jewes did wicckedly to put him to death: Good intentions excuse not our doing amisse: As the Midwives lie to Pharoah: Uzzas, ⟨putting⟩[d] his hand to stay the Arke from falling. The bloudy things &[e] massacres[e] approved by Popes &c on pretence of zeale for holy church: The B: Sacrament follow'd at which I received:

The Curate on 53 Isaia 4. 5. &c: concerning the bitter sufferings of Christ for us: I was exceeding drowsy:

8th: Our Viccar & Curate continue the same subjects.

15 On the same: [Karric firgus surrendred][f] 1 Lond derry after a wonderfull & brave holding out: Relieved.[2]

⟨18⟩[g] I went to Lond. to see severall of my friends: The Parliament adjourn'd 'til the 19: Octob:[3] Mantes taken by the Confederates,[4] D of Shomberg [arived in Ireland],[f] takes the passe at Eure:[5]

21[h] St. Mathews,[6] I went to visite the A Bishop of Cant: since his Suspension who received me with greate kindnesse: Dr. Stillingfleete promoted to Wooster, Dr. Patrick to

---

[a] Altered from *D-*.   [b] Altered from *God*.   [c] Altered from *in-*.
[d] MS. *putthing*.   [e-e] Substituted for *don*; reading doubtful.
[f] Interlined.   [g] MS. *28*; preceded by *18* deleted.   [h] Altered from *24*.

---

[1] *London Gazette*, 5 Sept. Carrick-fergus, surrendered 27 August.

[2] See above, p. 647 n. The siege had begun about 20 April.

[3] Ibid., 23 Sept. Parliament adjourned on 20 September.

[4] Ibid., 16 Sept. Mainz, surrendered 11 September, N.S.

[5] Ibid., 23 Sept. Newry (Nury), 'a very strong Pass' (ibid., 26 Sept.), abandoned by the Irish and oc-cupied by Schomberg on 5 September: *Cal. S.P., Dom., 1689–90*, p. 251.

[6] i.e. St. Matthew's Day. Sancroft had been suspended from 1 August in accordance with the act for the new oaths, 1 William and Mary, c. 8; it also provided for the eventual deprivation of the non-jurors.

Chichester, Dr. Lang being dead:[1] Dr. Tillotson made deane of S. Paules:[2]

I return'd this Evening: A very dreadfull fire happning in Southwark:[3]

22 Mr. *Meriton* preached on 2. *Cor:* 6: 1. concerning the Grace of the Gospel, and our obligations to receive & walke by it:

Our Reader[4] on 2. Pet: 3. 11 very well, concerning the greate worke of God in the creation for Conviction of Atheists &c: Especialy on the certainty of the final disolution of the world.

29 St. *Mich:* the extraordinary wett, &c kept us at home:

Afternoone, the Curate on *18 Luke*: the Repentance of the Publican:

Octob: 6 Our Viccar on 22: Apoc.   Concerning Angels, their ministry: we are not to worship them, Papists Error: A visite kept me at home in the afternoone:

9 Came to visite us the [young][a] Marquis de Ru⟨v⟩ignie[5] & one *Monsieur le Coque*[6] a French Refugiè, who left greate Riches for his Religion, a very learned civill person: he married the sister of the Dutchesse de la Force &c.

13 Our Viccar on his former subject, shewing that God was in Christ the onely object of all Worship, Christ, not Angels, our only Mediator, Pride & Ignorance being in the contrary Superstition.

Bonne after a tedious siege rendered to the Confederates.[7]

---

[a] Interlined.

[1] Lang is an error for Lake, who had died on 30 August. The warrants for *congés d'élire* for Stillingfleet and Patrick are dated 9 September: *Cal. S.P., Dom., 1689–90*, p. 247. They were consecrated, with Ironside, at Fulham on 13 October: *London Gazette*, 17 Oct.

[2] In place of Stillingfleet. His appointment dates from September, but he was not elected and installed until 19 and 21 November.

[3] See also Luttrell, i. 584.

[4] Presumably the Deptford lecturer: above, p. 563, &c.

[5] The elder Ruvigny had died on 26 July: Dumont de Bostaquet, *Mém.*, p. 247.

[6] François le Coq, sieur de Germain: Agnew, *French Protestant exiles*, ii. 326. His wife's sister was married to Jacques-Nompar de Caumont, Duc de la Force from 1678 to 1699: de la Chenaye-Desbois and Badier, iv. 873–4.

[7] *London Gazette*, 17 Oct. Bonn capitulated on 12 October, N.S.

Ottobone a Venetian Cardinal 80 yeares old, made Pope:[1]

20 Our *Viccar* on 4: *Philip:* 6: [Duty]ᵃ Necessity, & direction for continual Prayer. I went in the afternoone to the French Congregation at Greenewich, where preached a young man on 50 Psal: 13: Concerning the proportion of the Ritual & Mosaic Sacrifices in relation to that of Christ:

27 Our Viccar continued the same Argument of the duty of Prayers:ᵇ

29 To Lond.

31: My Birthday, being now 69 years old: Blessed Father who hast prolonged my years to this greate Age, & given me to see so greate & wonderfull Revolutions, preserved me amidst them, to this moment; accept I beseech thee the continuance of my Prayers & thankfull accknowledgements, and graunt to me the Grace to be working out my Salvation, & redeeme the Time, that thou mayst be glorified by me here, & my immortal Soule saved, when ever thou shall call for it, to perpetuate thy prayes to all eternity, in that heavenly Kingdome, where there is no more Changes, nor Vicissitudes, but rest & peace, & Joy & consummate felicity for ever: Grant this, ô heavenly Father, for the sake of the L. Jesus, thyne onely Sonn & our Saviour: Amen:

Nov 3 I received the H: Sacrament at St. Martines, Dr. Tenison preaching most excellently (as he allways dos) on: 3: *Luke* 5² Concerning Nichodemus his question, & our B: Lords Answer about Regeneration:

5 Bish: of St. Asaph Lord Almoner &c: preached before K. & Q: on 57: *Psal:* 7:[3] the whole discourse being almost nothing save an historical narrative of the C. of Englands several Deliverances, especialy that of this Anniversary, signalized, by that of the P: of Oranges Birthday,ᶜ & Marriage (which was on the 4th)[4] & of his Landing at Tor-bay

---

ᵃ Interlined.   ᵇ Or *Prayer:*   ᶜ Followed by *wh-* deleted.

[1] *London Gazette*, 24 Oct. (see also 17 Oct.). Pietro Ottoboni, 1610–91; elected pope on 6 October, N.S.; took the name of Alexander VIII.

² An error for St. John iii. 5.

[3] Lloyd's text was Psalms lvii. 6, 7; the sermon was printed this year.

[4] William was born in 1650 and married in 1677.

this day: which ended with a splendid Ball, & other festival rejoicings:[1]

In the Meane time, No, or not sufficient supplies, Ireland[a] gives greate apprehension of the successe of our Army there, under the D: of Shomberg, K. James, being more powerfull in Horse: & the Weather exceeding wet & stormy: [& we having miserably lost all the past summer for want of prudent menagement of affaires: The Convention vote a Tax of 2 Million &c:[2]][b]

Card: Ottaboni (a Venetian) chosen Pope:

7th: I returned home on the 7th.

10 Our Viccar on his former Text: the Curate on 6: John: 37. of our Saviours benignity in receiving those who came to him: &c: I received the B: Sacrament with my Wife at home, she as yet not daring to adventure in the cold, which now (after a very wett season) came on very severely:

17 Our Viccar proceeded, to shew how necessary faith, and our Endeavors to obtaine what we pray for, was in all our devotion: without which nor long, nor earnest prayers would be Effectual:

Pomerid: the Curate of Greenewich on: 11: Matt: 3 last verses, shewing how preferrable[c] our obedience to the Gospel, was above all other things, in order to our greatest satisfactions:

Hithertoo much wett, & cold, without frost, yet the Wind N & Easterly:

The Assembly at Lond, now begin (too late) to consider how miserably publique matters have ben maneiged;[3] especialy as to Ireland, the imbarging our Merchant ships now 15 moneths for want of Convoys[4] (which the Dutch afforded theirs with to the immense prejudice of our Trade,

---

a Followed by *posse-*? deleted. *the* deleted.   b Interlined.   c Followed by

[1] The ball was held on 4 November: *London Gazette*, 7 Nov.
[2] Resolution of the commons 2 November: *C.J.*, x. 279.
[3] The commons appointed a committee to examine the miscarriages

of the war on 1 November: ibid., x. 278.
[4] The merchants complained of the loss of ships and the cost of convoys: ibid., xiv. 285, 286, 288, 289; Grey, *Debates*, ix. 411–21, 430–6.

& advantage of theirs) besides the losse of so many of our best ships & other Vessells both by accidents, & pirates:

A Convocation of the cleargy meete, about the Reforming of our Liturgy, Canons &c: [obstructed by others of the Cleargy.]ᵃ¹

27 I went to Lond [with my family]ᵇ to Winter at Sohò in the greate Square.²

30 I went to the R: Society, where I was chosen one of the Council, my Lord Penbrok³ president, we dined together:

December 1: Dr. Tenison preached at St. Martin on 1. Tim. 5. 21. against partiality and the factions now exceedingly disturbing & threatning the publique:⁴ The H: Communion followed, at which I was participal,ᶜ⁵ praised be God.

I dind at Sir William Godolphins:

I spent most of thisᵈ following weeke in receiving and returning Visites:

8 Dr. *Herne*⁶ at St. Anns preached on 7 Luke 19, concerning the Messias's being come, which he proved by all the usual Arguments, Historical, prophetical, & as to that remarkable passage,⁷ of Christs presence in the 2d Temple, making its glory so much greater than the first, though as to its fabric & out-ward splendor and cost, it was so much superior: our B: Lords appearing in it, was such an impleation of that

---

ᵃ Added later.   ᵇ Interlined.   ᶜ Perhaps a slip or a contraction for *participant*.   ᵈ Followed by *next* deleted.

¹ The Convocation of the province of Canterbury met for business on 21 November and sat until 13 December, when it was adjourned until 24 January. Proposals for altering the liturgy, &c., to make them acceptable to the majority of the nonconformists, were to be submitted to it: T. Lathbury, *Hist. of the Convocation*, 2nd ed., 1853, pp. 325–32, and sources there indicated; Macaulay, iv. 1730–59.

² The square had been built in 1681. The south side was occupied by Monmouth House, which had been built for the late duke. In 1693 four earls were living in the square: Kingsford, *Piccadilly*, p. 69.

³ The eighth earl: above, p. 440, &c. He was president for one year only.

⁴ A sermon preached by Tenison on this text on 3 Dec. 1691, and published in 1691, may repeat part of the present sermon.

⁵ The only occurrence of this word recorded in *O.E.D.* dates from 1497. See critical note.

⁶ John Hearne, d. 1704; matriculated at Oxford 1653; D.D. 1687; rector of St. Anne's, Soho, 1686–1704: Foster.

⁷ Presumably Haggai ii. 9.

Prophesy, as is impossible, should ever be fullfilled here-after, as the Jewes dreame; since that 2d Temple[a] or Later fabric being utterly destroy'd, it can never be that their Messias should enter into that which is no more: The application was, that if we Christians believe Christ the Messias to be come, we should live as those who do believe it: and be our selves daily fullfilling those Prophesies, which[b] shew'd what successe & wonderfull effects were to follow it, & would be the effects of it: namely universal peace & unity, righteousnesse, sobriety, purity, humility and all other[c] angelical vertues; wheras men now live such wiccked lives, in warrs, persecution, Idolatry, laciviousnesse, oppression & other enormous vices, as[d] if the Messias were yet not come, or Christ had never had his gospel preached to us, & all were impostor: and this might (if any thing) be enough to harden the Jewes, & keepe them off from believing that Savior to be come, to which ther follows so little[e] of those prophesies fulfilled.

In the Afternoon preached the B: of Bangor:[1] on 37: Psal: 37: Perswading to a godly life, for the infinite benefit, & joy it would bring to be[f] upright at the end: The Bish: spake so low, that I could heare very little:

11 To Deptford to see my Grandson falln ill of a scarlet feaver at the French Schoole at Greenewich,[2] which, after blood letting so abated that by Gods mercy I left him in an hopefull way.

15 The Schoole Master of Leasam[3] preach'd on 5. Joh: 28. 29. concerning Judgement to come: In the Afternoone

---

a Followed by *being* deleted.
c Followed by *Chr-* deleted.
e Followed by *fruit* deleted.

b Followed by *were* deleted.
d Followed by *might* deleted.
f Or *the*.

[1] Humphrey Humphreys, 1648–1712; D.D. 1682; bishop of Bangor 1689 (consecrated 30 June); of Hereford 1701: *D.N.B.*

[2] A French school at Greenwich is among the schools listed in J. Houghton, *A Collection for improvement of husbandry and trade*, between 29 June 1694 and 25 Oct. 1695 (the list of schools appears only between these dates). No master's name is given.

[3] i.e. Lewisham. Presumably John Turner of Colfe's School: above, p. 591.

the Curate of Greenewich on 39 Psal: 14. strangers & pilgrimes in the world &c:[1]

16: I return'd to Lond: blessed be God, in good hopes of the Childs recovery.

[My Servant Jo: Brake a rib by a fall, but is I hope in good way also of recovery.][a]

22: The reader of St. Anns, preached on: 119 Psal: 67: very excellently, of the benefit of Gods Chastizements, & of the greate danger of prosperity:

25 A stranger preached at St. Anns on: 2[b] Luke 14:[b] the holy Commun. followed:

Afternoone Mr. Wake on 40: Isa: 3: both of the Birth of Christ, & proper for the day:

29 Dr. Tenison at St. Martin on 1. Joh: 4: 9. shewing the infinite obligation we lie under to Love God, who sent his Son, who so loved us: & that therfore every sin is ⟨inconsistent⟩[c] with the love of God, & that though we cannot allways be praying or actualy hearing, or doing works of Charity, because they depend upon circumstances of times, & places &c: yet a Christian may love God at all times, & be ready to shew his love upon all occasions:

Afternoone at St. Anns, a stranger on: 90: Psal: 12th: shewing the necessity of a Christians care in spending of the little time of his sejourne in this world, and[d] that this advise of Davids to number our dayes comprehended in it, all the Conversation of a Christian, in a pious, & virtuous life, as the greatest wisdome.

An extraordinary wet season, & stormy, greate losses by sea,[2] & much confusion & discontent among our selves:

---

a Interlined.   b-b Substituted for *40 Isaias: 9.*   c MS. *inconsistal*; perhaps a contraction for *inconsistent.*   d Followed by *the severall* deleted.

---

[1] The text is cited from the Prayer Book; see also Hebrews xi. 13.

[2] Wood notes the rains about Christmas: *Life and times,* iii. 320.

There was a storm involving some loss about Plymouth on 25 December: *London Gazette,* 2 Jan. 1690; an earlier storm, ibid., 30 Dec.

PRINTED IN
GREAT BRITAIN
AT THE
UNIVERSITY PRESS
OXFORD
BY
CHARLES BATEY
PRINTER
TO THE
UNIVERSITY